Biggles'
DANGEROUS MISSIONS

Biggles'
DANGEROUS MISSIONS

Captain W. E. JOHNS

PRION

This edition first published in 2008 by

Prion
an imprint of the
Carlton Publishing Group,
20 Mortimer Street,
London W1T 3JW

Biggles and the Secret Mission First published in 1937 as *Biggles Air Commodore*
Biggles – Secret Agent First published in 1940
Biggles – Flying Detective First published in 1947 as *Sergeant Bigglesworth CID*
Biggles in Australia First published in 1955

Copyright © W. E. Johns (Publications) Ltd.

A catalogue record for this book is available from the British Library

ISBN 978-1-85375-663-4

Illustrations by
Alfred Sindall and Studio Stead

Typeset by e-type, Liverpool
Printed in Thailand

Contents

Introduction

One of the many things that has brought an enduring popularity to the Biggles stories is the fact that the technical details about the aircraft involved in the adventures of Squadron Leader James Bigglesworth were factually accurate, giving the aviation yarns an air of authenticity that could only be supplied by a true expert. Captain W. E. Johns was an officer in the Royal Flying Corps during the First World War, a combat pilot who knew the capabilities and flying characteristics of the aircraft about which he was writing. When Biggles took to the sky in anything from a Sopwith Camel or a Spitfire to a Hawker Hunter jet fighter, you could be sure that whatever tricky manoeuvre he was required to undertake was possible – especially for a pilot of Biggles' proven skill and daring.

Johns' expertise helped to put boys of all ages in the pilot's seat, if only in their mind's eye, adding an extra element of excitement to his stories, but a Biggles adventure was never solely about soaring through the clouds. Johns was also a master storyteller, taking his hero through almost a hundred books over a period of more than thirty years from 1932 right up to his death in 1968. Biggles fought in both World Wars, joined an elite, airborne Scotland Yard crime-fighting team after the Second World War and turned his talents to espionage during the Cold War.

On most of his missions, Biggles was ably assisted by characters such as Algy Lacy and Ginger Hebblethwaite, Algy and Ginger becoming almost as famous as their flying ace boss. These characters embodied the spirit of the British fighting man, Johns cleverly tapping into the way that his readership wanted their heroes to behave. They had a very British way of going about their business; they were courageous and uncompromising in battle, yet still managed to retain a notion of fair play; they were highly-skilled professionals, adept at handling all manner of technical equipment, yet they could improvise ingeniously when all was not going to plan and they were left to survive on their wits alone; above all, they were thoroughly decent chaps who could always be relied upon to do the right thing.

Biggles and his team manage to achieve all of this without drinking or swearing, although they are not entirely free of vices, smoking rather too much by modern standards. This is just one of the areas that mark these stories as having been written in a different age. The Biggles books have been criticised in the modern era for presenting views and attitudes that are outdated or politically incorrect. This is almost inevitable given that the first of the Biggles stories appeared more than 75 years ago, but it does not detract from the fast-moving, action-packed nature of the books. A Biggles reader was never given much time to recover from one fight-or-die battle before he was plunged straight into the next.

Rarely was the breathless pace of Biggles' adventures more intense than in the four novels in this second epic omnibus which shows Biggles and his colleagues in action as special emissaries fighting a variety of dangerous enemies of the crown just before and just after the Second World War.

In *Biggles Secret Agent* they have to fly secretly into a small European country to rescue a distinguished British Scientist and prevent his vital invention falling into enemy hands. In *Biggles and the Secret Mission* (first published as *Biggles Air Commodore*), Biggles, Algy and Ginger tackle a mysterious gang that is sinking British ships in the Indian Ocean. In *Biggles Flying Detective* (first published as *Sergeant Bigglesworth CID*), he confronts a conspiracy of former military fliers who, in the aftermath of the war, have taken to stealing valuable jewels. In *Biggles in Australia*, Biggles foils a conspiracy led by his former arch-enemy, Erich von Stalhein to provoke a rebellion by aborigines in the Australian outback.

Sit back and enjoy the action!

BIGGLES AND THE SECRET MISSION

CHAPTER I

An Unusual
'Whether' Report

'A penny for 'em.' Captain Algernon Lacey, late of the Royal
Flying Corps,[1] looked across the room at his friend, Major
James Bigglesworth – more often known as 'Biggles' – with a
twinkle in his eye.

'A penny for what?' inquired Biggles, starting out of his reverie.

'Your thoughts, of course.'

'You're over generous; I don't think they are worth as much,'
smiled Biggles.

'You seemed to be cogitating with considerable concentration,'
observed Ginger Hebblethwaite, their protégé, who was passing
a wet afternoon usefully by pasting up some photographs in an
album.

'Since you're both so confoundedly inquisitive, I'll tell you what
I was thinking,' growled Biggles. 'I was thinking what a queer
thing coincidence is. I mean, I was wondering if it really is, after
all, coincidence – as we call it – or whether it is simply the wheel
of destiny spinning for a definite purpose. From time to time it

[1] Later renamed the Royal Air Force (RAF).

makes contact with two or more people, or events. If they have no connection with each other the incident passes unnoticed, but if they are in any way related the thing at once claims our attention and we call it coincidence.'

'Why this sudden transit to the realms of philosophy?' asked Algy casually. 'Is there a reason for it?'

'There is a reason for everything.'

'I see. I thought perhaps this perishing weather was starting a sort of rot in your brain-box. If it goes on much longer mine will start sprouting fungus.'

'I shouldn't be surprised at that,' returned Biggles evenly. 'Fungus thrives on things that are soft and wet – steady with that cushion, you'll knock Ginger's paste over. As a matter of fact, you are quite right. Something has happened, and since we've nothing better to do I'll tell you what it was. I've got a feeling—'

Ginger shut his album abruptly. 'Go ahead, Chief,' he prompted. 'When you get feelings it's usually a sign that something's going to happen.'

Biggles shook his head. 'I don't think anything will start from this,' he murmured. 'Still, you never know. But listen; I'll tell you. This morning, when I was going to the bank, who should I barge into but Tom Lowery. You remember Tom, Algy? He came to 266 Squadron just before the Armistice.[1] He stayed on in the service after it was all over, and I haven't seen or heard anything of him for years. He's a squadron leader now, stationed at Singapore, so he hasn't done so badly. Naturally, we swapped *salaams*, with the result that we ended up at Simpson's for lunch. Now follow me closely because the sequence of events is important.

[1] The armistice that ended World War 1, in 1918.

'While we were disposing of our steak and kidney pudding he started to tell me about Ramsay who, you may remember, was an ack-emma[1] in 266. He is now a sergeant wireless operator mechanic – still in the service, of course. Or perhaps it would be more correct to say that he *was* a sergeant, because he no longer wears three stripes. Apparently Tom thought a lot of Ramsay, for not only did he wangle him into his squadron, but he used to take him in the back seat of his machine during air operations. Now during one of these flights Ramsay picked up a wireless message out of the blue, and Tom had just got as far as that with his story when who should walk in through the door of the restaurant, looking for a seat, but Jerry Laidshaw, who is now in charge of "sparks"[2] at the Air Ministry. Naturally, Jerry joined us, and after all the "well, fancy seeing you's" had been exchanged, he invited Tom to proceed with his yarn while he studied the menu card. So Tom carried on telling me about Ramsay. Is that all clear?'

'Perfectly.'

'Good. Tom, then, proceeded with his tale. Why he made so much of it I don't know, but I fancy he was feeling pangs of remorse on Ramsay's account. However, that's by the way. It appears that while they were in the air Ramsay picked up this message that I've already mentioned, and he handed it over to Tom as soon as they were back on the ground at Singapore. I can't remember the exact words, but the message – which was really an S O S – was to this effect. It was from the steamship *Queen of Olati*, and the wireless operator was broadcasting for help because they were on fire. He gave the ship's position, and concluded with the words

[1] RAF jargon for air mechanic.
[2] RAF jargon for radio operator.

"weather fine, sea slight." Now you'll observe that the word "weather" occurs in that sentence, and upon that single word hung a power of mischief. Ramsay, in taking down the message – which came through, of course, in Morse – had spelt it w-h-e-t-h-e-r. Tom looked at it and said to Ramsay, "You should be able to spell better than that; you mean w-e-a-t-h-e-r." Said Ramsay, all hot and peeved, "No, sir. The word I took was w-h-e-t-h-e-r." Whereupon Tom told him to alter the message before it was handed in at the pay-box.'[1] Ramsay refused. An argument then started which, I am sorry to say, ended with Ramsay losing his head and saying things which in turn resulted in his losing one of his stripes for insubordination.'

'But I don't see where there is any coincidence in this,' put in Algy.

'Wait a minute, I haven't finished yet,' replied Biggles impatiently. 'The coincidence – we'll call it that – is about to be introduced. This is it. As Tom finished telling me his story, Jerry, who had been listening to the last part of it with interest, blurted out, "But Ramsay was right! I picked up the *Shanodah*'s message at the Air Ministry, and the word weather was spelt w-h-e-t-h-e-r. I can vouch for it, because I made particular note of it."

'At that, Tom gave him a queer look and said. "What are you talking about? I never said anything about the *Shanodah*; in fact, I've never heard of such a ship. I was talking about the *Queen of Olati* that went down in the Indian Ocean about six months ago." Jerry looked at him and looked at me. "Well, that's odd," he said. "I didn't catch the name of the boat when you were telling your tale, but when you mentioned the way the word

[1] Service slang for Squadron Office.

weather was spelt I thought naturally that you were referring to the *Shanodah*, which also – curiously enough – went down in the Indian Ocean, or the Bay of Bengal, which is practically the same thing. It would be – let me see – about five months ago. But she wasn't burnt. She hit an uncharted reef and went down with all hands.'

'"There were no survivors in the case of the *Queen of Olati*, either," put in Tom casually, and with that the conversation turned to something else, and no more was said about it. That's all.'

'Strange,' murmured Algy.

'Strange!' cried Biggles. 'I think it's more than strange when two mercantile wireless operators, both English, and presumably both educated men, misspell the same word – which, incidentally, is a word they must use more than any other. But when you add to that the fact that both ships foundered with all hands, in the same sea, within a month of each other, I should call it dashed extraordinary – too extraordinary to be either human or natural.'

'What do you mean?'

'Hasn't anything struck you?'

'No, I can't say that it has.'

'Well, this is the way I figure it out. The chances against two educated men misspelling the same word almost at the same time and place, and in practically similar circumstances, must be so remote as to leave one no alternative but to assume that they were both one and the same man.'

'But how could that be possible? The operator on the *Queen of Olati*, which went down first, was drowned.'

'He should have been, but there is something weak about that supposition.'

'Why not approach the shipping company and find out?'

'I have.' Biggles smiled. 'My confounded sense of curiosity was so intrigued that after I left Tom I went down to Tower Bridge and made a few inquiries.'

Algy threw him a sidelong glance. 'So that's where you were all the morning, is it? he growled. 'Well, and what did you discover?'

'That the name of the wireless operator was Giles, and that he was most certainly drowned. His next of kin was notified accordingly.'

'Why "most certainly" drowned?'

'Because his body was one of those picked up by one of the ships that raced to the rescue after the S O S went out.'

'Then that knocks your argument on the head right away.'

'It looks like that, I must admit.'

'What happened to the wireless operator on the *Shanodah*?'

'He was drowned, too; at least, he's never turned up, so he has been presumed lost at sea.'

'Then that must be the end of the story,' suggested Ginger in a disappointed tone of voice.

Biggles smiled mysteriously. 'Not quite,' he said. 'I was so chagrined at my theory all coming unstuck that while I was by the river I pursued my inquiries a bit farther. You may be interested to know that since the *Queen of Olati* and the *Shanodah* went down, two other ships have been lost with all hands – also in the Indian Ocean. Both sent out S O S's, but by the time rescuers were on the spot they had disappeared, leaving no trace behind – as the papers put it.'

'Was the word weather misspelt in those cases, too?'

'Ah, that I don't know. In each case the S O S was picked up by one vessel only. One of them was on the way to Australia, where she now is, but the other was homeward bound and docked at the Port of London this morning. She wasn't in when I came away, but she'll have paid off by now, and the crew gone home. Her name is the *Dundee Castle*, and the name of the wireless operator is Fellowes. Under the pretence of being an old friend I managed to get his address and his home telephone number from a very charming girl in the company's office.'

'You don't mean to say that you've got the infernal impudence to ring him up and ask him if the word weather occurred and, if so, how it was spelt?'

'That's just what I'm going to do – now. Pass me the telephone.'

'You're crazy.'

'Maybe, but my curiosity won't let me rest until I find out.'

'But suppose the word weather *did* occur, and *was* incorrectly spelt; what would that tell you?'

'A lot. It would be an amazing coincidence for two mercantile wireless operators to misspell the word they use most, but don't ask me to believe that *three*, all in the same locality, could do it. That is straining credulity too far.'

Biggles unhooked the telephone receiver and dialled a number. 'Hello, is Mr Fellowes at home, please?' he asked. 'What's that? Oh, it is Mr Fellowes. Splendid. Don't think me presumptuous, Mr Fellowes, but I believe you were the officer who picked up the S O S sent out by the *Alice Clair* about three months ago ... yes ... that's right. My name is Bigglesworth. I've just been having an argument with a friend of mine about that S O S. The word weather ... yes ... quite ... really! ... Thanks very much. That's just what I wanted to know – good-bye.'

Biggles hung up the receiver, put the instrument on the table, and took out his cigarette case.

'Well?' inquired Algy impatiently. 'Out with it. Not so much of the Sherlock Holmes stuff. What did he say?'

Biggles lit a cigarette. 'He said that now I mentioned it, it *was* rather odd that the wireless operator of the s.s. *Alice Clair* should spell the word weather, in a meteorological sense, W-H-E-T-H-E-R!'

Algy thrust his hands deep into his trousers pockets and stared at Biggles for a moment in silence. 'By the anti-clockwise propeller of Icarus! That certainly is a most amazing coincidence,' he got out at last.

'Coincidence my foot,' snorted Biggles. 'There's no coincidence about it. It's a bag of diamonds to a dud half-crown that those three messages were sent out by the same man.'

'But that isn't possible—'

'Of course it isn't. That's what worries me. How can an impossibility become possible? There is only one answer to that. The impossible is not, in fact, impossible at all. Work that out for yourself.'

'But how could three men, miles away from each other, and two of them dead, be one and the same?'

Biggles shook his head sadly. 'Don't ask me,' he murmured. 'I'm no good at riddles. There's just one more thing I should like to know, though.'

'What's that?'

'Just what cargo those ships were carrying.'

'Why not ask Colonel Raymond at Scotland Yard? I don't suppose he'd know offhand, but he'd jolly soon find out for you if you asked him.'

'That's a good idea! Let's try. What's the time? Four o'clock. He won't have left the office yet.' Biggles reached for the 'phone again and dialled Police Headquarters at Scotland Yard.

'Colonel Raymond, please,' he told the operator at the Yard switchboard. 'Name? Major Bigglesworth ... that's right.'

'Ah! Is that you, sir?' he went on a moment later. 'Yes, it's Bigglesworth here. I've an unusual question to ask, but I've a reason for it or I wouldn't bother you. It is this. Within the last six months four ships have sunk with all hands in the Indian Ocean. One by fire, one by fouling a reef ... what's that? You know all about it! Fine! Then you can no doubt quench my curiosity. What was on their bills of lading?'

The others saw his expression change suddenly. From casual curiosity it became deadly serious.

'Really,' he said at last. 'What? No, I don't know anything about it. Why did I ask? Oh, well, just a hunch, you know – no, perhaps it wasn't a hunch. I – no, I'd better not say anything over the 'phone. What about slipping round here for a cup of tea; it's only a few minutes ... Good ... that's fine. See you presently, then.'

Biggles hung up the receiver and eyed the others gravely. 'It looks to me,' he said slowly, 'as if we may have hit a very grim nail somewhere very close to the top of its sinister head. The *Queen of Olati* was outward bound for Melbourne, loaded chock-a-block with military aeroplanes for the Australian government. With her went down one of our leading aircraft designers and a member of the Air Council. The *Shanodah* was bound for Singapore with twenty Rolls-Royce Kestrel engines, spare parts, machine-guns, and small arms ammunition. The *Alice Clair* was bound for Shanghai with munitions for the British volunteer forces there; and the other ship – the fourth, which we haven't investigated – was coming home from Madras with a lot of bar gold. Raymond is on his way here now.'

A low whistle escaped Algy's lips. 'By gosh! There's a fishy smell about that,' he said softly.

'Fishy! It smells to me so strongly of fish, bad fish, too, that – but I believe that's Raymond at the door. Ginger, slip down and ask Mrs Symes to let us have tea for four right away.'

A minute later Colonel Raymond walked into the room.

'Nice to see you all again,' he smiled, after shaking hands all round. Then he sat down and turned a questioning eye on Biggles. 'Well,' he said, 'what do *you* know about this, eh?'

Biggles shrugged his shoulders. 'Nothing,' he said simply. 'I've been guessing, that's all.'

'And what have you guessed?'

'I've guessed that it would suit some people remarkably well if all British ships bound for the Far East and the Antipodes, with armament, never got there.'

Raymond stared. 'That's not a bad guess, either,' he said in a curious voice. 'By heavens, Bigglesworth, I always said you should be on our Intelligence staff. You're nearer the mark than you may suspect – a lot nearer; but how did you come to tumble on this?'

'And how did *you* happen to know all about it when I rang up? Shipping isn't in your department.'

'I was dining with the Commissioner and the First Lord of the Admiralty the other night. The Sea Lords are worried to death. So is the Air Council. But they know nothing – that is, they only know that these ships have disappeared. The public know nothing about these ships carrying munitions; naturally, we daren't let it get into the newspapers. But come on; this is very serious indeed. What strange chance led you to the trail?'

'Merely the fact that I have reason to suspect that the S O S sent out by each of the doomed vessels was broadcast by the same man.'

'Great heaven! How on earth did you work that out?'

'By so small a thing as a spelling mistake.'

Briefly, Biggles told his old war-time chief what he had told the others earlier in the afternoon.

When he had finished Colonel Raymond got up and began pacing up and down the room. Suddenly he stopped and faced Biggles squarely. 'Bigglesworth, if you'll give up this free-lance roving and join our Intelligence staff, I'll give you any rank you like within reason,' he declared.

Biggles shook his head. 'It's very nice of you, sir, but I should be absolutely useless in an official capacity,' he said slowly. 'I have my own way of doing things, and they are seldom the official way. If I got tangled up with your red tape I should never get anywhere. It is only because I've played a free hand that I've sometimes been – well, successful.'

'Yes, perhaps you're right,' agreed Raymond despondently. 'But tell me, have you formed any ideas about this business?'

'I've hardly had time yet, but my first impression is that some foreign power is operating against our shipping from a base in or near the Indian Ocean. They are sinking every ship which their spies inform them is carrying munitions to our forces in the Far East. Knowing that it is improbable that these ships could disappear without sending out any sort of message, they take control of the wireless room before the captain or crew suspect what is going to happen, tap out a false S O S, and then sink her, taking care that there are no survivors.'

'But Bigglesworth! They wouldn't dare!'

'Wouldn't they! It is my experience that people or nations will dare anything if enough is at stake. You should know that. In the old days we had plenty of examples of it.'

The colonel suddenly snatched up his hat. 'I must get round to the Admiralty,' he declared. 'They must know about this.'

'What do you think they'll do?'

'Do! They'll send a flotilla of destroyers, of course, and—'

'Tell the enemy – whoever it is – that their scheme is discovered,' smiled Biggles, with a hint of sarcasm in his voice. 'Which should give them plenty of time to remove themselves from the scene, or look innocent when the white ensign heaves up over the horizon. Why not write to them and have done with it? You might just as well: the result would be the same; all you'll meet will be suave faces and pained protests.'

Colonel Raymond bit his lip. 'Perhaps you're right,' he said shortly. 'That's for the Admiralty to decide. You stay where you are; you'll hear from me again presently.'

'What do you mean, stay where I am?'

'What I say. Don't go away. Don't go out.'

'But I'm not in the army now. I'm a citizen and a free man,' protested Biggles indignantly.

'So you may be, but you'll jolly well do what you're told, the same as you used to,' growled the Colonel with a twinkle in his eye. 'I shall rely on you.'

Before Biggles could reply he had gone out and slammed the door.

'You see what comes of nosey-parkering in matters that don't concern you,' Biggles told Ginger sadly. 'Let it be a lesson to you – ah, there you are, Mrs Symes,' he continued, as the housekeeper came into the room with the tea-tray. 'Sorry, but we shan't have a guest after all. He was in too big a hurry to stay. Never mind, no doubt Ginger will be able to manage his share.'

'There now,' was Mrs Symes's only comment as she went out again.

'Exactly,' murmured Biggles softly. '"There now." We shall be saying the same thing presently, or I'm a Dutchman.'

'You think we've stepped into the soup?' suggested Algy.

'More than that. Before many hours have passed we shall find ourselves up to the neck in the custard, or I'm making a big mistake,' declared Biggles.

CHAPTER II

An Important Conference

'If anyone asked for my opinion as to the location of the enemy base – assuming, of course, that there is one – I should say that if you took this as a centre, and combed the area within a radius of a hundred miles, you'd find it.'

As he spoke, Biggles carefully stuck a pin into the big atlas that lay open on the table, and then glanced in turn at the others who were seated on either side of him.

The tea things had been pushed on one side to make room for the book which, lying open at a double page entitled 'The Indian Ocean and the Dutch East Indies,' for more than an hour had absorbed their interest. Four red ink spots marked the last known positions of the ill-fated vessels, and from these lead-pencil lines radiated out to the nearest points of land, each line being accompanied by the distance in miles written in Biggles's small, neat handwriting.

'Mergui Archipelago,' read Ginger aloud, craning his neck to see the words that appeared on the map at the point which Biggles had indicated with the pin. 'What makes you think it is there?' he asked.

'Simply because it seems to me to be the most natural place,' replied Biggles without hesitation. 'It's the place I should choose

*Biggles carefully stuck a pin into the big atlas that
lay open on the table.*

were I asked to establish such a base for such a purpose. Look at the whole of this particular section of the globe, the Bay of Bengal, in or near which these ships went down. On the west it is bounded by India. That can be ruled out, I think. What hiding-places does it offer to a craft engaged in a murky business of this sort? Very few, if any. Not only that, but India is a thickly popu-lated country with excellent communications; a strange craft would certainly be noticed and rumour of its presence reach the ears of those whose job it is to watch such things. Admittedly, there are the Andaman and Nicobar Islands out in the middle of the sea. The base may be there, but somehow I can't think it is. If I remember rightly, the Andamans are used as a penal settlement for Indian political prisoners, and there are too many planters in the Nicobars to make it healthy for foreigners whose comings and goings would be bound to attract attention. Now let us go across to the other side of the bay. Here we have a very different proposition. Down the western seaboard of the Malay Peninsula there are a thousand places – creeks and estuaries – where a craft could lie concealed for months. The natives, such as they are, are very unsophisticated. Not only that, but the location is conveniently situated for the interception of ships bound for the Far East. They all call at Singapore, which is at the southern end of the Peninsula.'

'But what made you choose the Mergui Archipelago?' asked Ginger.

'Well, just look at it and consider the possibilities,' replied Biggles. 'Hundreds of islands – thousands if you count islets – lying at a nice convenient distance from the mainland – thirty or forty miles on an average – and spread along the coast for a distance of nearly three hundred miles. The islands are rocky, well wooded, with magnificent natural harbours. What more could a mystery ship ask for?'

'I've never heard of the place before,' confessed Ginger.

'Very few people have. I doubt if Algy and I would have heard of it but for the fact that we once flew over it for nearly its entire length, on the way home from New Guinea.'

'Are the islands inhabited?'

'Generally speaking, no, although I believe there is a strange race of Malay Dyaks, called Salones, who wander about from island to island in glorified canoes which they make their homes. Quite a bit of pearl fishing is done in the vicinity, chiefly by Chinese and Japanese junks during the north-east monsoon when the weather is fine and the sea calm. For the rest of the year, between June and October, when the south-west monsoon is blowing, it can be the very dickens, as a good many Australia-bound fliers know to their cost. We saw two or three junks when we flew over. Queer spot. Sort of place where anything could happen. Do you remember Gilson, Algy, that Political Officer who came to see us at Rangoon after the Li Chi affair? I have a vague recollection of his telling me that the islands are infested with crocodiles and all sorts of wild beasts that swim over from the mainland of Burma and Siam. The thing stuck in my mind because he told me that he once saw a tiger swimming across, which struck me as most extraordinary, because the picture of any sort of cat swimming in water seems wrong somehow. But there, what does it matter? We aren't likely to go there.' Biggles closed the atlas with a bang and rose to his feet.

'Pity,' murmured Ginger sadly.

'Pity, eh? My goodness! You're a nice one to talk. What about that African show, when we were looking for young Harry

Marton? You jumped every time you heard a lion roar. Africa is civilized compared with this place. I – hello, who the dickens is this, I wonder?' Biggles broke off and reached for the instrument as the telephone repeated its shrill summons.

'Hello,' he called. 'Oh, hello, sir ... It's Raymond,' he whispered in a swift aside, with his hand over the mouthpiece ... 'Yes, sir? What's that? Dine with you? Delighted, of course. You want me to dress formally? What on earth for? … where? Oh dear! that isn't in my line … Right you are, sir, I'll be ready. Good-bye.' He hung up the receiver and turned to where the others were watching him expectantly. 'He's picking me up in his car in half an hour,' he said. 'Ever heard of a place called Lottison House?'

'Heard of it!' cried Algy. 'Great Scott! You're not dining there, are you?'

'So he says.'

'But Lord Lottison is one of the head lads at the Foreign Office.'

Biggles started. 'Jumping mackerel!' he breathed. 'Of course he is. I thought the name seemed familiar. It begins to look as if my confounded curiosity has got me into a nice mess. Well, I shall have to go and get ready.'

'Didn't he say anything about bringing us?' inquired Ginger, frowning.

'No, not a word,' grinned Biggles.

'Then I call it a dirty trick.'

'Never mind, I'll bring you a lump of jelly home in my pocket,' promised Biggles. 'I shall have to hurry. I've only half an hour to dress, and it usually takes me twenty minutes to get my studs into that boiled horror misnamed a shirt.'

*

Nevertheless he was ready and waiting when the impatient shriek of a hooter in the street below warned him that Colonel Raymond had arrived, so with a brisk 'See you later' to the others, he ran down the stairs and took his place in the limousine that had drawn up outside the door.

'You haven't wasted any time,' he told the Colonel, who, in evening dress, was leaning back smoking a cigarette. 'I wish you'd left me out of it. I'm not used to dining with peers of the realm, so I hope you won't accuse me of letting you down if I gurgle over my soup.'

'You'll find Lottison is a very decent fellow,' the Colonel told him seriously. 'This dinner was his suggestion, not mine. He's a busy man, and couldn't manage any other time.'

There was one other guest, and Biggles realized the gravity of the situation when he was introduced to Admiral Sir Edmund Hardy, head of the Admiralty Intelligence Department. Little was said during the meal, but as soon as it was over Lord Lottison led the way into his library, and without any preamble embarked on the problem that had brought them together.

'Well, gentlemen,' he began in a clear, precise voice, 'I don't think there is any need for me to repeat what we all know now, although only suspected until Major Bigglesworth brought the matter of the misspelt S O S message to our notice. That gives us a clue, as it were – something concrete on which to work. Our munition ships bound for the East are not foundering by accident. If proof of that were needed I have it here in the form of a cable which I have just received from Australia in answer to one I sent when this wireless incident was first mentioned to me late this afternoon. The Master of the *Tasman*, the ship which picked up the S O S sent out by the *Colonia*, the fourth vessel to be sunk, reports that the word weather was spelt w-h-e-t-h-e-r. That, I think, settles any possibility of coincidence. What is happening on the high seas, and how it comes about that an unknown operator has access to British ships, we do not know. The question is, what are we going to do about it? It cannot be allowed to continue, but I need hardly say that any steps we take must be made with extreme delicacy. At all costs we must avoid a situation that might end in war, particularly if – as it seems – the enemy has already established a means of severing our Far Eastern communications. Now, Hardy, what do you suggest?'

The admiral studied the ash on his cigar thoughtfully. 'Well, I – er – that is – I'm prepared to do anything you like – on your instructions. I can't act on my own account, as you know perfectly well. If you're prepared to back me up and shoulder responsibility for anything that might happen, I'm prepared to go ahead and comb every sea-mile between Calcutta and Singapore.'

A worried frown creased Lord Lottison's forehead. 'I'm not anxious to take the risk of precipitating the country into a first-class row any more than you are,' he said frankly. 'If things go wrong, the government will be thrown out on its ear, and I shall be the scapegoat.'

Biggles fidgeted impatiently. 'May I be allowed to make a suggestion, sir?' he said.

'I should welcome one.'

'Very well, then, let us get right down to brass tacks,' proposed Biggles bluntly. 'Our ships are being sunk. Someone is sinking them, cleverly, secretly. Clearly, we've got to hoist the enemy with his own petard and dispose of him in just the same way – cleverly, secretly. Do you agree to that?'

'Absolutely.'

'Good! Now this private war is being carried on either by a surface vessel or an underwater craft. Whichever it is, it must be operating from a base which is being fed with supplies from the country that owns it. As I see it, we can do one of two things. Either we can sink the ship that is doing the dirty work, or we can wipe out the base. But if we merely sink the ship the people at the base, although they may be upset, may put it down to an accident and simply get another ship and go on with the job. So it is better to smash up the base than sink the ship. But when the base is smashed up it's got to be done properly. If it can be done in such a way that no one is allowed to go home to tell the tale, so much the better. That's the game they themselves are playing. Not that that is vitally important, because the country concerned can hardly ask us for an explanation without explaining what it was doing with an unauthorized base, anyway. Still, it's better to avoid complications if it can be arranged.' Biggles paused.

'Go on,' said Lord Lottison, looking at him oddly.

'If you are going to be content with sinking the ship, or submarine, as I suspect it to be,' continued Biggles, 'surely nothing could suit your purpose better than one of the "Q" boats,[1] such as were used during the war. All you have to do is to send a ship out to Singapore, and let it be known that she is carrying munitions. Man the ship with naval ratings and line her sides with concealed guns so that the raider can be given its *quietus* as soon as it shows up.'

'Yes, that could be done,' declared the admiral, almost eagerly.

'The only drawback to the scheme is that it might only half answer the question,' observed Biggles. 'It isn't much use killing

---

[1] A boat armed with hidden guns.

31

a wasp and leaving the nest. And, with all due respect to you, sir—' Biggles glanced at the admiral – 'the finding of that nest might be a job beyond your power, because it is pretty certain that the enemy will know what you're after as soon as your ships start nosing about in unusual places. In short, it's a job for aircraft.'

'Then we shall have to call the Air Force in,' declared Lord Lottison.

'They'd do the job all right,' admitted Biggles, 'but they'd be up against the same difficulty as the Navy. The enemy would know what was afoot. Moreover, you would have to take a lot of people into your confidence. You can't send out several aeroplanes to look for something without telling the crews what to look for. And if you tell the crews, everyone on the station will soon know, and it will only be a question of time before rumours reach the ears of the people we are up against.'

'Then what the devil *are* we to do?' burst out Lord Lottison irritably.

Biggles raised his eyebrows. 'Are you asking me that as a serious question, sir?' he inquired.

'You're an airman – something more than an airman, judging by what Raymond here tells me – so any suggestion you make will receive our earnest consideration. That, frankly, is why you're here.'

'Very good, sir. I was half prepared for this, so I've given the matter some thought, and this is my idea. It is a case where co-operation is necessary, but the co-operation has got to be worked in such a way that the fewest possible people know what is actually in the wind. The chief properties required would be an ordinary merchant ship, a destroyer, and an aircraft. The purpose of the ship would be to act as bait, a decoy. No one on board except the captain and the wireless operator need know that. The wireless operator would have to know because it would be necessary for him to keep in touch with the destroyer and the aircraft, in code, on a special wave-length. The enemy also has wireless, remember. Our decoy ship would, to all intents and purposes, be engaged on an ordinary job of work. The destroyer would primarily be nothing more than a supply ship for the aeroplane, although naturally it might be called in to do any other job that became necessary. Have I made myself clear so far?'

'Quite. Go on.'

'The destroyer, one of an old type for preference, to lessen the chances of its attracting attention, will keep close enough to the decoy ship to be effective in emergency, yet far enough away not to be associated with it. The aeroplane will operate between the two.'

'But surely the aircraft would be heard by the enemy?' put in the admiral quickly.

'I hadn't overlooked that possibility,' replied Biggles. 'The aircraft will be fitted with one of the new silencers now under experiment at Farnborough.'

'How the dickens did you learn of that?' cried Lord Lottison aghast.

'I know a lot of things I'm not supposed to,' answered Biggles imperturbably. 'As a matter of detail, the inventor sought my opinion on a technical question long before the device was submitted to the Air Ministry. But allow me to finish. Having equipped ourselves in the manner I have outlined, this is the order of progress. The decoy ship, its warlike cargo having been remarked in the press, will put to sea, followed shortly afterwards by the destroyer. Coincidental with their approach to the Indian Ocean, a long-distance flight will be commenced by a civil pilot. It is extremely unlikely that anyone, even the most astute enemy agents, will connect the three events. That the pilot will encounter unexpected difficulties between Dum-Dum Aerodrome, Calcutta, and Batavia, is fairly certain, for it is all in accordance with the best traditions of long-distance flights. It is also extremely likely that he will be blown off his course by contrary winds, and possibly lose his way. Thus, no great surprise would be felt if he were seen *anywhere* in the region of the Bay of Bengal. Naturally, what we hope will happen is that the raider will attack the decoy ship, whereupon the wireless operator will report what is going on to the aircraft, or the destroyer, or both, who will head in that direction.'

'And sink the raider,' concluded the admiral enthusiastically.

Biggles looked pained. 'Oh dear, no,' he exclaimed. 'The skipper of the decoy, being prepared for trouble, should be able to avoid it. Having enticed the raider out of its lair, he will have to escape as quickly as possible. The aircraft will pick up the raider and note the direction it takes with a view to ascertaining the approximate position of its base. It is pretty certain to head for home after its attack has failed. And here let me remind you that if it *is* a submarine, submergence will not conceal it from the aircraft, for the pilot will be able to see it as clearly under water as if it were afloat. If the skipper of the attacked ship can give the pilot the direction taken by the raider, all well and good; if he can't – well, no matter, he will have to pick it up as best he can. From twenty thousand feet a pilot can see over an immense area, you know.'

'And if everything works out according to plan, and the pilot discovers the enemy base, what then?' inquired Lord Lottison curiously.

A peculiar smile flitted across Biggles's face. 'Well, the base will have to be obliterated – blotted out; otherwise there is no point in finding it, is there?'

'No, I suppose not,' was the thoughtful answer.

'How do you suppose the pilot will be able to effect the blotting-out process?' asked the admiral.

'He'll have to use his own initiative,' declared Biggles. 'He might be able to do it by borrowing a torpedo or a load of bombs from the destroyer. It all depends upon circumstances, but if he is a resolute fellow he'll find a way of doing it somehow. Naturally, he wouldn't appeal to you, or Lord Lottison, for assistance, because neither of you would dare to give an order involving the complete destruction of the property of a foreign power. He would have to act as an individual.'

'It sounds a very hazardous business to me,' murmured the admiral doubtfully.

'I don't think anyone has suggested that it isn't, sir,' answered Biggles a trifle harshly. 'It's a matter of desperate cases needing desperate remedies, if ever there was one. Either we are going to wipe out this base when we find it, or we might as well stay at home. To be on the safe side—'

Biggles hesitated.

'Go on,' prompted Lord Lottison.

'Well, I was thinking, sir,' continued Biggles slowly. 'Supposing that when the pilot finds the base, for some reason or other he finds the job of destroying the whole works rather beyond him, he ought to be able to call for assistance.'

'How?'

'By asking an R.A.F. unit to come and do it. If they made a clean job there would be little risk of detection.'

'I don't quite follow that.'

'Well, put it this way. The thing might be made to look like an accident. After all, military aircraft carry out bombing practice regularly, and pilots are not to know that a secret submarine base had been established at the very spot selected for the bombing. What could the enemy do even if he was sure that his base had been deliberately bombed, anyway? You would simply look round, registering innocence, and say, "My dear sirs, we are very sorry, but how on earth were we to know that you'd got a lot of naval and military stores tucked away at so-and-so? What were they doing there?" What answer could they make? None, that I can see, without admitting their guilt. No, sir. If such a situation came about I fancy the enemy would have to take his medicine in silence.'

'By heaven, I believe you're right,' cried Lord Lottison. 'But tell me, who is to fly this aircraft you've talked so much about? Who could be entrusted with such a job?'

'Don't ask me, sir; I don't know,' returned Biggles promptly.

'There's only one man for the job,' put in Colonel Raymond quietly, speaking for the first time.

'And who's that?' asked Lord Lottison sharply.

'Bigglesworth.'

A smile spread slowly over the face of the Foreign Office diplomat, and he looked at Biggles good-humouredly. 'Why pretend, Bigglesworth?' he said softly. 'We all knew this from the beginning. The only question that remains is, will you undertake it?'

'Certainly,' replied Biggles without hesitation. 'If you can't find a better man, I can't very well refuse, even if I wanted to, the affair being a matter of national importance. But in order that there is no misunderstanding, I might as well say right away that I should demand certain – er – facilities.'

'Demand?'

'That's the only word I can use, since I would not undertake the job unless they were agreed to.'

'Well, let us hear them.'

'In the first place, I should stipulate that you gave me complete control of the whole expedition. It would be no earthly use my giving orders if they weren't obeyed.'

'Do you mean that you expect to be put in command of a destroyer?' asked the admiral incredulously.

'No; but the captain would have to act on my instructions.'

'But you can't expect a naval officer to take orders from a civilian.'

'It isn't a matter of what I expect, sir; it's a matter of what I should have to have. If the decoy ship, the destroyer, and myself, are going to act independently, we might as well wash out the whole project; you've only to look at your history book to see what has happened to expeditions when two or three people shared command.'

'But it's unheard of – a civilian in command of a naval unit,' protested the admiral.

'You can easily get over that,' smiled Biggles.

'How?'

'By giving me a commission in the Royal Navy, with rank superior to that of the skipper of the destroyer.'

The admiral stared. 'You're asking me to take a nice risk, aren't you?' he observed coldly.

'I suppose I am,' admitted Biggles. 'But what are you risking? Your appointment, that's all. I'm going to risk my life, if I know anything about it, and from my point of view that's a lot more important than your commission.'

The admiral glared, but Lord Lottison saved what threatened to become an embarrassing situation by laughing aloud. Whereupon they all laughed.

'I haven't finished yet, sir,' went on Biggles, looking at Lord Lottison dubiously.

'What else do you want besides a commission in the Navy?'

'A temporary commission in the Royal Air Force, with the rank of Air Commodore. You'd have to fix that up with the Air Council.'

It was the admiral's turn to laugh at the expression on Lord Lottison's face.

'It isn't a matter of personal vanity, sir,' went on Biggles crisply. 'I'm only thinking of the success of the show. I may need the Royal Air Force assistance, and what sort of reception do you suppose I should get if I, as a civilian, gate-crashed into the Royal Air Force headquarters at Singapore and demanded a machine, or even petrol or stores? I should be thrown out on my elbow; yet upon my request might hang the success or failure of the expedition. I've got to be able to get what I want without cables flying to and fro between the Air Ministry and Singapore. Let's be quite frank, sir. You wouldn't consider for an instant sending me on this job if there was any other way, or if you dared send a regular officer. But you daren't. You know you daren't, and I know you daren't; in case of failure or in the event of publicity – but I don't think we need go into that. I'm a civilian, and even if I had temporary rank it wouldn't matter what the dickens happened to me if things went wrong. You could have me hanged as a scapegoat if you felt like it, and I should have no redress. It might never be necessary for me to use my rank, but if I had it, instead of the delay which might prove fatal to the show, I should be able to walk into an R.A.F. depot, produce my authority, and demand what I required. Naturally, I should be fully alive to my responsibilities, and take care not to play the fool, or outrage the dignity of R.A.F. officers with whom I came in contact. It might be a good plan to warn the officer in charge of the Singapore station that I am about and that I might call upon him to undertake some unusual bombing operations.'

'Very well, if you think it is necessary I'll see what can be done; but by heaven, if you let me down—'

'Don't you think you'd better get somebody else to do the job, sir?' suggested Biggles coldly.

'No, no! No, no!' replied Lord Lottison quickly. 'You must see my difficulties, though.'

'I do, sir. I also endeavour to foresee my own,' answered Biggles quietly.

'All right. Then let us call it settled,' agreed Lord Lottison, glancing at the clock. 'By jingo, I shall be late; I've got to attend a Cabinet meeting at half-past ten. Draw up a plan of campaign as quickly as you can, Bigglesworth, setting down everything you require, and I will see to it that things are put in hand immediately. Will you do that?'

'Certainly, sir.'

'Good! We must break off the conference now. Don't forget to let me have that list.'

'You shall have it within twenty-four hours, sir,' Biggles promised as they all walked towards the door.

CHAPTER III

In the Nick of Time

Biggles sat on a water-worn breakwater on the outskirts of the primitive harbour at Tavoy, in Lower Burma, and gazed pensively through the masts of several Chinese sampans, a junk or two, and other odd native craft towards the Bay of Bengal. It was a beautiful morning, with the morning star still hanging low in the sky, and that first false dawn, which is only seen in the tropics, bathing everything in a weird, unnatural light.

'You know, Algy,' he said moodily, 'the anxiety of this job is getting me down. I don't think I quite realized until we got here just what we have taken on. The world seems such a whacking great place, and – well, dash it, one feels that it's futile to try and control anything. And this job is so indefinite, not in the least like the others we've undertaken.'

Three weeks had passed since the momentous decision in Lottison House, and each day had been one of intense activity as plans for the expedition had been pushed forward. Unexpected difficulties had been encountered and overcome, but the unnecessary delays – at least, they seemed unnecessary to Biggles – inevitable when dealing with government departments, had made him tear his hair and threaten to throw up the project.

However, in the end the preparations were concluded, and a general meeting of those chiefly concerned was held in an inner sanctum of the Foreign Office where, for the first time, those not acquainted with the real purpose of the campaign were informed and instructed in their particular duties.

Algy and Ginger attended in a secondary capacity in order that they might hear the plan unfolded in its entirety. The others present, beside those who had taken part in the preliminary debate in Lottison House, were: Air Marshal Sir Dugan Wales, Liaison Officer with the Air Ministry; Commander Michael Sullivan, R.N., Captain of H.M.S. *Seafret*, the destroyer detailed to act as a floating supply ship; Lieutenant Rupert Lovell, his Navigating Officer; Captain Angus McFarlane, of the *Bengal Star*, an old tramp steamer which had been selected as the decoy ship; and Chief Petty Officer Turrell, R.N., who was to act as the wireless operator on it.

Two speeches had been made, the first by Lord Lottison, who outlined the general plan in front of a huge wall map, and concluded by introducing Air Commodore Bigglesworth, the officer in supreme command of the operations. Biggles had, in fact, received a temporary commission with that rank from the Air Ministry, and notification of it had appeared in the *Gazette* under the broad heading of 'Special Duty'; naturally, the commission was to be relinquished at the end of the affair. He had abandoned his request for naval rank on the assurance of Admiral Hardy that Commander Sullivan would accept orders from him in his capacity of an Air Officer, the matter being made easier by the Admiralty 'loaning' the *Seafret* to the Air Ministry.

Biggles made the second speech. It was brief and to the point, and in effect merely a request for the loyalty and unswerving obedience to orders by which only could success be assured.

On the following day the *Bengal Star* put to sea, bound for Singapore via Calcutta. On mature consideration it had been decided that she should not carry munitions. Although a notice issued to the press stated that she was loaded with crated aeroplanes, actually there was nothing more romantic than good Welsh coal below her decks when she set sail. The *Seafret*, being faster, had given her two days' start, and another week had elapsed before the airmen set off after them with a prearranged rendezvous at Calcutta, from which point onwards the menace they were seeking might be expected to show up at any time.

The aeroplane they had chosen was a 'Storm' amphibian, aptly named *Nemesis*, fitted with two Rolls-Royce 'Kestrel' engines, and special tanks giving an endurance range of nearly three thousand miles. Personal luggage had been reduced to bare necessities in order that extra weight, in the form of a highly efficient wireless equipment and a powerful service camera, might not interfere with altitude performance. Altitude, Biggles claimed, was of paramount importance, for not only did it increase their range of vision, but it reduced their chances of being heard by the enemy; for although the special silencers had been fitted to the engines, there was no means of silencing the 'whip' of the propeller, or the vibrant hum of wires – both largely responsible for the noise made by aircraft in flight. A machine-gun of mobile type and automatic pistols completed their outfit, for with the *Seafret* in attendance anything else they required could always be obtained at short notice.

So far everything had gone in accordance with the scheme. The *Bengal Star* had proceeded on her way south-east from Calcutta, with the *Seafret*, in constant radio communication, following the coast but taking care to keep within reach should her presence be demanded. The *Nemesis*, in touch with both, officially on a long-distance flight to Australia, had followed in her own way, watching the *Bengal Star* from afar by day and lying at any convenient harbour during the night, refuelling when necessary from the *Seafret*. On two occasions, when the water had been dead calm, the airmen had spent the night on the open sea quite close to the decoy ship.

Biggles glanced at his watch. 'Well, come on,' he said. 'It's light enough to get away. Let's have another look at that chart, Ginger, before we go.'

He took the folded map which Ginger passed to him and opened it out flat on the breakwater. 'Now then, here we are,' he said, laying his forefinger on Tavoy. 'According to dead reckoning, the *Star* should be about here, and the *Seafret* here.' He pointed first to a spot about a hundred miles due north of the Andaman Islands, and then to a place much nearer the mainland, about fifty miles due west of the decoy ship's position. 'We mustn't let the *Star* get too far away from us,' he concluded as he folded up the map, 'although this cruising about all day and half the night gets pretty monotonous. I hate letting her out of my sight.'

'Turrell will always warn us the moment he sees anything suspicious, so I don't think there is any cause for anxiety,' murmured Algy as he moved towards the cockpit.

'That's true. In fact, that's my only comfort,' admitted Biggles, as he followed. 'It's the nights that give me the willies. We can't fly all day and all night, although we've jolly well nearly done that, but I'm always scared that something will happen when it's too dark for us to see what's going on. Start her up, Ginger, and then get to the keyboard and tune in.'

Five minutes later the *Nemesis* was in the air, with Biggles at the controls, heading south-west across the track of the decoy ship.

'What the dickens is Ginger doing?' asked Biggles presently, with a glance at Algy who was sitting beside him. 'He's a long time picking up the *Star*. You'd better go and see.'

Algy left his seat and went aft into the cabin. He was back in a moment, though, nudging Biggles impatiently. 'You'd better go and speak to him yourself,' he said in a normal voice, for owing to the silencers on the engines conversation could be conducted without shouting. 'He seems to be a bit worried about something.'

A frown of anxiety flashed across Biggles's face. 'Take over,' he said shortly and, leaving the joystick to Algy, ducked through the low doorway that gave access to the cabin.

Ginger was sitting at the radio, in the use of which he had had a concentrated course of instruction before leaving England, fingers slowly turning the tuning-in keys, but he desisted when he saw Biggles and slipped off his headphones. 'There's something wrong somewhere,' he said quickly. 'I can't get a sound of any sort out of the *Bengal Star*.'

'Have you spoken to the *Seafret*?'

'Yes.'

'What did they say?'

'They can't make contact, either.'

'Is that all?'

'Not quite. Lea, the operator on the *Seafret*, says he last spoke to the *Star* at five-thirty and got her position. Everything was all right then, and he arranged to speak to Turrell again at six o'clock if nothing happened in the meantime. Lea remained on duty, and five minutes to six, just as he was thinking of speaking again, he got the call-sign from the *Star*. It was repeated twice and came over very quickly as if it was something urgent. He picked up his pencil to take the message, but it never came. Instead, there was an uproar of atmospherics, or buzzing, that nearly blew his eardrums out. It went on for more than a minute and then cut out dead. After that there was silence, and he hasn't been able to get a sound since. He thinks something must have gone wrong with the *Star*'s equipment.'

'I don't,' muttered Biggles tensely. 'All right. Ask Lea for the *Star*'s last known position, and then send a signal to Commander Sullivan telling him to proceed at full speed to the spot. Let me know that position as soon as you get it.' Biggles hurried back to the cockpit.

'I don't like the sound of it,' he told Algy crisply. 'Neither Ginger nor Lea can get a sound out of the *Star*. No, don't move; you go on flying. Give her all the throttle and don't climb any higher; from this height we ought to be able to see the *Star* in about ten minutes.'

Ginger's face appeared in the doorway, and he handed Biggles a slip of paper on which he had jotted down the *Star*'s last position. Biggles passed it to Algy who, after a glance at his chart, altered his course a trifle.

Nothing more was said. The minutes passed slowly. Algy continued to fly, mechanically, depressed by a sudden sense of calamity that he could not throw off. Ginger remained in the cabin, still trying to make contact with the *Star*, while Biggles sat in the spare seat beside Algy, scanning the sea methodically, section by section, hoping to see the *Star*'s masts appear above the horizon.

Presently he glanced at the watch on the instrument board. 'She's gone,' he said, in a curiously expressionless voice.

'Begins to look like it,' admitted Algy, with fatalistic calm.

'Go on a bit farther,' Biggles told him, still hoping against hope that the *Star* had either altered her course or transmitted her position incorrectly. But when another five minutes had elapsed they knew it was no use trying to deceive themselves any longer. The *Bengal Star* had disappeared.

'Let me have her for a bit,' said Biggles, and changing places with Algy, he began to climb, at the same time turning in wide circles.

Suddenly Algy, who had opened the side window of the wind-screen and was staring down at the sapphire sea, caught Biggles's left arm with his right hand. 'What's that?' he said pointing.

Biggles, tilting the *Nemesis* over so that he could look down, followed Algy's outstretched finger. 'Wreckage, I fancy,' he said quietly, at the same time beginning to side-slip steeply towards it.

'It's wreckage, there's no doubt about that,' observed Algy, moodily, a minute later, when they were not more than a thousand feet above a number of miscellaneous objects that were floating on the surface of the tranquil sea. 'I think I can see oil stains, too. Is that a man? Look! Yes! By gosh! There's somebody there. I saw an arm wave. Down you go.'

'All right. Don't get excited. I'm going down as fast as I can,' replied Biggles, pulling the throttle right back and leaning over to see where he was going. 'We've only got to knock a hole in our hull on one of those lumps of timber to complete a really good day's work,' he added with bitter sarcasm, as he flattened out and prepared to land. 'Call Ginger to stand by to help you get him aboard,' he snapped, as the keel of the *Nemesis* kissed the water and cut a long creamy wake across its blue surface. The port engine roared, and the wake curved like a bow as the *Nemesis* swung round to come alongside the flimsy piece of timber to which the sole survivor of the ill-fated vessel was clinging.

'Look out! He's sinking!' cried Algy suddenly. 'I'll—' The sentence was cut short by his splash as he struck the water in a clumsy dive – clumsy because of the movement of the aircraft and the angle at which he had to take off to avoid a bracing strut.

He was only just in time, for the man had already disappeared beneath the water when he struck it. For a few seconds he, too, disappeared from sight; then he reappeared, catching his breath with a gasp, with the unconscious sailor in his arms. 'Quick!' he spluttered.

Ginger was already out on the wing, lying flat on his stomach, hand outstretched over the trailing edge. Still clinging to his unconscious burden, Algy seized it, and Ginger began to drag him towards the hull.

At that moment another movement caught Biggles's eye and he drew in his breath sharply. Cutting through the water towards the commotion was the black, triangular-shaped dorsal fin of a shark, the dreaded 'grey nurse' of the deep seas. He did not shout a warning, for Ginger was already doing everything in his power to get Algy into a position from where he might climb aboard, but in a flash he was out on the wing, drawing his automatic as he went. *Bang! Bang! Bang! Bang!* spat the weapon, as he opened rapid fire on the swiftly moving target. Whether he hit

He opened rapid fire on the swiftly moving target.

or not he did not know, but the killer swerved sharply and dived, showing its white belly as it flashed under the boat. Thrusting the pistol back into his pocket, he dropped on to his knees, and reaching down, caught the sailor under the armpits. 'You help Algy, Ginger,' he cried and, exerting all his strength, dragged the unconscious man aboard. The weight on the wing caused it to dip sharply, which made matters easier for Algy who, with much spluttering and grunting, pulled himself up and then rolled over on to his back, panting for breath and retching violently from the seawater he had swallowed.

He was not a moment too soon, for as he rolled over on the wing the shark swept past underneath it, so close that they could see its evil little eyes turned towards them. It passed on, but the danger was by no means over, for under the weight of the four men the wing dipped down at such an angle that they were all in danger of sliding down it into the sea. Biggles dropped on all fours and began dragging the unconscious man towards the hull. 'Come on, Algy! Come on, Ginger!' he cried desperately. 'Get aboard, or we shall tear the wing off the hull by the roots. I—' He broke off, staring at a broad crimson stain that meandered along the wing and trickled away between the ribs to the trailing edge, from where it dropped into the sea. 'Great heaven! Where's all this blood coming from?' he cried in a horror-stricken voice. Then he saw, and shuddered. The unfortunate sailor's right foot had been bitten clean off above the ankle.

Biggles's manner became peremptory. 'Ginger, go into the cabin; make it snappy,' he said curtly. 'Get out the medicine box. I want lint, iodine, a roll bandage, and a piece of cord. We shall have to get a tourniquet round that leg pretty sharp or he'll bleed to death. Algy, get into the cockpit and take off the moment I've got him inside. Make for the *Seafret* as fast as you can and land as near to her as you dare.'

Half lifting, half dragging him, he got the injured man into the cabin, where, on the floor, he applied rough but efficient first-aid. He was pale when he had finished, by which time the engines had been throttled back and the angle of the floor told him they were gliding down. He reached the cockpit just as the keel touched the water, and saw the *Seafret* standing towards them, not more than a hundred yards away. Clambering up on to the centre section as Algy switched off, he beckoned vigorously. '*Seafret* ahoy!' he roared. 'Send me a boat. Sullivan!'

The *Seafret's* commander appeared on the near side of the bridge. 'What's wrong?' he called through his megaphone.

'I've got a wounded man aboard. Tell your doctor to stand by for an amputation case.'

Quickly the two craft closed in on each other; a boat was lowered from the destroyer, and in a very short time Biggles was standing on her deck while the wounded man was lifted by many willing hands into the sick-bay.

Commander Sullivan looked at Biggles's strained face and dishevelled clothing with anxious, questioning eyes. 'Where did you pick that fellow up?' He asked.

'He's one of the crew of the *Bengal Star*,' replied Biggles quietly. 'In fact, he's the only survivor.'

The naval officer blanched. 'Good heavens!' he cried aghast. 'You mean—?'

'The *Star's* gone – sunk – sent to Davy Jones; a few sticks and this poor fellow are all that remain. We saw him in the water, but a shark took his foot off before we could get down to him. Your doctor has got to save his life so that he can tell us what happened. I expect I shall be on board for some time, so you might get your fellows to make my aircraft fast and keep an eye on her while the rest of my crew come aboard. They are wet, so they will probably want to change. Anyway, we shall have to have a conference. I'm afraid my first effort at naval co-operation has not been exactly successful.'

Algy and Ginger looked at Biggles askance as they came up the steps that had been lowered and joined him on the quarter-deck. For the first time they saw him really agitated. His face was pale, his manner almost distraught, and his hands were clenched.

'What a tragedy! What a tragedy!' he muttered, pacing up and down. 'It's my fault; I should have foreseen it.'

'That's nonsense,' put in Sullivan, a good-looking fellow in his early thirties, tapping an empty pipe on the rail thoughtfully. 'You're no more to blame than anyone else. How anyone – ah! here's the doctor. Hello, Doc, how's the patient?'

The doctor's face was grave as he hurried up to them. 'He's conscious,' he said, 'but if you want to speak to him you'd better come right away. He hasn't long, I'm afraid.'

At the last words Biggles grew white to the lips. 'Hasn't long?' he echoed. 'Why, his foot—'

'The foot's nothing; I could patch that up. But he's got a bullet through the stomach, and with the water he's swallowed that's more than I or any one else can cope with. Come on.'

'You fellows had better stay here,' Biggles told Algy and Ginger, as he turned to follow the doctor and the captain down the companion. 'It's no use making a crowd, and I can tell you afterwards what he says.'

The wounded man's eyes were on them as they walked into the sickroom.

'May I ask him a few questions, doctor?' enquired Biggles.

'Certainly; I've told him I was fetching you for that purpose.'

'What's your name, laddie?' asked Biggles in a kindly voice, noticing for the first time that he was little more than a boy.

'Ladgrove, sir.'

'Can you tell us what happened this morning? Don't hurry – just tell us quietly in your own words.'

'Yes, sir, or I'll tell you as much as I know of it,' answered the dying man in a weak voice. 'It was my watch, and I was in the bows, on look-out, when it happened. It was just before six, I should think. Everything was still and quiet, and I saw what I took to be a fish about a mile to starboard. It was still dark, or, at least, it wasn't light, and at first all I could see was phosphorescence on the water, like as if it was a shark's fin or something. Then I see a thing like a pole sticking out and I knew what it was. I didn't see no torpedo, or nothing. I'd turned round, and was just yelling "Submarine to starboard" when there was a terrific explosion amidships. I believe there was two explosions, but I ain't sure about that because the first explosion bowled me over and I 'it my 'ead a crack on the deck. As I lay there I seem to remember 'earing another explosion. If I was knocked out it couldn't 'a bin for many seconds, because when I got on me feet everything was just the same except that we'd got a bad list, and fellers were coming up from below. I see something else, too. Funny, it was. The wireless aerial was a mass of sparks, blue sparks, like lightning darting up and down. Our engines had stopped, and I could 'ear the skipper blindin' the submarine to all eternity and shouting orders.'

The wounded man paused for breath, and the doctor moistened his lips with a sponge.

'What happened after that?' asked Biggles.

'I see some fellers start gettin' into a boat, but just as they were goin' to lower away, the *Star* she gives a quick lurch and threw the fellers 'olding the ropes all of a 'eap. The rope slipped at one end and threw everybody in the boat into the sea, the boat being 'ung up by the bows, if you see what I mean. With that the ship gives another lurch and starts to go down fast by the stern. I see the bows come up clear of the water and steam come pouring out of the ports. I thought to get a lifebelt, but she was going down so fast that I daren't stay, so I jumped overboard and started swimming as 'ard as I could. I'd got about fifty or sixty yards when I saw the sub pop up not far away. I see people come out on the deck and 'eard them talking in a foreign lingo. When I turned my 'ead the *Star* had gone, but there were two boats on the water. One wasn't far away, so I give 'em a 'ail and they picks me up. I don't know who was in 'er, because just at that minute the sub opened fire on us with a machine gun.'

Biggles's nostrils twitched and he caught Sullivan's eye, while the doctor again moistened the dying man's lips.

'They fairly plastered us,' continued Ladgrove, 'and before you could say Jack Robinson the boat had sunk under us. I felt a bullet 'it me in the stomach somewhere, but it didn't 'urt much so it can't be very bad. I caught hold of an oar and 'ung on to it, and saw 'em deal with the second boat in the same way. Then for about twenty minutes they cruised round and round shooting at everyone they saw in the water. They must have shot a lot of fellers that way, the murdering swine. Every time they came near me I sunk under the oar and 'eld my breath till I thought my lungs would burst. At the finish the sub made off, so I let out a 'ail or two, but I couldn't make no one 'ear. Then it got light and

I could see that I was the only one left. I see the aeroplane coming and waved my 'and. A bit of luck it was for me and no mistake that you spotted me. I see that shark, too, while you was coming down. It had been 'anging about for some time, but I'd managed to keep it off by splashing, but suddenly the strength seemed to go out of my legs and I couldn't splash any longer. I felt the shark pull me under by the foot, and that's all I remember.'

'You've no idea what nationality the people in the submarine were, I suppose?' asked Biggles. 'I mean, you didn't recognize the type of boat or the language used by the crew?'

'No, sir, except that they seemed to be little fellows and rattled away like they might have been Japanese, or Chinese. Can I 'ave a drink, doctor?'

The doctor looked at Biggles. 'Any more questions?' he said quietly.

'Just one,' answered Biggles. 'Tell me, Ladgrove, did you happen to make a note of the course taken by the submarine when it went off?'

'Yes, sir, I can tell you that. It was due south-east. I know that because I watched it till it was out of sight, and it seemed to be going on a steady course.'

'Thanks,' nodded Biggles.

'I hope you're going ter get these blighters, sir,' called Ladgrove, as Biggles turned to follow Commander Sullivan towards the door.

'Yes, we'll get them,' smiled Biggles, and then, making his way to the deck, he stared with unseeing eyes at the blue water.

Ginger watched him curiously for a moment, and then nudged Algy in the side. 'Don't tell me the skipper's crying,' he whispered.

Algy glanced up. 'Shouldn't be surprised,' he said moodily. 'I saw him do that once before, in France. Heaven help these skunks who sunk the *Star* if ever he gets his hands on them; they'll get little mercy from him now. Better not speak to him for a bit.'

The doctor joined them on the deck.

'I suppose there's no hope for him?' asked Biggles quietly.

'He's dead,' answered the doctor shortly.

CHAPTER IV

'Reported Missing'

Half an hour later, after a hasty toilet and breakfast, they all forgathered in the captain's cabin to discuss a revised plan of campaign made necessary by the loss of the decoy ship. It was not a cheerful gathering, for the fate of the crew of the *Bengal Star*, in particular the captain and wireless operator whom they knew, weighed heavily upon them.

'Well,' began Sullivan, looking at Biggles questioningly, 'where do we go from here? I can see you're a bit upset, which is not to be wondered at, so I'll take this opportunity of saying that you can still count on me to the bitter end.'

'Thanks, Sullivan,' answered Biggles simply. 'We've started badly, but we haven't finished yet, not by a long shot. I have only one fear, and that is that the people at home will recall us when they hear what has happened. As a civilian I could ignore such an order, but not as a serving officer – and a senior one at that – as I am now.'

'You'll tell them, then?'

'We shall have to. A thing like this, involving loss of life, can't be kept secret. Naturally, the public will not be told the truth, for that would warn the enemy that his scheme is discovered; but I think we can leave that to the discretion of the Foreign Office. I expect they'll break the news gently by allowing it to be known that the *Bengal Star* is overdue, and finally report her missing, believed lost. But she hasn't been lost in vain. For the first time there is a survivor to say what happened, and give us the direction taken by the enemy craft. You'll notice they've changed their plan. Instead of sending out a false S O S they contented themselves with jamming Turrell's equipment so that he couldn't broadcast a message. You remember what Ladgrove said about sparks flying up and down the *Star*'s aerial? That would account for the terrible noise that startled your own operator. It was the submarine soaking the air with electricity. The Germans used to do that in France, to drown messages sent out by artillery co-operating machines – but that's immaterial now. The chief thing is, we know the direction taken by the submarine, which gives us a rough idea where to look for her, so the sooner we start the better. But first of all I think I shall run down to Singapore and have a word with the R.A.F. people there, to let them know we are about and that there is a chance we may need help.'

Sullivan suddenly sprang to his feet. 'By Jove! that reminds me,' he said. 'I'm sorry, but I forgot about it for the moment; I've a letter here for you.'

'A letter!'

'Yes, I picked it up at Akyab on the way down. It had been sent out by air mail, and the post office people there asked me if I had seen anything of you. They were going to forward it on to Singapore, but I told them I'd take it as I should probably be seeing you. Here it is.' He opened a drawer and passed the letter to Biggles, who raised his eyebrows wonderingly.

Tearing it open, he glanced swiftly at the signature at the end.

'Why, it's from Tom Lowery,' he cried. 'Lowery is an old friend of mine; he's a squadron leader in the R.A.F. stationed at Singapore,' he explained for the benefit of the naval officers. 'Pardon me; I'll see what he has to say.'

"My dear Biggles," he read, "This may reach you or it may not. If it doesn't there's no harm done, but having seen about your flight to Australia in the papers I thought it was worth trying. By the time you get this I shall be flying over the same ground on the way to Singapore. My leave is up, so I'm flying back the first of the new Gannet flying boats with which my squadron is to be equipped, and I thought there was a chance that we might meet somewhere. If you go straight on without trouble you'll be ahead of me, of course, but if you get hung up anywhere keep an eye open for me.

"By the way, I've been thinking about that conversation of ours at Simpson's. There's probably nothing in it, but a Chinese storekeeper in Singapore for whom I once did a good turn told me a funny yarn not long ago about something fishy going on in the Mergui Archipelago. Said something about certain people who don't like us very much having a wireless station there. I didn't pay any attention to it at the time, but lately I've been wondering if there was any connection between that and the message Ramsay picked up. Curiously enough, we were in that district when he picked up the message. Anyway, I mention it because, instead of flying straight down the coast, I shall probably fly down the Archipelago keeping an eye open for anything that's about, so if we miss each other that may be the reason. Still, we may meet at Alor or Singapore. Cheerios and all the best,

Tom."

'Have you seen or heard anything of an R.A.F. flying boat?' Biggles asked Sullivan casually. 'Tom is flying one down to Singapore.'

'No, I haven't seen anything like that,' replied Sullivan.

'Never mind. Judging by the date on the letter he'll be in Singapore by now, so no doubt I shall see him there. For the moment we've more important things to attend to. Now this is my plan. I shall fly down to Singapore today and come back tomorrow. While I am away I want you to find a quiet creek where you can hide up, on the coast, opposite the Mergui Islands.'

'Why there?'

'Because if the submarine stuck to the course it was on when Ladgrove last saw it it would make a landfall somewhere in the Archipelago. Anyway, that's where I'm going to start looking for it; and I shall go on looking while you have any petrol left. You may find it a bit dull just sitting in a creek with nothing else to do but keep me going with food and fuel, but I can't help that. Keep out of sight as far as you can; if once the enemy know you're here our task will be twice as hard. That's all. If you can make a better suggestion I shall be pleased to hear it.'

Sullivan shook his head. 'No,' he said, 'I don't think I can improve on that. Looking for a submarine from sea level in this part of the world would be like looking for a needle in a haystack, but with an aeroplane it becomes a different proposition. I have been here before, and I think I know a place where I can lie up with small chance of being seen. Here it is.' He got up and indicated a spot on the chart that lay on his table. 'If you don't get a signal from me you'll know that's where you'll find me.'

'Fine!' exclaimed Biggles, rising. 'All right, then; we'll get along to Singapore, and all being well we'll rejoin you tomorrow evening.'

The sun was sinking like a blood-red ball into the Malacca Strait when the *Nemesis* landed at Singapore, and Biggles, leaving the others in charge, wearing his new uniform for the first time, made his way to Station Headquarters, where he found a group captain in command, the air commodore being in hospital with an attack of fever. The group captain, who was still working in his office, looked at him curiously as he entered, and Biggles, rather self-conscious of his unorthodox appointment, lost no time in explaining the situation.

'My name is Bigglesworth,' he began, knowing that the other would perceive his rank by his uniform. 'You may have seen notification of my appointment in the *Gazette*, or you may have been told of it expressly by the Air Ministry.'

'Yes, I had a secret minute from the Ministry,' replied the other quickly.

'Good, then that makes things easier for me,' went on Biggles. 'No doubt you will wonder what is going on and what I am doing here. Well, I'm going to tell you. Frankly, if I obeyed my instructions to the letter, I shouldn't, but I think it's better that you should know because the knowledge will help you to silence any rumours that may get about the station. It may also help you to act with confidence and without hesitation if, in the near future, you get a message from me asking you to perform a duty so unusual that you might well be excused for hesitating, or even refusing to carry it out. Is that all clear so far?'

'Perfectly, sir,' replied the group captain, still looking at Biggles with an odd expression.

'Very well, then. This is the position. I'm on special duty. You probably know that, but what I'm going to tell you now you must never repeat except to the air commodore if he returns to duty. Somewhere in these seas an enemy submarine base has been established. Already it has sunk five British ships, three of which were carrying munitions. One, incidentally, was bringing you some new engines. I'm looking for that base, and when I find it I've got to wipe it out of existence. If I can find a way of doing that single-handed I shan't trouble you, but if I can't I shall send you a signal, and you'll have to do it for me with as many machines as you can get into the air. This is no case for half measures. You served in the war, I suppose?'

The other nodded, a light of understanding dawning in his eyes. 'Good,' continued Biggles. 'You remember the old Zone Call that we used to use to turn every gun in the line on to a certain target? If you get a Zone Call, beginning with the usual Z Z and followed by a pin-point, you'll act on it immediately. To make quite sure there is no mistake, the message will conclude with a password, which will be "Nomad". On receipt of such a signal you will put every aircraft you can into the air with a full load of bombs or torpedoes, and blot the pin-point off the face of the earth.'

'Have you any idea where it's likely to be? I only ask because I must consider the endurance range of my machines.'

'I'm not sure, but I think it will be one of the islands in the Mergui Archipelago.'

'That's a long way; I don't think we could get there and back, with war loads, without refuelling.'

'That's a matter I shall have to leave you to arrange, but in emergency you can refuel at my supply ship. It's a destroyer, the *Seafret*. Sullivan is in command, and I'll tell him to signal his position to you so that you'll know where to find him. He's got about eight thousand gallons of petrol on board which you can have with pleasure, for by the time you've done your job we shan't need it. Have I made myself perfectly clear?'

'Quite, sir.'

'Then that's that. Oh, and by the way, if it becomes necessary for me to call you out you'll have to warn all your officers about secrecy. I need hardly tell you that no one except those taking part must know what happens. I shall spend the night here and go back to Mergui in the morning. Is Tom Lowery about? I'd like a word with him.'

The group captain raised his eyebrows. 'You haven't heard, evidently,' he said quickly.

'Heard what?'

'Lowery is missing.'

Biggles stared. 'Missing!' he ejaculated.

'Well, he's four days overdue. No one has seen or heard a word of him since he left Rangoon a week ago.'

'Good heavens!'

'We've made a search for him, but I am afraid he's down. If he's down in the jungle on the mainland there is just a chance that he may turn up, but there seems to be no earthly reason why he should fly overland in a flying boat. No, I'm afraid he's down in the sea.'

Biggles looked out of the window, thinking swiftly. 'I wonder,' he breathed. Then he turned again to the group captain. 'Perhaps your mess secretary can fix us up for the night?' he suggested.

'Certainly,' replied the other promptly. 'I'll speak to him right away.'

'Good; then I'll be seeing you at dinner. Meanwhile I'll go and see my aircraft put to bed,' answered Biggles, turning to the door.

CHAPTER V

A Desperate Combat

Five days later, from twenty thousand feet, cruising on three-quarter throttle, Biggles and his companions gazed down on the sun-soaked waters of the Bay of Bengal. To their left, in the far distance, lay the palm-fringed, surf-washed beaches of Southern Burma, behind which a ridge of blue mountains marked the western boundary of Siam. To their right lay the ocean, an infinite expanse of calm blue water stretching away league after league until it merged into the sky. Below, the islands of the Mergui Archipelago lay like a necklace of emeralds dropped carelessly on a turquoise robe.

It was the fourth day of their search. Starting at the northern end of the long chain of islands, they had worked their way slowly southward, scrutinizing each island in turn, sometimes making notes of likely-looking anchorages, and sometimes taking photographs, which were developed on the *Seafret* and examined under a powerful magnifying glass. As each island was reconnoitred it was ticked off on their chart in order that they could keep a check on the ground covered, for with the number that awaited inspection it was by no means easy to commit them all to memory. Each day for eight hours they had remained in the air, but without result; and although they took it in turns to fly the machine, they were all beginning to feel the strain.

On this, the fourth day, they had seen nothing worthy of note except a junk that was moving slowly northward, leaving a feather of wake behind her on the flat surface of water to reveal that she had an auxiliary engine. Still proceeding on their way south, they reached the next island, a small one, unnamed on their chart, the first of a group of several, some large, but others no more than mere islets. Ginger was flying at the time, so Biggles and Algy were left to play the part of observers. Algy was using binoculars and, with these held firmly against his eyes, he gazed down at the irregular, tree-clad area of land which, from their altitude, looked no larger than a fair-sized wood.

Suddenly he shifted his position, readjusted the glasses, and looked again, while a puzzled expression crept over his face.

'Biggles,' he said sharply, 'can you see something – a speck of white, almost in the middle of the island?'

'Yes, but I can't make out what it is.'

'Try these.' Algy passed the glasses.

Biggles looked at the object for a long time with intense concentration. 'What did you think it was?' he asked at last, taking down the glasses.

Algy hesitated. 'The broken wing of an aeroplane,' he said. 'I thought I could just make out the ring markings on the end of it.'

'I'm inclined to think you're right,' replied Biggles quickly. 'We'd better have a closer look at this. Put her nose down, Ginger.'

Biggles studied the island inch by inch through the glasses as the machine glided down towards it, but there was no sign of life anywhere; in fact, the island was precisely the same as a hundred others they had already looked at, consisting of a few square miles of heavily timbered slopes rising to a cone-shaped hill in the centre, the seaward side ending in steep cliffs, and the inland, or mainland, side shelving down gently to numerous sandy coves and bays which suggested that the island had once formed part of the continent of Asia. For the most part the timber was the fresh green of palms, casuarina, camphorwood, and broad-leaved trees, but in several places dark patches marked the position of the mangrove swamps that are common features in tropical waters. One, larger than the rest, occupied the entire southern tip of the island.

At a little more than a thousand feet there was no longer any doubt; a crashed aeroplane was lying in the jungle about half-way between the eastern side of the island and the elevation in the middle, and the mutilated tree tops showed how tremendous had been the impact. One wing had been torn bodily from the machine and, impaled on the fractured crown of a palm, presented its broad side uppermost. But for this the wreck might have been passed over a hundred times without being seen.

Biggles now took over the control of the machine and landed smoothly in a beautiful little bay that lay at no great distance from the crash, afterwards dropping his wheels and taxiing up on to the clean, silver beach.

With firm sand under their feet they looked about them expectantly, hoping to hear or see some sign of the pilot whose accident had brought them down; but a significant silence hung over everything, and Biggles shrugged his shoulders meaningly.

'I think you'd better stay here, Ginger,' he said quietly. 'We may find something – not nice to look at. We shall have to leave a guard over the machine, anyway. Keep your eyes open and fire three quick shots if you need help, although I don't think it will be necessary. Come on, Algy.' Without another word he set off in the direction of the crash.

Before they had gone very far they found it necessary to draw the knives they carried in their belts, so thick was the undergrowth, and although it could not have been much more than a quarter of a mile to their objective, it took them nearly an hour to reach it.

At the edge of the clearing made by the falling plane they stopped, glancing furtively at each other, half fearful of what they knew they would find.

'I should say it's Tom,' said Biggles in a strained voice, pointing to the wreckage of a boat-shaped hull with the red, white, and blue ring markings of the Royal Air Force painted on it.

A cloud of flies arose into the air as they advanced again, and the details of the tragedy were soon plain to see. The pilot was still in his seat, held by the tattered remains of his safety belt, helmet askew, goggles smashed and hanging down. Biggles took one swift look at the face and then turned away, white and trembling. 'Yes,' he said, 'it's Tom.'

A second body, in air mechanic's overalls, lay a short distance away where it had been hurled clear, and Biggles pushed his way through the tangled wires, torn fabric, and splintered struts, towards it; the noise he made seemed like sacrilege, but it could not be avoided. A sharp cry brought Algy to his side, and he pointed an accusing finger at the dead man's forehead, where a little blue hole, purple at the edges, told its own grim story.

'That's a gunshot wound,' he said harshly. 'Tom was shot down. That is something I did not suspect. By heaven, if ever I get my hands on these swine they'll know about it. They're using aircraft besides submarines, evidently. Poor old Tom! Well, I suppose it comes to us all at some time or other,' he concluded heavily.

'What are we going to do? We can't leave them here like this.'

'Of course we can't, but it's no use our trying to do anything by ourselves. I feel we ought to take them to Singapore, but we can't do that without completely upsetting our arrangements. Perhaps there is really no point in it. I think we had better fetch the *Seafret* here and ask Sullivan to send a burying party ashore. Frankly, it's a task beyond me. I tell you what – you go down and join Ginger; take off, and as soon as you are in the air send a signal to Sullivan asking him to come right away. I'll stay and collect the things out of their pockets for evidence of identification, and then join you again on the beach as soon as you have got the signal off. How does that sound to you?'

Algy nodded. 'Yes, I think that's the best plan,' he said moodily. 'I imagine it has struck you that poor Tom must have gone pretty close to their headquarters – might even have spotted it – for them to shoot him down this way. I suppose he wasn't killed by a shot from the ground?'

'The bullet that killed the mechanic came out a lot lower than it went in; it could only have been fired from above.'

'Then that settles it. It's a good thing to know that the enemy have got a machine here somewhere. I'll go and get that message off to Sullivan; we'll see you on the beach presently. Don't be long; I've got a nasty feeling about this place.'

'I'm not feeling too happy about it myself,' replied Biggles as, with a nod in answer to Algy's wave, he set about his gruesome task.

Some time later, after he had recovered all the things from the dead airmen's pockets, he made them up into neat bundles in their handkerchiefs with the log books and maps that he had found in the wreck. He heard the engines of the *Nemesis* start up, and, subconsciously, heard the machine take off; and half regretting the necessity for sending it into the air simply in order to use its radio, he was in the act of covering the bodies with as much loose fabric as he could find when he heard another sound, one that caused him to spring to his feet and stare upwards in alarm. Above the subdued hum of the 'Kestrel' engines came the sound of another, and the scream of wind-torn wings and wires that told a story of terrific speed.

He saw the *Nemesis* at once, climbing seaward on a steady course, just having taken off and clearly unaware of its danger. Behind it, dropping out of the eye of the sun like a winged bullet, was another aircraft, a small single-seat seaplane not unlike the Supermarine of Schneider Trophy fame, painted red.

Breathless, he stood quite still and watched. There was nothing he could do … absolutely nothing. Except watch. And as he watched he realized that the end was a foregone conclusion, for the *Nemesis*, flying serenely on, was a mark that not even a novice at the game could miss.

In a sort of numb stupor he watched the pilot of the seaplane half pull out of his dive, swing round on the tail of the amphibian, and align his sights on the target. Indeed, so intense was the moment that he could almost *feel* him doing it.

At that particular instant the amphibian turned. It was only a slight movement, but it was enough to disconcert the pilot of the seaplane, who, at the same time, opened fire.

Biggles felt a cold perspiration break out on his face as the *Nemesis* swerved sickeningly. Whether or not the movement was accidental or deliberate he did not know, but when he saw the nose soar skyward and the machine swing round in a tight Immelmann turn, he knew that whoever was at the controls had not been hit, for the manoeuvre was one that could only be performed by a machine under perfect control.

Again the seaplane fired, and again the amphibian twisted like a snipe as the pilot strove to spoil the other's aim. And for a moment it seemed to Biggles that he succeeded, although he knew quite well that such an unequal combat could not be prolonged. 'Go down!' he roared, well aware of the futility of speech but unable to control himself any longer, for his one concern at this stage was that Algy and Ginger might save their lives regardless of anything else.

From the behaviour of the *Nemesis* it almost seemed as if the pilot had heard him, for both engines stopped and, with propellers stationary, the machine began to zigzag back towards the land, at the same time side-slipping, first to left and then to right, in order to lose height. The seaplane was round after it in a flash, little tongues of orange flame flickering from the concealed guns in its engine cowling, and streams of tracer bullets cutting white pencil lines across the blue.

With a wild swerve, and with the seaplane in close attendance, the *Nemesis* disappeared from sight behind the high ridge of trees on Biggles's right, so that he could only stand and listen for the sound he dreaded to hear. He clenched his teeth as the harsh, staccato chatter of a machine-gun palpitated through the still air. It was maintained for several seconds, and then followed a screaming wail that was cut short by a crash like that made by a giant tree when it falls in a forest. Then silence. Absolute silence.

In an agony of suspense Biggles waited for one of the machines to reappear; but he waited in vain. The echoes of the combat died away; the parrots that had circled high in the air in alarm at the unusual spectacle returned to their perches, and once more the languorous silence of the tropics settled over the scene.

Biggles had no recollection of how long he stood staring at the ridge of trees, but suddenly he seemed to come to his senses. Throwing the things he had collected into a heap, regardless of stings, tears, and scratches, he set off at a wild run in the direction of the hill behind which the machines had disappeared.

CHAPTER VI

Jungle-Bound

In spite of their recently acquired knowledge that a hostile aircraft was, or had been, in the vicinity, nothing was farther from Algy's thoughts as he pushed forward the master-throttle of the *Nemesis* and soared into the air. As a matter of detail, he was not even thinking of the message they were to send, but of the dead men who lay on the hill-side.

Ginger, having already worked out the position of the island, was inside the cabin letting out the aerial, at the same time carefully forming in his mind the context of the signal he was about to send.

He had tapped out the call sign, thrice repeated, and his position, and was about to follow with the rest of the message when, without the slightest warning, the whole apparatus blew up, or so it seemed to him. There was a tremendous crash and, simultaneously, a sheet of electric blue flame flashed before his eyes with a vicious crackling noise, while a smell of scorching filled his nostrils. Temporarily half-stunned with shock, he staggered up from the floor where he had fallen and tore the headphones from his ringing ears, only to be thrown down again as the machine heeled over in a vertical bank. As he clambered to his feet again a conviction took form in his mind that the aircraft had been struck by lightning, throwing it out of control, and he swayed through to the cockpit fully prepared to find Algy unconscious.

To his astonishment he found him very much alive, crouching forward, but looking back over his shoulder with a terrible expression on his face. At the same time, above the hum of the engines, Ginger heard for the first time the unmistakable *taca-taca-taca-taca* of a machine-gun and, looking back over the tail, saw the seaplane.

Such was his surprise that for several seconds he could only stare at it unbelievingly; but then, his brain at last taking in the full extent of the danger, he turned and ran back into the cabin in order to get their own machine-gun from the locker in which it was kept. Ran is perhaps not quite the right word, for it is impossible to do anything but roll in a machine that stands first on its nose and then on its tail. However, he managed to get to the armament locker, and to it he clung with a tenacity of despair while the *Nemesis* performed such evolutions that he became convinced it could only be a matter of seconds before she broke up. The thing that worried him most was whether or not Algy had been hit. From time to time he could still hear the rattle of the seaplane's machine-gun, and the sound seemed to drive him to distraction. Bracing himself against the side of the hull, in a passion of fury he flung open the locker and dragged out the gun. Seizing a drum of ammunition, he clamped it on and, at imminent risk of shooting his own pilot, he staggered through into the cockpit in order to get into the open.

He knew without looking that the *Nemesis* was going down; the angle of the floor told him that; but he was not concerned with it. At that moment he was concerned with one thing, and one thing only, and that was the destruction of their attacker, the man who, he guessed, must have been responsible for the death of Tom Lowery and his mechanic. He felt no fear; he felt nothing but an overwhelming desire to destroy the man who was shooting at them; he wanted to do that more than he had ever wanted to do anything in his life before. After that, he wouldn't care what happened.

Actually, although he was unaware of it, his reactions were precisely those of scores of air fighters in France during the war; and they were the reactions by which those fighters could only hope to achieve success, or even save their lives, for in air combat it is a case of kill or be killed.

Vaguely he saw the trees rushing up to meet them, was dimly aware that the engines had stopped. But neither of these things meant anything to him. He did not even hear Algy's frantic yell of 'Be careful!' With a fixed purpose in his mind, he scrambled up the back of the cockpit until he was standing on the hull just behind it, with the machine-gun resting on the main spar of the top plane. He saw the seaplane sweeping down over their tail; saw the pilot's helmeted head looking out over the side of his cockpit as he measured his distance; saw his head bob back and knew that he was squinting through his sights; knew that if he was allowed to fire at such point-blank range it would be the end.

As he glanced along the blue barrel of the gun a feeling of power swept over him, bringing with it a wonderful sense of satisfaction. Coolly and deliberately he trained the muzzle on the pointed nose of the other machine. His finger crooked round the trigger, pressed it down and held it down.

Instantly a stream of glowing white-hot sparks appeared.

They seemed to form a chain, connecting the two machines. In a curious, detached sort of way he saw the drum slowly revolving, in funny little jerks, while his ears were filled with a harsh metallic clatter and his nostrils with the acrid reek of burning cordite. The gun quivered like a live thing in his hands, but still he clung to it, his left hand clutching the spade-grip and his right forefinger curled round the trigger.

Suddenly the gun stopped moving; the noise ceased abruptly, and he looked at it reproachfully, unaware that he had emptied the entire drum. Looking back at the seaplane, he saw that it was behaving in an extraordinary manner. Its nose was dipping down – down – down, until it was nearly vertical. Why didn't the pilot pull out? The fool, he'd be in the trees ...

'Ah!' Unconsciously he winced as the seaplane struck the trees and instantly seemed to dissolve in a cloud of flying splinters. The terrible noise of the crash came floating up to him, and he looked at Algy oddly, feeling suddenly queer. For one dreadful moment he thought he was going to faint, but the feeling passed, and again he tried to catch Algy's eye. But Algy, he saw, was not taking the slightest notice of him, or the crash. He was levelling out over a stretch of black, oily water, surrounded on all sides by trees with which he felt sure they would presently collide.

For a few seconds it was touch and go, and Algy only saved the machine by a swerve, before it had finished its run, that nearly sent Ginger overboard. Then, in some curious way, the *Nemesis* was floating motionless on its own inverted image, while little ripples ruffled the water and disappeared under the dark trees that lined the water's edge.

'Good shooting, kid,' said Algy, looking up at Ginger and smiling in a peculiar, strained sort of manner.

'I got him, didn't I?' muttered Ginger, as if he still had difficulty in believing it.

'You can write number one on your slate just as soon as you get back to where you can buy yourself one,' answered Algy, standing up and looking around. 'Did you get that message off, that's what I want to know?'

'No, I only got the call sign and our position out when a bullet knocked the instrument to smithereens.'

Algy grimaced. 'Do you mean to say that our wireless is smashed?'

'It's in so many pieces that it would need a magician, not an electrician, to put 'em together again,' declared Ginger. 'Why did you come down?'

'For two very good reasons,' Algy told him shortly, still taking stock of their surroundings. 'In the first place I wanted to, and in the second I couldn't help it. I don't know what's happened, but a bullet must have hit something vital. Both engines cut out together. I switched over to gravity but there was nothing doing, so I made for the only stretch of water within reach that was big enough to land on. I'd have got back to the sea if I could, but I hadn't enough height. Poor old Biggles will be in a stew, I'll bet; he must have seen the whole thing.'

'He'll be on his way here by now,' announced Ginger firmly.

'No doubt he'll try to get here, but from what I can see of it, it isn't going to be too easy,' murmured Algy anxiously. 'It looks to me as if we're in the middle of that big mangrove swamp at the end of the island, and there isn't a way out to the sea; I noticed that from the air before I put her down.'

'How are we going to get out?'

'I don't think we ever shall unless we can fix things up and fly her out. I wonder if we can make Biggles hear us? Let's try a hail.' Cupping his hands round his mouth Algy yelled 'Biggles' two or three times, but the only answer was the screech of startled parrots and parakeets that rose into the air from the surrounding trees voicing their indignation at the intrusion.

'Nothing doing,' said Ginger, and resting his hands on the edge of the cockpit he regarded the boundaries of the watery glade with interest not unmixed with apprehension.

On all sides the sombre mangroves lifted their gnarled trunks on fantastic, stilt-like roots from the black waters and slime of the swamp from which, here and there, sprang rank growths of orchids and other exotic flowers, the only spots of colour in a world of desolation and decay. Except for an occasional humming-bird, or butterfly of gigantic size, nothing moved. Even the air, heavy with the stench of corruption, was still, and endowed the place with an atmosphere of sinister foreboding.

Ginger shivered suddenly. 'I don't think much of this place,' he said. 'I should say it's rotten with fever.'

'There will probably be a mosquito or two about when the sun goes down,' opined Algy. 'Well, looking at it won't get us anywhere; let's see if we can get the engines going.'

It did not take them very long to locate the damage. The gravity tank had been holed, and the petrol lead that fed both engines from the main tank had been severed in two places by bullets. Several had struck the machine, but as far as they could ascertain nothing else was damaged except the wireless gear, which was completely wrecked.

'Can you put it right, do you think?' asked Algy, looking at Ginger, who was examining the fractures with professional eye.

'Yes, but it will take some time to make an air-worthy job of it.

I could make a temporary job with tape, but I don't think we'd better risk it; if the vibration shook the join apart again just as we were taking off over the trees it would put the tin hat on the whole caboodle. The same applies to the gravity tank. Much better do the thing properly. Lucky you turned off the petrol when you did, or we should have lost all our juice.'

'Lucky! You don't flatter me, do you? That was common sense. As soon as I smelt petrol I couldn't turn it off, or the ignition, fast enough. I was afraid the main tank had gone, and the thought of fire put the wind up me. How long will it take to mend those holes?'

Ginger glanced at the sun, now sinking fast behind the tree tops. 'I shan't get it finished in time to get out of here tonight,' he said frankly. 'Personally, I don't mind that; it's the thought of Biggles dashing about not knowing what has happened to us that upsets me. I wonder if it's possible to get out of this swamp on foot? I can see one or two places where the ground seems fairly firm. What with that, and by clambering over the roots of these foul-looking trees, one might be able to make terra firma.'

'How can we reach the trees?'

'Oh, we can easily fix up some sort of paddle or punt pole. I wonder how deep the water is?'

A quick examination revealed that the stagnant water on which the *Nemesis* floated was not more than three feet deep. By splitting the cover of the armament locker and binding the ends together, they soon had a makeshift punt-pole, flimsy it is true, but quite sufficient to cause the lightly borne amphibian to move slowly in any desired direction; and as Algy poled carefully towards that side of the swamp nearest the place where they had left Biggles, Ginger got out his emergency repair outfit and prepared to mend the fractured parts.

'I tell you what,' said Algy suddenly, as the *Nemesis* grounded gently on the mud in the shade of the trees. 'How does this idea strike you? I can't do much in the way of helping you and, as you're going to be some time, suppose I work my way to solid ground and look for Biggles? With luck I might be able to do that and bring him back here – either that or we could fetch you and spend the night on the beach.'

'I think it's a good scheme,' agreed Ginger. 'Whatever else we do, I think we ought to make a big effort to let Biggles know how things stand. But be careful what you're doing in that swamp; it wouldn't be a healthy place to get stuck in. If the going gets difficult you'd better come back rather than take any risks.'

'I think I can manage it,' replied Algy confidently, crawling along the wing and letting himself down carefully on the twisted roots of the nearest tree, regardless of the clamour set up by a number of monkeys that were catching their evening meal of crabs and limpets a little farther along.

'Got your gun?' asked Ginger, watching him rather doubtfully.

Algy tapped his pocket and nodded. 'I don't think I shall need it, though,' he said cheerfully. 'It can't be more than a couple of hundred yards to dry land.'

'I should say it's nearer a quarter of a mile the way you're going,' argued Ginger, as he turned to go on with his work.

For a little while he glanced occasionally into the swamp where Algy was slowly picking his way over the roots, but after he had disappeared from sight he became engrossed in his task and concentrated on it to the exclusion of everything else.

In such circumstances time passes quickly, and almost before he was prepared for it he became conscious that darkness was falling. Looking up with a start he saw that a thin miasma of mist was rising slowly from the silent water about him and, leaving his work, he leaned over the side of the hull, peering in the direction in which Algy had disappeared. As he did so he became aware of something else, although at first he could not make out what it was. Somehow the scenery seemed to have changed. Then he saw, and drew in his breath quickly with a little gasp of consternation. There was no longer any land visible, nor any of the tentacle-like roots. It was as if the whole forest had sunk several feet, allowing the oily water to creep up the trunks; so much so that the branches of the nearest tree, instead of being several feet above the wing as they had been, were actually brushing it.

Then, with a flash of understanding, he perceived what had happened, and wondered why he had not anticipated it. The tide had come in, raising the level of the water several feet.

'Algy!' he cried loudly, in a sudden panic as he realized what the result might be if Algy had not succeeded in reaching the far side of the swamp. 'Algy!' His voice echoed eerily away among the trees.

There was no reply.

For some minutes he stood staring into the gathering darkness wondering if there was anything he could do; then, with a little gesture of helplessness, he picked up his tools and carried them through into the cabin.

CHAPTER VII

A Terrible Night

Algy had not covered a third of the distance that separated him from dry land when he became aware of the flowing tide, although at first he did not recognize it as such and, as footholds and handholds became more difficult to find, he merely thought that he had struck a difficult part of the swamp, possibly a more low-lying area than the earlier part. But when he noticed suddenly that the turgid water was flowing steadily past him, gurgling and sucking amongst the hollows in the roots, he realized just what was happening. Even so he was not particularly alarmed, although he was certainly annoyed, knowing that his task would not be made easier by the new conditions.

But when shortly afterwards he saw that he could get no farther in the direction in which he was heading and, stopping to look about him, saw that his retreat was completely cut off, he experienced a pang of real fear, for he needed no one to tell him that a mangrove swamp is no place in which to be benighted.

For a while he scrambled desperately, often dangerously, from branch to branch after the manner of the renowned Tarzan of the Apes, but he quickly discovered that this method of progress was much easier to imagine than put into practice, as the palms of his hands testified. To make matters worse, he knew that he had been clambering about regardless of which way he went, taking advantage of any handhold that offered itself; and now, sitting astride a fork to contemplate his predicament, he was compelled reluctantly to admit to himself that he had completely lost all sense of direction.

On all sides stretched the morass. Above, a gloomy tangle of interlaced branches, fantastic, bewildering; below, the sullen water, as black as ink in the fast failing light except where grey, spectral wraiths of mist were beginning to form and creep silently over the surface. All was still. The only sounds were the soft, sinister gurgle of the questing water, and the ever-increasing hum of countless myriads of mosquitoes that took wing at the approach of night. The heat was intense. Not the fierce, dry heat of the midday sun, but a clammy oppressive-ness that clung to the skin and made breathing difficult. Every now and then strange, foreign smells tainted the stagnant air: sometimes the noisome stench of corruption, and sometimes a perfume of glorious fragrance that seemed strangely out of place in such a setting.

He stirred uneasily, and in spite of the heat a cold shiver ran down his spine.

'Hi! Ginger!' he called, in something like a panic, and then waited tensely for an answer. But none came. 'Ginger!' he yelled again, but the only reply was the mocking screech of a monkey.

Looking down, he noticed that the water was still rising, for when he had lodged himself in the fork his shoes had been a good three feet above the level of the water, but now he saw with renewed misgivings that they were almost touching the surface. And presently, as he gazed downward with worried eyes wondering if he should climb higher, he became aware of a broad V-shaped ripple that was surging through the water towards him, and for a few seconds he watched it curiously, trying to make out what was causing it. Straight towards the trunk of the tree it swept, and only at the last moment did a purely instinctive fear make him jerk both his legs clear of the water.

He was only just in time, for as he did so a long black object broke the surface and rose clear. There was a rush, a violent swirl, and then a crash like the slamming of an iron gate as the crocodile's jaws came together.

A cry of stark terror broke from Algy's lips as he scrambled frantically to a higher branch. Reaching one that promised to bear his weight, he looked down, but all was quiet again and still, except for a ring of tiny wavelets that circled away from the trunk of his tree and lost themselves in the gloom.

With every nerve tense, his heart thumping like a piston and perspiration pouring down his face, he again examined his surroundings for a possible way of escape; but with the water still rising matters were getting worse instead of better, and a few minutes' investigation proved to him beyond all doubt that, far from finding a way out of the swamp, he could not even leave the tree in which he was precariously perched. Swimming was, of course, out of the question, and as if in confirmation of his decision in this respect a huge water-snake, its head held erect like a periscope and its forked tongue flicking, went sailing past. He watched it out of sight, shuddering.

By this time it was practically dark and, abandoning all hope of getting clear until the tide went down, he was making himself as secure as possible on his perch when his hands, which were gripping the branch, felt suddenly as if hundreds of tiny pins

A long black object broke the surface and rose clear.

were being stuck into them. Striking a match as quickly as his trembling fingers would permit, for the strain of his position was beginning to tell, he saw at once the reason: they were covered with thousands of the minute ants which, although he did not know it, were the dreaded *Semut apis*, the fire-ants of the Malay Peninsula. His lips went dry when, in the yellow glow of the match, he saw that the branch on which he sat was swarming with them; worse still, as far as he could see the whole tree was alive with them.

What to do he did not know: he was beginning to find it difficult even to think coherently. To stay in the tree and be eaten alive was obviously out of the question, yet to enter the domain of the horrors in the water was equally unthinkable. The burning in his hands ran swiftly up his arms and, driven to desperation by the irritation, he began to beat his arms against his sides in the hope of dislodging at least some of his undesirable tenants; but the only result was to bring down a shower of them from the branches above on to his head and neck.

Instinctively he started backing along the branch away from the trunk, which seemed to be the headquarters of the fiery army, but an ominous creak warned him that he was testing it nearly to the limit of its endurance. With his heart in his mouth, as the saying is, he began to work his way back again, but what with the irritants on his skin, the darkness, and haste, he missed his hold and slipped. He made a frenzied clutch at the sagging branch to save himself, but almost before he knew what was happening he found himself hanging at the full length of his arms with his feet only a few inches above the water. He could hear the branch creaking under his weight and, knowing that it would not support him for many more seconds, he strove with a determination born of despair to pull himself up again, performing extraordinary gymnastics with his legs as he tried to hook them round the branch in order to take some of the weight from his arms; but it was a feat beyond his strength, for the branch sagged lower and lower and eluded his ever groping legs.

The creaking became a definite crackle and, perceiving beyond all doubt what must happen within the next few seconds, he let out a yell of fear. It was still ringing in his ears when, with a loud crack, the branch broke off short, and the next moment, with a mighty splash, he, the branch, and the ants disappeared under the water.

He was up again in an instant, blowing and gasping, and with his toes curling with horror he struck out madly for the nearest tree. He could not have been more than a quarter of a minute reaching it, but to his distorted imagination it seemed like eternity and, clutching the rough bole in his arms, he went up it in a manner that would have been impossible in cold blood. Grabbing at a bough, he pulled himself on to it and, throwing a leg over it where it joined the trunk, he sagged limply, panting for breath, watching as in a nightmare the water dripping from him into the black stream below.

By this time he had reached that degree of misery that knows neither pain nor fear, a lamentable condition in which death appears as a welcome release; and it may have been due to this that at first he regarded a vague black shadow that appeared suddenly on the water a few yards away without any particular emotion. But as he watched it, knowing that although he could not see them two cold eyes were watching him too, a bitter hatred slowly took possession of him and of it a new idea was born. He remembered something. Feeling in his soaking pocket, he took out his automatic and, taking careful aim, pulled the trigger. *Bang! Bang! Bang!* Three times the weapon roared.

With a convulsive swirl the crocodile half threw itself out of the water, plunged back, and then disappeared from sight.

'Hold that lot, you ugly swine,' he growled viciously, as he stared down at the turmoil below him.

'Here, be careful what you're doing with that gun,' called a voice near at hand.

In his astonishment Algy nearly fell into the water again, but as he recognized the voice a little cry of relief broke from his lips. Peering into the darkness, he could just make out a queer-shaped mass moving smoothly over the oily surface of the water towards him. 'Hi! Biggles' he called joyfully.

'Where the dickens are you?' came Biggles's voice.

'Here – up a tree,' answered Algy. 'What on earth are you in – a boat?'

'I'm not swimming, you can bet your life on that,' returned Biggles tersely. 'A lot of very nasty people use this place as a bathing pool, as you may have noticed. What in the name of goodness are you doing up there?' he concluded, as he drew up underneath.

'What do you suppose?' replied Algy shortly. 'I'm not practising a trapeze act or anything like that.'

'It looks uncommonly like it,' grinned Biggles, as Algy lowered himself down into the boat. 'Hey! Go steady; this isn't a barge,' he went on quickly, clutching at the sides of the frail craft as Algy let go his hold. 'What's happened to Ginger? Where is he?'

'The last time I saw him he was in the machine, nailing up holes in the petrol tank,' answered Algy wearily.

'What machine?'

'Our machine, of course.'

Biggles stared. 'But I thought I heard it crash,' he muttered incredulously. 'I've been looking for the wreck ever since.'

'It was the other fellow who crashed, not us. Ginger fairly plastered him with a whole drum of ammo from about ten yards' range.'

'Where did he crash?'

'Somewhere over the other side of this swamp, which is about the nearest thing to hell that I've ever struck. Did you ever see such a foul place in your life? There's a sort of lake in the middle of it, and I managed to get the *Nemesis* down on it. By the way, where the dickens did you get this conveyance? It feels kind of soft for a boat.'

'It's the collapsible rubber canoe out of poor Tom's crash,' replied Biggles. 'After running about for hours like a lunatic looking for a way into this confounded bog, I suddenly had a brainwave and remembered that nearly all big service marine aircraft now carry collapsible boats. I went back and looked for it and there it was, although there were two or three bullet holes through it which I had to mend. It isn't too safe now, but it's better than nothing. Is the machine badly damaged?'

'No. I had a petrol lead shot away, so I had to get down as best I could and where I could. The only place was the lake I mentioned just now. Then, knowing you'd be worried, I set off to look for you while Ginger did the repairs, but I got marooned in this tree by the tide. Where were you bound for when you came along this way?'

'I was looking for you,' answered Biggles, 'although I don't mind admitting that I was lost to the world. The whole place looks alike, and I fancy I had been going round in circles when I heard you singing—'

'Singing my foot!' interrupted Algy indignantly. 'I was yelling with fright.'

'Well, it was easy enough to make the mistake,' protested Biggles, grinning. 'But let's try and get out of this. I'm not particular, but this strikes me as being neither the time nor place for a picnic. In which direction is this lake of yours?'

'I haven't the remotest idea.'

'Then we'd better set about looking for it. Hark! That sounds like Ginger,' went on Biggles quickly, as a revolver shot split the silence. 'He must have heard your shots and is trying to let you know where he is. From which direction do you think the sound came?'

'Over there.' Algy pointed vaguely into the darkness.

'I thought so, too,' declared Biggles, urging the tiny craft forward with its small paddle. 'We'll try it, anyway. Fire another shot and keep your eyes open for an answering flash. We ought to be able to see it in this darkness.'

Algy pointed the muzzle of his automatic skywards and pulled the trigger, only to cower down as a pandemonium of shrieks and barks instantly broke out over his head. 'What in the name of thunder is that?' he gasped.

'It sounds as if some of your pals up in the trees thought you were shooting at them,' murmured Biggles, moving the boat forward again as a flash showed momentarily through the trees some distance away, to be followed by another report.

After that it was only a question of time while they sought a way through the labyrinth of branches before they reached the open stretch of water on which the *Nemesis* rested; in the starlight they could see Ginger's silhouette standing erect in the cockpit, looking towards the trees. He let out a hail when he saw them.

'You've been a long time,' he observed, looking at Algy reproachfully as they drew alongside. 'I began to think you weren't coming back.'

'Curiously enough, I was thinking the same thing not long ago,' Algy told him meaningly as he climbed aboard.

'Never mind about that. We're here now, and that's all that matters,' murmured Biggles philosophically. 'Open up some of the emergency rations, Ginger, and let's have a bite of food. After that I think a spot of shut-eye is indicated. We shall have to be on the move as soon as it's daylight. If that fellow you shot down has any friends about they'll be looking for him bright and early. Besides, I want to find out where he came from.'

CHAPTER VIII

Shadows on the Shore

'Whereabouts did the seaplane hit the ground, Ginger?' asked Biggles, shortly after dawn the following morning as, standing on the hull, he sponged himself down briskly from a bucket of cold water. They had already discussed the details of the combat.

Ginger, who was putting the finishing touches to the fractured petrol lead, pointed to an adjacent tree-covered slope that rose just beyond the irregular outline of the mangroves. 'Somewhere over there,' he said. 'Why? Are you thinking of going to it?'

'I don't know yet,' replied Biggles thoughtfully, drying himself on a well-worn strip of towel. 'The first thing I want to do is to get out of this place and find the *Seafret*; it's bad, this being out of touch, although you were lucky to send her our position before that fellow in the seaplane shot your instrument to pieces; still, Sullivan will wonder what the deuce has happened to us. When we find her, if we do, I may go and examine what's left of the seaplane while his sailors are ashore burying poor Tom and his mechanic – that is, provided the place isn't too difficult to reach. I ought to have a shot at it, anyway, because it may furnish us with some important information.'

'Such as?' inquired Algy, who was anointing his ant-bites with boracic ointment from the medicine chest.

'Well, it would be something to know for certain the nationality of the people we're up against, wouldn't it?'

'By jingo, it would! I never thought of that,' confessed Algy. 'What do you suppose his people will think when he fails to return?'

'I don't care two hoots what they think. I only hope they didn't hear the shooting or see anything of the combat yesterday.'

Algy glanced back over his shoulder to where Biggles was standing watching Ginger at work. 'Good gracious! Do you think they may be as close as that?' he asked quickly.

'I don't think they can be very far away or surely there would have been no point in their shooting down Tom's machine. What I should very much like to know is whether the fellow in the seaplane spotted us flying around from his base on the ground, and came out deliberately to get us, or whether he was merely cruising about and lighted on us by accident.'

'He may have been searching for Tom's crash,' suggested Ginger.

'That isn't at all unlikely,' agreed Biggles, 'although had that been the case one would have thought that he would have been flying very low, instead of high up, as he must have been or we should have heard him before we did.'

'I suppose it is also possible that he was sitting high up over his base, doing a sort of aerodrome patrol as a routine job, on the look-out for strange ships or aircraft, when he saw us a long way off,' went on Ginger thoughtfully.

'Quite possible,' agreed Biggles readily. 'He may have been doing that when he spotted Tom.'

'I fancy Tom must have been pretty close to their base – might even have spotted it – or surely they wouldn't have killed him.'

'Oh, I wouldn't stake too much on that,' declared Biggles. 'After all, there was no reason why he shouldn't be shot down. He was an enemy, assuming that all British subjects are regarded as enemies by these people, as presumably they are; and don't forget that there was little or no risk of discovery. Tom's machine wasn't fitted with guns; I know that because I looked particularly to see. No doubt the guns would have been put on the machine when he got to Singapore. The seaplane pilot probably guessed he would be unarmed, as there is no war on, and that being so his task would be easy. In fact, Tom would merely provide him with a useful bit of target practice, quite apart from enabling him to destroy another piece of British property. If these skunks are out to sink British ships, there doesn't seem to be any reason why they shouldn't be equally glad to smash up British aircraft. But there, what's the use of guessing? Tom's dead, and the fellow who killed him is dead, or it looks that way to me, so neither of them can tell us anything. I suppose there's no doubt about the fellow in the seaplane being killed, Algy?'

'None whatever,' declared Algy emphatically. 'I saw him hit the carpet and I never saw a worse crash. The kite went to pieces like a sheet of wet tissue-paper in a gale.'

'I see,' replied Biggles. 'All right. If you fellows are through we'll see about getting away. There isn't a dickens of a lot of room. Have you finished, Ginger?'

'Yes, I think she's O.K. now,' answered Ginger, stepping down into the cockpit and turning on the petrol. 'We can test her, anyway. I've put some juice into the gravity tank; it isn't full, but there's sufficient to take us out of this place if the main tank doesn't function.'

Decks were quickly cleared; small kit and tools were stowed

away and everything made ship-shape for departure. Biggles took his place at the joystick with Algy beside him, while Ginger watched proceedings from the cabin door.

'I hope she'll unstick,' muttered Biggles anxiously, as he twirled the self-starter, and smiled his relief as both engines came to life at the first attempt.

Twice he taxied the full length of the lagoon, both to ascertain that the engines were giving their full revolutions and to make sure that there were no partly submerged obstacles in the way; and then, satisfied that all was well, he turned the machine round facing the longest run possible for the take-off.

With a muffled roar that sent a cloud of birds wheeling high into the air with fright, the amphibian sped across the placid water, leaving a churning wake of foam to mark her passage. With a normally powered machine it is likely that the take-off would have ended in disaster, for the *Nemesis* was loath to leave the water; but the extra horses under the engine cowling saved them, and, although they had very little room to spare, they cleared the trees, whereupon Biggles at once swung round towards the open sea.

The first thing they saw was the *Seafret*, cruising along near the shore at half speed, apparently looking for them. There was a bustle on her decks as the aircraft climbed into view, and as he swept low over her Biggles saw her commander wave to him from the bridge. There was no point in prolonging the flight, so he throttled back and glided into the little bay they had used on the previous day, and there, a few minutes later, the *Seafret* joined them and dropped her anchor.

'What the deuce are you fellows playing at?' roared Sullivan, half angrily, as he ran alongside.

'Send us a boat and I'll tell you,' grinned Biggles.

A boat was quickly lowered, and the three airmen, after making the amphibian fast to the destroyer, joined the naval officer on the quarter-deck.

Sullivan looked at them curiously. 'What's been going on?' he asked. 'We got the call signal, and your position, but that was all,' he declared. 'Since then we haven't been able to get a word out of you, so we concluded you were down somewhere, either in the sea or on one of the islands.'

'We were,' Biggles told him. 'Not that it would have made much difference if we'd been in the air.'

'Why not?'

'Because our wireless equipment is a nasty-looking heap of bits and pieces.'

Sullivan stared. 'How did you manage that?' he asked.

'*We* didn't manage it,' answered Biggles grimly. 'It was managed for us by a packet of bullets fired by a dirty skunk in a seaplane. Listen, and I'll tell you what happened, although we've no time to spare: there are several things we shall have to do before we leave, and I have a feeling that we're by no means safe here. We are close to the enemy stronghold, or my calculations are all at sea.' Briefly, he described how they had found the flying boat and its dead crew and how, while calling up the destroyer for assistance, they themselves had been shot down.

'It looks as if things are getting warm,' muttered Sullivan when he had finished.

'Warmish,' agreed Biggles, 'but they'll be warmer still presently, I fancy.'

'What's your programme; have you made one?'

'More or less. First of all, I want you to send a party ashore to bury poor Tom Lowery and his gunner. Get a report from the petty officer in charge to accompany mine to headquarters. He will find their personal effects lying near the crash where I dropped them when the *Nemesis* was attacked. They will be needed for the Court of Adjustment which I expect will be held at Singapore. While that's going on I want a couple of strong fellows, with cutlasses or billhooks, to help me find the seaplane. We may discover something important either in the machine or on the body of the pilot – maps – log-books – orders – you never know. As soon as we've done that you'd better push off back to the mainland out of harm's way while we get on with the job of finding the base. We shan't have far to look, if I know anything about it. It's going to be a bit awkward without wireless, but we shall have to manage without it for the time being.'

Biggles turned to Ginger. 'While I'm ashore, if Algy goes with the party to Tom's crash, as I hope he will, I shall leave you in charge of the machine. If by any chance you are attacked by another aircraft, run her up on to the beach and try to keep the fellow off with your gun until I get back. Don't attempt to take off. It's no use taking on a single-seater while you're by yourself in a machine of this size. Is that clear?'

'Quite, sir,' replied Ginger smartly, conscious of his responsibility, and that several pairs of curious eyes were on him.

A day of activity followed. It began with the destroyer's boat taking two parties ashore. The first consisted of Algy with a dozen bluejackets[1] equipped with picks and shovels, to whom had been allotted the dismal task of burying the two dead British airmen and collecting their effects. The second was smaller, being composed only of Biggles and two sailors who were to help him to

[1] R.A.F. slang for sailor.

cut a way through the dense jungle to the hill-side on which the enemy seaplane had fallen.

Ginger spent rather a lonely day, but he utilized the time by going over the *Nemesis* very carefully, examining the controls and other parts where the hard wear to which the machine had been subjected might be beginning to show. Later, in the afternoon, he refuelled from the *Seafret*'s store, a task he was just completing when a sharp gust of wind caused the *Nemesis* to yaw violently and send his eyes skyward. What he saw brought a slight frown to his forehead, and he finished his task hurriedly; but before he could return to the *Seafret* a hail made him look up, and he saw Lovell, the Navigating Officer, looking over the rail.

'What do you make of this breeze?' he asked with a hint of anxiety in his voice.

'That's what I've come to tell you,' replied the naval officer. 'The barometer's falling; not much, but it looks as if we might be in for some weather. The skipper says it's the tail end of a big blow centred somewhere near the Philippines, but for an hour or two it's likely to get worse instead of better. What are you going to do?'

Ginger thought sharply. 'I think I'd better run the *Nemesis* up on the beach,' he answered. 'She'll be safe enough there. If I stay here and a sea gets up she may smash her wing-tips to splinters against your side. No, I'll get her ashore. Biggles can't be much longer, anyway, and if he'd rather she rode it out on the water he can tell me to bring her back when he comes down to the beach.'

'Hadn't you better take a man with you in case you need help?' suggested Lovell.

'Thanks! I think that's a sound idea,' agreed Ginger. 'If the wind freshens I may have to peg her down.'

'All right. Stand by, I'll send you a hand.'

With a parting wave the naval officer disappeared and a few moments later one of the bluejackets who had been helping with the refuelling, a lad named Gilmore, ran down the steps and joined Ginger in the cockpit. It was the work of a moment to cast off, start the engines, and turn the nose of the amphibian towards the sandy beach that fringed the bay. As they reached it, Ginger lowered the undercarriage wheels, and the aircraft crawled ashore like a great white seal.

'That's O.K. – she'll do here,' declared Ginger, as he turned her nose into the slight breeze and cut the engines. 'I believe we've had our trouble for nothing, after all; the wind seems to be dropping already.'

'I expect we shall get it in gusts for an hour or two,' replied the bluejacket professionally. 'Are you going to tie her up or anything?'

'Not yet. There isn't enough wind to hurt at the moment, so I think I'll wait for my skipper to come back and leave the decision to him. You can take a stroll round if you like, but keep within hail. I had a bad night so I'm a bit tired, and I think I shall stay here and rest.'

'Then if it's all the same to you I'll have a stroll outside,' decided the sailor. 'We don't often get a chance of putting our feet on dry land.'

'That suits me,' agreed Ginger, preparing to make himself comfortable, while the other jumped to the ground and disappeared under the wing.

A few minutes later Algy and his party, looking rather tired and depressed, emerged from the bushes, and while he was waiting for a boat to take him to the destroyer he expressed surprise at finding the *Nemesis* on the beach; but he nodded agreement when Ginger told him the reason.

'I think you're right,' he opined, as the destroyer's boat grated on the sand. 'You'd better wait here until Biggles comes back; he can't be very much longer.'

'Right-ho! See you presently, then,' nodded Ginger, returning to the cabin as Algy departed.

For what seemed to be a long time he sat in the machine with his feet up on the opposite seat, contemplating the project on which they were engaged; then, happening to glance at the sky through the window, he saw that its colour had turned to that soft shade of egg-shell blue that often precedes twilight. It struck him suddenly that it was getting late and, wondering what could be delaying Biggles, he rose to his feet, yawning, and looked out through the opposite window, which overlooked the jungle, casually and without any particular interest. But as he gazed, a curious expression, in which incredulity, doubt, and alarm were all represented, stole over his face. He did not even finish his yawn, but allowed his lips to remain parted, while his eyes, from being half closed, slowly grew round with the intensity of their stare. The point on which they were focused was a narrow open space, not more than a couple of feet wide, between two clumps of fern-palm on the very edge of the jungle. It was already in deep shadow, but from out of its centre peeped an evil yellow face, flat, wizened, surmounted by a tightly fitting skull-cap. It was perfectly still, so still that it might have been a mask. The eyes did not even blink, but remained fixed so steadfastly on the aircraft that Ginger, still staring at it, with his pulses tingling, began to wonder if it was real, or whether his imagination was playing tricks with him. Shaking himself impatiently, he rubbed his eyes and looked again. The face was no longer there.

The shock of this second discovery moved him to action although, knowing how deceptive the half-light can be, he was still in doubt whether he had really seen what he thought he had seen. For a moment or two his eyes probed the edge of the jungle, scrutinizing every gap and clearing, but he could see no sign of life. He noticed that the wind had dropped, for everything was still, and the heavy silence that hung over the scene seemed to charge the atmosphere with a sinister influence. Then he noticed something else, or rather the absence of something. There were no monkeys on the beach, as there usually were on all the beaches of the island, seeking their evening meal of crabs and shellfish. Why? He remembered Gilmore. Where was he? What was he doing? Swiftly he made his way through to the cockpit and, without exposing himself, peeped over the edge.

The first thing he saw was Gilmore, lying on the soft sand under the wing, asleep. He seemed curiously still, ominously still, even for sleep. His position was an unusual one, too – more that of a person arrested in the act of stretching than sleeping, for his back was arched in an unnatural manner. Ginger could not see his face, but as he stared at him he felt a sudden unaccountable twinge of fear and shivered as if a draught of cold air had enveloped him.

'Gilmore,' he whispered.

The sailor did not move.

'Gilmore,' he said more loudly, a tremor creeping into his voice.

Still the man did not move.

Ginger moistened his lips, and lifted his eyes again to the edge of the jungle.

This time there was no mistake. For a fleeting instant he caught sight of a leering yellow face. Then it was gone. But he distinctly saw it go, merge into the dark background rather than turn aside. His heart gave a lurch, and while he hesitated, uncertain for the moment how to act, he heard a soft *phut*, as if a light blow had fallen on the fuselage just below him.

Even in that moment of panic his first thought was of Biggles, out there in the shadowy jungle. A swift glance over his shoulder showed the *Seafret*, motionless at anchor. It seemed a long way away. Turning, he was just in time to see a vague shadow flit across a narrow clearing.

He waited no longer. Drawing his automatic, he took aim at the bush behind which the shadow had disappeared and fired. He saw another bush quiver, and he blazed at it recklessly, emptying his weapon except for a single round which he saved for emergency.

As the echoes of the shooting died away everything seemed to come to life at once. Scores of birds rose into the air with shrill cries of alarm. There was a chorus of shouts and sudden orders from the direction of the destroyer, while at the same time there was a loud crashing in the bushes not far from the beach.

Ginger, wondering if he had done the right thing, saw with relief that a boat had been lowered from the ship and was already racing towards the amphibian; but before it reached the shore Biggles, gun in hand, followed by his two men, had burst through the bushes looking swiftly to right and left for the cause of the uproar. He started when he saw the *Nemesis* high and dry on the beach, and broke into a run towards it, only to slow down again with questioning eyes as Ginger jumped out.

'What on earth's all the noise about?' he asked sharply, almost angrily.

Ginger, who had not yet recovered from his fright, pointed at the jungle. 'Be careful,' he shouted, almost hysterically. 'Watch out – they're in there.'

'Who's in there? What's in there?'

'Natives! Savages! Something – I don't know,' answered Ginger incoherently.

The destroyer's boat reached the beach and, without waiting for it to be pulled up, Algy and several sailors armed with rifles leapt ashore and raced up to where the others were standing.

'What's going on?' asked Algy quickly, looking from one to the other in turn.

'I'm dashed if I know,' replied Biggles. 'Come on, Ginger, pull yourself together. What did you see?'

'Faces, in the bushes.'

'You haven't been dreaming, have you?'

Before Ginger could answer, a cry of horror broke from the lips of one of the sailors and, swinging round, the others saw him staring ashen-faced at Gilmore, still lying in the dark shadow under the wing. Ginger took one look at the bared teeth and staring eyes, and then covered his face with his hands.

Biggles shook him roughly. 'How did it happen?' he snapped.

But a Chief Petty Officer who had seen much service in the Far East had taken in the situation at a glance.

'Cover those bushes,' he cried tersely to the sailors who were armed, 'and shoot at anything you see move.' He turned to Biggles. 'It looks like Malay work to me, sir,' he said crisply. 'We don't want to lose any more men if we can help it. It's no use trying to fight them on their own ground, so we'd better retreat. Gilmore was killed by a blow-pipe – look at this.' He held up a tiny pointed dart, discoloured at the tip. 'One scratch of that and you're a goner inside ten minutes,' he declared. 'I've seen 'em before.'

'Where did you find that?' asked Biggles quickly.

'Stuck in the nose of your aeroplane.'

'Were you attacked, Ginger?' inquired Biggles.

'No. I only thought I saw a face, but it put the wind up me and, knowing you were still in the jungle, I fell into a panic, thinking perhaps a crowd of them were lying in wait for you.'

'I should say they would have had you, sir, if they'd known you were in there,' the Chief Petty Officer told Biggles seriously. 'They've cleared off now by the look of it, but they won't have gone far away. We don't want to be caught here in the dark, so I suggest that you give orders for everyone to return to the boat; and I'd take the aeroplane out, too, sir, or you won't find much of it left in the morning.'

'What made you bring her ashore?' Biggles asked Ginger as they started the engines.

'A breeze got up, and I was told that the glass was falling, so I thought she'd be safer ashore than on the water.'

'Yes, you were right there,' admitted Biggles, as he eased the throttle forward and ran down into the sea. 'It's a bad business about that sailor being killed,' he went on moodily. 'Sullivan will jolly soon be getting fed up with me. I don't know what's wrong, but nothing seems to be going right on this trip. We've had nothing but casualties since the time we started.'

'Well, it's no use getting depressed about it,' put in Algy. 'Let's get aboard and call a council of war.'

'I think that's the best thing we can do,' agreed Biggles despondently. 'It's getting time we did something. So far the enemy seem to have had things pretty well their own way.'

CHAPTER IX

A Nasty Customer

Sullivan awaited them with a gloomy face when, with the island a silent world of indigo shadows behind them, they returned to the destroyer, for the body of the dead sailor had preceded them. He did not speak, but his eyes rested on Biggles's face questioningly.

'Let's go below,' suggested Biggles curtly.

In single file they made their way to the commander's cabin, where the three airmen threw off their coats and sank wearily into such seats as they could find, for although the port-hole was wide open, the atmosphere was heavy and oppressive.

'I'm afraid you're beginning to feel that I am making a mess of this business,' began Biggles, looking at the naval officer, who had seated himself at his desk, and, with his chin cupped in his left hand, was moodily drawing invisible lines on the blotting-pad with the end of a ruler.

Sullivan glanced up. 'No,' he said. 'One can't make an omelette without breaking eggs, and one can't conduct a war without casualties; but I must admit that I'm beginning to wonder if we haven't taken on something rather beyond our limited resources.'

'I'm beginning to wonder the same thing,' confessed Biggles slowly, biting his lower lip and staring morosely through the open port-hole to where the distant, gentle swell of the sea was beginning to turn from navy blue to black. 'It's these casualties that depress me,' he went on. 'I'm not used to them. In the past we've taken many risks, willingly, even as we are prepared to take them now, but this losing of men—' He broke off and began walking slowly up and down the cabin. 'All the same, I don't think we can stop now whatever the cost may be,' he continued bitterly. 'I suppose you know as much as we do about what happened on the beach just now?'

'The Chief Petty Officer in charge of the shore party gave me a verbal report.'

'Where have these people come from suddenly? They weren't here yesterday, I'll swear.'

'Why are you so sure of that?'

'Because if they had been they would have molested us. Had they been here they would certainly have seen us land, and, scattered as we were, it would have been the easiest thing in the world to have bumped us off. Moreover, they would have been to Tom Lowery's crash, if only to look for plunder, yet nothing had been touched. I tell you, Sullivan, these people – whoever they are – came here today. Have you seen any native craft about?'

'I haven't seen a craft of any sort for days except a junk, beating north, well out to sea.'

'A junk! When did you see a junk?'

'This morning.'

'Was it under steam or sail?'

'Both, I fancy, judging by the speed she was moving, although she was too far away for me to say with certainty.'

'What sail was she carrying?'

'A mains'l and a jib – or what goes for them.'

'Was the mains'l red and the jib yellow, by any chance?'

Sullivan raised his eyebrows. 'Why, yes, that's right,' he answered quickly.

Biggles thrust his hands deep into his pockets, and, coming to a standstill, faced the commander squarely. 'I saw that same craft – let me see, when would it be? – yesterday morning. But it was a long way north of here. I don't understand—' He wrinkled his forehead as he pondered the problem. 'What course was this junk on when you saw her?' he asked.

'Mainly north, but I wouldn't swear that she wasn't making a little westerly.'

'Westerly, eh! That means that even if you had watched her you would have lost sight of her as she passed behind the next island – what's the name of it?'

'Lattimer Island.'

'That's right.'

'What are you trying to get at?'

'I'm trying to work out how a boat could have landed these toughs on the island since we came here without our knowing it. Mind you, even if that is what happened it doesn't neces-sarily follow that they are connected with the people we are up against.'

'Is it possible that they could have landed?'

'Certainly – if the junk beat back to the far side of the island after disappearing behind Lattimer Island.'

'Then you think the junk's still hanging about not far away?'

'I shouldn't be surprised.'

'Well, we can soon satisfy ourselves on that point,' declared

Sullivan. 'Let's have the anchor up and sail round the island. How does that strike you?'

Algy noticed that Biggles was staring at Sullivan with a most extraordinary expression on his face; heard him say 'No' in a detached sort of way, as if he were suddenly disinterested in the conversation. Then he appeared to recover himself.

'No, I don't think there's any necessity for that,' he exclaimed, in a firm voice. 'To tell you the truth, I'm half inclined to think that Ginger's imagination got away with him when he was ashore, and that Gilmore died from snake-bite.'

Ginger stared at Biggles incredulously, wondering what had suddenly come over him. His manner was most odd. Without looking at them, he had walked the full length of the cabin, turned at right-angles, and, with his eyes on the floor, was now walking back as close to the wall as possible. Near to the port-hole he stopped, facing them, as if grateful for the slight change of temperature the position afforded.

'What I hope most of all,' he continued, 'is that my staff have not lost their capacity for prompt action.' He spoke quietly, but there was a curious inflexion in his voice, and Ginger quivered suddenly as the full significance of the words dawned on him. Something was about to happen. But what?

'I don't understand you,' muttered Sullivan, frowning. 'What on earth are you talking about?'

'I'll show you,' answered Biggles, and whirling round, he thrust his right hand and arm far through the port-hole.

The others heard him catch his breath, saw him take a quick pace backwards, bracing himself as if to support a weight, at the same time jerking his arm inwards. They all sprang to their feet as a brown face, wearing an expression of astonished alarm, appeared in the circular brass frame of the port-hole. Biggles's fingers were twisted in the long, greasy hair.

'Outside, Sullivan,' he snapped. 'You'll have to get him from outside. Jump to it! Algy, get your hands round his neck – I daren't let go his hair. It's all right, he can't get his arms through.'

The whole thing had happened in an instant of time, but after the first speechless second the spectators moved swiftly. Sullivan darted through the doorway. There was a rush of feet on deck. Algy, as he had been bidden, took the eavesdropper's neck in his hands in a grip that threatened to choke him.

'Go steady,' said Biggles tersely. 'Don't throttle him. I shall want him to be able to talk presently.'

It was an extraordinary situation. The man, now snarling with animal rage, had his head through the port-hole and his shoulders jammed tightly against the frame, the rest of his body being outside. Clearly, the capture would have to be effected from without, for the port-hole was much too small for the man's body to go through it.

There came the splash of a boat on the water, and muffled words outside.

'All right, sir, let go; we've got him,' said someone.

Biggles and Algy released their grips. The face disappeared, and a moment later Sullivan walked back into the cabin, smiling.

'By gosh! That was smart work,' he exclaimed. 'How the dickens did you know he was there?'

'I saw his fingers as he pulled himself up,' answered Biggles. 'Or rather, I saw the reflection of his fingers in that mirror.' He pointed to a small square mirror on the opposite wall. 'They only appeared for a moment,' he went on, 'because once the fellow was up he could keep his balance in the canoe, or what- ever he was in, by just resting his hands on the outside of the destroyer. He was in a very nice place, too, because not only could he hear every word we said, but he could see us – or our reflections – in the mirror, without our seeing him. That's what made it so awkward. I daren't warn you by word or action for fear he bolted. That is why I didn't agree with you about making a search for the junk. I had just seen him, and I was afraid he'd be off to tell his pals what was afoot before I could collar him. I daren't leave the room either, in case he took it as a sign that he had been spotted; all I could do was make a grab in the dark and hope for the best. Luckily I managed to get him by the hair. What was he in – a boat?'

'Not he. A boat would have been seen by the watch, as he knew jolly well. He was standing on a length of tree-trunk; paddled himself here beside it with only his nose out of the water, I expect. No doubt he saw the light in the port-hole and made it his objective, which, as it turned out, was a pretty shrewd choice. What about this junk though?'

'Let's hear what the prisoner has to say for himself before we make any decision about that.'

'I doubt if he can speak English.'

'I should say he can, otherwise he wouldn't have been sent here. I mean to say, he was probably selected for the job on account of that qualification.'

There was a murmur outside the door, and a knock; it was then thrown open to admit four men: the Chief Petty Officer who had been in charge of the shore-party and two sailors who between them held the prisoner by the arms, although his wrists had been handcuffed behind his back. He was stark naked and dripping wet, and as Ginger gazed at him in morbid fascination, he thought he had never seen a more unpleasant looking individual.

Small, and thin to the point of emaciation, in colour he was a light brown, almost a tawny yellow, mottled by countless scars of some skin disease. Lank black hair hung half-way down his neck.

'Will you do the questioning?' invited Sullivan, looking at Biggles.

Biggles nodded. 'I'll ask him a few things first, and then, if there's anything else you want to know, you can have a go.' He sat down and fixed his eyes on the man's face.

'What's your nationality?' he asked, speaking very distinctly.

The man glowered and made no reply.

'Come on, you can speak English.'

Not by a single sign did the prisoner betray that he understood.

A hard glint came into Biggles's eyes. 'You heard me,' he rapped out sharply. 'Where have you come from?'

The man only stared at him sullenly.

Biggles nodded grimly. 'I see; it's like that, is it?' he said slowly. 'Listen here, my man. You're on a British warship, and if you behave yourself you'll have a fair trial, but if you try being awkward you'll find that we can be awkward, too. Now then. Who sent you to this ship?'

Still the prisoner did not answer.

Biggles glanced at Sullivan. 'Do you think your stokers could loosen his tongue?' he asked meaningly.

The commander nodded. 'Yes,' he said simply, 'they'd make a dumb man speak if I told them to.'

Two sailors between them held the prisoner by the arms.

'Very well. Let them take him below and see what they can do,' ordered Biggles harshly. 'And you can tell them that if they fail they needn't bring him back here; tell them to open one of the furnaces and throw him in.' Biggles's eyelids flickered slightly as he caught Ginger's gaze on him.

The prisoner stirred uneasily, and his little eyes flashed from one to the other of his interrogators.

'All right! Take him away,' said Biggles shortly.

'No! I speak,' gasped the prisoner desperately.

'You'd be well advised to do so,' Biggles told him grimly. 'My patience is at an end. What is your nationality.'

'No understand – nashnalty.'

'Where do you come from?'

'Me stay Singapore.'

'Where did you come from before that?'

'Manila.'

'I see. Who is your master?'

'He no name.'

'Where is he?'

The man hesitated.

'Come on!'

'He on junk.'

'Where is the junk?'

The prisoner's eyes switched nervously to the port-hole, as if he feared he might be overheard. 'Junk he lay offside island – round headland,' he whispered hoarsely.

Biggles half smiled at Sullivan at this piece of vital informa-tion. Then he looked back at the prisoner, who, he suspected, was a Malay Dyak with Chinese or Japanese blood in his veins. 'What is the junk doing in this sea?' he asked crisply.

The man screwed up his face. 'Not know,' he answered earnestly.

Biggles thought he was telling the truth and turned again to Sullivan. 'I don't think there's much point in prolonging this interview,' he said. 'Have you any questions for him?'

'No.'

'All right. Take him away. Keep him in irons and under guard,' Biggles told the Chief Petty Officer.

'I don't think we shall get any more information out of him,' he continued, as the prisoner was marched out, 'for the simple reason that he doesn't know what it's all about. I fancy he is just a deckhand sent over to listen because he knows a smattering of English. We shall do more good by having a closer look at this junk.'

'Absolutely,' agreed the naval officer promptly. 'Shall we move off right away?'

Biggles pondered for a moment. 'No, I don't think so,' he said. 'If they hear us or see the ship moving they'll know what we're after and perhaps give us the slip. If it's agreeable to you I'd rather put an armed party in the long-boat and try and take the junk that way. We should be able to creep along close to the shore – closer than you dare risk in the destroyer. In fact, we might get right up to the junk without being spotted.'

'I think perhaps you're right,' agreed Sullivan. 'How many men will you need?'

'A score should be enough. Serve them out with cutlasses and pistols.'

'Good enough. When will you start?'

'Just as soon as you can detail a party and put the boat on the water.'

Sullivan moved towards the door. 'Five minutes will be enough for that,' he promised.

His time estimate was not far out, for inside ten minutes the boat was on the water creeping stealthily towards the shore. Biggles sat in the stern with Lovell, for Sullivan could not, of course, leave his ship. Ginger, who with some difficulty had persuaded Biggles to allow him to accompany the party, sat just in front. Following the policy of always leaving a pilot with the *Nemesis*, Algy, much to his disgust, had been left behind.

The air was still. In the pale light of a crescent moon the silhouette of the island was very beautiful, and as they crept along the deserted shore, occasionally catching the perfume of the flowering shrubs that backed the white sandy beach, Ginger was enchanted with the peace and loveliness of the whole setting, and more than half regretted the business on which they were engaged. He would have much preferred to play at Robinson Crusoe for a little while, for there were many things of interest, both in the water, where brightly coloured fish swam unafraid amongst pink and yellow coral, and on the shore, where everything that lived was new to him.

The sailors rowed without speaking, for conversation had been forbidden, and in the fairy-like surroundings a curious feeling crept over Ginger that he was dreaming. But when, presently, rounding a headland, the bare masts and ungainly hulk of a junk came into view against the deep purple sky, a thrill ran through him, and he sensed the tension of the moment in the quick intaking of breath of the men in front of him.

'Easy all,' said Biggles softly, and then, as the sailors rested on their oars, he continued: 'Take it quietly everyone until I give the word, then put your backs into it. The boarding party will avoid bloodshed if possible. I hope the enemy will surrender, but if we meet with resistance, which we may take as proof of guilt, then use your weapons. Bo'sun, you know more about these things than I do. Select two good men, and the instant you get aboard make for the captain's quarters. It is important that he should not have a chance of destroying anything. That's all. Now then, gently does it.'

As the boat moved forward over the smooth surface of the water, leaving only a phosphorescent ripple to mark her passage, Biggles leaned forward and spoke to Ginger. 'You keep close to me,' he said severely. 'There's no sense in you getting your head sliced off by a crazy Dyak armed with half a yard of razor-edged steel. The sailors will attend to the fighting, if there is any.'

They were not more than a hundred yards from the junk when a shrill cry warned them that they had been seen.

'All right, my lads, let her go,' roared Biggles, abandoning all attempt at concealment. 'Junk ahoy!'

There was another shout. A firearm flashed and the missile ricocheted off the water not far away. The deep breathing of the sailors told of the efforts they were making, and within a few seconds of the alarm the boat had run alongside the larger vessel. There was a mighty swirl as the oars backed water, and then what seemed to Ginger a moment's confusion as the boarding party jumped to their feet and swarmed over the side, Biggles amongst them. There was a blinding flash and a deafening roar as a firearm exploded at point-blank range, and a sailor fell back into the boat, swearing fluently and clutching at his shoulder. Simultaneously a clamour broke out above, exaggerated in its volume by the preceding silence – shouts and screams punctuated by thuds and occasionally shots.

Ginger could stand it no longer. Grabbing at the loose end of a trailing rope, he went up the side of the junk like a monkey and threw his leg over the rail. All he could see at first was a confused mêlée of running men, but presently he was able to make out that there was a certain amount of order about it, and that the sailors were driving the crew of the junk before them into the bows. One or two of the orientals had climbed into the rigging, and he saw another deliberately dive overboard. The men in the rigging rather worried him; he wondered if the sailors had overlooked them, and with his automatic in his hand he had stepped forward to warn them when he saw Biggles leave the party and hurry towards the companion-way, evidently with the idea of following the bo'sun below, assuming that he had carried out his orders and rushed the captain's quarters.

Ginger saw that Biggles would have to pass immediately below the men in the rigging, so he shouted a warning. 'Watch out, Biggles – up above you!' he yelled, and to emphasize his words he threw up his pistol and fired without taking any particular aim. He did not hit any of the men aloft – not that he expected to – but the shot may have saved Biggles, for with a crisp thud a knife buried itself in the planking near his feet.

He leapt aside, calling to the sailors as he did so. Two or three of them broke away from the party in the bows, and pointing their weapons upwards, induced the natives to come down. It marked the end of the resistance, which had only been half-hearted at the best, and Ginger, following Biggles below, was just in time to witness the last act of a tragedy.

In the corner of a large, well-furnished room, evidently the captain's cabin, stood a modern steel safe with its door wide open. Below it, on the ground, lay a number of papers. Near by stood a small, dark-skinned man in blue uniform, covered by the revolvers of the two sailors who had been detailed by the bo'sun to accompany him. Such was the position as Biggles strode through the doorway with Ginger at his heels. But at that moment there was a muffled report. The dark-skinned man swayed for a moment, and then pitched forward on to his face.

The bo'sun, who had been kneeling near the safe collecting the papers, sprang to his feet. 'Who did that?' he cried.

'The fool shot himself,' answered one of the sailors.

The bo'sun looked at Biggles and shrugged his shoulders. 'I didn't think of him doing that, sir,' he explained apologetically.

'Couldn't be helped,' Biggles told him quietly. 'Pick up those papers will you, and collect anything that is left in the safe. Make a thorough search of the room and bring me any other papers you find. I shall be on deck.' Then, turning, he saw Ginger. 'What are you doing here?' he asked. 'I told you to keep out of the way. Still, it doesn't matter now; it's all over by the look of it. Let's get up on deck.'

At the head of the companion-way they met Lovell, who seemed to be labouring under a high degree of excitement. 'I was just coming to fetch you,' he exclaimed. 'Come and take a look at this.'

The others followed him quickly to where a hatch, with its cover thrown aside, lay like a square of black linoleum on the deck.

'Cast your eyes down there,' he invited them with a peculiar expression on his face, as a torch flashed in his hand, the beam probing the depths of the hold.

Biggles looked, and Ginger, taking a pace forward, looked too. At first he could not make out what it was upon which the yellow rays of the torch flashed so brightly; there seemed to be four long steel tubes, about a foot in diameter. His eyes followed them along to the end, and he saw that each terminated in a point.

'Torpedoes,' said Biggles, in a funny sort of whisper.

'Yes, they're "mouldies" all right,' grinned Lovell. 'There are also some cases of small-arms ammunition in the forward hold, and some shells, large ones and small ones that look like anti-aircraft tackle.'

Biggles glanced up to where the crew of the junk were huddled in the bows under the watchful eyes of the sailors. 'I think we had better get those beauties below and batten them down,' he suggested. 'You remain here with your fellows while I go back and have a word with Sullivan about this.'

Twenty minutes later he was telling the commander of the destroyer the result of the raid and what had been found on the junk. The documents from the safe, still unexamined, lay on the table.

When he had finished, Sullivan rubbed his chin reflectively. His face was grave. 'We're sailing in tricky waters, Bigglesworth, and no mistake,' he said anxiously. 'Goodness knows what might not happen if we make a blunder. I don't want to go down to posterity as the man who plunged the world into a war of destruction, and it might be as bad as that if we slip up. But there, you're in charge. It's up to you to decide on a course of action, and to that I have only one thing to add. You can rely on me to stand by you to the bitter end.'

'Thanks, Sullivan,' answered Biggles simply. 'I know how you feel about the frightful responsibility of this thing. In the ordinary way a matter as serious as this would be reported to the Admiralty and probably to the Cabinet. It's their pigeon really, but we simply haven't time to work through those channels. Finding those "mouldies" tells us what we want to know. These enemy operations are no myth. They're a fact, and we're within a few miles of the headquarters of the organization. I said I'd find it and blot it out, and those are the lines on which I'm going to proceed regardless of what the result may be. But first of all we've got to dispose of this junk and its crew. Obviously we can't let them go loose or the fat would be in the fire before we could say Jack Robinson. Frankly, as far as I can see there's only one thing we can do with them.'

'What's that?'

'Set them ashore here on this island. Maroon them. Without a boat they wouldn't be able to leave until someone picked them up, by which time we should either have finished the job or be where it wouldn't matter much whether it was finished or not.'

'And the junk?'

'Bring one of the torpedoes aboard the *Seafret* for evidence in case it is ever needed, and then scuttle her.'

Sullivan nodded. 'Yes, I think that's the best way,' he agreed.

'Then you'd better send a message to Lovell to ask him to bring the junk along. It's easier to do that than for us to go round to her because it means moving the aircraft as well. Now let's see what we've got here.' He turned to the papers still lying on the table, and gave an exclamation of disgust when he saw that they were all penned in Oriental characters.

'Any of your fellows able to read this stuff?' he asked Sullivan.

The naval officer shook his head. 'No,' he said. 'That's an expert's job, and a sailor who could do it wouldn't be serving in a destroyer.'

'Pity. You'd better put them in your safe, then, for the time being. I wonder if this will tell us anything.' He picked up a chart that the Chief Petty Officer had brought over with the other papers. 'Aha! Aha! What's this?' he went on quickly, pointing to a number of fine pencil lines that converged on a point amid a group of islands that he recognized instantly as part of the Mergui Archipelago. Indeed, he had looked at the same section of the globe so often of late that he could have drawn a chart from memory. He looked at Sullivan with eyes that held a sparkle of triumph. 'So it's Elephant Island,' he said quietly.

'Looks like it,' agreed the other. 'That's all we want to know, isn't it?'

'It *would* be, if we were quite sure,' answered Biggles cautiously. 'Unfortunately we daren't take anything for granted in this affair. After all, for all we know, this point—' he laid his forefinger on the chart – 'might merely be a sub-depot at which the skipper of the junk had been ordered to deliver his goods. We mustn't overlook that.'

'By jingo, yes. I'm afraid I had overlooked that possibility,' confessed Sullivan. 'That means—'

'It means that before we dare strike we've got to confirm that Elephant Island is, in fact, the base we are looking for.'

'How do you propose to do that?'

'I don't know,' answered Biggles frankly. 'I shall have to think about it. How far are we away from the place – forty miles?'

'Nearer thirty, I should say at a rough guess.'

'That's plenty close enough to be healthy,' declared Biggles. 'I'll think things over for a little while. Perhaps it would be better to sleep on it and have another conference in the morning. Meanwhile, let's get this business of the junk settled.'

'Right you are,' agreed Sullivan. 'Just a minute, though,' he went on quickly, as Biggles turned away. 'There's something I've been wanting to ask you, but what with one thing and another I haven't had a chance. What about that seaplane? Did you find anything of importance?'

Biggles nodded. 'I know who made the aircraft,' he said softly, giving the naval officer a queer look. He leaned forward and whispered something in his ear.

'Was there nothing on the pilot?' asked Sullivan.

'There wasn't any pilot,' replied Biggles grimly. 'The crocs – or a panther – got to him first.'

CHAPTER X

A Risky Plan

The pink of dawn was fast turning to azure the following morning as, watched by the three airmen and the entire ship's company, the junk sank slowly out of sight beneath the limpid blue waters of the bay, carrying with her the body of her dead captain, which had seemed the most befitting burial they could give him.

As the mainmast disappeared from view Biggles turned his eyes towards the island on which the crew had been put ashore, but not a soul was in sight. 'You gave them plenty of stores, I suppose?' he asked, looking at Sullivan.

'Ample,' was the brief reply.

'Good! Then that's that,' observed Biggles, turning away from the rail.

'Have you decided what you are going to do?' inquired the naval officer.

Biggles nodded. 'Yes,' he said, 'but to tell you the truth, I am not absolutely convinced that it is the right thing. It's rather a tricky problem, whichever way you look at it. As I see it, there are two courses open to us in this matter of getting confirmation that Elephant Island is the place we're looking for. I think you'll agree that we must do that before taking any action. I mean, it would be a dickens of a mess if we went and blew up a friendly village, or a bunch of innocent Salones, wouldn't it?'

'It certainly would,' agreed Sullivan.

'Very well, then. We're agreed that we've got to have a look at this place. There are two ways in which we can do it. One is to fly over it, and the other is to tackle it from ground level. At first glance the flying method might strike you as being far and away the easier, the same as it did me; but is it? If our friends know we're about, and I have an inkling that they do, they'll be watching the sky, that's certain. At the worst they might shoot us down, for while I am not without experience in the business of air combat, I don't feel in the least inclined to take on a bunch of single-seater fighters – or even one, if it comes to that – in an amphibian which, while it may be a good ship for our job, was never designed for fast combat work. Even one fast interceptor, flown by a determined pilot, could make things thundering uncomfortable for us; I've no delusions about that. Even if they didn't succeed in shooting us down they would know from the very fact that we were flying over their hide-out that we had spotted it, in which case they would either abandon the place forthwith and start again somewhere else, or else clean things up to such an extent that we should have no apparent justification for tackling them. You see what I mean?'

The others nodded.

'On the other hand,' continued Biggles, 'if, by scouting on foot, I could prove beyond all possible doubt that Elephant Island is the nest from which our ships have been sunk, the immediate result would be quite different. They would not know they had been spotted, and we should catch them red-handed, as it were.

If their suspicions *have* been aroused they'll be far less likely to expect us to land on the island than choose the more obvious course of flying over it, or sailing round it in a ship.'

'I'm not anxious to sail my ship round it,' declared Sullivan emphatically.

'You'd be a fool if you did, and deserve what you'd probably get,' Biggles assured him. 'That's why I vote for the "on foot" method, although, coming from a pilot, that may strike you as odd. In my experience, though, the unorthodox, the unexpected, is always preferable to the obvious.'

'It seems to be asking for trouble, to land on the very island that the enemy have made their perishing headquarters,' murmured Algy doubtfully.

'I suppose it is,' agreed Biggles, 'but then so is anything else that we could do. And, anyway, we expected that we should have to take risks when we started, didn't we? In fact, whenever a job has been offered us that involved no risk, you've usually been the first to turn your nose up. But we're wasting time. I'm going to Elephant Island.'

'What, alone?'

'No, I'm taking Ginger with me.'

'And what about me?' asked Algy.

'Oh, there'll be a job for you, don't you worry,' Biggles told him. 'Now listen; I've given a good deal of thought to this proposition and this is my idea. We lie low here until it gets dark, when, provided the weather remains fine, the *Seafret* will take us – that is, the *Nemesis* – in tow to Hastings Island. We shall then be a lot nearer to Elephant Island than we are here. According to Sailing Directions, which I have looked up, there is a lagoon with a good anchorage at the eastern end of Hastings Island that should suit us very well as a temporary base. It's rather close to the enemy, I know, and it would be out of the question for a prolonged stay, but I'm hoping that we shan't be there many hours. Anyway, it wouldn't do for the *Seafret* to drift about on the open sea, or the next thing will be a torpedo in *her* ribs.' Biggles glanced at Sullivan, who nodded agreement.

'I hadn't overlooked the possibility of that,' he observed drily.

'All right, then,' continued Biggles. 'Now somebody has got to stay with the *Nemesis*. That's definite. I'm going ashore, so it will have to be you, Algy. The next move will be made as soon as it gets dark, when the *Seafret* will steam slowly to within a mile or two of the south-east corner of Elephant Island, where she will lower a dinghy in which Ginger and I will row ashore. If you look at the chart you will notice that just off that particular piece of coast there are a number of small islets, bare rocks for the most part, I fancy. Some of them almost touch the main island. We – that is, Ginger and I – will make for those islets and find a good hiding-place. Having settled that, Ginger will then put me ashore, and afterwards return to the hiding-place, where he will lie doggo until he gets my signal to come and fetch me. You get the idea? We daren't risk leaving the boat on the actual beach of the main island in case anyone happens to come along. By parking it behind one of the islets it will be out of sight. Naturally, the *Seafret* will return to Hastings Island as soon as she has dropped Ginger and me in the dinghy. So the position will be this. I shall be ashore, scouting. Ginger will be with the dinghy hiding behind the islet waiting to pick me up. You, Algy, will be at Hastings Island with the *Nemesis*, where the *Seafret* will rejoin you as soon as she can.'

'And after that?' asked Algy.

'As soon as I discover what I hope to discover,' went on Biggles, 'I shall return to the beach and whistle for Ginger to pick me up, whereupon we return to the hiding-place behind the islet and remain there all day. As soon as it gets dark, and before the moon rises, the *Seafret* will come back and pick us both up.'

'But wait a minute,' cried Algy. 'I don't get the hang of this. Why not let the *Seafret* dump us all ashore and stand by until we've finished the job? It can then pick us up again and the whole thing will be over in one go.'

Biggles lit a cigarette. 'I expected you'd suggest that,' he murmured. 'Admittedly, at first glance there seems much to recommend that plan, but if you examine it closely you'll see that there are certain difficulties. In the first place, there is a time factor, and it is very important. The *Seafret* can only approach Elephant Island while there is no moon; it would be absolutely fatal for her to be within five miles of the place after that. You know what tropical moonlight is like as well as I do – we might as well go in daylight. Anyone on the island would only have to look out to sea to spot her. I don't think I could possibly hope to explore the island and get back to the boat in sufficient time to enable the *Seafret* to get over the horizon before moonrise.'

'Why not let her hide amongst those islets you've spoken about?'

Biggles frowned. 'Be reasonable, my dear fellow,' he said. 'It would take more nerve than I've got to ask Sullivan to take his ship amongst a maze of strange rocks and reefs, many no doubt uncharted, in the pitch dark. The *Seafret* would probably rip her bottom off inside five minutes, and that would just about put the tin hat on everything. I've taken all that into account, and that's why I'm of opinion that the plan I have outlined is the best.

Besides, Ginger and I in a little boat would make a very mobile unit, able to dodge about anywhere with very little risk of being seen.'

'Then there's nothing I can do?' asked Algy.

'I'm coming to that,' answered Biggles. 'Now if we – that is, Ginger and I – do our job, and the *Seafret* picks us up as per schedule, all so well and good. The *Nemesis* won't be needed for the moment. But suppose something goes wrong. Suppose I got delayed on the island for some reason or other. If the worst came to the worst you'd have to fly over and look for me. Naturally, if I was free to do so I should make for a place where you could get the machine down. I couldn't ask Sullivan to charge round the island looking for me, but at a pinch you could do that, although you'd be taking a tidy risk. It would be a case where you would have to use your initiative and act for the best, but I must say it would be a big consolation to me to know that if for any reason I couldn't get back to the boat, there was a second string to our fiddle in the shape of the *Nemesis*.'

'Yes, I see that,' admitted Algy; 'but I can't help feeling that there are a lot of loose joints in this scheme.'

'I know; that's why I'm not infatuated with it myself,' confessed Biggles. 'But it's the best plan I can think of. We've got to know what's happening on Elephant Island, and we've got to know pretty soon. It won't be long before the enemy will be wondering what has happened to the junk, which presumably was a supply ship, and while I don't think it's likely, there is always a risk of one of those natives we put ashore getting down to Elephant Island and spilling the beans good and proper – as they say on the films.'

'But how could he do that?'

'They might make a raft, or a dug-out canoe.'

'Then why did you turn them loose?'

'What else could we do with them? Had I been a hard-baked pirate I could have bumped the whole lot off, shot them, hung them, or sent them to Davy Jones in the hold of their junk; but wholesale murder isn't in our line, not even though we are virtually at war. There were too many of them to keep as prisoners on the *Seafret*.'

'Yes, I suppose you're right,' agreed Algy doubtfully. 'When is this programme due to start?'

'This evening, as soon as it's dark. As we're so close to the enemy's stronghold we should be crazy to start cruising about either on the water or in the air in broad daylight.'

'And suppose Elephant Island is the enemy stronghold, what then?' asked Ginger.

'Let's do one thing at a time,' suggested Biggles. 'It's always sound policy.'

CHAPTER XI

Horrors from the Deep

When Biggles and Ginger set out the following evening in accordance with the carefully considered plan of campaign, Biggles – although he did not say so – felt that the end of the affair might well be in sight, and he derived some relief from the thought, for both the importance of his task and the magnitude of his responsibilities weighed heavily upon him, and filled him with an unusual nervousness concerning the issue. The reason may have been that, whereas most of his adventures hitherto had been of a personal or private nature, the present one involved considerations so momentous that they appalled him. A single indiscretion might, he knew, embarrass the leaders of the Empire at a singularly inopportune time, and failure at the crucial moment would almost certainly precipitate a world war.

That was no doubt why he was inclined to be taciturn as he leaned over the *Seafret*'s rail watching the inky water glide past as the destroyer thrust her hatchet bows into the darkness in the direction of Elephant Island. Ginger, sensing his anxiety as he stood beside him, said nothing, but stared moodily at the bridge, on which the vague silhouette of Commander Sullivan's

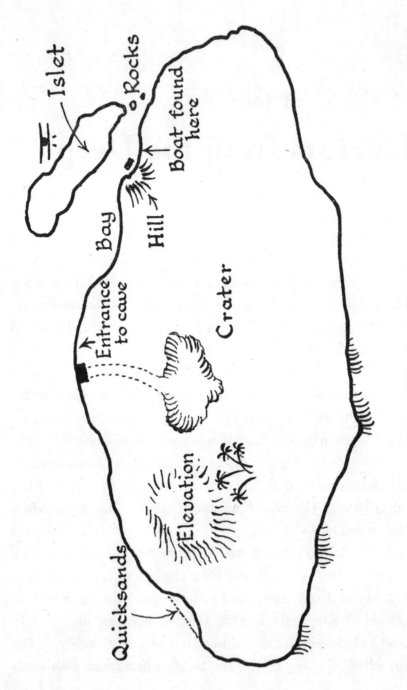

Islet

Rocks

Boat found here

Bay

Hill

Crater

Entrance to cave

Elevation

Quicksands

Map of Elephant Island.

head and shoulders could just be seen against the sky. Algy, as arranged, had been left behind with the *Nemesis* at the Hastings Island anchorage.

'What's the time?' asked Biggles at last. We must be nearly there.'

Ginger looked at his wrist watch. 'Twenty to ten,' he answered quietly.

'Another five minutes,' murmured Biggles, obviously glad that the time for action was at hand, for the sepulchral gloom that surrounded the ship, which, of course, was showing no lights, did nothing to enliven the proceedings.

A minute or two later the barely perceptible vibration of the destroyer's engines ceased, and Sullivan joined them.

'Here we are,' he said. 'It's as black as pitch. I'm afraid you're going to find things rather difficult until the moon gets up.'

'You put a compass in the dinghy?'

'Yes, with a tin of food and a beaker of water.'

'That's all right, then. We shan't miss the island, although I shall have to wait for moonrise before I start operations.' Biggles turned and walked slowly towards the davits where a number of sailors were preparing to lower a small boat. 'I shall expect you back about the same time tomorrow night,' he told Sullivan quietly as he climbed into the suspended dinghy. 'If it's very dark I may have to whistle for you; we daren't risk showing lights. If you *do* see me show a light you'll know things are pretty urgent.'

'Good enough. Best of luck', was the naval officer's farewell as the boat was lowered to the water.

Biggles picked up an oar and pushed the dinghy clear; then, after rowing for a short distance, he paused to make himself comfortable and arrange the compass on the seat in front of him.

Ginger, in the stern, could do nothing but sit still and watch him. When he next looked behind him the destroyer had merged into the black background of night. They were alone.

'We have some funny sort of picnics, don't we?' he murmured, for the sake of something to say, for the darkness, the silence, and the lap of water on the keel all combined to create an atmosphere of mystery that was by no means conducive to peace of mind.

'This hardly comes in the category of picnic, I think, and I shall be surprised if you haven't endorsed my opinion by the time the day dawns,' replied Biggles softly. 'Keep your eyes open and tell me if you see anything which looks like a rock or an island.'

For some time Biggles rowed in silence; then he looked up, resting on his oars. 'See anything?' he asked.

'I shouldn't be able to see a church if there was one an oar's length away,' declared Ginger. 'It's as black as your hat.'

'Then we'll take an easy until the moon wakes up and does its stuff,' said Biggles. 'We've only about another ten minutes to wait.'

He was quite right. In seven or eight minutes a faint luminosity in the sky provided enough light for them to see about them, and they were relieved to find that their position was as they intended it should be. Lying right across their bows lay the solid black mass of Elephant Island; nearer, not more than two hundred yards away, was the nearest of the rocky islets behind which they proposed to take cover. Several similar islets, all smaller, dotted the dark surface of the gently heaving waters.

Biggles dipped his oars again and the dinghy forged forward, leaving a gleaming trail of phosphorescence in her wake. The water that dripped from the blades of the oars each time they were raised flashed like molten silver, and Ginger watched it, fascinated; but he had no time to remark on it, for their objective was at hand, and reaching over the side he grabbed at a projecting piece of rock to steady the boat. There was no beach. The islet was just a mass of rock, roughly oval in shape, perhaps two hundred yards long and forty or fifty feet wide at the widest part. In most places it was low enough to enable them to step straight ashore, but towards the northerly or right-hand end, which was the end farthest from the island, it rose gradually to a maximum height of about ten or twelve feet. At this spot the rock, for the islet was little more than that, was some three hundred yards from the main island, but the other end, which tapered considerably, curved round until the tip was not more than thirty to forty yards from a spit of sand that jutted out from the beach, the sand deposit no doubt being caused by the islet's effect on the currents.

They pulled the boat into a fairly deep indentation in the rock and Biggles stepped ashore. For a moment he stood gazing at the island with speculative eyes. Then he turned back to Ginger.

'I think this place will suit us pretty well,' he observed, glancing around. 'The boat will ride here quite comfortably while you sit on the rock and keep an eye open for me to come back.'

'Right you are,' agreed Ginger. 'Where do you want me to put you ashore?'

'Anywhere on that beach will do,' replied Biggles, regarding a little sandy cove that lay immediately opposite the islet. 'It all looks the same, and there doesn't seem to be anyone about.'

The final remark may have been induced by the fact that the moon was now clear above the horizon, flooding everything with its silvery light. The beach to which Biggles had referred lay clear and white, with hardly a ripple to mark the water-line, but beyond it and at each end the jungle towered up steeply to the usual central eminence, black, vague, and forbidding.

'Well, I might as well be getting ashore,' announced Biggles getting back into the boat, and pushing it out again into deep water. He picked up the oars, and a minute or two later the keel grated quietly on the soft sand of Elephant Island. 'Well, so long, laddie,' he whispered softly, getting out again. 'Keep awake; don't show a light, and above all don't make a noise.' Then, with a cheery wave, he set off at a brisk pace along the beach.

Ginger watched him until he was swallowed up in the dense shadows where the sand gave way to rock at the extremity of the bay. Then he turned his eyes on the primeval forest, silent, brooding, sinister, unchanged through the years, untouched by human hands, as far removed from the surging crowds of civilization as though it were on another planet. Apparently it slept – but only apparently. Within its sombre heart moved – what? Things. Things that crawled. Nameless horrors of a thousand legs and stings of death waging a perpetual warfare in the rotting tropic debris that cloaked the steaming earth. Larger things: panthers – sleek, black as the night through which they moved; pythons – twenty feet of sinuous horror; crocodiles of unbelievable size, survivors of another age that had outlived the centuries.

Ginger shivered, oppressed by a sudden pang of anxiety for Biggles. Then, knowing that he could do nothing to help him, he rowed back slowly to the islet.

Several hermit crabs scuttled into the sea as he backed the dinghy into the tiny creek that was not much larger than the boat, and stepped ashore. He did not tie the boat, for one reason because there was nothing to tie it to, and, as the water was almost motionless, there seemed to be no reason why he should.

But he took the painter ashore, threw the end down near his feet, and, with his eyes on the pallid crescent of sand that fringed the bay, settled himself down to await Biggles's return.

A faint clicking noise made him turn again to the seaward side of the islet, and he saw that the crabs were coming back, crawling ashore on their ridiculous stilt-like legs in greater numbers than before. Some, already on the rock, were marching to and fro in small companies, for all the world like soldiers on parade. For a long while he watched them with interest, glancing from time to time at the beach, for there was something fascinating about the spectacle. Vaguely he wondered how long they had been carrying out their absurd exercises, and how long they would continue to do so.

Then, at last growing weary of them, he turned and watched the beach with a renewed interest, knowing that Biggles might return at any time. Occasionally a silver ripple would surge across the narrow strait that divided the islet from the island, a gleaming streak that threw two little waves on either side of it, and he was thankful that swimming formed no part of the programme. He could not see, but he could guess what caused the ripples. And when, presently, a small fish shot high out of the water and he saw the huge grey shape that flashed beneath it, he knew that his suspicions were correct.

It was a little while after this that he became aware of something different. Something had changed. Something that had been there was no longer there. At first he could not make out what it was. But then, suddenly, he knew. The crabs were no longer doing their exercises. The bony clicking of their long legs had ceased, and quite casually he turned to see why.

A glance revealed the reason. They were no longer there.

But it was not this simple fact that brought him to his feet with a startled cry. It was the discovery that the dinghy had drifted unaccountably away from its berth; already it was at the seaward end of the tiny creek, although fortunately the end of the painter still rested on the rock. But only just. He saw that in another moment it would be in the water, and he sprang forward quickly to pick it up; but even as he stooped, he stopped, staring. What was wrong with the boat? It seemed to be all lop-sided, as if a weight was pulling the side down into the water. He could see the weight, a dark, indistinct mass, hanging on the side of it. Then, as he stood staring, with his heart thumping strangely and his throat constricting, there was a swish in the air as of a rope when it is thrown. A dark, snake-like object curled through the air and fell with a soft thud across the rock on which he stood. It came so close that it grazed his ankle, and at the feel of it he leapt backwards, an involuntary cry of horror breaking from his lips.

He no longer thought of saving the boat. His only immediate concern was for his own preservation, and in a panic he ran towards the centre of the islet until, reaching what seemed to be a safe place, he turned and looked again. He was just in time to see the weight slide off the side of the dinghy, and the boat, thus released, right itself with a gentle splash.

His knees seemed to go weak, and he sank down limply on the rock, wondering with a sort of helpless horror how he was going to recover the boat now floating placidly some ten yards from the water's edge. To swim out for it with that ghastly creature about was unthinkable. He knew what it was, of course: either an octopus or a decapod, perhaps the most loathsome living thing in all creation.

His anxiety was nearly as great as his fear. Without the boat he was helpless; what was even worse, Biggles would be helpless, too, when he arrived on the beach, and he might be expected at any moment. Yet he could do nothing except stand and stare in an agony of despair, clenching and unclenching his hands in his extremity. Then he saw something that once more put all thought of the boat out of his head. The octopus was crawling out of the water on to the rock.

For a second or two the horror of it nearly overwhelmed him, for he could see it clearly now; a great pig-like body as large as a barrel, with two long tentacles protruding in front and a number of shorter ones behind. A decapod. Indeed, so far did his nerves collapse that it was all he could do to prevent himself from screaming. He could only hope that the creature would not see him, for without the boat escape seemed to be out of the question; the mere thought of voluntarily entering the water in an attempt to swim to the island turned his skin to goose-flesh. He did not forget his automatic, but the weapon seemed hopelessly inadequate against such an adversary, quite apart from which he shrank from making a noise which could hardly fail to rouse the entire island, to Biggles's undoing.

Then, farther down the islet, another of the creatures dragged itself out of the water, and began turning over pieces of rock as if searching for some sort of food that it expected to find underneath. At the same time the original decapod began to move slowly towards him, the two long tentacles groping with a soft slithering noise over the rocks in front of it.

Ginger fled. He dashed up the incline to the higher end of the islet, but a glance showed that there was no escape that way. To make matters worse, he saw that in another moment his pursuer would reach the foot of the slope and effectually cut off his retreat. He waited for no more, but in a condition that can only be described as blind panic, he tore back down the hill, leaping such obstructions as lay in his path, and raced to the narrow end of the islet, nearest to the island. Out of the corner of his eye he saw that the second horror had taken up the chase, and he distinctly heard its tentacles fall across the rocks behind him as he dashed past it.

Nearing the end of his run, a swift glance backward revealed both monsters not thirty yards behind, moving swiftly over the ground in a sort of rolling motion. The sight drove the last vestige of control from his paralysed faculties. He reached the absolute extremity of the islet, but he did not stop. A few yards away another rock, quite small, rose clear of the water, and he launched himself at it in a manner that in cold blood he would have regarded – quite properly – as suicidal. Miraculously he landed on his feet, and, stumbling to the top, saw yet another rock, half submerged. Again he leapt.

This time he was not so lucky. The rock, which was almost awash, was covered with seaweed, and few things are as slippery as seaweed-covered rock. His feet landed squarely, but they shot away from under him, and he ricocheted sideways into the water. He was up in a flash, catching his breath in a great gasp, and was overjoyed to discover that he could stand on what seemed a hard, sandy bottom. Instinctively he made for the island, deliberately splashing and making as much turmoil as possible in the water. Twice he went under as he stumbled into deep channels, and had to swim a few strokes each time; but his objective was not far away, and almost before he was aware that he had reached it, he was dashing through a cloud of spray of his own making up the firm, sandy beach to the softer sand beyond. Then, and not before, did he stop to look behind him. All was silent; motionless except for the glowing ripples on the water that marked the course of his berserk passage. Of the decapods there was no sign, and so unreal did the whole thing seem at that moment that he almost fancied he had been the victim of a particularly vivid nightmare. The dinghy he could not see because, as he realized, it was on the other side of the islet.

Panting, he sank down on to the dry sand to recover his breath and as much self-control as he could muster, clenching his hands to stop the trembling of his fingers, for although the danger was past, the shock had left him weak and shaken. Human enemies were something he understood, a natural hazard only to be expected, encountered, and outwitted; but these dreadful creatures of the deep—

He brushed his hair back from his forehead impatiently and rose to his feet, peering in the direction of the islet in the hope of seeing the boat drift beyond the end of it, for his only chance of recovering it was, he knew, the rather forlorn one of a current or slant of air carrying it to the shore.

Nothing would have induced him to go back into that monster-haunted water in the hope of retrieving it, not even the knowledge of what the result of losing it might mean to Biggles as well as himself. There were, he discovered, limits to what he was prepared to do for the success of their enterprise, although only a few hours before he would have denied hotly any such imputation.

He derived a modicum of comfort from the thought that perhaps the tide might bring the boat in to the shore, and he watched the water-line for some minutes trying to make out whether the water was advancing or receding. The wavelets were, he observed, a little below the high-water mark indicated by the usual line of seaweed and shells, but whether the water was advancing or receding he could not discover, for there was little or no movement.

It dawned upon him suddenly that, standing as he was in the middle of the white beach, he was exposed to the gaze of any living creature, human or animal, that might be prowling about, which, in the circumstances, was hardly wise. The nearest and easiest cover for him to reach was, of course, the jungle that rose up behind him like a great black curtain, but he regarded it with disfavour. The end of the bay where Biggles had disappeared was not very far away, and this made a much greater appeal, particularly as Biggles might reasonably be expected to return the same way as he had gone.

Without any loss of time, therefore, he set off towards it, and was presently relieved to find that, although the sandy beach petered out, it gave way to a sloping shelf of rock that rose gradually to a low cliff about fifty feet high and continued along the foreshore as far as he could see. The only vegetation on it consisted of a few stunted bushes and gnarled trees, which suited him very well, for these enabled him to conceal himself, yet at the same time permitted a clear view of the beach, besides giving a fairly open aspect of the cliff along which Biggles had presumably gone.

A little farther along a queer formation of small trees attracted his attention, and towards these he made his way with the intention of taking up his stand amongst them, there to await Biggles's return. Accordingly he turned his steps towards them, only to find on closer inspection that the trees were even more unusual than he had at first realized. Indeed, they almost looked as if they had been arranged by human hands instead of being a perfectly natural growth. Generally speaking, they occurred in groups of three or four, although in a few cases there were only two. But it was not the trees themselves that made his eyes grow round with wonderment as he approached, but what lay on top of them.

Another few paces and he saw beyond all doubt that even if the trees were natural, the burdens they bore were not; they were obviously artificial, although whether they had been fashioned by men, birds, or animals, he had no means of knowing. It appeared that across the lower forks of the trees, normally some ten or twelve feet from the ground, had been laid other slender branches. Across these, at right-angles, was a rough trellis-work of smaller branches, while on top had been piled a great mass of twigs not unlike a gigantic jackdaw's nest. But the nests were not round. They were rectangular, or roughly oval, being between seven or eight feet long but only two or three feet wide.

For some minutes he stood staring at this extraordinary phenomenon, completely perplexed. 'What the dickens is it?' he muttered, taking a few steps sideways in order to regard it from a new angle. 'Well, if birds built those, I only hope they're not at home, that's all,' he concluded, picking up a piece of loose rock and throwing it at the nearest 'nest'.

Nothing happened. The rock bounded back on to the ground with a clatter, and again the deathly silence settled over the scene.

'Well, I give it up,' he murmured, seating himself on a convenient boulder from which he could keep watch in both directions. It was a lonely vigil, and before long he found himself wishing fervently that Biggles would return; moreover, he was worried to death about the loss of the boat, and he wondered uneasily what Biggles would have to say about it when he knew. From time to time an unpleasant musty odour tainted the still night air and did nothing to add to his comfort; indeed, once or twice the stench was so bad that a wave of nausea swept over him. Still, he did not attempt to find the source of it, supposing that it was some sort of corruption in the forest.

For a long time he sat, sometimes staring at the beach, sometimes gazing the other way, and occasionally watching the moonbeams flicker on the rippling water that stretched away from immediately below him to the distant horizon. He could see the islet clearly, but there was still no sign of the boat.

Suddenly his reverie was disturbed by a sound that brought him to his feet with racing pulses. At first he could hardly believe his ears; it was quite faint, but it increased rapidly in volume and there was no mistaking it. It was the deep, steady throb of a powerful engine, but far too slow and heavy for an aero engine, to the sound of which he was accustomed. In startled alarm, he turned swiftly to each point of the compass in turn, trying to locate the noise, but he could not; it seemed to be advancing over the ground from the direction of the forest – which was, of course, impossible. For a few unbelievable seconds it seemed to beat against his feet as though it were passing underneath him. Then, as though the door of an engine-room had been opened, the sound was magnified ten times, and welled up behind him. He was round in an instant, eyes wide open, lips parted, prepared almost for anything except what he actually saw.

Straight from the base of the low cliff on which he stood was emerging, very slowly, a black torpedo-shaped object. For five breathless seconds he stared at it uncomprehendingly; then, as the unmistakable conning-tower came into view, he understood everything and dropped flat, quivering with excitement but completely self-possessed. It was a submarine, under way, heading out to sea.

The heads and shoulders of two men protruded from the circular super-structure, and a few words of a strange foreign language floated up to him.

In silent wonderment he watched the sinister craft, tense with the knowledge that the secret of the enemy's base was now his. Like a great fish with its back awash, it held on its course, leaving a flashing wake of disturbed water behind it, growing quickly smaller as, once clear of the islet, it increased its speed. The sound became a throbbing purr, then died away altogether, and the scene reverted to its former condition.

CHAPTER XII

Elephant Island

When Biggles had left Ginger and set off along the beach, his direction was not a matter of choice. The jungle which enveloped the whole island like a shroud was, he knew from previous experience of similar islands, practically impenetrable by day, and to attempt to force a passage through it by night would be a physical impossibility, quite apart from the very real danger of an encounter with one of the deadly beasts that dwelt in it and the noise that such a method of progress would inevitably entail. It was for these reasons, then, that he followed the beach, although he was aware that had he been able to reach the hill in the middle of the island, it might have been possible to command a view of the whole coastline, including his objective, in whichever direction that might lie.

What sort of country lay at the end of the little bay where the beach terminated he did not know, so he could only hope that the vegetation would not be so dense as to bar his progress. On reaching it he found to his relief that the sand gave way to a rising rocky foreshore on which the jungle had only been able to fasten an insecure hold. Through this he made fast time, keeping as near to the edge of the cliff as possible and stopping occasionally to listen. Once or twice he heard sounds in the undergrowth which suggested that wild creatures were pursuing their nocturnal tasks or pastimes, but as far as humanity was concerned, there was nothing to suggest that he was not alone on the island. On the right was the sea, calm, silent, deserted, gleaming wanly in the eerie light of the young moon. To the left, the forest, dark, inscrutable, heavy with an atmosphere of menace.

In this manner he covered what must have been three or four miles, seeing and hearing nothing to arouse his suspicions. Nevertheless, he did not relax his caution. He noticed that the moon was now behind him, and realized that in following the curve of the coastline he was now facing a different direction, and was able to estimate that he must have traversed nearly a quarter of the circumference of the island. Looking ahead, he saw that the cliff rose still higher, but intervening was another small bay, smaller than the one on which he had landed, but otherwise precisely the same in appearance. It was as if a giant dredge had grabbed a great lump out of the rock.

He reached the point where the cliff sloped down to it, and paused to scrutinize the open area, but a few moments' investigation revealed it to be as deserted as the other. Stepping carefully from rock to rock, he hastened down the slope and jumped lightly on the sand at the base.

As he landed there was an unpleasant squelch, and he sank into it over the ankles. At the same time the ground seemed to quiver and press tightly round his feet. Even so, it was not until he went to take a pace forward that he realized that he was in the grip of a quicksand.

He perceived afterwards that, had he stood still, even for a few seconds, when first he stepped on to the sand, he would certainly have died the most dreadful of all deaths; but, fortunately, such was his haste that only a barely perceptible instant elapsed between the time he jumped down and the time he started to move on, to discover that his feet were held fast. To say that he 'discovered' this may not be the literal truth. There was no time to discover anything, for, instantly, he began to fall forward, as was inevitable in the circumstances.

Even as he fell, the thought, 'quicksands', flashed through his brain, but the frantic grab that he made at an overhanging shrub was purely instinctive.

He managed to catch hold of it and hang on. For a few desperate seconds, as he began to haul on the branch round which his fingers had closed, it was touch and go whether it would stand the strain, or break and precipitate him bodily into a death-trap; but it held, and the crisis passing as his feet began to emerge from the treacherous sand, it was only a matter of another second before he lay gasping on the rock and not a little shaken.

For a short while he sat regarding the innocent-looking beach with cold, hostile eyes, memorizing the lesson he had just learned – that in the tropics it does not do to trust anything, however harmless it may appear. Then, drawing a deep breath, he prepared to resume his march.

This, he discovered to his dismay, was likely to be difficult, if not impossible, for the jungle ran right down to the sand and both appeared to be impassable. He tried to find a way through the fringe of the tangled vegetation, and to some extent succeeded, but then a deep ravine into which he did not feel inclined to venture barred further progress. So he returned to the rock from which he had started. Somewhat to his surprise, he found that it was possible to work inland by keeping to the most prominent outcrops of rock, and he reproached himself for not investigating this direction before, although, thinking it over, he knew that it was the innocent-looking beach that had lured him on at that particular point.

The ground now rose steeply and, to his great satisfaction, the vegetation opened out instead of becoming more dense as he expected; and a quarter of an hour's hard work enabled him to reach the peak of a fairly considerable hill, from which he was able to make a comprehensive survey of the whole island and its coastline. It was with the coastline that he was particularly concerned, for he supposed that a submarine base was hardly likely to be established anywhere except on the actual shore.

Quickly his eyes swept round the limited seaboard, but all he saw was a succession of beaches, screes, and cliffs. Mystified, he looked again, this time more carefully, but with the same result. At first he was incredulous and refused to believe it, and it took him the best part of ten minutes to convince himself that he was not mistaken.

'Well, that's that,' he mused fatalistically, concealing his disappointment even from himself. 'There doesn't seem to be any reason why I shouldn't have a smoke.' He took a cigarette from his case, tapped it thoughtfully on the back of his hand, and then lighted it. For a little while he lingered, surveying the landscape that was as destitute of life as on the day it had emerged from the sea in some remote age, wondering what the next move would be now that his plan had so completely fizzled out.

'Yet it's funny about those lines,' he soliloquized, thinking of the chart that had been taken from the junk. 'This must be a watering-place, or a halfway mark, or something of the sort, that's the only solution. Well, I'd better see about getting back.'

He turned away from the tree against which he had been leaning at the precise moment that a perfectly aimed *kris* struck it with a vicious *zip*. Where it came from he did not know; nor did he stop to inquire. For one fleeting instant, hardly under-standing, he stared at it in shocked amazement, the haft still quivering, the steel gleaming brightly in the moonlight. Then he bolted, ducking as he ran.

Out of the corner of his eye he saw a number of figures take shape, flitting through the trees like shadows not ten yards distant, and he swerved like a hare away from them. He did not waste time feeling for his automatic; his assailants were too numerous and too scattered. Time for that when he was cornered or overtaken, he thought, as he sprinted down the hill towards the cliff.

Shouts now broke out behind him, and he hoped fervently that Ginger would hear them and take them as a warning to be prepared to move quickly when the crucial moment arrived and he reached the beach – if he did manage to reach it. Dodging, twisting, ducking, and jumping, he sped on. Reaching the cliff, he turned sharply to the right and set off back along the way he had come, but in a very different manner. For some time he did not look behind him, but concentrated his entire attention on avoiding the numerous obstacles that crossed his path; but reaching a fairly open space just before the point where the cliff began to slope down to the beach, he risked a quick glance over his shoulder.

What he saw made him redouble his efforts, for his pursuers were in a bunch not fifty yards behind. He looked again as he reached the far side of the open space, and saw to his horror that they were even closer, apparently travelling faster than he was now that the way lay open and the quarry was in view.

Biggles gathered himself for a final spurt. A dead branch protruded like a paralysed arm from a tree in front, and he ducked. In doing so he failed to see a loose rock that lay directly in his path. The first he knew about it was when his toe struck against it. Stumbling, he made a tremendous effort to save himself, but to become unbalanced at the speed he was travelling could have only one ending. For a split second he still ran forward, arms outstretched, and then crashed heavily to the ground.

CHAPTER XIII

A Gruesome Refuge

Ginger was still lying on the cliff staring out to sea at the point where the submarine had disappeared when he heard another sound that brought him to his feet with a rush. It was a confused hubbub as of several voices shouting at once, calling to each other. It sounded unpleasantly like an alarm, and if this supposition was correct, it seemed extremely likely that Biggles had had something to do with it – as was in fact the case. And when, a few seconds later, the shouting died away, only to be replaced by the drumming beat of running footsteps coming in his direction, his fears became acute.

Still, he did not lose his head. In any case it was no use running, for, with the boat gone, there was nowhere in particular to run to, so he took the obvious course, which was to find a hiding-place. The huge nests on their prop-like supports suggested themselves immediately, and up the nearest one he went without further loss of time. He was conscious of an overpowering stench as he clambered up on to the structure at the top and lay flat, but he ignored it, for his attention was entirely taken up by the hue and cry coming nearer every second.

Soon the chase came into view. Sprinting along the lip of the cliff, jumping over loose rocks, and swerving round trees and bushes, came Biggles. After him, with the relentless determination of a pack of wolves, came a mob of Dyaks, or natives of some sort; the distance and the deceptive light made it impossible for Ginger to make out just what they were. Nor did he care particularly. As far as he was concerned, the fact that they were in hot pursuit of Biggles was all that mattered. And Biggles was sprinting for dear life towards his only hope of escape – the boat. There was no doubt of that. But the boat was not there!

It may have been the realization of this appalling fact that kept Ginger tongue-tied. His usual alert faculties seemed to be paralysed. What to do he did not know, and the very urgency of the situation only made him worse. In fact, he floundered in a horrible condition akin to stage-fright when he could only stare, incapable of lucid thought or action. Should he shoot? If he did, Biggles would probably stop, or at least hesitate, and that was something he could ill afford to do. Yet if he, Ginger, remained silent, Biggles would dash off down to the beach, only to find that there was no boat and no Ginger. What would he do then?

These were the thoughts that rushed through Ginger's brain as he watched the chase approach, but they did not occur in sequence. Rather were they a chaotic jumble of impressions – detached, incoherent.

Then, at the precise moment that Biggles drew level with the eyrie on which he was perched, so many things happened together that the result was pure nightmare. It began when Biggles caught his foot against a rock and took such a header that a moan of horror burst from Ginger's dry lips, and unconsciously he started forward in order to see if Biggles had hurt himself badly, as seemed by no means improbable. But either

the sticks that comprised the 'nest' were rotten, or else the structure had not been designed for such treatment, for with a sharp
cracking noise, the whole thing began to slip.

Ginger's reaction was purely automatic. Quite naturally he
clutched at the sticks to save himself, and he sent a fair number
of them flying in all directions before he succeeded. His fingers
closed over something soft, and simultaneously a stench at once
so awful, so nauseating, so completely overpowering filled his
nostrils that he looked down to see what he was holding.

What he saw can safely be described as the final straw that
broke the back of his already overwrought nerves. Staring up at
him was a face: a human face – or what had once been a human
face. It had not been a pretty thing to look at in life. In death it
must have been awful, but in the advanced stages of decomposi-
tion it was so utterly dreadful that any description of it would
fail in its object.

Ginger stopped breathing as he stared down into the glassy
eyes and the grinning mouth with its protruding teeth. He forgot
where he was. Forgot what he was doing. Forgot what was going
on below. Forgot everything. He even forgot Biggles. A screech
of stark terror broke from his lips as he sprang upright, arms
waving as he strove to balance himself. Then he jumped clear. He
was not in the least concerned about where he landed, or how.
Had a famished lion been underneath he would have jumped just
the same, for there was only one thought in his mind, which was
to vacate the gruesome sepulchre on which he had taken refuge
with all possible speed regardless of any other consideration.

Subconsciously he was aware of a number of men recoiling
away from the spot, of a confused noise of shrieks and groans;
then he struck the ground.

For a moment he lay still with the breath knocked out of him; then he staggered to his feet, swaying, glaring wildly about him. Not a soul was in sight. The men were gone. Biggles had gone. He was quite alone. It seemed impossible, but there was no doubt about it. He was still staring, trying to force his brain to comprehend that this was in fact the case, when, without warning, his recent refuge collapsed completely, throwing its grisly tenant clear on to the rocks.

If Ginger had needed an incentive to cause him to move, nothing could have succeeded better. With a noise that was something between a moan and a yell, he turned on his heel and made a beeline for the beach. Biggles's flight has been in the nature of a headlong rush, but it was not to be compared with Ginger's, which was stark panic.

But it did not last long. Rounding a corner at the point where the rock sloped down to the sand, he met somebody coming in the opposite direction. There was no time to dodge. There was no time to do anything. They met head on, and the result was instantaneous and inevitable. Ginger skidded sideways like a rugger ball on a greasy field, and collapsed with a crash into a convenient clump of bushes. Threshing and plunging like a salmon in a net, he fought his way out of the tangle, and then stopped dead, staring at Biggles, who was still sitting where he had fallen, muttering under his breath and rubbing his knee.

Ginger's relief was beyond words. 'Come on, Biggles,' he cried hoarsely. 'Let's get out of this perishing place.'

'That's what I'm aiming to do,' answered Biggles savagely. 'Where's the boat?'

Ginger faltered. 'There isn't one,' he muttered miserably.

'What do you mean – there isn't one?'

'It's – it's gone.'

'Gone! Who took it?'

'Nobody took it – I mean, it sort of went.'

'Went? Have you gone crazy?'

'An octopus took it,' explained Ginger.

'Don't talk such blithering nonsense,' snapped Biggles crossly. 'Are you asking me to believe that an octopus got into our boat and rowed it away?'

'No – that is, not exactly. You see—'

'Just a minute, just a minute,' broke in Biggles. 'Let me get this right. The boat's gone – is that it?'

'Exactly.'

'Fine!' muttered Biggles grimly. 'Now we know where we are. In a minute you can tell me how you came to lose it. Meantime, let's get down to the beach, or anywhere away from here, in case these pole-cats come back.'

'I frightened them, didn't I?' asked Ginger, as they hurried down to the beach.

'No! Oh, no! Frightened isn't the word. Supposing you were walking through a churchyard one night and a corpse pushed its tombstone over and leapt out at you with a yell – would you be frightened? I mean, you wouldn't stop to ask it questions?'

'No,' declared Ginger emphatically. 'I certainly should not.'

'Precisely!'

'But was that place a churchyard?'

'What goes for one in these islands. If they buried their dead, which couldn't be very deep on account of the primitive tools they've got, the crocs would dig them up. So they hoist them up in the trees. You must have found an empty grave.'

'Like fun I did,' snorted Ginger. 'He was at home all right, only

154

I didn't see him when I first climbed up; you can bet your life on that. That yell you heard was me making his first acquaintance – ugh!'

'I don't wonder those fellows who were after me were scared,' muttered Biggles, smiling at the recollection. 'I don't mind admitting that I was as shaken as they were, as you'd well believe if you'd seen me hoofing it as soon as I could get on my feet. But by the time I'd got down here I'd worked out what it was, and started back to fetch you. Wait a minute. I think this will do for a hide-out while we discuss what we're going to do.'

They had reached the beach, but instead of following the water-line, they worked their way to the edge of the jungle and pulled up in the inky shade of a giant casuarina tree.

'Now, then. Just tell me what happened,' invited Biggles. 'But make it short. It is known by now that there is at least one stranger on the island, and unless I've missed my guess, it won't be long before search parties are on the move.'

'They'll never find us in this darkness,' declared Ginger optimistically.

'Maybe not, but they'll watch every landing-place since they must know that whoever is here came by boat.'

'By the way,' asked Ginger suddenly, remembering the reason for the excursion and what he himself had seen, 'did you see any submarines?'

Biggles looked at him sharply. 'No,' he said. 'Nor did I see any place where one might expect to find one.'

'I have,' Ginger told him.

Biggles started. 'You've what?' he gasped.

'Seen a submarine.'

'Where?'

'Just along past the end of the bay – over there,' Ginger pointed.

'What, by that cliff!'

'The sub came out of the cliff.'

'Came *out* of it – talk sense.'

'I am. I tell you I saw a submarine come out of the cliff and put out to sea. There must be a hole there – a cave of some sort.' Briefly, Ginger described how he had first heard and then seen the underwater craft, and followed this up by describing his adventures from the time the first decapod had dragged the boat away from the islet.

'My gosh! You have had a night of it,' muttered Biggles when he had finished. 'No wonder you were getting a bit het up when you bumped into me. Well, what are we going to do? This is the place we're looking for, there's no doubt about that, but the information isn't going to be much use to us unless we find a way of getting back to our rendezvous.'

'Could we make a raft, do you think?' suggested Ginger hopefully.

Biggles regarded him sadly. 'Have you ever tried to make a raft?' he asked.

'Never.'

'Then don't. I did once. Oh, yes, I know it sounds easy in books, but don't you believe it. Anyway, quite apart from that, I don't fancy rafting about on an octopus-infested sea. A liner wouldn't be too big for me after what you've just told me. All the same, things are not going to be too cheerful on this island now we've been discovered; except for that I wouldn't mind staying and lying low for a bit. But as soon as these johnnies have recovered from their fright they'll be back, and I don't like the look of the weapons they carry.'

'What sort of weapon is it?'

'A thing called a *kris* – a cross between a cutlass and a cleaver. Nasty.'

'Hadn't they got firearms?'

'Apparently not, or they'd have had a crack at me.'

'What happened?' inquired Ginger. 'I mean, how did you come to barge into them?'

In a few words Biggles described his adventure. By the time he had finished the sky was beginning to turn grey, and he peered apprehensively along the beach.

'Look here, it's beginning to get light,' he muttered. 'We'd better find a better hiding-place than this in which to spend the day. First of all, though, let's make sure there's no chance of getting the boat. If we can get on to that rising land farther along to the right we ought to be able to see beyond the islet. Come on, let's go and have a dekko. Keep your eyes skinned.'

CHAPTER XIV

Where is the *Seafret?*

They set off along the beach, keeping as close to the edge of the jungle as possible. Biggles broke into a steady trot as soon as he saw the coast was clear, for the day was fast dawning, and in this way they soon reached the end of the bay, where the vegetation, curving round to meet the sea, brought them to a halt.

'Come on, we shall have to force a way through this stuff,' muttered Biggles, plunging into the undergrowth in order to reach the top of the high ground of which he had spoken.

The going was heavy, and several times they were compelled to make detours around fallen trees with their hosts of clinging parasites; but in due course, panting and dishevelled, they reached the crest and looked down.

A cry of triumph at once broke from Biggles's lips, and Ginger murmured his satisfaction, for there, high and dry on even keel on the sand just round the headland, where the flowing tide had apparently cast it, lay the dinghy.

'We'd better go and get it,' said Biggles quickly. 'If any one comes along we shall lose it for good.'

Again they set off, this time downhill, in the direction of the boat.

'What are we going to do with it?' asked Ginger as they reached it, and saw with relief that it was undamaged, with the oars still in place.

Biggles thought swiftly. 'We ought to get out behind the islet, as we arranged,' he answered, 'but I must say that I am tempted to go and have a look at this place where the submarine came out. There must be cave or a hidden creek there. It's a bit risky, but we've got to have a look at it sometime to see just what there is there. It's no use trying to blow up the whole blessed island, and we might go on bombing the trees for weeks without hitting the vital spot.'

'Well, if we're going, no time could be better than this, I imagine,' suggested Ginger.

'How long will it take us to get there?'

'About five minutes. Certainly not more than ten. It's only just across the other side of the bay.'

'Come on, then, let's have a shot at it,' decided Biggles, well aware of the desperate nature of the enterprise. But, as he had just observed, they would have to look at it at some time or other, and they could not hope for a better opportunity than the present.

They pushed the boat into the limpid water and scrambled aboard. Biggles picked up the oars, and in a few seconds they were skimming towards their objective, keeping close in to the shore in order, as far as possible, to avoid observation.

Reaching the far side of the bay, Biggles rested on his oars while the dinghy crept forward under its own way round the rocky headland. For a moment or two he looked ahead eagerly, expectantly; but then a look of blank wonderment spread slowly over his face as he stared at a plain wall of rock. Not a cleft or a cave showed anywhere in the cliff; from the rank green vegetation fifty feet above to the turquoise ripples at their own level, the wall fell sheer without an unusual mark of any sort.

Turning, he looked at Ginger with questioning eyes. 'Well, what do you make of it?' he asked, a faint hint of scepticism in his voice.

Ginger was nonplussed. Never in all his life had he felt so foolish. 'I don't know what to make of it and that's a fact,' he admitted.

'You're not going to try to persuade me that a submarine sailed straight through that chunk of rock?'

Ginger shook his head. 'No,' he said. 'That's solid enough. Nothing but an earthquake could shift it.'

'Well, what's the answer?' inquired Biggles, a trifle coldly.

'A lemon, by the look of it,' smiled Ginger, weakly.

'You're sure this is the right place?'

'Absolutely certain.'

'In that case, it looks as if we've gone back to the age of miracles,' declared Biggles sarcastically, dipping the oars into the water.

'What are you going to do?'

'I'm going back to the islet. There's no sense in sitting here gazing at a blank wall; there's a degree of monotony about plain rock that I find distinctly boring.'

Not another word was spoken while Biggles rowed back across the bay and took the dinghy behind the islet so that it was concealed from the main island.

'Don't forget that this place is alive with octopuses,' warned Ginger.

'Don't you mean octopi?' suggested Biggles.

'What does it matter?' protested Ginger. 'Had you been here last night and seen them you wouldn't have stopped to consult your pocket dictionary, I'll bet.'

'I think it will be safe enough during daylight.'

'What about when it gets dark?'

'We shall be gone by then,' answered Biggles. 'Let's haul the dinghy ashore; we can forget all about it then and pass the day in the shade of that rock.' He nodded towards the mass of rock that rose at the higher end of the islet.

The rest of the day was in the nature of a picnic. The sun shone brightly, but a little breeze from the sea tempered the heat to a pleasant temperature, while the food and water Sullivan had put into the boat staved off the pangs of hunger. For some time they talked of the mystery of the submarine. Biggles was sceptical and made no secret of it, and at the end even Ginger began to doubt himself.

'The fact is, you didn't see a submarine at all; you only thought you saw one,' concluded Biggles.

After lunch they slept in turn, one keeping watch while the other rested, but not once did either of them see or hear anything of the men who they knew must be somewhere on the island.

'I should say they were a tribe of seafaring Dyaks,' decided Biggles at last, as the sun began to sink towards the western horizon. 'The natives in these parts are a wild lot, I believe, and would murder anyone for a pair of boots. It begins to look to me as if we're all at sixes and sevens, and the people we're looking for aren't on this island at all, but— Strewth! What's that?'

He leapt to his feet with undignified haste as an aero engine roared – almost in their ears, it seemed. Ginger sprang round as if he had been stung, and peeping round the rock, they beheld a sight so inexplicable that for a time they could only stare speech-lessly. Floating on the blue surface of the translucent water at the far end of the bay, the reflection of her silver image distorted beneath her, was a small seaplane. How it had got there without being heard or seen was a mystery that defied all logical conjec-ture. Not that they had time to contemplate the matter calmly, for, with a roar that sent the parrots screaming into the air, the aircraft sped across the water in a cloud of glittering spray and soared into the sky.

Biggles dragged Ginger down with him as he flung himself flat. 'What do you know about that?' he gasped.

'About what?'

'That seaplane.'

'Seaplane! You didn't see a seaplane – you only thought you saw one,' mocked Ginger, getting his own back for Biggles's gibe earlier in the day.

The machine flashed across their field of vision, climbing for height, and hardly knowing what to say, they watched it until it was a mere speck in the blue. Then the hum of the engine died away suddenly, and they saw it coming down again.

'He's been up for an evening reconnaissance, I should say,' observed Biggles quietly. 'Not a bad idea, either. The fellow in that machine would be able to see fifty miles in all directions from his altitude – a lot better than scouting about in a boat.'

'Maybe he was looking for the junk,' suggested Ginger.

'Quite likely,' agreed Biggles. 'Look out! Keep your face down. You can see a face looking up at you easier than you can see a hundred men with their faces covered.'

Out of the corners of their eyes they watched the machine glide in, saw its long floats kiss the water and run to a stop not fifty yards from the cliff. There was a bellow of sound as the engine roared again and the machine disappeared behind the headland. The noise of the engine ceased, and they waited for it to start again, but in vain. Once more silence settled over the scene, now mauve-tinted with the approach of twilight.

Biggles started collecting the belongings that were scattered about at their feet.

'What's the programme?' asked Ginger.

'I'm moving off,' said Biggles quietly.

'That suits me,' declared Ginger warmly. 'It's getting near octopus time.'

As is usual in the tropics, night closed in around them swiftly, and by the time they were ready to depart it was nearly dark.

'Which way?' asked Ginger, taking his seat in the boat.

'I'm going to have another look at that cliff,' announced Biggles.

'You won't be able to see much in this darkness.'

'Enough, I fancy.'

Just what he expected to find Biggles did not say, but he expressed no surprise when the dinghy rounded the headland and the secret of the seaplane's disappearance was explained – as was the case of the submarine. Gaping in the face of the cliff, low down on the water-line, was a great black hole like the mouth of a tunnel.

'Fancy not thinking of that! Why, a half-wit would have spotted it,' grunted Biggles disgustedly.

'Spotted what?'

'That there was a cave, exposed at low water, but submerged at high tide. It was high water when we came round here this morning.'

'Pretty good,' was Ginger's vague reply. Whether he was referring to Biggles's solution of the problem or the cave itself was not clear. 'Are you going to have a peep in?' he added.

'No. I'd like to,' confessed Biggles, 'but I don't think it would be good generalship. We've got the secret now, and it's up to us to pass it back to Sullivan before we take any more risks, so that he can send the information back to the people at home in case anything unpleasant happens to us. After we've done that we'll certainly come back and have a snoop round, because then our precious lives won't be of such vital importance if we get into a jam.'

'You speak for yourself,' growled Ginger.

Biggles laughed softly as he pulled on the oars, and the island faded into the dark background.

'Are you going to look for Sullivan?' asked Ginger.

'I am,' declared Biggles tersely.

'We shall be a bit early.'

'No matter. It's no use blinking at the fact that we've had a bit of luck in spotting this dug-out, and I'm itching to get the information off my chest before anything happens to upset our apple-cart.'

'What can happen?'

'Don't ask riddles. How do I know? But it's time you knew that on these jaunts of ours something usually does happen at the crucial moment to throw things out of gear.'

Ginger said no more, but prepared to make himself as comfortable as possible during the wait.

In the pitch darkness, with nothing to do once they had reached the rendezvous, the time seemed to pass slowly.

'Time he was here,' muttered Biggles at last, staring into the gloom to seaward.

Another quarter of an hour passed and Biggles stirred uneasily. 'Funny,' he said, as if to himself. 'I suppose we couldn't by any chance have missed him?'

Ginger said nothing. Biggles had expressed his own thoughts and he had nothing to add.

The next half-hour was the longest either of them could ever remember. 'Begins to look as if I was right,' Biggles observed dispassionately, at last.

'How so?'

'About things going wrong.'

'But surely nothing could go wrong with the destroyer?'

'Then why isn't it here?'

'That, I admit, is something I can't answer,' was Ginger's only comment.

Another half-hour or so elapsed, and Biggles roused himself from the listening position in which he had been sitting. 'I don't think it's much use waiting here any longer,' he announced bitterly. 'Sullivan isn't coming, or he'd be here by now.'

Ginger barely heard the last part of the sentence. He had crouched forward in a rigid attitude, listening tensely. 'Hark!' he said softly. 'I can hear something. What is it?'

From somewhere far away out to sea a deep drone pulsed through the night; for a moment or two it persisted, rising to a crescendo, and then died away. A moment later the sound was repeated, and then again, slightly louder.

'What does that sound like to you?' asked Biggles in an odd tone of voice.

'If I were near a naval airport I should say it was a marine aircraft, taxiing over water,' replied Ginger slowly.

'Yes, I think you've hit the nail on the head,' agreed Biggles.

'You mean—'

'It's Algy taxiing here to fetch us. Something has happened to the destroyer.'

Ginger felt his heart go down like a lift. 'By gosh! I hope you're wrong for once,' he muttered anxiously.

'Well, we shall see,' was Biggles's pessimistic reply. 'One thing is certain,' he went on, as the sound moaned through the night comparatively near at hand. 'It's an aircraft, and if it isn't Algy we shall shortly be in the cart – up salt creek without a paddle, as the sailors say.'

The sound drew nearer, and it was quite easy to follow what was happening. Someone was sitting in the cockpit of an aircraft opening up the engine and easing back the throttle each time the machine gathered way.

'We don't want him to run us down,' exclaimed Biggles suddenly, rising to his feet.

He waited for one of the intermittent silences, and then, cupping hands round his mouth, let out a moderately loud hail.

A call answered them immediately. They recognized Algy's voice and rowed towards it, and a minute later the dark silhouette of the *Nemesis* loomed up in front of them. Biggles urged the dinghy forward until its bow was chafing the hull of the amphibian just below the cockpit.

Algy's head appeared over the side. 'Hello!' he said, switching off the engines.

'Hello yourself,' returned Biggles grimly. 'What in thunder do you think you're doing, buzzing about on the high seas? Where's the *Seafret*?'

'She was torpedoed this morning – at least, that's what it looked like.'

Biggles turned stone cold. 'Good heavens!' he ejaculated. 'Was she sunk?'

'No, Sullivan managed to beach her.'

Biggles balanced himself in a standing position. 'Tell me about it – quickly,' he invited.

'Nothing much to tell,' answered Algy simply. 'The *Seafret* was sitting in the little bay at Hastings Island – at anchor, of course. I had taxied the machine on to the beach and was giving her a look over when I was nearly knocked flat by an explosion. When I looked up I saw a cloud of smoke hanging over the destroyer. She had already taken on a bad list. Sullivan slipped his cable and ran her straight ashore not fifty yards from where I was.'

'No lives lost?'

'No.'

'Thank God for that, anyway. What's Sullivan doing?'

'Sitting on the beach cursing mostly. They've got plenty of stores ashore and have made a camp.'

'By heaven! These people must be pretty desperate to do a thing like that; anyone would think they were deliberately trying to start a war.'

'Not necessarily,' replied Algy. 'As Sullivan says, who's to say it was a torpedo? Nobody saw anything, either before or after the explosion. He says that in the ordinary way if he went home and said he'd lost his ship because she'd been torpedoed the Admiralty would laugh at him. People don't fire torpedoes in peace time.'

'Don't they, by James!'

'We know they do, but it would be hard to prove, particularly as we don't know whom to accuse of doing it.'

'That's true enough,' admitted Biggles. 'So Sullivan's still at Hastings Island?'

'Yes, and he's likely to be for some time.'

'Hasn't he called for assistance by wireless?'

'No. We decided that the enemy would pick up the S O S as well as our own people, so it might be better to lie low and say nothing for a day or two. We had a conference, and came to the conclusion that the first thing to do was for me to fetch you.'

'Quite right,' agreed Biggles. 'Did you see anything of the submarine yourself?'

'Not a thing. I did think of taking off and trying to spot it, but what was the use? I couldn't have done anything even if I had seen it, and had they come to the surface and seen me, they would then have known that I was there. As it was I don't think they could have suspected the presence of an aircraft. They just lammed a "mouldy" into the destroyer and made off.'

'Yes, I suppose that was about the size of it.' admitted Biggles.

'Well, if you'll get aboard we'll see about getting back.'

'Just a minute – not so fast,' protested Biggles. 'Let me think.'

For a little while he leaned against the side of the amphibian deep in thought. When he moved his mind was made up. 'No,' he said, 'I'm not going back with you.'

'You're *not?*'

'No.'

'What are you going to do?'

'Stay here. Listen, this is how things stand. Memorize what I say because you may have to repeat it to Sullivan. Elephant Island is the place we've been looking for. In the central face of rock on the eastern side – almost opposite us now – there is a cave. What it leads to I don't know, but inside there are submarines and aircraft. We've seen them both. If it's an underground lake, or something of that sort, then it's no earthly use bombing

168

it from above. That's why we've got to find out what it is. The
entrance is covered at high water, so whatever we do will have
to be done at low tide. This is my idea. The tide is down now. As
soon as the moon comes up Ginger and I will get into the dinghy
and go and have a look at this underground war depot. You stay
here, or better still, get behind the islet so that you can't be seen
from the shore, but don't get too close to the rock or you may find
an octopus in the cabin when you go to take off. And don't make
more noise than is necessary. They may have heard you for all
we know, but it can't be helped if they have. Well, how does that
strike you as a programme?'

Algy hesitated. 'I can't say that I'm exactly enamoured of it,' he
confessed, dubiously. 'I suppose it's imperative that you should
go poking about in this cave?'

'Absolutely,' declared Biggles. 'What is the alternative – if any?
As I see it, the whole Far East fleet of the Royal Navy could
hammer away at the island for weeks without hurting these
submarine merchants more than giving them a slight headache
from the noise. More direct methods will be demanded to hoist
them skyward, but until we know just what we've got to destroy
it is difficult to know how to apply them.'

'Yes, I see that,' admitted Algy. 'But what is Sullivan going to
think when we don't turn up?'

'He'll have to think what he likes.'

'I hope he won't do anything desperate.'

'So do I – but there, we can't let him know, so we shall have to
take a chance on it.'

'All right,' agreed Algy. 'If you're satisfied, then it's O.K. by me.
Let's get the *Nemesis* to this islet you talk about. Do you know
where it is?'

'Pretty well. Throw me a line. We'll tow the machine there – it isn't far. I'd rather you didn't start the engines again.'

The moon rose as they towed the *Nemesis* into position, and the final disposition of the aircraft behind the high shoulder of rock was made with some haste, for Biggles was frankly nervous about their being seen or heard by those on the island. It was not their personal safety that concerned him so much as the possible failure of their plans, for, as he pointed out to the others, with the aircraft at their disposal, ready to start at a moment's notice, if the worst came to the worst, they could always take flight with every prospect of getting away.

'Has anyone got the time?' he asked, as the *Nemesis* dropped her small anchor in thirty feet of water.

'A few minutes short of midnight,' answered Algy, glancing at his instrument board. 'Are you going to move off right away?'

'No, I don't think so,' answered Biggles. 'The hour before dawn has acquired a reputation through the ages for being the best time to catch people napping, and for all nefarious enterprises. I'll wait for a bit. Pass me down a torch, will you; we shall probably need one.'

Algy went through into the cabin and fetched a small electric torch, which he handed down to Biggles, who was still standing in the boat. 'Anything else you want?' he asked.

'No, I think that's everything,' replied Biggles slowly. 'We've got guns, but I don't think we shall need them – anyway, I hope not. With luck, tomorrow will see the end of this business, and I can't say I shall be sorry,' he added thankfully.

Two hours later he embarked on one of the most desperate adventures of his career.

CHAPTER XV

Trapped!

A gentle breeze, bringing with it the subtle aroma of spices, caused the water to ripple and gurgle softly against the prow of the dinghy as, under the stealthy impetus of the oars, it edged round the headland and approached the cave which, as they drew near, they observed was larger than they had at first supposed. Except for the incessant lapping of the tiny wavelets against the rock, and the occasional distant, choking grunt of a crocodile, there was no other sound, yet to Ginger the atmosphere seemed charged with hidden threats and the presence of things unseen.

Inch by inch they approached their objective. Biggles dipped his left oar deeply, and the boat crept nearer to the cliff until Ginger, by reaching out, was able to touch it. Another minute and the bows projected beyond the opening; another, and they sat staring into a cavity that was as black as the mouth of the pit. Neither spoke, knowing full well that in such conditions the sound of the human voice travels far.

Another stroke of the left oar and the nose of the dinghy came round until it was pointing directly into the void; an even pull and they were inside, swallowed up in such a darkness as

Ginger had never before experienced. It was not darkness in the ordinary accepted sense of the word, the darkness of a moonless night; rather was it an utter and complete absence of light, the darkness of total blindness.

A gentle click, and from the centre of the boat sprang a beam of light that cut through the air like a solid white cone as Biggles switched on the torch. He regretted having to use it, but further progress without illumination of some sort was, he felt, quite useless, if not impossible. He realized that if guards had been posted they would see the yellow glow of a match as certainly as they would the more powerful beam of the electric torch, so he accepted the risk as inevitable, and switched it on, half prepared for the action to be followed immediately by a signal of alarm.

But all remained silent. Slowly the round area of light travelled over the walls, to and fro, above and below, but it revealed nothing except a semi-circular arch of rock with a floor of still, silent water, which appeared to run straight into the very heart of the island.

There was another click as Biggles switched off the light, and a moment later Ginger felt the boat moving forward again. It was an eerie sensation, gliding through space in such conditions. The only sound was the faint swish of the oars as they dipped in and out of the water, and he wondered how long Biggles would be able to keep the boat on a straight course. It was longer than he expected, and some minutes elapsed before the side of the dinghy grated gently on the rough wall. Thereafter progress was slower, for rather than switch on the light again Biggles began to maintain a forward movement by using his fingers against the wall, taking advantage of any slight projection that he could feel. As soon as he realized what was happening Ginger joined in the task.

It was difficult to estimate how far they travelled in this manner, but it must have been several minutes later when Ginger's warning hiss caused Biggles to desist, for, as he had been at the oars, his back was towards the bows, and he was unable to see ahead. Turning quickly, he saw at once what it was that had attracted Ginger's attention. Some distance in front, just how far he was unable to tell, a half-circle of wan blue light had appeared, and he realized that it was the end of the tunnel.

Quickly he pushed the boat clear of the wall, picked up the oars, and in two or three strokes had completely turned it round, whereupon he began backing towards the light, which he soon perceived was cast by the moon. His object in turning the boat was, of course, that the nose might be pointing in the right direction for speedy retirement should an alarm be given.

The nervous tension of the next few minutes was so intense that Ginger clutched at the gunwale of the boat to steady his trembling fingers, at the same time craning his neck so that he could see what lay ahead, for he felt that anything, *anything* might happen at any moment. Somewhat to his surprise, and certainly to his relief, nothing happened. With infinite slowness the boat floated backwards until it was possible to see through the opening at what lay beyond. At first, owing to the deceptive light, it was rather difficult to make out just what it was, but as they gazed section by section of the scene unfolded itself.

Biggles realized instantly that he was looking into an old crater, the crater of a long extinct volcano, now filled with water which had come through from the sea presumably by the same channel through which they themselves had come, and which had, no doubt, once been a blow-hole bored by a colossal pressure of pent-up gas when the rock had been in a fluid, or semi-fluid, state. The island itself must have been the actual peak of the volcano which, with the cooling of the molten mass, had remained hollow.

The sides of the crater were not very high; they dropped sheer from heights varying from one hundred to a hundred and fifty feet to sea-level, where, of course, the water began. At one place only, not far from where the dinghy floated, the wall had crumbled away until the slope, while steep, could easily be scaled, and was, he perceived, the path by which the submarine crews travelled to and from their quarters, which were situated halfway up the cliff. Even now the dark bulk of a submarine rested motionless against a rough quay at the base of the incline.

At the back of Biggles's mind as he took in these general impressions was a grudging admiration for whoever had discovered the place and thought of turning it into a submarine base, for as such it was more perfect than anything that could have been fashioned by human hands. Another point he realized was that even if he had flown over the island, while he might have seen the gleam of water, he would merely have taken it for a lake, for the buildings, being built of the actual rock which formed the sides of the crater, or camouflaged to resemble them – he could not tell which – would certainly have escaped detection.

These buildings he now examined in detail with the practised eye of an aerial observer. No lights were showing. There were four in all. The lowest three were long, squat structures, evidently living quarters or storerooms; in fact, just the sort of accommodation one would expect to find. The top one, however, perched almost on the lip of the crater, was much smaller, square in shape, and he wondered for what purpose it was used until he saw the antennae of a wireless aerial outlined like a spider's web against the moonlit sky. That, so far as he could see, was all the information he would be able to pick up from an exterior view of the buildings.

There was only one object on the water besides the submarine already remarked. It was a seaplane which floated, with wings folded, near the foot of the path just beyond the underwater craft. It was easy to see how it was employed. It could not, of course, take off from the crater, but with its wings folded it could easily pass through the tunnel to the open sea where, with its wings rigged in flying position, it could operate at will.

There seemed to be nothing else worthy of note, and Biggles was about to turn away, well satisfied with his investigation, when Ginger, whose end of the boat had swung round some- what, giving him a slightly different view, touched him on the elbow and pointed. At first Biggles could not see what it was that he was trying to show him, but a touch on the oars brought him in line, and he was just able to make out a narrow cleft, or opening, in the rock wall not more than a few yards from where they sat. A slight pull on the oars brought them to it; another, and they had passed through the gap and were staring with astonished eyes at what met their gaze. The place seemed to be a sort of secondary crater, very small, not much larger in area than a fair-sized house, but in this case the walls were perpendicular. It was quite a natural formation, if somewhat unusual, but Biggles was only interested in what he saw on the surface of the water. There was no possibility of mistake. The round, buoy-like objects, with horns projecting at different angles, could only be mines such as are used in naval warfare. A little farther on, as his eyes became accustomed to the gloom, he could just discern, packed on ledges of rock which looked as if they had been cut by hand, a vast array of metal cylinders with pointed ends, and he did not have to look twice to recognize them as shells.

At this discovery the whole matter took a different turn. Not only was the place a submarine depot, but it seemed also that it was a naval armoury, an armament stores depot capable of supplying a fleet with material, to say nothing of laying a minefield around itself for its own protection. And the concentration of stores was apparently still proceeding, harmless-looking junks being used for the purpose. There was another dark area at the far end of the tiny crater which looked as if it might reveal further secrets, but Biggles had seen enough. He knew all he needed to know, and his one concern now was the destruction of the whole concern.

'My goodness! These people have got a brass face, if you like,' he breathed in Ginger's ear. 'Fancy having the nerve to put up a show like this on a British island!'

His eyes swept over the array of sinister-looking mines for the last time, and his oars were already in the water for immediate departure when an idea flashed into his head, so audacious that for a moment it took his breath away. Yet was it audacious? There was a submarine outside. Ginger had seen it go out. It could not have come back without their seeing or hearing it. It might return at any time. One mine in the tunnel! The submarine could not fail to strike it as it came in, whereupon, even if the tunnel did not completely cave in, as seemed likely, the submarine would sink in the fairway, effectually bottling up everything that was inside the crater. The R.A.F. machines could do the rest in their own time. All that was necessary was to place a mine in position, bolt back to the *Nemesis*, fly to the *Seafret*, and call up the military machines from Singapore on the destroyer's wireless. The plan, if successful, would, he saw, be more certain and conclusive in its result than simply calling upon the Royal Air Force to bomb the place, when it was quite on the boards that one or both of the submarines would escape, possibly taking the personnel of the island with them to report to their headquarters what had happened and perhaps start a similar scheme somewhere else.

All this flashed through Biggles's head a good deal faster than it takes to read, and as he turned the plan over quickly in his mind he knew that he was going to put it into action.

'What's the idea?' whispered Ginger, who was watching him closely.

'I'm going to lay one of these mines in the tunnel,' declared Biggles, in the incisive tones he always used when he was keyed up for action.

'A sort of miniature Zeebrugge, eh?' grinned Ginger.

'Exactly. Hang on while I see if these pills are fastened together. Don't run the boat against one of those spikes or we shall take a flight through space that will make Clem Sohn's show look like a half-fledged sparrow doing its first solo.'

The 'spikes' to which Biggles referred were, of course, the 'horns' of the mines, which, in effect, act like triggers, in that anything coming into contact with them depresses a firing-pin into a detonator, which explodes the bursting charge.

The mines were, Biggles quickly ascertained with satisfaction, merely roped together at equal intervals to prevent them from bumping against each other; and with far less trouble than he expected he untied one, and then ordered Ginger to 'hang on to it' while he picked up the oars.

Ginger obeyed promptly but without enthusiasm, for like most people who are unaccustomed to handling high explosive, he regarded any instrument containing it with deep suspicion and mistrust. However, leaning over the stern, he got his hand through the iron ring attached for that purpose, and in this position was rowed by Biggles back into the tunnel.

'Be careful you don't barge into the wall,' warned Ginger nervously. 'For the love of mike use your torch.'

'It's all right, you can let it go now,' replied. Biggles. 'Don't worry; I hate the sight of these things as much as you do. Two minutes and we shall be out.'

Ginger released his dangerous charge with a deep sigh of relief, and could have shouted with joy when, a moment later, with Biggles bending to the oars, the entrance to the tunnel came into view. He was watching the pale grey opening become lighter as they drew nearer to it when, to his surprise, it was suddenly blotted out. At the same moment a deep, vibrant roar filled the tunnel, and he knew what it was.

'It's the submarine!' he cried in a strangled, high-pitched voice. 'She's coming in!'

'It's the submarine!' he cried. 'She's coming in!'

CHAPTER XVI

In the Lion's Den

That was, without doubt, one of the most desperate moments of their many desperate adventures. Biggles gasped out something – what it was Ginger did not hear – and whirling the dinghy round in its own length, set off back down the tunnel with all the power of his arms. A light flashed from the bows of the submarine and illuminated the cave as brightly as broad daylight. Then a shout rang out.

Biggles did not stop. Strangely enough, in his frantic haste to race the submarine he forgot all about the mine, and Ginger let out a shrill cry of horror as they missed it by a foot, their wake setting it bobbing and rolling in the middle of the fairway.

'Keep your head,' snarled Biggles angrily. 'I'm going to make for the quay – it's our only chance. Try and keep together … we've got to get up that path … use your gun if any one tries to stop you.'

They shot through the end of the tunnel into the moonlit crater, Biggles grunting as he threw his weight on the oars, knowing that life or death was going to be a matter of a split second. In his heart was a wild hope that they might reach the quay before the mine exploded, but it was not to be. He had just ascertained from Ginger that no lights were showing in the buildings when, with a roar like the end of the world, from the mouth of the tunnel belched a sheet of flame that shot halfway across the crater.

Biggles continued rowing without a pause, but there was only time for two more strokes. Then something seemed to come up under the boat and carry it forward with the speed of a racing motor-launch. The oars went by the board as he clutched at the sides to prevent himself from going overboard; and before anything could be done to prevent it, the dinghy had crashed into the undercarriage of the seaplane with such force that the top was ripped clean off one of the floats and a hole torn in the dinghy's side. It began to sink at once. Ginger grabbed at the undamaged float and managed to drag himself across it. Biggles was not so lucky. He fell into the water, but managed to seize the end of the damaged float, to which he hung, trying to make out what was happening ashore. 'Hang on,' he choked. 'Don't show more of yourself than you can help.'

At the moment Ginger was far too concerned with keeping his place on his refuge to pay much attention to anything else, for around them the water boiled and heaved and foamed as, flung into a maelstrom by the explosion, it dashed itself against the cliff, only to be hurled back in a smother of spray to meet a wave receding from the opposite wall.

The effect of this on the heavy submarine was bad enough, for it rocked like a cork, rolling its metal plates against the quay with an appalling grinding noise; but the antics of the lightly floating seaplane were terrifying in their complete abandon. It reared and bucked and threw itself about like a newly roped wild horse, sometimes thrusting its propeller deep into the waves, and at others standing on its tail with half of its floats out of the water. Fortunately, this state of affairs did not last long, and once the first shock had passed the miniature tornado began quickly to subside.

But on the shore – if shore it could be called – things were happening. From each of the three lower buildings men began to run down towards the quay, some shouting orders as they ran. Lights appeared everywhere.

'Looks like the evacuation of Sodom and Gomorrah,' grinned Biggles, his curious sense of humour overcoming all other emotions even at this critical juncture. 'I wonder what they think they're going to do.'

This was apparently something that the men themselves did not know, for they merely crowded on the end of the quay nearest to the cave, talking and gesticulating as they tried to ascertain the cause of the explosion.

Presently, when they had all collected there, Biggles realized that no better opportunity of escape would ever be likely to present itself. The tunnel had, he felt sure, caved in, or had so far become choked with debris as to be impassable. In any case they had no boat, so their only avenue of escape lay in the cliff path down which the men had come. It was, he knew, a forlorn hope at the best, but there was no other way, and their chances would certainly not be improved by the broad light of day which could not now be long in coming.

'Ginger,' he said quietly.

'Ay, ay, sir,' answered Ginger, with the calm that comes of knowing that things are so bad that they can hardly be worse.

'I'm going to make a dash for the top of the hill while these stiffs are all down on the quay,' Biggles told him. 'It's our only chance. If we can make the top we might, by taking to the jungle, get back to Algy. Are you ready?'

'O.K., Chief.'

'Come on, then.'

They released their hold on the seaplane and swam the few yards to the nearest point where they could effect a landing. Unfortunately, it meant going nearer to the men clustered on the quay, but there was no other landing-place, for in the opposite direction the cliff fell sheer into the water.

At first their luck held. They dragged themselves ashore dripping like water-spaniels, and had actually succeeded in getting above the quay before one of the men, for no reason at all, apparently, happened to look round. Ginger, who had kept one eye on the crowd, saw him peer forward, evidently seeing or sensing something unusual in their appearance; he saw him call the attention of the next man, who turned sharply and looked at them. He in turn called out something which made several of the others look; then, with one accord, they started up the path. At first they only walked, but as Biggles and Ginger quickened their pace they broke into a trot. Biggles started to run, and that was the signal for the chase to begin in earnest. Above, the sky was already grey, flushed with the pink rays of dawn.

The climb would have been a stiff one at the best of times, being sharply sloping rock for the most part, with hand-hewn steps occurring in the worst places; to take it at a run called for considerable endurance, and before they had gone far both Biggles and Ginger were breathing heavily.

Biggles was thankful for one thing. It seemed that the entire population of the enemy camp had, as was not unnatural, rushed down to the quay to see what had caused the explosion, so there was no one to bar their path. Had there been, then their case would have been hopeless from the start.

Rounding a shoulder of rock in which a flight of steps had been cut, he saw something that brought an ejaculation of satisfaction to his lips. Beside the path, where the workmen had piled it rather than carry it away, was a stack of detritus, pieces of rock of all shapes and sizes, just as it had been cut out in the construction of the steps. He was on it in a flash, kicking and pushing with hands and feet. Ginger joined him, and a minor avalanche of rocks and dust went bouncing and sliding down the path.

There was a yell from below as their pursuers saw what was happening and dashed for such meagre cover as the causeway offered. Which was precisely what Biggles had hoped to achieve, for it gave them a fresh start of which they were not long taking advantage.

'We've done it!' he gasped, as they burst round the last bend and saw that they were not more than twenty yards from the top, with the enemy a good forty or fifty yards behind. But he spoke too soon, although it was not to be expected that he could foresee what was to happen next.

Over the brow of the cliff, beyond which they could just see the thatched, conical roofs of native huts, poured a stream of Dyaks armed with their native weapon, the *kris*, which, in the hands of an expert, can take a man's head from his shoulders as cleanly as a guillotine. Their appearance confirmed what Biggles had suspected the previous day, that the enemy had natives in their employment, brought possibly from their own islands in the China Sea.

There seemed to be only one hope left, and Biggles, without pausing in his stride, swerved towards it – the wireless building, a rock-built structure with a heavy door made of rough-hewn planks of island timber. Would the door open? If it was locked—

With Ginger facing the mob, gun in hand, he tried the door. It opened easily, and they both burst inside.

Two men, oriental in appearance, in gold-braided blue uniforms, who had been sitting at the desk in front of a magnificent modern wireless equipment, sprang to their feet with startled eyes as the two airmen burst in. For an instant they stared, their little dark eyes flashing from one to the other of the intruders; then the elder, his flat face with its high cheekbones clouding with suspicion, pulled open a drawer and whipped out a revolver.

Biggles's pistol spoke first, and the man crumpled up like an empty sack.

The other darted round the desk with the obvious intention of getting to the door. Ginger barred his path, but at Biggles's quickly-snapped, 'All right, let him go', he stood aside and the man disappeared.

Biggles slammed the door behind him, locked it, and slipped the bolt with which it was fitted. Then, with his back to it, his eyes swept the room. It was typical of him that the major issue still weighed more with him than personal considerations, as his next words showed, for he did not waste time discussing ways and means of escape from the trap in which they found themselves.

'Can you handle that set?' he rapped out.

'I don't see why not,' answered Ginger, reaching the apparatus in three quick strides.

'Then try and get Singapore – usual wavelength,' Biggles told him tersely. 'As soon as you get 'em let me know. If the *Seafret* interferes tell the operator to listen but not jam the air.' As he finished speaking Biggles threw up his automatic and blazed at a face that appeared at the only window the cabin possessed, a small square of light near the door. One of the panes flew to fragments and the face disappeared.

Ginger did not even look up; with the earphones clipped on his head, he was already revolving the black vulcanite controls.

Biggles took up his position close to him, facing the window, pistol ready for snap-shooting.

There was a short silence; then something crashed against the door. Occasionally a dark figure flashed past the window, but Biggles held his fire. Time was the one factor that mattered now. If he could hold the place until he had got a message through to Singapore he didn't care much what happened after that. He saw that it was now broad daylight, and he was wondering what Algy would be thinking, when there came a crash on the door that made the whole building shake. But it held. For how long it would stand up to such treatment he did not know, but obviously it could not last many minutes. Then, with a crackle as of wood being broken up with incredible speed, a stream of machine-gun bullets poured through it, sending a cloud of splinters flying across the room; but they were well out of the line of fire, and the shots spattered harmlessly against the opposite wall.

'Any luck?' he asked Ginger, quietly.

'I've got *Seafret* – strongly, too – but I haven't been able to hook up with Singapore yet.'

'Never mind Singapore then; give this message to Sullivan

and ask him to transmit it as quickly as possible,' said Biggles quickly, taking a map from his pocket and opening it on the desk. For a second or two he studied it closely; then, picking up the pencil that had been dropped by the operator, he wrote swiftly on a message block, disregarding the attack on the door which was now being prosecuted with increasing vigour. When he had finished he pushed the slip over to Ginger, picked up his pistol again, and resumed guard over the window.

It was as well that he did so, for at that moment a brown arm, holding a revolver, appeared through the broken glass, and a bullet ploughed a long strip of leather from the top of the desk. Biggles leapt aside just in time, and before the man could fire again he had taken two swift paces forward and blazed at the arm from point-blank range. There was a yell outside; the revolver fell inside the room, and the arm was withdrawn.

'O.K.', called Ginger. 'Sullivan's got the story. Have you anything else to say to him?'

'Tell him we're in a jam—'

'I've told him where we are.'

'That's fine. Tell him not to worry about us but get through to Singapore as quickly as he can.'

Ginger returned to his task, but a moment later looked at Biggles with puzzled eyes. 'That's funny,' he exclaimed.

'What is?'

'I was speaking to *Seafret* when the operator cut in and said, "Hang on! Stand by for—" And that's as far as he got when the instrument went stone dead. I can't get a kick of any sort out of it.'

'I should say they've cut the lead-in wire outside,' answered Biggles, without taking his eyes from the window. 'They'd be pretty certain to do that as soon as they realized that we might start broadcasting for help. I wonder what *Seafret* meant by telling us to stand by. What for? But there, it's no use guessing. I should like to know what's going on outside; they seem to have stopped banging on the door.'

'I suppose we can't hold out until the R.A.F. machines arrive?'

Biggles shook his head definitely. 'No,' he said. 'That's out of the question. They'll be hours. In any case, the last place we want to be when they start doing their stuff is here; believe me, life won't be worth living.' As he finished speaking, actuated by a sudden impulse, he snatched a quick glance through the window. It was only a momentary glimpse, but it revealed a lot. 'My good-ness!' he gasped.

Standing in the middle of the path, not ten yards from the door and pointing towards it, was a machine-gun on a tripod, a metal belt of ammunition hanging out of it like a long flat centipede. There was nothing surprising about that; on the contrary, it was just what he expected to see; but he certainly did not expect it to be deserted. A little farther down the path a large party of men, some in uniform, and others, the Dyaks, bare-skinned, were dragging a much heavier gun into position. Scattered about the rocks in various positions watching the proceedings were others, mostly officers, judging by their uniforms.

Biggles made up his mind with the speed and precision that comes from long experience in the air. 'I'm going to make a bolt for it,' he snapped. 'Keep me covered as far as you can.' With that he unfastened the door, flung it wide open, and raced to the machine-gun.

It is probable that this was the very last thing the people

outside expected. One does not look to a rabbit to leave its burrow voluntarily when a pack of terriers is waiting outside. Certain it is that not one commander in a hundred would have anticipated such a move, or made allowance for it. On the face of it, it was sheer suicide, but as so often happens in the case of unorthodox tactics, it was in this very factor that its highest recommendation lay. Biggles knew that, as well as he knew that indecision and procrastination could have but one ending, and upon his judgement in this respect he was prepared to risk all.

It was not remarkable that all eyes were on the heavy gun, and the ill-assorted team working on it, when he made his dash. What was inside the wireless hut may have offered food for speculation, but the exterior presented no attraction, so of the two subjects the gun offered most entertainment. Which again was all to Biggles's advantage, and he actually reached the machine-gun before he was seen. In the twinkling of an eye he had swung the ribbed water-jacket surrounding the muzzle in the opposite direction and squatted down behind it, thumbs on the double-thumbpiece. There was no need to take aim. The target was large and the range point-blank. Jabbing yellow flames leapt from the muzzle, and before the stream of lead the crowd disappeared like a waft of smoke in a high wind. Those who had been hit lay where they had fallen; the others raced for cover.

Biggles did not confine his attention entirely to the main body of the enemy. From time to time he slewed the barrel round and raked the surrounding rocks behind which the spectators had taken cover, and the scream of ricocheting bullets seemed to intensify the volume of fire. Suddenly the noise broke off short, and he knew that the belt was exhausted.

The target was large and the range point-blank.

'Come on,' he yelled to Ginger, who was crouching behind him, automatic in hand, and made a dash for the jungle not a score of paces distant. Ginger followed. So completely successful had the sortie been that he did not have to fire a single shot during the whole engagement.

CHAPTER XVII

Just Retribution

For a short distance they followed a narrow path through the bush, but then, knowing that they would be pursued by the Dyaks, who, at home in such surroundings, would soon overtake them, Biggles turned aside into the rank vegetation, taking care not to leave any marks that would betray them. Ginger, feeling with a queer sense of unreality that the clock had been put back a few years and he was once more playing at Indians, followed his example.

Within the forest a dim grey twilight still persisted, for the matted tree-tops met over their heads, shutting out the sunlight, while below, the secondary growth made the going difficult, and the only way they could keep moving was by constantly changing direction, taking the least obstructed path that offered itself. After the recent noise and commotion, it all seemed very still and quiet, but Biggles was not deceived; he knew that somewhere not far away the enemy would be seeking them.

Ginger realized suddenly that they were out of the trap – or nearly out – and so swiftly had the situation changed that he had difficulty in believing it. 'Where are you making for?' he whispered.

'So far, I haven't been making for anywhere in particular,'

answered Biggles quietly. 'I've been quite happy to go anywhere. But now we must try to get down to the beach; I only pray that Algy is still sitting tight behind the islet. If he's had to move – but let's not think about that. Come on, let's keep going. Hello! What's that? Listen!'

From somewhere not far behind them a wild shout had echoed through the trees, to be followed immediately by others, and the swish of undergrowth.

Biggles knew what it meant. The Dyaks had found their trail and were in hot pursuit. 'Come on,' he whispered. 'It's no use trying to move without leaving a trail in this stuff; it has got to be a matter of speed.'

Neither of them will ever forget the next ten minutes. At first they tried to move quietly, but it was impossible, and in a short time they had abandoned such methods and were making all the speed possible, regardless of noise. The stagnant air, combined with the flies that rose from the foetid ground and followed them in an ever-increasing cloud, did nothing to make their progress easier, and to Ginger the flight had soon resolved itself into a delirium of whirling branches and swaying palm-fronds; but he kept his eyes on Biggles's back and followed closely on his heels. Once they plunged through a mire in which several crocodiles were wallowing, but the creatures were evidently as startled as they were, for they crashed into the bushes, leaving the way clear. On the far side the ground sloped steeply down towards the sea, the deep blue of which they could now see from time to time through the foliage. Down towards it they plunged, slipping, sliding, falling, and sometimes rolling, grabbing at any handhold to steady themselves. Occasionally they heard crashes in the bush perilously close behind them.

They burst out of the forest at a point which Biggles recognized at once; it was a little to one side of the quicksands, fortunately the side nearer to their own bay. A few hundred yards to the right the gaunt uprights of the elevated cemetery straddled the rocks near the edge of the cliff, and as they swung towards them Biggles grabbed Ginger's arm with his right hand, pointing to seaward with his left.

'Great Heavens! What on earth is all that?' he gasped.

He need not have pointed, for Ginger had already seen them – a dozen or more machines in arrowhead formation, the point directed towards the island.

'They're Vildebeests!' he yelled exultantly, as he saw the blunt noses and queerly humped backs of the aircraft. 'How the – where the—?'

'Never mind how they got here, keep going,' panted Biggles, snatching a glance over his shoulder just as the Dyaks began to stream out of the jungle. They raised a shout as they viewed their quarry.

To Biggles, the appearance of the R.A.F. machines was as miraculous as it had been to Ginger, for it was quite certain that they could not have come from Singapore in the hour that had elapsed since they had signalled the *Seafret*; but there was no time to ponder the mystery. The Dyaks were gaining on them. They were not more than fifty yards behind, and the beach was still nearly a quarter of a mile away.

As they reached the cemetery, a *kris* flashed past Biggles's shoulder and glanced off the rocks in front of him, and he knew that to continue running was to court disaster, for the next one might bury itself in his back – or Ginger's. Subconsciously he was aware of the Vildebeests nosing down towards the centre of the island, the roar of their engines drowning all other sounds, and he knew that whatever happened now their mission had been successful. In a sort of savage exultation he drew his automatic and whirled round. *Bang! Bang! Bang!* it spat as he opened rapid fire on the mob. *Bang! Bang! Bang!* Ginger's gun took up the story.

The Dyaks, who were evidently well acquainted with firearms, split up like a covey of partridges going down a line of guns as they dodged for cover, and at that moment the first bomb burst.

Biggles grabbed Ginger by the arm and sped on, satisfied with the brief respite they had gained. With the roar of bursting bombs in their ears, they reached the place where the rocks sloped down to the bay, and Ginger let out a yell as the *Nemesis* came into view, her metal propellers two flashing arcs of living fire as she skimmed across the surface of the water towards them. They saw her nose turn in towards the shore and then swing out again as her keel touched the sandy bottom near the beach; saw the propellers slow down; saw Algy jump up in the cockpit and dive into the cabin, to reappear with the machine-gun, which he balanced on the windscreen. But that was all they saw for, at that moment, the whole island seemed to blow up.

Ginger afterwards swore that the ground lifted several inches under his feet, and Biggles admitted that he had never heard anything quite like it, not even during the war, although the explosion must have been similar to that of the famous Bailleul ammunition dump. It was just like a tremendous roar of thunder that went on for a full minute.

The force of it threw both Biggles and Ginger off their feet, and they finished the last twenty yards of the slope in something between a roll and a slide. And, as he lay on his back at the bottom, with the extraordinary vividness that such moments sometimes produce, a picture was printed indelibly on Ginger's brain. It was of a Vildebeest, against a background of blue sky, soaring vertically upwards and whirling like a dead leaf in a gale as the pilot strove to control his machine in such an up-current as would seldom, if ever, be encountered in nature.

Shaken, and not a little dazed, Ginger picked himself up and obeyed Biggles's order to get to the amphibian. Biggles himself, gun in hand, was looking back up the slope at the place where the Dyaks might be expected to appear. But they did not come, and presently he followed Ginger to the *Nemesis*.

Algy looked at him askance. 'If sounds are anything to go by, you *have* been having a lovely time,' he observed.

'Not so bad,' grinned Biggles. 'Where in thunder did all this aviation start from?'

Algy shrugged his shoulders. 'Don't ask me,' he answered shortly. 'I know no more about it than you do. I—' He broke off with a puzzled expression on his face, staring over Biggles's shoulder at the jungle-clad hill-side.

Ginger, following his gaze, saw a curious sight. From the centre of the island there seemed to be rising a pale green transparent cloud that writhed and coiled like a Scotch mist on an October day, and rolled in slow, turgid waves down the hill-side towards the sea. And as it rolled, and in silence embraced the forest, the foliage of the trees changed colour. The dark green of the casuarinas turned to yellow, and the emerald of the palm crests to dingy white.

As Biggles beheld this phenomenon he turned very pale and shouted one word. It was enough. The word was 'Gas', and almost before the word had died on his lips the three of them were falling into their places in the aircraft faster than they had ever embarked in all their travels.

Within a minute the *Nemesis* was tearing across the water, flinging behind her a line of swirling foam. The line ended abruptly as Biggles lifted her from the sea, and climbed slowly away from where the Vildebeests were now re-forming.

'Where to?' asked Algy.

'I think we might as well go home,' answered Biggles, glancing down through the green miasma at the flagging desolation of what had, a few minutes before, been a living forest. 'But before we do that we had better have a word or two with Sullivan,' he added, turning the nose of the *Nemesis* in the direction of Hastings Island.

Twenty minutes later he landed in the anchorage that had proved so ill-chosen for the *Seafret*, and taxied up to the beach near the stranded destroyer, where the ship's officers awaited them in a little group. From the far distance the drone of many engines rose and fell on the gentle breeze, and as he stepped ashore Biggles could see the formation of Vildebeests heading towards the island. He raised a finger and pointed to them, at the same time turning to the commander of the *Seafret*.

'Sullivan,' he said, 'can you satisfy my burning curiosity by telling me just how it happened that these aeroplanes arrived at this particular spot so opportunely?'

The commander smiled. 'That's easy,' he answered. 'I fetched them here.'

'*You* did?'

'Of course. You didn't suppose it was a fluke, did you?'

Biggles scratched his head. 'I didn't know what to think, and that's a fact,' he confessed. 'You certainly had a brainwave. What caused it?'

'The simple fact that Lacey didn't return. I don't mind telling you that it got me all hot and bothered. It seemed to be the last straw, our only mobile unit going west – as I thought. In the circumstances there was only one thing left for me to do, which was to get in touch with R.A.F. headquarters at Singapore and ask for assistance both for myself and you. We'd got to get away from here some time, and I didn't feel like abandoning you without a search. Squadron-Leader Gore-Alliston had just landed here with his pack of air-hounds, and I was just telling him the story when your message came through. Naturally, Gore-Alliston took off at once for Elephant Island. I hope he did his stuff all right.'

'He certainly did,' agreed Biggles gravely. 'There isn't a living creature left on the island, I'll warrant – human being, crocodile, or mosquito.'

Sullivan's face expressed incredulity.

'They're gassed, the lot of them,' explained Biggles. 'I didn't know our fellows carried gas-bombs nowadays—'

'Who told you they did?'

'It looks mighty like it to me.'

Sullivan shook his head. 'You've got it all wrong,' he said, 'but I can hazard a guess as to what happened. The Vildebeests were carrying ordinary hundred-and-twelve pound high explosive bombs, and they must have hit the enemy's gas-shell dump.'

'Gas-shells? Where did you get that idea?'

'When we brought the "mouldy" aboard from the junk, my gunnery officer thought it would be a good thing to have a shell or two as well, to try and find out the name of the firm who was supplying them. He tells me that they are all gas-shells – at least, all those he brought aboard the *Seafret.*'

'Jumping crocodiles! Do you mean to tell me that those skunks were going to use gas-shells if it came to a scrap?'

Sullivan nodded grimly. 'I don't suppose they were going to use them for ballast,' he observed harshly.

'Then it serves them jolly well right that they've got hoisted with their own blinking petard,' declared Biggles savagely. 'There seems to be a bit of poetic justice about what has happened that meets with my entire approval.' He turned to watch the Vildebeests land on the bay.

'What are you going to do now?' asked Sullivan.

Biggles glanced over his shoulder. 'I suppose they're sending a ship from Singapore to pick you up?' he asked.

'Yes, a destroyer is on the way.'

'In that case I'm going to hit the breeze for home,' Biggles told him. 'The people who sent us out on this jaunt will be anxious to know what is happening, and I don't think it would be wise to entrust such delicate information to ordinary lines of communication.'

'You're not going without telling us what happened on the island,' protested Sullivan.

Biggles looked pained. 'My dear chap, I wouldn't dream of doing such a thing,' he answered. 'How about a quiet bit of dinner tonight to celebrate the occasion? I can tell you all about it then.'

In Passing

Ten days later, early in the evening, the door of the sitting-room in Biggles's flat opened and Biggles walked in. He glanced at Algy and Ginger, who looked as though they had been expecting him, lit a cigarette, and flicked the dead match into the grate.

'Well, come on, out with it,' growled Ginger. 'What did he say?'

Biggles frowned. 'You mustn't call the Foreign Secretary a "he".'

'I'll call you something worse than that if you don't tell me what he said,' grinned Ginger.

'Very well, since you must know, he said, "Thank you!"'

Ginger blinked. 'He said *what?*'

'"Thank you!" Or, to be absolutely accurate, he said, "Thank you very much".'

'Is that all?'

'What did you expect? Did you suppose he was going to kiss me?'

'No, but – do you mean to tell me that was all he had to say, after all we've done?'

'Unless he wrote a song and dance about it, there isn't much more he could say, when you come to think about it, is there?'

'No, I suppose there isn't. But he might have done something – given us a gold watch apiece, for instance.'

Biggles shook his head. 'The government doesn't express its thanks by doling out gold watches,' he answered seriously. 'And, anyway, you've got something better than that. Your name is down on the Imperial archives for having rendered the state a signal service, and one day that may stand you in very good stead. When you've worked for the government as long as I have you'll know that virtue is expected to be its own reward.'

'Well, if that's all, we might as well go out and buy ourselves a bite of dinner,' declared Algy, rising.

'No need to do that,' replied Biggles, smiling. 'Lord Lottison has been kind enough to ask us all to dine with him, at his house, in order that certain members of the Cabinet may learn at first hand just what transpired during the operations of His Majesty's aircraft *Nemesis* in the Straits of the Mergui Archipelago. Go and put on your best bibs and tuckers, and look sharp about it; Cabinet Ministers don't like being kept waiting.'

BIGGLES –
SECRET AGENT

CHAPTER I

An Alarming Proposition

The Honourable Algernon Lacey rose slowly from the easy chair in which he had been reclining, yawned, and took up a position on the hearth-rug with his back to the fire, hands thrust deep into the pockets of a well-worn pair of grey flannel trousers. A frown lined his forehead as he turned his eyes to where Ginger was lounging in another chair with every indication of bored impatience. 'Where the deuce *is* Biggles?' he inquired in a manner which suggested that he did not expect an answer. There was more than a suspicion of irritation in his tone of voice.

'If you say that again I shall throw something at you,' answered Ginger coldly. 'How should I know?'

'He said that he would be back for lunch. He was emphatic about it.'

'He promised me that he would come to the flicks this afternoon – the new flying film at the Plaza. It's now after three o'clock. He isn't given to saying what he doesn't mean, from which we can assume, I think, that he has run into somebody or something important.'

'That's true,' agreed Algy moodily. 'I hope he hasn't run into a bus, or anything like that.'

'It wouldn't surprise me; the traffic is getting awful,' murmured Ginger in a resigned voice. 'I'm about sick of London. What did they say at the Aero Club when you rang up?'

'They said he'd been in, got his letters, and gone out again.'

'He didn't stay there for lunch?'

'No.'

'Oh, well, it's no use fretting. Flicks are out of the question, anyway. He'll be along presently, I expect.'

Ginger's expectation materialized about a quarter of an hour later, when the door opened and Biggles walked in. He tossed his hat carelessly on a side table and, sinking into an easy chair, regarded Ginger gravely. 'Sorry about the flicks, Ginger,' he said in an expressionless voice. 'I couldn't get back.'

'That's all right, Biggles,' returned Ginger casually, but with a sidelong glance at Algy. 'We waited lunch for you until two o'clock. I suppose you've had some?'

Biggles pulled himself together. He looked up and smiled. 'Yes, thanks; I had an excellent lunch.'

'What did you have?'

Biggles ran his fingers through his fair hair. A puzzled expression crept over his face. 'That's funny,' he said. 'Dashed if I remember.'

'Where did you go?'

Biggles smiled again. His hazel eyes twinkled. 'As a matter of fact I had lunch in a private room in Whitehall – in an annexe of the Home Office, to be precise.'

Ginger nodded slowly, and flashed another glance at Algy. He looked back at Biggles. 'I get it,' he said knowingly. 'I don't bet, but I'd risk a small wager that Colonel Raymond was there.'

'You win,' smiled Biggles.

'Who else?'

'Sir Munstead Norton.'

'Sir who—? Who the dickens is he?'

'Permanent Assistant to the Home Secretary.'

Algy whistled softly. 'So that's it, is it?' he murmured. 'Now we know why you were looking worried when you came in. What did they want?'

Biggles took a cigarette from his case, lit it, and flicked the dead match into the grate before he replied. 'They wanted me to do a job for them,' he said quietly.

'Not being altogether a fool – I hope – I had already gathered that,' muttered Algy with asperity. 'It's the only time Raymond stands any of us lunch.'

'Come now, he's a busy man,' protested Biggles. 'To be Assistant Commissioner of Police, Special Intelligence Branch, is no blind nut.'

'The point is, have you taken the job on?' asked Ginger.

'No – not yet.'

'Why not?'

Biggles drew at his cigarette and exhaled the smoke slowly. 'Because,' he answered, slowly and distinctly, 'it is not a job to be lightly undertaken.'

'Is that why you looked fed up when you came in?'

'Not altogether. I may as well be frank. I am worried about you two. We've always been in on these jobs together, and I know it's no use trying to keep you out. But this time it – well – it alarms me.'

'From which I gather that it involves a certain amount of danger,' put in Algy suavely.

Biggles looked him in the eyes. 'If I merely said yes to that

I should be guilty of understatement,' he said simply. 'Suicidal would probably be a better word.'

Algy frowned. 'Good heavens! That sounds pretty grim.'

'Grim it is!'

'Suppose you tell us about it?' suggested Ginger.

'That is my intention,' replied Biggles, knocking the ash off his cigarette onto the floor and putting his foot on it. 'I've only been giving myself a minute or two to settle down, to get the thing into some sort of order in my mind. I have permission to take you into my confidence, but – it's hardly necessary for me to say this, but I was asked to do so – what is said between these four walls this afternoon must never be repeated outside them. From that you will judge the matter to be of considerable importance. It is. The issue involves no less than the safety of the nation.'

'My word!' muttered Ginger.

Algy said nothing, but a grimace expressed his thoughts.

When Biggles continued his voice had dropped to little more than a whisper. 'Does the name Beklinder mean anything to you?' he asked. 'Professor Max Beklinder?'

Algy thought for a moment and then shook his head. 'No,' he said at last. 'I seem to recall the name vaguely, but I don't know in what connection.'

'I remember the name,' murmured Ginger, wrinkling his forehead. 'Isn't he an inventor of some sort?'

Biggles nodded. 'Professor Beklinder was the name of the man who invented Linderite, which is an explosive just about three times as powerful as anything previously discovered. That was only one of his inventions.'

'Queer name; what nationality is he?' asked Algy.

'Lucranian by birth, British by naturalization,' answered Biggles.

'Where the deuce is Lucrania?'

'You might well ask. I didn't know myself when the name cropped up. Apparently it is one of those little principalities, like Monaco and Liechtenstein, that linger on in Europe, officially independent and self-governing but in fact controlled by a powerful neighbour under whose military and economic protection they are allowed to survive. Lucrania is quite a small place, and is now almost entirely embraced by the new German frontiers. There are narrow corridors into France and Switzerland. The language spoken is German. The country comprises a central plain surrounded almost entirely by mountains forming the natural frontiers by virtue of which it has managed to retain its so-called independence. So much for the country in which Professor Beklinder was born. Twenty years ago he was practising – successfully, I understand – as a doctor; but he got mixed up in a political intrigue and had to flee for his life. He came here, leaving his wife – who subsequently disappeared – behind. I mention the wife for reasons which will presently become apparent.' Biggles lit another cigarette before he continued.

'I was saying,' he went on, 'that Beklinder, like most political refugees, came to England, where he soon settled down and made a name for himself as a research chemist, specializing in high-combustion explosives. Linderite put him at the top of the tree with our people, at whose invitation, about two years ago, he turned his abilities to the production of poison gas. Not a very pleasant occupation, you may say, but while other nations devote time and money to chemical warfare we must do the same. Beklinder apparently worked hard at his new job, so hard that he came near to having a breakdown. By this time, however, he had got on the track of a poison gas so deadly that he declared that the nation which alone possessed the formula could make itself master of the world – by the destruction or terrorization of the others. How far that is true, or an exaggeration, I am not in a position to judge; it is sufficient for me that our experts believe it. Very well. Encouraged by the departmental experts of this country he went on with his work. The secret was practically within his grasp when his health broke down. It became necessary for him to rest. And this is where the trouble started.

'I must now go back a bit to refer to an incident which may, or may not, have a bearing on what was to follow. About a year ago the Professor, possibly because he was run down, had a fit – a belated fit you will think – of remorse over the unfortunate wife whom he had, by force of circumstances beyond his control, left in Lucrania. He asked the British Intelligence people to try to locate her, or ascertain her fate; and although they were only too willing to oblige, they failed to discover anything, which was in due course reported to the Professor, who made no complaint, and appeared to dismiss the matter from his mind. But the fact that he made such an inquiry has now become significant.

'The Professor rested, and quickly recovered his health. He was almost fit enough to resume work when he suggested to the government that a fortnight on the Riviera was all that was needed to put him on his feet again. Naturally, our people would have preferred that he completed his formula; but he was, after all, a private individual, and it was not within their rights to refuse. To make a long story short, he went. That was nearly three months ago. He took his own car, a Morris Ten, across the Channel, with the avowed intention of following the *Route*

Nationale – the main highway – down to the Mediterranean. I say "avowed" intention because it now transpires that he did nothing of the sort – although how far this was due to the Professor himself we have no means of knowing. A Scotland Yard man had been detailed to watch him – for his own protection, of course – but he lost him in Paris. The story now becomes extremely interesting.

'Three days after Beklinder disappeared in Paris a story reached England through the usual news agencies that a motor-car accident had occurred at a village named Unterhamstadt, in Lucrania. A small car bearing a British registration plate had been involved in a collision with a lorry. The driver of the car had been killed on the spot. His papers revealed that he was a British subject named—'

'Max Beklinder,' murmured Algy.

'Exactly,' continued Biggles. 'This unfortunate man, the agencies reported, had been buried in the village churchyard. That was all. No more, no less. But you can imagine the effect of it on our people. The Home Office, the Foreign Office, the Poison Gas Experimental Station, and the Intelligence Service were thrown into a panic. It is easy to see how they were fixed. The story came through the British press in a perfectly normal manner. Max Beklinder might have been a Mr Brown, or a Mr Smith. To follow the story up too closely might have set the Lucranian government wondering what all the fuss was about – if, of course, they didn't already know the true facts of the case. *That* was the thing that turned our fellows' hair grey overnight. The Lucranian Intelligence people *might* know who Max Beklinder was, and what he was doing in England. On the other hand, they might not, considering that the man had been in England for nearly twenty years. Naturally, all his work had been carried on in secret, but spies have a way of ferreting out these things. In short, the government went into what we should call a flat spin. Was the thing an accident – or was it not? What was the Professor doing in Lucrania, anyway? Had he gone there of his own free will, or had he been taken there by force? These were some of the questions with which our people were faced, and the answers weren't easy to find. Then somebody remembered the business about his wife, and a motive for his presence in Lucrania was discovered – but it didn't help much. The situation as it stood was bad enough, but worse was to come.

'About seven weeks ago, three weeks after the alleged accident, out of the blue came a piece of news that rocked Whitehall to its foundations. A British secret agent in Prenzel, the capital of Lucrania, reported that at a certain place and time he had seen Professor Beklinder driving in a motor-car with the Chief of the Lucranian Secret Police. Just reflect on that for a moment, and see what it meant – if the report was correct. Beklinder dead was bad enough, but alive in the hands of a potential enemy power was worse – a lot worse. The accident business began to look very fishy. And things began to look fishy for this country, for if Lucranian agents had got hold of poor old Beklinder it would only be a question of time before they forced him to divulge what he had been doing, and disclose the formula for the poison gas. The upshot of this news was to put the government into about the worst jam of its career. And that is how things stand now. The trouble is, it has been impossible to get confirmation of the British agent's report. The fellow is in London now. He admits that he doesn't know Beklinder very well, but he *thought* it was him. It was only a passing glance. It might have been him. But the bare possibility of it is enough to keep our people awake at nights. It comes to this. If the man in the car *was* Beklinder, then the accident business was all a frame-up, and there wouldn't have been any frame-up unless the Lucranian agents had known what the Professor was doing in England. And if they did know, with the Professor in their hands the formula is as good as theirs. When they get it – if they get it – it is good-bye to the British Empire. And after hearing that you won't wonder any longer why I looked worried when I came in just now.'

'But do you mean that they want *you* to go and investigate this?' asked Ginger incredulously.

'That's the idea.'

'But in heaven's name, why *you*?' cried Algy. 'Surely they have got plenty of people of their own, capable—'

Biggles held up his hand. 'Just a minute,' he said quietly. 'Our Intelligence people aren't fools. They had a man planted in the country within twenty-four hours of the information being received, with instructions to report progress every three days. Not a word has been heard of him since he crossed the frontier. A week ago they sent another man – one of the best they have, with similar instructions. He went forewarned, but that did not save him. He's gone.'

'Where were these men actually making for?' asked Algy.

'Unterhamstadt – but it's unlikely that they got as far as that. Our people are of opinion that they were caught on the frontier.'

'Is there any reason to suppose that they wouldn't catch *us* on the frontier?' inquired Algy.

Biggles looked up. 'Yes,' he said softly.

'Why?'

'Because we shouldn't go in that way.'

'Ah! I see,' murmured Algy. 'I begin to understand why they sent for you. They suggested that you avoided frontiers by the expedient of flying over them?'

'Precisely,' agreed Biggles. 'Our Intelligence people have established that frontier control has been so tightened up that it would be impossible for a mouse to get through without being marked down. A stranger entering the country is watched from the moment he puts foot past the Customs House.'

'Which suggests that Lucrania has something valuable to guard.'

'Our people haven't overlooked that. It all goes to confirm that the alleged accident to Beklinder was a plot to cover what really happened.'

'So what?'

'Sir Munstead Norton, advised by Colonel Raymond and Intelligence experts, is of the opinion that the only way a man could get into the country is by flying in. Regular air transport is no use, of course; airports are watched as closely as stations on the frontier. Oh, I can see plainly enough why they got hold of me – I was just leaving the club – and asked me to go to Unterhamstadt.'

'Why there, particularly?'

'Because it's the only loose end in this very tangled ball of string.'

'What exactly do they hope you will achieve when you get there?'

'Find out, first of all, whether the Professor is alive or dead. That, clearly, is the crux of the situation. If he is really dead, then that's the end of it.'

'And just how would you propose to establish that?' asked Ginger slowly, his eyes on Biggles's face.

Biggles rose from his chair and paced slowly up and down the hearthrug. He stopped abruptly. 'It would be futile to tour the country on the off-chance of seeing the Professor. If he is, in fact, dead, it would be running an appalling risk unnecessarily.'

'Yes, but *is* there a way of ascertaining definitely whether he is alive or dead?' insisted Algy. 'I can't think of a way.'

'There is only one way – one way of making *quite* sure,' said Biggles in a curious voice.

Ginger nodded. 'I get it,' he said.

Biggles regarded him steadily. His face was set in hard lines. 'Where would *you* start?' he asked shortly, almost harshly.

Ginger faltered. 'In the – the – churchyard,' he stammered.

Biggles drew a deep breath. 'That's it,' he murmured.

'You mean – you'd go to look for the tombstone?' put in Algy.

Biggles shook his head. 'It would hardly do to trust to a tombstone,' he said slowly. 'In fact, there's almost certain to be a tombstone. A grave will be there, whether it contains the Professor's body or not; I don't think we need have any doubt about that. Even if the alleged accident was a fake, Beklinder's death was officially reported to the press, so the Lucranian agents would hardly overlook the necessity for providing such an elementary piece of evidence as a grave. Frankly, I have an open mind as to what it may contain—'

'Just a minute,' interrupted Algy tersely. His eyes had opened wide, and an expression of disgust, almost of horror, had settled on his face. 'You mean—'

'I perceive that you have at last realized just what I do mean,' put in Biggles evenly. 'Finding the grave is only the first step. We should have to open it up to see what it contained. That is the *only* way – to make sure; and guesswork won't do in a case like this. There's no alternative.'

Silence fell. Biggles lit another cigarette. Algy stared into the fire. Ginger gazed thoughtfully at the hearthrug, chewing the end of a dead match, while the clock on the mantelpiece ticked out the seconds and dropped them into the past.

'Is this – churchyard business – what was suggested to you?' asked Algy at last.

Biggles nodded.

'Having established that fact, one way or the other, you could then come home?'

'That would depend on what we – found.'

'You mean, if Beklinder was alive?'

'We should have to try to find him.'

Algy stared aghast. 'By heavens! That's a tall order,' he exclaimed indignantly.

'If you will cast your mind back you will recall that I pointed that out in the beginning. Well, what do we do about it?'

Ginger walked across to the bell-push.

'What are you going to do?' asked Biggles.

'Ring for some tea. The fact that Mr Beklinder has disappeared seems to be no reason why we should all starve to death. On the contrary, the statement that we're all likely to be gassed to death in the near future suggests that we should make the most of things while the going's good.'

The remark relieved the tension in the atmosphere. Biggles smiled. 'I quite agree,' he said. 'We'll have a pot of tea and then go into things a bit more closely.'

CHAPTER II

Ways And Means

'While the tea things were still on the table Biggles reopened the conversation. 'Assuming that we agreed to take on this proposition, let us try to work out how we should have to go about it. I gave it some thought on the way home, and this is the way it looks to me. First of all, let us be under no delusions as to the risks; if we're caught, or if our mission is so much as suspected, we shall be – to use the popular expression – bumped off. In no circumstances whatever would the British government come to our assistance; on the contrary, they would, in accordance with international tradition in such matters, disclaim all knowledge of us. It would be impossible for them to do anything else. I don't know how you feel about it, but my own reaction to all this is something like relief, because it permits no introduction of half measures. If we go, we go the whole hog all the time. The question of mitigating circumstances would not arise. Knowing that failure could have only one ending we should go to any lengths – *any* lengths – to prevent it. In other words, knowing that our opponents would not hesitate to kill us, I should not hesitate to proceed on the same principle.

'Now about getting there. As I see it, the machine required would be a four-seater with manoeuvrability as the first consideration. We shouldn't need anything of outstanding performance. Something stable, easy to fly – bearing in mind that the actual flying would be done at night – something that could be put down in a small field, on rough ground, is what we should want. That means something light, with wheel brakes to pull up quickly, and a wide landing chassis to prevent the machine turning over if a wheel hit an obstruction.'

'Something like the Wessex "Student"?' suggested Ginger.

'That's the machine I had in mind,' declared Biggles. 'All right. Let us imagine that we are starting. Obviously we couldn't operate from England. It's too far away. The ideal base would be a small aerodrome in north-eastern France. At the moment we are good friends with France, so Colonel Raymond could probably arrange that. Right! We are now at the aerodrome. We go over into enemy country on the first fine Saturday night – and here we strike the first snag; there's no way round it that I can see. There can be no question of landing in Lucrania except in the case of extreme emergency, because while it's possible to get down without making a noise, it's unfortunately impossible for a machine to take off except under full throttle, and you know what that means. We daren't risk being heard. With the state of vigilance the country is in, one rumour of a machine taking off at night would make further operations impossible. No! There's only one way. It means taking the machine up to twenty thousand feet outside the frontier and gliding over. Some one will have to stay in the machine; the other two will go down by parachute. The machine, still gliding, will then go back across the frontier without having opened its engine inside Lucrania.

Algy, I should ask you to fly the machine. Ginger and I would go down into what we may regard as enemy country.'

Algy nodded. 'That's all right with me,' he said lightly.

'It's the getting out that is likely to worry us,' continued Biggles. 'And this is where we shall have to do some serious thinking. It means working to a time-table. You would have to glide over at prearranged times and watch for signals. Fortunately, we all know the Morse code, so in emergency those on the ground could flash a message to the machine. That may not be necessary, though. Coloured lights are simpler. For example, a red light would mean "keep away"; a green light would be "come down and fetch us." Do you follow?'

'Yes, that's quite straightforward,' agreed Algy.

'Good! Now for the landing-ground. In my pocket I have a tracing of a large-scale map of the Unterhamstadt district. I got it at the Foreign Office. There isn't a proper aerodrome near the village – nor would it be desirable to work too close, anyway. The village itself lies in a valley with wooded hills on either side. Incidentally, the churchyard is about a quarter of a mile from the centre of the village. Apart from the church, there happens to be a conspicuous landmark near by – Unterhamstadt Castle. It's only a ruin of crumbling towers and walls, so I understand, but it stands on a knoll and rises above the surrounding trees. It seems to be one of those romantic-sounding old places that inspired Grimm's fairy tales. Lucrania and Bohemia are full of them – relics of the days when knights were bold and slew stray dragons to please beautiful princesses. I fancy we shall have something far more dangerous than dragons to contend with.

'Beyond the hills the country is open, most of it under cultivation. There are several places where a machine could get down at a pinch, but four miles due north there's a large grazing area which would suit our purpose admirably. Ginger and I would aim to hit that when we go over with our "brollies". Another point arises here. We can't float about Lucrania without any luggage. We should have to adopt the role of tourists – this being, as far as I can see, the only excuse for an Englishman to visit the country.'

'You mean – you wouldn't actually hide up?' asked Ginger.

'I don't see how we could. We may be there for some time, and we've got to eat. Sooner or later somebody would be bound to see us, and a report of two strangers slinking about in the woods wouldn't make our task any easier. This is my idea, and you'll see the reason for it presently. Bear in mind that I have been into this pretty closely with the Foreign Office people, who were able to give me a lot of useful information. Ginger and I would arrive at Unterhamstadt ostensibly as tourists. Having disposed of our parachutes we should, of course, arrive on foot. Now tourists seldom walk about Lucrania, or anywhere else in Europe for that matter, carrying their own suitcases. When they have suitcases they arrive at the railway station, and either drive or walk to their hotel, in which case the hotel porter fetches the luggage. Alternatively, they arrive at a place by motor-car. I say alternatively, but there is, in fact, another fairly common way of travelling nowadays when a lot of people are going abroad on the cheap. They walk, carrying their kit in a rucksack. If, therefore, Ginger and I arrive at the hotel in Unterhamstadt in shorts or flannel bags, carrying rucksacks, we should, I think, pass for a type of tourist which is becoming increasingly common on the Continent. As you know, I speak German fairly well, which should be a great help.'

'You said *the* hotel,' put in Algy.

'Yes, there's only one, but it is a good one. I gather that it is one of those big old coaching stations which still hang on in France and Germany. I believe a number of tourists use it, artists, plant hunters, hikers, and so on. We can be artists.'

'I see – go on.'

'Very well. Ginger and I arrive at the hotel. Assuming that our arrival passes without comment, we shall have exactly seven days to do our job and get out of it.'

'Why seven days?'

'When we arrive we shall have to register, which reminds me, we shall have to forge frontier control stamps on our passports for the hotel proprietor's benefit. As you know, one has to register everywhere in Europe. The hotel proprietor checks the registration forms with passports. In Lucrania, every seven days – every Saturday, to be precise – the forms are sent to police headquarters. I suspect that when the forms bearing the names of two Englishmen are received at headquarters the police will be along hot-foot. You see, quite apart from the fact that they'll want to have a look at us anyway, their anxiety will be stimulated when they discover – as they certainly will – that there are no corresponding entries in the frontier books. Naturally, they will want to know how we got into the country, and that's a question we should not be able to answer. And that, I may say, is looking at the thing in the best possible light. In other words, that is what we might reasonably suppose would happen were the circumstances merely normal. Unfortunately a factor arises here which will make our task much more hazardous, although to some extent it cuts both ways. The circumstances will *not* be normal.'

'What do you mean by that?' asked Algy.

Biggles smiled, a curious smile in which there was little mirth. 'You will remember that when I mentioned the incident of Beklinder being seen by a British agent in Prenzel, he was accompanied by the Lucranian Chief of Secret Police.'

'Yes?'

'There is nothing surprising in the fact that this official is a German, Germany being the country most concerned with the welfare or otherwise of Lucrania. Many of the leading civil and military appointments are held by Germans.'

'Go on. You're not going to tell me that we know him?'

'We do. By a curious chance which at first sight may seem remarkable, but which, when all the circumstances are considered, becomes a feasible likelihood, this gentleman happens to be one whose path we seem destined to cross – at least, while we both make a business of espionage. I mean Erich von Stalhein.'

There was a moment of profound silence. Then Ginger sprang to his feet. '*What?*'

Algy sat bolt upright in his chair. His eyes narrowed. 'That oily-tongued swine?' he exclaimed in a hard voice.

Biggles made a deprecatory gesture. 'You choose your words carelessly, Algy,' he protested. 'There is nothing oily about von Stalhein. Acid-tongued, if you like. And why a swine? Be fair. The man serves his country as we try to serve ours. Apart from which he is the most efficient German I have ever met. Had he been in command of German Intelligence in the Near East during the last war I should now be a handful of mouldering earth under the desert sand. He knew I was a fake – but his boss didn't believe him. He was brilliant, and only I know how lucky I was to beat him. We ran into him again in that gold racket. Again it was touch and go. At the finish the cards fell in our favour. No, von Stalhein is a gentleman at heart. If his methods seem harsh, remember that he is a German, and was trained in a school where ruthlessness is essential to success. Personally, I have a sneaking regard for him; and, if we knew the truth, he probably feels the same about us. That would not prevent him from killing us, nor us him, if circumstances demanded it. But I wouldn't call a man a swine on that account. Now let us get back to the point. Von Stalhein knows us by sight. We also know him – that is what I meant when I said that it cuts both ways. The fact that he is where he is makes our task more difficult. There is just a chance that he, personally, may not see the hotel registration forms when they are sent in from Unterhamstadt, but if he does – well, I need say no more. If we arrive at the hotel on Sunday morning those forms should not reach police headquarters until the following Saturday afternoon. Now you know what I meant when I said that we have seven days to do the job and get out.'

'Why not use false names?' suggested Ginger.

Biggles shook his head. 'That would only complicate matters,' he answered. 'It would mean false passports.'

'That could be arranged, too.'

'No doubt; but one slip and we shouldn't have a leg to stand on. We might arouse suspicion where none existed. After all, if our plan goes right, we *might* be tourists. But if we are found to be carrying dud passports we might as well admit that we are spies. Our records are in the German archives, don't forget. They've probably got our photographs filed there, too.'

'Couldn't we disguise ourselves?' offered Ginger.

'I'm all against this melodrama stuff,' replied Biggles emphatically. 'Unless a disguise is absolutely perfect, it is worse than useless. We're not experts at that sort of thing. I should prob-

223

ably forget my wig and leave it on the dressing table, or drop my false whiskers into the soup, or something equally daft. My feeling is that all these tricks are out of date. They belong to spy books of the last generation. My principle is, and always has been, simplicity. It has worked so far, and I don't feel inclined at this juncture to switch on to cheap detective stuff. Let us make a straight bid for what we are after. We ought to have a clear week to do the job. If we haven't done it by then, the chances are that we never shall do it.'

'That's O.K. by me,' agreed Ginger.

'What happens next?' inquired Algy.

'When we arrive in the country we shall have to take certain equipment, which we must dispose of before arriving at the hotel,' went on Biggles. 'As we agreed just now, after that our immediate objective would be the churchyard. If we are lucky enough, or clever enough, to discover what the grave contains, the first vital step would be to report to London. If we can do that, no matter what happens to us we shall have done a good job. We may be able to get out of the country and report in person, but, on the other hand, a hundred things might happen to prevent us from doing that. I propose, therefore, to take a Foreign Office pigeon. Once it is released with a message it will be a lot harder to catch it than us.'

Algy nodded thoughtfully. 'That's a good idea,' he agreed. 'But tell me – how do you propose getting into this grave?'

'I'm coming to that,' replied Biggles. 'Obviously, we shall need tools – a couple of spades would probably do, since the earth will have been newly turned.'

'But you can't take things like spades with you. You'll be cluttered up quite enough with your rucksacks and pigeon basket for safe parachute work.'

'We shall have to put them on a special parachute and throw it overboard at the same time as we ourselves jump.'

'Yes, that sounds the only way.'

'Having collected the spades, we hide them, with the pigeon basket, in the woods, if possible somewhere near the churchyard. We then proceed to the hotel. After that we shall have to take our chance.'

'Do you imagine that you can get into a churchyard and dig up a grave without leaving signs of what has happened?' Algy's tone of voice was frankly sceptical.

'Surely that depends on where the grave is?' returned Biggles without hesitation, which suggested that he had not overlooked the point. 'If the grave is in a conspicuous place, say near the porch, obviously any interference would be noticed by people passing by. But if it is in a remote corner, which seems more likely, nobody may go near it for some time; in which case, as it is the spring of the year, the herbage will soon overgrow any mess we make. That is one of the things we have got to take a chance on. But even if the grave were right by the church door we should have to investigate it, otherwise we might as well stay at home. To start looking haphazardly for the Professor, even in a small country like Lucrania, would make looking for a needle in a haystack child's play by comparison; and that is assuming he's alive.'

'That's true enough.'

'Well, that's the story, and the broad basis of the only practicable scheme the Intelligence experts, in conjunction with myself, can work out. The only saving grace about it is, money is no object. The security of the nation is at stake, and we can spend as much as we like on equipment, bribes, or anything else. The only question that remains to be answered is – do we take it on? We are under no compulsion to do so, nor any obligation. The risks being what they are, and the government fully aware of them, it is essentially a volunteer show. But once started there's no going back. Now, how do you feel about it? Your lives are your own; they are the only ones you're likely to have this side of eternity so they are not to be thrown away lightly. You've risked them before, I know, more than once, and so have I; but maybe we've all been lucky, and luck is a mistress not to be relied upon. We shall need her to smile on us this journey, make no mistake about that. Never before has the peril been so real, so deadly, so cold-blooded, from the very outset. If we go, we go with our eyes open. If you'd rather not, don't hesitate to say so. Now, what about it?'

'We've never turned down a job yet, and considering what is at stake, this strikes me as being the wrong time to start jibbing,' said Algy slowly.

Biggles turned to Ginger. 'What about you, laddie?'

'I'd as soon be bumped off trying to do something useful as flattened out by a lunatic in a motor-car while trying to cross the road in this bedlam of a city,' replied Ginger carelessly.

'Good enough. Then that settles that. You'd better make yourselves familiar with this.' Biggles took a photograph from his breast pocket and laid it on the table. 'That is a portrait of Professor Beklinder,' he said. 'It's an interesting face; with that high forehead and long hair. He looks more like a musician than a chemist, doesn't he? Get his face fixed in your memory, because we cannot take the photograph with us. I'll let Raymond know we're going.' Biggles reached for the telephone.

CHAPTER III

A Drop In The Dark

'**W**ell, what do you think of it?' It was Algy who spoke, addressing Biggles, who, hands in his pockets, was gazing reflectively at a few wisps of filmy cloud that appeared to be drawn slowly across a starlit sky by an unseen hand.

. 'I think it's all right,' returned Biggles after a moment's hesitation. 'The weather report is good, anyway. If we don't go tonight it will mean waiting another week. I think we'll get along. Are you feeling all right, Ginger?'

'As right as rain,' answered Ginger carelessly.

'All right, then; let's go,' murmured Biggles, and turning, walked towards where the black silhouette of a hangar rose sharp and clear against the sky.

Ten days had elapsed since their momentous decision to enter Lucrania in an endeavour to ascertain the truth concerning Professor Beklinder's mysterious disappearance. They had been busy days, for there was much to arrange, and Biggles had been meticulous in his preparations. The others had never seen him pay so much attention to even the minutest details. 'We can't afford to take one single risk that can be reduced or discounted by ourselves before we start,' was all he had said when Algy had once questioned his care over a matter of such triviality that it hardly seemed worth troubling about.

There had been no difficulty in getting the machine they required, a Wessex 'Student'. The government had merely commandeered a new one that had just been built to the order of a private individual. What the owner thought of this they did not know, for they had heard no more about it. A special branch of the Foreign Office had attended to its own part of the proceedings, the preparation of papers, passports, and permission to use an aerodrome in France from which operations could be conducted without fear of awkward questions being asked by the local authorities. It was only a small place, no more than an emergency landing-ground for east-bound air liners, but it suited their purpose well enough. Here they had arrived two days previously, and after making final arrangements they had nothing more to do than wait, with some anxiety on account of the weather, the time for departure. Now the hour had arrived. The weather was fair. It might have been better, but it could have been much worse.

Just before they reached the hangar Biggles stopped and turned to Algy. 'There's just one other thing,' he said in a low voice. 'I haven't mentioned it before, and – well, perhaps there's really no need to mention it now. Maybe I'm a bit keyed up. It's about that ground engineer here – Brogart.'

'What about him?'

'Nothing really tangible – but—'

'I thought he was a nice chap.'

'He may be. But be careful. I wouldn't trust him too far. Perhaps he's just one of those cheerful busybodies who is a nosey-parker without knowing it, or without meaning any harm, but it has struck me that he is very interested in us. I am going on what I know of the French temperament. Mechanics, particularly French mechanics, don't stick around on their jobs when they are off duty and when there is an *estaminet* handy. I know Brogart is a cheerful fellow, very willing and obliging and all that, but I've noticed that he's always about when we are. Once I caught him looking through the side window of our machine. I admit that may have been natural curiosity because the door was locked. He may be all that he pretends to be. On the other hand, he may not. We don't know, and we're not likely to find out. He may be an interested – er – spectator, acting on behalf of the French government. He might even be a British agent. He might be anything. But my advice to you is to keep your eyes open and your mouths shut. If he turns up here tonight – seven o'clock on a Saturday night, when his pals are sipping vermouth in the local pub – I shall say that he is unusually industrious.'

'I'll keep an eye on him, but I think you're unduly suspicious,' opined Algy.

'It's better to be suspicious now than sorry later,' returned Biggles curtly. 'Ginger, walk down to the end of the shed and watch the road while Algy and I get the machine out.'

'O.K.' Ginger walked briskly away on his errand.

Between them, Biggles and Algy folded back the hangar doors and pulled the 'Student' out into the open. They had just closed the doors when Ginger hurried up.

'There's somebody coming,' he said in a low voice. 'I think it's Brogart.'

Biggles muttered something under his breath. 'All right. We can't put the machine back. Confound the fellow.'

A moment later the French mechanic came round the corner of

the hangar. He stopped abruptly when he saw the machine, and the motionless figures awaiting him. Then he came on again.

'*Bon soir, messieurs*,' he cried cheerfully. 'You make the night flight – yes?'

'Yes, we're going to visit some friends,' growled Biggles.

'Ah, you go to Paris – my lovely Paris? Its cafés! And the girls! Ha!'

'Perhaps,' returned Biggles coldly.

The Frenchman was not abashed by Biggles's manner. 'I thought I could help to make the start. *Voilà!*'

'Why? What made you think we were likely to fly tonight?' inquired Biggles evenly.

The mechanic hesitated for an almost imperceptible fraction of a second. Then he shrugged his shoulders. 'I see you come this way, so I say, *voilà*, they will fly. That is the good sense, yes?'

'Your sense is so good that it almost amounts to telepathy,' murmured Biggles.

'Telepathy? What is zis?'

'Never mind. It's all right, Brogart. We shan't need any help. We'll see you later.'

The Frenchman lit a cigarette. '*Bien*,' he exclaimed, flicking the dead match aside. 'You are mechanics as well as pilots? *Bon*. Zat is good. You send for me if something is wanted. I tink I will take a cognac with my leetle girl at the *Cochon Rouge. Au revoir, messieurs*.' The mechanic bowed, raised his beret, and humming softly to himself, walked away in the direction from which he had come.

As he rounded the corner of the hangar Biggles caught Ginger by the arm. 'After him,' he breathed. 'Watch where he goes – but don't let him see you. Don't leave the aerodrome.'

Brogart leaves the aerodrome.

Algy looked at Biggles. 'Well?' he grunted.

'Let's get started up. We can't waste any more time.'

'Can he possibly know what we're doing?'

'Of course not. There isn't the remotest chance of that. But all the same I'd bet my life he knows that we're up to something unusual, and he would like to know what it is. Whether that's for his own private information, or for somebody else who is interested, we don't know and we're not likely to. You'll have to be careful with that fellow, Algy,' Biggles concluded, as he unlocked the door of the machine, and after a quick look round to see that all their equipment was inside, turned again to wait for Ginger.

He returned in about five minutes. 'He's gone,' he said.

'Are you sure?'

'Pretty sure. I watched him walk down the road. He was still walking when I last saw him, although he looked back once or twice as if he thought he might be followed.'

'Good! Then let's get away,' announced Biggles. 'Be careful how you get into that parachute, Ginger.'

In a few minutes they were ready, for they had discussed this moment so often that they were all word-perfect in the parts they were to play. They took their places, Algy at the joystick, Biggles beside him with a map on his knees, and Ginger in the tiny cabin behind.

Algy reached for the self-starter, and the engine caught immediately, for it had been tuned up to as near perfection as it is possible for a piece of machinery to be. For five minutes they sat still, nobody speaking, while the engine ticked over with the precision of a well-oiled sewing-machine as it warmed up.

'All right,' said Biggles at last. 'Let her go.'

Instantly the 'Student' began to move forward. Algy took it

well out into the aerodrome before turning into the slight breeze; he regarded the skyline intently for a moment; then the engine roared as he slid the throttle open and the 'Student' sped across the darkened aerodrome towards the distant boundary. For a few seconds the machine quivered as its wheels raced over the rough turf; then the vibration ceased abruptly and it climbed steeply into the night sky. For a thousand feet Algy held the machine straight; then, still climbing, he turned slowly until the 'Student' was on its compass course for their destination.

For half an hour nobody spoke. There was nothing to say, for every possible contingency had been discussed on the ground. They had climbed to 18,000 feet and were still climbing.

Ginger stared out of the window; not that there was much to see, for the earth was no more than a vague black shadow at the bottom of an immense void, dotted with innumerable pinpoints of light, sometimes in clusters and sometimes isolated, marking the position of villages and lonely dwellings. Above and around the stars shone hard and clear from a cloudless sky.

Algy looked from the watch on his instrument board to Biggles's face. His eyes held a question.

Biggles nodded. 'Better ease her,' he said. 'We're nearing the frontier.'

As if in answer the noise of the engine faded to a soft purr. The nose of the machine tilted down.

'You're sure we're all right?' asked Algy.

'Yes, I'm watching it. See the river ahead? Turn right and follow it when you get to it.'

Algy nodded, throttled right back and began a long steady glide.

Another quarter of an hour passed. The 'Student', moving at

little more than stalling speed through a lonely world of its own, was down to 14,000 feet and still losing height slowly.

Biggles stared long and intently at the ground. 'I can see the village,' he said. 'At least, I think those are the lights, over on the right. Come round to the left a little, to bring us over the plain.' Then, as the nose of the machine crept round, 'Hold her,' he called. 'You'll do. Keep her there. Are you ready, Ginger?'

'Ay, ay, sir.'

'Right! Give me five seconds to get clear after I jump.' Biggles picked up a large bundle from the floor of the cabin, opened the door and crept carefully out on to the port wing. The bundle disappeared into the void. Three seconds later he followed it, the machine rocking as he slid off the trailing edge of the wing. He disappeared from sight instantly.

Ginger, who was already on his feet, immediately crept out on to the wing. 'I'd as soon be kicked in the teeth as jump into that hole,' he growled into Algy's ear as he passed him. Closing the door behind him, he gripped the rip ring firmly in his right hand and took a deep breath. Then he launched himself into the void.

There was no sensation of falling, although the wind was bitterly cold as it beat against his face. One – two – three, he counted and tugged at the ring. An instant later the jerk of his harness told him that the parachute had opened; looking up he could see it billowing above him like a great black cloud. He looked around. There was no sign of Biggles; the sky was so clear that he thought he ought to be able to see him, although he knew well enough how difficult it is to see a moving body in the air when it is dark. Everything was still – silent. The silence was uncanny. He could not even hear the still-gliding 'Student', now on its way back to France. A horrible feeling began to creep over him that he was not falling at all, but was suspended in space from some invisible object. He whistled, hoping that Biggles might hear, but there was no reply. He looked down. For the most part the earth was wrapped in profound gloom, but the tiny cluster of lights that marked the village of Unterhamstadt gleamed more brightly. Presently he could see vaguely the shape of the hills surrounding them. On the crest of one there appeared to be a clearing, grey in the dim light. He remembered the castle of which Biggles had spoken and stared at it with interest. He was about to turn his eyes away when a light flashed from the edge of the pile. So quickly did it appear and disappear that he found himself wondering if he had really seen a light. He recalled what Biggles had said about the place being a ruin. However, he dismissed the matter from his mind, for he knew he must be nearing the ground and gave his entire attention to the business of landing; for when one is falling at several feet a second it is an easy matter to sprain an ankle; and such a mishap in the circumstances would be in the nature of a disaster.

The end came suddenly. The ground seemed to rush up to meet him, and he was thankful to see that he was clear of obstructions. He braced himself for the shock of landing; hardly had he done so than he was on the ground, with the soft silk burying him under its voluminous folds.

He rolled clear, slipped off his harness and looked around anxiously. Seeing nothing, he whistled softly, and drew a deep breath of relief when it was answered from a short distance away. Satisfied that everything so far had gone according to plan he began rolling up his parachute; by the time he had finished Biggles was standing beside him, half buried under his burden of parachute, rucksack, pigeon basket, and digging implements, also with their parachute attached.

'Everything all right?' inquired Biggles.

'Yes, we don't seem to have broken anything,' Ginger told him.

'Good! Then let's get rid of this junk. There's the wood, over there. The village is on the other side of the hill.'

Ginger gathered the unwieldy bundle of his parachute under his arm and set off at Biggles's side across the open ground towards the place where they had decided to conceal their questionable burdens.

They moved quickly but quietly, although there appeared to be nothing to fear. Not a sound broke the silence. Five minutes' sharp walking brought them to the edge of the wood. It was pitch dark under the pines, but Biggles groped his way inside. Then he took out his flashlamp, and finding a comparatively level spot, dropped his burden. 'It feels like sandy soil under foot,' he said quietly. 'I hoped it would be. It will be easy to dig,' he went on, cutting the digging utensils clear of their parachute, and setting about the task of making a hole large enough to bury them in.

Even though the ground was soft it took them the best part of half an hour to finish the job to their satisfaction. The digging tools, a spade and a small military entrenching tool with a pick at one end, were laid on the top of the pile, and the last covering of earth was put on by hand, the whole site of the excavation finally being carefully smoothed over and strewn with pine needles. It took Biggles a few minutes to find a satisfactory place to hide the pigeon basket, for this, of course, could not be buried. In the end he decided to put it under a thick holly bush, and cover it lightly with leaves.

'Thank goodness that's done,' he murmured as he rejoined Ginger. 'Now for the village. We've a good two miles to go, I reckon. We had better get on the road; we can reach it by keeping to the edge of the wood. Incidentally, we had better mark this spot down from the outside; we should look a pair of fools if we couldn't find the place again.'

Ginger agreed, so after memorizing the place as well as they could in the starlight, they set off along the edge of the wood towards the road. As they walked Biggles submitted Ginger to a sort of catechism of questions, questions such as how long they had been in the country, where they had come from, their last place of call, their business, when they were returning, and the like, for it was part of their programme that their stories should coincide should they ever be questioned separately.

'We might have brought a couple of good ash walking-sticks with us,' remarked Biggles as they neared the village. 'Most hikers carry sticks. As a matter of fact, I did think of it before we started, but we were already so cluttered up that I didn't like adding any more to our kit. No matter; we shall probably be able to buy a couple here. This looks like the beginning of the village, and where our troubles begin – if we are going to have any. It may all turn out to be a lot easier than we think. Anyway, whatever happens, we can console ourselves that we have left as little as possible to chance.'

By this time they had reached the village, which, in the wan light of a newly risen moon, they saw was little more than a single street of old houses, most of them half-timbered, with overhanging eaves and numerous gables, in typical central-European medieval style. Some of the timbering was quaint in design, some almost fantastic; and as many of the houses had either been built out of true, or had warped under the heavy hand of time, the effect was what Ginger described, aptly, as Christmas-cardish.

'I should say that in the ordinary way this is a nice old place,' murmured Biggles appreciatively. 'It's got a pleasant old-world air – the real thing, not imitation, as one so often sees at home. Things have probably changed very little here during the past five hundred years. I've seen villages in Bavaria and Bohemia very much like it. Left alone, there's nothing wrong with the people, but with the political stew Europe is in they are probably getting a bit sullen, although they have to take care not to show it. However, we shall see. I – hold hard a minute.'

Biggles had caught Ginger by the arm and drawn him back into the black shadow of a dilapidated barn. 'Take a look at that,' he whispered, indicating a low-fronted tumble-down house that stood by itself on the opposite side of the road. Several windows had been broken.

'What do you mean – the broken windows?' asked Ginger quietly.

'Partly, but look what is written on the door.'

Peering forward, Ginger could just make out the word '*Jude*' crudely chalked across the entrance. 'What does that mean?' he asked.

'The owner of the place is a Jew. Apparently this is one of the places under the influence of anti-Jewish propaganda. He's evidently a tradesman. That's his name over the door. What is it – Simon Kretzner? *Beerdigungs-Institut*. By Jove! He's the local undertaker. I wonder how much *he* knows about this business – or if he knows anything. I wonder if we could find out.'

'How could we do that?'

'There's only one way, and that is by asking. It's risky, but if it came off it might save us a lot of trouble.'

'Is there anybody there? I don't see a light.'

'That looks like a workshop in front. There might be a light at the back. Let's go and look.'

After a quick glance up and down the road to make sure there was nobody about, they crossed it, and lifting aside a broken wicket gate that gave access to a narrow path, they walked quietly to the end of the house and looked round.

The reflection of a feeble orange light glowed on an overgrown tangle of bushes that had encroached far into what had once been a kitchen garden. But even as they looked the light went out, leaving the bushes to the bluey-grey moonlight.

'He heard us. We've scared him,' whispered Ginger.

'Then he must have pretty sharp ears – unless he was on the watch,' muttered Biggles. 'I'm going to knock on the front door. Behave naturally if he answers it. I'll do the talking.'

Retracing their steps down the path to the front door, Biggles rapped sharply on it with his knuckles.

CHAPTER IV

The Jew Of Unterhamstadt

Possibly on account of the fact that the house was in darkness, or because of its forlorn appearance, the knock had an eerie, almost sinister sound, altogether unlike the announcement of the arrival of an expected guest. It seemed to break sharply into an attentive silence, as if it were awaited, yet feared. As the sound died away to a hush more profound on account of its having been broken, the two airmen listened intently for a reply. But they listened in vain. All remained as silent as the grave.

'I have a feeling that there's something wrong about this place,' muttered Ginger, glancing around apprehensively.

'Nonsense,' retorted Biggles impatiently. 'Why should there be? You're getting nervous. Somebody is at home; we know that because we saw the light. Evidently they think we're footpads.' He knocked again, more loudly this time.

The knock was answered instantly by a faint cry from within, a curious whimpering sound that might have been made by an animal.

'That's got somebody on the move, anyway,' murmured Biggles, as there came a soft shuffling noise from behind the door, which, after a rattling of chains and scraping of bolts, was opened a few inches. Who had opened it was not evident, however, for the room beyond was in darkness.

'*Guten Abend*,' said Biggles, in a cheerful tone, calculated to allay suspicion if in fact it existed. Continuing in the same language he went on, 'We are Englishmen and strangers to this place. Is this the village of Unterhamstadt?'

For a brief moment there was no reply; only a long indrawn breath, almost a shudder, as of infinite relief. '*Ja, ja, meine Herren*,' came a thin, quavering voice. The door started to close again, but Biggles put his foot against it. 'Have you any walking-sticks for sale?' he inquired.

The voice replied in the negative.

'May we come in and rest for a minute or two?' persisted Biggles. 'We have come far, and would like to ask some questions about accommodation in the village.'

This request did not immediately produce an answer. It was as if the man behind the door suspected that it was only an excuse to gain admittance – as indeed it was.

'You need have no fear of us,' continued Biggles, in a low voice. 'We are English travellers – and friends of the Jews.' Biggles did little more than whisper the last few words.

The door was opened slowly and the voice invited them to enter.

With Ginger following, Biggles stepped across the threshold. Standing in utter darkness, they still could not see the man whose privacy they had invaded, and thus they stood while the door was closed, shutting out even the feeble moonlight. Ginger was conscious of a pricking sensation down the spine as there came again the curious shuffling sound, accompanied by a low muttering. He started violently as, with a scratching noise, amplified no doubt by the darkness, a match flared up disclosing the scene, and, for the first time, their host, who was in the act of lighting a cheap tallow candle from the match which he had struck.

Ginger regarded with a mixture of disgust and sympathy an old man whose back was bent by years, by labour, or by suffering, or, perhaps, by a combination of all three. His hair, had it been clean, would have been white; long and tangled, it hung far down over the back of his collarless neck, and down his cheeks until it became part of the unkempt beard that concealed the lower part of his face. His old-fashioned jacket and shapeless trousers, once black, were green with age, and dirty beyond description, as were his hands and that part of his face which was not covered with hair. His movements were slow and uncertain; indeed, his fingers trembled to such an extent that it was only with diffi-culty that he brought the wick of the candle and the flame of the match together.

Biggles caught Ginger's eyes. 'Observe what persecution and the fear of death does to a man in time,' he said softly, in English. 'Poor devil. He is just an animated piece of terror.' Then, more loudly, he went on in German, 'Do not worry about us, Father. You have nothing to fear.'

'I have no money here – none,' said the old Jew, in a dull, heavy voice, raising his hands, palms outwards in a characteristic gesture of hopelessness, and regarding his visitors with anxiety and suspicion.

Biggles smiled reassuringly. 'We have more than we need,' he said gently. 'We may even have some to spare,' he added signifi-cantly.

The old man's deep-set eyes regarded Biggles broodingly. 'So,' he breathed. 'It would be better for me – and for you – if we did not talk here. Follow me.' Turning, he led the way into a small room at the rear. It was filthy beyond description. A heavy foetid smell hung on the air, and judging from the heaped-up rags on a couch that occupied one side of the room, it was plain that the old man lived in it. Indicating a wooden bench, he invited his visitors to be seated; then, after standing the candle on a table littered with dirty crocks, he himself sank down on the rag-covered bed.

'What can I do for you?' he asked nervously, looking from one to the other. 'You were not wise to come here.'

'Why not?' asked Biggles.

'I am a Jew.'

'Do they treat Jews so badly?'

'You have seen,' said the old man simply.

'Why do you stay here and suffer?'

'How can I go? I have no money – none.' The old man's eyes darted from door to window, and back again to his visitors. 'They have had it all,' he said softly, but there was a world of hate behind his tremulous voice.

'Have you anywhere to go – if you had money?' inquired Biggles.

'I have a married daughter in Switzerland. Fortunately she left before the trouble began.'

'And if you had – shall we say – two thousand marks, you could join her – yes?'

Surprise joined the smouldering fear in the old man's eyes. 'Where is there so much money?' he scoffed.

'I can give you that – and more – if you can furnish me with the information I seek,' said Biggles deliberately, his eyes squarely meeting those of the Jew.

Again there was a short silence. Again the old man's eyes flashed from door to window, almost, it seemed, from very habit. 'What is it you want to know?' he asked at last.

Biggles had gone too far now to dissemble. He decided there and then to take the downright course. 'Not long ago a learned doctor was injured here in a motor-car accident, so that he died,' he murmured, quietly but distinctly. And even as he spoke he saw the old man's flabby muscles stiffen.

The Jew crouched back, an arm over his face as if he feared a blow. 'No!' he gasped. 'No – not that!' His tongue licked his lips as again his eyes darted from door to window. 'No!' he panted, his voice breaking into a whimper.

Biggles's face hardened. His manner became cold and direct. 'Listen, old man,' he said in a terse whisper, 'I will pay you to tell me what you know.'

'I know nothing.'

Biggles took out his wallet and slowly counted out twenty-five hundred-mark notes. 'Will those restore your memory?' he asked grimly. 'With those, tomorrow you could leave this place for ever. Now tell me. Did you bury the doctor's body?'

The Jew stared at the notes as if they fascinated him. 'No,' he insisted.

'But you are the undertaker here.'

'Yes, but it was not I. It was—' The man broke off abruptly, as if he realized that he was saying too much.

'Who was it?' Biggles's voice was as cold and hard as cracking ice.

'My son. He, too, is of my trade. His workshop is nearer the middle of the village.'

'Is he there now?'

'No.'

'Where is he?'

'Gone.'

'Gone? Gone where?'

'They took him away – afterwards.'

'I see,' said Biggles slowly. 'Did you see him – afterwards?'

'No'

'Don't lie.'

The old man quivered. 'I do not – lie.'

'Then if you did not see him how did you know about this?' asked Biggles sharply.

'He told his wife that night. The next day they took him away. She told me,' gasped the old man, his eyes on Biggles's face. It was as if Biggles was dragging the information out of him against his will.

'That night? What night?' demanded Biggles.

The Jew shook with terror. His eyes were never still, and the trembling of his hands was such that he had to grip the bed to steady them.

Biggles began picking up the notes. 'I am wasting my time,' he said grimly. 'Will you tell me what I want to know or shall I pursue my inquiries elsewhere?'

The funeral director's agitation was pitiful to behold. 'I will tell you,' he gasped at last, holding out his hand for the notes.

But Biggles withdrew them. 'Tell me first and they shall be yours,' he promised.

The old man moistened his lips with his tongue. 'I will tell you everything,' he said desperately. He was nearly inarticulate with terror, and Ginger marvelled that a man could be reduced to such a lamentable condition.

'After the accident the man was brought here, to the Kleishausen, which is the big hotel—'

'Where did the accident happen?' interrupted Biggles.

'Ah! That I do not know.'

'Very well, go on.'

'It was this way. My son was just sitting down to his supper when two storm-troopers came into his house and told him that he was wanted for work in the hotel. My son thought it was for carpenter's work, and said that he would go tomorrow; but they said that would not do; a man had been killed and a coffin was wanted at once. So my son took his rule to measure the body, and went to the hotel. The body was in a great bedroom, which has the number seventeen, and he was surprised at this, for he could not think why they should take a dead man into the best room. This, you understand, is what he told Greta, his wife, when he returned home.'

'Did he see the body?'

'Yes – and no. A doctor whom he did not know was there, with the body on the bed, but it was so wrapped up in bandages that he could not see the face. There was blood on the bandages, and on the bedclothes, but when he asked about this the doctor bade him sternly to take the measurements and ask no questions. So he took the measurements and departed, with instructions to work all night and make the coffin. Which he did. Just before noon the next day it was finished, and he, helped by the storm-troopers, took it across. He did not come back; not that day, nor the next; nor has his unhappy wife seen him since.'

'You mean – he disappeared?'

'That is what I mean.'

'But did not his wife make inquiries?'

'Yes. She was told that he had gone away, but would return later. If she asked questions she would never see him again. The head of the storm-troopers also asked her if her husband had spoken about what he had seen the night before, and she, fearing for herself, and him, said "No, nothing". They told her threateningly to speak to no one about what had happened. Nor has she, except to me, to whom she came in her grief.'

'But what of the funeral? Did she not see it?'

'No. It was all done very quietly and secretly, at the break of dawn.'

'How do you know that it was at dawn, if it was so secret?' demanded Biggles instantly.

'Because my daughter-in-law, hearing a noise, went to the window of her room and saw the coffin brought out – the hotel being in view of her house. So she sent Joachim, her little boy, to see if he could see his father. From the woods he saw the funeral, but he did not see his father. There were only the storm-troopers there, and they put the coffin in the vault on the western side, near the tower.'

Biggles started. 'In the *what*?'

'The vault.'

Biggles was silent for a moment. 'Then it was not an ordinary grave?' he said slowly.

'No. The church is very old, and there are vaults, although it is long since they were used.'

'How are the entrances to these vaults sealed?'

'I do not know that. It is not my church. Only once was I there, many years ago; but if I remember, the vaults are behind slabs of stone. That is the truth, and that is all I know. And now spare an old man's anguish and be gone, for if anyone should find you here it would be very bad for both of us.'

Biggles nodded. 'Yes,' he said, 'we will go. We shall forget we ever saw you, and you will forget that you have seen us.' As he spoke he handed the money to the old Jew, who seized the notes eagerly and thrust them far down inside his ragged shirt.

He had not yet withdrawn his hand, and Biggles was in the act of rising to leave the room, when a sound broke the temporary silence. It was so slight that in the ordinary way it would not have been noticed; nor would it have been audible had the conversation persisted. It was merely the slight creak of a door.

Biggles turned like lightning. The door was open perhaps an inch. Yet it had, he knew, been closed and latched after they had entered. The old man had seen to that.

The Jew's terror was pitiful to behold. A faint moan broke from his ashen lips, and he nearly collapsed. His eyes, saucer-wide with fear, stared at the door. His lips moved noiselessly.

Biggles's mouth set in a hard line. He motioned Ginger to remain still. 'Thank you very much, Father,' he said in a loud voice. 'I think we shall be able to find our way now.' But as he spoke he tiptoed towards the door with cat-like tread. Reaching it, with a swift movement he jerked it wide open.

A girl, young, good-looking, dressed in a neat brown tweed costume, stood on the threshold.

Ginger stared unbelievingly at the pale face, surmounted by golden hair. Whatever he had expected, it was certainly not this.

Biggles, too, stared. But his hand went slowly to his head, and he raised his cap with a little bow. 'Good evening, Fraulein,' he said pleasantly. 'Have you, like us, lost your way?'

The girl did not answer immediately. She seemed as taken aback to see Biggles as he was to see her. 'Yes – yes, yes,' she stammered at last.

'Then you had better ask the old man your way,' continued Biggles evenly, trusting that the Jew had recovered himself sufficiently to be able to speak. 'He has been kind enough to tell us what we wanted to know. We are just going.' Then, turning, 'Good-night,' he called over his shoulder to the old man, and beckoning to Ginger, made ready to depart.

The girl stepped aside to allow them to pass.

Biggles whistled softly as he walked down the path towards the gate, and so out on to the road. Not until he had taken some fifty paces did he speak. 'Well, laddie,' he said, 'that little interlude has given us something to think about.'

'What was that girl after?'

'Heaven alone knows. She was just about the last sort of person I should expect there.'

'She was listening.'

'Yes, I think she was. A funny business.'

'What was the old man talking about all that time? I wish to goodness I could speak German.'

'Let's go to the hotel; then I'll tell you all about it,' said Biggles. 'That looks like it, just ahead on the left. Handsome place, isn't it?'

'Let's hope it's a case of "handsome is as handsome does",' murmured Ginger aptly.

CHAPTER V

Under the Castle Walls

A s they walked slowly up the deserted village street towards the hotel, Biggles gave Ginger the gist of his conversation with the old Jew; for, as it had been carried on in German, he had not understood a word of it. 'This business of Beklinder being buried in a vault instead of a grave fairly staggered me for a minute, I can tell you,' he said. 'It will alter our plans. It may make the exhumation easier or it may make it harder; that's something we shan't know until we see the vault. Still, it's a very good thing we found out about it, otherwise we should have wasted a lot of time looking for a grave that doesn't exist, and so possibly have arrived at an incorrect conclusion. We shall have to go and take a look at this vault at the first opportunity – probably tonight, if our room is so situated that we can get out without being seen. But here is the hotel. Let's go in and get things fixed up. It will be interesting to see what sort of reception we get; we shall soon know whether we are welcome or otherwise.'

The hotel was a large, rambling, but rather impressive building, obviously medieval in its inspiration. Surmounted by a tower, the roof was broken by innumerable gables, each complete with diamond-paned windows, and decorated with much ornate timbering, as was, in fact, the whole building, in the style now commonly referred to in England as 'black and white'. An imposing timber porch, carrying the insignia of several international touring associations, protected the main entrance.

Biggles opened the door and they went into a long, low-ceilinged reception hall. A log fire smouldered sullenly at one end. As they stood in momentary hesitation, looking for the reception office, a heavily built man, typically German in appearance, arose from behind a counter at which he had been sitting and came towards them. 'At your service, gentlemen,' he said in English with a strong foreign accent, at the same time drawing himself up and making a stiff little bow.

'You are a good judge of nationality,' smiled Biggles.

'I should be a bad judge if I did not recognize English clothes,' returned the man smoothly.

Biggles nodded, knowing that what the man had said was true; there was nothing particularly clever in his assumption, after all. 'Am I speaking to the proprietor?' he asked.

'Yes, sir.'

'Good,' answered Biggles. 'We are on a walking tour, and we should like to stay here for a few days if you can accommodate us.'

'For how long?'

'Two days – three days – perhaps a week. We have no definite plans. If we like it here we may even stay longer. You have some rooms?'

'But certainly. We have few visitors so early in the year. You require two rooms?'

'No,' replied Biggles quickly. 'We would prefer a large room with two beds.' As he spoke an idea came into his mind. 'The best you have,' he added.

'Of course – of course,' agreed the proprietor. 'I can show you a room of much excellence.' He walked stiffly to the key-rack that almost covered the wall behind the reception counter and unhooked the one that hung below a disk bearing the figure 18.

'What about number seventeen?' suggested Biggles casually.

The man stopped dead in what he was doing. Then he went on again. It was as if the words had for an instant bereft him of the power of movement. There was a curious timbre in his voice when he asked, 'Why that number?'

Biggles had his answer ready. 'Oh, it just happens to be my lucky number, that's all,' he answered nonchalantly.

'Number seventeen is not a double room,' said the man slowly, but with unmistakable deliberation.

Biggles passed the matter off as if it were of no account. 'That's all right,' he said lightly. 'Any number will do.'

'You will find that number eighteen is a room most comfortable,' announced the proprietor, laying the key on the counter; then, taking two forms from a sheaf that stood in a letter-rack, he placed one before each of his visitors. 'Please to fill in these forms,' he said. 'Have you baggage?'

'Only what you can see,' Biggles told him.

'Then I must ask you to pay a deposit in advance.'

'With pleasure.' Biggles took a thousand-mark note from his wallet and laid it on the counter. 'Please tell me when that is exhausted,' he said.

The hotel proprietor's manner changed when he saw the note. It became obsequious. It was obvious that if he had judged his visitor's nationality correctly, he had been in error over their financial status. 'Will you please to fill in the forms now,' he said again. 'I regret, gentlemen, but this is the regulation, you know.

Just at the top part will be sufficient. If you will leave me your passports I can fill in the rest.'

Biggles nodded. 'You speak English very well; have you been in England?' he inquired, as, picking up a pen, he filled in the questions concerning his parents' nationality, his last stopping-place, and other details which could not be completed from his passport.

'Yes, for five years I was a waiter in London,' admitted the man.

Biggles judged him to be about fifty years of age. That was before the War, I suppose?' he suggested.

'Yes.' The man's manner changed again. It became almost curt, suggesting that he was not interested in personalities – at least, those which concerned himself.

'Are there any other English visitors here?' asked Biggles, as the man picked up the key and invited them to follow him towards a sweeping wooden staircase, black with age, that led upwards from a corner of the entrance hall.

'No,' was the short response. 'Mind your head on the beam, if you please.'

After traversing a long corridor on the first floor he stopped. The number plate attached to the key jangled as the door swung open. He stood aside to allow his visitors to enter.

'Yes, this will do very well,' agreed Biggles, glancing around appreciatively, for the room was spacious and furnished in excellent, if old-fashioned, style.

'I thought you would like it. You will require dinner – yes? It is rather past the usual hour, but—'

'Yes, we should like something to eat,' Biggles told him. 'Shall we say in about ten minutes?'

'Very well. The bell is here by the door. Should you require anything ring once for the waiter and twice for the chamber-maid. Will you take breakfast in your room?'

'No, thanks – we shall probably come down for it.'

The hotel proprietor bowed and withdrew.

'Everything seems all right so far,' murmured Biggles as soon as he had gone. 'Frankly, I quite expected to find that we were unwelcome, but I couldn't detect anything in mine host's manner to suggest it – although he shied a bit when I mentioned room seventeen. But let's have a wash and go down for a bite of food; I can do with some.'

They were not long taking such things as they required, pyjamas and toilet requisites, from their rucksacks, and after a quick wash and brush up they went down to the dining-room, which, in keeping with the rest of the building, they found to be in the nature of a baronial hall. An elderly waiter in a white apron and napkin on his arm came forward to meet them and showed them the table that had been laid for them.

But Ginger barely noticed these things, for his attention was entirely taken up by the only other person in the room. It was the golden-haired girl in brown whom they had last seen at the Jew's house. She was just beginning her soup, and it was obvious from her manner that she was a guest at the hotel. For a moment she stared as hard at the new-comers as they at her.

Ginger looked up and caught Biggles's eye. There was a curious expression on Biggles's face. 'That gives us something else to think about, doesn't it?' he murmured dryly.

'She's having a jolly good look at us,' said Ginger, in a low voice.

'I've noticed it. She's evidently staying here – alone, too. What was she doing prowling round the Jew's house, I wonder? I mean, her movements were a good deal more like those of a burglar than ours were. We did at least knock on the door.'

'She behaved like an eavesdropper,' declared Ginger, as he pulled out a chair and sat down at the table.

'She certainly did. I wonder how much she heard of our conversation – not that guessing will help us. We shall have to keep an eye on her. The odd thing is, although I cannot help feeling that it must be pure coincidence, her face seems vaguely familiar.'

'I didn't like to say so for fear that you would accuse me again of being nervous, but since you mention it I don't mind admitting that the same thought struck me,' declared Ginger.

'Hm,' mused Biggles, 'a funny business. But let's get on and finish the meal. I'd like to have a stroll round outside before turning in – unless you're too tired.'

'Me tired? Not in the least,' asserted Ginger. 'Let us stroll, by all means.'

They hastened the meal to a conclusion, although they took particular care not to make this obvious, after which they went back upstairs for their caps. Biggles slipped an electric torch into his pocket at the same time, after which they made their way back to the entrance hall.

The proprietor was standing at his desk, reading a paper. 'You are going walking again tonight?' he asked, in a not unfriendly manner.

Biggles shrugged his shoulders. 'Just a stroll round the village to get our bearings before turning in.' Which, in the circumstances, he thought not unreasonable. And with that they passed on into the street.

'Where are you going – to the churchyard?' whispered Ginger as soon as they were outside.

'Not yet. Later, perhaps. We shall have to make a pretence of going to bed, so we can't very well stay out for a couple of hours. That would look a bit *too* odd.'

They stood for a moment or two looking about them. The moon was now well up and they could see their surroundings fairly clearly. 'Let's have a look in here,' said Biggles, indicating what no doubt had originally been a coach entrance, but was now the way to the garage.

There was nobody about, so they strolled slowly round the extensive outbuildings unquestioned. Beyond them there was a wide kitchen garden, walled on one side, with a dilapidated lean-to greenhouse occupying part of its length. The other part was taken up by a shed. Biggles, after an apparently casual but in reality penetrating glance round to make sure that they were not observed, walked slowly towards it. 'With luck we may find in here something we shall need,' he said.

'What's that?'

'A crow-bar, or a stout piece of timber. I imagine we shall need such an instrument to get into the vault.'

The shed was not locked, so there was no difficulty about gaining admittance. Biggles's torch cut a wedge of light into the darkness, and rested, as he had hoped, on an array of gardening tools, old wheel-barrows, a rusty lawn-mower and other garden furniture, none of which looked as if it had been touched for years. Against the wall, amongst a litter of old spades, rakes, hoes, worn-out brooms, and an axe with a cracked shaft, they found what they sought. There were, in fact, several pieces of iron of various lengths which in emergency might have suited their purpose. 'Good,' murmured Biggles. 'Had we not found one in here we should have had to ask the old Jew to help us again, and I'd rather keep away from him.'

'He'd rather we kept out of *his* way, too,' murmured Ginger.

Leaving the tools where they were, they made their way back to the road and walked unconcernedly down the middle of it in the direction opposite the one by which they had entered the village, until at last they came to the point where it disappeared into the forest. Biggles noticed a lane winding uphill on the left-hand side. 'That, I fancy, leads to the castle,' he observed.

'That's the direction, anyway,' agreed Ginger. 'By the way, that reminds me, as I was coming down on my brolly I thought I saw a light there.'

Biggles stopped dead. 'In the castle?'

'Yes.'

'Are you sure?'

Ginger hesitated. 'It's hard to be certain. I thought I saw a light, but it was gone almost at once.'

'Hm. That's queer. My information was that the castle was a ruin. Let's stroll along a bit; it isn't far, and if anyone sees us it can hardly be said that we are behaving suspiciously.'

As Biggles said, their manner was that of casual tourists; at least, in that they made no attempt at concealment. It was dark under the trees, which closed in on the lane on both sides, but sufficient moonlight penetrated for them to advance without using the torch. After about a quarter of an hour's walk the lane steepened; then the forest terminated abruptly and the massive pile of the castle loomed up grotesquely in the moonlight before them. Not a light showed anywhere. A little breeze had got up and moaned dismally through the pines.

'A grim-looking sort of spot,' murmured Ginger.

'Yes, I should say some dirty work has gone on here in the past,' agreed Biggles, walking closer to the mighty bastions which girded the castle itself. 'This is as far as we can get, apparently,' he continued, when the roadway ended at a broad gateway of heavy, iron-studded timber, which was closed.

'Let's walk along here for a bit,' suggested Ginger, indicating a narrow, weed-covered track that skirted the bastion on their right. 'There seems to be a sort of building on the top of the wall there – stables, or something,' he went on. 'There's a window, too. If one could get up to it it might be possible to get on the wall and drop down on the inside.'

'I don't think it's the ideal moment to start exploring the castle,' murmured Biggles. 'I doubt whether it is likely to produce anything of interest to us anyway, although we might have a look at it sometime. That window up there is barred, isn't it?'

Ginger strained his eyes upwards. 'I think so,' he said. 'By standing on your shoulders I could just about reach it. Lend me the torch and give me a bunk up – I'll have a look inside.'

Biggles glanced up and down the path. There was nobody in sight. 'Right you are,' he said, handing Ginger the torch and making a 'back' for him to mount on.

Ginger, holding the torch between his teeth, climbed up on his unsteady perch. As Biggles straightened his back and thus brought him nearer to the window he gripped the bottom bars with his left hand to take as much weight as possible off Biggles's shoulders. When his eyes grew level with the opening he took the torch from his teeth and directed a shaft of light inside. For perhaps fifteen seconds he remained thus. Then he flicked out the light and dropped back to the ground. He was slightly breathless.

'What is it?' asked Biggles tersely, sensing from his manner that he had seen something.

'There's a car there.'

'A car? What sort of car?'

Ginger drew a deep breath. 'It looks to me like a Morris Ten.'

There was a moment's silence. 'By thunder! That puts a different complexion on things,' breathed Biggles. 'Beklinder's car was a Morris Ten. If that isn't his then it's an uncanny coincidence. Was it damaged?'

'Not a mark on it that I could see.'

Biggles whistled softly. 'We'll look a bit closer into this,' he breathed. But before he could suit the action to the word there came a sound from farther along the path that sent them both with one accord scuttling into the dense shadow of the trees on their right, for at this point the forest approached nearly to the castle walls. It was only a slight noise, but it was significant; the mere rattle of a piece of stone against another. Slight as the sound was they both knew that it could only have been caused by human or animal agency, for stones do not move by themselves.

Biggles, holding Ginger by the arm so that they would not lose each other in the darkness, backed farther into the trees until there was a good ten yards between them and the path, but in a position from which it could be seen. A few moments later the dark outline of a man appeared round a bend in the moonlit path, and it was clear at once from his dress and manner that he was a guard, or sentry. In breeches, military field boots, and a shirt of dark-coloured material, he wore no jacket, but a leather belt with revolver holster attached gave him the appearance of an irregular soldier. He came slowly on, looking about him in an inconsequential manner, as if he had performed the same duty many times before and did not expect to see anything of interest.

When he reached the junction of the path and the roadway he stopped and squatted on a large piece of fallen stone.

'I hope he isn't going to sit there long,' breathed Biggles in Ginger's ear. 'We couldn't move without him hearing us.'

The sentry sat long enough to cause them some anxiety, but at the end of about ten minutes he rose, and after looking at his wrist watch walked up to the heavy door upon which he struck a heavy blow, twice repeated.

Almost at once it was opened, and a second man, dressed in a similar uniform, joined him. Thereupon a conversation was begun, but in tones too low for Biggles to hear what was being said. This went on for several minutes when the distant sound of a Klaxon horn galvanized them to sudden activity; the first man marched up and down in a brisk, soldier-like manner, and the second man threw the gates wide open, keeping them in that position with two heavy stones. A moment later a car could be heard coming up the roadway. Its blinding headlights threw the scene into high relief in a curiously flat manner, so that the picture thus presented was like a piece of stage scenery.

The car, a large dark limousine, drove straight through the gateway without stopping. The gates were then closed, with the two guards on the inside.

Biggles and Ginger remained still for several minutes, not daring to move; but when the guards did not reappear they began to edge towards the roadway. They did not step out on to it, however, but, keeping parallel with it, began to make their way back towards the village. Not until they were once more in the main street did they breathe freely.

'My goodness! We nearly walked into something that time,' muttered Biggles. 'Whatever it is, there is more going on behind

*The car drove straight through the gateway
without stopping.*

those grey walls than appears on the outside. But come on, we must get back to the hotel or the proprietor will wonder what the dickens we are up to. He must know that something is going on at the castle.'

They hurried back to the hotel, where they found the proprietor sitting at his desk, a newspaper in his hand. He looked up as they entered, glanced at the ornate wooden clock which hung on the wall, folded his newspaper and laid it aside.

Biggles took the key of their room from its hook. 'Good-night,' he said.

The proprietor inclined his head. 'Good-night, gentlemen. At what time would you like to be called in the morning?' he asked suavely.

'Oh, you'd better wait until we ring. We'll see how we feel,' returned Biggles, and with a nod passed on to the staircase. Reaching their room, he was putting the key in the lock when a movement made him glance down the corridor. A door was slowly closing. He said nothing, however, until they were inside their room and the door shut. 'That young lady seems to be extremely interested in our movements,' he said quietly.

'Was it her?' I couldn't quite see—'

'I think so. Apparently there is nobody else in the hotel, so it must have been her.' Biggles locked the door on the inside and dropped the key on the dressing-table. 'We shall have to be careful what we say, even in here,' he whispered, as he sat down on his bed. 'We *might* be overheard – if somebody was sufficiently curious to listen.'

'I'll remember it,' agreed Ginger, in an undertone. 'For the first evening we haven't done too badly. What's the next move?'

'I feel like keeping the ball rolling while the coast seems

reasonably clear,' replied Biggles. 'We shall have to stay here and rest, I think, until everyone has settled down for the night. Then, if we can get out of the window, as no doubt we can, we'll go and have a look at the churchyard. There is a moon, and I'd rather go now than in broad daylight, when people might be about. We must get back before dawn, though. We can sleep on in the morning if we're very tired. In fact, if those blackshirts, or brownshirts, or whatever they are, are prowling about, we may be safer indoors than outside.'

'That suits me,' agreed Ginger, kicking off his shoes, and making himself comfortable on the bed.

Somewhere downstairs a clock chimed the midnight hour.

CHAPTER VI

What Happened at the Vault

An hour and a half later Biggles got up from his bed, put a pair of light tennis shoes on his feet, and began collecting certain articles together on the table. From his rucksack he took a thin, but strong cotton rope, knotted at intervals; beside it he laid a screwdriver and the electric torch. 'Time to be moving, laddie,' he told Ginger, who had fallen into a doze.

Ginger sprang to his feet. 'Phew, I was nearly asleep,' he said in a startled voice. 'Is everything O.K.?'

'I think so. The house has been quiet for some time.' Biggles went to the window, and quietly opened one of the lattice diamond-paned frames which overlooked the courtyard just inside the coach entrance. They were on the first floor, so the distance to the ground was not far, a matter of a mere fifteen feet. He looked up and down, listening intently, but there was no sound. Even the breeze had died away, leaving the atmosphere heavy and humid, as if it might rain. A tenuous veil of mist half obscured the moon.

'I think it's all clear,' he whispered, turning back into the room. 'Give me a hand to move the bed right up to the window. We shall have to pass the rope round the bedpost to let ourselves down; there doesn't seem to be anything else firm enough. I'm afraid it's going to be a bit of a job getting the rope back on it to pull ourselves up when we return, but we daren't leave the rope hanging in case any one happens to pass, and sees it. No matter. If we put the bedpost right up against the window so that we can see it from outside we should be able to manage it all right. In any case, it's only a matter of ten or twelve feet. They built these old places with low ceilings – as you have probably noticed. If the worst comes to the worst you could pretty nearly reach the windowsill by standing on my shoulders. We shall have to leave the window open, but I don't think that matters; being English, they would expect us to sleep with our window wide open, anyway.'

Preparations for departure were soon complete, Biggles stowing his equipment, with the exception of the rope, in the big inside pocket of the sports jacket he was wearing. 'Ready? You go first,' he ordered.

Holding the rope to steady himself, Ginger crawled backwards through the window and lowered himself hand over hand to the ground. Biggles followed, and, drawing the rope clear, coiled it and put it in his pocket. Then, keeping close to the wall, their rubber-soled shoes making no sound on the cobblestones, they made their way to the tool-shed where Biggles collected the crowbar. This done they retraced their steps and continued on to the village street, now silent and deserted, and set off at a brisk pace for the churchyard. Not a light showed anywhere.

Not until they were clear of the houses did Biggles speak again. 'We've tackled some queer jobs in our time, but this is about the grimmest,' he said quietly. 'In fact, I've never set about anything with less enthusiasm; but there's no way out of it. No matter. In an hour or two, with any luck, the first part of our job will be done.'

The road that led to their destination was desolate, and, as they expected, deserted; only the distant barking of a dog, and the occasional melancholy stirring of the pines, broke the silence. The track, for the way could hardly be called a road, was sandy, so they made no sound as they trudged along. Rounding a bend the pines straggled out on to open ground, and the dark silhouette of the church, looking huge in the deceptive light, loomed up before them.

Examination revealed that the churchyard was surrounded only by a low stone wall, so ignoring the elaborate wicket gate they vaulted over the low obstruction and went on towards the church, picking their way between the mounds of earth that marked the last resting-place of generations of simple villagers. Few of the graves carried a headstone. One or two could boast of a rough wooden cross, in varying stages of dilapidation. Nothing moved.

One thing is pretty certain,' remarked Biggles, with a mirthless little laugh. 'We are not likely to be interrupted. Most people give churchyards a wide berth at this hour – the days of body snatchers being over.'

'I feel a bit like a body snatcher myself,' grumbled Ginger. 'I never did have much time for churchyards at night. If anything moves I shall probably let out a yell. I find this a most depressing business.'

'I'm not exactly bursting with hilarity myself,' admitted Biggles seriously. 'Let's keep going. If the Jew was right the vault is at the foot of the tower, on this side.'

'I'm not going down into any spooky vault,' growled Ginger.

'Please yourself. If there are any spooks about they are just as likely to be on top as underneath,' bantered Biggles.

By this time they had reached the west wall of the church tower, so Biggles stopped and, taking out his flashlight, started examining the wall closely, looking for the entrance to the vault. It was not difficult to find, for there was only one, and it showed signs of having been recently disturbed. Actually, the entrance was not in the wall; the stone that closed it rested on a few courses of brickwork sunk into the ground at right-angles to the wall. Biggles's flashlight rested for a moment on the slab. 'Ah,' he said quietly, 'I thought they wouldn't overlook that.' Incised on the stone, in clear letters, was a name. It was M. Beklinder. Under the name was a date, followed by the customary letters R.I.P. Switching off the torch, he put it in his pocket and allowed the end of the crow-bar to drop gently on the slab, so that it gave out a hollow booming sound. 'When I prise the stone up with the bar you grab it and hang on to it until I can help you,' Biggles ordered. 'I'll try to fix the bar at an angle so that it keeps the entrance open. There is no need for us to lift it off altogether, because it might be difficult to put it back so that if fits exactly. We only need an aperture wide enough to get through.'

Ginger glanced apprehensively round the melancholy scene and shivered. 'O.K.,' he said, 'go ahead. Let's get the ghoulish business finished.'

'What's the matter, are you afraid of something?' inquired Biggles.

'I certainly am.'

'Of what?'

'Spooks.'

'Spooks my grandmother! Where did you get such ideas? For

my part, I should be most interested to see one, because I've never seen one yet – and I never shall.'

'You may get your wish presently,' muttered Ginger.

Biggles laughed. 'Rot! Believe me, we're a lot safer here than we were up at the castle. I observed that those fellows in the dark shirts carried guns, and doubtless they would have used them had they seen us; but I can't imagine a spook cluttering itself up with such material things as firearms. According to what I've read they rely on hollow groans and clanking chains—'

'Will you shut up and get the lid off this death hole?' snorted Ginger. 'The sooner I'm back in my little cot at the hotel the happier I shall be.'

Biggles said no more, but driving the sharp end of the crow-bar under the edge of the slab, raised it sufficiently for him to get a more secure grip. Then, putting all his weight on the iron, he levered the stone cover several inches into the air. Ginger grabbed it and held on while Biggles allowed the bar to fall and seize the other side. 'Now,' he grunted, and the stone came up on end, steady on its own weight. 'Hold it like that for a minute,' went on Biggles quickly. 'For heaven's sake don't let it fall.' He drove the bar diagonally into the ground so that by allowing the slab to come forward again it rested on the blunt end and remained in that position. 'Good,' said Biggles, 'I think that's done the trick. Will you go first?'

'Not on your life,' declared Ginger, starting back.

Biggles chuckled and took out his torch.

'This seems to strike you as funny,' sneered Ginger.

'No, frankly, it does not,' Biggles told him earnestly. 'But surely it is better to treat the thing lightly than take it too seriously, or we might both get the screaming heebie-jeebies, which would be silly now that we're actually on the spot.'

As he spoke Biggles knelt down and directed the ray of the torch into the vault. The yellow light revealed a flight of steps leading down into a gloomy recess, the limits of which could not be seen. Without any more ado he slid through the opening and made his way carefully down the steps. His voice came up to Ginger, who was also kneeling, peering into the vault. 'It's all right. I'm standing on the floor.'

Ginger followed Biggles down the steps, ultimately finding himself in what might be best described as a large, rectangular room. It was, of course, entirely devoid of furniture, but round the walls, laid lengthways in niches built for their reception, rested what were unmistakably coffins. Above each, let into the wall, was a metal plate bearing a name.

Biggles walked to the nearest, read the name, and then began to move slowly along the line. 'These are all pretty ancient,' he observed. 'Hm. There seems to have been a lot of nobility living hereabouts at one time – at the castle, I expect. Counts and countesses – barons – why, here is even a prince, eighteen years old; he died in the plague of 1660.'

'Never mind about him; find the one that matters and let's get out,' urged Ginger.

Biggles went on along the line. 'Ah!' he exclaimed. 'Here are some more recent dates. We're in the eighteenth century now. What's this one – 1815. That was the year of Waterloo, if I remember my history.'

And so Biggles went on, although he did not linger anywhere, for it was possible to judge in a moment from the condition of the name-plate how long each coffin had been there. 'It still puzzles me why they buried Beklinder here, instead of in an ordinary grave,' he remarked. Almost immediately afterwards he found the name he sought, and announced it triumphantly. The name-plate was new, as was the coffin below it. 'We shan't be long now,' he declared. 'You take the torch and stand over there, and throw the beam in my direction so that I can see what I'm doing. You'd better look the other way – in case of accidents; but if my guess is right we're likely to find in this coffin anything but what that name-plate says it contains.' So saying, he handed Ginger the torch, and taking the screwdriver from his pocket, set to work on his odious task.

'I'll tell you another thing,' he went on presently. 'The fellow who put these screws in was either a rotten undertaker – or else he wasn't an undertaker at all. They're all loose.'

Ginger, staring into the darkness, heard the scraping of the coffin lid as Biggles gently withdrew it. His nerves tingled as Biggles laughed softly.

'It's all right,' came Biggles's voice. 'Come and take a look at poor Max Beklinder.'

Ginger swung round. 'Books!' he gasped.

'A good way of getting rid of your old books and magazines,' said Biggles dryly. 'They weigh heavy just about as heavy as a body. Well, that's all we want to know. I'll soon have this lid on again.' With that, Biggles pushed the lid back into place and began replacing the screws.

'Do you know what made me laugh when I looked in the coffin?' he asked, as he worked.

'No – unless it was relief.'

'It wasn't that; it was the title of the top book.'

'What was it?'

'*Grimm's Fairy Tales*. If this deception isn't like a fairy tale, I don't know what is.'

Biggles mopped his forehead with his handkerchief as he finished his task and took the torch from Ginger's hand, for he had been working with almost furious speed and the atmosphere in the vault was stuffy. 'Thank goodness that's over,' he announced. 'We'll get along home – ssh! What's that?' He broke off and switched out the light so that they were in absolute darkness. His hand gripped Ginger's arm like a vice.

Ginger's blood seemed to freeze as from somewhere not far away came a curious soft swishing sound. It stopped, and then came on again, the sound appearing to come from the entrance to the vault, which in the utter darkness now showed as a narrow strip of dark grey light.

'What – what is it?' gasped Ginger.

Biggles did not answer. On the contrary he shook Ginger's arm impatiently for silence. And thus they stood while the seconds ticked by at a speed infinitely slower than the spasmodic thumping of Ginger's heart. Then, as they stared at the opening, it was suddenly blotted out as if something had filled it.

To Ginger, time seemed to stand still. There was no future, no past; only the dreadful present. The suspense was such that only by clenching his teeth could he prevent himself from crying out aloud. Then, whatever it was at the mouth of the vault moved aside, and the grey strip reappeared.

Biggles cupped his hands round his mouth close against Ginger's face. 'There is somebody out there,' he breathed. 'Don't move.'

Slowly the seconds passed, and became minutes, each minute seeming like an eternity. But whatever it was that had passed the opening did not return.

'I've had enough of this; I'm going to have a look outside,' whispered Biggles at last. 'We can't stay here all night.' Moving a few inches at a time he began to make his way towards the exit.

Still nothing had happened by the time he reached it. Not a sound came from outside. Again Biggles halted; Ginger joined him and they remained motionless while two or three more minutes passed; then, with infinite caution, Biggles began to creep up the steps, with Ginger, fearful of being left alone, keeping pace with him; for the steps were wide enough to admit two, no doubt for the more easy access of the coffin-bearers.

On hands and knees they reached a step high enough for them to get a view of the moonlit yard outside. There was nobody in sight. With a deep gasp of relief Ginger began to move forward, and had half emerged from the vault when what he had taken to be a headstone suddenly came to life. With a wild screech something white fluttered into the air, and then swept swiftly over the graves.

Ginger did not see what became of it. His cry of horror was drowned in the screech and he fell back into the vault. Biggles's fist caught him in the ribs. 'Keep your head,' he said, angrily. 'It's gone. Let's get out.'

'Where did it – where did it go?' panted Ginger.

'It jumped the wall, and as far as I can make out disappeared down the road.'

'My gosh! I nearly died of fright,' muttered Ginger weakly, passing a trembling hand over a clammy brow. 'Who said there were no such things as spooks, eh? Now what about it? If that wasn't a spook, what was it?'

'Obviously, I don't know who it was, but you can take it from me that it was no spook. It was a human being.'

'It didn't look much like a human being to me,' asserted Ginger emphatically. 'Didn't you see that white thing fluttering?'

'I did,' agreed Biggles curtly.

By this time they had emerged from the vault and were standing erect. Biggles switched on his torch and directed the beam to the ground at the place where the figure had been standing when they had first seen it. 'Take a look at that,' he said, pointing to a spot where the dew-soaked turf had been trampled down. 'Spooks don't trample down the grass, nor do they leave a trail. Look, you can see the way the fellow ran across the grass.'

'By jingo, you're right,' declared Ginger. 'It begins to look as if somebody followed us here.'

'I don't know about that,' replied Biggles, 'but one thing is certain; there was somebody here in this churchyard tonight besides us, close against this vault, somebody dressed in a manner well calculated to frighten anyone else who came along. It was rather a clever idea to dress up like a ghost. We might have done the same thing had we thought of it. One day we may discover who it was, but at the moment it isn't much use guessing, although at the back of my mind I have the glimmering of an idea – but come on; let's get this slab back into place. We've done pretty well, I think, although this spook business is a bit disconcerting. There certainly is something very funny going on around here, although how far it has to do with the Professor is a question we can't answer.'

Without any difficulty they lowered the slab back to its original position. Satisfied that there was nothing to betray that it had been moved, they brushed their clothes, and after concealing the crow-bar under a nearby yew, in case it were needed again, they set off back towards the hotel, moving with caution and keeping

to the side of the road as far as it was possible in case their movements were being watched. But if such was the case they saw
no signs of it, and in due course reached the hotel yard without
seeing a soul. Keeping close against the wall, Biggles took the
rope from his inside pocket, and making a wide noose in the end,
undertook the rather tricky job of catching it round the bedpost.
After several failures he succeeded, and the rest was easy. Biggles
went up the rope first. Ginger followed him. As he stepped inside
he tapped Biggles on the arm. 'I'll tell you something,' he said.

'What?'

'The girl next door saw us come in.'

'The dickens! How do you know? There was no light in her
room.'

'Maybe not, but I saw the curtain move.'

Biggles shook his head as he pulled in the rope and closed
the window. 'That's a pity,' he said, turning back into the room.
'I can't get that girl placed at all. It seems as if she is watching
us, but, somehow, I don't see how she can be – or rather, why she
should be. Her arrival at the Jew's house must have been purely
coincidental with ours, for until that moment she could not have
been aware of our existence, any more than we were aware of the
Jew's existence.'

'She might have been watching the house, and saw us go in,'
suggested Ginger.

'That's true,' admitted Biggles. 'If that assumption is correct,
it leads to the question, on whose behalf was she watching the
house? She doesn't look the sort of person who would be engaged
by those concerned with the Professor's disappearance, or the
storm-troopers whom we know are at the castle. It seems equally
unlikely that she can be working on her own account; yet it must

be one or the other – unless, of course, our caution has made us take an exaggerated view of her actions, and she is only an ordinary tourist, after all.'

'She doesn't strike me that way,' said Ginger slowly, shaking his head.

'Nor me, I must admit. It will be interesting to see how she reacts when she suspects that we are watching *her*.'

'*Are* you going to watch her?'

'Possibly, if it doesn't retard our own plans. If she is watching us we shall certainly have to keep an eye on her, for she becomes a danger. At the rate things are going we shall probably pick up a clue presently, that will put us on the right track. But actually, I am more concerned about that spook than I am about the girl. I can't make head or tail of that affair. What the deuce was the person playing at? Why play the spook? Only a lunatic does that sort of thing without a good reason. Had there been a storm-trooper on guard I could have understood it – but a spook, no. The people concerned with the Beklinder affair would surely not play fool tricks like that. Can you imagine von Stalhein countenancing such childish methods, because I can't? But there, we might sit here all night asking ourselves questions without being any the wiser.'

'Questions – such as?'

'Did the spook know we were in the vault?'

'It certainly saw us come out.'

'Yes, and from the way it gave tongue it was as startled as we were. Well, maybe things will work themselves out in due course; we shall see. We ought to see about getting some sleep. We've had a long day, and there is no doubt that things have gone exceptionally well for us. I hope they'll go as well tomorrow.'

'What's the next move?'

'We'll get the pigeon away first thing in the morning. But now I come to think of it there is just one more little job that we ought to do tonight. We shall probably have to do it sometime and the present moment seems as good as any. There's nothing like following up your luck when it is going well.'

'What are you contemplating?'

'I'd like to have a look in the room next door – number seventeen, the room the Jew told us Beklinder was put in. There might be something to learn there, and it would be dangerous to try to get in in the daytime. The key is on the rack downstairs, and so far as I can see there is nothing to prevent us from using it.'

'Shall I go down and get it?' suggested Ginger, watching Biggles coil the rope and hide it under the mattress of his bed.

'Yes. Take the torch – and watch your step. Don't for the love of Mike knock anything over.'

'Leave it to me,' murmured Ginger, picking up the torch and crossing over to the door. Taking the greatest possible care to ensure silence, he unlocked it and went out into the corridor. All was silent, so after a moment's hesitation he began to make his way towards the head of the stairs.

There was nothing particularly difficult about his task, although the profound silence, and the heavy, old-fashioned panelling and furniture, created an air of brooding mystery that caused his nerves to tingle. However, he reached the hall without anything happening and turned the beam of the torch on the rack. As the hotel was practically empty all the keys were in place – except three; their own, number fifteen, which he realized must be the number of the girl's room, and number seventeen. The key he had come to fetch was not there. For a moment he stared at the vacant hook, taken aback by this unexpected turn of events and what it portended. Then, realizing the full significance of his discovery, he hurried back to where Biggles was waiting for him. 'The key's gone,' he breathed.

Biggles's response to this information was a '*tck*' of surprise.

'It looks as if the proprietor takes it with him when he goes to bed,' murmured Ginger.

'Or is somebody using the room, after all?' suggested Biggles. 'I think we must look into this. Were any other keys missing?'

'Only number fifteen, which I imagine is the girl's room.'

'Ah! I wonder if she's in her room?'

'You can't very well find out.'

'Can't I, though?'

'How?'

'By trying her door.'

'By gosh! You've got a nerve.'

'If she's inside it will be locked for a certainty.'

'And if it is not locked?'

'If that is the case I should say she is not in her room.'

'But suppose she does happen to be in her room, with the door unlocked?'

'In that case, when she sees the door opening, or hears it opening, she will probably make a sound of some sort. Then, all we have to do is to return here with all speed, and no one will know who tried her door.'

'What's the idea of this?'

'If my guess is right, I think I know who has borrowed the key of number seventeen. Stay where you are, there's no need for us both to go,' went on Biggles quickly. He crossed over to the door, opened it quietly, and peeped out into the corridor. With cat-like tread he went on to the door of number fifteen. His hands settled lightly on the brass knob and turned it. Only when it had turned as far as it would go did he put a gentle weight against the door. It opened easily. He peeped inside. A candle was burning near the head of a bed which had not been slept in. Moving quickly but quietly he closed the door and returned to Ginger. 'It is as I thought,' he said. 'She isn't there. It is a hundred to one that the girl is in number seventeen. I'm just going to make sure.'

'How?'

'By trying the door.'

'You're taking some chances.'

'I expected to when I came here.'

Again Biggles opened the door and crept out into the corridor.

With his pulses racing, Ginger watched him from the threshold of their room. There was just enough moonlight from a window at the end of the corridor for him to see Biggles's form creeping towards his objective. It was only a matter of four or five steps.

Reaching the door of number seventeen, again Biggles's hands closed lightly over the knob. Slowly he turned it, and pressed gently. But this time he was not so fortunate. The door squeaked. It was only a slight sound, but in the dead silence it was enough to make Ginger catch his breath. The sound was followed instantly by a faint cry of alarm from inside the room. Quite calmly Biggles closed the door again and came back swiftly down the corridor. Ginger stepped back. Biggles came into the room, but he did not quite close the door; he left it open perhaps half an inch. Motionless he stood with an eye to the crack. The silence was such that the ticking of the clock in the entrance hall could be heard distinctly. Then, along the corridor came a sound so faint that a mouse might have made it. Biggles, seeing nothing pass, opened the door a few inches wider and looked out. He was just in time to see a shadowy figure disappear down the stairs that led to the hall. 'She's gone to put the key back,' he whispered, for Ginger's benefit.

Still watching, a moment later the figure reappeared. With no more noise than a shadow it glided down the corridor towards him. He held the door closed while it passed and then looked out again. It was too dark for him to see anything clearly, but the quiet opening and closing of a door, and the sudden ray of yellow candlelight, told him all he wanted to know. He turned to Ginger. 'It was the girl,' he said. 'She's gone back to her room. We have learnt this, anyway; she knows about Beklinder; that can be the only reason for her interest in room number seventeen.'

'She may have overheard the Jew telling us.'

'That is more than likely.'

'Shall I go and get the key of number seventeen?'

'Not now. I think it's dangerous. She may be watching us, and there is no knowing what she might not do. I think I have a better plan.' Biggles went over to the wall that separated them from the room next door – number seventeen. It was half timbered, but as is usual with such construction the spaces between the beams had been filled with plaster. Satisfied with his inspection he fetched the screwdriver, and after carefully arranging a towel on the floor to catch any loose pieces of plaster that might fall, he began boring a small hole through the wall. Soft as the plaster was it took him some time to complete the task. The screwdriver told him when he was through. He applied his eye to the hole, but, as he expected, the room on the far side was in darkness and he could see nothing, so after plugging the hole with a tiny wad of paper he returned the tool to his rucksack and began to undress. 'That will have to do for today,' he said. 'We shall have to turn in. It's no use overdoing it.'

Ginger yawned. 'I've had about enough for one stretch,' he admitted.

CHAPTER VII

Strange Birds in the Forest

It seemed to Ginger that he had no sooner closed his eyes than he was wide awake again, every nerve alert, listening for a repetition of the sound which had awakened him. It is not easy to locate a sound when it is heard during sleep, but he retained in his mind a sort of echo of a gentle tap-tap, as if someone had knocked lightly on the door. Indeed, as he raised himself on his elbow and stared into the darkness in the direction of the door, he became so convinced that this was the case that he almost called 'Come in'. But a swift movement from the other bed told him that Biggles was awake, and had evidently heard what he had heard; so he did nothing. Another instant and Biggles was bending over him. 'Keep quiet,' he breathed.

'What is it?' whispered Ginger.

'I think it is somebody in the next room.'

Again came the soft tap – tap; it seemed to come from the wall in which Biggles had bored the hole, and in which direction Biggles now crept.

As Ginger swung his legs out of bed the darkness was pierced by a minute ray of light which started about half-way up the wall which divided their room from number seventeen and lost itself in a vague halo on the far side. It was immediately blotted out, but Ginger realized that Biggles had uncovered the hole he had made and was now peeping through it into the next room. As only one person could use the spy-hole at a time he continued sitting on the edge of his bed, waiting with lively expectation for the report which he knew Biggles would presently bring him. Several minutes passed, during which absolute silence reigned, before Biggles crept back again. 'Take a look,' he breathed.

Ginger made his way silently to the tiny source of the light and applied his eye to the hole. The room into which he found himself looking was not illuminated as brightly as he expected it would be, for which reason it took him some seconds to comprehend fully what was going on. The first thing he made out was the light itself, a small electric lamp which stood on a bedside table and cast its glow over a section of the room which included part of a sheet-covered bed and a light-coloured object on the floor – something that moved slowly. Concentrating his attention on this, he soon perceived that it was a human form in night attire; or, to be precise, in a nightdress. At this moment the face looked up, almost as if the owner of it was suspicious of the wall; then it turned down again as the figure continued to pursue what seemed to be a close scrutiny of the polished floor boards. But the brief glimpse of the face had been sufficient for Ginger to recognize the girl whose mysterious movements had already aroused their curiosity. Wonderingly he watched the girl crawl slowly over the floor, examining it inch by inch and occasionally sounding it with her knuckles, making the gentle tapping sound which had awakened him. And while he was still watching he saw the conclusion of this extraordinary performance. The soft tap – tap had suddenly changed its note. Simultaneously the girl's movements became more rapid. With something bright which she held in her hand she appeared to be working on one of the boards; then, surprisingly, a section of the floorboards moved slowly upwards, disclosing a black hole some two and a half feet square. The girl's gasp of triumph came distinctly to Ginger as he stepped back and groped for Biggles, whom he knew was standing at his elbow. 'Look!' he breathed, and stood aside to allow Biggles to take his place.

There was another interval of silence. Then Biggles retired to where Ginger was again sitting on the edge of his bed. The ray of light no longer gleamed through the hole. 'She's gone,' he said quietly. 'Having found what she was looking for, she's gone back to her room.'

'You saw the trap-door?' queried Ginger.

'Of course.'

'She must have known it was there.'

'Obviously.'

'She seems to know a lot more about this place than we do.'

'I had already suspected that.'

'There must be a subterranean passage under the hotel. Where does it lead to, that's the question.'

'It can hardly be a subterranean passage because it's on the first floor,' murmured Biggles. 'But we shall know more about it when we've explored it. This girl is certainly making things complicated, but I am beginning to feel that she is working on parallel lines to ourselves; if she is we might both do better to compare notes, but I must confess that I jib at the idea of approaching her direct. She is suspicious of us as it is. Well, I'm afraid we can't do any more about it at the moment. What's the time?' Biggles reached for his watch. 'Quarter to six,' he continued. 'We haven't had much sleep, but a little is better than nothing; I don't think it's worthwhile going back to bed; it's just beginning to get light. I'm anxious to turn that pigeon loose. I shall breathe more freely when that's done.'

'Is there any reason why we shouldn't go along right away?'

'It's early to be about – a bit too early for normal tourists.'

'What about getting out of the window?'

Biggles shook his head. 'We mustn't do too much of that,' he argued. 'It would be better if we used the door, except in cases of emergency. Let's lie down for a bit; I'll have a cigarette and think things over. Then we'll take our time getting dressed and so arrive downstairs at a reasonable time. There will be nothing suspicious about it then if we go for a hike.'

'Good enough, chief.' Ginger threw himself back on his bed, and with his hands under his head stared unseeingly at the spiral of Biggles's cigarette smoke as he turned over in his mind the events that had occurred since their arrival in Unterhamstadt. Not the least remarkable thing about the girl was her vague resemblance to somebody whom he knew, he pondered. That this was not merely imagination was borne out by the fact that Biggles had thought the same thing. Which meant that it was somebody known to both of them. Yet who could it be? They knew very few women. Was it a film star whose face had become familiar by constant publication in newspapers and magazines? No, he decided. Yet just behind his consciousness was the link which he felt was there but could not grasp. Then, quite suddenly, it came to him. He knew. He did not know how he knew – but he knew. And the knowledge sent him bolt upright on the bed. 'Jumping rattlesnakes!' he gasped aloud. 'I think I've got it!'

Biggles raised his eyebrows. 'Got what?'

'That girl.'

'What about her?'

'I know who she's like – or am I crazy?'

'Tell me, and I'll give you my opinion.'

'Beklinder!'

Biggles stiffened. His eyes opened wide and an extraordinary expression swept over his face. Then, with a single movement, he was on his feet. 'You're right,' he snapped. 'That's it. Beklinder. That's the likeness. It's more a similarity of expression, though, than a likeness of the features.' Biggles paced up and down the room in his agitation. 'Can it be coincidence? Is it possible?'

'It might be,' murmured Ginger dubiously.

'Surely not. Hang it all, there must be a limit even to coincidence,' muttered Biggles impatiently.

'Did the people at home say anything about Beklinder having a daughter?'

'No – nor any other relation except his wife.'

'It couldn't be his wife, I suppose?'

'Of course not. This girl can't be a day more than twenty. No, if Beklinder had a daughter then he was unaware of it, of that I'm certain.'

'Why should he tell anybody – even if he knew?'

'On the other hand, why not? What need was there for secrecy? He told the Foreign Office everything about himself. Why conceal the fact that he had a daughter – if he had one? Unless – unless – yes, that may be the answer. It might have been a trap to get him here. Ginger, I feel that we're on the scent of something, and we're getting warm. There is only one thing to do; I'm going to find a way of getting into conversation with that girl. It's a risk, but it's worth taking. She knows something that might be invaluable to us, and I'm going to find out what it is. How goes the time? Nearly half-past six. Let's get dressed; it will be after seven by the time we get down. We'll free the pigeon and then try to make contact with the girl. That's our plan for the moment.'

Ginger said no more, and they set about their toilet. As there was no hot water available, shaving took rather longer than usual, and the clock in the hall had struck seven by the time they were ready to move off. But early as it was, footsteps and the rattle of crockery told them that the hotel staff was already afoot.

Biggles opened the door and stepped out into the corridor. Ginger followed, and as they stood there an old, cheerful-looking chambermaid came along carrying a pile of dirty linen over her arm.

'*Guten morgen*,' Biggles greeted her cheerfully, but his eyes were on one of the sheets which the woman was trailing over her arm. Clearly imprinted on it was a footmark. He made a grimace. 'What!' he exclaimed. 'Do your guests go to bed in their boots?'

The old woman frowned. 'That young gad-about does, it seems,' she declared. 'Twice this week I've had to change her sheets.' She nodded towards the door of the only other guest in the hotel, which was, of course, that of the girl. 'I don't know when she sleeps at all,' she continued. 'She goes to bed late and she's gone off this morning already.' With a sniff that expressed strong disapproval of such behaviour the woman swept on down the corridor and round the corner. They could hear her heavy foot-steps going down the stairs.

'Quick,' snapped Biggles, and made a dash for the girl's room, the door of which had been left wide open. 'Keep *cave*,' he said, tersely, and disappeared inside.

Within two minutes Ginger could hear the chambermaid returning. '*Cave!*' he hissed, just loud enough for Biggles to hear.

Biggles rejoined him, and they walked on down the corridor just as the old woman came in sight carrying a supply of clean sheets. The proprietor was sweeping the entrance hall when they reached it, and Biggles asked if it was too early for coffee. On receiving a reply in the negative he sat down at one of the small tables to await its arrival.

'Well, did you learn anything?' asked Ginger, pulling up a chair.

'A little,' replied Biggles. 'Anyway, we've laid the ghost that gave you such a fright in the churchyard.'

'You mean – it was the girl?'

'Of course. She used one of the sheets off her bed to play the part – and trod on it, probably when she was running away from us.'

'What was her idea, I wonder?'

'Much the same as ours, I should say.'

'What did you see in her room – anything interesting?'

'Yes. The room had been tidied up, and in the short time at my disposal I hadn't much time for Sherlock Holmes stuff. The flashlamp was on her bedside table – a natural place for it, I suppose – and a book. The title caught my eye. It was *A History of Unterhamstadt from the Earliest Times*, a sort of guide book, but a very old one, one that might be difficult to pick up in the ordinary way, but easy enough in a local second-hand bookshop. There was a bookmark in it, so I had a quick look to see what she had been reading. The particular chapter was about the castle, and she had been indiscreet enough to make a pencil mark against a special paragraph. I could well understand it interesting her.

I can't remember the actual words, but it was something to the effect that legend claims that in the bad old days underground passages connected the castle with the hostelry and the monastery of San Stefan, the site of which has been lost.'

Ginger started. 'By gosh!' he exclaimed. 'I was right about that passage in Number Seventeen. It must go underground to the castle.'

Biggles nodded. 'I don't think there is much doubt about it. That trapdoor must open into a passage that goes right through the room below – or maybe there is a concealed closet, or double walls. They were experts at that sort of thing years ago.'

'The girl must have learned of the existence of it from the book.'

'Probably, but I could see nothing in the paragraph to indicate where the passage began. In fact, according to the book, the underground passage story was only a legend. Yet she evidently knew where to look for it. At any rate, she found it. That could hardly have been luck. How did she know the entrance was in number seventeen? That takes a bit of explaining, doesn't it? As we have already agreed, this young lady knows as much about this place as the proprietor – if not more.'

'The thing is certainly getting into a bit of a tangle.'

'It is sorting itself out fairly well, I think.'

'Where on earth could she have gone so early?'

'Ah! That's something – ssh! Here comes the coffee.'

The same waiter who had served them with supper set a tray of coffee and rolls on the table between them, and on these they now focused their attention, although only a few minutes were needed to consume them.

'Well, it is certainly a grand morning,' murmured Biggles, as they closed the door of the hotel behind them and went off down the road in the direction of the wood in which they had concealed the pigeon basket. Overhead the sky was a dome of unbroken blue towards which the wooded hills rose sharply from misty valleys. The air was sweet and fresh, faintly tinctured with the refreshing perfume of pines, while over all hung the pleasing silence of an unspoilt countryside.

For some time they walked without speaking, Biggles deep in thought, pondering over the problems that confronted them, and Ginger hesitating to interrupt; but reaching a bend Biggles stopped, and after a quick glance up and down the road, entered the dim aisles of the fir forest on their right. 'I think we can cut through here to reach the place,' he said, and again they walked on, their feet making no sound on the soft carpet of generations of fir needles. Except for an occasional rabbit which scuttled across their path, or a squirrel that eyed them inquisitively from a tree, the forest appeared to be deserted, although larger tracks, which Biggles said he thought were those of wild boar, were sometimes discernible. From the point where they had entered the forest to the place where they had concealed the pigeon was, they agreed, about two miles, and they had covered half this distance when Biggles said quietly, 'Has it struck you as odd, that although we continually hear birds we never see one?'

Ginger looked up sharply, realizing that there was more behind the words than casual observation. 'Now you mention it, I have noticed it,' he answered. 'The birds seem to be calling and answering each other.'

'Precisely,' said Biggles dryly. 'And although birds of a species have the same note, there is a curious similarity with these. Quite apart from which, although I do not profess to be an ornithologist, I know of no bird that makes such a peculiar whistle.'

'You think they are *not* birds?' said Ginger quietly.

'I may be alarming myself unnecessarily, but it is my opinion that we are being followed,' declared Biggles. 'Keep walking, and on no account behave as if we suspected anything.'

'Crikey!' muttered Ginger. 'Hadn't we better confirm this before we go anywhere near the pigeon?'

'We most certainly must,' Biggles told him. 'Do what I do.'

For a little while they strolled on, remarking loudly about the trees, and the forest generally, as if they were walking aimlessly. Once Biggles picked up a fir cone and threw it at a grey squirrel, and they both laughed as it bolted higher into the tree. Then, 'This way,' said Biggles softly, and they turned down into a small dell-hole, one side of which was fringed with a thick clump of holly. 'Let's sit down here,' he went on. 'We may see something. Sit still and behave naturally.' He took out a small sketching block, which he had brought with him to support his claim of being an artist, and began making a sketch of a glade which could be seen beyond the far side of the dell. Almost at once came the whistle on which Biggles had remarked, to be answered by another some distance farther on. Even making allowances for imagination, Ginger felt that there was something unnatural about them.

Five minutes passed, and then his muscles tensed, and he turned his eyes to the rim of the dell just above them and to their right. Something was coming. Biggles, too, was watching. A moment later a dog appeared on the rim. It was an Alsatian. It pulled up dead when it saw them, gazing down with keen, intelligent eyes. And while it stood watching them in a manner curiously and unpleasantly human, making no attempt to approach nearer, the whistle, now very close, echoed through the quiet aisles of the forest. Instantly the hound turned and disappeared.

Biggles glanced at Ginger, laid a finger on his lips, and went on sketching. Again for a short time there was silence. Then, not far away, two men carried on a conversation in low tones. Again silence. Presently a twig snapped, and Ginger felt his skin creep, knowing that in the apparently deserted forest men were moving about for a purpose that was not difficult to guess. Biggles was proceeding with his sketch as if he had neither seen nor heard anything. Then a movement caught Ginger's eyes. Without speaking he touched Biggles on the knee, keeping his eyes fixed on the object. A broad figure in the sinister uniform of a storm-trooper was walking slowly across the glade, looking about him intently as he crossed the open space. Ginger noticed that his shirt was not brown, as he had supposed it to be, but a dark greeny-grey. Somewhere a little distance away another twig cracked. A bird whistled.

Ginger looked at Biggles, alarm in his eyes. 'This is a bit trying,' he breathed. 'They seem to be all round us.'

'Yes, but I think they've lost us, temporarily at any rate,' returned Biggles. 'We can only sit still for a bit and hope that they lose us altogether. By hook or crook we have got to get to that pigeon; but if we're seen with it—' He broke off and made a grimace.

After that neither spoke for some time. Twenty minutes, which seemed to Ginger like an hour, passed, during which time there had been no sound beyond an occasional whistle in the far distance.

'I think we might risk getting a bit nearer,' said Biggles quietly, rising to his feet. 'In any case, so far there has been nothing definitely suspicious about our actions, so even if we are seen I do not see how we can be accused of anything.'

'You don't think they were actually looking for us to arrest us?'

'No. I think it is more likely that they received information that we were at the hotel, and decided that they had better keep an eye on us while we were here.'

They walked on, not directly towards their objective, but on a meandering course which, nevertheless, took them ever nearer to it; and, in this way, without seeing anything more of the storm-troopers, they came to within sight of the edge of the forest, on the side where they had first entered it to conceal their parachutes and the pigeon basket.

'I think we've struck the edge a bit too far down. Bear to the right a bit,' said Biggles softly. His manner was inconsequential, but his eyes were never still for a moment. 'Yes, that's the place, just ahead,' he went on a few minutes later. 'There's the holly bush. There is no desperate hurry now we're so close. I think it might be a good thing if we sat down for a little while – in case we are being watched. Keep your eyes and ears open.'

'We used to play games like this when I was in the scouts,' muttered Ginger, sitting down on the soft mat of pine needles. 'I never thought I should be doing it in reality. It's more nervy work than I thought.'

Hardly had he spoken the words when, from between the trees some distance beyond the holly bush which concealed the pigeon basket, appeared an Alsatian, either the one they had already seen, or another. Behind it, carrying its lead, came a storm-trooper. When it first appeared the dog's manner was normal, as if it were merely being taken for a walk. But suddenly it stopped, and threw up its head, nostrils twitching. For a moment it remained thus; then, with its muzzle close to the earth it began quartering the ground swiftly. The storm-trooper, seeing the animal's manner change, also became more active, and urged it on in a low, tense voice.

Biggles muttered an exclamation of annoyance. 'It's got our taint,' he said. 'It's no use running. He'll see us if we stand up. We shall do better to sit still and see what the fellow has to say.'

Meanwhile, the storm-trooper had put a whistle into his mouth and sent a fair imitation of the notes of a bird ringing through the forest in a series of short, sharp trills. Immediately it was answered from several places.

'My goodness! The forest is full of them,' grunted Ginger. 'Look – look!'

There was no need for Ginger to explain his final ejaculation. The Alsatian had suddenly run straight into the holly bush, to reappear at once with the pigeon basket in its mouth, at the same time worrying it furiously, putting its feet on the wicker-work and tearing at it with its teeth.

For a brief moment Ginger prayed that the dog might succeed in wrenching off the lid, thus allowing the bird to escape; but he was doomed to disappointment. The storm-trooper, seeing what the animal had found, dashed up and snatched the basket away.

'That's done it,' muttered Biggles. 'We've got to get away from here. It will be all up if they find us near that bird.'

He was already on his feet when the drama took another unexpected turn. Running like a deer out of the heart of the forest, panting with exertion and wide-eyed with alarm, came the girl in brown. She swerved like a Rugby player when she saw the storm-trooper and made off in a fresh direction. But the man had seen her and shouted a peremptory order to her to stop. But she ignored it and sped on, her brown dress twisting and turning through the trees like a woodcock. The storm-trooper snatched out his revolver and fired three times, the crashing reports of the shots shattering the silence like thunderclaps. Another storm-trooper appeared higher up the bank and he, too, fired. Whether or not the shots took effect Ginger did not know, for Biggles had grabbed him by the arm, and with a crisp 'Come on', set off at a sprint in the direction opposite to that taken by the girl. As he ran he cut diagonally down the gentle slope that led to the edge of the forest; but he did not emerge into the open; keeping just inside the cover of the trees he ran like a hare parallel with the edge. ''Ware rabbit holes,' he flung back over his shoulder, a necessary warning, for in places the bank was honeycombed with burrows.

For the best part of a quarter of an hour they ran at racing speed, but then, as there was neither sound nor sign of pursuit, they steadied their pace, and presently slowed down to a fast walk. 'I don't think they're following us,' panted Biggles. 'In fact, I don't think they saw us. That wretched girl showed up at a lucky moment for us, and got all the attention.'

'What swine those storm-troopers must be,' muttered Ginger disgustedly. 'They didn't hesitate to shoot, even at a girl. Did they hit her?'

'I don't think so.'

'They'll credit her with the pigeon affair.'

'Probably. Without wishing her any harm, I hope they do. This business is too serious for gallantry. As far as I'm concerned she'll have to take her luck.'

*The storm-trooper snatched out his revolver
and fired three shots.*

'She must have followed us – or was it a fluke that she happened to be in the same part of the forest as ourselves?'

'I think it's more likely that she deliberately got down early, watched us go out and then followed us. But never mind about that now. We're well out of it, but it's a tragedy about the pigeon. That's our messenger gone west.'

'We look like going west ourselves if we aren't jolly careful,' muttered Ginger. 'They're watching us more closely than I thought. If they find us again they won't take their eyes off us after what has happened.'

'Well, it's something to know that we *are* being watched,' opined Biggles. 'I had a feeling that things were too quiet to be true. Let's keep going. The farther we get away from here the easier I shall feel.'

'How are we going to get a message home now we've lost the pigeon?'

'Algy – I'm afraid it's the only way.'

'That means he'll have to land.'

'Yes, it's unfortunate, but it's vitally important that the information should be got home. Wait a minute, though, there is just a chance—' Biggles stopped, and taking his map from his pocket studied it closely for a minute or two. 'We daren't risk sending a message by post from Unterhamstadt,' he went on thoughtfully. 'But there is another village about six miles down the valley called Garenwald. We can send a postcard from there to a private emergency address which I know would find Raymond, wording it in such a way that it would convey our meaning without being suspected by the censors at the Lucranian frontier. For instance, if we merely said that the box was empty Raymond would know what we meant. The postcard might get through; after all, there must be hundreds of tourists sending postcards home; in any case, I don't see that it would do any harm. Furthermore, a visit to Garenwald would give us an alibi if we are questioned when we get back to the hotel as to where we have been.'

'All right. Then let's do that,' assented Ginger. 'I have a nasty feeling that we are skating on pretty thin ice, and it would be a pity if, having got as far as this, we couldn't let Raymond know about the Professor.'

'That's how I feel about it,' agreed Biggles, and without further ado set off at a brisk pace along the edge of the forest towards the village he had named.

CHAPTER VIII

Enter Von Stalhein

The sun was fast falling towards the pine-clad hills to the west, when, with dusty shoes, they trudged back into Unterhamstadt, having carried out their emergency programme of sending home from Garenwald an ordinary picture postcard bearing a message, innocent enough in its context, but significant in its real meaning. They had lunched well at the village restaurant, after which they had strolled about for an hour, staring tourist-fashion at what few features of interest the place had to offer, and generally making themselves conspicuous before starting back, unhurriedly, for their hotel. On the way they had, of course, discussed the situation in its new light. The discovery of the carrier pigeon, the purpose of which would certainly be realized at once by the storm-troopers, had, they agreed, made their task much more hazardous by bringing to the notice of their enemies the fact that a secret agent was in the locality. Indeed, but for the opportune arrival on the scene of the girl in brown, and her incriminating behaviour of resorting to flight even when she was under fire, Biggles was of the opinion that to return to the hotel would have been more than their lives were worth. But in the circumstances he took the view that while they would unquestionably be regarded with suspicion, the hiding of the pigeon would be credited to the girl.

In any case, it was now clear that their presence had been well noted by the storm-troopers, or whoever was in charge of the secret police of the district, otherwise they would not have been followed when they set off through the forest earlier in the day. Biggles was inclined to think that there was nothing personal about this; he took the view that *any* stranger arriving at the hotel would at once be placed under police surveillance; which, as he pointed out to Ginger, was fairly conclusive proof that something unusual was going on in the district. As far as the girl was concerned, her particular mission – if she had one – remained a mystery, although it was now apparent that she was not on the side of the secret police.

The result of a long debate on the situation was a decision by Biggles to take the risk of returning to the hotel; and the chief factors that guided him were, in the first place, the increased suspicion that would undoubtedly fall on them if they failed to return, which might end in a hue and cry, and secondly, the necessity of remaining in the district in order to keep in touch with Algy and the aeroplane in which lay their only hope of escape from the country when their work was finished. As to what would happen when they walked into the hotel, Biggles had an open mind, for he realized that much depended on whether or not the girl had been hit by the shots fired at her, or captured. Had she been captured she would certainly be forced to speak, in which case she would at once disclaim all knowledge of the pigeon, and at the same time probably reveal all she knew about the suspicious behaviour of the two Englishmen, such as their visit to the Jew's house and their nocturnal excursion.

Biggles eyed the hotel dubiously as they approached it. 'Well, we shall soon know how we stand,' he murmured, half humorously. 'Behave naturally when we go in, as if nothing unusual had happened. If anyone asks questions we shall just look blank and say that we have walked to Garenwald and back.'

There was no one in the entrance hall when they went in. All was quiet. Biggles glanced through the glass panel of the adjacent dining-room door as they passed it. The dining-room, too, was empty. 'Good! It rather looks as if it's all quiet on the western front,' he murmured, as he took their key from the rack and passed on up the stairs.

They reached their room without seeing anyone, and as Biggles closed the door behind them Ginger sank on his bed with a deep breath of relief. 'Phew! that's better,' he exclaimed, relaxing. 'I don't mind admitting that as you pushed open the front door I had a very nasty moment. There is something about those storm-troopers that gives me the willies – I think it must be the uniform.'

Biggles smiled. 'I was prepared for anything myself,' he confessed. 'The nice tranquil atmosphere was a bit too suggestive of a storm about to break. Even now I am not altogether convinced that things are as calm as appearances would suggest, but we can only go on playing the part of two innocent tourists. I should like to know what happened to that girl, though. If she got back to the hotel – and I don't see where else she could go – she must be in her room. I noticed that her key was missing from the rack, although it doesn't necessarily follow that she is in the hotel; she might have taken it with her. Well, we'll have a wash, I think, and then go down for a drink while we are waiting for the dinner gong. After that we'll have a conference. I don't think it's much use forming a definite plan until we are satisfied that things here are really as quiet as they seem to be.'

'What about Algy, if he comes over?' asked Ginger quickly.

'Well, as you know, the arrangement was that he was to come over as often as weather permitted, but if he got no signal from us he was to go straight back. Actually, once every two or three days would probably have been sufficient, but, naturally, he rather feels that he has been left out of things, so he might as well come over. It gives him something to do, apart from which I suppose he is anxious about us – and when one is worried it's beastly having nothing to do. It looks like being a fine night, so no doubt he will come over, but if we are being watched, and I am pretty sure we are, it would be folly to risk spoiling our line of communication for no particular reason. It would be much better to keep clear of the machine until an emergency arises. He'll come over, but getting no signal he will tootle off back again.'

They both washed, and Ginger was drying his hands on the towel, humming quietly to himself as he did so, when, happening to glance through the window down into the courtyard, he stopped dead. The tune died away on his lips. 'Biggles,' he said, in a low, tense voice, 'come over here.'

Biggles, sensing danger, was at his side in an instant, eyes probing the twilit courtyard.

'Over there on the right, by the garage,' muttered Ginger. 'Isn't that a storm-trooper standing close against the wall – under the steps that lead up to that loft?'

'By thunder! You're right. It is.' Biggles's voice was hard. 'There's another along there by the tool shed – two, in fact. It begins to look as if they waited for us to come in before closing the ring on us. Stay where you are. Keep away from the window,' he concluded crisply.

Ginger, still watching the man by the garage, heard Biggles go out and close the door quietly behind him.

In two minutes Biggles was back. 'They're all round the hotel,' he said calmly. 'There's one under the tree at the back; I saw him from the window at the end of the corridor. There are several in the street near the front door. I'm afraid we've walked into a trap.'

'So what?'

Biggles sat on the edge of Ginger's bed and lit a cigarette. 'As you rightly say – so what?' he murmured. 'Frankly, I don't see that we can do a thing except stay where we are. It's obvious that we cannot get out of the hotel without being seen, so to do that would only expedite trouble – if it's coming.'

'Then it looks as if they've got us caged,' muttered Ginger bitterly.

'I should be a liar if I denied that,' agreed Biggles.

'What are we going to do? Try to shoot our way out?' suggested Ginger.

Biggles smiled faintly. 'We might as well commit suicide where we are,' he said sarcastically. 'We couldn't get through that ring; there are too many of them. Even if we did, we shouldn't get a mile before we were captured, certainly not out of the country. We might last the night, but by tomorrow there would be a thousand storm-troopers round the whole district. I'm sorry if I seem depressing, but we must face facts. If we stay where we are there is just a chance—'

'I hate the idea of just sitting here waiting for them to come in and arrest us,' declared Ginger impatiently.

'No more than I do. But *force majeure* won't help us now.

Indeed, to attempt it would only supply the evidence they need to hang us. Bluff is more likely to get us – hark!'

Ginger stiffened as footsteps came down the corridor outside – swift, nervous footsteps. One could almost sense the agitation of the person who made them. A key jangled in a door. Ginger looked at Biggles questioningly.

'That sounds like the girl – bolting to her room,' whispered Biggles. 'She, too, has evidently seen the gentry outside.'

'This is awful, sitting here doing nothing.'

'Very well. Suppose we take the bull by the horns and stroll downstairs?' said Biggles, with a curious smile. 'No doubt they will come up here and fetch us as soon as they are ready, so we shall lose nothing by going down. Put your passport in your pocket.' And with that he went to the door and opened it.

The corridor was empty. All was silent.

'Let's go down,' said Biggles, closing the door behind Ginger. He put the key in his pocket and walked unconcernedly down the stairs.

The lamp had been lighted in the entrance hall, but the room was empty. Not even the proprietor was at his desk. Biggles walked over to one of the small tables at the far end, and, sitting down, rang the bell. He caught Ginger's eye and winked significantly as he inclined his head slightly towards the window that overlooked the street. It was nearly dark outside, but two vague forms could just be seen.

The proprietor appeared. His manner was nervous, almost to the point of agitation. He looked at Biggles inquiringly.

'A glass of beer and a lemonade,' ordered Biggles.

The proprietor nodded. '*Ja*,' he said. 'You will take them in your room?'

'No, we'll have them here,' Biggles told him.

The man hesitated. He glanced apprehensively towards the door, and then started visibly as a powerful car came slowly to a standstill outside with a faint squeak of brakes.

'Is there any difficulty about having a drink before dinner?' asked Biggles evenly.

'*Nein – nein.*' The proprietor, now pale in his embarrassment, after another furtive glance towards the door, hurried from the room.

'I wish somebody would throw a bomb, or do something,' growled Ginger. 'This sitting here doing nothing is like waiting for a parachute to open.'

'Don't be in a hurry,' Biggles told him smoothly. 'Just keep calm and let things take their time. There will be plenty of action presently, if I know anything about it – ah! This is where the play begins, I fancy.'

Biggles's eyes were on the front door. Ginger, following them, saw that it was slowly opening. Suddenly it was pushed wide open, and a grey-shirted storm-trooper entered the hall. He glanced around swiftly, allowed his eyes to rest for a moment on Biggles and Ginger, and then said something in a low voice to somebody behind him. Three more troopers followed him into the room. The last one closed the door behind him. The first, who appeared to be the leader, spoke again, quietly, and then, his black field boots squeaking, strode over to the key rack. It seemed that one glance told him what he wanted to know. He gave an order and walked briskly towards the staircase. The other three followed him in single file.

As the four men disappeared from sight Ginger turned startled eyes to Biggles. 'What the deuce—?'

There was a queer expression on Biggles's face. 'Sit tight,' he said, through his teeth. 'I don't think they're here for us, after all.'

'You mean – the girl?'

Biggles nodded.

'What do we do?'

'Nothing.'

'But the girl?'

'That's her affair. We've enough troubles of our own without indulging in any fancy knight-errantry at this stage.'

The sound of insistent knocking now came from upstairs. There was a crash, followed by a sharp cry of fear, cut short by what was unmistakably the noise of a struggle. A moment later the sinister sounds approached the head of the stairs. A treble voice began crying out, shrilly.

'Sit quite still and appear to take no notice,' ordered Biggles firmly.

Ginger leaned back in his chair, but his eyes were on the stairs. And as he watched a strange procession came into view – four storm-troopers, holding between them the girl in brown, who struggled violently and kept up what were obviously alternate cries of appeal and abuse.

As the party reached the foot of the stairs the girl's eyes fell on the other two guests, still sitting at their table. 'Spies! Spies!' she screamed in English, struggling with such violence that she almost broke free. And in the struggle an extraordinary thing happened. Her blonde hair suddenly came away and fell to the ground, disclosing a dark, close-cropped head. Curiously enough, this appeared to cause no surprise to the storm-troopers, for one of them, with a grim smile, snatched it up before taking a fresh hold on the prisoner.

'Swine – swine – murderers!' screamed the prisoner, in German. 'You murdered my father. I know – I know! You killed him. Cowards—' The prisoner was bundled through the door. It was slammed, but the cries could still be heard outside.

Biggles had not moved a muscle. 'Not a pretty scene,' he said in a low voice. 'Still, we have learned something from it. So it wasn't a girl, after all – but our guess was not far wrong.'

'It is Beklinder's son.'

'*Ssh*! That's how I read it. The story begins to unfold. What a pity we did not know before – but there, it's no use thinking about that now.'

Outside the cries had ended abruptly. The hotel proprietor came into the room with the drinks which Biggles had ordered on a tray. 'There has been a little trouble,' he said, setting the tray down shakily, 'but it is over now.'

Biggles made a deprecatory gesture with his hand. 'These things will happen,' he said casually.

'*Ja, ja*, they will happen,' agreed the proprietor, obviously relieved at Biggles's attitude, and, with yet another glance at the door, hurried away.

Biggles had picked up his glass, and was in the act of raising it to his lips, when the front door opened again, and a man in a dark uniform entered. He was obviously of superior rank. From where he was sitting Ginger could not see his face, but he saw Biggles stiffen.

The man strode straight to the reception desk and struck the bell.

The hotel proprietor almost fell into the room, bowing and scraping as he came when he saw his visitor. His agitation now was almost ludicrous.

The new-comer asked a question, sharply. There was a ring of authority in his voice.

The proprietor answered, and although he spoke in German Ginger caught two words which gave him a fair idea of what the question had been. The two words were 'Bigglesworth' and 'Hebblethwaite', from which he assumed that the new-comer had asked for the names of the other guests in the hotel.

The proprietor's reply had a curious effect on the new-comer. He swung round on his heels and raised a monocle to his right eye.

Ginger recognized him instantly and went cold all over. It was Erich von Stalhein, one-time German Intelligence agent on the Imperial Staff, now chief of the Lucranian Secret Police, officially known as the *Grospu*.

For perhaps half a minute von Stalhein stood stock still, regarding the two Englishmen with an expression which changed rapidly from incredulity to something like amused reproach. 'Well, well, well, my dear Major Bigglesworth – and, yes, it is our young friend with the difficult name,' he said cheerfully, in fault-less English. 'Tch-tch-tch. Believe me, I had no idea that you had honoured us with a visit.'

'I can well believe that,' said Biggles smiling. 'Won't you sit down and have a drink?'

'Still as courteous as ever – yet there are people who say that the English are a rude race,' murmured von Stalhein, advancing towards them.

Biggles pulled up another chair. 'What can I order for you?' he said evenly.

'Perhaps – yes – a cognac.'

'A cognac,' Biggles called to the proprietor, who hastened to obey the order.

Ginger looked with fascinated interest at the man whom he knew was their deadliest enemy. His hair was slightly greyer at the temples, otherwise he was unchanged since he had last seen him. The same slim figure; the same keen, alert, handsome face; the same cold eyes; immaculate, the same half-foppish manner; the same hard, grimly humorous expression.

The proprietor brought the brandy and placed it on the table. His eyes were round with wonder, and it seemed to Ginger that he regarded them with a new respect.

Von Stalhein raised his brandy glass; his eyes, like bluey-grey steel, gleamed coldly just above the brim. He murmured the German national toast 'Prosit'.

Biggles picked up his half empty glass. 'Prosit,' he echoed seriously.

'And you have been here – how long?' asked von Stalhein, replacing his glass on the table.

'We arrived last night,' Biggles told him.

'Just a friendly visit to see this beautiful country?'

'Of course – what else?'

'Of course – of course,' almost crooned von Stalhein, but there was an undertone of subtle sarcasm in the way he said the words. 'But for mere chance, an extraordinary coincidence, I should have been here last night to welcome you,' he went on suavely. 'I am staying not far away, so naturally I take a great interest in all our visitors – particularly English people, for whom, as you know, I have a great regard. Notice of all new arrivals is sent straight up to me, but yesterday morning I had to go at a moment's notice to Prenzel, so I was unaware that you were here. As a matter of detail, I have only just returned. It happened that I had to call in here on my way home, to attend to – well, no doubt you saw what happened here just now. An unfortunate business.'

'Very unfortunate for the girl – or rather, boy,' observed Biggles dryly.

'A boy masquerading as a girl,' declared von Stalhein. Ginger nearly gasped aloud as he continued, with surprising frankness, 'You know, we had an unfortunate accident here a short time ago. Perhaps you remember it. One of the people of this country, but long resident in England, came here on a visit – you may recall the affair, for I believe it was noted in your newspapers.'

Biggles wrinkled his forehead. 'I seem to remember something about it,' he said. 'What was the name?'

'Beklinder – Professor Beklinder,' prompted von Stalhein smoothly.

'Ah, yes. That was it,' nodded Biggles. 'I remember now.'

'He was driving his own car; approaching the village he collided with a lorry and was killed. He had a son in the country, and unfortunately the shock affected his brain, so it became necessary to keep him under observation in a nursing home. Due to the carelessness of his – er—'

'Keepers,' suggested Biggles.

Von Stalhein pursed his lips. 'That is a hard word, but we will call it that if you like. At any rate, the boy escaped, and by disguising himself as a girl, with an ingenuity I should not have believed possible, succeeded in reaching this place, presumably in the hope of carrying out investigations on his own account – although why he should question the coroner's verdict is more than I can understand.' Von Stalhein shrugged his shoulders.

'Remarkable.' There was the faintest suspicion of a sneer in Biggles's voice.

'As you say, remarkable,' murmured von Stalhein imperturbably.

'Possibly the boy had arranged to meet his father, and was disappointed that he did not see him before the accident?' suggested Biggles.

'Naturally.'

'Had the boy arranged to meet his father?'

Von Stalhein hesitated for a moment. 'There is no secret about the affair,' he went on casually. 'There is reason to believe that the unfortunate Professor, who often stayed here in his young days, arranged to meet the boy in this very hotel; he was on his way here, and had, in fact, nearly reached his destination when he was killed.'

'Very sad. Very, very sad,' said Biggles, in a melancholy voice.

'Do you intend to stay long?' inquired von Stalhein, suddenly twisting the trend of the conversation.

'No, there does not appear to be anything of particular interest here,' murmured Biggles. 'Still, I am glad we came this way or we should have missed seeing you.'

Von Stalhein nodded. 'It would be wise, I think, if you moved on,' he said. 'In some curious way this seems to be an ill-fated place for visitors – particularly English visitors. There have been two or three accidents lately.'

'Accidents?'

'Yes, not long ago – since the Professor was killed – an English tourist – actually an employee of your Foreign Office on holiday, I believe – was climbing about on the rocks near the castle when he fell and fractured his skull.'

'Do you live at the castle, by any chance?' inquired Biggles blandly.

Von Stalhein almost smiled. 'Yes, as a matter of fact, I have had a wing made habitable and use it as a shooting-box,' he admitted, with disarming frankness. 'You may have time to come up and see me before you leave. You may be sure I will do my best to make you welcome.'

'I am sure you will,' nodded Biggles pleasantly.

Von Stalhein finished his cognac and glanced at his wrist watch. 'I must be getting along,' he said rising. 'There are some urgent matters that need my attention.' He bowed stiffly from the waist. But instead of going he appeared to hesitate, regarding Biggles quizzically. 'You know, Bigglesworth,' he said, in a curious voice, 'there are moments when I could wish that you were on my staff.'

'Coming from you, von Stalhein, I appreciate the compliment.'

Von Stalhein nodded slowly, almost sadly. 'I even find myself regretting that you came to Lucrania.'

'Come, come,' protested Biggles. 'Surely it is a little early to talk of regrets?'

'You have a saying, "The pitcher that goes most often to the water in the end gets broken."'

Biggles smiled. 'We have another which says, "Don't count your chickens before they are hatched."'

Von Stalhein smiled, but there was no humour in his eyes. He bowed again. His heels clicked together. 'Good-bye – for the time being,' he said, and turned towards the door. Reaching it, he turned again. 'You won't forget that I am looking forward to seeing you again?' he called.

'Whatever else I may forget you may be sure that it won't be that,' answered Biggles.

The German went out, and an instant later his car could be heard speeding up the road.

Biggles moved swiftly. 'We've got about five minutes to get clear,' he said crisply.

'Why didn't he arrest us then?' asked Ginger, who had not for an instant been deceived by the casual cross-talk.

'He daren't risk it single-handed. He knew that we'd be armed. He's gone off to get his gang of greyshirts. We've got to move quickly.'

'It means bolting for it?'

'Yes – but not into the country. Von Stalhein could call up a regiment if he wanted to – or a whole blessed army corps if it became necessary. He's not going to let us get out of the country if human power can stop us. We've only one chance now that I can see.'

'What is it?'

'The castle.'

'The *castle*?'

'That's it. Von Stalhein lacks one quality and that's imagination. Though he searches the whole country – and he will – there is one place in which he will not expect to find us, and that is in the castle.'

'But how—?'

'We've no time to stand talking,' snapped Biggles. 'I'll show you. Come on.'

Four swift paces took him to the key rack. He unhooked the key of number seventeen and sped up the stairs; but he did not immediately use the key that he held in his hand. Instead, he went into their own room and filled his pockets with the most vital articles of their equipment, including the rope which he took from under the bed. Then he opened the window wide. This done, he went back into the corridor and locked the door of the room on the outside, after which he unlocked the door of number seventeen. He turned to Ginger. 'Listen carefully,' he said. 'This is what you've got to do. Lock me in here. Go down and hang the key in its proper place. Then go out of the front door and come round into the courtyard. I shall be waiting at the window with the rope to pull you up into number seventeen. Hurry! Every second counts.'

Ginger did not question the orders. Biggles had already gone into the forbidden room. Ginger locked the door and hurried downstairs. The proprietor had not returned. It was the work of a moment to replace the key on its hook, after which he went quietly out of the front door and walked swiftly round into the courtyard. Biggles was already waiting for him at the open window of number seventeen. 'Lay hold,' he said, dropping an end of the rope. Ginger seized the rope and was hauled up into the room.

'Good!' muttered Biggles, closing the window. 'I think that gives us a good start. If my calculations are right this will be the last room they will search. Hark! Here they come.'

From the road leading to the castle came the sound of a motor-car being driven at high speed.

Biggles took his screwdriver from his pocket and prised up the trap-door. 'This is the way we go,' he said cheerfully.

CHAPTER IX

A Grim Discovery

Ginger stared at the inviting hole, while Biggles, dropping on his hands and knees, turned the beam of the torch into it. The light revealed a flight of stone steps leading downwards.

Ginger almost fell into the hole as there came a rush of heavy footsteps along the corridor.

'It's all right. We've plenty of time now,' said Biggles calmly. 'They'll make for our own room first, and the door being locked will probably hold them up for a minute or two. Then, when they find the window open, they'll think we've bolted into the country. Even if they ransack the hotel for us this is the last room they will search.'

As he finished speaking there was a splintering crash which seemed so close that for a dreadful moment Ginger thought that it was the door of the room they were in that was being forced.

'There goes the door,' remarked Biggles. 'We had better get along. You go first – I'll close the trap after us. If my guess is right, the last thing that von Stalhein would imagine is that we know about this bolt-hole,' he added reassuringly.

Taking the torch Ginger went slowly down the steps, peering

fearfully in front of him in case there was a sudden drop. He waited until Biggles had closed the trap door, and then handed the torch back to him. Biggles took the lead and went on down. It was not very far. About twenty steps and the descent came to an end, finishing in a gloomy cave, which, from its bricked arches, was obviously artificial. It was damp; in places it was wet, for the moisture had seeped through the roof to fall on a slimy green floor, or into patches of grotesque fungus that clung to the walls.

Biggles examined the floor closely. 'Hm, as I thought,' he said. 'This tunnel has been used recently.'

'You're pretty sure that it goes to the castle?' asked Ginger.

'I can't imagine anywhere else that it would be likely to end.'

'There was mention of a monastery in the book, don't forget.'

'I haven't forgotten that, but if this tunnel goes to the monastery then it is unlikely that the site of the monastery would have been lost. Apparently nobody knows now where the monastery stood. However, we shall soon know where the tunnel ends. Let's go on. Keep close to me and be careful you don't slip on this stuff on the floor. It's like grease. And don't touch the walls; they look pretty rotten to me; we don't want to bring the roof down on us.' Picking his way carefully, Biggles began to walk along the tunnel.

'That was a bit of bad luck, von Stalhein barging in when he did,' observed Ginger, as they proceeded on their way, for the recent events were still running through his mind.

'I don't think it made much difference,' answered Biggles. 'I was an optimist to suppose that we should get a clear week to work in. I should have known von Stalhein better than that. You heard what he said – he has a list of visitors sent up to him every night. He would have known about us before but for the fact that he had to go to Prenzel – at least, so he said, and I fancy he was telling the truth. No doubt our names were sent up, but as von Stalhein was away the names did not convey anything particular to whoever received them. By jove! Did you see him start when the hotel proprietor told him who was staying in the hotel? That gave him a shock. He was certainly speaking the truth when he said he had no idea that we were here. Maybe it's as well things happened as they did; at least it gave us a chance to get away. Had he gone to his office and found our names on his desk we shouldn't have got such a chance, you may be sure.'

'I suppose Algy will be on his way by now?' was Ginger's next remark. 'After what has happened it seems a pity that we can't get in touch with him.'

'There's a chance that we may. We'll see how things go, although I imagine that von Stalhein's telephone is buzzing by now.'

'What are the chances of the Professor being at the castle, do you think?'

'Very good. I can't think of any other reason for von Stalhein and his gang being here. You can be pretty certain that he would not be down here if he was not handling something very impor-tant in the district, and what could be more likely than the Professor?'

'They'll probably take the son up to the castle, too.'

'For the time being, at any rate. It is a great pity we didn't know who he was before, or we might have compared notes. Another few hours and I should have spoken to him – but there, it's no use thinking of that now.'

'Didn't it strike you as odd that von Stalhein should tell us as much as he did?'

'The fact that he did so is pretty conclusive proof that he was certain that we could not get away. Otherwise he would not have been so frank – that is, if it was frankness, and not a cock-and-bull story to mislead us. But somehow I don't think it was.'

They continued on down the tunnel, the only sound being the soft squelch of the slime underfoot, or the sinister drip of water from the roof. In more than one place the brickwork had caved in, leaving the bare earth exposed, and such places they passed with extreme caution, for it seemed not unlikely that a touch, or even the vibration of their footsteps, might cause a collapse with results not pleasant to contemplate.

To Ginger the tunnel seemed interminable, but at long last, after rising steeply for a short distance, it came to an abrupt end at a point where there had been a more than usually heavy subsidence, beyond which was a massive looking door, barred with iron.

Biggles examined the door closely in the light of the torch, but there was no handle or other means of opening it. Further examination revealed that it opened inwards; that is to say, towards them, but it was prevented from doing so by a heavy lock on the other side, the bolt of which was home. 'I'm afraid there's no getting past that,' he said slowly, still looking at the door.

'We must have arrived at the castle,' suggested Ginger.

'I don't think there is any doubt about that,' replied Biggles. 'I suspected that we were nearing the end when the floor started to slope upwards.'

'What are we going to do?'

Biggles shrugged his shoulders. 'Obviously, since we can't go on we shall have to go back the way we came.'

'We could wait here for awhile. If the tunnel is being used somebody might unlock the door.'

'Even so, the door would be locked again, so that wouldn't help us much. Apart from that, we might have to wait here for days, and that is something I don't feel inclined to do.'

'There's absolutely no way of getting the door open?'

'None. I've satisfied myself on that point. If we tried to batter it down we should merely bring everybody in the castle to the spot, so that won't do. I'm afraid it means going back. There's no particular hurry. In fact, I think our best plan would be to wait for a time to allow the storm-troopers time to search the hotel, and clear off. I think I'll have a cigarette and think things over.' Biggles took out his cigarette case and sat down on a broad piece of fallen masonry.

Ginger flicked out the torch to save the battery and sat down beside Biggles. Silence fell, utter silence except for the persistent drip – drip – drip of water. And there they sat, while Biggles, his chin cupped in his right hand, and his elbow on his knee, smoked his cigarette. When it was finished he tossed the butt on the floor and ground it into the slime with his heel. But still he did not get up. Another ten minutes passed and he drew a deep breath.

'Yes, it's all very difficult,' he murmured in a low voice, as if to himself.

Ginger stiffened as a slight sound echoed down the tunnel. 'Did you hear that?' he breathed.

'I did,' answered Biggles. 'What did it sound like to you?'

'It sounded to me like the trap-door in the bedroom being allowed to drop back into place.'

'And to me. Hark!'

Faintly, so faintly as to be little more than a distant echo, from the direction of the hotel came the low murmur of voices.

'By thunder! Would you believe that?' grated Biggles. 'Somebody is coming down the tunnel – and certainly more than one person.'

'They'll find us.'

'Inevitably.'

'We can't go on, and we can't go back without meeting them.'

'Just a minute. Give me the torch.' Biggles took the torch and sprang to his feet. The beam cut a wedge of bright light through the darkness and moved slowly over the highest point of the fallen masonry at the base of which they had been sitting. 'I may be mistaken, but there seems to be some sort of cavity up there,' he went on, tersely.

'You mean on top of the bricks?'

'Yes – but whether it is big enough to conceal us, I don't know. You are lighter than I am; climb up and have a look, but for heaven's sake be careful; don't start a landslide – and don't make any noise or we shall be heard.'

Ginger took the torch, and with infinite care, on hands and feet, felt his way to the top of the sloping pile of bricks and mortar. Reaching the top he turned the light of the torch into the recess. His voice came down to Biggles in a sibilant hiss. 'There's plenty of room. I believe there's another tunnel at the back.'

Biggles crept up the treacherous pile and joined him.

By lying flat they found that they could worm their way through a low cavity that existed between the top of the masonry and the earth above, beyond which there was a recess, the extremities of which the torch failed to reach. Ginger held his breath as he squirmed through, for he had an uneasy feeling that the roof might cave in at any moment and crush him. However, nothing of the sort happened, and Biggles joined him on the other side.

'You're right,' grated Biggles. 'There's another tunnel along there. *Ssh*, keep still.'

The warning was necessary, because it was clear from the sounds on the far side of the barricade of debris that the other users of the tunnel were nearing the spot. Actually, the sounds were amplified by the silence, and the narrow confines of the tunnel, and it was some time before the newcomers drew level, and halted while a sharp double knock was made on the door. Of whom the party consisted neither Biggles nor Ginger knew, for the masonry obstructed the view and neither dared risk climbing up to look for fear of the movement betraying them. That there were at least two or three people, however, was obvious from the low mutter of voices which echoed weirdly along the tunnel. A bright light gleamed on the roof. They heard the lock turn and the door open. The party moved on again and the door closed with a dull clang. The lock turned. Again silence fell. Water dripped slowly from the roof, like a clock ticking in a bedroom at night.

'Well, they've gone,' breathed Biggles at last. 'Before we think about returning to the hotel I think we'll have a look to see where this tunnel goes, because it may alter the whole situation. I don't know how long it is since that brickwork caved in, but I shouldn't think any one has used this tunnel since. With luck it might take us to another exit. They made regular labyrinths under these old castles; it was all a part of the stratagem in medieval times.' As he spoke he began to grope his way forward.

The tunnel in which they now found themselves was a good

deal narrower than the previous one; indeed, it could more correctly be called a corridor than a tunnel. Presently a short flight of steps led upward, and Ginger noted that the walls were no longer of brick, but of stone. Further, the floor and roof were dry. Shortly afterwards, to his surprise, the stone wall on the left-hand side, along which he had been groping with his hand, gave way to wood. Biggles had apparently noticed this, too, for he had stopped, and was examining it, section by section, in the light of the torch.

As Ginger watched breathlessly he became aware of something else; it was a confused murmur, almost a hum. For a moment it puzzled him, then he realized what it was. It was a human voice speaking rapidly beyond the wooden partition. He turned questioning eyes to Biggles. 'We must be in the castle,' he whispered.

Biggles nodded.

Ginger turned his attention again to the partition. Close against his feet was a square stone, not unlike a milestone, or one of the 'mounting' stools which are still sometimes to be found outside old road-houses, and which were used in days gone by to enable horsemen to mount more easily. On this Ginger climbed, and placed his ear to the woodwork in a vague hope that he might be able to hear what was being said. But in this position he was not very steady, and he reached up with his left hand to a small, oblong panel of wood which he thought might help him to maintain his balance. The movement was purely instinctive, and he had no other motive, so he was entirely unprepared for what happened next. The wooden panel, instead of being a fixture, as he had naturally supposed, was fixed to the wall only at one end, so that under the pressure of his hand it moved bodily, as on a pivot, so that he nearly lost his balance. Startled, but retaining his perch with an effort, he turned his eyes upwards, and was astounded – and not a little alarmed – to see a beam of yellow light pouring through a small round hole in the wall. Simultaneously, the sound of talking changed from a distant hum to a comparatively clear conversation.

For perhaps ten seconds he could only stare at the hole in utter amazement. Then, slowly, with his body pressed close to the wooden panelling, he raised his eyes to the level of the hole.

The room into which he found himself staring with bated breath was a magnificently appointed hall, or dining-room, although it was now furnished as an office. So much he realized subconsciously, for he did not examine it in detail, his eyes being drawn irresistibly to a huge carved desk in the centre of the room, and four men who were disposed about it. Electric light revealed the scene clearly.

Behind the desk, in a high-backed chair carved in the same manner, was Erich von Stalhein. Standing facing him on the other side of the desk were two grey-shirted storm-troopers. Between them was a man in a leather flying jacket, obviously a prisoner. It was Algy.

It was Algy.

CHAPTER X

Von Stalhein Plays
a Trump Card

Algy's voice reached them clearly. It was coldly dispassionate. 'Perhaps you will explain the meaning of this,' he said.

'Surely the boot is on the other foot, as you English say,' returned von Stalhein, studiously polite. 'I await your explanation as to why you, knowing well the international regulations, make an illegal and surreptitious landing in a foreign country.'

Algy's answer was a revelation to the listeners behind the panelling. 'I landed because your gang of thugs signalled to me to do so,' he answered icily.

'I quite appreciate that when you landed your surprise at finding my men waiting for you must have been complete. Why dissemble, Captain Lacey? You expected to find your friends. Oh yes, I knew all about them coming here. I was waiting for them when they arrived, so they, like you, are under arrest,' lied von Stalhein easily.

Ginger, quivering with rage, was tempted to throw the lie back at the German, but prudence prevailed and he restrained himself.

'You seem to know all about it,' said Algy, with more than a suspicion of a sneer in his voice.

'It is my business to know,' purred von Stalhein.

'Where are my friends now?'

'You came here to answer questions, not to ask them,' von Stalhein pointed out coldly.

'Well, I'm answering no questions,' grated Algy.

'My dear Captain Lacey, your discourtesy pains me,' murmured von Stalhein sardonically. 'Why not be frank? I can be frank with you. Would you not be interested to hear the circumstances that have resulted in your arrival here?'

'Go ahead,' invited Algy. 'I'm not stopping you.'

'You see, it was like this,' went on von Stalhein smoothly. 'Immediately it was known that your friend the Major was here, it was quite obvious that two accessories could not be far away. The first was yourself, and the other, an aeroplane. Naturally, it required no great mental effort to deduce that the aeroplane, with Unterhamstadt as its objective, would operate from a point as conveniently near as possible; so friends of mine, who have control of such things, immediately broadcast a radio message to all those who work for us outside our country, asking if a British aeroplane, with a crew of three, had been observed on their particular aerodrome. By this means we were able to establish the base from which you were operating. A straight line drawn from there to Unterhamstadt on the map gave us the probable line of flight of the aeroplane. The rest was easy. An extremely delicate sound detector – our latest invention in this department, by the way – picked you up. As your friends were already here we knew that it could only be you flying the machine. After that I simply posted men at all available landing-grounds within a reasonable area, and when you arrived over that nice plain so conveniently near Unterhamstadt, they, acting on my instructions, flashed a message that you were to land. It was obvious, even to my limited intelligence, that such an arrangement must exist between you and your accomplices on the ground – unless, of course, you were both equipped with wireless apparatus, which I could not believe. But the ruse worked. So you see, it was all perfectly simple.'

And, as he stated it, so it seemed, thought Ginger, appalled by the cunning way in which the German had anticipated and countered their plan.

'Well, having flattered your vanity by letting me know how clever you are, what are you going to do about it?' asked Algy nonchalantly.

Von Stalhein was lolling back in his chair, his monocle in place, smoking a cigarette held in a long holder. It was obvious that he was enjoying the situation. 'You know, Captain Lacey,' he went on, ignoring Algy's question, 'great as is the admiration I have for your friend Major Bigglesworth, I fear that on this occasion he has committed a grave error of judgement in undertaking a task beyond his capacity. It is a pity.'

'Must I stand here and listen to you patting yourself on the back?' growled Algy belligerently. 'Don't laugh too loudly. Unless you have already killed him, Bigglesworth will give—'

Von Stalhein interrupted him with a short laugh. 'I shall take no risks, of that you may be sure,' he murmured. 'Is there anything more you wish to say? When it was reported to me that you had been brought in, naturally I felt obliged to accord myself the honour of renewing our acquaintance.'

'What you really wanted to do was to gloat,' declared Algy

bluntly. 'Well, have your little gloat while the going's good. It's time you knew that you won't have it all your own way all the time.'

'Silence!' Von Stalhein's pose broke under the strain of Algy's contemptuous jibe. He sat bolt upright in his chair, eyes flashing coldly, lips pressed together in a straight line. He barked an order. The grey-shirted storm-troopers took Algy by the arms and marched him from the room. The door slammed behind them.

Ginger continued to watch von Stalhein, who began to pace up and down the room with his head bowed in thought. His manner was by no means so assured as it had been for Algy's benefit, and Ginger guessed the reason. He and Biggles were still at large, although the information the German had volunteered to Algy was to the contrary, and he was worried about it. For a minute he continued pacing up and down; then, as if he had suddenly reached a decision, he sat down again and pressed a bell on his desk. The door was opened immediately by a storm-trooper. Von Stalhein rapped out a curt order, of which Ginger caught one word – 'Beklinder'. He turned away from the spy-hole. 'I believe he has sent for the Professor,' he whispered.

Biggles moved Ginger aside and took his place. A few seconds later a man whom he had never seen, but whom he recognized instantly, was brought into the room by a single guard. It was Professor Beklinder.

Von Stalhein dismissed the guard and pulled out a chair near the desk with an exaggerated exhibition of courtesy. 'Sit down, Professor,' he said.

'I prefer to stand,' replied the Professor bitterly.

'And you would prefer to speak in English?'

'That is my own language.'

'You are English only by naturalization.'

'Have you brought me here again to reopen this fatuous argument?'

Von Stalhein allowed his monocle to drop from his eye. He settled himself back in his chair. 'No,' he said, 'I brought you here to congratulate you on your wisdom in bowing to the inevitable. Believe me, Professor, I was delighted for your sake when I was told that you were at last working and exercising your unique talents in the laboratory which my government has provided for you.'

'You may have been delighted, but it was certainly not for my sake.'

'Let us not quibble about that. You have, I am told, made a small quantity of the – er – mixture, in which we are interested.'

The Professor took a small round bottle from his pocket, and holding it up to the light turned it so that a yellow oily liquid with which it was about half filled crept sluggishly towards the other end of the receptacle. 'Yes, no doubt this will interest you,' he said. 'The question naturally arises, what are you going to do with me now that I have submitted to your demands and presented you with my formula? You promised that I should be allowed to return to England.'

'Yes, that is true – but not immediately.'

'Why not?'

'There will be certain matters to arrange.'

'Yes, so I suspected,' said the Professor, in a curious voice. 'And no doubt the arrangements will take a very long time to make. In fact, the truth is, you have no intention of allowing me to return to England, have you?'

'You do me an injustice, Professor,' said von Stalhein in a tone of pained reproach.

'I observe that you avoid my question. Will you swear to me on your oath that I am to be allowed to return to England?'

Von Stalhein hesitated.

'No, you will not.' The Professor answered his own question. 'Can you possibly suppose that for one single moment I was deceived by your lies?' he went on quickly, with a rising inflexion in his voice, a flush of anger staining his pale cheeks. 'Can you think that I do not understand your methods – you cheat?'

Von Stalhein rose swiftly to his feet, the corners of his mouth drawn down. 'Such insulting remarks will not help you,' he snapped.

The Professor shook his head sadly. 'As if anything could have helped me – except perhaps the British government – once I was in your hands. Oh, I had no delusions. From the moment I knew that I was in your power I realized that I was doomed. It is a bad thing for a man to know that he is doomed, Hauptmann von Stalhein. Bad for him and bad for others, because it moves him to desperate measures. But you, for all your cunning, have made a grave mistake. You put me in a laboratory – me, the inventor of Linderite.' The Professor laughed bitterly. 'I have been very busy in the laboratory, and my work is now complete. But what I have in this bottle is not what you so earnestly seek. Could you think that I should be *such* a fool?'

'What is it?' jerked out von Stalhein sharply.

'It is an explosive infinitely more powerful than Linderite,' announced the Professor. He almost purred the words as he held up the bottle again and gazed affectionately at the contents.

Von Stalhein's hand crept towards his pocket, but the Professor saw the movement. 'Shoot – shoot by all means,' he said, calmly. 'Doubtless you are aware of what happens when nitro-glycerine is dropped – or even moved violently. It explodes. I believe the compound which I hold in my hand to be so deadly that any severe vibration – such as would occur if I allowed it to fall – would be sufficient to cause it to detonate. If such a thing occurred I should only have one regret – not that there would be much time for regrets, you understand? I should not live to see exactly how devastating would be the result. But it would be considerable, I assure you. Very little would be left of the castle. As for you and me, why, nothing would remain to show that we had ever been. A fitting end for a research chemist like myself – and for a liar like you.'

During this long oration von Stalhein had lit another cigarette. He puffed at it jerkily, nervously. 'But why do you call me a liar, Professor?' he asked.

'You brought me here, to Lucrania, by appealing to a man's most primitive instinct – paternity.'

'You came here entirely on your own initiative in order to meet your son.'

'The whole thing was a plot arranged by you.'

Von Stalhein shook his head. 'I am sorry that you should so misjudge me,' he said mournfully. 'Naturally, I did not want to take your mind off your work. The pleasure of meeting your son I reserved until your work was finished.'

'You persist in the deception?'

'It is no deception, Professor. Your son is here now.'

The Professor turned questioning eyes to von Stalhein. 'It would be a simple matter to prove that,' he said.

Von Stalhein smiled as he reached for the bell. 'You shall have proof immediately,' he promised.

A storm-trooper answered the summons. Von Stalhein gave an order, and as the trooper retired he got up and came round the desk towards the Professor. 'My dear Professor,' he said silkily, 'In a few moments you will be apologizing for the hard names you have called me.'

'I will reserve my judgement till then,' was the curt rejoinder.

The door was flung open again and the storm-trooper reappeared. With him was the pseudo-girl in brown who had been at the hotel, now in masculine attire. The boy stopped dead when he saw his father; then, with a glad cry, he ran forward, arms outstretched.

The Professor's hand trembled as he stood the bottle on von Stalhein's desk. He was staring at his son, so he did not see von Stalhein, with a swift movement, pick up the bottle and place it on a shelf in a full-length safe that stood against the wall.

Father and son spoke quickly in tones so low that Biggles could not catch the words, although he heard the boy make some reference to his mother. They spoke for some time, but at last von Stalhein interrupted. 'Well,' he said.

The Professor swung round. There were tears in his eyes and his face was working with emotion. His embarrassment was almost painful to see. 'I apologize,' he said huskily. 'This is my son.'

Von Stalhein's manner changed abruptly. 'Very well,' he said coolly. 'The interview has lasted long enough. You will now return to your rooms – you, Professor, until you have completed what is required of you.'

'Am I not to be allowed to see my son?'

'Afterwards.'

The Professor seemed to come suddenly to himself. His eyes went to the desk. 'Where is the bottle?' he asked.

'Where it can do no harm,' von Stalhein told him mockingly.

The Professor nodded slowly. 'So,' he said, 'again you have been too clever for me.'

Von Stalhein shrugged his shoulders. 'I trust that you now have an incentive to be more obliging,' he murmured.

The Professor bowed. 'I understand perfectly,' he said.

The storm-trooper parted father and son and ordered them to follow him. They went without a backward glance and the door closed behind them.

Von Stalhein sank down in his chair. There was a curious smile on his lips as he reached for the telephone. He spoke briefly. A few moments later an *unterofficier* of the storm-troopers appeared and, marching with military precision to the desk, saluted.

'The two Englishmen?' said von Stalhein crisply. 'Is there any news yet?'

'*Nein, Herr Commandant.*'

'Why not?'

'We cannot yet find which way they have gone.'

Von Stalhein frowned. 'So,' he said vindictively. 'It would be a good thing if they were soon found – a good thing for yourself – you understand?'

'*Ja, Herr Commandant.*'

'That is all.'

The storm-trooper saluted and marched out of the room.

Von Stalhein, after a few moment's reflection, picked up his cap and followed him.

Biggles drew a deep breath and relaxed. He closed the spy-hole and stepped down into the corridor.

'What the deuce is going on?' asked Ginger.

'We'd better not talk here; let's go farther along and I'll tell you all about it,' replied Biggles.

CHAPTER XI

Desperate Measures

As they moved carefully along the corridor, holding their arms in front of their faces to shield them from countless cobwebs, they saw other mounting stones with more spy-holes like that in the panelling of von Stalhein's room. They looked through each one, hoping they might discover the room in which Algy or the Beklinders were confined; but this, as Biggles pointed out, was too much to expect. In each case the room into which they peeped was in absolute darkness, and as there was no sound they assumed they were now in a part of the castle which was not used.

'My goodness! They didn't trust each other much in the old days,' whispered Ginger. 'Fancy building a place with all these spy-holes!'

'They're not uncommon,' Biggles told him. 'No doubt they were needed in the days when these places were built. There was usually a conspiracy of some sort going on, and a fellow was lucky indeed who could trust even his friends. Few did, with the result that they took precautions to hear what was being said behind their backs. In addition to the spy-hole, there are probably secret doors in this panelling if we knew where to look for them. Never mind about that now. Where the dickens are we getting?'

'Where are you hoping to get?'

'I've no idea,' admitted Biggles. 'Our job is to get Beklinder out of this place and out of the country; and, of course, Algy – if we can. The arrival of Beklinder's son on the scene hasn't made our job any easier. I don't suppose for a moment that the Professor will go without his son, or the son without his father. Unless they are together somewhere that is bound to complicate matters. Algy is in no position to help us; he's in a bad way himself. The unfortunate thing is that he doesn't know the facts. He thinks we are prisoners, so his chief concern will be to get into touch with us. Meanwhile, our own position isn't too bright. We've got to find a way out. I'm pretty certain that this passage connects with at least one room in the castle, but whether we can find it is another matter. We can't do anything until we find out where this passage ends. If it comes out inside the castle we might be able to do something. If it emerges outside the wall – well, I'm afraid we should never get in through the gate.'

They went on, walking slowly, examining the walls as they went, but they were blank on either side. The spy-holes no longer occurred, the reason being, as Biggles pointed out, that the panelling had given way to stonework so that the walls on either side were of heavy blocks of roughly hewn masonry. Then, suddenly, a door, pointed at the top in the manner of a Moorish arch, and studded with huge iron nails, barred their way. There was a handle, however, in the form of an enormous iron ring, rusty with age.

Biggles handed the torch to Ginger, and, taking the ring in both hands, attempted to turn it. At first it defied his efforts, but by wrapping his handkerchief around it he managed to raise the latch. He put his shoulder to the door and pushed. With a fearful

334

groaning of rusty hinges it yielded. He pushed it open wide enough to permit their passage, and again taking the torch from Ginger, went through. 'Heavens above!' he whispered, as Ginger joined him. 'What have we here?'

Ginger saw they were in a large vaulted chamber. 'It looks pretty grim to me,' he murmured.

Very slowly Biggles turned the beam of the torch on to the walls, the ceiling, and the floor, and on to certain strange-looking furniture which stood about. At intervals in the walls there were deep recesses, littered with mildewed straw. In several places there were chains fastened by enormous staples to the walls. From the roof hung pulleys, the ropes, rotten with age, drooping to the floor.

'This looks like a forge,' said Ginger in a puzzled voice, laying his hand on a metal stand on top of which was a heap of cinders. He picked up a curious doubled-ended poker. 'What on earth is this thing?' he asked.

Biggles was examining another piece of furniture. 'I don't think there is much doubt about where we are,' he said, in a strained voice. 'This thing gives it away.'

'What do you mean?'

'This is – or was – the torture chamber.'

'Great heavens!' Ginger stared, aghast.

'This is the rack,' went on Biggles. 'You've heard of poor brutes being broken on the wheel – well, there's the wheel over there. Those pretty little cages round the walls were presumably where they kept the prisoners, so that they could see what was in store for them, or what other poor devils were getting. That poker affair you picked up was either a brand, or the tool they used to put people's eyes out. Look, there's the block and the axe.

I'm afraid this devil's den once resounded with the shrieks and groans—'

'Shut up,' gasped Ginger. 'Let's get out of here. Even von Stalhein's worst jail would be a nursery compared with this chamber of horrors.'

'An antiquarian would find it very interesting,' murmured Biggles dryly.

'He might. I don't,' snorted Ginger. 'There's another door over there. Let's go on. If the boss of this place made a habit of coming down to watch his prisoners being tormented, it should lead to his private sitting-room.'

'I think there's a good chance of it,' agreed Biggles, picking his way through the dreadful furniture to a doorway on the far side of the chamber, similar to the one through which they had entered. 'Hello, it's a spiral staircase,' he observed. 'Watch your step.' Keeping the beam on the floor in front of him he began to mount, with Ginger following close behind. He had thought that the staircase would be only a short one, leading from one floor to another, but when it went on, and on, and on, winding ever upwards, he voiced his surprise.

'If we go on at this rate much longer we shall soon be on the roof,' declared Ginger, stopping to look through a narrow slit in the wall at a star which had suddenly caught his eye. Not until then did he realize how high they had ascended. 'My word! We are already above the castle,' he said. 'We must be in the main tower. I'm looking down on the roof.'

Biggles came back a step and looked through the loophole. 'By jingo, you're right,' he said. 'We're in the keep. We might as well go on to the top now that we've come so far, although there ought to be a doorway opening into the castle yard at ground level.

We must have passed it.' And with that he went on upwards, muttering that the flapping sounds which preceded them were caused by birds vacating their roosting places.

They were both out of breath by the time they reached the top, finally emerging on to a flat, leaded area bounded by a castellated parapet. Overhead the stars gleamed brightly from the blue dome of heaven. On all sides the country rolled away until it merged into the night, with tiny points of light marking the position of dwelling-houses. A cluster of such lights showed where the village nestled at the foot of the hill. Below them lay the castle and the central courtyard, the whole surrounded by the wall. They were, in fact, on the roof of the central tower.

Biggles, testing each step before he moved his weight, advanced cautiously towards the parapet. Ginger took one look down and drew back hastily. 'I should feel happier if I had a parachute,' he declared. 'I'm no bird.'

'Ssh,' cautioned Biggles, who was staring down into the court-yard.

'For heaven's sake be careful of that parapet,' warned Ginger. 'It looks to me as if you'd only have to cough to send the whole works overboard.'

'I'm watching it,' replied Biggles in a low voice. 'Something seems to be going on below. I'm glad we came up here; it has given me a good idea of the layout of the place. It is easy to see from the lights which is the wing that von Stalhein has had made habitable – as he told us, you remember? Algy and the Beklinders must be somewhere in there, but I am afraid that there are too many people about at the moment for us to do any scouting – even if we can find a way out. Wait a minute, something seems to be happening.'

Ginger crept forward like a cat walking on hot bricks and saw that what Biggles had said was true. A door had been opened, allowing a path of light to fall across the wide, stone-flagged courtyard. Three men were in view. Orders were being called. Then, suddenly, one whole side of the castle building was floodlit in a brilliant white glare, as if a searchlight had been turned on. A big limousine crept slowly from an unseen garage and came to rest almost immediately below them, and they saw that the light came from its headlamps. The door of the car opened and a storm-trooper chauffeur got out. Another trooper walked briskly towards him from the lighted doorway, speaking loudly as he came, so that the words floated up clearly to the watchers on the tower.

Ginger heard Biggles choke back an exclamation. 'What did he say?' he asked.

For a moment Biggles seemed nonplussed. Then, 'They're going to take the Beklinders away,' he breathed in a horrified voice. 'If they do, we're sunk. If they once take them away from here we shall never find them. That's von Stalhein. He's lost his nerve. He knows that we are still hanging around and he is afraid of us. We've got to stop them. If von Stalhein once gets them through that gateway we shall never see them again.'

Ginger said nothing. There seemed to be nothing to say.

'We've got to stop them,' muttered Biggles again, in a low, tense voice.

'There's no way—' began Ginger.

Biggles cut him short. 'There is *always* a way,' he snapped. 'I have told you before that there's always a way – if only you can think of it. I've got it. Stand back. Get back to the staircase.'

'What are you going to do?'

'Bust the car. Hold your ears because there's going to be a big noise. This should send the balloon up.' And with that, to Ginger's unspeakable horror, Biggles began pushing at the parapet. It looked flimsy enough, but apparently in places the mortar still held. Biggles put his foot against the mass and thrust at it.

'You'll go over,' Ginger nearly screamed. 'Give me your hand and lean back.'

Ginger reached forward and gripped Biggles's fingers with his own. He heard Biggles grunt as he pushed again. The mass swayed. Then it disappeared from sight. He was nearly right when he said that Biggles would go over. They both nearly went. But Ginger hung on like grim death to the edge of the opening behind him, and they both fell panting on the lead roof.

Biggles started to speak, but his voice was drowned in the crash of the falling stonework. Coming as it did in the silence it sounded to Ginger as if the whole castle had collapsed. He flinched under the shock. 'This is madness,' he thought wildly.

From below there came the banging of doors, shouts, and other sounds of alarm.

'I fancy that's queered their pitch,' whispered Biggles, quivering with suppressed laughter.

'You nearly queered ours, too,' panted Ginger. 'Did you get the car?'

'Couldn't miss it. It was right underneath.'

'What about the chauffeur?'

'I think he'd gone to meet the chap who was shouting to him. If he didn't – well, it was just too bad.'

'Did any one see you?'

'No. At least, I don't think so. I don't see how they could. I was flat on the roof before they could look up.'

'Great Scott!'

'What's the matter?'

'The other car.'

'What other car?'

'Beklinder's – Beklinder's own car. They could use that.'

Biggles was silent for a moment. 'I'd forgotten all about that,' he admitted bitterly. 'It's a four-seater. They could only – I wonder. Just a minute, stay where you are.' Lying flat Biggles wormed his way to the now sheer drop, and looked down.

Ginger could hardly bear to watch. 'Well?' he asked as Biggles crept back.

'I'm afraid you're right,' Biggles told him. 'Von Stalhein is there, cursing like a madman. The car is as flat as a sardine tin, but I just heard him shout to somebody to get the other car out.'

'Then that's stumped us.'

'Not yet it hasn't,' declared Biggles grimly.

'What—?'

'Don't talk. Let's get down the stairs. I'll go first. Be as quiet as you can because somebody may be looking up to see where our snowball came from. For that reason we daren't use the torch, so for goodness' sake watch where you're putting your feet.' With that Biggles set off down the winding staircase.

Ginger thought the steps would never end. It had seemed a long way up, but, probably on account of the darkness, which made the descent difficult if not dangerous, the way down seemed interminable. He made the best speed he could, but even so Biggles widened the distance between them. They collided at the bottom.

'Just a minute,' said Biggles. 'What's this? Shading it with his hands he switched on the torch for a moment; the brief flash was sufficient to reveal a number of large square stones placed loosely one on top of the other so that they blocked up what had once been a doorway. It was the roughness of the inside of these stones that had attracted his attention. It was not an easy matter to move the first one, but, by using the screwdriver as a lever he managed it, and peered through the gap thus created. It was, of course, dark, but there was sufficient reflected light from the other end of the courtyard for him to see that they were at the opposite end of it, near the outside wall, which information he passed back to Ginger, before lifting out five more stones which made an opening large enough for them to emerge. 'You'll have to pass the stones out to me,' he told Ginger, as he climbed through; 'we daren't leave the hole open or they will find it, and so discover our corridor.'

From the far side he took the stones which Ginger passed out to him, after which Ginger himself came through and they quickly pushed the stones back into place.

They were now in the courtyard. The far end of it was still brilliantly lighted, but this did not affect them for they were at the other extremity, and still in the black shadow of the tower, which they had just descended. A quick survey of the position revealed that they were about fifteen paces from the encircling wall of the castle, although, from the inside, this was little more than a parapet some three feet high, due to the fact that the courtyard had been built up to a much higher level than the terrain outside – doubtless to allow a defending garrison plenty of room to move about, and at the same time look down on the attacking force, which would find itself faced by a wall needing scaling ladders to surmount.

Biggles peeped round the tower towards the lighted end of the courtyard, and what he saw spurred him to a fresh effort of speed. 'Quick,' he said. 'They're getting the car out.' And with that he made a dash for the parapet. Ginger followed close behind him.

Looking down, he saw that it was a drop of some twenty feet to the track that skirted the bottom of the rampart, and he hung back in dismay until he saw Biggles take the rope from his pocket, for such a drop might easily mean a broken leg or a bad sprain. While Biggles was looping the rope round one of the battlements Ginger threw a glance over his shoulder, and saw that although the place where they crouched was in darkness, the far end of the courtyard was still illuminated by several lights, including the headlamps of another car, which he thought was the Professor's Morris. Several people were standing near it. He thought he saw the Beklinders among them, but he was not sure, and had no time to confirm it, for Biggles had already started down the rope and was telling him urgently to follow. This he lost no time in doing. As soon as he was on the path Biggles jerked the rope clear, and, looping it into a rough coil, stuffed it into his pocket again. Simultaneously there came the noise of the car being started up.

Whipping out his automatic, Biggles set off down the path at a run towards the road that led from the village to the main gate of the castle, but before reaching it he turned aside into the trees. 'Keep going!' he panted. 'It's our only chance and it's going to be a close thing.'

For the best part of a hundred yards, until he was certain that he was out of view of the gate, he kept inside the forest; then he struck diagonally towards the road, and on reaching it, after a quick look in both directions, continued down it for a further two hundred yards, where he stopped with a panted, 'Good! We've done it!' At the same time he broke off a piece of dead wood from the lower part of the nearest tree.

Ginger could not imagine what he was about to do. With wondering eyes he watched Biggles place the twig in the middle of the road. Then, switching on the torch, he adjusted it until it showed a red light, and placed it against the twig in such a way that the red light pointed up the road towards the castle gates – which, of course, could not be seen from where they were. The torch was one of the triple-light type, for it had been primarily intended for signalling purposes in accordance with their prearranged plan of sending messages to Algy in the machine.

Biggles returned to Ginger, who had watched all this from the edge of the road. 'I'm going to hold the car up,' he said. 'It's a ghastly risk, but there's no other way. We *can't* let the Beklinders go. Von Stalhein may be in the car or he may not. In any case, if the two Beklinders are there it is unlikely that there will be more than two guards. I reckon there will only be von Stalhein, with a storm-trooper driving, in the front seats, and the Beklinders in the back. We ought to – hello, that was the gate. The car's coming now. Get your gun out but don't use it unless you have to. Stay here. I'll take the far side. If by any chance the car doesn't stop, do nothing; otherwise act when I do.'

Biggles would have said more, but there was no time, for already the headlights of the car were turning the treetops to silver. He darted across the road and disappeared into the trees.

CHAPTER XII

Forestalled

The car came on, slowly, as was necessary on account of the state of the road. Ginger held his breath. The driver could not fail to see the red light – but would he stop? Ginger thought he would, for only a foolhardy driver would go on in the face of such a warning signal. And he was right. His heart leapt when the brakes were applied and the vehicle ran slowly to a standstill five or six yards short of the ruby glow. An instant later the front door on the driving side swung open and a man got out, walking towards the light, so that he came at once into the glare of his own headlamps. He was a storm-trooper.

Ginger, watching, waited until he saw Biggles, pistol at the ready, move swiftly into the road beside the unsuspecting storm-trooper; then, automatic in hand, he himself made a dash for the car. An instant later he was looking into the surprised face of von Stalhein.

'Keep your hands in front of you and keep 'em still,' snapped Ginger.

A split second later two shots rang out so close together that they almost blended as one.

Ginger's nerves vibrated like banjo strings, but he was too wise

344

to take his eyes from von Stalhein. He heard soft footsteps on the road; his lips went dry as he wondered whose they were, but he did not turn his head. Then a voice spoke. It was Biggles.

'I'm sorry I had to shoot your man, von Stalhein,' he said. 'He shouldn't have gone for his gun when he saw that I had mine already covering him. Step out, please, quickly. Ginger, get round to the other side.'

Ginger dashed round to the other side of the car and opened the door.

'Quickly, I said,' repeated Biggles. 'I should be sorry to have to shoot you, but I hear your fellows coming down the road, so in the circumstances you will pardon the urgency.'

Von Stalhein stepped out on to the road.

'Keep your hands still,' ordered Biggles, taking a pace towards him and running his hands over his pockets. He took a small automatic from the German's hip pocket and put it in his own. 'You would be well advised to do precisely as I tell you,' he went on. 'Start walking back towards the castle.'

Von Stalhein hesitated.

'I can give you just two seconds,' grated Biggles.

Von Stalhein shrugged his shoulders, turned about, and started walking slowly up the road towards the castle gate, whence came the sound of running footsteps.

Neither of the Beklinders had spoken. 'We're British agents,' was all Biggles said as he slipped into the driving seat.

'In you get, Ginger,' he ordered.

'Have you picked up the torch?'

'Yes.'

Ginger crawled swiftly into the seat beside Biggles and slammed the door. Biggles slammed his. The car moved forward, swerving round the fallen storm-trooper, who was sitting up near the side of the road. He shouted something as they passed but they could not catch the words.

'He seems to be annoyed about something,' murmured Ginger.

'A brave man but a fool,' said Biggles curtly, as he accelerated. 'Apparently he had the absurd idea that he could unfasten his holster, pull out his revolver, aim, and fire, before I, with my gun in my hand, could pull the trigger. I had to shoot him through the arm. He will know better next time.'

'Where are we bound for?' asked Ginger, as they reached the junction of the castle road and the village street, and Biggles put his foot hard down on the accelerator. The car raced forward.

'I've no idea,' replied Biggles. Then raising his voice a little, but without turning, he said, 'Professor Beklinder, I want you to be good enough to do exactly as you are told; we are going to try to get you out of the country. I take it that that meets with your approval?'

'Most certainly,' answered the Professor. 'But I will not go without my son,' he added.

'I appreciate that,' Biggles told him. 'Have you your passport, by any chance?'

'No.'

'Neither of you?'

'No.'

'Then it's no use our trying to get across the frontier in the ordinary way. With passports there was just a chance that we might have managed it within the next couple of hours; after that I'm afraid every frontier guard will be on the look-out for us. But it's no use trying it without papers. Every telephone in the country will start buzzing as soon as von Stalhein gets back to the castle.'

'How shall we get out of the country, then?' asked the Professor anxiously. He spoke with just a suggestion of a foreign accent.

'I can think of only one way,' replied Biggles, 'and that is by using the same means as we came in. That is, by aeroplane.' He suddenly applied the brakes, and, pulling the car to a skidding standstill, turned to Ginger. 'We'd better get things clear,' he said. 'First and foremost, we've got to get the Professor and his son out of the country.'

'What about Algy?' asked Ginger quickly.

'That, for the moment, becomes a side-issue. We shall have to come back for him afterwards. He'll understand that. As far as the immediate present is concerned I don't think we dare risk rushing about in this car. Von Stalhein will have its number, and within a couple of hours every policeman and storm-trooper in the country will be on the watch for it. We've got to try to get hold of Algy's machine. It was dark when he landed, and, as it seems unlikely that it would be dismantled or flown away before morning, it should still be where he left it. There will be a guard over it, of course, but we can't help that. We've got to get it, even if it means a fight. I can think of no other way of getting out of the country. And we've got to work fast. If ever they get hold of the Professor again, or ourselves, knowing that we know the truth about the faked accident, it will be good-bye. Hark!'

Far behind them, from the direction of Unterhamstadt, came the vibrant hum of a high-powered car.

'You see?' said Biggles. 'They've got another car on our track. There must have been one in the village. The pursuit is up.' As he spoke he started the Morris forward again, but cruised along

slowly, half leaning through the open window as if he was looking
out for something. Then, as if finding what he sought, he turned
the car off the road and allowed it to run quietly between the
trees of the forest that hemmed them in on both sides. Not until
the car was a good fifty yards from the road did he apply the
brakes and switch off the lights. As the car stopped he got out,
asking the others to do the same. And hardly had they complied
when round the corner came a big open car, driven at racing
speed. The seats were packed with storm-troopers. It tore on, and
disappeared from sight round the next bend in the road.

'You see what we're up against?' said Biggles. 'That car would soon
have overtaken us. We shall do better on foot, across country.'

'You mean, you're going to try to reach the landing-ground?'
inquired Ginger.

'Unless you can think of a more promising scheme.'

'No, I can't.'

'There is bound to be a guard, in which case there is likely to
be some shooting; nevertheless, we shall have the advantage of
surprise on our side. I have two spare weapons – von Stalhein's,
and the one belonging to the storm-trooper whom I had to shoot,
so we are all right for equipment. One of us ought to get through
– and it only needs one of us to fly the machine. If you find yourself in the machine with the Professor and his son, take straight
off. Don't wait for me. That's an order – you understand?'

'Perfectly.'

'Good!' Biggles turned to the Professor. 'Professor Beklinder,' he
said gravely, 'as you must have gathered from our conversation,
although we have got you out of immediate danger the position
is still serious. We had an aeroplane ready to fly you to England,
but unfortunately the pilot was captured, and we assume that

the machine is under guard. My plan is to attempt to take it by force, but I cannot jeopardize your life without your consent. Do you agree, or would you prefer to try some other way?'

'If there *was* another way I should prefer to try it,' admitted the Professor frankly. 'Not for myself, you understand, but on account of my son.'

'Have no fears for me,' declared the boy, stoutly. He turned to Biggles. 'Did I hear you say that you had a spare pistol?'

Biggles smiled faintly. 'You did.'

'Then please give it to me. You seem to forget that I have scores of my own to wipe out.'

Without a word Biggles passed him the revolver which he had taken from the wounded storm-trooper, and gave the Professor von Stalhein's automatic.

'Be careful with that, Gustav,' said the Professor, nervously, and thus the others learned the boy's name. 'In case the plan miscarries, there is one thing I should like to say,' he went on, turning to Biggles.

'Yes?'

'It is how much I appreciate what you, personally, are doing on our behalf, and the British government—'

'Oh, don't think about that now,' broke in Biggles. 'The British government looks after those who serve it, anyway. My only regret in this matter is that we did not make contact with your son earlier; he would have been a useful ally. But we've no time to waste. If we are all agreed, let us push on. Every hour will make our task more difficult.'

Leaving the car as it stood, they set off through the forest in the direction of the landing-ground, which was, Ginger judged, about two miles away.

They said little as they walked, for the night was still, and, well aware of the distance at which the sound of human voices can be heard in such conditions, Biggles requested silence. So they walked on, Biggles taking the lead, his brief remarks being confined to warnings against obstructions, such as low-hanging branches. They were, of course, travelling across country – if a forest can be so described. It was one which they had not previously seen, and the close-growing trees offered perfect cover. But after going about a mile Biggles suddenly called a halt, and the reason was at once apparent to the others. They had reached the edge of the forest. Strictly speaking, it was not the edge; the trees ended, but began again on the other side of what was, in effect, a wide strip of cultivated land that had swept far into the forest. The distance to the trees on the far side of this clearing was about two hundred yards, but in the whole of that area there was no cover of any sort.

'What do you think about it?' whispered Ginger.

'I think it is the sort of place that might be watched,' replied Biggles.

'I don't see anybody.'

'You wouldn't be likely to. A man keeping guard would hardly be such a fool as to stand in the middle of the field. He'd keep back in the trees so that he could not be seen.'

'That looks to me like a footpath running down the middle there,' observed Ginger.

'It is,' put in Gustav. 'I once walked to the edge of the wood yonder; I remember the place well,' he added by way of explanation.

'It would take us over a mile out of our way if we had to go all round the edge of the wood,' remarked Biggles. 'We can't spare the time to do that. We shall have to go straight across, and risk it.'

The words had barely left his lips, and he had, in fact, taken a pace forward with the object of continuing the march when from out of the forest, at the extreme end of the cultivated land, travelling away from Unterhamstadt, came a fast-moving object, which, as it drew nearer, resolved itself into several component parts.

'Keep quiet,' breathed Biggles, stepping back farther into the trees.

It was soon possible to make out the details of the approaching figures. There was a storm-trooper on a bicycle. Beside him, controlled by leads, ran two Alsatian dogs. The man made no sound, but, pedalling fast, went on down what Ginger had rightly supposed to be a path and finally disappeared into the dim distance. Nobody spoke until he was out of sight.

'That gives us an idea of how careful we shall have to be,' murmured Biggles.

'Where was he off to, I wonder?' said Ginger.

'If that path bears round to the right it would take him some-where near the open country where Algy landed – that is, if my bump of locality is correct,' answered Biggles.

'Yes, I think the path does go round that way,' put in the Professor, his voice heavy with anxiety. 'What had we better do?'

'We've got to get across this field before we do anything else,' declared Biggles. 'We can't afford to lose a minute. Let's make a dash for it. If we're challenged, go on running, but keep together. Everybody ready? Good. Let's go.'

They broke from the sombre trees and set off at a steady run for the opposite side of the clearing, where, at the foot of a low hill, the trees began again. They could just see the silhouette of the hill against the sky. At every moment Ginger expected to hear a challenge ring out, but nothing of the sort happened, and he voiced his relief when they once more plunged into the welcome cover of the trees. The Professor was out of breath. 'I am not so young as I was,' he said apologetically, as they waited for him to recover before they went on again.

Groping their way, stumbling over roots, and colliding with unseen obstacles, they pushed on, and they had nearly reached the top of the hill, which began to take the form of a ridge, when a sound split the silence – a sound that pulled them up short. There was no possibility of mistaking it. It was the sound of an aero engine being started up.

'He's done us,' grated Biggles through his teeth, as he ran on to the top of the ridge.

'Who?' asked Gustav.

'Von Stalhein. He's afraid of us. He guessed that we should make for the machine, and he daren't even trust his guard. He's removing our only link with France – look, there it goes.'

By this time they had all reached the top of the ridge, where an outcrop of rock prevented the growth of trees. There was no need for Biggles to amplify his remark, for what had happened was plain for all to see. The ridge overlooked the stretch of open country which they had chosen for a landing-ground. On the side of it nearest to them was a little group of lights. The machine was in the air, heading eastward. The noise of the engine diminished rapidly – became a hum. Some of the lights on the field went out. Figures began to move towards a waiting motor-car. The car went off, and disappeared round the shoulder of a neighbouring hill. Silence fell.

The machine was in the air, heading eastward.

'Well, that's that!' said Biggles in a resigned voice.

The Professor sank down and buried his face in his hands.

'Here – here, just a minute, Professor,' chided Biggles.

'It's hopeless now.'

'Hopeless?' Biggles laughed quietly. 'If you'd been through what I've been through in my time – and Ginger, too, for that matter – you'd know that nothing is hopeless until you're dead – and buried. You were supposed to be dead and buried, don't forget – but here you are.'

'But surely there is nothing we can do, is there?' asked Gustav miserably.

'There are plenty of things we can do,' answered Biggles. 'It's just a matter of choosing the best one.'

'That's right enough,' agreed Ginger, with a bigger show of cheerfulness than he felt in his heart.

Biggles took him aside, and, choosing a sheltered place among the rocks below the ledge, took out his map and the torch. He studied the map for a moment without speaking. Then he placed the index finger of his left hand on a spot a little to the north of the village. 'Look here, Ginger,' he said in a low voice, 'we've got about one chance left – but it wouldn't do to let the others know that things are as bad as that. I'm afraid they are depressed. If they lose heart altogether we shan't be able to do anything with them, so behave as if it were all plain sailing.' Biggles glanced at his wristwatch. 'It's nearly ten o'clock,' he continued. 'Now this is what I want you to do. You see this place on the map?'

Ginger dropped on his knees to see more clearly the place Biggles was indicating. 'Yes,' he said.

'I want you to be there, with the Beklinders, at twenty minutes past twelve precisely.'

'You're not going with us?'

'No. There's no time for answering questions, but I'm going to try to pull off the cheekiest coup of my life. You be on that field at twelve-twenty. Wait until twelve-thirty. If I am not there by then you can reckon that I shan't be coming. If that happens, forget about me and try to get out of the country as best you can. It's a thousand to one against your doing it, but you can only try; anyway, there will be nothing else left for you to do. Make for the French frontier. You know the tricks. Take cover by day and travel only by night. Remember it is better to lie in open fields of crops than in ditches. Your greatest difficulty will be food. Do without it if you can; don't go near houses unless you are absolutely compelled to. People in the country keep dogs, and dogs bark, and by tomorrow the whole country will be looking for us. One bark will be enough to bring a pack of storm-troopers to the spot. But I hope it won't come to that. The place where I hope to meet you is less than four miles from here, which means that if you started now you would be there in an hour – which is rather too soon. Yet with these storm-troopers all over the place it's going to be dangerous for you to hang about in the open.'

'We shall have to pass near the churchyard on the way to this new rendezvous; what's wrong with us hiding in the vault until it's time for us to go on to it?'

'That's a good idea,' declared Biggles. 'You ought to be safe there. I should say it isn't more than a couple of miles from the vault to the rendezvous—'

'What *is* this rendezvous?' asked Ginger puzzled.

'It's a big field. Before we started I looked at it with a view to using it as a landing-ground, but I decided that it was a bit too near the village. Had it become necessary for Algy to land he might have been heard taking off again. That was why I chose the other place – that and because it was larger. I'm going to try to get hold of an aeroplane. If I can't get a 'plane, I'll get a car. I've no time to tell you more than that now. Is everything clear?'

'Absolutely. We'll be at the field at twelve-twenty.'

'That's right. Stay in the vault as long as you can – but don't be late. If I don't turn up – well, you know what to do.'

'What about Algy?'

'While either of us is alive we'll try to get him out. He knows that. But we've got to get the Beklinders away first. Algy is a personal matter – they are a national matter.' Biggles got up and went back to where the Beklinders were waiting. 'I shall have to leave you now,' he said quietly. 'In the meanwhile I want you to do exactly as Ginger orders. Your safety will depend upon it.' And with that he walked away through the trees.

Ginger beckoned to the Professor and his son. 'Follow me, please,' he said.

CHAPTER XIII

Ginger Goes Back

As they made their way towards the churchyard Ginger explained the situation as far as he was able to the Beklinders, who accepted it philosophically and agreed to accompany him to the vault. They avoided roads, and even footpaths, in which matter both the Professor and his son were better informed than Ginger. Indeed, the Professor knew every inch of the country, having – as he said – stayed in the district many times when he was a young man.

In this way they reached the churchyard without trouble; there were one or two alarms, such as when a whistle was blown on a road near to which they happened to be passing; that was all. On reaching the churchyard Ginger recovered the crow-bar from where Biggles had hidden it, and, prising up the stone slab, they descended into their hiding-place. The time then, by Ginger's watch, was ten-thirty.

'I'm afraid we have rather more than an hour to spend here,' he told the others.

'What does your friend hope to do?' asked the Professor.

'Beyond the fact that he is going to try to get an aeroplane or a car, I do not know,' answered Ginger, who then went on to describe the rendezvous.

'I am afraid he will have a job to get an aeroplane in Lucrania,' said the Professor, shaking his head.

Ginger switched off the torch. 'Getting into Unterhamstadt was a job – but we got here,' he observed. 'Getting hold of you was a job – but we got you. In fact, nearly everything we do seems to be a job – but somehow we manage to do it. So while getting hold of an aeroplane may be a job, it doesn't mean that Biggles won't get one.'

'I know the field well,' remarked the Professor.

'Good! That ought to make things a bit easier, at any rate.'

'I could go straight to it,' declared the Professor. 'I have walked over the whole district many times.'

'While we are waiting you might tell me why you came back to this part of the world,' invited Ginger. 'Wasn't it rather unwise?'

'Yes, I suppose it was even worse than that; it was the height of folly,' admitted the Professor. 'But you see, I had a good reason for coming. It began like this. Some time ago I received an anonymous letter from Lucrania, from a man who signed himself "A Friend", informing me that my wife was dead, but my son, who was born after I had left the country, was living at an address in Prenzel. Needless to say I was astonished and delighted at the letter, although I should have been more sceptical of its authenticity had it not been for the fact that the notepaper bore a secret mark – the mark of the society to which I once foolishly belonged. It was when the activities of this society were exposed, twenty years ago, that I had to leave the country. You must understand that I did not even know of the existence of my son. I did not reply to the letter. That would have been too dangerous. Instead, I hired an agent to spy out the land for me, but either the man was a rogue or else he was in the employ of my enemies; I do not know which; I only know that he betrayed me. He came to me, and after telling me that my son was indeed alive, asked me if I would like to meet him, and on my assurance that I would, he invited me to suggest a meeting-place. At the same time he pointed out that it would be easier for me, carrying a British passport, to come to Lucrania, than it would be for Gustav to get out of that country, for everybody leaving is suspect. As I have already told you, I often came to Unterhamstadt when I was a young man; at that time I was interested in archaeology, and stayed at the hotel, which was handy for the castle which I wished to explore. I was actually writing a paper on my discoveries when I had to fly from the country.'

'Yes, I know that,' put in Gustav.

'How?' asked his father quickly.

'Because after mother died I found the papers, and read them,' answered Gustav simply.

'Of course. It was silly of me not to think of that,' resumed his father. 'Well, to conclude, it was not unnatural that I should arrange to meet my son at the place which held for me so many pleasant memories. You see, I spent my honeymoon here. But alas, the whole thing was a fraud to trick me into coming to the country. Even as I approached the village I was apprehended. They took me to the hotel where I was kept in a semi-conscious condition by means of drug injections.'

'I wonder what their object was in taking you to the hotel at all,' mused Ginger. 'And, for that matter, why they buried you in a vault instead of a grave.'

'I think that is something we shall have to assume, for von Stalhein is never likely to explain his actions to us,' returned the Professor. 'I imagine that von Stalhein knew about the tunnels

– possibly they were discovered when the castle was being reno-
vated. It might not have suited him had I merely disappeared,
for that would have led to inquiries. He preferred to pretend that
I had been killed in an accident. By using room seventeen at the
hotel he was in a position to move me – or anyone else – without
being observed, even by the village people. I was carried through
the tunnel to the castle. I can only suppose that by placing my
coffin in the vault he was in a position to recover it immediately
should he ever find it necessary. One way or another the tunnels
suited his purposes very well. Had you been captured at the
hotel no doubt you would have been taken to the castle that way,
for had you been seen in custody by someone in the village the
matter might have been reported to England.'

Ginger nodded. 'Yes,' he said thoughtfully. 'They must have
taken Algy to the castle via the tunnel. I fancy we were there
when he was brought along.'

The Professor continued. 'Once in the castle I was ordered
under pain of death to go on with the work I had been undertaking for the British government. I refused to do this, for
in my disappointment at not finding my son I cared little
whether I lived or died. Many interviews I had with that man
von Stalhein, who made vague promises about my son, none of
which materialized.'

'Then presumably Gustav knew nothing about this?' suggested
Ginger.

'No.'

'Then what brought him here?'

Gustav answered for himself. 'By the merest accident I saw in
the public library at Prenzel, in an English newspaper, a report
of the accident. You see,' he explained, 'knowing from my mother

that my father was in England, and hoping one day to join him, I made myself proficient in the English language so that I might one day get work in England. It was to find the appointments vacant columns that I was reading the paper, and so came upon the account of the accident to my father.'

'Ah, now I begin to understand,' murmured Ginger.

'I did not believe the story,' continued Gustav. 'I don't know why, yet somehow I felt that my father was still alive. I suspected that there may have been a plot to get him back into Lucrania – for our police never forget or forgive. The fact that the accident was supposed to have happened at Unterhamstadt was significant. I recalled what I had read about the castle and the secret tunnels in my father's papers, and I thought that, armed with this information, I might perhaps find him. So I determined to come to Unterhamstadt. But all the time, although I did not know it, I must have been watched by the *Grospu*, the secret police. I was arrested, certified insane, and placed in a mental home. But I escaped, and, disguising myself as a girl, came here.'

'That was a plucky thing to do,' declared Ginger.

'Not pluck, but love of my father whom I had never seen.'

'How long were you here before we came?'

'Two days.'

'What were you doing in the Jew's house – where we first saw you?'

'I thought I would risk asking him some questions – the very questions that I heard you ask him.'

'Ah – so you were listening?'

'Yes, although it was an accident that I arrived just after you. I dared not, of course, go near the house in daytime, for fear of being seen and bringing suspicion upon myself. So I waited until it was dark, and everything quiet. I was standing in a shadow watching the house, making sure that no one was in sight, when I saw you enter. Thinking that you might be agents of the secret police I crept across to listen to what you were saying.'

'That explains the whole story,' said Ginger. 'You were the ghost in the churchyard, weren't you?'

'Yes.'

'You nearly frightened me to death.'

'You were not more frightened than I.'

'What were you thinking of doing?'

'Getting into the castle.'

'The *castle*?'

'Yes. You see, my father in his explorations had found the tunnels and made a plan of them. One went from room number seventeen at the hotel. I looked for that one first, but for a long time I could not find the entrance, and it was dangerous work looking for it; for, as I think you know, the room was always locked. So I thought I would try the entrance in the monastery – it would be safer.'

'The monastery? But what has the monastery to do with the churchyard?'

'This is the monastery – or it was.'

Ginger gasped. 'What fools we were! We never suspected it.'

'Why should you? The monastery has been gone hundreds of years. The church was built from the ruins.'

'That will certainly interest Biggles,' declared Ginger. 'That's my chief's nickname, by the way. Good heavens!' he cried in a startled voice, as a new thought struck him. 'Do you mean to say there is a tunnel from here to the castle?'

'Yes, there is.'

'Where does it start?'

'In here – in this vault. One of the stones is a sham. It hides the entrance. But why do you ask?'

'Because a friend of mine is still a prisoner in the castle. We had to forsake him in order to try to get you away.' Ginger switched on the torch and looked at his watch. 'It is only a quarter to eleven,' he said quickly. 'I've still got over an hour – there is just a chance that I might find him – are you sure about this tunnel?'

'Most certainly,' replied the Professor. 'It joins the one from the hotel to the castle, somewhere about half-way.'

'When we went up the tunnel from the hotel to the castle we did not see an opening.'

'Nevertheless, it is there. I have been through it.'

Ginger rose to his feet. 'Do you mind if I leave you for a little while?' he said.

'Why should you stay with us?' answered the Professor. 'In any case, we know perfectly well where we are to meet your friend. I know the place even better than you do.'

Ginger made up his mind. 'Then I am going to the castle,' he declared, rather breathlessly. 'If I don't come back you know what to do. Whatever happens you must be at the field at precisely twenty minutes past twelve, and watch for Biggles to come. He may come in an aeroplane, in a car, or on foot – I don't know. But you must be there when he arrives.'

'We will do that.'

'I hope to get back before you leave, but in case I don't, will you give him a message from me? Tell him about the passage and say that I have gone to try to find Algy – he'll understand.'

'Very well. We shall obey your instructions to the letter.'

Ginger picked up the crow-bar. 'Show me the entrance to this tunnel,' he said grimly.

The Professor walked straight to a marble panel set low down in the wall. Its inscription, if ever there had been one, had been defaced by the ravages of time, but the remnants of some carved scrollwork remained. The Professor inserted his fingers under the carving and tugged. The panel swung open, disclosing a hole large enough to admit a man on hands and knees.

'How on earth did you discover that?' Ginger could not help asking.

'I did not discover it from this end, you may be sure,' returned the Professor. 'I came the other way.'

'From the other tunnel?'

'Yes.'

'How far is it from here to the other tunnel?'

'I do not remember exactly; perhaps a quarter of a mile, more or less.'

'Thank you.' Ginger crawled through the entrance. 'I shall try to get back,' he said again, 'but if I am not here by ten minutes to twelve you go on to the field.'

'We shall keep the appointment on time.'

'Good – *au revoir*.' Turning, Ginger went on down the tunnel, picking his way by the light of the now rather feeble ray of the torch, for the battery was beginning to show signs of exhaustion.

The tunnel was smaller than the one which connected the hotel with the castle, from which he judged that it was only a secondary line of communication. Even in the perilous circumstances in which he found himself he could not help wondering to what sinister purposes the tunnel had been put in days gone by. Thus he pondered as he hurried along, only to have his reflections suddenly cut short when he found himself face to face with a brick wall. He searched the walls of the tunnel on either side, but soon had to admit to himself the fact that he could not continue. The tunnel had been blocked up. Closer inspection of the brickwork which blocked the tunnel revealed it to be of more recent nature than the rest, and he guessed what had happened. The tunnel had been deliberately closed not very long before. He struck at the brickwork with the crow-bar. It gave back a hollow sound, from which he judged that it was not very thick. He struck again, harder, and had the satis-faction of seeing a brick move. After that it was only a matter of time; he propped the torch on the ground in such a way that it threw its light on his work, and then, with both hands free, he set about the wall in earnest. The brickwork crumbled before his furious onslaught, and after ascertaining with the bar that all was clear beyond, he soon had a hole large enough to get through. Picking up the torch, and still carrying the bar, he climbed through the hole and found himself in the tunnel which led from the hotel to the castle. He saw at once that they might have used the tunnel a hundred times without suspecting that the other passage was there, for after it had been blocked up the mildew and fungus had secured a hold so that there was little difference between it and the older brickwork. Hurrying on, he went towards the castle.

He was by no means clear in his mind as to what he was going to do when he got there. It would, he told himself, depend upon what he found; but nevertheless he determined to take any steps, however desperate, to secure Algy's release, for he realized only too well that such an opportunity as the one of which he was now trying to take advantage, would be unlikely ever to occur again. Von Stalhein would see to that.

He reached the end of the tunnel only to find – as he expected – that the door was locked. He wasted no time, but forthwith climbed up over the fallen masonry until he found himself in the narrow corridor in which occurred the spy-hole looking into von Stalhein's office. He went straight to it, intending not to do anything more than look in, for at the back of his mind he had a vague idea of effecting an entrance to the castle by breaking down the panelling of one of the rooms farther on – rooms which he thought, and hoped, were unused.

Von Stalhein's voice reached him even before he opened the spy-hole. A moment later he saw at a glance that the German was in a cold rage, lashing with his tongue about a dozen storm-troopers who stood stiffly to attention in front of him. Ginger could not, of course, understand a word of what was being said, but from mention of Biggles's name he thought that von Stalhein was rating his men for not having found the two *Englanders*. Von Stalhein concluded his invective with a sharp word of command. The men turned, and in single file marched stiffly from the room. Whereupon von Stalhein went quickly to the telephone, had a brief conversation – which again Ginger could not follow – slammed down the receiver, and, picking up his cap, followed the storm-troopers out of the room, leaving the light on.

Ginger did not know what to do, but remembering Biggles's remark about the likelihood of a sliding panel, he switched off his torch and endeavoured to locate it by seeking for a crack through which the light inside the room would show. He did not find exactly what he sought, but he found a minute glimmer of light, and he pressed against this with the sharp end of the

crow-bar. To his horror the bar went straight through the panelling into the room, the worm-eaten wood crumbling before the
iron. Nevertheless, a tiny line of light suggested that an opening
was there, if he could only discover the catch that controlled it.
Listening for von Stalhein's returning footsteps he searched dili-
gently for the catch, but he failed to find it. Indeed, he convinced
himself that there was not one, for the inside of the panelling
was as smooth as a board, and had there been any projection, or
a sunken finger grip, he could not have failed to find it.

Hardly pausing to consider what he was doing, in sheer desperation he wedged the sharp end of the crow-bar into the thin line
of light and attempted to lever the panel aside by brute force.
He succeeded beyond his expectations. There was a loud crack
followed by a sharp splintering sound, and before he could take
his weight off the bar a large section of the rotten woodwork had
broken off and fallen with a crash into the room. The corridor
was, naturally, instantly flooded with light from the room.

Ginger stared at the gaping hole, petrified with horror and
alarm, for the noise had seemed to him sufficient to bring
everyone in the castle to the spot, and if anyone entered the room
the hole in the wall would instantly be seen.

His first lucid thought was that he must get the panel back
into place before von Stalhein returned, or his corridor would be
discovered and his capture assured. With this object in view he
scrambled through the hole and jumped down into the room, a
distance of a mere two or three feet. Not until he was there did
he realize that what he had hoped to achieve was impossible. He
could not get back into the tunnel and temporarily fix the panel
in place from that side. He could put the panel roughly into position from where he now stood, as he quickly ascertained; but he

was, of course, on the wrong side of it. And while he stood there, his brain racing, almost overcome by dismay, he heard footsteps approaching.

Prompted now by instinct rather than by deliberate thought, he pushed the panel roughly into place and dived for the only cover the room offered, which was behind the tall door of the safe, which von Stalhein had left open. As he passed in front of it he saw the Professor's bottle of high explosive standing on a shelf, and with a wild idea of blowing the whole place to pieces if the worst came to the worst, he snatched it with his left hand, at the same time taking out his pistol with the other. 'If there is going to be a rough house I am at least well armed,' he thought grimly.

He was rigid behind the safe door when von Stalhein came back into the room. He held his breath, fully expecting the panel to fall down under the vibration of the German's heavy footsteps. But it remained in place, and von Stalhein sat down at his desk, in which position his back was turned to Ginger, who remained where he was, for he had no wish to start trouble against odds which his common sense told him were too heavy. He noted with satisfaction that von Stalhein's nerves seemed to be on edge, for he rapped irritably on the desk in front of him with a lead pencil. He reached for the telephone, changed his mind, and slammed the receiver down again. Ginger's prayer of thankfulness – for he was afraid that the German was again going to summon his men – was cut off short when the man in front of him picked up the instrument and snapped what was clearly an order. But Ginger's heart leapt, for he had caught the word *Englander*, which in the circumstances he took to refer to Algy.

Von Stalhein continued drumming on his desk with his pencil, and thus the situation remained for two or three minutes, which seemed like an eternity to Ginger, who was terrified that von Stalhein might decide at any moment to close the safe, in which case they would meet face to face.

Heavy footsteps outside the door sent him huddling closer against the wall behind him. The door was flung open. Two storm-troopers entered. Between them was Algy. All three took up a position in front of von Stalhein's desk.

'Lacey, I have decided to send you away,' said von Stalhein harshly.

'Why, what's the matter – lost your nerve?' asked Algy coolly.

Von Stalhein fixed his monocle in his eye and regarded Algy with a hostile glare. 'You would be wise to remember where you are,' he said frigidly.

Algy smiled. 'Von Stalhein, you're a liar,' he said evenly. 'You haven't got my friends or you wouldn't behave like this.'

'Silence!' Von Stalhein brought his fist down with a bang on the desk.

Ginger shuddered, and this time his fears were justified. The panel fell with a crash into the room.

There was dead silence as all eyes switched to it.

Ginger knew that for better or worse the end had come. He left his hiding-place, and with Indian-like tread advanced swiftly to the desk. As he took the last step a board creaked, and all eyes flashed to him.

Ginger's automatic was up. 'Keep still, everybody,' he jerked out. 'Von Stalhein, tell your men to—'

He got no farther. One of the storm-troopers reached for his revolver. Ginger's automatic spat. The man stared at him foolishly for a moment and then sank to the floor.

'The door, Algy – lock the door!' cried Ginger shrilly, knowing that the shot would be heard all over the castle. 'Keep still, von Stalhein, or you'll get yours,' he went on crisply, his face as white as death.

The second storm-trooper started to reach for his revolver holster, but the muzzle of Ginger's weapon swung round on him and he remained motionless, his hand poised in mid-air.

Algy had dashed to the door. He locked it an instant before the handle was turned and a weight thrown against it. There was a sound of hammering and many voices. He hurried back to the motionless group at the desk.

'Get that fellow's gun,' ordered Ginger.

Algy took the storm-trooper's revolver from its holster.

'Now von Stalhein's.'

Algy complied.

'That's the second pistol of mine you've taken tonight,' said von Stalhein whimsically.

'I think it's as many as we shall need,' Ginger told him smoothly. 'Come on, Algy, it's time we went.'

'Which way?' asked Algy, as there came a thunder of blows on the door.

'Through the hole where the panel fell out. Get a move on. When you get there, keep these fellows covered until I can join you.'

Algy ran to the corridor and turned about, a weapon in each hand. 'Come on!' he shouted above the clamour outside the door.

Ginger dashed to the hole and ducked into it just as the door crashed inwards. 'This way!' he shouted, and set off down the corridor.

Now until this moment he had completely forgotten the bottle which he still clutched in his left hand. In the other he held his automatic, leaving no hand free to hold the torch. In the darkness he was fearful of dropping the bottle, so as a last resort he put it into his pocket rather than take the risk. His left hand was now free to hold the torch, and with the fast-expiring beam making only a feeble glow in front of them, they hurried on.

As they reached the fallen brickwork there were shouts behind them. Ignoring them, they squirmed through into the main tunnel, Algy turning on the top to fire three quick shots down the passage behind them. 'That ought to discourage 'em,' he said lightly.

'Buck up!' cried Ginger, in a panic, for he heard the lock turning in the big door, which he realized, of course, that Algy knew nothing about.

Algy ran – or rather skidded on the slippery floor – after Ginger, who was making the best speed he could up the tunnel. And it was not until then, when the door was flung open, that he perceived the danger. The tunnel was filled with a medley of sounds.

'Is it all clear at the hotel?' shouted Algy.

'We're not going to the hotel,' Ginger told him.

'This tunnel goes to the hotel; I know that because they brought me up it not long ago.'

'Keep going, I'll show you another way,' panted Ginger, as a shot zipped along the wall.

He reached the side turning, and with a gasp of relief ducked through it as several more shots whizzed down the tunnel, the reports nearly deafening them. Algy followed.

With Ginger still leading they ran on, their pursuers never far behind them. Fortunately the tunnel was on a slight bend, which kept them just out of sight of the men who came storming along; what was more important, it prevented any direct shooting. Nevertheless, Ginger was more than a little worried, for a glance at his watch showed him that the time was a quarter to twelve, which left him in doubt as to whether the Beklinders had started for the rendezvous. They might have started, or, on the other hand, they might only be on the point of leaving; either way, he was leading a red-hot trail to their hiding-place, which was bad, for the escape of the Beklinders was more important than their own. Had it been possible he would have laid a false trail, but there was no alternative route, so he could only go on, well aware that if the Beklinders were still in the vault, the precipitate arrival of pursued and pursuers would be bound to cause a panic and perhaps jeopardize all Biggles's work.

'How much farther?' panted Algy.

'We're nearly there,' answered Ginger, stumbling, and breaking into a cold perspiration as he remembered the bottle, and thought of what might happen if he fell.

'Here's the end,' he gasped, as the opening into the vault came into view.

'Is Biggles here?'

'No.'

'Where—?'

'He's gone on. We've got to meet him. But the Professor may be here.' Ginger realized that as Algy knew nothing about what had happened during the last few hours this was an inadequate explanation, but there was no time for details.

They reached the entrance to the vault and scrambled through. One glance showed Ginger that the Beklinders had left, for which he was thankful, but as they knew nothing of the hue and cry, if he failed to overtake them and warn them of it, it was likely that they would be recaptured. A desperate expedient occurred to him and he resolved to take the chance. 'Get outside,' he told Algy frantically. 'There are the steps – get outside and lie down – hurry.'

He dashed back to the entrance to the tunnel. 'Help yourselves to that,' he yelled, and hurled the bottle with all his might. The instant it had left his hand he whirled about and made a dash for the churchyard, hoping to reach it before the explosion occurred. He almost succeeded. He managed to get to the top step when a blast of air, almost solid in its force, shot him out like a champagne cork. Following the blast came a streak of electric blue flame. For a split second it spurted through the vault entrance like a blow-lamp; then the earth shook with an explosion so violent that to Ginger it felt like the end of the world. Half dazed, a smell of scorching in his nostrils, he staggered to his feet, and saw Algy doing the same thing close at hand.

'What was that?' gasped Algy.

'One of the Professor's little squibs,' answered Ginger. 'Let's keep going; we've a long way to go.' He set off at a run across the churchyard in the direction of the rendezvous.

Vaulting over the wall they went on without stopping to look behind, and as they ran Ginger gave Algy a sporadic account of what had happened and the situation as it now existed.

'The Beklinders shouldn't be far – in front of us – then?' puffed Algy.

'We ought to overtake them before they get to the field,' Ginger told him.

'Can't we – slow down – for a bit? I don't think – anyone is – following us.'

'Von Stalhein would hear the explosion, and he would probably guess what caused it,' answered Ginger, easing the pace to a fast walk. 'He might even see the flash from the castle, and that would give him our position. His entire pack will be after us by this time. It's going to be touch and go.'

They both swerved violently as a figure stepped suddenly from behind a clump of bushes which they were at that moment passing.

'It's all right; it's only me,' said Gustav. 'We heard somebody coming and hid until we saw who it was.'

The Professor also emerged from his hiding-place. 'What was that explosion?' he asked.

'It was that little bottle of syrup which you mixed to blow von Stalhein up with,' Ginger told him. 'He took it away from you and put it in his safe, you remember? A mob of his greyshirts were on our trail so I tossed it back for them to play with. By the way, this is Algy Lacey – he's one of us; but postpone the "How-d'ye-do" stuff until later on. We're all right for time, I think, but the farther we get away from this locality, the better. Professor, you know the way, so will you please take the lead?'

In single file they resumed their journey. They saw no one, but more than once they heard sounds which told them that a hue and cry was in progress – shouts, whistles, and the honking of motor-car horns.

'They'll have a job to find us,' declared Algy confidently; 'in country like this, with so much timber about, looking for anybody would be worse than trying to find a pin in a cornfield.'

'I'd agree with you except for one thing,' muttered Ginger anxiously.

'And what's that?'

'They've got dogs.'

'Phew! I didn't know that.'

'I should feel easier in my mind if *I* didn't know. They're not ordinary animals; they're trained for the job; I've seen them at work.'

'I don't think we need worry, we are nearly there,' put in the Professor. 'The field is just beyond the belt of trees in front of us.'

They trudged on, and had just reached the trees when, from far away in the direction whence they had come, one of the most sinister of all sounds floated to their ears on the still night air. It was the deep-throated bay of a hound.

'It sounds as if they've got the dogs on the job,' murmured Algy.

'They'll have to travel fast to catch us,' said Ginger confidently, looking at his watch. 'It's twelve-fifteen. We have only five minutes to wait.'

They went on again through the trees.

'This should be the place,' announced the Professor, as they forced their way through the undergrowth and emerged into the open country beyond.

'You're quite sure about that?' said Ginger. 'I've left it to you.'

'Yes, this is it.'

Ginger looked round the boundaries of the big field in front of him. 'Yes, it must be,' he said. 'Anyway, it's big enough to get a machine in, and there can't be many fields of this size about here.' He whistled quietly and listened for a reply; but there was none. 'I was hoping that Biggles might be here a bit early,' he explained. 'But apparently he isn't here yet,' he added, looking again at his watch. 'Twelve-eighteen,' he announced. 'Two minutes to go.'

The sudden shrill of a whistle sent them all facing the way they had come. A dog barked furiously. There was another whistle, followed by a shout.

'I should say they are within half a mile of us,' murmured Algy.

'Well, if they arrive before Biggles there is only one thing we can do,' declared Ginger, holding up his pistol and stepping backward a few paces so that he could see the top of a slight rise in the ground behind the belt of trees. 'The result will depend on how many there are of them. We'll do our best to make things warm for them, however many there are.'

'It is twenty past twelve,' announced the Professor. He may have tried not to show it, but his voice was heavy with disappointment.

'Your watch is probably a minute fast,' Algy told him cheerfully.

'I'm afraid your friend isn't coming.'

'That's because you don't know him as well as we do,' said Ginger. 'Look – here come the greyshirts over the hill.' He started to count as figures, silhouetted against the sky, began to appear. 'That seems to be the lot,' he said, when he had counted up to ten. 'Ten and two couple of hounds. "Ten little greyshirts standing in a line, a bad boy plugged one and then there were nine,"' he misquoted glibly.

'This is no time for joking,' said the Professor severely.

'Personally, that's where I think you are wrong, Professor. We—'

'Would it not be better if we ran on?' broke in Gustav.

'I'm not doing any more running,' stated Ginger emphatically. 'Biggles said meet him here, so here I stay. I'm tired, anyway.'

'Yes, I'll bet you are,' said Algy quietly, looking at Ginger, whose eyes were heavy for want of sleep.

The figures could no longer be seen on the ridge. The rustle of bushes on the far side of the trees indicated plainly where they were.

'It looks as if we shall have to fight for it,' said Algy calmly. 'Keep together, everybody, or we shall be plugging each other in the dark.'

There was a soft pattering among the dry leaves under the trees. It stopped abruptly. A dog growled.

CHAPTER XIV

Biggles Goes to Prenzel

When Biggles had left the others after seeing Algy's machine take off, he knew what he was going to do – or, rather, what he was going to try to do. Searching his brains for another means of escape, it was only natural that he should dwell first on the chances of getting an aeroplane. There was, he knew, an air force in Lucrania, but, never having been concerned with it, he could not recall where the military aerodromes were located; nor had he any means of finding out. Then, suddenly, he remembered that there was a regular service operated by Planet Airways, running between Prenzel and Croydon, via Hamburg. A passenger machine left each terminus at nine in the morning, and a mail plane at twelve midnight. As soon as this thought occurred to him his mind was made up. Somehow – he did not know how – he would use the mail plane. There was just a chance that he might recognize the pilot, in which case he would endeavour to enlist his services by telling him frankly what the position was; but whatever happened he would use the mail plane, even if he had to purloin it. Prenzel was about forty miles away, which meant that he would have to return to the car which they had abandoned in the wood. There was no other way of getting to Prenzel before the machine left.

It was with the project still fluid in his mind that Biggles told Ginger of his intention of leaving the party. The revelation of his plan would, he knew, involve lengthy explanations, possibly a long debate, and as every minute was precious it was for this reason that he departed hurriedly without divulging the details.

Stopping occasionally to listen, he got back without incident to the place where the car had been left. It was still there. The road, or as much as he could see of it, was deserted. Before getting into the car he kicked off the 'G.B.' plate with his heel, and picking up a handful of moist earth rubbed it over the number-plate so as almost to obliterate the registration letters. Then he started the car, and backed, not without difficulty, to the road. Putting his pistol on the seat beside him, he sped down the road in the direction of the capital city of Lucrania.

He had not gone many miles before he was provided with proof of how far he had been right when he had said that the police would be on the look-out for the Morris. Going through the village of Garenwald a red lamp was waved in front of him. He could just discern two uniformed figures behind it. He did not stop. On the contrary he slammed the palm of his hand on the electric horn, and at the same time pressed his foot on the accelerator. He smiled grimly as the red light fell into the road and the two figures flung themselves aside. He felt his mudguard graze one. Instinctively he bent low over the steering-wheel; and it was a good thing that he did, for a bullet ripped through the coachwork behind him and bored a neat round hole through the windscreen just over his head.

He did not turn, but went straight down on the main road that led to Prenzel. He was tempted to leave it and take to secondary roads, and he would have done so had he known the country better; but he dared not run the risk of losing his way. So he raced on, glancing behind him at frequent intervals to see if there were any signs of pursuit.

Five minutes later, on a long straight piece of road, he saw behind him the blazing headlights of another car, following at a speed which told him that he was the object of it, for the needle of his own speedometer was over the sixty mark.

For the next two or three minutes he had to concentrate on the road, for there were several bends, but when he looked behind again he saw to his annoyance that the following car had lessened the gap between them. It was obvious that it must presently overtake him if he did nothing to prevent it. Ahead were the lights of a small town, and his common sense told him that he could not hope to get through it without trouble, for the police at Garenwald would have telephoned to their colleagues along the road the news that the 'wanted' car was coming in their direction.

A knowledge of continental road signs now stood him in good stead. His headlights flashed on one. It was a small black locomotive against a white background; below, a number of red lines had been drawn round the upright post. The sign warned him that he was approaching a level crossing; four red lines told him that it was two hundred metres ahead. Knowing that the chances were that it would be closed against him, he switched off his lights and swung down a side turning to the left; he groped his way along it until he came to a turning on the right, which once more took him in the direction of the town. Watching the road he had just left he saw the headlights of the pursuing car flash past the side turning, and knew that it would be suicidal to go on in the Morris. However, ready to jump out at an instant's notice, he clung to it for the time being, and so reached the town. A few cars were standing against the pavement on either side of the road, and he was about to attempt to exchange his own for one of them when he saw something that suited him even better. A short distance down the street was a cinema, with a car park adjacent. In it were perhaps forty or fifty cars.

He drove straight in, took his car to the place indicated by the attendant who came forward, and then made a pretence of arranging something inside the car until the man had gone. Putting his automatic in his pocket, and satisfied that all was clear, he selected a big car of unknown make, and, after a swift glance around, tried the door handle. It was locked. Three more cars he tried in turn before he found one which had carelessly been left open by its owner. It was a big car, and again of a make unknown to him, but he did not trouble about that. He got in, started the engine, and made slowly towards the exit. Out of the corner of his eye he saw the car-park attendant running towards him, waving an arm; but he did not stop. He turned into the road and promptly accelerated. Relying on his sense of direction he took the next turning on the right, and, as he had hoped, found himself back once more on the main road, apparently in the centre of the town. A group of storm-troopers and local police were standing there, deep in earnest conversation; they glanced at the approaching car, and then, to Biggles's infinite relief, resumed their conversation. He went on towards Prenzel, driving carefully until he reached the outskirts of the town.

He was just congratulating himself on having got clear when he saw in front of him two policemen in the act of putting a pole across the road; they had just laid it on the ground, preparatory to placing it on two trestles, one on each pavement. Seeing the car coming they paused in what they were doing. One raised a hand.

'You're just too late,' muttered Biggles, as he screeched his horn and put his foot down on the accelerator. The policemen leapt aside as the car bore down on them, and Biggles settled down into his seat as he saw an open road ahead. A signpost told him that he was now only twenty-two kilometres from Prenzel. He had never been to the airport, but he knew that it was four or five miles out of the city, and on the western side, for easy communication with the capitals of western Europe. He was now travelling north-east, so he reckoned that only about twelve miles separated him from his objective. He covered six of these at racing speed, and then saw another village ahead. Had there been a side turning he would have avoided the village, but there was none, so he could only go on; but he slowed down, staring through the windscreen for the police patrol which he felt certain would be there.

At the entrance to the village street he saw what he was afraid he might find – a barricade. As far as he could make out it comprised, as had the previous one, a round pole placed across the road, each end resting on a trestle. There was a small group of people on either side. His headlights flashed on the metal buttons of police and stormtroopers.

There was no question of stopping. It did not occur to him to do so, for that, he knew, would be the end of the affair as far as he was concerned, and probably the end of him, too; he was still cruising at about forty miles an hour, but the speed-indicator needle swung upwards as his foot came down on the accelerator – and stayed there. His hooter wailed a warning of his intentions.

Then he gripped the steering-wheel with both hands. His lips parted in a cold, mirthless smile.

At the last moment before the impact he saw the spectators fling themselves aside as they realized what he was going to do. With a splintering crash the radiator hit the pole. The car swerved violently, mounted the kerb, grazed a shop front – tearing off a headlight – and ricocheted back on to the road. Biggles clung to the wheel. To make matters more difficult for him the second headlamp had been knocked sideways, but did not break off; strangely enough the light remained on, but, blazing at an angle of forty-five degrees from its correct position, gave him a false sense of direction, with the result that he knocked an approaching policeman off his bicycle before he could switch the light off and get back on the crown of the road. Two shots hit the back of the car as he roared on down the street, hooting frantically, for there were several people about, and he had no wish to kill an innocent party. Possibly because of the danger of hitting civilians, no more shots were fired.

Still on the look-out for further obstructions he roared on out of the village. Once more the road lay clear ahead. On he raced, occasionally glimpsing a signpost which gave him the direction of the city. Presently he saw its lights in the distance, and he knew that he must be somewhere near the airport. Another minute and he saw the red glow of a neon beacon on his left front. As near as he could judge it was about two miles away. He also saw something else. Coming towards him down the road, but still some distance away, were the headlights of three cars, close behind each other. Looking over his shoulder he saw more lights behind him, and knew that at last he was caught between two parties of the enemy. The road ran across open, hedgeless fields, so, after running close to the side to make sure that there was no ditch, he swung the car off the road into a field of growing corn. The wheels sank deep into the soft earth, but he ploughed his way on for about a hundred yards. Then he stopped, jumped out, and ran on towards the beacon.

Glancing back as he ran, he saw the cars on the road meet and stop about a quarter of a mile beyond the place where he had turned off. A group of figures moved vaguely in the headlights. Hoping that it would take them some time to find his abandoned car he ran on, and without trouble reached the boundary lights of the aerodrome, but was still some distance from the airport buildings. Looking at his watch he saw with alarm that it was ten minutes to twelve. He dared not trespass on the aerodrome both on account of getting in the way of machines landing and taking off, and for fear of attracting attention to himself; he had to follow the wire boundary fence, with the result that it was five minutes to twelve before he found himself near the hangars.

Several machines were standing on the tarmac, but only about one were there any signs of activity. It was a twin-engined Lockheed Electra, bearing British registration letters; on its nose were the 'arrow and globe' insignia of Planet Airways. The fact that the engines were ticking over was all the confirmation he needed that it was the machine he hoped to find – the London-bound mail plane. Two men were standing near the wheels, holding the cords attached to the chocks. Another, evidently the mechanic who had started the engines, was walking back towards the brightly illuminated booking hall from which two uniformed figures had just emerged and were strolling slowly towards the machine.

Biggles climbed over the fence and walked towards the

machine. He was standing near the cabin door when the two pilots arrived. Seeing him, they broke off their conversation and looked at him curiously.

'Who are you – what do you want?' asked one.

Biggles did not recognize either of them. 'I'm sorry,' he said, 'but I hoped to find somebody whom I knew.' He dropped his voice. 'I need your help,' he went on. 'I'm a British agent. I have vital information to get home, and the frontiers are closed.'

'Sorry, but we can't get mixed up in that sort of business,' declared the first officer curtly.

'Just a minute – have you any proof of what you say?' asked the captain.

'No, I haven't,' Biggles was forced to admit.

'Then I'm sorry, but there is nothing doing,' returned the captain. 'The continent is rotten with refugees all trying to get into England. We've been tricked before, and we're not having any more of it. If you get to London they'll only send you back.'

'They won't send *me* back,' announced Biggles grimly. 'I tell you I'm an agent.'

'What do you want – a lift to London?'

'More than that, I'm afraid,' murmured Biggles apologetically, 'I've got to pick up three more people from Unterhamstadt.'

'Where's that?'

'It's a village near the frontier – about forty miles from here.'

'I've never heard of the aerodrome.'

'There isn't one.'

'You're not suggesting that I land my ship in a field, are you?'

'That's what it means.'

'You must be off your head. Look out of the way, we're due off.'

Biggles glanced towards the airport buildings. He did not move a muscle as he saw several police walk out of the booking hall and stand on the tarmac, staring towards the Electra. There was a shout.

Biggles looked at the two pilots. 'I think those people are calling you,' he said calmly.

Both the captain and the first officer turned. 'Yes, I think you're right,' said the captain. 'You'd better stay here until we come back, then I'll have another word with you.'

To Biggles's joy both pilots started walking quickly towards the group of officials now coming towards the Lockheed. He did not hesitate. Ducking under the wing, he came up in front of the machine and without warning hit the nearest mechanic under the jaw. He staggered backwards, dragging the chock with him. The second man bolted as Biggles rushed at him. He dropped the cord he was holding. Biggles snatched it up, tore the chock aside, and made a dash for the cabin. It was nearly his last movement on earth; for the first time in his life, although perhaps it was excusable in the circumstances, he forgot the whirling steel propellers. As he ducked under the wing he felt a blast of air on his face, and knew that a propeller blade had missed him by inches. The shock turned his lips dry, but he did not stop.

Before he had reached the cabin door a crowd of men, the two pilots among them, were racing towards the machine. The leader was not more than twenty yards away.

Biggles did not bother about closing the door. He made a dash for the cockpit. And not until then did he see that there was somebody already in the machine. A man in a neat blue uniform, with earphones clamped over his head, jumped up from the instrument at which he had been sitting. It was the wireless operator.

Without warning he hit the nearest mechanic under the jaw.

Biggles did not speak. He pushed his hand into the man's face and flung him backwards into his seat. Then, dropping into the pilot's seat, he pushed the master throttle open. As the machine began to move forward the wireless operator came up and grabbed him from behind.

'Look out, you fool, you'll kill us both!' yelled Biggles.

Which was true enough, for the machine was gathering speed every instant. The wireless operator evidently realized this, for he released his hold. His face was pale with fright. 'What do you think you're doing?' he shouted.

'Taking off – it's time you knew that,' snarled Biggles. 'Sit down before you get hurt.'

'But—'

'Shut up! Sit down, I tell you.'

'Who are you?'

'You can ask the police that when we get home,' said Biggles curtly, as the machine became airborne. 'I'm a British agent, and I've got to get out of the country – quick.'

'Can you fly this kite?'

'If I can't, it's going to be just too bad for you,' snapped Biggles, bringing the machine round on a course for Unterhamstadt.

The wireless operator, after a helpless shake of his head, sat down at his instrument and picked up the fallen earphones.

'You'll soon be picking up some interesting scraps of news on that thing,' smiled Biggles, as he settled down into his seat.

CHAPTER XV

Reunion

Ginger might not have admitted it, but when two minutes had gone by after the appointed time his heart began to sink. Biggles had not come; and with each succeeding second his advent seemed even more unlikely. That in itself was bad enough, but the fact that the storm-troopers would certainly arrive at the place where they were waiting within the next five minutes made the whole position seem hopeless. Still, he did not say so. He could still hear the dog in the bushes; from time to time it uttered a low growl, but it did not show itself, possibly because it was too well trained.

'I think we'd better surrender ourselves without causing further trouble,' suggested the Professor, in a resigned voice. 'Otherwise it will only be all the worse for us.'

'Don't you believe it,' growled Algy. 'We'll give these thugs something to remember us by, anyway.'

As he said the words there came a sound in the still night air that caused Ginger's heart to leap. 'He's coming!' he said, in a tense voice. It was only with difficulty that he restrained himself from shouting the words. 'Listen!' he went on. 'It's a plane. Can't you hear it?'

'Your faith in your leader is praiseworthy, but even if it is an aeroplane, is there any reason to suppose that he is flying it?' remarked the Professor despondently. 'It might be just a passing machine.'

'It might be, but it isn't,' declared Ginger confidently. 'There you are, what did I tell you?' he went on quickly. 'It's coming this way.'

'That sounds like a twin-engined job to me,' murmured Algy dubiously.

'I don't care if it's an Empire flying-boat, I'll bet Biggles is at the stick,' asserted Ginger firmly.

There was a sudden crashing in the bushes behind them, for they were now standing out in the field, staring up at the sky whence came the roar of the approaching aircraft. The commotion in the bushes increased; a shot was fired. It was followed by a rapid conversation.

'They are calling attention to the behaviour of the dogs,' translated the Professor. 'They are now coming on again.'

Algy took charge of the situation. 'Lie down, everybody,' he ordered. Then, as they obeyed, he addressed the Professor. 'I can't speak German,' he said, 'so will you shout to them and tell them that the first man who shows himself will be shot? Tell them that we are armed, and that we will fight.'

The Professor shouted something in German.

It was as well that they were lying down, for a volley of shots rang out, the bullets zipping viciously through the undergrowth.

Algy fired back at the flashes. 'Watch for the machine, Ginger,' he shouted, for there was no longer any point in remaining silent.

'The machine's landing,' called Ginger.

'Take the others with you and run for it as soon as his wheels are on the ground,' roared Algy, without looking round.

'What about you?' returned Ginger.

'Never mind me – I'll be along. Give me the Professor's gun – he won't need it.'

Ginger handed Algy the weapon, so that he now had a gun in each hand. Curiously enough, they had both belonged to von Stalhein. One had been taken from him in the car, and the other Algy himself had taken from the German when Ginger had rescued him. Seeing that the others had gone he started a rapid fire into the trees, in the direction of the approaching storm-troopers, moving his position after every shot. Ginger's voice reached him. He was shouting that the machine was now on the ground.

'Get aboard!' shouted Algy.

Ginger emptied his revolver into the bushes. Then, shouting to the Beklinders to follow him, he ran like a deer towards the big machine which was now taxiing towards them. The noise of its engine drowned all other sounds. An unknown man in a blue uniform was standing at the cabin door when he reached it.

'Get in!' shouted the stranger, who seemed to be beside himself with excitement. 'Your boss is at the stick. I shall get fired for this when I get back—'

'You'll be lucky to get back,' Ginger told him, as he bundled the Professor and his son into the cabin. Looking round for Algy he saw him running a zigzag course towards the machine. A number of men had appeared at the edge of the wood. Spurts of orange flame showed that they were shooting.

Panting, Algy reached the machine. Ginger helped him in.

They fell in a heap on the floor. 'All clear,' shouted Ginger from where he lay.

By the time he was on his feet the machine had swung round and was bumping over the uneven ground for the take-off. The wireless operator was staring foolishly at his hand, from which blood was dripping.

'Something hit my hand,' he gasped.

'You're lucky it didn't hit your head,' grunted Ginger as he hurried forward to the cockpit where Biggles was sitting. He grabbed a seat to steady himself as the machine swerved slightly; then the bumping ceased and he knew that they were in the air.

'I've got Algy,' he yelled triumphantly in Biggles's ear.

'You've *what?*'

'I've got Algy.'

At first Biggles looked incredulous; then a smile broke over his face. 'Masterly work,' he said. 'Make yourselves comfortable while I take you home.'

Looking down the lighted cabin Ginger saw that the others were already sitting or reclining in the seats in various stages of exhaustion following the last few hectic minutes. He dropped into the seat next to Biggles. 'By gosh, we've done it, after all,' he cried jubilantly.

Biggles did not take his eyes off the windscreen. 'I believe you're right,' he said. 'But it doesn't do to pat yourself on the back too soon – not in flying, at any rate. Look ahead.'

Ginger had been so taken up with what was going on inside the cabin that he had paid no attention to anything else. Realizing that there was a definite reason for Biggles's remark he peered ahead through the windscreen, and stared at what he saw. The sky was divided into many clean-cut sections by the white beams of searchlights. He gazed at them for a moment or two without speaking, noticing that the lights were set in a long, straggling line. 'That's the frontier, I suppose?' he said thoughtfully.

'That's it,' returned Biggles briefly.

'They'll have guns there.'

'You bet your life they will.'

'Well, we've got to get through 'em.'

'Right again,' said Biggles. 'We should find this sort of thing whichever way we tried to get out of the country.'

Ginger glanced at the altimeter and saw that they were at four thousand feet. 'We're a bit low, aren't we?'

'I daren't risk climbing any higher,' said Biggles, glancing through the side window on his right.

'Why not?'

'It would take time. I'm going to charge straight across – or try to.'

'But couldn't we turn back? With a light load like this you could take the machine up to twenty thousand, cut the motors, and then perhaps glide across without being spotted.'

'Take a look over to the right,' murmured Biggles, without taking his eyes from the windscreen.

Ginger looked, and saw a number of twin pairs of lights at about their own altitude. His heart missed a beat. 'They're machines,' he said.

'Fighters, by the rate they're travelling.'

'They're after us.'

'I don't suppose they're just roaring around for the fun of it.'

'Shouldn't we do better to put our lights out?'

'Yes – I was only waiting until Algy had tied Sparks's hand

up. I think he got a shot through it. He's just finished, I think.'
Biggles turned a switch and plunged the machine into darkness
– except, of course, the instrument board.

'One of them is getting close; he's trying to work round behind
us,' observed Ginger, who was still staring through the window
at the enemy machines.

'I'm watching him.'

'I wish we had a gun,' said Ginger wistfully.

'The trouble about wishing is, it doesn't get you anywhere,'
murmured Biggles dryly.

'That fellow's closing in. I believe he can still see us.'

'He's close enough to see our exhausts. Tell me when he gets
within range. Maybe I can show him something.'

'How far are we from the frontier?'

'Ten miles. She's taking all I can give her, so we ought to be
across in two or three minutes.'

'Look out! He's shooting!' yelled Ginger suddenly.

The words had barely left his lips when the machine banked
steeply and then plunged downward. He had to clutch at his
seat to remain in it. He lost all sense of direction, and even the
relative position of the machine with the ground. Hardened air
traveller though he was, his stomach seemed to come up into his
mouth.

Quivering, the machine returned to even keel.

'Gosh! If you do that again I shall be sick,' gasped Ginger,
looking around for the searchlights in order to find out which
way they were travelling. The lights were straight ahead,
groping towards them.

'Can you see that fellow who was shooting at us?' asked
Biggles.

'No – yes, there he is. The searchlights have just picked him up. He's miles above us.' Ginger glanced again at the altimeter and saw that they were down to two thousand feet. Half a dozen searchlights were now stabbing the air around them.

The noise of the engines died as Biggles cut the throttle. The machine banked vertically to the right and began gliding parallel with the line of lights. Looking back, Ginger saw that the beams had concentrated on the area they had just left. The sky was filled with crimson flashes, and he knew that the guns were in action.

The nose of the machine tilted down.

Ginger looked at Biggles. There was a curious smile on his face. He appeared to feel Ginger looking at him, for he glanced up and caught his eyes. 'This is like old times,' he said cheerfully.

With the machine still gliding Biggles began picking his way with uncanny skill through the beams. 'Tell everybody to hold on to something if a light picks us up,' he told Ginger. 'If that happens I shall make a rush for it, but I may have to throw the machine about a bit.'

Ginger obeyed the order and returned to his seat. 'My goodness, we're low,' he said, looking down.

'When there are guns about, if you can't get high, keep low,' muttered Biggles. And at that moment a groping light swung round and caught their wing-tip. It overshot, but the operator had evidently seen them, for the beam swung swiftly back towards them.

The Lockheed's engines burst into a bellow of noise. The nose tilted down steeply. Down – down – down.

Ginger held his breath, torn between looking at the jagged bursts of flame outside, and the air-speed indicator, the needle of which had crept up over the three hundred mark. He flinched when something struck the machine with a harsh, tearing crash.

Biggles eased the stick back. Again the machine quivered as something struck it. 'Are the others all right?' he asked calmly.

Ginger peered down into the darkened cabin. 'Yes,' he said. 'The Professor's got his hands over his face. He looks frightened to death.'

'So do you,' grinned Biggles.

'You don't look so good yourself,' snorted Ginger, marvelling at the way Biggles threw such a big machine about, for it was never on the same course for more than a moment. Looking around he saw that the lights were no longer in front of them. A black mass seemed to rise up on their left. 'What's that?' he cried in alarm.

'Only a mountain,' Biggles told him. 'I shot through a pass.' He brought the machine to even keel, but continued to bank steeply, first one way and then the other.

'The lights are behind us,' said Ginger.

'Quite right,' replied Biggles. 'We've crossed the frontier. We are over France.'

'They are still shooting at us.'

'The French will soon be shooting at them if they don't pack up,' growled Biggles, sitting back in his seat and taking a deep breath. 'I think the worst is over,' he murmured.

Ginger put his head out of the side window. 'The lights are going out,' he said as he drew it in again. 'Where are you going to make for?'

Biggles tried the controls carefully and studied the instrument board before he replied. 'Croydon,' he said.

'Croydon!'

'Yes. I'm not landing anywhere this side of Dover if I can prevent it. When I step out of this machine I want to feel good English soil under my feet.'

'The same as you,' nodded Ginger. 'I've had all I want of the continent for a bit.'

'Take a message to the wireless operator.'

'Yes.'

'Tell him to call up Croydon control tower. He is to say that he has a message for X.I.I., Whitehall. The message is, "All's well. Meet us at Croydon about three." Sign it "Bigglesworth". Got that?'

'Yes. Who is X.I.I.?'

'Colonel Raymond.'

'I get it,' nodded Ginger, making his way aft.

Conclusion

That is really the end of the story of how Professor Beklinder was snatched from a position which might have had far-reaching effects at a critical time in British history. Indeed, it would be no exaggeration to say that had Biggles and his two comrades failed in their quest, the result might have been disastrous, not only for the Professor personally, but for the British Empire. Naturally, no word of the affair ever reached the newspapers beyond a belated and curiously worded denial that the Professor had been killed in a motor accident. Only those actively concerned with the rescue knew the truth of the rumours which subsequently leaked out both on the continent and in London.

The shell-torn Lockheed reached Croydon a few minutes after three o'clock in the morning. The passengers found two cars awaiting them. Colonel Raymond was there with two bowler-hatted gentlemen whom Ginger did not know.

Colonel Raymond made only one remark to Biggles as he stepped out of the machine, before turning to Professor Beklinder, with whom, naturally, he was more concerned at the moment. Smiling, he shook his head. 'Good work, Bigglesworth,' he said. 'How do you do it?'

'Oh, just low cunning, with a bit of luck thrown in,' grinned Biggles wearily.

They all went in the two cars to a famous London hotel where Colonel Raymond had arranged for the Professor to stay pending a secret inquiry into the whole affair.

They all got out.

'I expect you fellows want to get home,' said Colonel Raymond, looking at Biggles, Algy, and Ginger in turn.

'That sounds a good idea to me,' admitted Biggles. 'I shall be available if you want me. I'll send you a long report in due course.'

'Good,' nodded the Colonel. 'James, my chauffeur, can drive you home. He knows where you live.'

'Thanks. Good night, sir. Good night, Professor; we'll have lunch together one day in the near future and congratulate ourselves.' Turning, Biggles got into the car with the others. He slammed the door. 'Home, James – and don't spare the horses,' he said, yawning.

BIGGLES – FLYING DETECTIVE

Foreword

Only those directly concerned realised the problems facing those who, at the end of a long war, found themselves in 'civvie street' not only without work but without a trade or profession. Many, who were doing something when the fuss started, had their jobs kept open for them; but there were others not so fortunate, notably those who went straight from school to war. At the age of perhaps twenty-four or twenty-five, with nothing to show but battle scars and medal ribbons, a sudden switch to peace was bound to leave them insecurely poised on the wreckage of the war. They could never recapture the years they had lost.

There were, of course, many cases where war-time friendships came to the rescue, those in good positions helping less fortunate comrades to get on their feet; for no associations are more enduring than those forged in the heat of conflict.

It was such an association that determined the future career of Squadron Leader James (Biggles) Bigglesworth, D.S.O., M.C., D.F.C., although, to be sure, for this his war record was largely responsible. Moreover, as a pre-war freelance pilot he was not unknown to certain departments in Whitehall, having on more than one occasion, when the employment of serving officers might have lead to embarrassing consequences, been useful to them.

What happened, therefore, when his war-time Higher Authority, Air Commodore Raymond was appointed to the post of Special Assistant Commissioner at Scotland Yard, for the purpose of forming an Air Police Force, was natural and almost automatic. The Air Commodore sought the services of those officers under his command on whose ability and integrity he had often had to rely, notably for those duties that come under the broad heading of Intelligence. In war-time, special missions, as they were called, were never easy, and usually highly dangerous. Biggles had often undertaken such missions, and the fact that he was still alive when 'cease fire' blew was the measure of his success. To the Air Commodore he was a Chief Operational Pilot ready to hand.

In the turmoil of the immediate post-war world it is unlikely that the ordinary citizen, busy with his own affairs, gave any thought to the impact aviation might have on criminal transactions. But those whose business it is to know about such things were aware that sporadic outbreaks of crime follow a war as surely as night follows day. They must have suspected that with tens of thousands of war-trained pilots thrown into the melting pot the aeroplane would come into their particular picture to give them another headache. It did.

Linked with crime is transport. It always has been. The life of the old-time highwayman depended on the speed of his horse. In 1946 the new-time highwayman had at his disposal a vehicle that could not only move him five thousand miles in twenty-four hours, but – even more important – could by its very nature cross frontiers, both land and sea, without being observed. Or if it was observed it could not be stopped and its occupants arrested. It was both obvious and inevitable that the aeroplane would make things easier for the law-breaker, and, conversely, more difficult for those who sought to catch him. So, as it takes an airman to catch an airman, the Special Air Police came into being with Headquarters at Scotland Yard.

There is another factor that should not be overlooked. It was certain that from now on the police would find themselves seeking not only the regular professional criminals whose faces and methods of operation were known to them. There would be an amateur criminal type, the ex-service man who, mentally unbalanced by war and unable to settle down, would risk his liberty as much for the excitement of it as for financial gain. And what of those airmen who loved the game and now found themselves grounded? Would they not do anything to get back into the air?

For such a man the post-war laws and regulations regarding currency, travel, import and export duties, and the general shortage of saleable commodities, played right into his hands. The market was there and waiting. A watch bought in Switzerland for £1 could be sold in London for £10. A pair of silk stockings costing a few shillings in Italy were worth a pound or more in England. There were people in Europe ready to buy £1 notes for £2 in another currency. All light-weight stuff that could be carried in bulk in an aeroplane. Never before had there been such opportunities for making 'easy money'. No need to bust banks or knock people on the head. All that was needed was a light plane and someone able to fly it. Well, there were plenty of both.

More smuggling went on, and still goes on, than most people imagine. Night after night in Europe planes carrying prohibited drugs, precious stones, gold, and all sorts of heavy-dutiable articles (to say nothing of secret agents) glide quietly across frontiers – not necessarily to land, but to drop their cargoes to waiting confederates. The truth is, it is almost impossible to stop this traffic. The profits are so high that the top men (who stay well clear of trouble) can afford to dole out large sums in salaries and bribes.

It was as a counter-measure that the International Police Commission, of which Biggles became British Air Member, was formed.

So in the first place it was to combat the winged law-breaker that the Special Air Police Force was inaugurated, with Air Commodore Raymond as its administrative head and Sergeant Bigglesworth as Chief Operational Pilot. Behind him, as his assistants, were Police Pilots 'Algy' Lacy, Lord 'Bertie' Lissie and 'Ginger' Hebblethwaite.

Now let us see how they got on.

W.E.J.

*T*his story tells of the initiation of Biggles and his war-time comrades into the Special Air Police. In it also, in what may be called his first assignment, is revealed the sort of crime with which the Air Police were likely to be confronted and the type of men to whom they would be opposed. No small-time housebreakers or smash-and-grabbers, these, but men of technical ability and organised efficiency who were not concerned with chicken feed but played for the big money. In a word, a new type of criminal produced by modern conditions, able to exploit modern methods to cash in on information acquired during the war. Men, too, with a grudge to work off.

It is unlikely that at this juncture Biggles realised fully what he had let himself in for. Indeed, as he himself averred, he was shaken by the magnitude of the schemes and the imagination shown in putting them into practice. That war-fostered hatreds should come into the picture was only to be expected.

He quickly perceived how futile it would have been for an ordinary policeman or detective – meaning one without a knowledge of technical aviation – to even attempt to cope with the situation. Indeed, as will be seen, it was only on account of his wide flying experience, coupled with a natural resourcefulness that had been sharpened by that most deadly of all human employments, air combat, that he was able to get on terms with his men.

This was his first job as a probationary police officer, and the fact that he found the going hard and dangerous may have made it more to his liking than the routine civil pilotage to which he had expected to return. For him, he found, the war was still on, and another, to become known as the Cold War, was on the way. But he did not know that at the time.

CHAPTER I

Crime à la Mode

The station headquarters of 'Biggles's Squadron,' R.A.F., wore an air of abandoned disorder, like a cinema when the last of the audience has gone and only the staff remain. Cupboard doors gaped, revealing bare shelves; the blackout blind sagged at one end; ashes of the last fire littered the grate; books and papers, tied in bundles with string, made an untidy pile in a corner.

Squadron-Leader Bigglesworth, known throughout the R.A.F. as 'Biggles', tilted back in a chair with his legs on the desk from which the letter trays had been removed. Flying-Officer 'Ginger' Hebblethwaite had perched himself on a corner of it, one leg swinging idly. Flight Lieutenant Algy Lacey sat in reverse on a hard chair, elbows on the back, chin in his hands. Flight-Lieutenant Lord Bertie Lissie leaned out of the open window regarding the forsaken landing-ground with bored disapproval. Biggles took out his cigarette-case, selected a cigarette, and tapped it on the back of his left hand with pensive attention.

'Well, chaps, I think that's all,' he remarked. 'The war's over. We can either proceed on indefinite leave while the Air Ministry is sorting things out, or we can ask for our demobilisation papers, go home, and forget all about it. I must admit that this feeling of anti-climax is hard to take. There doesn't seem to be any point in doing anything. I feel like a cheap alarm clock with a busted mainspring.'

'We shall have to do something,' observed Ginger moodily.

'You've said that before,' reminded Biggles, wearily.

'There will be civil flying,' put in Algy.

'The only excitement you're likely to get out of that is dodging the ten thousand other blokes who'll be doing the same thing,' sneered Biggles.

'They've shot all the bally foxes, so there won't be any huntin' for a bit,' sighed Bertie from the window. He leaned forward, gazing up the deserted road. 'I say, chaps, there's a jolly old car coming,' he observed. 'I can see a bloke in a bowler.'

'Some poor sap got off the main road and lost his way,' suggested Algy without enthusiasm.

'No, by jingo, you're wrong old boy – absolutely wrong,' declared Bertie. 'Strike me horizontal! If it isn't the Air Commodore, Raymond himself, no less. Coming to see that we're leaving everything shipshape and what-not, I suppose.'

'If he's in civvies he must be out of the service already,' said Biggles, with a flicker of interest.

Air Commodore Raymond stopped the car, got out, and strode to the door of the squadron office. For a moment he stood on the threshold, smiling faintly as he regarded the officers in turn.

'What's this?' he inquired. 'An undertaker's parlour?'

Biggles took his feet off the desk and pulled up a vacant chair. 'Take a pew, sir,' he invited. 'We're all washed up and browned off. Apart from an N.C.O. and a small maintenance party, what you see is all that remains of the squadron. Nice of you to run down to say good-bye. We should have departed an hour ago had we been able to think of somewhere to go.'

'Haven't decided on anything yet, then?' murmured the Air Commodore as he sat down.

'We've got to do something,' interposed Ginger.

Biggles considered him with disfavour. 'If you say that again I'll knock your block off,' he promised.

'Well, what *are* you going to do?' inquired the Air Commodore.

'That,' returned Biggles slowly, 'is a question that should baffle the Brains Trust.'

'Why?'

'Because there isn't any answer – at any rate, not at present. No doubt something will turn up, sooner or later.'

'I may have brought the answer,' suggested the Air Commodore softly.

Biggles's eyes narrowed. 'Are you kidding?'

'No,' answered the Air Commodore evenly. 'By the way, you may be interested to know that I'm back at my old job at Scotland Yard – Assistant Commissioner.'

'Congratulations,' offered Biggles. 'You didn't lose much time getting out of your war-paint.'

'There wasn't any time to lose,' was the terse reply. 'My chief was shouting for me, so the Air Ministry let me go right away.'

'Has this anything to do with your coming down here?'

'I didn't rush down to gaze at a row of empty hangars,' declared the Air Commodore. 'I've got a proposition.'

'We're listening,' asserted Biggles. 'Almost anything, bar directing the traffic in Trafalgar Square, will suit me.'

'Good. I've got a job I think you can handle. Suppose I run over the main features?'

'Go ahead, sir,' invited Biggles.

'When I went to the Yard last Monday to resume my duties, I soon discovered why the Commissioner was shouting for me,' began the Air Commodore. 'Before an hour was out I had taken over a case that is unique to the point of being startling. Naturally, even while the war was on I realised that as soon as it was over we should have flying crooks to contend with. With fifty thousand men – and women – of different nationalities, able to fly aeroplanes, that was pretty obvious; but I confess I didn't expect a racket to start so soon; nor did I visualise anything on the scale that I shall presently narrate. In view of my air experience, the Commissioner hinted some time ago that he would ask me to undertake the formation of a flying squad – in the literal sense. The idea was to start with a few fully trained men and build up. We've some good officers at the Yard, but, of course, they're not experts in technical aviation. We shall have to start with youngsters and teach them aviation as well as police procedure. But that's by the way. My flying days are past, I'm afraid, so my position is really that of organiser.' The Air Commodore took one of Biggles's cigarettes.

'Obviously, the formation of such a force as we envisage will take time,' he continued. 'In the meanwhile, a smart crook, or a gang, is gathering a nice harvest with comparative impunity. The thing is urgent, and serious – so serious that I have slipped down to ask you if you would co-operate with me until we can get properly organised, equipped to deal with the new menace. You had better hear the story before you commit yourselves.'

'Let me get one point clear, sir,' interposed Biggles. 'Should we handle this job as officers of the R.A.F., or as civilians, or police – or what?'

'For pay and discipline you would come under the Yard, so it would mean leaving the Air Force. If you were willing I should enrol you in the Auxiliary Police, special service branch, attached to my department at the C.I.D. It would mean a drop in rank, *pro tem*. The best I could do for you would be detective-sergeant.'

Biggles smiled. 'That would be fun,' he murmured. 'Just think how my lads would laugh to see me sporting three stripes.'

'You wouldn't necessarily have to wear uniform,' the Air Commodore pointed out.

'Plain-clothes men, what-ho,' said Bertie softly.

'You've been reading thrillers,' accused the Air Commodore. 'You can call yourself what you like as far as I'm concerned if you'll nab these winged highwaymen. But really, this is no joking matter. If you're interested I'll run briefly over the facts.' The Air Commodore settled back in his chair.

'The thing started three weeks ago, before the ink on the peace papers was properly dry, so to speak,' he resumed. 'From that fact alone we may assume that the scheme was already cut and dried. It began in the Persian Gulf – of all places; and here we see at once how aircraft are going to enable crooks to extend their range of operations. As you probably know, Bigglesworth, once a year the big Indian jewel buyers go up to the Persian Gulf ports to bid for the pearl harvest. Between them they buy all the best stuff. Having done so they return by steamship to India, handing their parcels of pearls to the purser for safe custody. The purser tags a number on each bag and puts it in his safe. Over many years this has become an established procedure, and up to the present there has never been any trouble. For that reason, precautions against theft may have got a bit slack. At any rate, such precautions as did exist were definitely obsolete. The run from Basra to India, in the *Rajah*, which is quite a small vessel, and very old – she has been doing the trip for years – takes ten days. When the *Rajah* docked at Bombay it was discovered that the back of the purser's safe – an old-fashioned affair not much better than a tin box – had been cut out. The pearls had gone – the entire year's catch, nearly half a million pounds' worth.'

Ginger whistled softly.

'Nice going, by Jove!' murmured Bertie.

'But surely no one could unload on the market such a quantity of pearls without the police hearing of it?' muttered Biggles. 'I mean, with such a parcel of pearls adrift the big dealers would be on the watch for them?'

'In the ordinary way, yes,' agreed the Air Commodore. 'But not in this case. Not only were the pearls – except the outstanding ones – disposed of before the theft was discovered, but a check-up reveals the almost incredible fact that the pearls, without going through customs, were offered for sale in the United States a week before the *Rajah* docked. In other words, the pearls were in America within three days of the *Rajah* leaving Basra. The thieves had a clear week in front of them to dispose of the swag before the robbery was discovered.'

'By gosh! That *was* quick work,' remarked Algy.

'You can imagine what a shock the Bombay police had when the facts were ascertained,' went on the Air Commodore. 'They were still searching the ship for the missing pearls, detaining the passengers, when it was learned that the gems had already been sold in America. The *Rajah* hadn't touched anywhere, so the thief must have dropped overboard at a pre-arranged rendezvous, where presumably he was picked up by an accomplice, either in a boat or a marine aircraft. Obviously, an aircraft comes into the picture eventually, because the only way the pearls could have got to the States in the time was by air – and not by a regular airliner. There was no public service running from the Middle East to Europe, and on to the States, in that time. Anyway, no commercial aircraft could have covered the distance so quickly. Moreover, all airliners have to go through customs. It must have been a private plane – and no ordinary plane at that.'

'You're right there,' agreed Biggles, who was scribbling figures on a pad.

'It was the slickest job ever pulled off,' declared the Air Commodore. 'We rather felt that after such a nice haul the mastermind behind the robbery would lie low for a bit. But we were wrong – unless two crooks have had the same sort of brainwave. A week later, the South African Government plane that flies the diamonds – uncut stones – from Alexander Bay to Capetown, failed to show up. This also is a regular run, made only once or twice a year. The plane carries an armed guard and is escorted by a fighter. A search was made. The missing machines were found, crashed, within a few miles of each other. Judging by the line of flight the escort must have been disposed of first – riddled from behind. The pilot was shot through the back. It seems unlikely that he even saw his attacker. It had become a routine job and he may have been caught off his guard. The pilot and guards of the transport plane were also dead. The diamonds, three hundred and thirty thousand pounds' worth, had vanished. We have no evidence that the job was done by the same gang that looted the pearls, but a similarity of methods suggest that it might have been. Here again the stones were sold before the loss was discovered. The South African Air Force was fifty hours finding the crashes. The diamonds had just been disposed of in

Buenos Aires and Rio de Janeiro. An interesting point is that, as in the case of the pearls, the best gems were retained. Maybe the gangsters decided they would attract too much attention if they were sold in the open market.'

'Suffering skylarks! Their plane must be something exceptional, both in speed and range!' exclaimed Biggles.

The Air Commodore nodded. 'You will begin to see what we're up against,' he said grimly. 'Here we have a crook who can transport himself, and his swag, to the other side of the world in a few hours. He could do a job in London tonight, and by dawn be six thousand miles away – in any direction. The police are on a spot. It looks as if we shall have to establish a network of radio-location observation posts all round the Empire to watch for this mystery plane. That will cost a tidy penny.'

While the Air Commodore had been speaking the telephone had rung. Biggles picked up the receiver, listened, and passed it to the senior officer. 'For you, sir,' he said.

'I told the Yard they'd find me here if I was wanted,' remarked the Air Commodore. Then, in the phone, 'Hello – yes, Raymond here,' He listened for two or three minutes. 'All right, thanks,' he said quietly, and hung up. Turning to Biggles, he went on: 'That was the Yard. Yesterday, the pilot who flies the pay-roll from Nairobi, in Kenya, to the Jaggersfontein Copper Mines, in Northern Rhodesia, was shot down and killed. The plane was burnt out. He carried forty-three thousand pounds, most of it in silver, to pay the native workmen. The silver may have melted in the heat – but it's gone.'

'Holy Icarus! This chap is certainly hot stuff,' averred Biggles. 'But just a minute! To pick up the silver – and the diamonds, for that matter – the outlaw plane must have landed. That must have been a nasty risk, in wild country.'

'In each case,' answered the Air Commodore bitterly, 'the shooting occurred over open country, terrain on which an emergency landing would be possible. That wasn't luck. This bandit knows his job. He chooses his spots.' The Air Commodore stubbed his cigarette viciously.

'One thing puzzles me,' murmured Biggles. 'You can't operate a high-performance aircraft without a base, and you can't run a motor without oil and petrol. Where's this chap getting his fuel and lubricant? He must have used a devil of a lot already. Only the big operating companies, apart from the Air Force, carry supplies on that scale. What have the airports to say about this? Haven't they seen the plane?'

'We've checked up,' asserted the Air Commodore. 'None of them has seen a strange plane. The queer thing is, oil and petrol are still under the control of the Allied Nations. A certificate is needed to buy a large quantity. None has been released to an unauthorised person. Certainly none has been sold.'

'Hm. This gets curiouser and curiouser,' murmured Biggles. 'Obviously, the chap is getting juice somewhere. If we could locate the spot we should be on his track.'

'How are you going to locate it?' inquired the Air Commodore, a trifle sarcastically. 'It might be anywhere between the North Pole and the South Sea Islands.'

'It certainly isn't easy to know where to start looking,' agreed Biggles.

'Personally, I haven't an idea,' confessed the Air Commodore.

Biggles raised his eyebrows. 'So you ask me? What do you think I can do about it? I'm no magician.'

'You're a technical expert on aviation as well as a pilot, and only a man with those qualifications has any hope of catching up with this bandit on wings,' declared the Air Commodore. 'Moreover, when you set about a thing seriously you have a knack of getting to the gristle, sooner or later. With all your experience, if anyone can do the job, it's you. As an inducement I can tell you that the insurance companies, who are getting worried, are offering a reward of ten thousand pounds for the information leading to the conviction of this crook, plus ten per cent of the value of the gems or money recovered.'

'Should we be eligible for that – as official policemen?' asked Biggles shrewdly.

'I'll put it in the contract if you like.'

Biggles's face broke into a smile. 'That does make a difference,' he admitted. Turning to the others, 'How do you feel about it?'

'Top hole – absolutely top hole,' assented Bertie warmly.

'I don't think you need consult Algy and Ginger,' the Air Commodore told Biggles. 'Where you go they'll go. It's up to you.'

'All right, sir, I'll have a shot at it,' decided Biggles. 'Our enlistment into the police force will only be temporary, of course. There's a question I'd like to ask – an obvious one. I assume no one has seen this mystery plane, otherwise you'd have mentioned it?'

'We've made inquiries, but so far we've had only one report – and that isn't very promising. Of course, several people must have seen the machine, unless it was flying at a tremendous height; but how could we contact them? With so many aircraft in the sky the average man barely troubles to glance up when one goes over. The report I spoke about reached us in a curious way. On a ship, a collier, outward bound from Cardiff to Montevideo, there happened to be a man who *was* interested in aircraft. He was the first officer. During the war he served in the R.N.V.R. as a plane spotter. On the day following the shooting down of the diamond plane – which, of course, this chap knew nothing about – he was on deck when the sound of an aircraft made him look up ... sort of semi-professional interest, I suppose. He was just in time to see a plane, travelling at high speed, pass across a break in the clouds. He could not identify it, and this so worried him that to satisfy his curiosity he radioed the Air Ministry asking them to identify the aircraft. From his description the design must have been very unorthodox – so unusual that the Air Ministry couldn't identify it either. According to this man's description the machine had no fuselage. It was a twin-engined job, the two power eggs projecting far in the front of the nacelle. This nacelle was tapered down aft to a single boom which carried the tail unit. The fin was exceptionally long, and narrow. It began halfway down the boom, and ended in a balanced rudder that was almost a perfect oval. That's all. It might have been the mystery plane, or an experimental job that we know nothing about.'

'Queer arrangement,' murmured Biggles. 'I'll bear it in mind. By the way, what are we going to do for aircraft?'

'The Air Force has more machines than it needs at the moment, so you can help yourself. I've already fixed that up with the Air Minister. He will provide us with documents that will enable you to refuel at any R.A.F. station, and call on service personnel for maintenance. That's a temporary arrangement. The police will need an air force of their own. I'm busy on that now. For the moment we have been allocated a hangar at Croydon, so you'd better regard that as your base. I don't suppose I shall see much of you, but officially, your headquarters will be at the Yard, so I'll fix you up with an office.'

Ginger grinned. 'Imagine me, a copper!'

The Air Commodore rose. 'Go and see what you can cop,' he invited. 'Now I must be getting back. I'd like you to make a start as soon as possible, otherwise the regular operating companies will set up a scream. The public may jib at flying in machines that are liable to be shot down, and if they did we could hardly blame them. Good-bye for the present. Come and see me when you check in at the Yard.'

The Air Commodore went out to his car.

CHAPTER II

Purely Technical

Biggles sat for some minutes deep in thought, watching the grey thread of smoke that rose from his cigarette to the ceiling.

'There's one point about this Raymond didn't mention,' he said slowly. 'You'll notice that these jobs were directed against British concerns. The *Rajah* is a British ship, so the pearls would be insured with a British company. The diamonds were the property of the South African Government. Jaggersfontein Mining Concession, Limited, is a British company. Why pick on Britain? – or was that just a fluke? After all, other countries fly valuable freight, but apparently they have had no trouble. That these are no ordinary crooks we can judge by the size of the stuff they go for. They think in millions, and they've hit us a tidy crack already.'

'You mean, the bloke behind the scheme may have his knife into us, so that apart from the swag he has the satisfaction of revenge?' suggested Algy.

'It was just an idea,' returned Biggles thoughtfully. 'But let us for a start tackle the thing from the technical angle. That's our only advantage over the regular police. I can well understand that they don't know where to begin on a case like this. Normally, they rely largely on the type and method of the crime to give

421

them a slant on the cracksman. But the man pulling these jobs doesn't come into the category of the common thief. He may not even have a police record. After all, think of the qualifications he must hold. He must be a first-class pilot, navigator, and mechanic.'

'A lot of fellows hold those qualifications today,' reminded Ginger.

'True enough,' agreed Biggles. 'But they do at least limit the possibilities. Men with those qualifications can earn good money. Most men turn crook when they can't pick up cash any other way. Why should this chap go off the rails? It comes back to the point I made just now. There is more behind this than mere money. The chap made a fortune out of his first crack – the pearls. Why does he go on?' Biggles lit another cigarette.

'We can line up one or two facts right away,' he resumed. 'One. This bloke has a base aerodrome. Two, it is hidden away in some remote place beyond the view of possible spectators. Remember, after a machine has taken off, while it is climbing for height, it can be seen from a long way round. Three, the chap has access to a considerable quantity of petrol and oil. He isn't getting it from a public airport, so he must have a private dump. We may assume that the landing-ground is near the dump – or vice versa.'

'And the dump might be anywhere on the face of the globe,' put in Algy cynically.

'I don't altogether agree with you there,' argued Biggles. 'Here again there are certain limitations – but we'll come back to that presently. I'm most interested in the aircraft. Forget the description of the unidentified plane reported by that sailor and run over those you know; by a process of elimination you'll soon see that there aren't many machines with the speed, range, and adaptability of this particular kite, which can hop from the Middle East to North America and from South Africa to South America. The plane may, or may not, have landed in America. It might have dropped the swag to an accomplice and flown straight back to its base. Much would depend, of course, on where it started from, but I can only think of two machines with such a performance.'

Algy stepped in. 'Our latest long-distance fighter, the Spur, which was just going into production when the war ended, has an outstanding range, so they say.'

'That's one of the two I had in mind,' acknowledged Biggles. 'But there is only one Spur, and that's still under test. Had it been pinched we should have heard about it. Apart from that, I visualise something larger, because there is reason to suppose that at least two or three men are engaged in this racket.'

'The Spur is a two-seater,' Algy pointed out.

'I know,' answered Biggles, 'but in this racket several specialised jobs are involved. First, there is the crew, although I admit that the pilot, navigator, and mechanic might be one man. It takes more than one to handle a heavy engine, though; I should say there are at least two airmen. Then there must be someone who knows the jewel trade pretty well. Not only would such a man be needed to dispose of the gems, but only a fellow who has had some association with the precious stone business would know about the pearl harvest in the Persian Gulf, and the times and the method of transporting diamonds from Alexander Bay to Capetown. Then what about the safe in the *Rajah*? The back was cut out. It may have been an old safe, but that job couldn't have been done with a pair of pliers. It sounds more like the work of a professional crook, one who has handled safes before.'

'These people may be using more than one aircraft,' suggested

Ginger. 'There is certainly a fighter, or a machine fitted with guns, in the party. Having done a job, say, in Africa, there would be no point in carrying guns and ammunition all the way to America. A transport plane could do that – unless the fighter returned to its base and dismantled its military equipment before going on to the States.'

Biggles nodded. 'There may be something in that,' he assented. 'In fact, that theory hooks up with the other machine – or rather, machines – I had in mind. Just before the war ended there was a rumour in the service – it must have leaked out from Intelligence, as these things do – that a new German designer named Renkell, Ludwig Renkell I think it was, had two red-hot jobs under test. From all accounts they were something super. One was a twin-engined two-seat fighter with some novel features that gave it an extraordinary turn of speed – both fast and slow. The other was a modification of the same type, also a twin-engined job, in the light bomber class, on the lines of our Mosquito, but slightly larger. They didn't get into production, but both prototypes whizzed through their tests – at least, so our agents reported. I wonder what happened to those machines? I should have thought our people would have taken them over, but come to think of it I haven't heard a word about them.'

'Why not ring old Freddie Lavers at Air Intelligence?' suggested Bertie. 'He might know something about them.'

'I think I will.' Biggles reached for the phone and put the call through on the private wire.

'Is that you, Freddie?' he began. 'Biggles here. I want a spot of pukka gen about those two super prototypes that rumour alleged were under test at Augsburg ... a new bloke named Renkell designed them ... yes ... yes. Well, I'll go hopping?' Biggles fell silent, listening. Twice he threw a curious glance at the others. Occasionally he murmured, 'Ah-huh.' Finally, he said, 'Many thanks, Freddie. See you sometime. So long.' He hung up with irritating deliberation and turned slowly in his chair.

'What do you know about that?' he said softly. 'Both machines have disappeared. At any rate, our people haven't been able to lay hands on them. They say they can't be found. They had gone when our people arrived to take over the aerodrome. When questioned, the workmen just looked blank and said they knew nothing about such machines.'

'Something fishy about that, by Jove!' swore Bertie. 'Dirty work at the cross-roads, and so on. What about the blue-prints?'

'They can't be found, either,' Biggles smiled, a peculiar smile. 'Neither can Renkell be found, or his test pilot, a chap named Baumer. Of course,' he went on quickly, 'it would be silly to jump to conclusions. Several machines disappeared from Germany after the last war before we could get hold of them. One designer had the brass face to admit, some time afterwards, that he took his machines away because he considered that they were his personal property.'

'Absolute poppycock,' declared Bertie, polishing his eyeglass. 'They belonged to the German Government, so they should have been handed over to us.'

'Of course – but people are like that,' murmured Biggles dryly. 'To get back to the point, Freddie said that as far as he knew, Renkell was a genuine designer. He also said he knew nothing about Baumer except that before he became a test pilot he was with Rommel in North Africa and that he was pally with Julius Gontermann, the Nazi liaison officer between Hitler and the Luftwaffe.'

'Surely Gontermann is one of the Nazis our people are still looking for?' said Algy quickly. 'He's wanted for crimes in Poland and in Czechoslovakia. I read something about it in the paper within the last day or two.'

'I believe you're right,' returned Biggles quickly. 'Gontermann would know, or guess, that he was on our black list, so he was pretty certain to bolt when Germany cracked. If Baumer was a pal of his he might well ask him to fly him out of the country, If Baumer agreed, nothing would be more natural than for him to pinch the best machine in his charge – with or without Renkell's permission. They might have taken Renkell along with them.' Biggles shrugged. 'Of course, we may be barking up the wrong tree, but this is worth following up. I wonder where we could get particulars of Gontermann's history and private life? Raymond would know, but he can't have got back to his office yet.'

'There was quite a piece about Gontermann in the paper I mentioned,' said Algy.

'What paper was it?'

'*The Times.*'

'Can you remember what it said?'

'I didn't read it,' admitted Algy. 'I just saw the headline, that's all.'

'The paper should be in the salvage bag, if it hasn't been collected. See if you can find it.'

Algy went off, and presently returned dragging a sack. 'I saw the notice within the last two or three days, so the paper should be near the top,' he announced. He picked up several newspapers and glanced at the dates. 'This should be it,' he went on, spreading a crumpled copy of *The Times* on the desk. He glanced through the pages. 'Here we are!' he cried. 'I'll read what it says:

'No news has been received concerning the whereabouts of the Nazi party chief, Gontermann, against whom there is a long list of indictments. Julius Hans Gontermann was born at Garlin, Mecklenburg, in 1902. He was destined for a military career, but as a cadet he was dismissed for some misdemeanour and went into politics. In this he was also unsuccessful, and was next heard of as an associate of Max Grindler, German-born Public Enemy No. 1 in the U.S.A. When Grindler was run down by G-men Gontermann turned State's evidence and got off with a light sentence. On his release from prison he took up crime on his own account, specialising as a jewel smuggler between Europe and America. For this, in 1930, he served a three year sentence and was then deported. Returning to Germany he joined the Nazi party, and his subsequent advancement may have been due to a streak of ruthless cruelty which first manifested itself during the Spanish Civil War, when he was attached to the Condor Legion, and later, in Czechoslovakia and Poland. In March 1942 he was decorated by Hitler with the Knight's Insignia of the Iron Cross for his work in the First Air Fleet under Generaloberst Keller, and was shortly afterwards promoted to Hitler's personal staff. Gontermann is good-looking, but tends to ostentation in his dress and manners.'

Algy looked up from the paper. 'That's all.'

'Well – well,' murmured Biggles. 'How very interesting. So Gontermann was a crook. There's an old tag, "once a crook always a crook". If he was attached to the Condor Legion in Spain he must know quite a bit about flying.'

'A pukka jail-bird, by jingo!' chuckled Bertie.

Biggles nodded. 'Baumer must have known about his murky

record, which tars him with the same brush – otherwise he wouldn't have associated with him. Of course, there is still no hook-up between this bunch and the gang we're after, but we've got to start somewhere, and the Gontermann-Baumer alliance offers possibilities, if only on account of their combined qualifications. Even if they are not our birds we can safely assume that they're up to no good.'

'Where do we start looking for them, old warrior?' inquired Bertie.

'Suppose we start by eliminating the countries where they are *not* likely to be,' answered Biggles. 'If they've bolted out of Germany, and presumably they have, there aren't many countries where they'd be safe – certainly not in Europe. Gontermann would hardly dare to show his face in Spain, or any of the late occupied countries. Nazis are not popular even in Italy. Yet they would certainly have a definite objective, a parking-place, in mind, when they bolted, and it would not be unreasonable to suppose that it is a place where one of them has been before. In fact, the existence of a suitable hide-out may have led to the flight. They could only know of it from personal experience. But we may be going a bit too fast. I'll think this over while we're getting organised. Let's go to town. In the morning I'll go to the Air Ministry about equipment. We'll also inspect the new office Raymond has promised us. Then I think we'll take a trip.'

Ginger opened his eyes wide. 'A trip? To where?'

'To Germany,' replied Biggles. 'I think we'll start at Augsburg. That's where the Renkell prototypes started from. We might strike what, as policemen, we should call a clue.'

'Ha! Fingerprints and what-not?' murmured Bertie.

'Not exactly,' returned Biggles, smiling. 'Nowadays, even

second-class crooks know better than to make such elementary blunders. Aside from that, it would hardly be surprising to find Renkell's fingerprints in his own works. But we may find something – and when I say that I'm still thinking on technical lines. We've done enough guessing. Let's get along.'

CHAPTER III

The Yellow Swan

The following afternoon two aeroplanes glided down to land on the aerodrome at Augsburg. Both were obviously military machines, although the identification markings were British civil registration letters. The faint outline of red and blue concentric rings could just be followed under a new coat of sombre grey. One machine was a Mosquito, a type that had become famous during the war for its daylight 'skip-bombing' raids. The other was the Spur, a twin-engined, two-seat high-performance fighter that was only prevented from making history by the termination of the war. Together, the two aircraft taxied to the control building. From the Spur emerged Biggles and Ginger. Algy and Bertie dropped from the Mosquito and joined them. All wore civilian clothes. There had been some discussion as to whether they should all go to Germany. Biggles had pointed out that four made a large party, but in the end he had decided to take the two machines, the Mosquito being in the nature of a 'spare' should one be needed.

On the way to the office he paused for a moment to indicate a group of buildings on the right. 'Those are Willy Messerschmitt's works,' he observed. 'Those on the left must be the Renkell outfit.

They weren't here the last time I came over.' He walked on until he was halted by an R.A.F. sergeant who inquired his business.

'Detective-sergeant Bigglesworth, of the C.I.D., to see Wing Commander Howath,' answered Biggles.

'This way, sir,' said the sergeant. 'The Wing Commander is expecting you.' He led the way to a room where an officer in R.A.F. blue, wearing the badges of rank of a wing commander, was sorting out some papers.

Smiling, the wing commander held out his hand in greeting. 'Hello, Biggles. What the devil's all this about?' he asked. 'I got a signal from the Air House to say you were on the way. They tell me you've gone over to the police force, to try to recover some jewels or something. It should be rather fun, if they pay you well—'

'The bloke at the Air House who told you that has got the wrong idea,' interrupted Biggles coldly. 'At the moment my new job is neither funny or profitable; but if I am successful I shall get more out of it than amusement and cash. You see, some people have been murdered, two pilots among them. I didn't know these chaps, but as they are in the same line of business as ourselves something ought to be done about it. I know that murder, to most people who like to read about it, means a gory body in a dismal cellar. Being shot down in an aircraft may lack the blood-curdling thrill of throat-cutting on a dark night, but it's murder just the same. In this case the murderer shot his unsuspecting victims through the back, which makes it worse. I aim to catch this skunk. That's all. Now let's get on.'

'Sorry,' muttered the wing commander contritely, his eyes on Biggles's face. 'Sit down. Have a cigarette? What can I do for you?'

'I'm looking for the Renkell prototypes,' answered Biggles bluntly.

'You won't find them here,' asserted the wing commander. 'They've gone – if they ever existed.'

Biggles looked up sharply. 'What do you mean – if they ever existed? Are you suggesting that our Intelligence people were talking through their hats?'

'Er – no – not exactly,' answered the wing commander, awkwardly.

'Sounded like it to me,' returned Biggles. 'Either the machines exist, or they do not. Intelligence say they do, and that's good enough for me.'

'Okay. Go ahead and find them,' invited the wing commander. 'All I can tell you is there's no trace of them here. We made a thorough search. First thing we looked for.'

'What about the workmen? What have they to say?'

'Most of them had gone by the time we got here. A few stayed on. I questioned them. They say they know nothing about such machines. They admit Renkell was working on new types, but swear they never got beyond the drawing-board.'

'What are these men doing now?'

'Just looking after things, presumably.'

'Who pays them?'

The wing commander raised his eyebrows. 'I've never inquired. It's no business of mine. The works' manager pays them, I suppose.'

'Who pays the works' manager?'

'How the hell should I know? I've never asked him. I've only spoken to him once. He told me they were turning over the plant to light plane production. He's got a machine of his own in the shed – useful-looking job.'

'Then this chap is a pilot?'

'Yes. He served in the Boelcke staffel[1] in nineteen-eighteen. Says he was too old for war flying in the last fuss.'

'What's this man's name?'

'Preuss – Rudolf Preuss.'

'What sort of fellow is he?'

The wing commander frowned. 'Look here, Biggles, the Ministry told me to give you all the assistance possible, but aren't you flogging a dead horse?'

'I've nothing else to flog at the moment,' answered Biggles imperturbably. 'Tell me about this fellow Preuss.'

The wing commander shrugged. 'He's a typical square-head. Prussian, I should say. About forty-five – tall, flaxen, blue-eyed, stalwart type, has one of those aggressive moustaches. Efficient-looking bloke.'

'Where can he be found?'

'Either in the works, or in his office.'

Biggles rose. 'I'd like a word with him. By the way, you haven't mentioned to anyone why I'm here?'

'No.'

'Please don't. You can give it out that I'm a British manufacturer with his technical staff having a look round for likely types to build under licence.'

'As you say. Like me to come with you?'

'That's not a bad idea. You can introduce us. After that, leave the talking to me.'

The wing commander put on his cap and led the way to the Renkell works.

---

[1] The Boelcke Squadron, named after a German fighter pilot of World War One.

They found Preuss in his office, and saw at a glance that the wing commander had given a fair description of the man. His manner, when the introductions were effected, was curt to the point of rudeness, but Biggles took no notice. It was understandable. After an exchange of formalities Biggles asked, casually, 'What happened to the two prototypes you had here?'

Preuss stiffened. 'I have already made a report. There are no such machines,' he said harshly, in good English. 'I am the manager. I should know.'

'What were you building when the war ended?' asked Biggles.

'Seeing the end of the war in sight, Herr Renkell was developing a civil type, in the light plane class.'

'In that case, why did Renkell leave?'

'He did not tell me,' sneered the German sarcastically.

Biggles nodded. 'I see. We'll have a look round while we're here, if you don't mind?'

'The works have already been examined,' said Preuss, in a surly voice.

'Look, Preuss, I understand how you feel about this,' replied Biggles quietly. 'But I've come a long way, and I might as well see what there is to be seen. You can stay here and talk to Wing Commander Howath. We'll find our own way round.' Biggles beckoned to the others, who followed him out into the corridor. He closed the door.

'Bad-tempered cuss,' muttered Algy.

Biggles did not answer. He had stopped before a door marked private. Under the word was the name, Kurt Baumer. This must have been the test pilot's office,' he said softly, as he tried the handle. The door opened and he went in.

There was little to see. It was evident that the room was no longer used. Only the furniture remained. The cupboard was empty, as was the locker. Biggles tried the desk. That, too, had been thoroughly cleared. The only paper in the room was in the waste-paper basket. Biggles emptied it on the desk and ran through the contents – one or two old newspapers, some blank forms, and a few odds and ends. Two screwed up pieces of paper turned out to be bills, both from tailors in Augsburg. Lying together were several snapshots of a Messerschmitt, in each case the same machine.

'That must have been Baumer's war-horse,' observed Biggles. 'That's probably him in the cockpit, but it's too small to give us much idea of what he looked like. I'll keep one and have it enlarged when we get back. Hallo, what's this?'

He had picked up another snapshot, this one a head and shoulders of a saturnine young man in an Italian Air Force uniform. On the back a few words had been written in Italian. Biggles translated, reading aloud: 'Souvenir of good comradeship, Libya, 1941. To Kurt, from his friend, Carlos Scaroni. Escadrille 33.'

'Hm. Baumer must have got thick with this fellow Scaroni when he was in Libya with Rommel,' went on Biggles. 'It seems likely that they served on the same aerodrome, since they got to know each other so well. It may mean nothing, but we'll remember it.' He put the photo in his pocket, swept the other papers into the basket and replaced it in its original position. 'Now let's have a look at the works,' he suggested.

When they entered the machine shop some half a dozen men were standing together, talking; they fell silent when the newcomers entered. Biggles nodded to them and then strolled on through the workshop, his eyes taking in every detail. There were the usual lathes and presses, but nothing unusual. He examined several of the presses. 'These are all new jigs and patterns,' he said quietly. 'It's no use asking Preuss what they were using before these were put in. We shan't find anything here – the place has been cleaned up. Let's try the scrap-heap; there's bound to be one. If I know anything about aerodromes it will be at the back of the hangar.'

Leaving the workshops they went on to the rear of the one large hangar, where, as Biggles predicted, they found the usual accumulation of waste material – fabric, timber, and both sheet and tubular metal. Biggles turned over several pieces.

'Take a look,' he said grimly. 'Nearly all this stuff has been flattened under a press. Why should they go to that trouble? You can guess the answer. Preuss is thorough all right, but here he has gone too far. The fact that he has been to the expense of smashing everything makes it quite certain that he had something to hide.' Stooping, he pulled out a flattened mass of tubular metal. 'Straighten that out between you, and see what it looks like,' he ordered.

Leaving them to the task he went on delving into the pile, and presently drew out a short length of steel tubing that had escaped the press. Then a cry from Algy brought him round. Looking, he saw that the tubing had taken rough shape. It now formed the rough outline of a rudder. The shape was nearly oval.

Biggles whistled softly. 'By thunder!' he exclaimed. 'An oval rudder. That sailor who spotted the machine crossing the South Atlantic was right. This stuff must have been the original mock-up.[1] All right. We've seen enough. Buckle it up and throw it back.

---

[1] Before a new type of aircraft is built, a rough, non-flying, full-sized model is made from the drawings, to give an idea of what the machine will look like, and to enable adjustments to be made, where necessary. This is called a mock-up.

Look at this piece of tubing I've found. No aircraft, even a heavy bomber, has longerons that size. It could only be one thing – a boom. This is a piece cut off it. That sailor was certainly right in his description. We haven't wasted our time after all. One of those prototypes, if not both, crossed the Atlantic. Whether it's still there or not is another matter. Let's see what's in the hangar.'

As they entered the big building, occupied by a single aircraft, a small civil type painted an ugly ochre yellow without registration marks of any sort, Preuss appeared, walking quickly. His face was slightly flushed.

'Hello, I thought you were with Wing Commander Howath,' said Biggles easily.

'He has returned to his office,' snapped Preuss. 'This is not a military machine. It is a private plane. What are you doing?'

Biggles shrugged. 'We've hardly had time to look at it. This is your machine, I understand?'

'Yes, it is mine,' assented Preuss in a hard voice.

'Mind if I have a look at it?'

'You won the war, so I suppose you can do what you like,' almost spat the German.

Biggles's expression did not change. 'Talking in that strain won't help to mend our differences,' he said evenly. 'If you must talk about the war, you should remember who started it. But let us not go into that.' He turned back to the machine. 'This is one of Herr Renkell's designs, I imagine?'

'What makes you think that?' asked Preuss sourly.

'Because designers tend to adhere to certain fixed ideas, with the result that their products usually have one or more features in common. That applies particularly to tail structures. One can tell who designed almost any machine by the shape of its tail – as you probably know. The rudder of this machine of yours is nearly oval. I gather that Mr Renkell is partial to that shape?'

Preuss was staring hard at Biggles. 'Where did you see one of Herr Renkell's machines?' he inquired, with venom in his voice.

Biggles puckered his forehead. 'I can't remember. Perhaps someone described one to me.'

Preuss did not answer.

Biggles walked up to the machine, opened the cabin door and surveyed the interior. He invited the others to look. 'You must admit that the Germans are thorough,' he remarked. 'Take a look at that instrument panel. They've worked in every conceivable gadget. Roomy cabin, too.' He glanced over his shoulder. 'You've installed a big petrol tank for a light plane, haven't you?' he inquired.

'We take the view that long range will be demanded by private owners,' answered Preuss. 'If one has to keep landing to pick up fuel, paying landing fees every time, private flying will be expensive.'

'That sounds a reasonable argument,' agreed Biggles. 'Presumably you're thinking of putting this type on the market?'

'After some modifications have been made,' returned Preuss. 'As usual with a new type, there are teething troubles. The plane is still in the experimental stage. We are not ready to sell.'

Biggles nodded. 'I see.' He closed the cabin door. 'Let me know when you're putting the machine on the market,' he requested.

'Very well.'

'Tell me,' went on Biggles, pointing to a name that had been painted on the engine cowling, 'why did you call this machine Swan, and then paint it that dirty yellow?'

Preuss hesitated. 'It can be painted any colour,' he answered.

'That's true,' agreed Biggles carelessly. 'Well, I think that's about all. We'll be getting along. Good afternoon, Mr Preuss.'

The German bowed stiffly.

Leaving him in the hangar Biggles walked towards the control office. For a little while he was silent, deep in thought. Then he said, 'There are points about that machine that excite my curiosity. To start with, if it was intended for a private owner, as Preuss asserts, the price would limit sales. I doubt if it could be turned out under a couple of thousand pounds, and not many people have that amount of money to spend on what is still a luxury vehicle.'

'The price could be dropped by discarding some of the equipment,' Algy pointed out.

'Then why install it in the first place?' argued Biggles. 'What about that main tank? With all due respect to the plausible Mr Preuss, few private owners would demand a range of two thousand miles. His argument about economy in the matter of landing fees is bunk. It would be cheaper to pay a landing fee here and there than haul that weight of petrol around. No, I can't accept that.'

'What did you mean by that crack about the dirty colour?' asked Bertie.

'It would be hard to think of a more unbecoming colour for a private plane,' answered Biggles. 'It was certainly not put on for appearance. If it was not put on for appearance then it must have been for a purpose. I can think of only one purpose. They painted planes, and tanks, that colour, for the Libyan campaign, to make them hard to see against the sand. Baumer served in Libya. Unless I'm mistaken we're going to have desert sand gritting in our teeth before this job's over. I'll tell you another thing about Mr Preuss's Swan. With all that equipment he forgot something really necessary. Radio. Or did he forget? Did you notice the thickness of that bulkhead? Did you ever know a designer to pack in unnecessary weight like that? I never did. There's something in that bulkhead. I should say it's a radio. Why hide it? There may be a good reason, but the one that comes to my mind is, because like everything else in that machine, it is a more efficient and expensive outfit than the type could possibly warrant. The more I think about it, the more convinced I am that that kite was never intended for the popular market. The original conception might have been – but not that machine.'

'You think Preuss is in the Gontermann-Baumer plot?' queried Algy.

'If he's not actually in the scheme I'm pretty sure he knows where the missing machines are,' returned Biggles. 'Gontermann and Baumer would need an inconspicuous communication aircraft to keep them in touch with things at home, and that bilious-looking Swan could do the job very well. It would be interesting to know, too, who is paying Preuss to keep the works running now the boss has disappeared. We'll keep an eye on this bird.'

Biggles went into the office.

CHAPTER IV

Preuss Plays a Card

The Wing Commander was putting on his cap. 'Find anything?' he asked cheerfully.

'Nothing to speak of,' answered Biggles cautiously. 'What time do you usually knock off work?'

'About four-thirty. It's that now. I'm just going.'

'Where are you staying?'

'I've got quarters in the town – at the Colon Hotel.'

'How about your lads, the care and maintenance party?'

'They live in billets round the aerodrome.'

'Do they knock off when you go?'

'Yes, usually.'

'I see. So after four-thirty there's no supervision here?'

'That's right. There's really nothing for us to do, you know, now we've finished taking an inventory of the place. We shall probably be withdrawn altogether very soon. Are you chaps going back to London?'

'I haven't made up my mind yet,' averred Biggles.

'There's plenty of room in the hangars for your machines, if you want to stay.'

'Thanks. I'll decide later. Don't let us keep you.'

'All right. If you don't need me I'll push along. Leave the key of the office with the sergeant.' With a nod the Wing Commander departed.

'If we are going back to England we can just do it in daylight, if we start fairly soon,' Algy pointed out.

Biggles did not answer. He was staring through the window. Suddenly he made a dash for the door. He did not speak.

After a startled glance the others followed, wondering what had happened. By the time they were outside Biggles was walking briskly along the tarmac to intercept a man in work-man's overalls who had just left the vicinity of the two British aircraft. The man, a small, dark, ill-nourished-looking fellow in the early twenties, saw him coming, and quickened his pace; but Biggles overtook him.

'Just a minute,' he said, speaking in German.

The man stopped, glancing apprehensively in the direction of the Renkell works.

'What were you doing over there by those machines?' asked Biggles curtly.

'I was just looking at them, sir,' answered the man, nervously.

'Are you one of Mr Preuss's men?'

'Yes.'

'So you're interested in flying, eh?'

'Of course.'

'Good. I always like to encourage young fellows who are inter-ested,' said Biggles pleasantly. 'Come on, I'll take you up.'

The man did not move.

'What's the matter – don't you want a joy-ride?' asked Biggles.

The man moistened his lips, and glanced again at the works. 'No,' he blurted.

Biggles's manner changed. 'What have you been up to?' he asked crisply, his eyes on a pair of pliers that projected from the man's pocket.

'Nothing.'

'In that case a joy-ride won't hurt you.' Biggles took the man firmly by the arm. 'Come on.'

Protesting, the man was taken to the Spur.

'Get in,' ordered Biggles grimly.

The man hung back. His face was white. Beads of sweat were standing on his forehead. 'No – no!' he cried.

'But I say yes,' rasped Biggles, thrusting the man towards the machine. 'I am going to fly this aircraft and you're coming with me.'

Again the man's tongue flicked over his lips. 'No,' he panted.

'Why not? Not nervous are you?'

'We – I – we should both be killed.'

'Ah!' breathed Biggles. 'I thought so. What did you do? Speak up.'

The man's breath was coming fast. Clearly, he was badly scared. 'I cut the aileron control,' he gasped.

'Why did you do that? Come on, let's have the truth or I'll have you sent to prison for life, for sabotage and attempted murder,' promised Biggles. 'Why did you try to kill me?'

'I didn't want to do it – I swear I didn't,' pleaded the wretched man, whose nerves seemed to have gone to pieces.

'Then why did you?'

'He made me.'

'Who made you?'

'Herr Preuss. For God's sake don't tell him I told you or he'll kill me.' The man's terror was almost pathetic.

'So you're afraid of Preuss?' Biggles's remark was more a statement than a question.

'He's a man to be afraid of,' was the answer.

'I see. Well, having gone so far you might as well make a clean breast of the rest. Where are the two machines that disappeared from here?'

'I don't know, and that's God's truth, sir,' declared the German.

'But they *were* here?'

The man betrayed himself by hesitation.

'Come on – I'm waiting,' snapped Biggles.

'Heaven help me if Preuss ever finds out I told you,' moaned the man. 'Yes, they were here. I helped to build them.'

'A fighter and a light bomber?'

'Yes.'

'What's your trade – fitter?'

'Yes.'

'Did you help to fit the undercarriages?'

'Yes.'

'Then you'd know the dimension of the wheel track of the bomber?'

'It was four metres. I didn't fit the Wolf – that's what they call the fighter – but it was slightly less.'

'Where did these machines go?'

'I don't know. I wasn't told. I don't think anyone knew except Preuss. He and Herr Baumer were always whispering together.'

'So Baumer flew one of the machines?'

'Yes.'

'Who went in the party?'

'There were five of them. The machines went together, at night. The only people I knew were Renkell and Baumer. Herr

Renkell seemed upset. Baumer flew the fighter, taking Herr Renkell with him.'

'What about the bomber?'

'It has been converted into a transport. I didn't know the man who flew it. He only arrived the day before. I think he was an Italian. Baumer called him Carlos.'

Biggles glanced at Algy before continuing. 'Who were the passengers?'

'From pictures I've seen of him I think one was Herr Gontermann. The other was a stranger, an American by his accent. He— But here comes Herr Preuss. He's seen me talking to you. For God's sake don't let him know what I've told you.'

'All right. You can trust me,' promised Biggles. 'It will be worth your while to do so. Tell me this. Preuss saw the two machines off, eh?'

'Yes.'

'What's you name?'

'Schneider – Franz Schneider.'

'Where can I find you if I want you? Preuss is heading for trouble, so if you want to keep out of the mess you'd better be honest.'

'I live at number forty Unterstrasse, Augsburg. I have a room on the top floor.'

'If Preuss attempts to leave the ground in his machine, I want you to ring me up at once and let me know. We've no time for more now. Get in touch with me at the Colon Hotel and we'll fix an appointment. Ask for Sergeant Bigglesworth.'

'Yes, sir.'

Preuss came hurrying up, his expression heavy with suspicion. 'What's the matter here?' he demanded.

'Nothing to get upset about, surely,' returned Biggles calmly. 'This lad was interested in my machine. I was telling him a few things about it. Any objection?'

'I don't like my staff talking with strangers,' said Preuss brusquely. 'Get back to your work, Schneider.'

The mechanic walked off, looking servile in the presence of a superior.

'Anything else you want to say, Mr Preuss?' asked Biggles quietly.

'No.'

'Then don't let us keep you.'

Preuss clicked his heels, bowed, and departed.

With a pensive expression in his eyes Biggles watched him go. 'A typical bullying Nazi, if ever there was one,' he observed. 'A potential murderer, at that. He sent that lad to sabotage the plane. Lucky I spotted him, otherwise we should have scattered ourselves all over the aerodrome when we tried to take off. Preuss knows what we're after. I fancy there's more in this affair than even Raymond suspects. A dangerous type, is Mr Preuss. He'll watch us from his office. When he sees us repairing that severed cable he'll know his plan for bumping us off has failed. I imagine he'll let Gontermann and Co. know that we're around. One thing is certain. We couldn't get back to England before dark even if we wanted to – and I'm not sure that I want to. I'd like another word with that fellow Schneider. He has no stomach for this job, and he's ready to talk, to save himself. He's scared stiff of Preuss, there's no doubt about that.'

'You told Schneider you'd be at the Colon,' reminded Ginger.

'I spoke on the spur of the moment, but I think I will stay there,' answered Biggles. 'We'll get the Spur into one of the empty hangars and repair the damage. Algy, you'd better have a good look round your machine, too. I've got a little job for you and Bertie.'

'Have you, by Jove?' murmured Bertie. 'What is it?'

'I want you to take a quick trip to the Persian Gulf,' answered Biggles casually.

Algy started. 'To *where?*'

'You heard me.'

'What's the idea?'

Biggles lit a cigarette. 'Because it's the thing to do,' he went on, smiling faintly. 'If murder novels and cinema thrillers are to be believed, the first thing the best detectives do is to visit the scene of the crime. The first crime of our series was the pearl robbery in the Persian Gulf. I didn't rush straight off there, but had we drawn a blank here I should have had a look round. We now have something definite to look for. Somehow – it doesn't matter how – the man who pinched the pearls left the *Rajah* and reached the coast, where a plane must have been waiting to take the swag to America. Naturally, the plane would wait on the side of the Gulf nearest to America. That's Arabia. I doubt if a plane could land on the other side, the Persian side, anyway, because it's mostly cliff and rock. The Arabian coast is flat sand. You could put a machine down almost anywhere, but you couldn't do it without leaving wheel marks.'

'But just a minute, old boy,' put in Bertie. 'If Baumer is as smart as he seems to be, he might have erased the tracks after he landed.'

'So he might,' agreed Biggles. 'But he'd be a thundering clever man to erase the tracks he made taking off. The machine took off again after picking up the pearl thief.'

Bertie made a gesture of disgust. 'What a bally idiot I am. Never thought of that, by jingo. You're absolutely right.'

'As I was saying,' went on Biggles, 'unless there has been a sand-storm, somewhere along that coast there are wheel tracks. There's no likelihood of their being obliterated by traffic because there isn't any traffic. It's Arab country, and most of the Arabs are in the towns – and there aren't many towns, anyway. I don't suppose anyone walks that coast once in a blue moon. I want you to go down and find the tracks. Cruise along the coast, low. On that unbroken sand, tyre marks should stand out like tank traps. Having found what you're looking for, land, measure the wheel tracks carefully, and then come home. Those tracks can tell us a lot, which is why I asked Schneider about them. He says the wheel track of the Renkell bomber – or, rather, transport – is four metres. That's a trifle over thirteen feet – thirteen feet one and a half inches, to be precise, if I haven't forgotten my arithmetic. If you find two grooves in the sand thirteen feet apart we shall know where the Gontermann-Baumer syndicate went when it bolted from here, and why. You've a longish hop in front of you – close on three thousand miles the way you'll have to go – so you'd better get cracking. If I were you I'd go via Malta and Alexandria, so that you can pick up petrol at R.A.F. stations. By taking turns at the controls you ought to be able to run right through. You should be at Basra, at the head of the Gulf, about dawn. Have a rest and a bite while the boys are servicing the machine, then go on. Unless you get a signal from me at Alex or Malta on the way back, go straight home to Croydon. Unless something happens in the meantime I shall be there myself by then.'

Algy nodded. 'Okay. We'll get off right away. Watch your step with Preuss. He's a nasty piece of work. Come on, Bertie.'

They went out, leaving Biggles and Ginger alone.

'You get busy on that repair job,' ordered Biggles. 'I'll ring Howath and ask him to mount a guard over the aircraft all night. I don't feel like giving Preuss a second chance to try any funny tricks. I'll ask Howath to book a couple of rooms at the Colon at the same time. We'll sleep there tonight. After dinner we'll try to get in touch with Schneider. I fancy he knows more than he had time to tell us. Even if this Renkell gang was not responsible for the robberies the authorities will be glad to have information about them. They're up to something, and it's something pretty big. If Schneider is to be believed, and I feel pretty sure he was telling the truth, there are at least six of them in it – Renkell, Gontermann, Baumer, Preuss, Carlos the Italian, and an unknown American. Carlos must be Carlos Scaroni, Baumer's pal, the chap who inscribed the photograph we found in Baumer's office. But how an American comes into this is a puzzler.'

'And that isn't the only thing that puzzles me,' remarked Ginger. 'How are we going to arrest six men, even if we find them? Suppose we did – what then? Even if they are engaged in skyway robbery, how the deuce are we going to prove it? If we found them tomorrow what evidence should we have against them? How are you going to get evidence? How can you prove that a plane went to any particular place, when it leaves no trail in the air?'

'The ideal thing would be to catch them red-handed at something,' returned Biggles thoughtfully.

'But in that case they'd be in the air,' argued Ginger. 'You can stop a surface vehicle without hurting the occupants, but you can't stop a plane forcibly without knocking it down and killing the passengers. Should we be justified in doing that?'

'I don't know,' admitted Biggles. 'Raymond doesn't know, either. I asked him that very question. He said something about challenging, and shooting if the plane refused to go down.'

'Challenging? That implies the use of the radio. You can't talk to another machine any other way. While we were requesting them to put their wheels on the ground they'd probably be popping at us with their guns. Shoot first and challenge afterwards, I should say.'

'The whole of this air business bristles with difficulties,' asserted Biggles. 'There will have to be new legislation to deal with it; until there is, we shall just have to use our discretion. There's nothing else we can do, as far as I can see.'

'If this chap Preuss is a sample of what we're up against, I'm glad we brought our automatics,' declared Ginger.

'I had a feeling we might need them,' murmured Biggles. 'But this won't do. Push on with the job. I'll give you a hand as soon as I have spoken to Howath.'

CHAPTER V

Preuss Tries Again

Later in the evening, Biggles and Ginger were just sitting down to dinner in the Colon Hotel when a waiter informed Biggles that he was wanted on the telephone.

Biggles put down his napkin. 'That'll be Schneider,' he said softly to Ginger, and followed the waiter to the instrument.

He was away about twenty minutes. When he came back his manner was alert. 'Schneider,' he said quietly, in reply to Ginger's questioning glance, as he dropped into his chair. 'Things are moving fast. Preuss has had his machine pulled out and filled up for a long trip. He hasn't left the ground yet, but he's all set to go. If it were daylight I'd try to shadow him, but it's no use trying to follow him in the dark. I've done a deal with Schneider. The poor little devil is scared stiff of Preuss, and of this crooked business he's engaged in. He's afraid Preuss suspects he told us more than he should this afternoon. Before he would tell me anything he asked me to give him a thousand marks, which would, he said, enable him to clear off to another town and find a new job.'

'Did you say you would?'

'Yes. It seemed a reasonable request. I told him he could come here to collect the money at eight o'clock; we shall have finished

451

eating by then. He said he'd come. He had something on his mind that he daren't say over the phone but he told me a few things. Preuss has been away twice before, taking a fairly heavy load with him. On each occasion he left here overnight, with a full tank, heading south, and arrived back from that direction at dawn, with a nearly dry tank, looking as though he had been up all night. Schneider doesn't know where he went; as far as he knows, Preuss told no one; but if he headed south he must have gone to Italy, or North Africa.'

'He couldn't have got to North Africa and back without refuelling,' put in Ginger.

'There might have been petrol available at the other end,' returned Biggles. 'Let's work it out. The Swan can probably kick the air behind it at around two-fifty miles an hour. Preuss was away twelve hours. Allowing an hour at the objective he could have covered getting on for three thousand miles. Beyond that, it's guesswork.'

'Where the deuce does he get so much petrol at this end?' demanded Ginger.

'I asked Schneider that. He says there's a concrete underground tank near the top end of the Renkell hangar. The valve is under a pile of rubbish. It was put in by the Nazis – emergency war stores. Preuss should have declared it to Howath, but he didn't. He told the staff to keep their mouths shut about it.'

'We could collar him for that.'

'It wouldn't do us any good. I'd rather Preuss were free. We shall learn more from him that way than by locking him up. Now we know where Preuss gets his petrol at this end, we could at any time keep the Swan on the ground by seizing the petrol – but I don't think the time is quite ripe for that.'

'Did Schneider tell you anything else?'

'Very little. He got on the phone as quickly as possible to let me know about Preuss going off. It looks more and more as if the Swan is running a private communication line between Gontermann and Co. and Germany.'

'Did it take Schneider twenty minutes to tell you what you've just told me?' asked Ginger incredulously.

'No, as a matter of fact it didn't. After he had finished I put a call through to the Yard. I managed to get hold of Raymond, and asked him to do one or two things for me.'

'Such as?'

'For one thing I asked him to get the B.B.C. to keep an ear to the air for unofficial signals. I told him I was particularly interested in South Europe and North Africa. He said he thought he could get service operators at Malta and Alexandria to listen, too.'

'Didn't he wonder what you were up to?'

'Probably. But Raymond knows me too well to waste time asking premature questions. He was a bit shaken though, judging from his voice, when I asked him to query the United States Federal Bureau if Max Grindler was at large.'

Ginger started. 'Grindler!'

'Grindler, you remember, was the big-shot gangster with whom Gontermann worked when he was in the States.'

'But Gontermann squealed when Grindler was caught. Judging from what I've seen on the flicks, and read in the papers, American racketeers take a poor view of that sort of thing. Grindler's only reason for contacting Gontermann would be to bump him off.' Ginger spoke with warmth.

Biggles nodded assent. 'I agree. But according to Schneider, there's an American in this party over here, and Grindler is the only American crook who, as far as we know, has been associated with Gontermann or his confederates. Of course, it might be another member of the Grindler gang, but we've no way of checking up on that. We can check up on Grindler. It's a shot in the dark, but I thought it was worth trying.'

'From the way you speak of Gontermann and Co., although the machines belonged to Renkell I take it you regard Gontermann as the head of this thing?'

'I should say he's the boss by now, if he wasn't at the beginning. Gontermann is that sort of man. He'd have to be, to get as high as he did in the Nazi party. I can't imagine him taking orders from Renkell, or Baumer, or this Italian, Scaroni. By the way, I also asked Raymond to try to get particulars of Scaroni, and his unit, which from the photo seems to have been Escadrille Thirty-three. He said he thought he could, although it might take a little time, because it would mean getting in touch with the Italian Record Office.' Biggles glanced at the clock. 'It's nearly eight. Schneider should be along any minute now. When he comes we'll ask him to join us over coffee. That should make him feel at home. I confess to some curiosity about this item of news he daren't mention over the phone.'

Another quarter of an hour passed. Biggles began to fidget.

'He's late,' he remarked, with a trace of anxiety in his voice. 'We'd better order some more coffee – this is nearly cold.'

Very soon he was looking at the clock every few minutes. At twenty past eight he left the dining-room, taking Ginger with him, and went into the vestibule, finding a seat that commanded a view of the swing doors. Still there was no sign of Schneider.

At eight-thirty Biggles got up. 'I don't like this,' he said bluntly. 'It begins to look as if he isn't coming.'

'Perhaps he's changed his mind,' suggested Ginger.

'A man in Schneider's position doesn't change his mind when there is a sum of money to be collected,' answered Biggles. 'I'm going to find out what's happened. We can leave word with the hall porter that if Schneider comes he is to wait. Let's go.'

A taxi not being available, a horse-cab took them to the Unterstrasse, which turned out to be an insalubrious thoroughfare in a poor quarter of the town. Biggles asked to be put down at the corner, where he paid the cab and dismissed it. Then he walked along the pavement, checking the numbers on the doors.

It did not take long to find number forty, which turned out to be a tall apartment house. The door stood ajar, revealing in the light of a dusty electric globe, a stone-paved hall, cold, dreary, depressing. There was no janitor.

'He said his room was on the top floor,' reminded Ginger.

'Let's go up.'

Biggles led the way up four flights of stone stairs. There they ended. There were two doors, one on either side of the landing. One stood ajar, as if the room was unoccupied. Ginger struck a match and saw that the other door was closed. On it a piece of pasteboard had been fastened with two drawing-pins. He held the match close, to see more clearly a name that had been written on it in block letters. 'F. Schneider,' he read aloud. 'This is it.'

Biggles knocked quietly on the door.

There was no reply.

He knocked again, louder.

Still no reply.

'He's out, apparently,' remarked Ginger. 'Probably gone round to the hotel.'

A horse-cab took them to Unterstrasse.

'No,' replied Biggles in a hard voice. 'At any rate, someone is inside – or has been. There's a light shining through the keyhole. That means there's no key in the lock. Why not, I wonder? Schneider didn't strike me as the sort of chap to live in a room that he couldn't lock.' As he finished speaking he reached for the handle, turned it, and pushed the door open.

For a moment he remained motionless, rigid, staring first at something that lay on the floor, then at a chaos of overturned furniture, or as much of it as could be seen in the feeble light of the candle that stood on a draining-board beside the sink.

'Good God! What a mess,' he breathed, and stepped into the room. 'Careful – don't touch anything,' he said in a brittle voice to Ginger, who followed him.

There was no need for Ginger to ask what had caused Biggles to exclaim. Across the floor lay a man in an attitude so shockingly grotesque that it could only mean one thing. The knees were drawn up into the stomach, and the hands were raised, with fingers bent like claws, as if to protect the face. The head rested in a pool of blood. Blood was everywhere. It had even splashed on to the whitewashed ceiling.

Something inside Ginger seemed to freeze, yet, impelled by a horrid fascination, he took another pace forward and looked down at the face. One glance at the bared teeth and staring eyes settled any hope that the man might still be alive. It was Schneider, although he was only just recognisable.

'Poor little devil,' said Biggles grimly. 'He put up a fight for it, but he hadn't a hope against a brute the size of Preuss. Admittedly, I don't see anything to indicate that Preuss was the murderer, but knowing what we know, I haven't any doubt about it. Preuss must have been suspicious, and followed him to the phone, no doubt, and then back here. Schneider's fears were justified. Whether Preuss overheard the telephone conversation or not is something we are never likely to know, but he must have been pretty sure that Schneider had squealed to make a mess like this. Only a man blind with rage batters another man's brains out. Killing wasn't enough. Schneider's head is smashed to pulp. Preuss must have gone on bashing him after he was dead. No wonder Schneider was scared of his boss; he knew him better than we did.'

'We know now,' murmured Ginger.

Biggles nodded. 'I shan't forget it, either.' He glanced round the room. 'I don't see the weapon, so the murderer must have taken it away with him. It must have been something pretty heavy, a tool, probably – a hammer, or spanner, or something of that sort. Well, it's not much use staying here. We shall never learn from Schneider what it was he wanted to tell us. Let's get out of this shambles.'

'Just a minute!' cried Ginger sharply. 'I think he's got something in his hand.'

Stooping, Biggles disengaged a small object from the fingers of the dead man's right hand. 'Hair,' he said. 'Fair hair. Quite a tuft. He must have torn it from his assailant's scalp in the struggle.'

'That supports the Preuss theory,' said Ginger. 'His hair is fair.'

'So is the hair of several million other Germans,' Biggles pointed out. 'If it did come from Preuss's head it must have been from the front, because if I remember rightly the back is close-cropped, Nazi style.'

'Are you going to take that hair away with you as evidence, or hand it over to the police?' inquired Ginger.

'Neither,' answered Biggles. 'I've no intention of getting mixed up with the German police. They'd probably be prejudiced against us from the start. On the other hand, in fairness to them, we've no right to remove anything from the scene of the crime. I'll leave the hair in Schneider's hand, just as we found it.' Biggles replaced the evidence, but retained one or two loose hairs, which he put in an envelope in his note-case.

'Aren't you even going to tell the police that a murder has been committed?' queried Ginger.

'No. It would do more harm than good. One thing would lead to another, and we should find ourselves faced with a choice of telling lies or answering embarrassing questions. Our reason for being in Germany would come out, and that wouldn't do at all. We'll leave the German police to work it out for themselves. They might resent our interference. I don't think there's much chance of their dropping on Preuss, and, in fact, I hope they don't, because, as I said just now, I'd rather he were free. Another aspect we mustn't overlook is this. If it became known in Germany that there was, in fact, an ex-Nazi gang, operating outlaw-fashion against the victorious nations, the head of the thing would be regarded by some Germans, not as a criminal, but as a national hero. We must avoid that. It's happened before. Robin Hood, who made himself a thorn in the side of the Norman conquerors of Britain, provides a good example. To those who were trying to establish law and order he was a bandit; to the defeated Britons he was the cat's whisker. We'll behave as though we had never been here, although, of course, I shall report the incident to Raymond in due course. Later on, when we see more clearly how things are going, he may drop a hint to the German police.'

While Biggles had been speaking, Ginger's eyes, roving round the room, had come to rest on a small mirror over the mantel-piece. It may have been that a movement had attracted them. At all events, his glance was arrested by a movement; and he noticed that the door, which had been left open not more than a few inches, was ajar. And that was not all. Something – he could not at first make out what it was – was being projected into the room. It stopped, and at that instant he understood. With a shout of 'Look out!' he flung himself against Biggles with such violence that they both reeled across the room. Simultaneously there came a sharp hiss, and the mirror, with which Biggles had been in line, splintered into fragments that radiated from a central hole.

Ducking low Biggles made for the door, snatching out his pistol as he went. But he was just too late. The door was snapped shut from the outside. A key grated in the lock. Keeping his body clear Biggles turned the handle and wrenched hard, but it was no use. The door remained closed.

'Of all the blithering idiots, I ought to be kicked from here to London,' he said bitingly. 'I noticed the key had gone, too. Thanks, laddie. You saved my bacon that time.'

He broke off and stood listening. For a little while there came a curious rustling sound from the other side of the door, then silence.

'He's gone,' breathed Ginger. 'For a moment, that silencer on the end of his pistol had me baffled. I spotted what it was just in time. We should have watched the door.'

Biggles shrugged. 'It's easy to blame yourself afterwards for being careless, but until you know just how far the enemy is prepared to go, it's hard to think of everything. Well, now we know. These people don't trouble to bluff, or threaten. They're killers in the best American gangster style. While we were standing here talking the murderer was in that room opposite all the time. Or was he … I wonder? Schneider must have been dead by eight o'clock or he would have come to the hotel. It was half-past eight by the time we got here, which means that Schneider must have been dead for at least half an hour. Would the murderer hang about here for half an hour after he had committed the crime? I doubt it. Why should he? He couldn't have known we were coming here. On second thoughts I think it's more likely that Preuss, assuming he is the murderer, came along to the hotel to see what we were doing. Or he may have watched the house from the other side, to see if we came. Either way, there's no doubt that he saw us arrive, and crept up on us.'

'But what's his idea, locking us in?' asked Ginger wonderingly.

'I don't know,' answered Biggles. 'Maybe it was to keep us here with the corpse until the police came, and so saddle us with the murder – having failed to put a bullet through me,' As he spoke Biggles crossed to the window, and lifted the blind at the corner, looked down.

Ginger joined him, and saw that the room overlooked the street. A man was just leaving the house, but what with the gloom, and the dark overcoat he was wearing, recognition was impossible. The man walked to a car that stood against the kerb a little higher up the street. He paused for a moment to look up; then he got in and drove away.

Ginger turned back into the room. As he did so his eyes fell on a line of smoke that was curling under the door. 'Hi! Look at this!' he cried. 'He's set the house on fire. That's why he locked us in.'

'In that case we'd better see about getting out,' returned Biggles. 'It shouldn't be difficult – at least, not if he left the key in the lock. The woodwork in a cheap lodging-house like this is usually pretty flimsy. It'll mean making a noise, but, that can't be prevented.'

This confident prediction turned out to be justified. Without much trouble Biggles was able to drive the leg of a chair through one of the thin panels of the door, choosing the one nearest to the lock. This done, it was the work of a moment to put his hand through and turn the key. By this time a brisk fire, consisting mostly of old newspapers, was burning on the threshold; but there was no danger or difficulty in getting through. Biggles used the hearth-rug to smother the flames.

'No doubt it would suit Preuss if the whole building was gutted, because that would effectually obliterate everything,' he remarked, as he splashed water from the sink bowl over the smouldering embers until he was satisfied that the fire was really out. 'I think that'll do. With one thing and another this top floor should provide the German police with a pretty puzzle. One day we may explain what really happened. Come on.' Biggles set off down the stairs.

Apparently the residents of the establishment were accustomed to noise, for none of them appeared, and the street was reached without an encounter.

'Now what?' asked Ginger.

'We may as well go back to the hotel,' decided Biggles, after a moment's reflection.

'What? You mean – you're going to let Preuss get away with this?'

Biggles shrugged. 'I don't see much point in following him to the aerodrome, assuming that's where he's gone. Even if we found him there, what should we do?'

'We could accuse him of killing Schneider.'

'A fat lot of good that would do. When all is said and done, Preuss isn't much more than a stooge. My only interest in him is that he may lead us to the people we're really after. I doubt if we should find him at the aerodrome, anyway. He's probably in the air by now, in his ugly Swan. According to Schneider, when he makes these trips he's gone about twelve hours.' Biggles looked hard at Ginger. 'That gives me an idea. We might have a look round Preuss's office while he's away. If he's flying a compass course it's ten to one he made some calculations before he went – or at any rate, made some notes about his line of flight. Few pilots trust to memory. There's a wall map in his office, too. If he's in the habit of referring to it there may be some interesting pencil marks.'

'Preuss would lock his office before he went,' Ginger pointed out.

'Perhaps,' agreed Biggles. 'I'll tell you what we'll do. We'll go back to the hotel for a rest, and make a start before dawn – say, around four o'clock. I want to be on the aerodrome when Preuss comes back. You see, we've got to find these Renkell machines, and we shan't find them by cruising round the world haphazard. The only man who knows where they are – as far as we know – is Preuss. He's working from here, so here we stay.'

As they went in the hotel the hall porter handed Biggles a cable. Biggles went over to one of the small tables, sat down and ripped the envelope. As he perused the flimsy sheet that it contained a ghost of a smile lifted the corners of his mouth.

'It's from Raymond,' he said softly. 'This is what he says. Max Grindler, sometimes known as The Pike, while serving a life sentence escaped from New York State Penitentiary two months ago, and hasn't been seen since. The Federal Bureau is still looking for him, but admits that it is baffled. Description: Age, forty-nine. Medium height and build. Black hair and grey eyes. Nose slightly bent. Little finger left hand missing.' Biggles folded the slip and put it in his pocket. 'Unless I'm wide of the mark, the American police are wasting their time,' he murmured. 'I'm not a betting man, but I'd risk a small wager that this particular fish is this side of the Atlantic. But let's try and get some sleep. I'll give you a shake about a quarter to four.'

CHAPTER VI

Getting Warmer

At a quarter to four Ginger was awakened by Biggles shaking his shoulder.

'On your feet,' ordered Biggles. 'We shall have to walk to the aerodrome.'

They arrived about half an hour later, and went first to the hangar that had been taken over by the R.A.F., where they found the Spur in charge of two airmen, in accordance with the arrangement made by Biggles with the wing commander. They had nothing to report. From them Biggles learned that an aircraft, presumably the Swan – they had heard it but not seen it – had taken off the previous evening about nine o'clock.

While they were talking at the hangar door Biggles more than once glanced curiously across the aerodrome in the direction of the Renkell works, whence came sounds of activity. An engine of some sort could be heard running.

'What goes on over, there?' he asked the senior of the two airmen.

'We've often wondered that, sir,' was the answer.

'Often?' queried Biggles. 'Do you mean it's a regular thing?'

'Well, of course, we're not up here every night, so we couldn't

465

say that,' replied the airman. 'But whenever I've been near the aerodrome at night someone has been hard at it in the Renkell machine shop.'

'I don't see any lights showing,' observed Biggles.

'I reckon they can't have taken their black-out blinds down yet,' suggested the airman.

'I see,' said Biggles slowly. 'All right, you fellows, stay here and look after the machine.'

'Very good, sir.'

Accompanied by Ginger, Biggles walked on towards the Renkell workshop – not directly, but keeping close against the buildings that lined the aerodrome boundary.

'What do you make of it?' asked Ginger.

'Queer business,' returned Biggles. 'The Renkell works are supposed to be doing nothing, yet here they are, running a night shift. Where's the money coming from to pay these chaps? And why the black-out? I'd say the two things go together. Something is going on in the works that outsiders are not intended to see, which means that it's fishy.'

'Making spare parts, perhaps, for the Renkell prototypes?' suggested Ginger.

'Either that, or they're building a new machine. Anyway, it rather upsets my plan. I expected to find the place quiet, closed down for the night. Still, there may be no one in Preuss's office. We shall have to find a way in without being seen.'

'That won't be by the door,' asserted Ginger. 'It opens straight into the workshop.'

Biggles went on, and after making a detour to locate the heap of old fabric that concealed the valve of the undeclared petrol store, he arrived at the workshop door. Cautiously, he tried the handle.

'Locked,' he said laconically. 'Let's go round the side and try the window of Preuss's office. I marked it down when we were in there.'

It turned out that this, too, was secured, but by climbing on Biggles's shoulders Ginger managed to make an entrance through another small window. He found himself in a lavatory. Leaving Biggles outside he went into the corridor and made his way along to the door that bore the manager's name, intending to open the window so that Biggles could enter. It was locked, but the door of the adjacent room, which turned out to be a small drawing-office, was open, so after closing the door behind him he crossed the room and unfastened the window, remarking, as Biggles joined him, 'Preuss's office is locked. This is the room next to it. There's a connecting door.'

This, too, was locked. With his penknife Biggles ascertained that the key had been left in the lock on the other side, but he was able to get it by the old trick of sliding a sheet of paper under the door and pushing the key out of the lock – again using the blade of his penknife – so that it fell on the paper. The paper was then withdrawn, bringing the key with it. Another moment the door was open, and they had reached their objective – Preuss's office. After a glance at the window to make sure that the blinds were drawn Biggles switched on the light. He paused to make a general survey of the room, and then walked to an overcoat that hung from a hook on the inside of the door.

'This is one of the things I expected to find,' he said quietly, as he felt in the side pockets. 'It isn't the sort of garment one would fly in, so I thought Preuss might leave it here!' He withdrew his hand and held it out for Ginger to see. It was moist, and stained – red. 'That settles any doubt as to who killed Schneider,' he resumed. 'Preuss got rid of the weapon, but until he did he carried it in his pocket. We'll remember this coat if ever we need evidence.'

A quick examination of the room yielded only one more item of interest. In a small toilet attached to the office Ginger found shaving kit that had recently been used. Judging from the state in which it had been left the user had been in a hurry. Biggles recovered a number of long fair hairs from the grid at the top of the grid waste pipe.

'A man doesn't shave his head,' he observed. 'It looks as if Preuss has taken off his moustache.'

'That won't be much of a disguise,' sneered Ginger.

'I don't think that was the idea,' returned Biggles. 'Remember the tuft of hair in Schneider's hand? We assumed it was torn from Preuss's head, but in view of this I'd say it came from his moustache. Rather than walk about with lopsided whiskers Preuss has made a clean job by taking the lot off – at least, that's how it looks to me.'

A close scrutiny of the wall map did not reveal the pencil marks Biggles hoped to find. Nor was there anything of interest in, or on, the desk, which was furnished with the usual office equipment. The only unusual object – not unusual, perhaps, considering the proximity of the drawing-office – was a pair of dividers, which lay on the blotting-pad with legs wide apart. Ginger would have picked them up, but Biggles stopped him.

'Just a minute,' he said. 'We may have something here. I've used a pair of dividers a good many times to plot a course – so have you. Preuss probably used these for the same purpose. The trouble about using dividers is that one is apt to prick the map, particularly at one's base, which is always the central point – for which reason maps captured from airmen are highly esteemed by the Intelligence Branch. If the distance between the points of this instrument are in relation to the scale of the map, Preuss has gone a long way – not less than a thousand miles, for a guess. Let's try our luck.'

Crossing to the map he lifted it from the nail, and standing behind it held it up against the electric light globe. 'Ah,' he breathed. 'Now we're getting somewhere. Come and look at this.'

Joining him, Ginger saw a number of tiny points of light where the map had been punctured, most of them grouped closely around one that was larger than the rest. At some distance lower on the map there was a single isolated puncture.

'The large hole will, of course, be Augsburg,' said Biggles. 'It's larger than the rest because whatever journey is intended it is always used. Those surrounding it are so close that they must be other aerodromes in Germany. Bear in mind that over a period of time several people have probably used this map. The hole that interests me is this little fellow all by itself, way down south.' Biggles applied the dividers, and clicked his tongue triumphantly when the points of the instrument precisely covered the gap between it and Augsburg.

The back of the map was, of course, plain; there was nothing to indicate the geographical position of the localities marked. But these were soon ascertained. Biggles ordered Ginger to go round to the front of the map and name the places where a point of the dividers appeared.

'That should be Augsburg,' he averred, making his first point.

'Quite right,' confirmed Ginger.

'What about this one?' Biggles inserted the point in the lower puncture.

'You're in Africa – North Africa,' answered Ginger in a tense voice.

'North Africa is a big place – kindly be a little more precise,' invited Biggles.

'Tripolitania – close to Tripoli,' said Ginger. 'By gosh! I've got it. It's Castel Benito aerodrome.'

'We're getting warm,' declared Biggles. 'I'm not interested in the other places – they're all more or less local. I don't think the map will tell us any more.' He re-hung it on the wall.

'You think Castel Benito is the base from which the gang is operating?' inquired Ginger eagerly.

Biggles shook his head. 'No. They may use it – in fact, that seems certain. But so do other people use it. I should say it's more likely that Castel Benito is the jumping-off place for the real hide-out. No matter, we're on the track.'

'How about running down to Castel Benito on the chance of finding Preuss there?' suggested Ginger.

'If he follows his usual procedure he will already be on his way back,' Biggles pointed out. 'Apart from that, we can't leave here until we get the message from Algy. We'll wait for Preuss to come in – we may learn something. We could always run down to Tripoli later on. But let's get out of this while the going's good.'

They left the office as they had entered, locking the door behind them and leaving the key in the lock. As they dropped through the window to the tarmac the hum of the power plant in the workshop died away. Dawn was just breaking.

Biggles glanced at his wristwatch. 'Six o'clock,' he observed. 'The men are knocking off work.'

'Aren't you going to try to find out what they are doing?' asked Ginger.

'I don't care much what they're doing,' answered Biggles. 'The knowledge wouldn't help us. These fellows are only accessories; they may not even know what the gang is doing. Neither do we, for certain, if it comes to that. Let's go over to our hangar and get out of sight.'

'If we've got to search the whole of Tripolitania looking for the Renkells we've got a big job in front of us,' remarked Ginger, as they walked on.

'I'm hoping it won't come to that,' replied Biggles. 'When we know where Baumer and Scaroni served during the North Africa campaigns I fancy we shall be on the right track. I'll tell you what. There's no need for both of us to stay here on the aerodrome. You stick around and watch for the Swan to come back. Make a note of what Preuss does and try to get a dekko at the machine. If it's been in the desert there should be sand stuck on the oil stains, for instance. I'll go down to the hotel and wait for the messages. If I see Howath I'll ask him to use his private wire to get a signal through to Alexandria asking Algy and Bertie to stay there pending further instructions. There's no point in their coming all the way back. If I miss Howath, you can ask him to send the signal when he comes in. I also want to get in touch with the Yard, to see if they've discovered anything about Scaroni. I'll join you later. Call me on the telephone if Preuss comes back.' Biggles departed.

It was nine-thirty when he returned to the aerodrome, and he raised his eyebrows in surprise when Ginger told him that the Swan had not shown up.

'In that case I'll take over while you slip down to the hotel for breakfast,' suggested Biggles. 'When you're through, you may as well pay the bill and check out.'

'Then you're leaving?'

'Yes.'

'What about the messages?'

'I've got them. Algy found the wheel marks on the sand about twenty miles north of Bahrain. He landed and measured the track. It was four metres, which confirms, definitely, that the Renkell prototypes are the machines being used by the crooks. I never had much doubt about it, but now we have concrete evidence. The chance of another machine with that wheel track – even if one exists – landing on the shore of the Persian Gulf, is so remote that we needn't consider it. I saw Howath, and got him to send a signal to Alex to hold the Mosquito there until we get in touch. Another interesting item of news I got from the Yard is, Scaroni was an officer of the regular Italian Air Force. Nearly all his service was in North Africa. He was supply and transport officer attached to Escadrille Thirty-three, which fought in Abyssinia, and was later stationed at Benghazi, Castel Benito, and El Zufra.'

'Where the deuce is El Zufra?'

'I looked it up. It's an oasis right down in the Libyan desert. The Italians must have used it during the fighting there. The most interesting thing about that is, if Scaroni was in charge of transport and supplies, he would have the handling of the petrol. Maybe he alone knows where a lot of it was hidden when the Italians were pushed out of their African Empire. Anyway, it's a million pounds to a brass farthing that it is from such a dump that the Renkell machines are getting their oil and petrol. The thing begins to fit together. Baumer had the machines. Scaroni had the petrol. Gontermann, who is wanted by the British authorities anyway, has knowledge and experience of the jewel trade, and crook methods of disposing of gems. Preuss, in the Swan, runs a communication machine between the gang and civilisation, in case anything is urgently needed. Just how Renkell fits in we have yet to find out – unless he's a sort of general mechanic.'

'What about this alleged American?' queried Ginger.

'That's a puzzler,' confessed Biggles. 'As I see it, one of two things happened. Either Gontermann, thinking he could use him, got him out of jail, or else Grindler – if it is Grindler – got out on his own account and came over here gunning for Gontermann – the man who had squealed on him. Having caught up with him he learned about the new racket; so instead of bumping Gontermann off, and returning to the States, broke, and a hunted man into the bargain, he joined the gang, which gave him a chance of keeping clear of the police and making a packet of money at the same time. By the way, I've told the Yard that we shall be leaving here shortly.'

'Did the B.B.C. pick up anything on the air?'

'No – not so far. They're still listening.'

'Have you decided definitely to go to Africa?'

'Yes. I want to see Preuss land, first, though.'

'Okay,' agreed Ginger. 'I'll slip down for some breakfast and bring the kit along.' He went off.

When he returned an hour later Biggles was still sitting in the hangar. He looked perplexed.

'Isn't Preuss back *yet*?' cried Ginger.

'Not a sign of him,' answered Biggles. 'Apparently, either something has happened to keep him at Castel Benito, or wherever he's gone, or else he's had a forced landing.'

'Perhaps he isn't coming back. Maybe he's got the wind up, and bolted?' offered Ginger.

'That didn't occur to me,' admitted Biggles. 'I must admit it's a possibility, although I can't think it's likely. I made a mistake in assuming that he was coming straight back because he has always done so in the past. It's time I knew that it doesn't do to take anything for granted. His non-return certainly makes a difference. For one thing, it means that unless he's also going to break his rule about daylight flying he won't start back until this evening, in which case we could get to North Africa before he leaves. We'll give him a little longer. If he isn't back by noon we'll make a fast run down to Castel Benito in the hope of catching him there.'

'With what particular object?'

'It would confirm that Castel Benito is being used by the gang.'

'He'll see us, and tip off the gang not to use the aerodrome any more.'

'What of it? They can't have many landing-grounds available, and by scotching them off we shall cramp their style.'

When noon came, and still Preuss did not show up, Biggles climbed into his seat, took off, and headed south.

The Spur covered the twelve hundred miles between Augsburg and Tripoli at cruising speed in a trifle over four hours, arriving in sight of the hot, dusty aerodrome shortly after four o'clock. While they were still some distance away Ginger noted two aircraft on the ground. Both were painted yellow. One was the Swan. It was just taking off. He shouted, but Biggles had also seen it, and swerved away to the west, into the glare of the sinking sun, to avoid being seen. The Swan held on a straight course due north.

'He took off in daylight after all!' cried Ginger.

'It will be dusk by the time he reaches the far side of the Mediterranean,' Biggles pointed out.

Ginger turned to look at the second machine, and saw that it was streaking across the aerodrome towards the south-east. He uttered a cry of amazement, for although he had never seen the machine before he knew from its unorthodox lines that it was the Renkell transport.

'By gosh! We've got it!' he cried.

'Got what?' asked Biggles evenly.

'The Renkell! Aren't you going to follow it?'

'Look at the petrol gauge,' invited Biggles.

Ginger looked, and saw with dismay that they were down to the last few gallons. He groaned.

'I don't mind taking risks,' went on Biggles, 'but I draw the line at starting off across the Libyan desert with an empty tank.'

'We can fill up at the aerodrome.'

'By the time I've got this aircraft on the ground, and refuelled, the Renkell will be a hundred miles away,' answered Biggles dryly.

'Then what are we going to do?' asked Ginger, in a disappointed voice.

'We'll get some juice in the tank for a start,' replied Biggles, as he took the Spur down and landed, finishing his run near the control building, adding another little cloud of dust to those that had been thrown up by the departing machines.

As they climbed out, an unshaven man in a faded, untidy Italian uniform, came to meet them. Apart from him the aerodrome was deserted. The buildings still showed marks of the war.

'Are you in charge here?' asked Biggles in English.

'I am da manager,' was the curt reply, in the same language.

'I need some petrol,' announced Biggles.

'No petrol.'

Biggles started. 'What! What about those two machines that just took off? You filled them up with petrol didn't you?'

'*Si, signor*, but they had special carnets,' was the suave reply.

'Is that so?' murmured Biggles frostily, looking hard at the man. 'Now you listen to me, *amico*, I've got a special carnet, too, so trot out your petrol, *presto*.'

The Italian affected a look of distress. 'But the *meccanos* – they are resting.'

Biggles tapped him gently on the chest. '*Signor*,' he said softly, 'I'm on British Government business. If my machine isn't refuelled by the time I've had a cup of coffee – say, twenty minutes – I shall make a report that there is an obstructionist at Castel Benito. If I do that you can start looking for a new job. Now, do I get the petrol?'

'*Si, signor*,' muttered the Italian.

'I shall keep an eye on you through the window,' cautioned Biggles, and walked on towards a door conspicuously marked *Ristorante*.

'From that fellow's attitude I should say he's in the racket,' remarked Ginger.

'Of course he is,' agreed Biggles. 'Or at any rate, he's on the payroll. There's no other reason why he should deny us the petrol. No doubt he would have produced some eventually, but he had no intention of doing so until those crook machines were well on their way. The Renkell, I imagine, has departed for its base, and from the line it took that might be El Zufra. The oasis lies southeast from here. The two machines met on this aerodrome. Was that, I wonder, a previous arrangement, or did Preuss dash down to warn the gang that inquiries were being made at Augsburg?'

'Either way, no doubt he's tipped them off,' asserted Ginger.

'He's bound to have done that,' agreed Biggles. 'How much he has told them depends on how much he himself knows about us. One thing is certain. We're a lot nearer to the headquarters of the gang than we were at Augsburg. I don't suppose there will be anybody in here, so we'll talk things over.'

Biggles pushed open the door of the restaurant and went in.

On this occasion he was wrong. A man, a youngish, dark-skinned man, dressed in slovenly tropical kit, was sitting at a small table drinking coffee. A peculiar feeling came over Ginger that he had seen him before, but he could not remember where. For a moment he groped in the mist of uncertainty; then in a flash, he knew. He had seen the man, but not in life. He had seen his photograph, and he had seen it too recently for there to be any mistake. It was the Italian ex-officer whose portrait Biggles had found in Preuss's office – Carlos Scaroni.

Ginger glanced at Biggles, knowing that he, too, must have recognised him. But Biggles's face, as he pulled out a chair at another table and sat down, was expressionless. However, after a moment or two his eyes met Ginger's. He winked.

'That's something I *didn't* expect,' he murmured.

Scaroni took not the slightest notice of them, which puzzled Ginger not a little, because even though the Italian had never seen them before, he must have watched the machine land; and if Preuss had mentioned them he would certainly have described the aircraft that had landed at Augsburg, particularly an outstanding aircraft like the Spur. At least, so thought Ginger.

His cogitations were interrupted when an inner door was opened and a second man appeared. He was immaculately, if somewhat loudly, dressed in ultra-smart European clothes. Ginger was astonished when he joined the Italian, for they were an ill-matched pair. The table, he now noticed, was laid for two. Then the newcomer spoke to his companion.

'Say, why don't you run your ships on time, like we do in the States?' he drawled irritably.

Ginger stiffened when Biggles addressed the American – it was so unexpected.

'Excuse me,' said Biggles, 'but I couldn't help overhearing your remark. Do I understand that a regular service runs through here?'

'Sure,' was the easy reply. 'The dagoes[1] have got a line running from Rome to Alex, via Tripoli and Benghazi. We're waiting for it, but like everything else in this goldarned country, it's late.'

'Thanks,' acknowledged Biggles.

At this point the Italian said something to his companion in a low voice, so low that Ginger did not catch the words. Whatever it was, it altered the expression on the American's face. His right hand moved slowly inside his coat towards his left armpit, and his eyes, pale and cold like those of a fish, came round to rest on Biggles's face.

'You figgerin' on staying in these parts, mister?' he asked, in a thin, dry voice.

'Maybe,' answered Biggles noncommittally.

'I wouldn't,' drawled the American.

'Why not?' inquired Biggles.

'It's bad country – bad for the 'ealth,' was the cold reply.

Ginger was conscious of a dryness in the mouth. He heard the conversation, as it were, from a distance. For his eyes were on the American's left hand. The little finger was missing.

[1] Offensive slang for Spaniards, Portuguese etc.

CHAPTER VII

Gloves Off

To Ginger, certain things were now clear. The American was Grindler. Of that there was no doubt. The description tallied. And Grindler knew who they were. He had not known when he returned to the room, but Scaroni had known. Naturally, he being a pilot, would recognise the aircraft, a description of which had evidently been furnished by Preuss. To Grindler, a layman, one aircraft was much as another, but Scaroni had lost no time in making him acquainted with the true state of affairs. There was no need to wonder what Grindler carried under his left arm, that he should so automatically reach for it.

When the shock of this disconcerting discovery had passed, and Ginger's nerves returned more or less to normal, Biggles was ordering coffee from a slatternly Italian waitress. Except for a ghost of a smile Biggles's expression was unchanged; but as soon as the waitress had gone he said softly, 'Okay, I've seen it. We're on thin ice, but take it easy.'

Grindler and Scaroni were also engaged in low and earnest conversation. Grindler – his hand was still under his jacket – appeared to be emphatic about something. The Italian looked nervous.

'I fancy Grindler is advocating a little gun-play, to settle any further argument,' murmured Biggles.

'What if he has his way?'

Biggles shrugged. 'I'm afraid there would be casualties. In America a gangster doesn't climb to the top of the tree unless he's pretty snappy with a gun. It only needs a spark to set things alight.'

'That's comforting,' grunted Ginger sarcastically.

At this juncture Scaroni left the room abruptly. Through the window Ginger could see him in serious conversation with the airport manager. The gangster lolled in his chair, picking his teeth nonchalantly with a match-stalk; but his eyes never left Biggles.

The waitress brought the coffee. She, too, was obviously nervous. Then Scaroni, after a glance at the sky, hurried back to the restaurant. The drone of an aircraft became audible. The airport manager came in and presented Biggles with a bill for the petrol, which he paid in English money rather than display his official carnet.

The plane, a Caproni bomber adapted for commercial use, landed, and this broke the tension. Scaroni and Grindler picked up their luggage – two small suitcases – and walked to the door, where the American turned.

'Remember what I said about your 'ealth,' he said, and followed the Italian to the Caproni. No passengers alighted, so they went straight on board. The aircraft took off again, heading east.

Ginger drew a deep breath. 'Phew! When we barged in here we bit off plenty,' he asserted. 'I didn't like that atmosphere at all. What's the programme? Not much use staying here, is it?'

'No use at all,' returned Biggles. 'What in thunder are Scaroni and Grindler up to, going to Egypt in a civil plane? That's a poser. We may as well push along that way ourselves. We'll keep an eye on them, and make contact with Algy and Bertie.'

'It looks to me as if we've sort of stirred things up,' opined Ginger. 'As I see it, Preuss came here to meet the gang. Baumer must have been flying the Renkell. Scaroni obviously recognised our machine, which means that Preuss must have told him about our arrival at Augsburg. As the Swan and the Renkell were here together, Baumer, as well as Scaroni, must have heard what Preuss had to say. Scaroni put Grindler wise when he came in. In short, the whole bunch now knows about us. What puzzles me is, why did the Renkell bring Scaroni and Grindler here, when it might as well have taken them to Egypt – presumably to Alexandria.'

'The probable answer to that is, it wouldn't do to have the Renkell seen flying over Egypt, where it could hardly fail to attract attention. Scaroni and Grindler prefer to arrive at Alex in a manner less conspicuous. As far as the police are concerned they are two ordinary, well-behaved, passengers. We know they're crooks, but knowing isn't enough; we've got to prove it, and that's something we can't do – yet. They made this the rendezvous because the manager here is on their pay-roll. He made that clear by the way he argued about petrol until the two machines were well on their way. Well, we shan't find out what Scaroni and Grindler are up to in Alex by sitting here. Let's push on. We shall be there long before they are.'

They paid the bill for the coffee, went out to the Spur, and took off. Biggles headed west.

'Here, you're going the wrong way!' cried Ginger.

'For the moment,' replied Biggles. 'I don't want that airport

481

manager sending word along to Scaroni and Grindler that we're following them.'

Biggles edged towards the sea, but as soon as the landing-ground had dropped below the horizon he swung round and raced east in the track of the Caproni. Flying high, they passed Benghazi at sunset, giving the aerodrome a wide berth in order not to be seen should the Caproni be there. They went on and landed at Alexandria in the light of the brilliant Egyptian moon. Having checked in and parked the machine they made their way to the aerodrome hotel, where they found Algy and Bertie, looking extremely bored, waiting for a message.

Without delay Biggles gave them a concise résumé of events.

'I've got a job for you two,' he concluded. 'In a few minutes the Caproni will land. This isn't the time to start a rumpus, so Ginger and I will keep out of the way; but neither Scaroni nor Grindler knows you, so you should be able to keep an eye on them without arousing suspicion. I want to know what they do. You've taken rooms here, I suppose?'

'Of course,' confirmed Algy.

'All right. Ginger and I will do the same. Let us know what happens. You'll find us in our rooms. I've done enough flying for one day, so I shan't move unless something startling occurs. This tearing round the world is hard work.' Crossing to the office, finding that there were no single rooms available, he booked a double room for Ginger and himself.

Half an hour later they were lying on their beds discussing the situation, when Bertie entered hurriedly.

'You're soon back,' remarked Biggles, looking surprised.

'Back? We haven't been anywhere, old boy,' declared Bertie. 'No need. Scaroni and Grindler are staying right here in the hotel – and when I say staying I mean staying. They're in their rooms now. We heard them giving orders that they were not to be disturbed. They're to be called at eight-thirty in the morning, to catch the nine o'clock plane.'

Biggles sat up. 'Catch what plane?'

Bertie rubbed his eyeglass briskly. 'I know it sounds silly, and all that, but they've booked passages to London.'

'The deuce they have!' ejaculated Biggles. 'By what line?'

'Our own – British Overseas Airways, or whatever they call it now. They travel in the *Calpurnia*, the Empire flying-boat that leaves at nine.'

Biggles thrust his hands into his pockets. 'That beats cock-fighting,' he declared. 'What on earth can they be going to do in London? I should have made a thousand guesses as to where they were bound for – and been wrong every time. Bertie, you and Algy will have to go with them. Slip down and book two seats.'

'I say, what fun,' murmured Bertie, and departed.

In five minutes he was back. Algy came with him. 'Nothing doing,' he informed them. 'The boat's full. Every seat has been booked.'

Biggles lit a cigarette. 'This has got me completely cheesed,' he confessed. 'All right. There's only one thing to do. You'll have to follow them right through to London in the Mosquito. Find Raymond, and tell him I want these two men shadowed. Cable me any news. Ginger and I will hang on here, in case they come back.'

'Okay,' agreed Algy.

'You'd better go and get some sleep,' advised Biggles. 'Tell the office we all want calling at eight o'clock sharp. We'll have break-fast in our rooms.'

Biggles had a restless night, and he was up, dressed, at eight o'clock, when breakfast was brought in. Shortly afterwards Algy and Bertie arrived.

'The more I think of this development the less I like it,' averred Biggles, walking about with his coffee in his hand. 'I swear there's a trick in it somewhere, but I'm dashed if I can see it.'

'Is this trip to London a red herring, to lure us off the scent?' suggested Algy.

'I've considered that, but I don't see how it can be,' answered Biggles. 'This trip must have been planned before we arrived on the scene. At any rate, Scaroni and Grindler had arranged to come to Alex. They booked to London the moment they got here, so that must have been part of the plan. No, I'm convinced that this was all fixed up some time ago. Scaroni and Grindler don't know we're here, so they're going on with their scheme – whatever that may be. We'll come down with you and watch the machine out, to make sure they actually travel in it. If they do, you Algy, and Bertie, can waffle along to England. You needn't hurry. In the Mosquito you'll be there before they are.'

'Right you are,' agreed Algy.

At a few minutes to nine, from a safe distance, they watched Scaroni and Grindler join the *Calpurnia* and take their places. At nine-five the flying-boat had still not taken off, and there appeared to be a consultation between the officials.

'What's the argument about, I wonder?' murmured Ginger.

'Some of the passengers haven't turned up,' answered Biggles. 'I've seen only six people get into that machine, not counting the crew. Ah! It looks as if they've decided to go without them,' he concluded, as the *Calpurnia* was cast off.

The engines came to life; the big aircraft taxied majestically into position for its take-off, and in a few minutes was in the air, heading west.

'Well, they're on board, that's certain, so we may as well be getting along, too,' suggested Algy, and Biggles agreed.

'I still don't understand it,' Biggles told Ginger, some little while later, after the Mosquito had taken off. 'Even if a few of the passengers had been on board before we arrived, that flying-boat took off with half its seats empty. Yet when we tried to book we were told that every seat had been taken. It's not an unusual thing for one, or perhaps two, passengers, to cancel, but that a dozen should do so strikes me as being too odd to be reasonable. I'm going to have a word with the traffic manager. Come on.'

In a few minutes they were in the traffic manager's office. Biggles showed his credentials.

'What can I do for you?' queried the official.

'Last night we were told that the nine o'clock plane for London had been booked to capacity,' asserted Biggles. 'It took off half empty. What went wrong?'

The traffic manager looked nonplussed. 'I don't know,' he admitted. 'I've never seen anything like it. Occasionally we get a cancellation, but these bookings didn't trouble to cancel. The passengers just didn't turn up, so they won't get a refund on their tickets. In the end we had to go without them. We can't hold up the air mail.'

A peculiar expression came over Biggles's face. 'Do you mean you carry the London mail?' he asked.

'Yes.'

'Was there anything particularly valuable in it?'

'Not as far as I know,' answered the official. 'There was the usual bag of registered letters, of course. Why do you ask?'

'Because,' replied Biggles, 'there happens to be an expert jewel thief among the passengers. He has a partner with him, too.'

The manager sprang to his feet in agitation. 'Good God! You don't tell me such a thing!'

'That's what I am telling you,' rapped out Biggles. 'What's wrong?'

The colour had drained from the official's face. 'I must get to the signals-room and get in touch with the radio operator at once,' he said in a voice hoarse with alarm. He started for the door.

'Just a minute,' snapped Biggles. 'Why the sudden anxiety?'

'Because,' answered the traffic manager, 'there are jewels in that aircraft worth a king's ransom. It's the regalia of the Rajah of Mysalore. His Highness is already in London for the Empire Conference. He offered to lend his regalia to some exhibition in aid of the Red Cross.'

'How were these jewels being carried?' asked Biggles, in a brittle voice.

'By special courier. The little man in the dark overcoat was carrying them in an attaché-case. Look out of my way, I must radio—'

'I'm afraid anything you can do will be too late,' broke in Biggles. 'I see the scheme, now. Those seats were never intended to be occupied. They were booked by the crooks to keep the machine empty. We'll do what we can. The best thing you can do is try to get in touch with that Mosquito that followed the *Calpurnia* out. It's flown by one of my men. Tell him to try to pick up the *Calpurnia* and keep it in sight. Come on, Ginger.'

Biggles ran to the hangar and ordered the Spur out. He was still panting when he climbed into his seat, and sent the machine roaring into the air.

'I'm losing my grip,' he told Ginger furiously. 'I should have suspected something of the sort. It was all so simple.'

'But I don't see what the crooks can do,' demurred Ginger. 'Suppose they get the attaché-case? How can they get away with it? The Renkell isn't an amphibian. It can't land on the water to pick them up.'

'You haven't by any chance forgotten that Scaroni is a pilot?' grated Biggles. 'Once Grindler has disposed of the crew, Scaroni can take the *Calpurnia* anywhere. I'm going to gamble that he'll head for the beach on the African side in order to make contact with the Renkell at some pre-arranged spot. We'll chance it, and follow the coast. We couldn't do anything over the sea, even if we picked up the *Calpurnia*.'

For nearly an hour, flying on full throttle, Biggles followed the flat sandy beach of the North African coast. On the right hand lay the Mediterranean, an expanse of colour representing every shade of blue and green, according to the depth of the water. To the left, the barren earth, still littered with the debris of war, rolled back until it merged into the haze of the far horizon. The haze was unusual, but the weather had deteriorated some-what; banks of fleecy cloud were drifting up from the west. The shattered remains of Mersa Matruh, Sidi Barrani, and Sollum, villages of poignant memory, flashed past below, and Biggles had just remarked that Tobruk came next when he moved suddenly, leaning forward in his seat.

'There they are!' he exclaimed. 'Both machines are on the beach. I'm afraid we're going to be just too late.'

Looking ahead, Ginger saw the great flying-boat on its side in shallow water. It appeared to have been driven ashore at high speed regardless of damage. A short distance away, on the smooth, dry sand, just beyond the reach of the foam that made a lacy pattern on the beach, stood the Renkell transport, its idling airscrews flashing in the sparkling atmosphere. Even as Ginger watched he saw two men jump from the flying-boat and run towards the Renkell. One carried a small, black attaché-case. He threw a glance at the approaching aircraft and then raced on, and Ginger knew they had been seen.

In the Middle East distance is deceptive, and the Spur was still a mile away when the Renkell took off. The instant its wheels were clear of the ground, it banked steeply and sped away towards the south, racing low over the wilderness.

'We've got the height; we ought to be able to catch him,' said Biggles tersely.

'You'll use your guns?' queried Ginger.

'You bet I will, if he won't go down,' answered Biggles. 'This is a better chance than I dared to hope for – to catch them red-handed, with the swag on them.' His thumb covered the firing button on the control column. 'Keep your eyes on the sky,' he ordered. 'The other Renkell, the Wolf, may be prowling about in those clouds.'

The words had hardly died on his lips, and Ginger had started to turn, to man the gun-turret, when above the roar of the engines came the harsh grunting of machine-guns. In a flash Biggles had dragged the control column back into his right thigh, sending the Spur up in a wild zoom; but quick though he had been, several bullets struck the machine. Ginger felt the vibration of their impact. As he grabbed for his guns the Wolf tore past, pulling up at the bottom of its dive, so close that Ginger flinched, thinking they had collided. He heard Biggles's guns snarling, and then a douche of ice-cold spirit on his legs wrung from him a cry of dismay. He clawed his way to Biggles. It was necessary to claw, literally, for not for an instant was the Spur on even keel.

'He got us!' he yelled. 'The tank's holed. There's petrol all over the place. Hold your fire, or we shall go up in a sheet of flame.'[1] He dropped into his seat, and through the windscreen saw the Wolf vanishing into the cloud. The transport had already disappeared.

Biggles cut his engines and turned back towards the beach. His face was pale with anger and chagrin.

'I'm game to go on if you are,' offered Ginger.

'There's no sense in committing suicide,' rasped Biggles. 'I should have guessed that the Wolf would act as escort to the transport. I took a look round, but it must have been in those infernal clouds. He got the first crack at us. Baumer knows his job all right.' Biggles glided down towards the area of the beach off which the flying-boat lay.

'But just a minute!' exclaimed Ginger. 'This means they've got three pilots. Scaroni was in the *Calpurnia*. Baumer could have flown the transport or the Wolf, but not both.'

'That's pretty obvious,' agreed Biggles, as he went on down and landed on the sand.

Another machine, flying high, was just coming in from the sea. It was the Mosquito.

---

[1] In air combat, petrol vapour can easily be ignited by the flashes from the muzzles of the guns.

CHAPTER VIII

Biggles Follows On

On the ground, all was tragedy and disaster, and the hard frosty look that Ginger knew so well, came into Biggles's eyes.

In the wrecked flying-boat both the first and second pilots lay dead, shot through the head. The wireless operator lay asprawl his instrument. He, too, was dead. The courier to whom the jewels had been entrusted was just expiring. An automatic close by his hand suggested that he would have put up a fight had he been given the opportunity. One of the passengers, who turned out to be an officer going home on leave from India, sprawled in a seat, deathly pale, a shattered arm dangling horribly. The steward and the four other passengers – two elderly tourists with their wives, one British and one American – had made their way to the beach, where they stood talking. They were shaken, but unhurt. After giving first aid to the wounded officer it was from one of these that Biggles presently got the story, a story that caused his lips to compress in a thin hard line.

By this time the Mosquito had landed. In a few words Biggles explained what had happened. Algy, in turn, revealed that they had picked up the radio message sent out by the traffic manager

490

at Alexandria. They had found the *Calpurnia* off its course, heading south, but had lost it in the cloud. By following its last known course, southward, they had arrived in sight of the coast, and were following it back to Alexandria when they spotted the flying-boat grounded in the surf.

The story of events in the *Calpurnia*, told by the passenger, were much as Biggles expected.

The thing began, he said, when the wireless operator came into the cabin, and going to the courier whispered something in his ear. (From this Ginger realised that the operator must have picked up the alarm signal sent out by Alexandria. He had warned the courier of his danger, which was all he could do.) The wireless operator – went on the passenger – had returned to his compartment. Two men then got up and walked to the forward bulkhead, to the door that gave access to the cockpit. Through this they disappeared, although a notice proclaimed that entry was prohibited. A moment later there came the sound of a shot. The passenger explained that he was not sure of this at the time; he thought it might be one of the engines misfiring. Apparently this was the shot that killed the wireless operator. Then came two more shots. At the same time the flying-boat swerved. This, the listeners realised, must have been the moment when the pilots were murdered in cold blood. Up to this time none of the passengers had reason to suspect that anything serious was afoot. The first indication of that came when one of the two men reappeared, an automatic in his hand. Standing in the doorway he covered the passengers and informed them that he would shoot the first person who moved. This man, asserted the passenger, spoke with an American accent. In spite of this threat the courier had jumped to his feet and pulled out a pistol. The gunman promptly shot him, unnecessarily firing a second shot into him after he was on the floor; whereupon another passenger – the officer – had flung a book at the murderer and then tried to close with him. But this, while brave, was foolish, and all he succeeded in getting was a bullet through the arm that shattered the bone. The other passengers, helpless, sat still, for which they were hardly to be blamed. Thus matters had remained for some time. The course of the aircraft had been altered from west to south. Later, with the gunman still keeping the passengers covered, the *Calpurnia* had been landed, and taxied to the beach where another machine was waiting. The gunman, who had already picked up the courier's attaché-case, with his companion, then changed machines and flew off. That was all.

'I see,' said Biggles quietly, when this grim recital was finished. 'For your information – but please keep this to yourselves for the time being – the little man who was shot was carrying a parcel of very valuable jewels. His assailants were jewel thieves.'

'Even so, there was no need for them to commit murder,' muttered one of the women passengers.

'To the people behind this affair murder is nothing new,' returned Biggles. 'But we mustn't stand talking here any longer. I have one serviceable aircraft, and although I need it badly myself I shall have to use it to get the wounded officer back to Alexandria. He is in urgent need of medical attention. Unfortunately, the machine will only carry one passenger, so the rest of you will have to wait until a relief plane arrives.' Biggles turned to Algy. 'I had better stay here,' he went on. 'You take the Mosquito and fly this officer to Alex. Explain what has happened, and ask for a relief plane to be sent to pick up the passengers. It had better bring a working party along; there may be a chance to do some

Standing in the doorway he covered the passengers.

salvage work on the *Calpurnia*. They'd better bring some petrol, too. Get back here as quickly as you can.' Biggles took Algy out of earshot of the passengers. 'You might ask the authorities to keep the story out of the Press as long as possible. In any case, in no circumstances do we want our names mentioned in connection with the affair. That's important.'

'Good enough,' agreed Algy, and in a few minutes was in the air, with the wounded officer as passenger, heading east.

After that there was nothing the others could do but wait. The steward waded out to the *Calpurnia*, and managed to produce a substantial lunch, which in the ordinary way would have been served on the machine.

The sun was well past its zenith when Algy returned, bringing the traffic manager with him. Biggles had to take him into his confidence, and explanations occupied some time. A relief plane, said the official, was on the way. It was bringing mechanics and petrol.

'I'd be obliged if you'd let your men repair the Spur before they start on the *Calpurnia*,' requested Biggles. 'I shall want to use it.'

To this the manager agreed.

'What are you going to do?' Algy asked Biggles.

'I'm going to make a reconnaissance while the trail is still warm,' answered Biggles. 'There's nothing else we can do that I can see. I'll take the Mosquito and have a look at this place El Zufra. The oasis is due south from here, and the Renkell's headed in that direction. Ginger can come with me. As soon as the Spur is serviceable, fill up with petrol and follow on. I doubt if that'll be this side of nightfall, though. If you can't get away before sunset you'd better wait for dawn, rather than risk missing the oasis in the dark. This is assuming that we're not back by then.

Of course, if there's nothing at Zufra we shall come straight back and contact you here.'

Bertie broke in. 'I say, old boy, what are you going to do if you find the Renkells at this beastly place, Zufra?'

'I shall endeavour to shoot them up, to ensure that they stay there,' answered Biggles grimly. 'Come on, Ginger, let's get cracking.'

By this time it was nearly five o'clock, with the sun sinking like an enormous toy balloon towards the western horizon.

Biggles walked over to the Mosquito, collecting his map from the damaged Spur on the way. In the cockpit, with Ginger sitting on his left, he opened the map and put a finger on a name printed in tiny italics, conspicuous only because it occurred on the vast and otherwise blank area of the Libyan desert.

'That's Oasis El Zufra, our objective,' he said. 'Don't ask me what there is there because I don't know. I expect it's much the same as any other Libyan oasis – a few sun-dried palms round a pool of brackish water.'

'It looks a long way from here,' observed Ginger.

'Roughly four hundred miles,' returned Biggles, folding the map. 'It will be nearly dark by the time we get there, but as it's the only green spot between here and French Equatorial Africa, it shouldn't be hard to find.'

In three minutes the Mosquito was in the air, climbing for height on a course due south, over what is generally acknowledged to be the most sterile area of land on earth. As soon as the altimeter registered five thousand feet Biggles settled down to a steady cruising speed of three hundred miles an hour.

In an hour and a quarter by the watch on the instrument panel the oasis crept up over the southern horizon. In all that time the scene had remained unchanged – a flat, or sometimes corrugated, brown, waterless expanse, occasionally strewn with loose rock, and more often than not spotted with areas of lifeless-looking camel-thorn shrub. Nothing moved. The scene was as motionless as a picture.

'Is this oasis inhabited?' asked Ginger.

'I don't know for certain, but I should say it's most unlikely,' replied Biggles. 'Generally, only the very large oases have settled populations, although nomad Arabs on the move call anywhere if there is water to be had. Hallo! I can see something moving ... a camel. Apparently there are Arabs here now.'

By this time the Mosquito was circling over the oasis, losing height as Biggles throttled back and put the machine in a glide. There was little to see. In shape, the oasis was roughly oval, perhaps a mile long and half that distance wide, set about with straggling palms. It appeared to stand on a slight eminence, with shallow wadis, or dry water-courses, radiating out at regular intervals. The sand lapped like an ocean, so that it was possible in one stride to step from a land of death to a fertile haven. There was no sign of aircraft. Near the centre there was a clearing in which had been erected what seemed to be a rough bough-shelter of dead palm fronds – a structure commonly found at oases.

'It looks as if we've drawn a blank,' muttered Biggles.

'I can't see anything,' said Ginger.

Biggles opened the throttle a little and continued to circle at about a hundred feet, all the time staring down at the depressing scene below. For some minutes nothing was said. Then Biggles remarked, in a curious voice, 'Is that a dead camel lying down there on the sand?'

'I see what you mean,' answered Ginger. 'I was just looking at it. It must be a camel, but it's a funny shape. What's that bundle of rags lying beside it – two bundles, in fact?'

'If the rags weren't so scattered I'd say they were dead Arabs,' mused Biggles. 'But why should Arabs die there, just outside the oasis? Where's that live camel?' He swung round towards the beast that was making its way slowly, and apparently with diffi-culty, towards the palms. 'From the way it's limping that poor brute has got a broken leg,' he went on sharply. 'What the deuce goes on here? I don't understand it at all.'

'Why not land and find out?' suggested Ginger.

'That's a practical suggestion,' acknowledged Biggles, and proceeded to adopt it.

As far as space was concerned there was no difficulty. On all sides between the wadis stretched the desert, flat, colourless, depressing in its dismal monotony. The sand, as far as it was possible to judge from the camel tracks, was firm. There was no wind, so choosing a line between two wadis that would allow the machine to finish its run reasonably close to the oasis, Biggles throttled back, lowered his wheels, glided in and touched down. The injured camel was about forty yards away, still limping towards the palms. Neither Biggles or Ginger paid much attention to it at the time. There was no reason why they should, for the risk of collision did not arise.

Just what happened after that – when Ginger was able to think again – was a matter of surmise. There was a blinding flash. With it came a thundering explosion. A blast of air hit the Mosquito and lifted it clean off the ground. For perhaps three seconds it hung in the atmosphere, at an angle to its original course, wallowing sick-eningly. Then it settled down, struck the ground with one wheel, bounced, swerved, and came to rest with its tail cocked high.

Dazed, his ears ringing, in something like a panic Ginger

pushed himself back from the instrument panel against which he had been flung, and tried to get out. The door had jammed. Biggles's voice cut in, it seemed from a distance.

'Sit tight,' he ordered.

Ginger looked at him and saw that he was removing a splinter of glass from his cheek. There was blood on his face. He looked shaken.

'What happened?' gasped Ginger.

'Nothing – only that we've landed in a mine-field,' returned Biggles.

'Mine-field? What are you talking about?' ejaculated Ginger.

'Look at the camel – or what's left of it,' invited Biggles.

Ginger looked, and through the side window saw a tangled mess of skin, hair, and blood, lying beside a shallow crater from which smoke was still rising sluggishly.

'That camel trod on a land mine; it couldn't have been anything else,' declared Biggles. 'The area must have been mined during the war, probably when the Italians were in occupation, and nobody has troubled to clear it up. A mine must have killed that other camel, and the two Bedouins. This poor brute was probably with them, but got away with a broken leg,'

'That's beautiful,' muttered Ginger bitterly. 'It'll be a long time before this machine flies again – if it ever does. How are we going to get back? Thank goodness you told Algy to follow us. We can wait at the oasis. I—'

'Not so fast,' interrupted Biggles. 'You appear to have over-looked one or two details. The first is, between us and the oasis there is a hundred yards of sand under which, for a certainty, there are more mines. Personally, I've never walked through a minefield; I've never had the slightest desire to do so, but it looks as if the time has come when I shall have to try it. Well, it'll be a new sensation. The second point that occurs to me is – supposing we are lucky enough to reach the oasis in one piece – what is going to happen when Algy arrives? He'll see the crash, and he'll promptly land. If he doesn't land on a mine he'll probably run over one as he taxies in – although the chances of that, of course, depend on how thickly the mines are sown.'

'We shall have to wave to keep him off,' suggested Ginger gloomily.

'He'll probably think we're beckoning,' asserted Biggles. 'He's certain to land. We've been in some queer messes, but this one is, as the boys say, a fair knock-out.'

'What are we going to do?' demanded Ginger.

'I'll tell you what *you're* going to do,' answered Biggles. 'You're going to stay here. I'm going to the oasis.'

'But that's preposterous,' objected Ginger hotly.

'We should be very foolish indeed to walk together,' went on Biggles imperturbably. 'To start with, two pairs of feet would double the chances of striking a mine. If either of us stepped on one we should both go up in the air and come down in fragments, in which case there would be no one to tell the story. No, that won't do. Sitting here won't get us anywhere, so I may as well find a path to the oasis. That will be something to go on with. I can get halfway safely by stepping in the hoof marks of the camel. For the last fifty yards I shall have to take my chance. You'll sit here and have a grandstand view of the proceedings. If I get through, you can join me by following in my tracks. If I don't – well, follow my tracks till you come to the crater, then it will be your turn to take a chance.'

'And if we get to the oasis?' queried Ginger.

'We shall either have to work out some sort of signal to keep

Algy off the ground, or poke about with sticks, like the sappers had to do in the war, to locate the mines. With luck – with a lot of luck – we may be able to mark out a runway and arrange a visual signal that will induce Algy to land on it. He'll have to land if we are to get home. One thing is quite certain; we can't walk it. We're four hundred miles from the nearest blade of grass, remember. Fortunately, we've plenty of time. Algy isn't likely to be along yet. I doubt if he'll get off the ground much before dawn. Well, it's no use messing about.'

As he finished speaking Biggles forced the door open and stepped out on to the sand. 'Don't move until you get the okay from me, then walk in my tracks,' he commanded.

The rim of the sun, a thin line of glowing crimson, was just sinking into the eternal wilderness. With its going, a veil of purple twilight was being drawn across the scene. Biggles turned towards the oasis.

With his heart in his mouth, as the saying is, Ginger leaned forward in his seat to watch. The strain was such that he found it difficult to breathe. He derived some slight relief when Biggles reached the tracks of the unfortunate camel, and then proceeded at a curious gait, imposed by the necessity of putting his feet in the oddly spaced hoof marks. The relief did not last long. Biggles reached the crater by the dead camel. He turned, waved, lit a cigarette, and then, to Ginger's utter consternation, strode casually towards the oasis as if he were out for an evening stroll.

Ginger held his breath. Knowing that every step Biggles took might be his last he watched with an agony of suspense that drove beads of perspiration through the skin of his forehead, He began to count the number of paces Biggles would have to take to reach safety – ten – nine – eight—

CHAPTER IX

Gontermann Makes a Proposal

Having reached the crater Biggles wasted no time – to use his own expression – messing about. Like a diver on a high board, the temptation was to hesitate; but this would be procrastination, and could avail him nothing. If a mine lay in his path, walking slowly would make no difference should he put his foot on it. So he walked normally. Nevertheless, he advanced with his eyes on the ground, seeking disturbed areas of sand that might betray the location of a mine. Long years of flying had taught him to be master of his nerves, so while the sensation was anything but pleasant he was not unduly perturbed, deriving a crumb of comfort from the knowledge that if he did step on a mine he would be unlikely to know anything about it.

In spite of all this it was with considerable satisfaction that he saw he had nearly reached his objective, the nearest point of the oasis, an area of coarse, wiry grass, from which the palms sprang. As he took the last pace, from the sand to the grass, a voice close at hand said, 'Congratulations.'

The sound, coming as it did in the hush of twilight, made

Biggles start. He was utterly unprepared for it. Looking up, he saw, leaning against the bole of a palm in an attitude so elegant that it was obviously a pose, a man whom he had never seen before, but whom he recognised at once from photographs he had seen in the press. It was the tall, austere, good-looking ex-Nazi chief, Julius Gontermann, dressed immaculately as though for a ceremony in a tight-fitting, dove-grey suit of semi-military cut. Smoke spiralled from a cigarette in a long, gold-and-amber holder. His expression was one of cynical admiration and satisfaction.

He was not alone. Near at hand, in attitudes of idle interest, were Scaroni, Grindler, and Baumer, whom Biggles also recognised from his photograph. Grindler was the only one who openly displayed a weapon; he dangled an automatic from his trigger finger. There was one other man, a man whom Biggles certainly did not expect to see; but his presence explained the mystery of the third pilot. It was von Zoyton, a pilot – and, incidentally, an ace – of the Luftwaffe, against whose *Jagdstaffel* he had fought a bitter duel over the Western Desert during the war.[1]

Von Zoyton smiled icy recognition.

Biggles shook his head sadly, and addressed him without malice, in English, which he knew von Zoyton spoke well.

'I'm surprised to see you mixed up in a graft like this. Perhaps you couldn't help being a Nazi, but you can help being a crook. I suppose they pulled you in because you knew the country?'

'Hit the nail right on the head, as usual,' conceded the German, who seemed amused about something.

'Is there anything funny about this – or have I lost my sense of humour?' inquired Biggles.

---

[1] See *Biggles Sweeps the Desert*.

'It is the winner's privilege to laugh,' answered von Zoyton. 'I've just won a hundred marks from Scaroni – who, by the way, produced and planted the fireworks. So proud he was of his effort that he laid me odds of ten to one that you wouldn't reach the oasis intact. I, gambling on your usual infernal luck, wagered that you would.'

'I'm glad you won your bet,' replied Biggles dryly.

Grindler interrupted with a snort. 'Say, what is this, a kid's party?' he snarled. 'If this guy's a cop I know how to handle him.'

'Plenty of time for that,' put in Gontermann. He, too, spoke in English, an affected, pedantic English, with an exaggerated Oxford accent through which ran an American drawl. 'I'd like a word with him first,' he added. 'Let's get up to the house. Come along, my dear Bigglesworth. Oh, by the way, you won't mind if I ask Baumer to take over any hardware you may be carrying – merely a precautionary measure against accidents, you know.'

Covered at close range by Grindler's gun, without a word Biggles passed over his automatic. Resistance, in the circumstances, was useless.

A short walk took them to the structure that Biggles had observed from the air, and he perceived at a glance that what he had seen was camouflage, clever camouflage, concealing a roomy, portable hutment of military design. The interior was simply but comfortably furnished, and illuminated by a hanging oil-lamp.

'Sit down my dear fellow,' invited Gontermann. 'May I offer you some hospitality? Get the drinks out, Scaroni; our guest will be thirsty after his trying ordeal.' He turned back to Biggles. 'You were foolish to come here, you know.'

'Surely that remains to be seen?' returned Biggles evenly.

Gontermann shrugged. 'What can you do? The age of miracles

has passed, my dear fellow.' He glanced at Baumer. 'You'd better finish the business as we arranged.'

As Baumer withdrew Biggles wondered what this business was. He did not guess it.

'Now let us get down to what you English call, I believe, brass tacks,' suggested Gontermann. 'There is no need for me to tell you what we are doing here. Conversely, we know what you are doing. Preuss is rather a dull fellow, but he was able to find out. Are we clear so far?'

'Quite clear,' agreed Biggles.

'In that case you must be wondering why we have permitted you to go on living,' went on Gontermann, smiling faintly.

'I must confess to some curiosity on the point,' admitted Biggles, who, in actual fact, was thinking of something quite different. He was wondering what Ginger would make of his disappearance.

'An hour or two, more or less, is of no consequence now that you are here,' said Gontermann lightly, pushing the cigarette box over to Biggles. 'I've heard about you, of course. Your name was often mentioned in the Wilhelmstrasse, during the war, notably by my good friend, Erich von Stalhein, of the Gestapo. I gather you caused him a good deal of inconvenience?'

'I'm gratified to hear it,' murmured Biggles.

'Von Zoyton also had quite a lot to say about you,' continued Gontermann. 'And that brings me to the point of this interesting debate. You're the sort of man I should like to have with us. Our programme is going splendidly and there is no reason why it should not be expanded, if we can find suitable personnel. We can also do with one or two more machines, which, in your official capacity, you could acquire. You could also serve a useful purpose by keeping us informed as to the measures being taken against us.'

Incredulity puckered Biggles's forehead. 'Are you making this suggestion seriously?'

'Of course,' averred Gontermann. 'I'm not a man to waste time.'

Biggles sipped the drink that had been set before him, and lit a cigarette. 'You amaze me,' he said softly. 'You really do amaze me. Just as a matter of interest, what should I get out of this?'

'Money, my dear chap; and the satisfaction of exerting power over those who think they can run civilisation their own way for their own ends. The world is bursting with wealth. Why not have some of it? There are two sorts of people in the world, my dear Bigglesworth – the mugs and the others. The mugs accept what is doled out to them. The others, to which class we belong, help themselves. Here, take a look at these, for example.'

Gontermann picked up a black attaché-case, the property of the late courier, and carelessly tipped the contents on the table. Such a stream of jewels gushed forth that Biggles caught his breath in sheer admiration. There were ropes of pearls, strings of rubies, cut and uncut diamond and emerald rings and earrings, set as single stones and in clusters. Gontermann ran his fingers through the heap until it gleamed and flashed and flashed again as though illuminated by some unearthly fire.

'Pretty, eh?' he said slyly. 'Not bad, for a day's work? And there are plenty more where these came from.'

'I begin to see the force of your argument,' said Biggles slowly. 'But what,' he went on, 'leads you to suppose, that having been allowed to leave here, I should not double-cross you?'

'That's my argument,' growled Grindler.

'Not bad for a day's work.'

Gontermann ignored him. 'You would merely have to give me your word that you would not do so.'

'You'd accept that?'

'Of course. The word of a British military or civil servant is one of the few stable things left in a tottering world. Nevertheless, it is one of the weak spots in the British character, for it enables others, like myself, who have a more flexible code, to make our plans with a good deal of certainty. With men of your type, for instance, your word is a sort of fetish; you would suffer untold hardships, even die perhaps, rather than break it. Conditions in the world today, my dear fellow, do not justify such conceit. Give me your word that you accept my offer and you shall be as free as the vultures that otherwise will have the pleasure of dining on you.'

'Now I call that a really pretty speech,' sneered Biggles. 'You have the brass face to sit there and accuse *me* of conceit, when—'

He broke off suddenly, as from outside came a sound which astonished him not a little, although a moment later, on secondary consideration, he realised that there was nothing remarkable about it. It was the sound of twin aero motors being started up.

'What's that?' he demanded.

'Only the Wolf, growling,' answered Gontermann with a smile. 'Baumer is about to give it a little exercise. He won't be long. You did not suppose that we had stranded ourselves here without air transport?'

'I hadn't thought about it,' returned Biggles, wondering how the machine, or machines, had been so cleverly camouflaged that his reconnaissance had not revealed them. 'What's Baumer going to do?'

'Finish the job you began so efficiently a few minutes ago. Your aircraft is rather conspicuous as it is. Being of wooden construction it should burn briskly.'

'But why use an aircraft to do that?' inquired Biggles.

'Because, my dear chap, the reaction of a land mine is precisely the same regardless of who treads on it. The area round this oasis is so thickly sown with mines that none of us feel inclined to use it as a promenade. There is, of course a gap, known only to ourselves, for the purpose of taking our machines in and out.'

'Do you mean that Baumer is going to shoot the machine up?' cried Biggles, with a rising inflection in his voice.

'The only safe way to reach it is by air,' explained the German.

'But just a minute! He can't do that,' snapped Biggles. 'My second pilot is in it.'

'Ah! That's a pity,' murmured Gontermann smoothly. 'I'm afraid he is – how do you say? – out of luck. It's too late for us to do anything about it.'

This, clearly, was true, for the Wolf had already taken off, and now, to Biggles's unspeakable horror, came raking bursts of machine-gun fire.

'Stop him!' he shouted, and made a dash for the door.

Grindler raised his pistol, but Gontermann knocked it aside. 'Put that thing away,' he said irritably. 'You won't need it.'

Biggles went on until he had a clear view of the desert, and then stopped dead. The wrecked Mosquito was already enveloped in flames.

'Baumer is a very good pilot,' remarked Gontermann from his elbow.

Biggles started forward.

'Steady, Bigglesworth, steady,' said the Nazi. 'You can't do any good. Of course, if you choose to risk another trip across the mine-field I shouldn't dream of stopping you, but your luck might not be so good this time. At least give Scaroni a chance to recover his money with another little bet.' It was clear from the cynical banter in Gontermann's voice that he was thoroughly enjoying himself.

Biggles went on to the edge of the sand and then stopped. A wide area was lit up by the flames, but on it nothing moved. One thing was certain; anyone in the machine must already be a charred cinder. Gontermann had spoken an obvious truth when he had said, 'you can't do any good.' Biggles heard the Wolf land, but he did not see it. He could not take his eyes from what, he knew in his heart, must be Ginger's funeral pyre. It was with difficulty that he maintained his composure. He had no intention of giving his enemies the satisfaction of seeing his distress.

'Well, I suppose it's no use staying here,' he said evenly.

'I hoped you'd see it in that light,' answered Gontermann. 'Come back to the mess and have another drink. That crude fellow Grindler is agitating to shoot you, but it has always been my policy to preserve anybody or anything that might be useful to me.'

They walked back to the hut. Baumer came in, with the air of a man who has done a good job. Biggles looked at him.

'You deliberately killed that boy,' he accused.

'Of course,' answered Baumer, quite casually. 'There was no point in leaving him out there to die of thirst. We had to burn the aircraft, anyhow. It might have been seen. He wasn't a relation of yours, was he?'

'No.' Biggles shook his head. 'No, he wasn't a relation. By the way, who shot down the diamond plane?'

'I did,' replied Baumer promptly, and with some pride.

'And the pay-roll plane from Nairobi?'

'Me,' Scaroni answered.

Biggles considered them with frosty, scornful eyes. 'It must be a source of infinite satisfaction to you, to know that you shot a couple of unarmed pilots through the back,' he said, with iron in his voice. 'Grindler murdered three men in the flying-boat – three quite ordinary fellows just doing their jobs. But there, he's used to that sort of thing. It seems he is in good company.'

Grindler rasped out a curse. Baumer started forward angrily, but Gontermann waved him back.

'As our guest, your remarks are not in the best of taste, my dear Bigglesworth,' he said suavely. 'It would be better to avoid personalities.'

'From your point of view, you are definitely right,' grated Biggles.

'This mine-field idea was a good one, don't you think?' went on Gontermann, switching the subject. 'That, and the desert, makes the oasis a perfect retreat, and at the same time, a prison that requires neither wire nor iron bars. Scaroni knew of the mines; indeed, he hid them when the British advanced during the war; but I take credit for putting them to practical use. Incidentally, Scaroni has some other useful equipment, too. By the way, should you go outside, keep away from the water-hole. The verge positively bristles with mines – a double row of them. You see, by this means, we have provided an almost unbreakable line of defence. Should anyone be so fortunate as to reach the oasis during our absence which occurs from time to time, it is exceedingly unlikely that they would profit by it. After crossing the desert they would naturally make straight for the water, in which case ...' Gontermann made a significant gesture.

Biggles flared up. 'That's a scandalous thing to do,' he protested hotly. 'What about the Arabs? They've probably used this oasis for centuries. They haven't harmed you.'

'Nevertheless, my dear fellow, they might be tempted to report what they had seen,' returned Gontermann casually. 'Besides, what is an Arab, more or less? You British are the most extraordinary people, always worrying about someone else. It impairs your efficiency. We do not allow ourselves to be hampered by such humanitarian scruples.'

'I've noticed it,' answered Biggles shortly.

'Well, what do you think of the scheme?' queried Gontermann.

Biggles did not answer. He was finding it hard to hold himself in hand. What had been a mere desire to bring these men to justice as a matter of duty, was now an obsession. The matter had become personal.

Gontermann hazarded a guess as to what was passing in his mind – and guessed wrong.

'I can give you until the morning to think it over,' he offered. 'We are leaving here at dawn. We use this place only occasionally, as an advanced landing-ground.'

Grindler broke in. 'What's that? Leaving here? Are we going back to that goldarned sanseviera?'

Gontermann flashed a scowl at him. 'Never mind where we're going,' he said curtly, and turned back to Biggles. He was smiling again, but Biggles could see that he was annoyed by Grindler's remark. 'Very well, my dear fellow,' he said airily. 'Let us leave it like that. The oasis is at your disposal. We sleep in the open – it's cooler. You can have a camp bed under the palms.'

Biggles raised his eyebrows. 'Aren't you going to tie me up or something?'

The German affected a look of reproach. 'To what purpose, old chap? If you feel like trying your luck again in the mine-field we shall be most interested spectators; but it is only fair to warn you, that in the unlikely event of your getting through, you would find the long walk across the desert to Sollum, without food or water, rather exhausting. It's a good four hundred miles, you know. There's no cover, and we should find you quite easily. But why discuss it? I'm sure that you, with your reputation for intelligence, would not be so ill-advised as to attempt the impossible.'

Biggles did not argue.

'Just one other thing,' concluded Gontermann. 'At the moment there are two aeroplanes here. You would find them quite easily. They are in a slight depression under a sand-coloured awning. I mention this because you might be tempted to try your hand at the controls. Resist it. The ground around them is so thickly sown with mines that I confess to some nervousness every time I approach by the narrow path which was left for our accommodation. You'll forgive me if I don't show you the path?'

'I shall bear it in mind,' promised Biggles.

CHAPTER X

Ginger Takes a Walk

Sitting in the cockpit of the Mosquito, Ginger had let out a gasp of relief when Biggles took the final step from the death-sown sand to the supposedly safe terrain of the oasis. He wiped the sweat from his forehead with a hand that trembled and sank back limply to recover.

Of course he kept his eyes on Biggles, expecting him to turn at any moment and give the okay signal. When this did not come he sat up again, not a little puzzled by Biggles's behaviour. There was no suggestion of a signal. Biggles was standing still, staring into the palms as though mesmerised. That in itself was odd. What was even more extraordinary, Biggles appeared to be talking to somebody – unless he was talking to himself, a most unlikely event. The trouble was it was nearly dark, and although some light was furnished by a rising moon, it was deceptive, and certainly not enough to probe the shadows of the palms.

When Biggles suddenly walked on and disappeared from sight Ginger was dumbfounded. He could not imagine anything that would have such an effect. It could hardly be possible that Biggles had forgotten him. Yet the fact remained, there was no signal. His orders on this point were clear. He was to remain in the aircraft until he received the okay to proceed. So he stayed, convinced that Biggles would presently reappear.

Minutes passed. Nothing happened. The oasis remained silent, with the deep stillness of death. The afterglow of the setting sun faded, and in the darkness that followed, the moon shone more brightly. Ginger continued to wrestle with a problem for which he could find no reasonable answer. If it seems strange that he did not guess the truth, it must be remembered that as a result of the air reconnaissance he had quite decided in his mind that the oasis was abandoned. So firmly had this conviction estab-lished itself that it remained unmoved. Nothing happened to imply that he and Biggles might have been mistaken in their assumption.

But when, shortly afterwards, the clatter of aero engines being started up shattered the silence, he moved with alacrity, and with some agitation. For the obvious explanation of his problem did not come to him gently; rather did it burst upon him like a thunderclap. The Renkells – or one of them – was at the oasis after all. If the machine was there, then it followed that the crew were there. Clearly, Biggles had walked into a trap, and that being so, it did not take Ginger long to decide that orders given before this fact was known were automatically cancelled.

As he jumped down on to the warm sand he saw the aircraft take off. It was not the transport, as he rather expected, but the Wolf, which suggested that the whole enemy party was at the oasis. It began to look very much as if the oasis was, in fact, the enemy's headquarters. The Wolf, he observed, did not take off across the open sand; it chose for its run a shallow *wadi* that emerged from the eastern side of the oasis. Only too well aware that the sand was mined, Ginger guessed the reason.

There was bound to be a gap in the mine-field, and the *wadi* provided it.

Actuated by this new peril, Ginger started running towards the *wadi* with the object of getting into the oasis. In his anxiety to discover what had become of Biggles he forgot all about such things as mines. Not until he was halfway to his objective did he remember them, and the effect produced was a sinking feeling in the stomach. But he did not stop. He daren't. In sheer desperation he ran flat out, and fairly flung himself over the rim of the *wadi*, where he lay panting, not so much from exertion as shock.

By this time the Wolf was in the air. He wondered where it was going, and why, so he lay still to watch. He could see it distinctly, for at no time was it more than a hundred feet from the ground, a performance that puzzled him considerably. Nor was his curiosity allayed when the machine banked steeply and came tearing back over its course. He wondered what it was going to do, for there appeared to be no reason for such an evolution.

What happened was the last thing he expected. The nose of the Wolf suddenly dipped in line with the Mosquito and a stream of tracer bullets lacerated the sky, so that the sand round the damaged machine was torn and lashed with metal. Not all went into the sand, some must have penetrated the tank, for a flame shot up. Another minute and the machine was wrapped in fire. The bullets in the Mosquito's guns began to explode.

Ginger was about forty yards away – too close to be comfortable. He started running down the *wadi*. This, as he quickly realised, was a blunder, for in the light of the blazing aircraft the pilot of the Wolf saw him. This information was conveyed by a burst of bullets that sent him scrambling, flat on the ground, under the lee of a dune. The Wolf roared over him at a height of not more than ten feet, and then zoomed as Ginger knew it must. He was also aware that the pilot would turn to confirm that he had hit his mark. Obviously, he must provide the pilot with a mark to shoot at. In a moment he had torn off his jacket, and flinging it down where he had been lying, made a dash for a clump of camel-thorn that clung to the side of the *wadi* at no great distance.

He reached it just as the Wolf completed its turn, and at once dropped its nose towards the jacket, which lay conspicuously on the open sand. Again came the vicious snarling of multiple machine-guns. In the lurid glow of the burning Mosquito, Ginger saw his jacket leap into the air, and then go bowling down the *wadi* as though impelled by a jet of water from a pressure hose. With this he was quite content, thankful that he was not inside it. Had he been, he reflected, its spasmodic movements would have been much the same. He did not stir. From the flimsy cover of the leafless bushes he watched the pilot turn again and land, using the same *wadi* from which it had taken off. The machine taxied in. The clamour of its motors died away. There were a few odd noises, then silence fell. The glare of the burning Mosquito began to fade. Petrol-soaked wood and fabric burns quickly.

Ginger sat still long enough for the flames to die down, and to recover from a series of shocks that had left him slightly bewildered; then he walked along the *wadi* to his jacket. It was shot to ribbons. With some difficulty he put it on, not so much because he wanted it as because he was loath to leave it where it might be seen in daylight, for this would expose his ruse. If the enemy wondered what had become of his body – well, they would have to wonder. He then returned to the camel-thorn to consider the situation.

His first inclination was to reconnoitre the oasis forthwith, approaching by the *wadi* which the Wolf had used as a runway, for this, as far as he knew, was the only safe passage. Desperate though the circumstances were, he had no desire to test his luck in the mine-field if it could be avoided. Then he remembered Algy and Bertie, who would be coming along in the Spur, and this threw him into a quandary. Although it was unlikely that they would arrive before dawn, there was a chance that they might turn up at any time. Even now they might be on the way. On arrival they would most certainly land, in which case the Spur would probably follow the Mosquito to destruction. If it were not blown up, it would probably be shot down by the Wolf in a surprise attack. That would not do. At all costs the Spur must be preserved, otherwise, whatever else happened, they would all eventually perish in the desert. The Spur was now the only link with civilisation.

Still pondering, Ginger also saw that even if the Spur delayed its flight until dawn, it would be futile to try to save it within sight of the oasis. If he stood up in the open desert where he could be seen by Algy, he would also be seen by the enemy. That would be fatal. If it became known that he was still alive, steps would be taken to finish more efficiently the task the Wolf had just attempted. At present he was presumed dead, and if anything was to be done to save Biggles – assuming he was still alive – that impression must remain. He dare not risk going to the oasis to look for Biggles in case the Spur should arrive while he was there.

As far as he could see there was only one chance of saving the Spur, himself, and, eventually, Biggles. This was to go to meet the aircraft. Out of sight of the oasis he would be able to take up a position in a conspicuous place, where there was a fair chance that Algy would see him. Being the only moving thing in the desert he would stand out like a fly on a tablecloth. To make sure, he might even make smoke, for he had a box of matches in his pocket. If the machine came over before daylight he would have to light a fire, using such materials as were available. If Algy or Bertie failed to see him it would be just too bad, he decided. At all events, he would have done his best.

Feeling better now that he had a fixed plan, he turned his face towards the north, and started walking, keeping in the *wadi* for as long as it ran in the right direction. It gave him an uncomfortable feeling to recall that in front of him lay four hundred miles of desert. He had neither food nor water. It was better, he told himself, not to think about that. He knew all about the risks of becoming lost. Once before he had been lost in the wilderness, and he had no desire to repeat the experience. However, while the stars remained visible this should not happen. He walked on.

The moon climbed over its zenith, shedding an eerie light over the vastness around him, and still he walked, a speck in the centre of a round horizon. An hour passed, and still there was the same circle of sand around him. He was tired, but he dare not rest in case he fell asleep, and the Spur passed over while he slumbered. In his hand he carried his matches, a few odd letters from his pocket, and some strips of rag torn from the lining of his jacket, all ready to make a tiny blaze should a drone in the northern sky herald the approach of the Spur.

An eternity of time passed – or so it seemed. Sometimes

his feet sank into soft sand, sometimes they rustled harshly on rough volcanic ash. Once he crunched through an area of gleaming salt, evidently the dry bed of a lake. He tried talking to himself to keep awake, but the sound, in the loneliness, frightened him, so he soon gave it up. The night wore on. To his weary brain the outlook became ever more melancholy. He began to fear that even though he made contact with Algy and Bertie they would be too late to help Biggles. In the long night hours anything could have happened, he reflected gloomily.

More time passed. The moon ran its course across the heavens, and sank, as silently as a stone in a deep pool, into the distant world beyond the horizon. A period of darkness followed, and what with this, and sheer weariness, he was constrained to take a rest upon a little mound of sand. Around him the horizon was still the same unbroken circle, and a sinister feeling came over him that he was the only living creature left on earth.

But all things have an end, and for Ginger it came when the first faint flush of the false dawn lightened the eastern sky. The sun, of course, had not yet shown its face. Ginger stood up, and as he did so there reached his ears the sound for which he had so long waited – the drone of a high-flying aircraft. The sound came from the north, so that he knew it could only be made by the Spur. It was difficult to fix its precise position. But after a while, as he gazed up, he suddenly saw a living spark of fire moving across the dome of heaven. He had seen the phenomenon before, so he was not altogether surprised; but he was thrilled. He knew that the speck of orange light was a ray from the still invisible sun striking upwards, to be caught, and flung back, by the under-surfaces of the aircraft's wings. The world around him was still in sombre darkness.

In a moment, with fingers that shook a little from the knowledge of the tremendous consequences involved, he lighted his little fire. The flame of a match seized the paper hungrily, and devoured it all too quickly, almost before he could get the rag alight. He flung himself on his face, and coaxed the flame with his breath. To his great relief the rag caught, but at best the fire was but a puny affair, and his heart went cold with apprehension. The plane droned on with awful deliberation through the crystal clear atmosphere.

Then came the daily miracle of dawn. First, the stars lost their brilliance. Then long pale fingers swept upwards, like beams from a battery of ghostly searchlights, to shed a mysterious radiance over the waste of sand. The light became tinged with colour, pink, green and gold. The colours faded, and it was day. The aircraft was no longer a spark, but a black speck speeding across a ceiling of eggshell blue.

Ginger threw up his arms and waved. He danced, and ran about, hoping by this means to attract the attention of the pilot. And it seemed that he succeeded, for to his unspeakable joy the aircraft began to turn, and a change in the note of the engines told him they that had been throttled back. But he continued his gymnastics, swinging his tattered coat about his head, until he was convinced that he was the objective towards which the descending machine was heading. Then, quite exhausted by his efforts, and feeling rather foolish, he ran up and down the sand to make sure that it was firm, and that there were no obstructions such as rocks to spell final calamity.

The Spur landed, and it had hardly run to a standstill before he was on the wing, gesticulating, and making incoherent noises.

Bertie pushed back the 'lid', and adjusted his monocle regarding him with frank alarm. 'I say, old boy, are you all right?' he inquired earnestly.

'No, far from it,' snapped Ginger, who was in no mood for pleasantries.

'You're not loony, or anything like that, from thirst?' queried Bertie.

'No!'

'Then what have you been doing to yourself? I've heard of people getting all worked up and rending their jolly old garments—'

'Never mind what you've heard,' broke in Ginger. 'Get out, both of you. I've got a tale to tell.'

Bertie jumped down, followed by Algy. 'What is it?' he asked anxiously.

'They've got Biggles,' announced Ginger.

'Who's got him?'

'I don't know exactly,' confessed Ginger. 'Let me tell you all about it.' And he forthwith plunged into an account of the things that had befallen since the Mosquito left the coast.

'Beastly things, mines – if you know what I mean?' muttered Bertie when Ginger broke off.

Algy was still staring at Ginger. 'What in thunder are we going to do?'

Ginger shrugged helplessly. 'I don't know. I hadn't thought as far ahead as that. My one concern was to get hold of you.'

'How far are we from this perishing oasis?'

'I'm a bit hazy about that,' admitted Ginger. 'Somewhere between ten and twenty miles, for a rough guess.'

'If we fly over the place they'll see us,' went on Algy. 'If we land in that *wadi* they'll shoot us up as we come in, so that's no use. If we try to reach the oasis any other way we're liable to be blown up. Suffering Spitfires! What a kettle of fish.'

'We've got to do something,' declared Ginger.

'Absolutely … absolutely,' murmured Bertie, polishing his eyeglass.

'Don't stand there burbling like a bally parrot,' snarled Algy. 'Think of something.'

'How about shooting the beastly place up, and all that sort of thing?' suggested Bertie. 'Borrow some bombs from the boys in Egypt and fan the whole works flat. That would tear their Renkells for them.'

'And tear Biggles at the same time,' grated Algy.

'By Jove! Yes, I didn't think of that,' confessed Bertie contritely. 'How about fetching some troops – punitive expedition, and so on, if you see what I mean?'

'And launch the attack somewhere about next Christmas?' sneered Algy, with biting sarcasm. 'Think again.'

'If we go on sitting here, the Wolf will probably come prowling along and find a nice sitting target,' muttered Ginger. He squatted on the undercarriage wheel and cupped his chin in his hands. 'We ought to be able to think of something. What would Biggles do in a case like this?'

'What would Biggles do in a case like this?'

CHAPTER XI

Biggles Takes To Water

Biggles passed one of the longest nights that he could recall. As Gontermann had promised he had been given a bed, actually a palliasse, outside the hut; but he slept badly, if at all. As the night wore on, rather did he fall into a state of half oblivion, in which he was yet conscious of what was happening.

Ginger's presumed fate weighed heavily on him; indeed, it overshadowed everything, and, as is usual with death, created an atmosphere of unreality. Lying there, with nothing between his face and the stars, an immeasurable distance, the drama seemed all the more poignant. The silence, too, was uncanny. Strain his eyes, and listen though he would, everything seemed still and lifeless, as though he were alone on some forgotten world that had got adrift in space.

In spite of all that Gontermann had said, he could not believe that he was not being watched. If he was, he saw no sign of the watcher. Not that it mattered. He was content to lie and think. He wanted to think. He was worried about Algy and Bertie. Sooner or later they would arrive. Gontermann and his confederates knew nothing of that, but he did not see how he could

524

turn their ignorance to advantage. The Spur would probably be blown up when it attempted to land. There appeared to be no way of preventing that. If he told Gontermann, it would come to the same thing in the end. On the face of it, nothing could prevent a melancholy conclusion to a mishandled affair. That the enemy was possessed of war stores, not normally available to civilians, and therefore unsuspected, was, to Biggles, no excuse. He could not shake off a feeling that he had shown a lamentable lack of foresight, with the result that he had blundered badly.

With the approach of dawn the air grew cooler. As the stars began to pale, unable to bear inaction any longer, he determined to find out if he was under surveillance. He was lying fully dressed, so the question of clothes did not arise. First he sat on the edge of the bed. Nothing happened, so he stood up. Still nothing happened, so with infinite caution he moved away among the palms, making no more noise than the moon passing across the heavens. At last the silence was broken by a curious sound that could only be described as a snort. Advancing in the direction whence it came he saw Scaroni, sitting with his back against a log, a rifle across his knees, as though he had been detailed to keep guard, but had dozed. Biggles eyed the rifle. It seemed too good to be true. But before he could move Scaroni started, yawned, and rubbed his eyes. It was clear that to attempt to get the rifle now would only result in a general alarm.

With no definite plan in mind, but hoping to make a discovery that could be turned to good account, Biggles edged away. Time was now important. At any moment the Spur might arrive, or Gontermann might appear to insist on an answer to his proposition, a proposition which, Biggles knew quite well, was really an ultimatum. It was an issue he preferred to avoid.

He came upon the water-hole. Remembering the mines, he regarded it from a safe distance. It was larger than he expected – a silent pool of stagnant, dark-coloured water, of unknown depth, perhaps fifty yards long and varying in width from twenty to thirty feet. There were large patches of greenish scum, particularly round the papyrus reeds that in several places fringed the bank. He considered these reeds thoughtfully. They were too sparse to offer a place of concealment even if they could be reached; but as he gazed at them the germ of an idea was born in his mind. At the far end of the pool the palms straggled nearly to the edge of the water. One had almost fallen, so that the trunk lay far over, the sagging fronds hanging within three feet of the placid surface of the pool.

This palm presented possibilities that Biggles was not slow to observe. The trunk offered a passage, a rather risky passage, by way of a bridge, over the mined area surrounding the pool. Having reached the crown, it should be possible, he thought, for a man to slide down the fronds into the water without a great deal of noise. It would be futile to suppose that anyone afloat in the water would not be seen by a person standing on the bank; but there was a trick ...

His ruminations were interrupted by a cry. He recognised Scaroni's voice. The Italian shouted, 'He's gone!' A moment later Gontermann answered: 'He can't have gone far. See if you can find him.'

Biggles was already on the move. He did not need to be told whom Scaroni was to find. There was this about the situation; his fate, when he refused to join the gang, was a foregone conclusion; so he stood to lose nothing by taking the most desperate risks to avoid a showdown.

In a moment he was astride the trunk of the fallen tree, working his way quickly towards the crown. His only fear was that Scaroni would arrive before he had accomplished his objective, but apparently the Italian went first to the edge of the oasis to survey the desert, now grey with the advent of another day.

Reaching the crown, Biggles took a firm grip on one of the twenty-foot long fronds that hung nearly to the water, and lowered himself hand over hand to the extremity. The palm sagged under his weight, and as his feet touched the water he released his hold. The water at once closed over his head, which surprised him; he had not expected it would be so deep. He was pleased to find it so, for it suited his purpose. He swam into the nearest reeds. As these were stationed near the bank, the water shallowed, perhaps to a depth of three feet. The bottom was soft mud, which he was careful not to disturb. Breaking off a hollow reed, he took one end between his teeth and sank under the water, leaving the other end of the reed clear. Through this improvised tube he was able to breathe, not so easily, but for short periods of time without serious discomfort.

He did not really hope to get away with this simple ruse, which is practised by the native races practically all over the world. He was afraid Grindler would tumble to it, because in the old days of the United States it was brought to a fine art by escaping slaves, as the only efficacious way of eluding the hounds that were commonly employed to run them down. Biggles had often heard of the trick, but this was the first occasion he had attempted to put it into practice.

It had, he found, one big disadvantage – an obvious one. While under water it was impossible to see or hear what was going on outside, so to speak. He dare not look for fear of disturbing the water. A single ripple might betray him. He knew that his entry into the water must have caused some turbulence, but as time passed, and nothing happened, he had grounds for hope that the water had settled. The main difficulty was to keep submerged; his legs would float up, and it was only by clinging to the weeds that he was able to keep them down. Apart from that, he learned that he could not remain below the surface indefinitely; the strain was too great; it was necessary from time to time to take a deep breath. As nothing happened, this method of breathing became more frequent, and after a time he risked a cautious survey of the bank.

Not a soul was in sight, so he remained in this position, prepared to take cover should anyone appear. So long elapsed before this happened that he could only conclude that his enemies had left the pool out of account as a possible hiding-place, doubtless on account of the mines.

The sky was turning pink when Gontermann, Scaroni, and Grindler appeared, walking quickly, and having a lively altercation. Biggles dare not watch. With the reed in his teeth he sank quietly under the water and waited. It was disconcerting, not knowing what was happening, but there was no way of getting over this without taking risks that hardly seemed justifiable.

He endured this final submersion for about five minutes. When he could stand the strain no longer he allowed his face to 'surface', slowly increasing his range of vision when no danger threatened. There was no one in sight. Gontermann and his accomplices had presumably walked right on. He supposed they were still looking for him, and derived some slight satisfaction from the knowledge that he was at least causing them some trouble. He now began to hope that they would think he had risked the mine-field, made a successful passage, and had fled into the desert.

He eased his position still more, going so far as to sit up, prepared, of course, to submerge instantly. Now that his ears were clear of the water he could hear voices. It sounded as if a violent argument was going on, with Grindler playing a major part. Biggles could imagine his wrath at the escape of the prisoner. This state of affairs persisted for several minutes, when he distinctly heard Gontermann say, in German, in a voice raised in anger, 'So! He's gone, but he will not get far. He will die in the desert. Say no more about it. Let us go.'

Voices continued to mutter, but very soon afterwards, they were lost in the roar of aero engines being started; and when presently, the din was intensified, Biggles knew that both aircraft were about to leave. It became manifest that the bandits were sticking to their programme of departure regardless of the escape of their prisoner, although they might make a reconnaissance of the desert in the hope of spotting him on its bare surface. That is, if they got off. With a rifle it might be possible to do something....

At this juncture Biggles made a mistake, one that might well have had fatal results. So anxious was he to see what was going on that, forgetting the mines, he started to drag himself out of the water in the manner of a crocodile. Then he remembered, and with a grunt of disgust at his folly, he slid back. At the same time he perceived a contingency for which, in his haste to get into the pool, he had made no provision. How was he to get out? The frond from which he had dropped, which had sagged under his weight, was now far out of reach. With a shock he realised that he was, quite definitely, a prisoner in the pool – at any rate, for the time being.

While he was still occupied with this problem there was a roar as one of the Renkells took off. The other followed, and very soon he could see them both climbing into the blue. As he expected, they circled once or twice, evidently looking for him; then the transport straightened out and headed south-east, and soon afterwards the Wolf followed it.

With this state of affairs Biggles was well satisfied, even though his escape might only be temporary; for he realised that the departure of the aircraft, leaving him to his own devices, was not as casual as it might appear. From Gontermann's point of view, even discounting the mines, his complete escape from the oasis, surrounded as it was by four hundred miles of sand, must seem utterly impossible. This supposition was justifiable; no man, not even a Bedouin, could hope to make the journey. Only a fully equipped and properly provisioned expedition could traverse that awful wilderness without disaster. For the rest, the mines would take care of any casual visitors during the absence of the Renkells.

The drone of the aircraft died away.

Now that there was no longer any need for caution Biggles directed himself entirely to the business of getting out of the pool, an operation which, with ample time, would present no great difficulty. But minutes, even seconds, were now of importance. The Spur might arrive at any moment, and if it landed in the mine-field only a miracle could save it. Should the machine be wrecked, then he would be a prisoner indeed.

There was only one way of getting out of the pool, and that

was by locating and clearing sufficient mines to form a gap. There was no alternative. He was glad Gontermann had stated specifically that there was a double circle of mines; this was valuable information; it meant that he had only to remove two mines in line to make a way through the circle.

He started work at the nearest point of land, digging with his hands. The sand, damp from the proximity of the water, was soft, and he made good progress. In five minutes his questing fingers had come in to contact with the first metal instrument of death. It looked like two saucepan lids fixed face to face. He laid the mine on one side and proceeded. He hoped that the two rings of mines would be set close together, but in this he was disappointed, and he had to burrow a distance of four feet before he came upon the next one. The discovery gave him a nasty moment, for the mines were not in line, as he had supposed; they were staggered, making it impossible for anyone to reach the water. Should approaching feet by good fortune miss the first line, they would inevitably encounter the second. Unaware of this, he had been working with one elbow resting on the sand within an inch of the second mine.

He lifted the horror to one side, and with a deep breath of relief stood up to wipe the sweat from his face. He was in time. No distant drone had as yet announced the approach of the Spur. There was no need to hurry, so from his elevated position he made a casual survey of the oasis, or as much of it as could be seen. Not that he expected to see anyone. That was the last thing in his mind. Consequently, his nerves twitched with shock when a movement attracted his eyes.

He saw a figure sneaking towards the dust-coloured camou-flage muslin under which the aircraft had been parked. Stalking would perhaps better describe the manner of approach. The figure was crawling swiftly from palm to palm. Already it was so close that Biggles realised it must be on the fringe of the mine-field which, according to Gontermann, surrounded the aircraft park.

For more reasons than one he nearly choked when the figure half turned, and he saw who it was. Oblivious to his own danger from further mines he dashed forward with a yell. 'Hi! Ginger! Stop!' he shouted.

Ginger stopped, staring, as well he might.

'For the love of Mike, don't move,' went on Biggles, still advancing. 'You're on the edge of a mine-field.'

There was no need to repeat the order. Ginger did not move. His jaw sagged. 'What – what shall I do?' he gulped.

'Retrace your steps, carefully.'

Ginger lost no time in acting on this advice. When he was at a safe distance he remarked, 'If there are mines about we had better warn Algy.'

Biggles blinked. 'Algy! Is *he* here?' He did not wait for an answer. Spinning round, he saw Algy advancing on a line that would take him to the pool. He let out another shout. 'Keep clear of that water!'

Algy backed away from the pool. Then, making a detour, he came to where the others were standing. He looked Biggles up and down.

'What in thunder have you been up to – having a mud bath?' he inquired.

'You bet I have,' answered Biggles grimly. 'I'll tell you all about it presently. How did you both get here? I thought Ginger was killed last night.'

'So did I,' admitted Ginger with a wry smile. 'But I shed my coat, and they shot that up instead.'

'But how did you both get into the oasis?' demanded Biggles in an amazed voice.

Ginger explained. 'I got away and made for the desert, heading north, to intercept the Spur. I lit a fire. Algy spotted it and came down. We talked the position over. I saw the Wolf take off last night, so I knew the way in and out of the oasis. We taxied the Spur into a *wadi* about five miles off, and leaving Bertie in charge, walked the rest of the way. We daren't taxi any nearer for fear of being heard. We were about a mile away when we saw the two Renkells go off; we lay flat until they were out of sight; we didn't know what was going on here. We came on to see. Are you here alone?'

'All by myself,' declared Biggles.

'Where's the gang?'

'Gone.'

Ginger shook his head. 'I don't get it. Why did they leave you here?'

'Sit down,' invited Biggles. 'I'll tell you.'

It did not take Biggles long to tell his story. When he had finished Algy asked: 'You don't know where these skunks have gone, then?'

'I haven't the remotest idea,' admitted Biggles.

'What do we do – wait here for them to come back?' put in Algy.

'I don't think we can do that,' replied Biggles. 'They may be away for weeks. It's hard to know what to do and that's a fact. The difficulties of competing with air bandits become more apparent as we go on. In ordinary crime, a cop can shadow his man, no matter whether he travels by road, train, or steamer. On the ground there is always plenty of cover. You can't do that in the atmosphere because you have the sky to yourselves. Again, the ordinary detective usually has some idea of where to look for his man. At any rate, there are limits to the zone of operations. The people we're after have the whole blessed world at their disposal, and I'm just beginning to grasp what that means. The world is still a biggish place. I don't think Raymond realises what we're up against. It was fairly certain that the up-to-date crook would use aircraft, perhaps a private plane, to make a getaway. That's a different thing from this, which is sheer piracy; but whereas the old buccaneers ambled over the waves at a nice steady four knots, these blighters hit the breeze at four hundred miles an hour – which makes them rather more difficult to catch. I'm more than ever convinced that the best way, perhaps the only way, to stop this racket, is by finding the base aerodrome and wiping it out. That would cut off the petrol supply. But talking won't get us anywhere. We'd better bring Bertie here for a start. We can't leave him to fry in the sun. Algy, I think you'd better go; Ginger has done enough walking. You can fly back here in the machine. In the meanwhile we'll look for some breakfast. I imagine there is a food store here somewhere.'

'Okay,' agreed Algy. 'Watch where you're putting your feet. This place gives me the jitters. Every time I take a step I expect to hear a loud bang.'

'It isn't exactly the place to gambol about,' agreed Biggles, as Algy set off for the *wadi*.

It was getting on for three hours before Algy returned to where the others were waiting in a state of acute suspense. He came alone, on foot. He looked up at Biggles.

'He isn't there,' he said wearily.

'What do you mean?' asked Biggles sharply.

'What I mean is,' answered Algy, 'the machine's gone!'

CHAPTER XII

Bertie Flies Alone

Bertie was sitting under the port wing of the Spur, with his back against an undercarriage wheel, regarding the sea of sand around him with bored disfavour, when the distant drone of aircraft brought him scrambling to his feet with alacrity. For the sound came from the south, which could only mean that the Renkells were taking the air.

His first thought was for his own aircraft, and the subsequent events hinged on that factor. What had happened to Biggles, of course, he did not know. Algy and Ginger had gone to find out, and at that juncture the very last thing in his mind was to leave them marooned on the oasis. But he realised that if the Renkells were in the air he could not remain where he was, for should the Spur be spotted it would present a sitting target for the enemy to shoot to pieces at leisure. It was primarily in order to prevent this that he tore into the air, and then, prepared to give combat, edged away to the east into the cover provided by the blinding glare of the newly risen sun. This achieved, he surveyed the southern sky with the efficiency that comes of long practice.

His eyes soon found what they sought – two black specks climbing away from the oasis, which could now be seen, towards the south-cast. The slight pressure of his right foot on the rudder-bar was also automatic, and before he had seriously considered what he was doing he was in pursuit. At first, his intention was the natural one of shooting the machines down, or attempting to do so, to prevent their escape and it was not until some seconds had passed that he perceived a serious objection to this course. It occurred to him, in the light of what Ginger had said, that Biggles might be a prisoner in one of the machines; indeed, if the Renkells were leaving the oasis this seemed highly probable – always assuming, of course, that the bandits had not killed Biggles out of hand. In view of this possibility it became obvious that aggressive tactics were, for the time being, at least, out of the question.

Still following the two machines, climbing for more height, but taking care to keep in line with the sun, Bertie observed further disconcerting prospects, factors that induced a state of indecision. If he shadowed the enemy aircraft, Algy and Ginger would certainly be left on the oasis without any means of getting away from it. On the other hand, if he abandoned the pursuit he might be throwing away a golden opportunity to discover what Biggles was most anxious to learn – the bandit's secret base. The fact that the Renkells were heading due south-east, on a dead straight course without any deviation, was significant; it seemed certain that they were making for a definite objective, and what could be more likely, he reasoned, than that this objective was their base depot? He made careful note of the compass course.

Broadly speaking, Bertie's geography of the district was good, because he had served both in Egypt and Aden. He was aware, therefore, that if they held straight on, they would come to the Anglo-Egyptian Sudan. He was also aware that there was nothing but desert between their present position and the southern extremity of the River Nile. This was still some hundreds of miles away – precisely how far he did not know. It seemed unlikely that the Renkells would be going to the Sudan, and a vague idea formed in his mind that they were making for another oasis, perhaps at no great distance. So he decided to follow, telling himself that it would be an easy matter to return to the oasis when his object was achieved. Keeping as far away from his quarry as he dare, without actually losing sight of them, he flew on.

An hour passed, and he began to get worried, for the Renkells were still streaking across the trackless blue as if they had no intention of stopping. Not that there was anything to stop for. At any moment Bertie expected to see an oasis creep up over the horizon, but this expectation did not materialise. Below, and on all sides, the sand rolled on, and on, and on, to more sand, and still more sand. There was nothing to indicate a boundary, but he knew they must be over the fringe of the Western Sudan. Nothing changed; only the sun climbed higher, to strike down with shafts of white light at the winged invaders. The air quivered in the heat and the Spur rocked on an invisible swell. Even the engine seemed to moan.

Another hour passed. The sun climbed higher, the machine rocked, the engine moaned, and the frown that lined Bertie's forehead deepened. Where was this crazy chase going to end? Had he known that it was to last as long as this he would have thought twice about following, he reflected bitterly. They had now covered some six hundred miles, and he looked more often at his petrol gauge. He was alarmed at the thought of going on, yet he dare not turn back. True, he still had enough petrol to reach the oasis, but that was not enough. It was no use arriving back at Zufra with an empty tank. There would be another four hundred miles to cover – the distance between the oasis and the North African coast, the nearest point of civilisation. Already he had overstepped the margin of reasonable safety for such a trip – a trip on which it would be the height of folly to risk a forced landing. So he went on, not a little worried, with an increasing conviction that he had behaved rashly, to say the least of it.

Another hour passed. The sun climbed into its throne; the machine rocked sickeningly in the tortured air, and still the desert rolled away on all sides, to eternity, it seemed. The Spur was like a fly hanging over the centre of an enormous bowl of gleaming sand. The heat was terrific, and as so often happens in such conditions, a haze, a deceptive invisible haze began to form. The hard line of the horizon became a distorted blur, and at the risk of being seen Bertie had to close up with his quarry to avoid losing them. If either of the enemy crews saw him they gave no sign of it.

The Spur's petrol was now so low that it was with heartfelt relief that Bertie observed a ragged fringe of palms across his bows. As he drew nearer, a broad river, which he knew could only be the Nile, came into view. He had only a very vague idea of what part of the river it was, but that, for the moment, did not matter. It was pleasant to see again something green. Now, surely, the Renkells would go down.

The Renkells went on. Bertie glared; he muttered; but it made no difference. To give up the pursuit, after such an extended chase, would be maddening, but prudence counselled a halt while there was still a little petrol in the Spur's tank. He wavered, and while he did so his problem was answered for him. The Renkells, still on their original course, disappeared into the haze. Bertie made a half-hearted attempt to find them, but he soon gave it up. Just what lay ahead he did not know – except, as far as he could see, the desert. Clearly, it would be suicidal to go on. The Spur had been handicapped in the matter of range by starting from the coast with a tank that was not full. Then there had been the flight to Zufra, which had lowered the gauge still more. The Renkells had obviously started from the oasis with full tanks, which suggested that petrol, probably in a concealed dump, was available at Zufra. Bertie made a mental note of it, and turned back to the river, over which he had passed.

Hot, tired, and disgruntled, he followed its course northward, and was pleasantly surprised when, after a further twenty minutes in the air, he saw a town of flat roofs that he recognised as Khartoum, with its aerodrome and big R.A.F. depot. Down to the last pint of petrol, he landed, and reported to the Duty Officer, a youthful pilot officer who, judging from his manner, regarded him with not unpardonable suspicion.

'What cheer,' he greeted.

'What cheer yourself,' returned Bertie.

The lad looked at the Spur. 'That isn't the sort of machine I'd expect a civilian to be flying,' he observed shrewdly.

Bertie considered him through his monocle with sympathetic toleration. 'In this world, a lot of things will happen that you don't expect, young feller-me-lad,' he responded. 'I'd like some petrol – and all that sort of thing.'

'Is that so?' inquired the duty officer, sarcasm creeping into his voice. 'What do you think this is – a public garage?'

'I,' said Bertie deliberately, 'am a policeman.'

The pilot looked incredulous. 'Are you kidding?'

Bertie frowned. 'Don't I look like one?'

The lad looked Bertie up and down. 'No. In fact, I can't recall ever seeing anything less like one,' he remarked, with the ingenuous frankness of youth. 'Got any papers on you?'

With mild consternation Bertie realised that he had not – or none that would help him. Biggles carried the official documents. He made this confession.

'You're coming with me to see the C.O.,' decided the duty officer, with some asperity.

'All right – all right – there's nothing to get excited about,' returned Bertie. 'Who's in command here?'

'Group Captain Wilkinson.'

'Not the chap they call Wilks?'

'That's him.'

'That's marvellous – absolutely marvellous,' murmured Bertie. 'Astonishing luck, and all that. My troubles are over.'

'Is he a pal of yours?' inquired the pilot.

'No – but he's a pal of a pal of mine – if you see what I mean?' declared Bertie.

'I don't, but never mind. You can tell your hard luck story to him,' consented the pilot. 'But I warn you,' he added, 'he takes a poor view of aviators who waffle about the Sahara with dry tanks. Come on.'

In a few minutes, having introduced himself, Bertie was telling his story – or as much of it as was appropriate – to the Group Captain, whom he had never met, but whom he knew had for years been a close friend of Biggles, who always referred to him as Wilks.

'Well, well. So Biggles is an airborne cop?' murmured Wilks when Bertie had finished. 'He's tried most things, but this is something new. And you say you don't know where he is?'

'If he wasn't in one of those two Nazi kites, then he's still at Zufra – alive or dead,' answered Bertie.

'It would surprise me very much if he were dead,' returned Wilks, with a faint smile. 'By rights he should have been killed years ago, but he seems to be one of those chaps who have the knack of slipping through the clammy clutches of Old Man Death every time. But what's your idea now – I mean, what do you propose doing?'

'There's only one thing I can do,' decided Bertie. 'If you'll fill me up with juice I'll claw my way back to Zufra and have a dekko round the jolly old date palms.'

Wilks looked serious. 'You can have the petrol, of course, but it seems to me that there are several snags in that arrangement. First of all, it's bad country, and there's a deuce of a lot of it between here and Zufra.'

'I noticed it,' murmured Bertie.

'Down here we don't like machines flying alone too far afield,' went on Wilks. 'We prefer to fly in pairs, at least, the idea being that if one has trouble, and has to go down, the other can pick him up, or pin-point the spot so that we know just where he is. Another snag; you say Algy Lacey and young Ginger Hebblethwaite are at Zufra. If Biggles is there, there will be four of you. You couldn't all pile into the Spur. You would have to make at least two journeys to get them out. I can't see any necessity for that. Why not take a big machine, or better still, have one of my Lankies[1] go along with you. You could then evacuate the whole party at one go.'

'That's a stupendous idea – absolutely terrific,' declared Bertie. 'Jolly sporting of you, and all that.'

---

[1] R.A.F. slang for the Lancaster Bomber.

'I'm a bit worried about these mines,' went on Wilks. 'We can't leave the infernal things lying about for the Arabs to trip over. They'll have to be cleared up.'

'Absolutely,' agreed Bertie. 'But not by me. No bally fear. I'm frightened to death of the beastly things.'

'I wasn't thinking of you,' replied Wilks. 'I'll have a word with the political officer about it. It's really his pigeon. We've got some Askaris[1] here – the Fourth Pioneer Corps. They are trained in mine detecting – had plenty of practice chasing Rommel in the Western Desert during the war. They could go out in the Lanky when you go.'

'Absolutely. By Jove! Yes,' said Bertie, warmly. 'Then, if the crooks were still in occupation at Zufra we could mop the whole place up – what!'

'I'll suggest it to headquarters at Cairo,' promised Wilks. 'We should have to get their okay. I'll tell you what. Leave this to me. You trot along to the mess and tear open a tin of bully. By the time you get back I shall have got a decision on the matter. If it's okay to proceed I'll organise the sortie.'

'That's the tops, sir, absolutely tophole,' declared Bertie. 'Biggles always said you were the king-pin. Thanks, and all that.' Feeling better, Bertie went off to the mess.

When he returned, an hour later, he found that the station commander had wasted no time in keeping his promise. With him was a flying-officer, and a spick and span, dark-skinned, Askari sergeant.

Wilks introduced the R.A.F. officer. 'This is Collingwood,' he said. 'Colly, for short. He'll fly the Lanky. Unfortunately, Jones

[1] African soldiers in European armies.

of the Askaris is down with fever, so I got in touch with Cairo myself. They say the mines must be cleared immediately, and the Fourth Pioneers are to do the job. They'll take mine-detecting gear with them, and stay at Zufra till the work's finished. It'll probably take two or three days. I've told Collingwood that there's no need for him to stay there; Sergeant Mahmud is quite capable of taking charge. Colly will go back in a day or two to bring the working party home. If you can show Sergeant Mahmud roughly where the mines are, he'll do the rest.'

'I'm not sure about the position of the mines myself, but Ginger knows all about them,' remarked Bertie.

'In that case you'd better land both the Spur and the Lanky well clear of the oasis, and march in,' suggested Wilks.

'Absolutely,' agreed Bertie, emphatically.

'If you do happen to meet any opposition at Zufra the Askaris will handle it – not that I think that's likely, since the Renkells have fled elsewhere.'

Bertie concurred.

'If Biggles is at Zufra with the others you could all come back here together,' went on Wilks. 'As the crooks have gone some-where south-east of here I imagine that this place would suit you as well as anywhere for a temporary base.'

'That's what I was thinking,' rejoined Bertie. 'The final decision about that, though, will rest with Biggles, if he is still at Zufra.'

Wilks nodded. 'Good enough. Your machine has been refuelled, so you may as well get off right away. That should get you to Zufra before sundown. You could either come straight back here or wait till morning. There's a moon, so if you take my tip you'll make a night flight – it's a lot more comfortable than flying across that devil's cauldron in the sun.'

'I'll remember it, and thanks again for your co-operation. It makes it all easy.' Bertie turned to Colly. 'I'm ready to push off, if you are.'

They went out to the aerodrome, where Bertie watched a dozen efficient-looking Askaris, under Sergeant Mahmud, in full desert equipment, file into a Lancaster that stood waiting. Colly climbed into his cockpit. As the motors growled, Bertie walked over to the Spur.

In a few minutes both machines were off the ground, thrusting north-west through the sun-drenched air above the scintillating sea of sand.

CHAPTER XIII

Events at El Zufra

It did not take those left at the oasis long to force the door of the hut and help themselves to the ample supply of tinned food and mineral waters which they found there. Their immediate requirements satisfied, they selected a shady position under the palms, one that commanded a view of the desert to the north, and sat down to wait for what might befall. There was nothing else they could do.

Naturally, their conversation was practically confined to one subject – the mystery of Bertie's disappearance. Algy stated positively that the Spur had not been attacked on the ground, or there would have been evidence of it, such as bullet-marks in the sand, which he could not have overlooked. After debating the subject from all angles they were unanimous in the opinion that the most obvious solution was probably the correct one – that Bertie had seen or heard the Renkells take off, and had followed them. Biggles asserted that he could think of no other reason why Bertie should leave the ground.

As the day wore on what did puzzle him was why the Spur should remain away for so long. It gave rise to a fear – although he did not mention this – that Bertie had attacked the Renkells, found trouble, and was down somewhere in the desert. When four hours had elapsed, and still the Spur did not show up, he inclined more and more to this view. Knowing the endurance of the aircraft, he remarked that wherever the machine might be, it was no longer in the air, for the simple reason that its petrol must be exhausted.

'One thing is quite certain,' he averred. 'We can't get back on our feet. Four hundred miles would be a tidy jaunt on a macadam road with a tavern at every corner. Across that' – he nodded towards the glowing sand – 'it couldn't be done. Gontermann was right about that. The only thing we can do is wait. If the Spur doesn't come back, then we'll stay here and fight it out with the crooks when they return, as they are almost sure to, sooner or later. If the Spur does come we can't all get into it. I'll fly up into Egypt with Bertie and try to get another Mosquito to replace the one we've lost. Which reminds me: if Bertie comes back he won't dare to land near the oasis for fear of putting his wheels on a mine. The chances are that he'll land at the place from which he took off. He knows that's safe, and that's where we shall look for him. But we can't sit out there all day in the sun. One of us will have to go out and leave a note to let him know that we're waiting here, at the oasis. If we fix it on a piece of stick he can hardly miss seeing it. We'll tell him to taxi towards the *wadi*, when one of us will go out to show him the way in.'

'He knows there's a safe runway along the *wadi*, because I told him so,' put in Ginger.

'Never mind. We'll go out to meet him. This is no time to take chances,' asserted Biggles.

'What beats me is, why the Renkells left here, and where they could have gone,' muttered Algy.

'They probably left here because it's no sort of a place for an extended stay,' answered Biggles. 'They only use the oasis as an advanced landing-ground; they told me so; which means that their permanent hide-out is tucked away still farther in the back of beyond.'

'When they talked about leaving in the morning, they didn't drop any sort of hint as to where they might be going?' queried Ginger.

'Come to think of it, they did – or rather Grindler did,' murmured Biggles thoughtfully. 'I can't remember his exact words, but he said something about going back to that goldarned Sanseviera – or some such word. It sounds like the name of a place. I've never heard of it, but if it is, we ought to be able to find it. Now I think we ought to see about fixing that note in case Bertie comes back.'

'I'll take it,' offered Ginger. 'This sitting here doing nothing gives me the willies.'

'Be careful not to lose your way – it's pretty hot out on the sand,' warned Biggles.

'Don't you worry about that,' returned Ginger grimly. 'I shall follow our tracks out and back. You write the note.'

Biggles wrote the message on a leaf of his note-book, and selecting a dead palm frond, stripped it until only the spine remained. In the end of this he made a slit to hold the paper, and passed it to Ginger, who took it, and with his tattered jacket on his head departed on his errand.

Biggles and Algy sat in the shade where they could watch him, still talking over the strange turn of events, grim evidence of which lay before them in the shape of two dead Arabs, the remains of two camels, and the blackened area that marked the burnt-out Mosquito. None of these could be approached, of course, on account of the mines.

Time passed, probably the best part of two hours. They saw Ginger coming back, a microscopic figure in the vastness, making for the entrance to the *wadi* which, as far as they knew, provided the only safe path through the mine-field. They watched him without any particular interest; and perhaps because their eyes were on him they failed for some time to see another movement away to the west. In fact, their attention was only called to it by the behaviour of Ginger, who suddenly stopped, staring across the sand, shielding his eyes with his hands. At that time he was about four hundred yards away.

'What's he staring at?' muttered Algy, with quickening interest.

Biggles uttered an ejaculation and sprang to his feet. He did not speak. There was no need. Also advancing towards the oasis, on a line that would intercept Ginger before he reached it, from a fold in the ground had appeared a group of camels, mostly with riders, a dozen all told, with long rifles slung across their shoulders.

'Arabs,' said Algy.

'Touregs,' said Biggles, noting the blue veils that covered the faces of the riders. There was a suspicion of uneasiness in his voice, for he knew that while the nomad Touregs seldom interfered with white travellers, they resented their intrusion, and on that account were not entirely to be trusted. Still, he did not think they were in real danger. Neither, evidently, did Ginger, for after a good look at the newcomers he walked on towards the oasis.

Biggles's only real fear at this stage of the proceedings was that the Touregs might inadvertently attempt to cross the mine-field; not for a moment did it occur to him that they might know about the mines; and it was with the object of preventing an accident that he started forward. At the same time the riders whipped their camels into a run, directly towards Ginger who, seeing that he was their objective, stopped to wait for them. In any case he could not hope to outrun the camels to the oasis. Wild yells from the Touregs now made it plain that their intentions were not friendly.

'You stay here, Algy,' snapped Biggles, and began running along the *wadi* towards the group out in the desert.

By the time he had reached it Ginger had been surrounded, and was now being driven in a hostile manner towards the oasis.

The party halted and silence fell as Biggles ran up, hands raised to show that he was unarmed. Dark, sullen, inscrutable eyes, looked down on him. He spoke first in English, but receiving no answer, tried French. Upon this, at a word of command, one of the camels 'couched', and its rider, a leader by his bearing, dismounted. He was tall, bearded, lean, with fierce eyes, a true son of the desert and a magnificent specimen of manhood. He answered Biggles, in guttural French, with a question.

'Why have you done this?' he demanded harshly, indicating the desert with a sweep of his arm.

At first Biggles did not understand. Then he saw the Touregs looking at the dead men and beasts that lay drying in the sun, and it needed no effort of the imagination to guess the cause of the natives' belligerent attitude.

'We did not kill them,' he said quickly.

'You have put the bombs in the sand,' accused the sheikh.

All was now plain. 'These men who were killed were of your tribe?' queried Biggles.

'One was my son,' was the grim rejoinder. 'My brother lost an arm, but was able to reach my tents. You fired at him with rifles as he ran across the sand.'

This was worse, much worse, than Biggles expected. He did not doubt that the chief spoke the truth, and he mentally cursed Gontermann for his foul work.

'We did not shoot, and we did not put bombs in the sand,' he asserted. 'Not knowing that you knew of the bombs I ran out to warn you not to cross the sand. The men who did this evil thing are our enemies; we came here seeking them; that, O sheikh, is the truth, and the government at Cairo will bear witness.'

The Toureg's hard expression did not change. 'What does it matter who put the bombs? The faces of the men who did this thing were white, so they were of your tribe.'

Biggles realised the futility of trying to explain to the savage that all white men were not of the same 'tribe'. 'There are bad men, and good, in every tribe,' he said earnestly. 'The men who put these bombs in the sand are outlaws, fleeing from justice. They tried to kill us, too, but we escaped.'

The sheikh was not impressed. 'Where are your camels?'

'We have no camels,' answered Biggles.

'Then how did you get here?'

'We came through the air in one of the machines that fly.'

The sheikh drew in his breath with a hissing sound, and there was a note of triumph in his voice when he challenged. 'The men who put the bombs came here in a flying-machine. You must be the same. Allah, the Merciful, has delivered you into our hands. We shall kill you. Go.' The chief pointed to the oasis.

'Wait!' cried Biggles. 'I say again that the men who put the bombs in the sand were our enemies, enemies that we came here to seek. If you kill us they will go free, for you cannot follow them into the air. We are your friends, and to prove this I warn you that when you reach the oasis, keep away from the water, for there are more bombs in the sand around it. Stay away, too, from the large tent, where there are yet more bombs; but this, I swear, was not our doing.'

'What does it matter who did it?' returned the sheikh with primitive but deadly logic. 'My son is slain. White men are all the same. They bring death to where there was only peace.'

Biggles looked at Ginger and shrugged his shoulders. 'I'm afraid there's nothing we can do about it. I sympathise with these chaps. We can't blame them for taking this line. Were we in their sandals we should probably feel the same way as they do about it.' To the sheikh he said, 'Keep in the *wadi*; it is the only safe way.' And with that, followed by the rest, he walked back to the oasis.

Algy was waiting at the fringe, his right hand behind his back. Knowing that it held a pistol – he himself was unarmed – Biggles shook his head. 'Put it away,' he said quietly. 'If you show it it will only make matters worse. We can't fight this bunch. Our only hope is to try to placate them by argument. They think we laid the mines – the sheikh's son was killed by one.'

Algy returned the pistol to his pocket. 'May the devil run away with that hound Gontermann,' he snarled. 'One skunk like that undoes all the good our people do.' He joined the party, which proceeded to an open area among the palms, close to the water-hole.

There was nearly a nasty accident forthwith, for the camels strained to get to the water, and it was only with difficulty that they were held back. Biggles shouted, and pointed to the two mines which he had unearthed, as proof of his allegation that the pool was a death-trap.

'If you need water I'll fetch it for you,' he offered. And he did, in fact, fill the Touregs' leather buckets and water-skins, going to and fro through the narrow path he had cleared to escape from the pool. The natives watched him with cold, expressionless eyes.

When the camels had been watered and tethered the Touregs formed a rough circle in the clearing, and the sheikh addressed them in their own tongue. It was a long speech. No one interrupted. What he said, of course, the prisoners did not know, although it was obvious that their fate was being discussed. They sat together, watching, Biggles smoking a cigarette. The question of escape did not arise, for there was nowhere to go except into the desert, which offered only an alternative form of death. The Touregs were well aware of this and took no notice of them.

When the sheikh finished talking the others at once broke into a violent argument among themselves – or so it appeared.

'I wish I knew what was going on,' muttered Ginger.

'I think it's pretty clear,' replied Biggles. 'The sheikh has told the story of the mines, with all the gory details, after the manner of a judge summing up. He has now left it to his men to decide what shall be done with us. That's the usual Arab way of doing things. The sheikh's own opinion no doubt carries a good deal of weight, but with these wandering bands it isn't final. A man is chosen as chief, but he only holds that position while the majority agree with him. The true Arabs refuse to be dictated to by anyone; they obey their chief as long as it suits them; but if they disagree with him they get over the difficulty by choosing another sheikh. The fact that these fellows are arguing is a good sign. It means that some of them, including the sheikh, I fancy, are against doing anything drastic in a hurry.'

At this point the sheikh came up to Biggles and asked, 'Where is the machine that flies?'

Biggles stretched a finger towards the charred remains of the Mosquito. 'Our enemies, your enemies, those who put the bombs in the sand, set fire to it and fled, leaving us to perish, as you may see for yourselves.'

The sheikh obviously repeated this information to his warriors, and it seemed to make a good impression. As Biggles had said, the point of his argument was there, on the sand, for all to see.

Biggles decided to follow up the ground he had gained. He addressed the sheikh. 'If you kill us,' he said, 'the bombs will remain in the sand for all time, and the oasis will be a place of death for every Arab who passes this way. Help us to cross the desert and we will return with soldiers who will clear away the bombs and make the place safe for man and beast. *W'allah!* It is for you to decide.'

The sheikh repeated this statement, again with good effect, for the advantages of the plan to the Arabs could hardly be denied. Only one or two of the warriors were irreconcilable, handling the hilts of their long-bladed knives in a manner that left no doubt as to the course they would have preferred. Nevertheless, they were a minority; the chief harangued them, and Biggles ventured to predict that everything would be all right.

And so it might have been but for a tragedy that overwhelmed all the good that had been gained by fair argument. One of the warriors, moved by some impulse known only to himself, strode towards the water-hole. No one noticed him for a moment. Then Biggles caught sight of him out of the corner of his eye and let

'It is for you to decide.'

out a yell, but he was too late by a split second. The shout was lost in a deafening explosion that threw everyone flat. The man who had stepped on the mine lay where he had been flung, a horrid heap of quivering flesh. Another warrior was trying with his hands to stop blood that was spurting from his leg. Another clutched at his face, that had been torn open by a splinter.

Silence fell – a deadly, ominous silence.

'That, I'm afraid, has sunk us,' remarked Biggles evenly.

The Touregs, for a moment stricken dumb by shock, found their tongues in a howl of rage. There was no longer any talking, only savage muttering. All eyes were on the prisoners. Knives swished from their leather sheaths. Only the sheikh stood aloof. The circle began to close in, not quickly, but slowly, as though there was some doubt as to who should strike the first blow.

'This is it,' said Algy, and drew his pistol.

'I object to being butchered like a sheep,' declared Ginger. He, too, drew his automatic.

The Touregs halted, tense, some half crouching, checked for the moment. The atmosphere was electric, like the lull before a storm.

CHAPTER XIV

Back to the Trail

Into this dramatic scene anti-climax arrived like a thunderbolt – although with less noise.

'Hi! Hi! Hi! there,' said a voice in a tone of gentle reproof. 'You fellows mustn't do that sort of thing, really, you know.'

Again silence fell. All movement stopped except at one place. Bertie, monocle in his eye, a cigarette between his lips, smiling a rather foolish, almost an apologetic grin, walked slowly into the scene as an actor steps on a stage from the wings. He tapped the ash off his cigarette. 'Hallo everybody,' he greeted. 'Sorry I've been away so long. It looks as if I've arrived in the jolly old nick of time – what?'

'You've arrived just in time to get your jolly old throat cut,' muttered Ginger.

Bertie stopped. 'Really? I say, that's too bad.'

'Don't stand there looking like a fool,' grated Biggles. 'There's going to be a rough house.'

The Touregs stared at Bertie. They stared at Biggles. They stared at each other, dull amazement on their faces. Bertie's miraculous arrival evidently upset them. It may have been the calm manner of it as much as the actual event. At any rate, shock took the sting out of them, if only temporarily. The sheikh spoke to Biggles, pointing at Bertie.

'Who is the man who wears a window in his face? Is he your friend, or an enemy?'

'A friend,' answered Biggles.

'Is he alone?'

It did not occur to Biggles that this could be otherwise, but he put the question to Bertie.

'Alone? No bally fear,' answered Bertie. 'We're quite a party. You wait and see. I walked on ahead.'

There came a sound of voices, and a moment later another actor appeared on this curious stage. It was Flying-Officer Collingwood, in uniform.

'What cheer,' he said casually. 'What's going on?' He glanced at the Touregs. 'You've got company, I see.'

Before anyone could answer, Sergeant Mahmud and his twelve Askaris appeared at the edge of the clearing. They halted, and at a word of command, 'ordered arms' smartly. The comical part of this was, that after a curt nod of greeting to the sheikh, Sergeant Mahmud took no further notice of the Touregs, who, suddenly confronted by this display of armed force, continued to stand and stare. One by one they sheathed their knives.

Biggles shared in their surprise. He, too, stared, mostly at the Askaris. 'Bertie, where in heaven's name did you pick up this army?' he asked in a dazed voice.

'Pick it up? I didn't pick it up,' declared Bertie. 'The Higher Command has sent them along to clear up these beastly mines.'

Biggles passed a hand over his eyes like a man who doubts his senses. 'Where the deuce have you been?'

'Khartoum,' answered Bertie evenly.

Biggles started. '*Where?*'

'Khartoum. You know, the jolly little place on the Nile.'

'But that's a thousand miles away.'

Bertie smiled wearily. 'It seemed more like ten thousand to me – I've just been there and back.'

Biggles leaned limply against a palm. 'I'm going crazy,' he muttered. 'It must be the sun.'

'I wasn't sure about the mines, so we parked our kites on the sand and walked in.'

'Kites?' queried Biggles. 'Don't tell me you've brought a squadron here?'

'No. Colly hoisted the soldiers here in a Lanky.'

'Oh,' said Biggles.

The different parties on the oasis now began to sort them-selves out. Naturally, the white men drifted together. The Askaris began forthwith to clear the mines away from the water-hole. The Touregs watched for a time, and then silently faded away into the desert that was their home, heading in single file towards the setting sun. Biggles had told the sheikh that in a few days the oasis would be safe.

Explanations followed. Biggles narrated briefly what had happened on the oasis, and Bertie, at greater length, told of his flight to Khartoum, and of his meeting there with Wilks.

'Bit of luck finding Wilks there,' observed Biggles. 'He's a good scout. I think you did quite right to follow the Renkells. What I'm most pleased about is your getting their compass course. If we follow that line it ought to take us to Gontermann's base camp – that is, if he wasn't laying a false trail, which in the circumstances seems unlikely. My map was burnt in the Mosquito, or I'd plot the course right away to see where it leads.' He turned to Collingwood. 'How long have you been in Upper Egypt?'

'Six months.'

'Ever hear of a place called Sanseviera?'

Colly shook his head. 'Never – and I know most of the country round Khartoum. Of course, I haven't been any great distance to the east, because we don't patrol over Abyssinia.'

Biggles started. 'Abyssinia! Of course! By thunder! – that's the answer. Scaroni served in Abyssinia during the campaign. He probably knows every inch of the country. Abyssinia would be a central point for striking at the Persian Gulf, Kenya, and the Mediterranean. Scaroni has got another of his secret dumps there – buried the stuff, no doubt, to prevent it from falling into our hands when we pushed the Italians out. We'll get along to Khartoum right away, and take up the trail again from there. Are you going to stay here with the Askaris, Collingwood?'

'No my orders are to leave them here to clean up, and collect them in a day or two. I'm going back to Khartoum. There's plenty of room for everybody in my Lanky.'

'Any objection to starting right away?'

Colly smiled. 'I'd rather do that than sweat across this blistering desert tomorrow morning in the sun.'

'That's fine,' declared Biggles. 'Let's get cracking. Bertie, you must be tired; you go in the Lanky and snatch a snooze. Algy, you'd better go with him. Ginger can come with me in the Spur.'

And so it was decided. Biggles made a tour with Sergeant Mahmud to show him the approximate position of the mines, and then, rejoining the others, they all walked up the *wadi* to the aircraft, which had been left some distance out, Bertie having landed at the spot from which he had taken off, and followed the instructions contained in the note, which he had found. Darkness was settling over the wilderness, so without further discussion they disposed themselves as arranged. The two machines then took off and set a course for Khartoum.

The flight was uneventful, and it was just eleven o'clock when they arrived over the aerodrome and received permission to land.

In a few minutes, at Station Headquarters, Biggles was shaking hands with Wilks. Algy and Ginger took part in the reunion, for they, too, knew the Group Captain, although he had not reached that high rank when they last saw him. Wilks had been expecting them and a late supper had been laid in the mess. While this was being enjoyed, and over the coffee that followed, Biggles took his old comrade into his full confidence. This was necessary, if only because his close co-operation would be required if the pursuit of the bandits was to be pushed on without loss of time.

'I heard about the affair of the *Calpurnia*,' said Wilks, when Biggles had finished. 'In fact, Egypt is buzzing with it. They say there's an unholy row over the loss of the rajah's jewels.'

'So I imagine,' returned Biggles. 'I shall have to get in touch with the Yard right away to let Raymond know that we're doing something about it. He hasn't the remotest idea of where we are or what we are doing. I'll bet he's tearing his hair out in handfuls. That isn't our fault; things have happened too fast for me to keep him informed. I doubt if even he realised that this chase was going to take us halfway across the world. What are the chances of getting a cable through from here?'

'You can send a cable in the ordinary way from the post office,' answered Wilks. 'But as this is something of a national matter, and confidential, I feel justified in sending a signal through, in code, to the Air Ministry, who will pass it on to Raymond.'

'That's fine,' asserted Biggles. 'The difficulty is to know how much to tell him. I think, as matters stand, all we can say is that we're on the track, and expect results shortly. Another thing I must do is get a spare machine, a Mosquito if possible, from the aircraft park at Heliopolis. They have some there. If they say I can have one, perhaps you wouldn't mind one of your lads flying Algy and Bertie up to fetch it?'

'Not in the least,' agreed Wilks. 'But do you really expect results?'

'It all depends on how my two clues pan out,' replied Biggles. 'The first is the compass course on which the Renkells were flying. That should give us the general line. We can plot it in the map room. The other is a place called Sanseviera – or something like that; Grindler happened to mention it in the course of the conversation. By rights, it should be on the course the bandits were flying. Did you ever hear of a place of that name?'

Wilks shook his head. 'Never – although there's plenty of it not far from here. There's a lot in the Sudd – you know, the swamp higher up the river.'

Biggles looked puzzled. 'I don't understand. A lot of what?'

'Sanseviera.'

Biggles stared. 'What the devil are you talking about?'

'I'm talking about sanseviera.'

'Listen, old boy.' murmured Biggles, 'I'm trying to remain calm. Will you please tell me, in plain, simple English, what is this sanseviera?'

'I mean the stuff that grows.'

'*Grows?*'

'Yes, it's a plant.'

Understanding dawned in Biggles's eyes. 'Good Lord!' he breathed.

'Didn't you know?' inquired Wilks.

'What gave you the idea that I was a professor of botany?' demanded Biggles. 'Horticulture isn't my strong suit. Tell me more about this stuff.'

'Frankly, I don't know much about it myself, except that it's something to avoid,' answered Wilks. 'The common name is bow-string hemp. It's a tall, spiny bush, rather like a cactus. I believe there are different sorts, but the stuff around here sprouts up a bunch of leaves that look like flattish cylinders, mottled, about six feet high. You find it all over East Africa. In fact, I hear they are cultivating it now in Kenya – they make ropes out of the fibres. There's a whole forest of it, hundreds of square miles, just over the frontier in Abyssinia. I happen to know that because during the war, on a reconnaissance, one of my lads, a chap named Saunders, made a forced landing in the blasted stuff. It took him a fortnight to find a way out. He reckoned he never would have got out had he not been found by some Samburus – the local natives. Saunders told me that the place was mostly swamp, crawling with crocodiles, snakes, and bugs of all shapes and sizes. He was nearly torn to pieces by mosquitoes.'

During this recital Biggles sat staring at Wilks's face. 'Well, I'm dashed! So *that's* it?' he muttered at the finish. 'What a set-up. I should never have guessed. Now we're getting somewhere. It looks as if Gontermann's permanent hide-out is somewhere in that cactus patch.'

'If it is, you're going to have a lovely time trying to find it,' opined Wilks.

'If the compass course crosses it, and I'm willing to bet my brolly that it does, by following the line we ought to hit the camp.'

'That may be so,' agreed Wilks. 'And then what?'

'I see what you mean,' said Biggles slowly. 'If we fly over it we shall be seen, and if we are seen the blighters will know we're on their track.'

'Exactly. How are you going to get at them?'

'How about dropping a bomb or two on them, to stir them up – if you see what I mean?' suggested Bertie. 'Scatter them, and all that.'

'A direct hit would also scatter the rajah's jewels,' Biggles pointed out. 'Apart from that, we're policemen now, not war flyers, and a policeman isn't justified in dishing out his own idea of justice even though he may shoot in self-defence. I aim to catch this skunk Gontermann, and deliver him, alive, to those who will see that he answers for his crimes with a nice piece of new rope round his neck. Shooting is too good for him.' Biggles turned back to Wilks. 'All the same, remind me to borrow a gun from you – in case. I wonder if we could get into this sanseviera stuff on foot?'

'I should be sorry to try that,' declared Wilks. 'Abyssinia is a wild country, and since the natives were sprayed with poison gas by the Italians they take a pretty dim view of white men, regardless of nationality.'

'But Gontermann and Co. are there,' argued Biggles.

'They probably keep the natives at a distance with machine-guns,' returned Wilks. 'You couldn't play that sort of game. Another point you appear to have overlooked is, you'd have to get permission to fly over Abyssinia. People are getting particular as to who waffles about their territory.'

'Who's going to stop us?'

'The Abyssinian Air Force might – the Emperor has one, you know, at Addis Ababa. If you start scrapping with them you'd be liable to start another war. This is really a matter for the Foreign Office.'

'I'm afraid you're right,' agreed Biggles. 'We don't want to start another rumpus. I'll tell Raymond that we've located the crooks in Western Abyssinia, and ask him to get permission for us to go in from the Abyssinian Minister in London. That should keep us safe from the political angle.'

'Whatever you do, you'll always be faced with the difficulty of making an air reconnaissance without being seen, and once you're spotted you'll be handicapped from the start,' said Wilks pensively. 'I don't see how you can get over that.'

'There's always a way of getting over an obstacle – if you can find it,' remarked Biggles. 'That's one of my little axioms.' A twinkle came into his eyes. 'I think I've got it. You say Abyssinia has its own air force?'

'Yes.'

'What machines do they use?'

'I'm not sure about that,' answered Wilks. 'We had a formation over here a week or two back on a courtesy visit; but they were trainers – Tiger Moths.'

'Have you any Tiger Moths here?'

'Yes, we've a couple. We use them for co-operation with the Askaris.' Wilks looked suspicious. 'What's the bright idea?'

'From what you tell me,' explained Biggles, 'it wouldn't be a remarkable thing if an Abyssinian Tiger Moth flew across this sanseviera area. I mean, Gontermann wouldn't take any notice of that.'

Wilks looked puzzled. 'I don't get it. We haven't got an Abyssinian Tiger Moth, and if you're thinking of going to Addis Ababa to borrow one you'll have grey hair before you get back. Our Tigers wear R.A.F. ring markings.'

Biggles grinned. 'Did you never hear of a stuff called paint? They say you can't make a leopard change his spots, but we could make one of your Tigers change his stripes by painting out our own nationality marks and substituting those of the venerable land of Ethiopia.'

'Hey! Wait a minute,' cried Wilks. 'Do you want to get me court-martialled?'

'Frankly, I don't care what you get, old bloodhound, as long as I get these infernal crooks,' returned Biggles lightly.

'You always were a calculating son-of-a-gun,' growled Wilks. But humour glinted in his eyes. 'All right. I'll do it. All the same, you owe it to the Foreign Office to let them know that you propose to cruise over a prohibited area, in case you run into trouble or have a forced landing.'

'Now you're talking,' declared Biggles. He grinned again. 'No use having pals if you don't use them sometimes.'

'You write out your message for Raymond and I'll see that it's transmitted by radio right away,' invited Wilks. 'Then, if you don't mind, I'll get some sleep. I've work to do tomorrow.'

'Now you remind me, I could do with a spot of shut-eye myself,' said Biggles, yawning.

CHAPTER XV

The Sanseviera

The air police were at breakfast the following morning when the answer to Biggles's signal to Air Commodore Raymond was received. Wilks brought it into the mess, and delivered it personally. He was smiling.

'I should say your remark about Raymond tearing his hair out was understatement rather than exaggeration,' he observed. 'Here's your answer – I've had it decoded.'

'Read it,' requested Biggles, reaching for the coffee. Wilks's smile broadened as he read:

'Owing to Calpurnia affair matter has become a political issue in Parliament stop I shall be on the mat unless you end racket stop Go where you like and do what you like as long as you get crooks stop Leave subsequent explanations to me stop R.A.F., Middle East Command, has been ordered by Secretary of State for Air to co-operate without limit stop Signed Raymond.'

A smile spread slowly over Biggles's face. 'Strewth! Raymond must be in a sweat to send a message like that. I like the last part – that relieves you of any responsibility, Wilks.'

Wilks folded the message. 'It looks as if you'd better get cracking, my merry sleuth,' he advised.

'You can get *your* boys cracking with their paint pots, on a Tiger Moth, for a start,' requested Biggles. 'I'm going to cast an eye over this sanseviera jungle.'

'They're already on the job,' answered Wilks.

'Good. In that case you can go and ring up Heliopolis to see if I can borrow a Mosquito.'

'It's done,' announced Wilks. 'The machine is on the tarmac waiting for someone to fetch it. Collingwood is standing by to fly Algy and Bertie up, as soon as they've finished wolfing my last pot of marmalade.'

Biggles chuckled. 'You always were one for keeping pace with things. Get moving, Algy, and make it snappy.'

'What do we do when we've got the Mosquito?' asked Algy, rising, with a piece of toast still in his hand.

'Bring it here – that's all for the time being. I'll take Ginger with me on this jungle jaunt; we ought to be back before you are. What we do after that will depend on what we find. We can't do anything until we locate Gontermann's hide-out.'

'Okay,' said Algy. With a wave Bertie followed him to the door.

Biggles also rose, and tossed his napkin on the table. 'Come on, Ginger, if you want to sit in my spare seat. I'm all agog to run an optic over this botanical bunk-hole.'

'Anything more I can do?' asked Wilks.

'Yes, you can get me a nice big automatic and a couple of spare clips of slugs,' answered Biggles. 'I'd better have a pocket compass, too.' He went out to the aerodrome where a placid-looking Tiger Moth was receiving the final touches of its transformation.

In ten minutes, while the paint was still tacky, Biggles was in the air, flying south-east on the compass course that Bertie had given him, towards the Abyssinian border. This was well over two hundred miles distant, or a two hour flight each way, and the Tiger, even with a special long-range tank, had an endurance of just over five hours, it only left an hour – allowing a margin of safety – for the actual reconnaissance. Fortunately, the sanseviera area began not far from the border.

When this was reached, the country below, while bearing no resemblance to the desert, was nearly as depressing. The tangled mass of undergrowth, which Biggles knew must be the sanseviera, occurred first in scattered outposts; but these soon became larger, and eventually merged into one vast, dull green panorama, stretching as far as the eye could see, undulating rather than flat, with outcrops of gaunt rock sometimes breaking through the higher parts. There were numerous pools of water, frequently linked together by winding channels, and an occasional open space, or group of flat-topped trees, caused presumably by a change in the nature of the soil. If there were any paths through this hideous blemish on the earth's surface, they could not be seen. Yet, as Biggles pointed out, it was fairly certain that there must be paths, for twice he went low to examine the source of smoke which curled upward, and on each occasion it came from a primitive native village.

Biggles surveyed the gloomy picture with disfavour. 'What a place – what a mess,' he muttered. 'Fancy getting lost in that lot.'

Sometimes circling over suspicious-looking areas, but always returning to the original compass course, Biggles went on and at the end, after covering nearly seventy miles of it, came to the far side of the sanseviera jungle. The growth gave way to arid, rocky hills. By that time he was near the limit of his petrol range, so, without finding what he sought, he was compelled to fly straight back to the aerodrome. He made no secret of his disappointment.

Bertie and Algy were not yet back, but they landed some time later in the new Mosquito.

The same afternoon Biggles made another five-hour reconnaissance, again without result. He went out the following morning as soon as it was light, and returned, disgruntled, to report no progress. Algy and Bertie went out, using the same Tiger Moth. They, too, came back depressed, with nothing to report.

'I know what the trouble is,' said Biggles savagely, as they dressed on the third morning. 'They've got the place camouflaged – too well camouflaged. But there, I suppose that was only to be expected. No doubt they all know something about camouflage, but Scaroni, as a transport and supply officer, is probably an expert. I'm sick of flying up and down over the cursed stuff, but there's nothing else for it. What worries me is, if we go on like this Gontermann will realise that the Tiger isn't just a casual machine passing over; not being a fool he'll know that somebody is looking for him. Come on, Ginger, let's have another shot.'

The Tiger went off. Collingwood also went off, to Zufra, and returned later with the Askaris, who had finished their job of mine clearing. Biggles wasn't interested in mines, or Zufra. The reconnaissance had revealed nothing, and he was getting desperate. His state of mind was not improved when a signal was received from Raymond, demanding in no uncertain terms to be informed what he thought he was doing.

Biggles looked at the others, with eyes weary and bloodshot

from long hours in the air. 'He wants to know what we are doing,' he said plaintively. 'I don't know what to tell him, and that's a fact.'

'You can tell him we're all going nuts, looking for a needle in a haystack a hundred miles square,' muttered Algy.

Wilks was sympathetic, but had no suggestion to make.

Biggles turned towards the mess. 'Let's have some lunch. I'll try again this afternoon.'

Half an hour later, surprisingly, another signal was received from Raymond. This time it contained information, and Biggles whistled joyfully when he read it. 'Listen,' he said. 'I'd completely forgotten that I'd asked the B.B.C. to listen for signals. Raymond says they've picked up something; they can't decipher it; all they can say is, something is coming over the air from an unknown source in Africa. They've sent us the bearing, in case it is any help to us.'

'Is it?' asked Bertie, vaguely.

'I'll say it is!' cried Biggles. 'That is, if it is Gontermann signalling to Preuss, as I hope. It's the answer to my prayer.'

'How do you work that out?' asked Algy.

'Because, if we strike this bearing from London across Africa, and then plot the course the Renkells took from Zufra, the point where the two lines meet – if they do – will be the place we're looking for. Let's go to the map room.'

After a few busy minutes with a pencil and ruler Biggles let out a cry of triumph. 'We've got it!' he declared, stabbing the map with the point of his pencil.

His enthusiasm was not without justification, for the two lines he had drawn cut across each other in the middle of the sanseviera.

'And now what are you going to do?' asked Wilks dispassionately. 'You must have flown over that spot before. If you fly over it again it's ten to one you'll still see nothing.'

'I'm not going to fly over it,' asserted Biggles grimly. 'I'm going to land.'

'In the sanseviera?' cried Wilks, aghast.

'In the nearest clearing that I can find to this spot.'

'You're crazy.'

'Maybe, but I shall soon go crazy, anyway, if I go on flying over that perishing jungle.'

'And suppose Gontermann and his gang *are* there?' inquired Wilks. 'What are two of you going to do against that bunch?'

'There'll be four of us,' retorted Biggles. 'We'll borrow the other Tiger.'

'And what if you bust them trying to get down?'

'If we make crash landings we'll clear a proper runway, so that you can fetch us out with a Lanky.'

'Suffering Icarus!' cried Wilks. 'What do you think this is – a circus? By the time you've finished you'll have my machines scattered halfway across the blinking continent.'

'That'll give you something to do – picking 'em up,' persisted Biggles. 'Come on, don't stand there blowing through your whiskers. Trot out that spare Tiger. Never mind about painting fresh colours on it – I'm in a hurry.'

'It's taken me twenty years to climb to Group Captain,' muttered Wilks in a resigned voice. 'By the time you've finished running my station I shall be back to aircraftman, second class.'

'Then you can start to climb up again,' said Biggles, grinning. 'Now you've had some practice you ought to be able to do it in nineteen years. Come on, chaps, let's get cracking. Algy, you follow in the second machine. If I can find a clearing without too many obstructions I'll go down first; if it's okay for you to follow I'll give you a wave.'

'Good enough,' agreed Algy cheerfully. 'Thank goodness things are looking up at last.'

'You'll probably change your mind about that when you've trodden on a snake or two, or tripped over a crocodile,' growled Wilks.

'Don't take any notice of him,' scoffed Biggles. 'He always was a pessimistic cove.'

Wilks's sunburned face flashed a smile. Then he became serious. 'Will you take a tip from me?'

Biggles noticed the change in his manner. 'I'll always take a tip from the man on the spot,' he assented.

'Take Sergeant Mahmud with you – he's back from Zufra.'

'For what purpose?'

'He may save you a packet of trouble if you encounter hostile natives. He speaks Amharic, the local lingo.'

'I see,' said Biggles slowly. 'It'll mean leaving one of the others behind, but I think you've got something there, Wilks. Sergeant Mahmud will fly with Algy. Sorry, Bertie, old boy, but you'll have to stand down. Wilks is right; it's in the best interests of the expedition.'

Bertie's face fell, but he was too well disciplined to argue. 'Pity, and all that,' he sighed. 'Isn't there something else I can do?'

'Yes, as a matter of fact, there is,' returned Biggles. 'We should look silly, shouldn't we, if one of the Renkells – or both of them for that matter – decided to pull out, leaving us staggering about in a couple of Tigers. You take the Spur and patrol the frontier. Keep high and you'll be able to watch a lot of sky. Should one of the Renkells try to break out, go for him.'

Bertie polished his eyeglass without enthusiasm. 'As you say, noble chief. Since birth it has been my fate to hold the dud end of the stick.'

'You never know which is the dud end until afterwards. You may have all the luck,' predicted Biggles, with unsuspected accuracy as it turned out. 'Well, we'll push along. Cheerio, Wilks. See you later.'

'You hope,' murmured Wilks.

In a few minutes the two Tigers were in the air, Biggles and Ginger in one, and Algy, with Sergeant Mahmud as passenger, in the other.

In spite of his inconsequential manner Biggles was under no delusion as to the dangerous nature of the task in front of him. The landing in the sanseviera, a hazardous expedient, was only the beginning. After that there would be the bandits, and that they would fight with all the weapons they possessed was not to be doubted. By this time he knew the general configuration of the country, and such landmarks as there were; and although he made straight for the pin-point indicated by the crossed lines on his map, he had no intention of flying over it, knowing that if he did he must inevitably be seen by the bandits, who, if not actually suspicious of this prowling Tiger Moth, would be on the alert. He wanted, if possible, to take them by surprise. He hoped to find a landing-ground, one of the several comparatively open areas in the sanseviera, a few miles short of his objective – not too close, in case they should be heard. He recalled that there were some, but he did not know which was the best for his purpose, for he had never examined them with this object in view.

He circled low over half a dozen before he made his choice.

The first four were too small, or too narrow, and the fifth had a native village in the middle of it. The sixth, which he reckoned to be about five miles from the pin-point, was the best, so far. It was by no means an ideal landing-ground and would have been out of the question for a heavy machine, being narrow, slightly on the slope, with a rough surface; but he thought it unlikely that he would find anything better, so he decided to take a chance.

The aircraft bumped and rocked when he put it down, and all but turned over when a wheel encountered a low bush; but it finished on even keel, so he taxied on to leave a clear run in for the following machine. Before signalling to Algy to land he went out and tore up the bush that had nearly turned him over. A quick survey of the clearing also enabled him to indicate the best area. With this advantage Algy landed without mishap. Both machines were now put in position for a quick take-off should one become necessary, after which Biggles produced the compass, without which progress on foot through the jungle would have been sheer guesswork.

The value of Wilks's tip was at once proved, for there now appeared from the jungle a figure dressed in half-native, half-European style. That is to say, he wore a *shamma*, which looked like a dirty piece of sheet wrapped round his body, and over it, incongruously, a Sam Browne belt. A dilapidated slouch hat, much too large, that had once obviously been the property of an Australian soldier, covered his head. His legs were encased in gum-boots, the origin of which was not so plain. In his left hand he carried a long spear, the butt of which rested on the ground, so that he was able to use the shaft as a support for his left leg, which in some curious way appeared to be curled round it. The impression created was of a one-legged man. A rifle sloped across his right shoulder.

'A Danakil,' said Sergeant Mahmud, and called to the man in what, presumably, was his own language.

A brief long-distance exchange of words followed. At the end the native advanced, reluctantly, and Sergeant Mahmud, acting as interrogator and interpreter, extracted this information. The native, as he had already conjectured from his habit of standing on one leg, was of the Danakil tribe. His name was Burradidi, and he was a hunter by profession. He was then out on a hunting trip. In answer to a question as to whether there were any white men in the vicinity, he answered emphatically that there were, at the same time pointing the direction with his spear. It was on this account that he had been nervous about coming forward, for until Sergeant Mahmud had declared himself to be a British soldier he had feared that the newcomers might be friends of these same white men. Asked if he would guide the party to these other white men, Burradidi refused point-blank, declaring that this was impossible. No native would go within miles of the place on account of the 'air that killed'. This 'air that killed' puzzled Biggles for some moments, until he realised that the man was talking about poison gas.

'Gontermann mentioned to me that Scaroni had provided them with other weapons besides mines,' he said in a hard voice. 'Poison gas bombs must be one of them. That, apparently, is how they keep the natives at a distance. The more I learn about these thugs and their methods the more delighted I shall be to see them strung up.' To Sergeant Mahmud he said, 'Explain to this chap that we have come to capture these users of air that kills. If he will help us to do this, the country will be well rid of them, and he shall have a hundred dollars into the bargain.'

At first the Danakil demurred, but a hundred dollars was a big sum of money, and in the end avarice gained ascendancy over fear. He offered to show them a path by which the camp of the white men could be reached; he would go part, but not all the way.

This suited Biggles, who, as a preliminary measure, merely wanted to find out the exact location of the bandits' base, and ascertain how the flying part of it was organised – why it was, for instance, that no landing-ground was visible from the air.

The Danakil struck off into the jungle on a course that tallied with the pin-point, much to Biggles's satisfaction. For the first time he was able to appreciate all that Wilks had said about the sanseviera. Burradidi had mentioned a path, but knowing the usual native idea of a path Biggles was astonished to find a passage more in the nature of a road. There was no surface to it, but swampy areas were made passable by 'corduroy' tracks of tree-trunks lain side by side. The ugly sanseviera had encroached, and in place almost met overhead, which accounted for the fact that the road could not be seen from the air.

'I don't understand this,' remarked Biggles. 'This isn't a native path. It looks more like an abandoned military road. By thunder! I've got it. Of course – what a fool I am. The Italians must have made this track during or after their conquest of the country, when they were trying to subdue the outlying tribes.'

Sergeant Mahmud questioned the Danakil on this point, and found that this was the case.

'It's Zufra all over again,' declared Biggles. 'Scaroni was with the Italians, and used this track for the transport of stores and petrol. No doubt he told Baumer about it. It wouldn't surprise me if we found a serviceable landing-ground, suitable for military aircraft, at the end. No wonder our fellows never found the petrol dump. Scaroni wouldn't have to go to much trouble to hide it, in this stuff.' He glanced at the scene around them.

It was all that Wilks's informant, the pilot Saunders, had said of it – and more. The ground was little better than a swamp – enormous tussocks of coarse grass with pools of black, stagnant, evil-looking water, between them. From the tussocks sprang the coarse, mottled leaves, or rather spines, of the prevailing sanseviera. Rustlings in the grass, and soft furtive plops in the water, suggested a wealth of reptile life. Enormous black flies, as well as mosquitoes, rose in clouds. The air was hot, humid, and heavy with the stench of rotting vegetation. The travellers sweated copiously as they marched, striking at the flies that swarmed about them, and tried to settle in their eyes. The great wonder to Ginger was how Saunders had managed to live for a fortnight in such horror without going mad.

For about an hour the party went forward through a never-changing scene. Then the Danakil stopped, and pointed with his spear. He would go no farther.

Biggles took the lead. 'Come on,' he said softly. 'No more talking.'

The Danakil stopped, and pointed with his spear.
He would go no farther.

CHAPTER XVI

The Poison Belt

Almost imperceptibly the scene began to change. The vivid green of the jungle turned slowly to a rusty yellow. The sanseviera still reared its octopus-like arms, but they were dead, and remembering what the Danakil had said it did not take Biggles long to guess the reason.

'Poison gas did that,' he whispered. 'If Gontermann has used it against the natives he won't hesitate to use it against us. Quietly now.'

They moved forward, slowly, picking their way with care, and in this manner reached the outer fringe of the enemy camp. By that time they were all gasping for breath, and Biggles understood why Grindler had prefixed the word sanseviera with a curse. There was something about the steaming atmosphere that was not only oppressive, but positively suffocating. The place stank with the acrid smell of vegetation that had grown and died and rotted in successive layers through centuries of time. An occasional skeleton lying in the tangle of undergrowth did nothing to enliven the scene.

'Probably natives who were gassed,' said Biggles, referring to them, as he paused to wipe the sweat from his face.

It was at this stage that Algy made a remark which was to have far-reaching results, although he was unaware of it. Sergeant Mahmud was quietly preparing for action, and in the course of this he took from his pocket a pair of hand grenades and hung them on his belt. Algy looked at them with disapproval which he made no attempt to hide.

'Look what the sergeant's produced,' he growled. 'He wouldn't have flown in my machine with those in his pocket if I'd known about it.'

'Very good,' said Sergeant Mahmud, imperturbably, tapping a grenade.

Biggles turned to look. 'You be careful what you're doing with those things, Sergeant,' he warned.

'Very good, sahib,' acknowledged the sergeant, who was a man of few words.

There was not a soul in sight; all was silent except for the constant buzz of the flies, so with the others following Biggles now made a cautious reconnaissance. It occupied some time, but by the end he had grasped the general lay-out of the place, which was so plain for all to see that it hardly called for comment. It confirmed his conjecture that the camp had been originally a war-time emergency landing-ground. Skilfully designed by army engineers, particular care had been taken against aerial observation, and it was now easy enough to understand why the flights had failed to reveal it.

There was no exposed runway. A central building of wood frame construction, loop-holed for defence and thatched with layers of sanseviera, formed, as it were, the hub, of a wheel; from it, like spokes, aisles had been cut in the jungle towards the four cardinal points of the compass. Over these aisles, camouflage netting, threaded with the eternal sanseviera, had been spread in such a way that they could be drawn aside to permit air operations on a small scale. It was really quite simple, yet effective, even though the camouflage, bone dry and withered from long exposure to the sun, showed signs of falling to pieces. This also applied to the central hutment which, from the cover of the jungle, Biggles surveyed from a distance of about fifty yards. He could get no closer without exposing himself, for the intervening space was open, in the manner of a parade ground, although even this had been strewn with dry branches of sanseviera to prevent detection from the air.

'Well, this is it,' said Biggles quietly. 'I should say the part of the hut we're looking at is the living accommodation; the machines are probably parked under that big awning carried out on poles from the far side.'

'Just what are you aiming to do?' asked Algy.

'I want to catch these criminals alive, arrest them in the regulation manner, if possible,' replied Biggles. 'The place seems so quiet that I feel inclined to try to take it at a rush, before Gontermann can organise a defence.'

'If we could put the machines out of action for a start we should definitely make an end of their pirate pranks, whatever else happened,' suggested Ginger. 'That would fix them in this area, and put a stop to this gallivanting round the globe.'

'I think there's something in that idea,' assented Biggles. 'If I could get across to the hut without being spotted I could work my way round it to the awning. We've got to cross the open, anyway, to reach the place. No doubt it was to prevent a surprise attack that the jungle was cleared. I'll try it. You fellows stay here and keep me covered in case I bump into opposition.'

He had taken the first step into the open, and was crouching for a dash across, when an unexpected factor altered the entire situation. Round the end of the building came a gaunt, mangy, Alsatian dog. It moved quietly, as though prowling with no particular object. Biggles froze. The dog stopped abruptly. Its nose went up, feeling the air, as though it had caught a suspicious taint. Its head came round and it looked straight at Biggles. It stiffened and bared its teeth, growling deep in its throat; then it broke into a clamour of furious barking which was all the more devastating on account of the previous silence. Inside the hut somebody shouted. Feet thudded on the bare boards.

Seeing that it was now impossible to proceed with his plan, Biggles backed hastily into cover, and with a crisp, 'Come on,' to the others, started to work his way round the clearing, away from the point where the animal had located them. He had no fixed plan. Indeed, in his heart he knew that now the alarm had been raised the odds were all against them, but he still hoped that it might be possible to reached the Renkells and put them out of service. This hope was short-lived. The dog followed, barking, and to complete the pandemonium a machine-gun came into action. A burst of bullets raked the spot they had just vacated.

Biggles blundered on, heedless of the thorns and spines that tore at his clothes; but he pulled up short when a metal object, about the size of a cricket ball, came bounding across the clearing. It exploded with a sullen bang, splashing in all directions a black, oily fluid, from which vapour drifted sluggishly.

'The air that kills. No good,' muttered Sergeant Mahmud.

'Mustard gas,' rasped Biggles, as another gas bomb exploded. 'I can't see where the infernal things are coming from. It's no use, chaps. We can't fight that stuff. Let's get out of this before we're skinned alive. Back to the path!' His face was pale with chagrin.

They had started to retire when, as if he had suddenly remembered something, he caught the sergeant by the shoulder. 'Just a minute, Sergeant,' he said tersely. 'I hate letting them have things *all* their own way. Give me those grenades.'

Sergeant Mahmud handed them over. 'Very good,' he said.

Biggles's face was set in grim lines as he forced a way to the edge of the clearing, where he crouched for a moment while he tore the safety-pins from the grenades with his teeth. Then he made a short rush and flung the missiles in quick succession. The first landed on the roof of the hut; the second struck the side of the awning and dropped among the debris at the bottom. The two explosions merged. He did not wait for the smoke to clear to observe results, as the enemy continued to fire blindly through the smoke and the bullets were coming dangerously close. Moreover, another gas bomb came lobbing across the clearing. He dashed back to where the others were waiting, and shouting, 'Run for it!' and plunged on towards the path by which they had approached.

'That confounded dog upset the apple-cart,' he panted, as he ran on. Shots were still being fired from the hut, and the bullets came slashing through the mushy sanseviera. Not until they were some distance down the path did he ease the pace.

'I imagine this is what the papers call being repulsed in confusion,' grunted Ginger.

'Not having respirators or gas-proof equipment there was no sense in staying where we were,' returned Biggles. 'Once we were discovered it was all up. We couldn't see them, but they could evidently see us.' Biggles went on at a steady dog-trot.

'What are we going to do?' asked Algy.

'Get back to Khartoum as fast as we can,' replied Biggles. 'We'll come back with the Mosquito and the Spur and prang this place off the map. The rajah's sparklers will have to take their luck.'

'Look!' cried Ginger, pointing.

All eyes were turned behind and upward, to where a column of smoke was rising in the air.

'By gosh! It looks as though something has set fire to the sanseviera – perhaps the camouflage,' exclaimed Biggles. 'It must have been one of the grenades. Come to think of it, that stuff was like tinder. It should make the place easy to find when we come back. Let's keep going.'

They ran on. Ginger had never plumbed the extent of Biggles's endurance; nor did he now, although he ran until his heart pounded in his ears and his knees felt like jelly. Towards the finish, the journey to where the Tigers had been left became a nightmare of mud, and sweat, and flies – and sanseviera.

Not until they reached the machines did Biggles stop and look back. The pillar of smoke had become a mighty cloud that rolled up and up towards the blue dome of heaven.

'It looks as if we've given them something to think about, something to keep them busy, anyway,' he muttered.

'I should say we've done more than that,' declared Algy, still staring at the signs of a considerable conflagration. 'They may be smoked out.'

'The fire may reach their petrol,' puffed Ginger.

'Wishful thinking won't get us anywhere,' contended Biggles. 'Let's get home and fetch a load of high explosive – something to *really* warm their hides.'

Both machines took off without mishap, and flying low for maximum speed set a course for the aerodrome. From time to time Ginger looked back to note the progress of the smoke, and was pleased to see that the volume was increasing rather than diminishing. He passed this information on to Biggles, observing that Algy's prediction about the enemy being smoked out was now a real possibility.

They had just crossed the frontier, where the jungle gave way to typical Sudan desert, when Ginger, who again happened to glance back, let out a cry so shrill with alarm that Biggles turned sharply to see what was amiss.

'The Renkells!' shouted Ginger. 'They're coming this way – both of them.'

Biggles raced on. It now seemed certain that the enemy had been smoked out, or driven out by the fire – not that it mattered which – and he was by no means pleased. This evacuation was premature, and altered his plan. While the enemy were in the sanseviera he did at least know where they were, but now they might be going anywhere. It looked as if they might escape, after all, for his aircraft was neither equipped to catch the Renkells, or stop them. There were no guns in the Tiger Moths, and the comparative speeds were as a hen and a hawk. This irritating handicap so occupied his mind that it never struck him seriously that the Renkells might attack. If he thought about the possibility at all it was in an abstract sort of way; he assumed, rather, that even if the two Moths were seen, which was by no means certain, the gang would be in too much of a hurry to bother about them.

The first warning of peril came from Ginger, who suddenly shouted, 'Look out!' and Biggles, looking over his shoulder, saw the Renkells coming down like eagles on a pair of lost lambs. Their intention was instantly apparent, and making sure that Algy was aware of the danger he prepared to take evading action, which was all he could do. Even so, he did not think much of his chance. The Tiger Moths were so far below the Renkells in speed and manoeuvrability that they would be easy marks for beginners; the enemy pilots, far from that, were experienced men of war. All he could do was skim the desert sand, keeping one eye on the enemy, nerves and muscles braced to move like lighting the instant their guns flashed.

He noted that the Wolf had picked him out, and from his own experience he could judge when the pilot would fire. At that moment he turned at right angles, so that the bullets flashed past his wing-tip to plough up the sand, and a split second later the Wolf had to zoom sharply to avoid hitting the ground. It was rather like a greyhound snatching at a hare, and just missing it on the turn.

This happened three times, and each time Biggles got away with his trick; but he did not deceive himself; he knew that it could not go on. Now that his tactics were revealed, the pilot of the Wolf would presently forestall him. Still watching his opponent, he had braced himself for the next move in the grim game of aerial 'tag', when Ginger let out a yell, shrill with excitement.

'Bertie! It's Bertie! Good old Bertie!' he shouted delightedly.

Biggles dare not take his eyes from the Wolf. He hoped, without much confidence, that the pilot would not see the Spur; but he was not surprised when the Wolf swept up in a beautiful climbing turn, no longer the attacker, but the attacked. The Spur flashed into view, coming down like a winged torpedo.

Now, for the first time in his life, Biggles had the doubtful pleasure of watching a dog-fight from the air without taking part in it. Indeed, having no petrol to spare, he resumed his course for the aerodrome, whilst Algy, who had managed to dodge the transport, took up a position near his wing-tip.

At first Biggles was rather worried on Bertie's account, for he had two opponents, either one of which, considered on performance, would have been a fair match; and the transport had turned, as if the pilot intended to make the duel between the Spur and the Wolf a three-cornered combat. But then, to Biggles's utter amazement, it suddenly straightened out, turned, and sped away across the desert, the pilot clearly having decided to save his machine while its consort engaged the Spur.

'Did you see that!' cried Ginger. 'The transport's packed up. What a pal! What a pal! I wonder who's flying it?'

Biggles was wondering the same thing, but he felt pretty certain that Gontermann was in the escaping machine, probably with his friend Baumer.

The combat between the Spur and the Wolf did not last long. As far as the machines were concerned, odds were about even, but Bertie, without indulging in any wild aerobatics, out-manoeuvred his opponent. In fact, he only fired twice, each time from short range, whereas the pilot of the Wolf revealed anxiety by shooting frequently from outside effective range, evidently hoping for a lucky hit – which, admittedly, happens sometimes, but not often.

The first time Bertie fired, after a clean, calculated turn, he shot a piece off the Wolf's tail unit. The Wolf flashed round in profes-sional style and fired back, whereupon the Spur rocketed, fell off on its wing and went down in a spin. Not even Biggles knew if this was accidental or deliberate. Anyway, the Wolf followed it down, and thereby made a fatal blunder, for the Spur recovered, and coming up under its adversary raked it from nose to tail-skid.

'Got him!' yelled Ginger, in a voice hoarse with excitement.

He was right. The Wolf went on down, obviously in difficulties. Near the ground it managed to flatten out, without having lowered its wheels. It struck the desert with a crash, throwing up a cloud of dust, and rolled over and over, cart-wheeling, breaking up and flinging pieces of fabric, wood, and metal, all round the fractured fuselage.

Biggles side-slipped down to the stricken machine and landed. He jumped out, and was running over to the wreck when he saw the Spur coming down, wheels lowered, also with the obvious intention of landing. Feeling that this was an unnecessary risk he waved Bertie away; but the Spur ignored his signals and landed heavily. Biggles paid no further attention to it, but with Ginger keeping him company ran on to the Wolf. The first thing he saw was Scaroni, who had been thrown clear, with his head twisted under him at a ghastly angle.

'Poor devil,' said Biggles. 'He's got what he had coming to him. We needn't waste time there.'

Von Zoyton was the other occupant. He was still in his seat, held in place by the safety belt. His eyes were dull, but recognition gleamed in them for a moment as they fell on Biggles. His lips moved, parting in a cold, sardonic smile, and he muttered: 'If the fools hadn't left us – we could – have got you – Bigglesworth.'

'Who left you?' asked Biggles quietly, unfastening the safety belt.

'Gontermann – always for himself.'

Biggles nodded. 'Baumer was no friend of yours, or he'd have stayed.'

'He would do – what Gontermann – ordered,' was the laboured reply.

'Is Grindler with them?'

'Ja.'

'What about Renkell?'

Von Zoyton did not answer. He was obviously on the point of collapse, so Biggles and Ginger, between them, got the wounded man out of his seat, and into the meagre shade of a tattered wing.

'I warned you to get clear of that bunch of crooks,' said Biggles sadly.

'Your friend – flies well,' muttered von Zoyton.

Biggles smiled. 'You've met before – in the desert.'

'Ah. Which one – was it?'

'Lord Lissie.'

'With the eyeglass. I remember him.'

'Why did you take off?' asked Biggles.

'Had to. You burnt – us out. I told Gontermann that stuff – was too dry … but he wouldn't – listen. You won't get the jewels, though, Bigglesworth. He's got them – with him.'

Biggles started. 'Where's he bound for?'

'America. *Ach!*' The German's face twisted with pain. '*Mir deht … nicht sehr gut,*' he gasped.

'Hang on. We'll get you to hospital,' promised Biggles. He glanced up as Algy's voice came across the silence. 'What's Algy shouting about?' he muttered.

Algy had also landed, and seeing that Bertie had not left his machine went over to congratulate him. His frantic shouts took Biggles and Ginger over at the double.

'Bertie's stopped one – in the thigh, I think,' greeted Algy urgently.

Biggles climbed up into the cockpit. Bertie was still sitting in his seat. His face was ashen, but his monocle was still in his eye. He smiled weakly. 'Got my leg in the way – silly ass thing to do. Sorry – and so on.' And with that he fainted dead away.

'Let's get him out,' said Biggles curtly.

They got Bertie out of the cockpit and found an ugly wound in the upper part of his right leg. He had lost a good deal of blood, but using the bandages from the first-aid kit they managed to stop the bleeding.

'Scaroni's dead,' Biggles told Algy. 'Von Zoyton is in a bad way. I fancy he's got broken bones. I want to get on after Gontermann, but we shall have to get him to hospital as well as Bertie. I'll tell you what,' he went on, clipping his words. 'I'll fly Bertie to Khartoum in the Spur. Algy, you follow with von Zoyton. Ginger, you fly the other Tiger. Sergeant Mahmud will have to stay here to keep the hyenas away from Scaroni's body until the ambulance comes out. I shall be at Khartoum first so I'll tell Wilks what has happened. Ginger should have arrived by the time I've finished, so we'll push right on after Gontermann. You can follow in the Mosquito, Algy. You'll be last in, so I shan't wait for you; make for Zufra; failing that, Tripoli; von Zoyton says Gontermann is heading for America, but he'll have to refuel somewhere before starting across the Ditch. From what Bertie told us there must be petrol at Zufra, so the transport may make for the oasis. I shall go there first, anyway. Let's get cracking. The transport's got ten minutes start as it is.'

They lifted Bertie into the spare seat of the Spur and made him as comfortable as possible. Von Zoyton, who had now lost consciousness was carried to Algy's Tiger. Biggles then took off in the Spur. He was followed by Ginger, flying solo. Algy, with his limp passenger, then took the air, leaving Sergeant Mahmud standing at attention by the wreck, a lonely figure in the wilderness.

CHAPTER XVII

Gontermann Does it Again

Biggles landed at Khartoum and taxied tail-up to the tarmac where his yell brought everyone within hearing running towards the Spur, including Wilks, who was in station headquarters. Within thirty seconds the ambulance was alongside, and Bertie, now conscious, lamenting his enforced retirement from the affair, was raced away to hospital.

'I shall be back just as soon as this business sorts itself out,' Biggles promised him.

He then turned to Wilks and asked him to get the Spur refuelled in the shortest possible time. Wilks gave the order, and while mechanics were busy on the machine Biggles gave him a concise account of what had happened.

'You'd better send a vehicle out for Sergeant Mahmud,' he concluded. 'Please yourself what you do about the Wolf. Perhaps you'd better bring the pieces in – Air Ministry experts may want to look at them.'

'Pity you couldn't have got the transport at the same time,' murmured Wilks. 'It looks as if the four ringleaders have got away after all.'

'Three of them have – so far,' replied Biggles. 'I don't know about Renkell, but I imagine he's in the party. I shall push on as soon as Ginger comes in. For your guidance, should anything go wrong, my first objective will be Zufra. If I don't catch up with them there I shall go on to Tripoli. Beyond that, I don't know.'

'The transport's got a good start; do you think you'll catch it?' asked Wilks anxiously.

'Yes, I do, because it can't get off this continent without refuelling,' answered Biggles 'Somewhere it will have to lose the time I'm losing here. Apart from that I should say the Spur is a trifle faster than the transport. Ah! Here comes Ginger now.'

'You're not stopping for food?' queried Wilks.

'I'm not stopping for anything once Ginger's on the ground,' declared Biggles.

As soon as Ginger landed Biggles called him over and climbed back into the Spur. Algy's Tiger Moth could be seen in the distance, but Biggles did not wait for him. He took off at once and headed out over the desert on the long flight to El Zufra. Naturally, he watched the sky ahead, although he hardly expected to overtake the transport, even if he had correctly predicted its destination.

During the entire flight neither he nor Ginger saw anything except an implacable sky of lapis lazuli overhead, and the pitiless distances on all sides. The sun toiled wearily across the heavens, splashing gold with a lavish hand and striking the ground with silent force. At last the oasis crept up over the horizon, like an island in a sea that had been suddenly arrested in motion.

'Are you going to land?' asked Ginger.

'I don't know, yet,' answered Biggles as, with his eyes surveying the ground he roared low over the palms.

'They're not here,' said Ginger in a disappointed voice.

'We shall have to make sure,' replied Biggles. 'The machine

may be under that awning, in which case we shouldn't be able to see it. Naturally, they'd keep out of sight when they heard us coming. I'm going down. If they're here, not knowing that the mines have been cleared, they'll expect us to land in the *wadi*, so that's where they'll have their guns trained. It should give them quite a shock to see us land on the other side without being blown up. Five minutes will be time enough to settle whether they are here or not.'

Lowering his wheels, he landed, not in the *wadi*, but on the opposite side of the oasis, allowing the machine to run on until it was near the fringe of palms.

'You stay here and look after the machine, in case of accidents,' he ordered. Leaving the engine ticking over he jumped down and walked briskly into the oasis.

As he strode on towards the depression over which the awning was spread he noticed a piece of paper in a cleft stick, erected in the manner of a notice-board, but at the moment he was too occupied with other matters to make the detour that would have been necessary to see what it was. Automatic in hand he ran up a slight eminence, the top of which he knew commanded a view of the awning. Even then there was good reason to suppose that his guess had been correct. The bandits were there; at any rate, somebody was there, for to his ears now came an urgent buzz of conversation. Metallic noises suggested that a vehicle was being refuelled in haste.

Had it not been for a warning shout from Ginger he might have collided with Grindler. Ginger, it transpired, caught sight of the gunman running along the fringe of the oasis, just inside the palms, from the direction of the *wadi*, as though he had waited there to intercept the crew of the Spur; but perceiving his error, he was now attempting to rectify it. He carried an automatic in each hand.

At Ginger's warning shout Biggles swerved to a tree and stopped. An instant later Grindler came into sight, taking advantage of the meagre cover available by dodging from palm to palm. The gunman saw Biggles at the same moment, and in a flash had fired two shots from the hip. But the range was long for accurate pistol work – about forty yards – and intervening palms made shooting largely a matter of luck. One bullet struck such a tree; the other whistled past the one behind which Biggles stood.

Biggles saved his ammunition. He stood still, waiting, hoping that Grindler would come on; but the gangster, while confident of his shooting, was evidently not as confident as all that, for he, too, jumped to a palm and remained still.

When two or three minutes had passed without a move being made by either side, it slowly dawned on Biggles why Grindler was apparently content with this state of affairs. His job was simply to keep him at a distance while the transport was being refuelled. If this was to be prevented, it meant that he, Biggles, would have to take the initiative. To advance in the face of Grindler's guns, while the gunman remained in cover, was clearly a project of considerable peril, for Biggles had no doubt about his opponent's ability to handle his weapons with speed and accuracy. Still, as Grindler stood between them and the spot where the transport was being refuelled there was nothing else for it. He jumped to the next tree in the line of advance. In the instant of time occupied by the move two bullets had zipped past his face, and he knew that he was taking a desperate chance. Grindler had not shown himself; and as he held the cards there was no reason why he should.

Biggles jumped to the next palm, firing two shots as Grindler's right hand appeared, more to spoil his aim than with any real hope of hitting him. They were now not more than thirty yards apart.

Grindler sneered: 'Come on, Limey; what are you stopping for?'

How the affair would have ended had there not been a diversion is a matter for conjecture, but at this juncture there occurred an interruption which gave the situation a new twist, one that evidently surprised Grindler as much as it did Biggles. The transport's engines came to life, and it rose to a crescendo which could only mean that the aircraft was about to take off.

It did not take Biggles long to perceive the shrewd cunning behind this move. Even though the Renkell's tanks had not been filled it was ensuring a clear start by leaving those on the oasis fully occupied with each other. Grindler was being abandoned. This was so much less weight for the machine to carry, and would result in an improved performance. A ghost of a smile flickered over Biggles's face at the thought of the gunman being left, as they say, to hold the baby. At the same time, even though he was dealing with crooks whose lack of scruples had already been proved, he was astounded at such unbelievable treachery. Not that Grindler deserved better treatment.

Biggles knew that those in the transport must have been refuelling from cans, or drums – a long process. They had not had time to completely refuel, which meant that they hoped to 'top-up' somewhere else. There was good reason to suppose that this would be Tripoli, where the airport manager would oblige them. Biggles could see the machine through the trees, heading north-west, a course that tended to confirm this theory. He heard the Spur's engine rev up, and fully expected Ginger to take off in case he should be attacked; but when it became clear that those in the transport had no such intention the Spur's engine dropped back to its low mutter.

All this had taken place much faster than it can be told, and Grindler had not been idle. When the truth – and it must have been a paralysing truth – struck him, that he was being deserted, his feelings in the matter found expression in a yell of fury. Spitting obscene vituperation he raced to the edge of the palms, and as the transport's tail lifted, blazed away at it with both guns. His chances of hitting it were, of course, remote, and he must have known it. He fired probably in sheer blind rage. Anyway, the transport gave no indication that it had been hit, and proceeded on its way.

Biggles was not so much concerned with Grindler as with the transport, because while the aircraft could continue operating without the gangster, the gangster could not go on without the aircraft. Grindler could wait, a prisoner on the oasis. All Biggles wanted was to get in the Spur in order to go on after the transport. He started backing away, but Grindler opened up such a fusillade that he was compelled to take cover in a hurry. He could not remember precisely how many shots the gunman had fired, but it struck him that the magazines of both pistols must be nearly empty. In order to find out if this were so he tried a bluff.

'You can drop those guns, Grindler, they're empty!' he shouted, at the same time emerging from cover.

'Who says they are?' snarled Grindler, also advancing.

Biggles knew he was taking a big chance, but he kept on. 'So your pal Gontermann has let you down again,' he scoffed.

Grindler choked; Biggles had never seen a man's face so distorted with fury. 'That dirty, double-crossing Nazi rat,' stormed the gangster. 'I came over here to get that squealer, but he made a sucker outa me by offering to let me muscle in on this airplane racket.'

'I don't see that you've anything to complain about,' returned Biggles evenly. 'You left the Wolf to shift for itself.'

'That was Gontermann did that,' growled Grindler.

'I wonder Herr Renkell didn't stand by you,' resumed Biggles. 'He's got a clean record.'

Grindler jeered. 'That sap! He wasn't with us.'

'Not with you?'

'You bet he wasn't. We left him in that weed swamp.'

Biggles was genuinely shocked, and he looked it. 'Spare my days! You *are* a bright lot,' he sneered. 'Are you coming quietly?'

'Who said I was coming any place?' snarled Grindler.

'Please yourself,' returned Biggles. 'But make up your mind because I'm leaving. Stay here if you'd rather have it that way. You can't leave the oasis – you know that.'

'Is that so?' replied Grindler with ominous calm. 'I guess you're right, at that. Now let me tell you something, wise guy. I've got one slug left, and if I'm staying I reckon that should be enough to see that you stay, too.'

Before Biggles had fully grasped the threat that lay in the words, Grindler had spun round, and twisting like a snipe was racing towards the Spur.

Biggles fired, and missed. Before he could fire again Grindler had disappeared behind some palms. 'Look out, Ginger!' he shouted, as he set off in pursuit, aware that if the gunman did succeed in reaching the Spur one shot in a vital place might well immobilise it – a bullet through one of the tyres would do it, for instance.

Dodging and ducking among the trees Grindler sped on. He topped a rise, and before Biggles could fire, leapt into a sort of small dell-hole beyond. Suddenly he screamed clutching at a tree; but his hand slipped, and his impetus carried him on.

The scream was cut off short by an explosion of such violence that Biggles was hurled to the ground by the blast, momentarily stunned. Smoke swirled. Sand, pebbles, and pieces of palm frond pattered down. Still half dazed Biggles picked himself up and staggered to the stump of a shattered palm to get a grip on himself; then, breathing heavily, he walked on to the scene of the explosion. Just as he reached it a piece of paper came floating down. Automatically he reached for it and picked it up. On it, under a bold heading, a single line had been written in three languages—English, French, and Arabic: 'WARNING. *Beware of land mines in hollow*' it read. It was signed '*Sergeant Mahmud, King's African Rifles.*'

Biggles climbed to the rim of the crater and looked down. Except for a few shreds of clothing, and some suggestive red stains, there was no sign of Grindler. He went on towards the Spur with some anxiety, fearing that it might have been damaged, although he hoped that an intervening dune would have saved it from the blast. It had. Ginger, looking pale and shaken, was standing in his seat.

'What in heaven's name was that?' he gasped.

'It was Grindler, falling into a nest of mines,' answered Biggles slowly. 'Sergeant Mahmud dumped them in that hollow. I suppose he had to put them somewhere, and in the ordinary way that place was as good as any. He put up a notice, but Grindler was in too much of a hurry to stop to read it. He fell into the dump and got the full benefit. What's left of him isn't worth picking up. He probably helped to plant the mines in the first place, so it's a nice example of poetic justice. Anyway, I'm not shedding any tears for that thug. Is the machine all right?'

'I think so,' answered Ginger. 'It danced a bit from concussion, but I fancy the worst of the blast went over us.'

'Thank God for that,' said Biggles fervently. 'We'll push on after Gontermann. The transport has taken in some petrol, but not much, I think. We barged in a bit too early for them. I should say it's making for Tripoli to top up before striking across Algeria and Morocco on the way to the States. Let's go. We haven't a lot of daylight left.'

'Personally, I haven't much of anything left,' averred Ginger. 'This show is just one place after another. Where is it going to end?'

'It will end,' answered Biggles deliberately, 'where the transport hits the carpet.'

Looking travel-stained and weary he climbed into the cockpit, and in another minute the Spur was in the air again, heading north-west on the trail of the transport.

CHAPTER XVIII

The Last Lap

Biggles knew that by cutting in on the transport while it was refuelling he had decreased its lead by some minutes. In the case of a slow-moving vehicle, minutes, translated into terms of distance, may not amount to much; but with aircraft, able to cover the ground at seven or eight miles a minute, even seconds count. Against this advantage he had to offset the handicap that the transport had taken in an unknown quantity of fuel, so that if the chase became a test of endurance the transport would in the end outrun the Spur. He did not think it would come to that, unless Gontermann had another secret landing-ground; if he had, it seemed probable that he would now make for it, leaving the Spur with the hopeless task of finding it. Biggles did not consider this possibility seriously, because he felt that had the bandits possessed a secret refuelling station near the North African coast they would never have used a public airport like Castel Benito, at Tripoli.

As the Spur roared on, with the shadows of the dunes beginning to lengthen towards the east, Biggles perceived that the hunt was fast becoming a matter of geography. The transport was, in a manner of speaking, an outlaw, and laboured under the usual disadvantages of that condition, particularly now that it was on the run. It could only go into hiding, and obtain supplies, where friends were prepared to take the risk of accommodating it. Ruling out secret hiding-places, it was practically certain that Castel Benito aerodrome, where petrol was available and where the manager was in the swim, would be the next port of call. From there Gontermann might head north for Germany, where he would certainly have friends among the ex-Nazis prepared to offer him sanctuary. He might have to dispose of the aircraft, but he would get away with the loot. Or he might carry on due west for America, as von Zoyton had declared. America would probably suit him very well, reflected Biggles, particularly as he had now got rid of such a dangerous companion as Grindler, who was wanted by the Federal Police. But could he get there in one hop? Tripoli was still a long way from the Atlantic. The Renkell would have to have a tremendous range to take the northern Sahara in its stride, and then cross the ocean. Biggles had not forgotten that the machine had already crossed the Atlantic, but then its starting-point was unknown.

It all came to this. If the transport was able to jump from Tripoli to America, unless the Spur could catch it at Tripoli it would probably get away, because the Spur, even with full tanks, had nothing like that range; and its tanks, far from being full, were nearly empty. If the Spur had to stop to refuel at Tripoli, the transport would obtain such a lead that it would be hopeless to try to overtake it; and if the Spur went on without refuelling it would have to run the risk of running out of petrol somewhere over the desert. The immediate future, therefore, was very much in the air – literally.

Reluctantly the sand gave way to shrubs and rocky hills, while the valleys filled with verdant almond trees and silvery-grey olives. The aerodrome came into view, and Ginger surveyed the tarmac swiftly, eagerly, shielding his eyes with his hands to see the better, for they were flying almost into the orb of the setting sun, and the glare was dazzling. When he saw the unmistakable outline of the transport his satisfaction found outlet in a whoop of exultation.

'She's there!' he cried. 'We've caught her refuelling again.'

'There's another machine in the shadow of the hangar,' remarked Biggles. 'By Jupiter! It's the Swan. Preuss must be there. That's it! Now we know the meaning of the R/T signal the B.B.C. picked up. It *was* Gontermann getting in touch with Preuss, asking him to come here for some reason or other. Maybe Gontermann has an idea of dropping the transport and slipping into Germany in the Swan.'

The Spur roared on, nose down, and the aerodrome seemed to float on invisible rollers towards it; but before Biggles glided in over the boundary fence, engine idling, feverish activity was apparent round the stationary machines, although it was hard to make out just what was happening. It was obvious, however, that the arrival of the Spur had caused a commotion. A man in mechanic's overalls jumped off the transport's centre-section. Gontermann, bag in hand, dashed out of the restaurant, and started running towards the Swan; then he appeared to change his mind and made for the transport, behind which a swirl of dust revealed that its engines had been started.

At this juncture it would have been a comparatively simple matter for Biggles to shoot the transport up, but there were reasons why he hesitated to do so. The men in it were not convicted criminals, for they had not yet been tried in a court of law. Castel Benito was not the sanseviera; it was a public aerodrome; there would be spectators, witnesses who would say that the attack on the grounded machine was made without provocation – for so it would appear – and in such circumstances, if he killed the men he would be accounted little better than a murderer. Such an incident might cause a political crisis. Again, even if the men were not killed, the authorities might make a fuss over the deliberate destruction of an aircraft which, with some justification they could claim as their property. And finally, should the Renkell catch fire, the British Government might be embarrassed by the irreplaceable loss of the rajah's jewels. Had the Renkell taken off and attacked the Spur the position would be altogether different. In short, while Biggles was prepared to use his guns to prevent the escape of men whom he knew were criminals and murderers, although it might not be easy to prove this, he decided first to try other methods.

The transport had swung round to face the open aerodrome, and was moving forward, slowly as yet, but with the obvious intention of taking off. To prevent this Biggles landed across its nose – or rather, it would be more correct to say that he attempted to do so. His wheels were already on the ground, so it seemed a simple matter to taxi on and block the transport's chosen runway. And no doubt it would have been, had it not been for the intervention of the Swan, which now took a hand.

Concerned primarily with the transport, after making a mental note that he could catch up with the Swan if it attempted to get away, Biggles had forgotten all about it. But the yellow plane now appeared on the scene, playing the Spur's own game. That was Biggles's first impression; but he soon saw that the pilot intended more than that; for the Swan, instead of slowing down as it cut across his bows, suddenly swung round on one wheel to which the brake had been applied, and charged straight at him.

It was a clever, unexpected move, and not so dangerous to life as it might appear. The Swan had only to collide with one of the Spur's wings and the British aircraft would be grounded for an indefinite period. The collision could afterwards be described as an accident. In the meantime the transport would get clear away.

All this flashed through Biggles's mind as he took the only course open to him if collision was to be avoided. He knew that if he swerved to left or right the Swan had only to do the same to achieve its object of ramming him. So he flicked the throttle wide open, and as the Spur gathered flying speed he snatched it off the ground. It was a desperate expedient, for had his wheels failed to clear the Swan the result would have been utter and complete disaster; as it was, they missed the obstruction by a margin so narrow that the corners of Biggles's mouth were drawn down in a wave of cold anger, which was aggravated by the fact that the transport, quick to take advantage of his preoccupation, had succeeded in getting off.

As soon as he was clear, regardless of any subsequent inquiry, Biggles whirled the Spur round, and dropping his nose, slashed the Swan with a burst of fire. The pilot, presumably Preuss, might well have crashed the Spur, and that was more than Biggles was prepared to accept without retaliation. Preuss may have expected some such move, for he had stopped the Swan, jumped out, and was sprinting for the aerodrome buildings. As it happened, these were in line with Biggles's attack. For a few seconds he ran on, with bullets tearing up the sand around him; then he crashed headlong, and after rolling over and over like a shot rabbit, lay still.

'That should stop *him* laughing in church,' muttered Ginger.

'He asked for it,' grated Biggles. 'The airport manager will probably say we murdered him; which means we've burnt our boats; we've got to get the others with the swag on them, or we may find ourselves in the custard up to the neck.' Coming round in a climbing turn as he spoke, he made out the transport heading westward, having got a start of about three miles. 'We've got just one hour in which to catch them,' he remarked.

'Why an hour?' asked Ginger.

'Because, in the first place, I've got only an hour's petrol left; and secondly, in one hour from now it will be dark,' answered Biggles. 'Apart from petrol, they could give us the slip in the dark – always bearing in mind that the transport must have a lot more juice in its tanks than we have,' Biggles settled down to the chase.

In point of fact, Ginger knew that the fate of the transport would be decided in less than an hour. It would be settled in five minutes. If, in that time, they had closed the gap to any appreciable extent, they would overtake the fugitives within the hour. If the gap was not closed, it would prove that the speed of the Renkell was at least equal to their own, in which case it would certainly get away. For this reason it was with no small anxiety that he kept his eyes on the enemy aircraft.

When five or six minutes had elapsed he drew a deep breath. 'We've got 'em,' he declared, a note of triumph in his voice.

Biggles did not answer.

The Spur was on even keel at a thousand feet. The Renkell was higher, nearer two thousand, and seeing that it was being overtaken it had dropped its nose slightly. This gave it an increase of speed that enabled it to forge ahead again. But Biggles was not perturbed. Both machines were now at the same height, so the advantage gained by the transport was only temporary. The manoeuvre could not be repeated successfully. Gradually the gap closed. The transport sacrificed a little more height for speed, but Biggles merely did the same, so in the end the German gained nothing by the move. All it really did was reveal its inferiority.

When twenty minutes had elapsed the distance between the two machines was less than a mile. Both were at the same height, flying directly into the sun, which now appeared to rest on the western horizon like an enormous crimson ball, casting a lurid glow across the arid waste.

Ginger looked down with some apprehension, for he knew they were running across the northern fringe of the Sahara desert, which varies a good deal in its formation. The area below appeared to have been swept clean, except for innumerable little stones which gleamed as though they had been highly polished – as, indeed, they had been, by the wind and sun. The horizon was a hard, unbroken line. It was no place to run out of petrol, and Ginger began to wonder what would happen when their tanks petered out, as they would in the near future. Biggles made no move to turn back.

Over this scene, naked and helpless in its desolation, the two machines roared on, the distance between them closing slowly. Ahead, Ginger was relieved to see, the horizon was at last broken by low hills, and an occasional group of palms; but the sun had nearly run its course, and it was impossible to make out precisely what lay in front of them.

Only a quarter of a mile of heat-distorted air divided the two machines; and still the distance closed. Biggles sat quite still. His face was expressionless. Never, not for an instant, did his eyes leave his quarry.

Ginger moistened his lips, thankful that he was not in the Renkell. There was something so implacable, so relentless, about Biggles, when he was in his present mood. He knew that whatever happened he would not turn back. He would go on to the end, even if their petrol ran out and left them stranded in the heart of the Sahara.

His soliloquy was interrupted by the behaviour of the Renkell. It turned suddenly on its port wing-tip and headed south; and looking for the reason for this unexpected move Ginger saw a belt of mist hanging over a long valley, down the centre of which ran an area of swamp, or salt-marsh. The mist was not coming from anywhere; it was forming in the air, now that the sun was setting, due to the difference of temperature between the sun-soaked sand and the water-cooled marsh. With a pang of alarm he realised that should the transport reach the miasma it would disappear from sight, and by changing course, lose them. Then he caught his breath with relief, for Biggles had also turned, and by cutting across the angle, brought the transport within striking distance.

After that the end came quickly. Slowly, with calculated deliberation, Biggles took the objective machine in his sights. His thumb slid over the firing button. Tracer flashed across the gap. Instantly, the transport, seeing that it could not escape, whirled round and came back at them, flecks of flame spurting from its guns, revealing for the first time the type of armament it carried. Biggles pressed his left foot gently on the rudder-bar and the transport's tracer streamed past his right wing-tip. The Renkell hurtled past. The Spur was already turning, and in a split second Biggles was on the transport's tail. Again his tracer flashed, the shots converging on the target. The Renkell zoomed wildly, and turned vertically at the top of its climb; but it made no difference; the Spur was still behind it, firing short, vicious bursts.

Then a strange thing happened. The escape hatch of the transport opened and a man's figure dropped earthwards. An instant later a parachute mushroomed.

'Gontermann. He can't take it,' said Biggles, and went on after the transport, which was now barely under control. It went into a dive that became steeper and steeper, and Ginger could hear the scream of its airscrews above the roar of their own. He bit his lip, knowing what was going to happen. He had seen it happen before. Biggles was no longer firing.

The dive of the stricken machine steepened until it was going down vertically. Ginger flinched when the crash came. With the languid deliberation of a slow-motion screen picture the aircraft seemed to disintegrate, and spread itself over the desert. He knew that no one inside the machine could have survived such a fearful impact.

Biggles circled once or twice, losing height, and then, flying a few feet above the sand, went on after Gontermann who, still carrying his bag, was running towards the swamp.

'To the last, all he thought about was himself,' said Biggles grimly. 'He hadn't the guts to see it through. What a skunk the fellow must be.'

He landed the Spur between the swamp and the running man, jumped down, and after walking a few paces, took out his pistol and waited.

Gontermann also stopped, snatching a glance at the desert behind him.

'Go that way if you like,' sneered Biggles. 'Your carcass should poison the vultures, when they find you.'

Gontermann hesitated.

'Come on – come on; you've got a gun,' invited Biggles. 'Use it or drop it, I don't care which.'

Gontermann advanced a few paces. 'Listen, Bigglesworth,' he called in a high-pitched voice. 'What I've got in this bag will make us the two richest men on earth. I'm willing to split two ways. All I ask is, you give me a lift—'

'Shut up,' snapped Biggles. 'You make me sick. Drop that bag and get your hands up.'

Gontermann stood the bag on the desert sand. All the arrogance had gone out of him. 'Don't shoot,' he pleaded.

'Put your hands up and keep walking,' said Biggles coldly.

The Nazi walked forward, slowly, nervously. 'All right. I'll come quietly,' he said. 'I know when I'm beaten.'

'Okay.' Biggles returned the pistol to his pocket, or had started to do so, when Gontermann moved with the speed of light. His hand flashed to his side and came up holding a heavy calibre Mauser.

Biggles's gun spat, and the Nazi seemed to stiffen. Yet he managed to get his pistol up and fire. But Biggles had sidestepped. Again his gun cracked. Again Gontermann stiffened convulsively. The muzzle of the Mauser sagged; it exploded into the ground, making the sand spurt; then the weapon dropped with a gentle thud. The man who had held it sank to his knees, and then slid forward, like a swimmer in smooth water.

Biggles stood still for a moment, watching, before walking forward to look at the fallen man.

'Pity,' he said quietly to Ginger, who now came running up. 'I would rather have taken him alive – but perhaps it's better this way. I daren't take a chance with him in a place like this. He was as crooked as a dog's hind leg; even at the finish he tried to spring one on me. Well, it's spared the country the expense of a trial, and saved the hangman a job. Let's see what's happened over here.' He walked on to the crash. Now that Gontermann was dead his anger seemed to have burnt itself out like a wisp of paper.

As they expected, there was only one man in the wreck – Baumer. He was dead.

'I still don't understand why they left Renkell in the sanseviera,' said Biggles. 'He may still be alive. When we go back to Khartoum to see how Bertie's getting on we'll see if we can find him.'

'What I should like to know,' said Ginger, 'is how we're going to get out of this devil's dustbin with empty tanks.'

'Not quite empty,' reminded Biggles. 'We've still a drop in hand, and I reckon we're not many miles south of the French Air Force landing-ground at Touggourt. There's another one, Ouargla, a little to the south. As a matter of fact, there are quite a bunch of desert aerodromes in front of us – Colomb Bechar, Beni Abbes.... Hallo! What's this coming?' He broke off, gazing into the darkening eastern sky, whence came the drone of an aircraft.

'Mosquito,' said Ginger. 'That'll be Algy. He must have had a word with the manager bloke at Castel Benito, and ascertained the course we took. He can't miss seeing us on this blistering billiard table.'

The Mosquito came on, roaring at full throttle a few hundred feet above the sand.

'Poor old Algy,' said Biggles, smiling. 'He still hopes to be in at the finish. Ah-ah! He's seen us.'

The Mosquito had altered course and was now standing

directly towards them. The bellow of its engines died away; its wheels came down, and very soon it was on the sand, taxiing towards the Spur. Algy leapt out.

'What's happened?' he asked quickly.

'It's all over,' answered Biggles. 'Baumer stuck to his ship and went into the deck fast enough to break every bone in his body. Gontermann baled out. He tried to plug me, so I had to let him have it. I aimed at his arm, but hit him in the chest. My shooting must be getting shaky.'

'After the flying you've done today I'm not surprised at that,' asserted Algy. 'What are we going to do?'

Biggles thought for a moment. 'We shall have to leave things here as they are. I don't see what else we can do – unless you feel like turning your kite into a hearse. We'll make for Algiers – that's the nearest airport – and send a cable to Raymond from there. No doubt he'll ask the French authorities to take care of this mess. In the morning I'll push on to London in the Mosquito, taking Gontermann's collection of sparklers with me. They should cure Raymond's headache. You two can drift back to Khartoum in the Spur, in your own time, to see how Bertie's getting on. We'd better be moving, before it's quite dark.'

He walked over to Gontermann's bag, and opening it, gazed for a moment at its scintillating contents. 'While this sort of rubbish clutters up civilisation I suppose there will always be crooks,' he remarked. Then a smile spread slowly over his face. 'Still, ten per cent of that little lot should keep us in cigarettes for a day or two.' He closed the bag, stood up, and passed his hand wearily over his face. 'Strewth! I'm tired. Let's get along.'

*

The story of a chase should end with the death or capture of the quarry, but in this case one or two points remain to be cleared up.

By noon of the day following the final affair in the desert Biggles was at Scotland Yard. As a matter of detail he had slept at Gibraltar, from where he had been able to send a signal through service channels to Air Commodore Raymond, who was at Croydon Airport to meet him. At the Yard, an inventory was made of the contents of Gontermann's bag, which, besides the rajah's regalia, included the best of the pearls of the Persian Gulf affair, and the South African diamonds.

'Ten per cent, sir, I think you said?' murmured Biggles blandly.

The Air Commodore looked up with a twinkle in his eye. 'I doubt if any policeman earned so much in so short a time. You'd better stay in the Force and make your fortune.'

'It has to be shared four ways, don't forget,' reminded Biggles. 'Still, I'll think about your suggestion,' he added.

After writing a detailed report on the whole operation, he had a bath, changed, and later dined with the Commissioner of Police, and his assistant, Air Commodore Raymond. That night he had his first unbroken sleep for some time.

In the morning he started back for Khartoum to see how Bertie was faring. He found him out of danger, although the doctor predicted that the injured leg might shorten a trifle, so that he would probably limp for the rest of his life.

'I asked him to cut a piece off the other, to get 'em the same length again – if you see what I mean?' complained Bertie. 'But the silly ass wouldn't do it. Said he might slice off too much, and then I should go into a permanent bank the other way – or some such rot.'

Algy and Ginger had flown on into the sanseviera. They came back some time after Biggles's arrival, bringing with them Herr Renkell, whom they had spotted wandering in the swamp. The aircraft designer declared that far from having any hand in the disappearance of his prototypes, he had been abducted by the bandits and forced to act as mechanic on his own machines, the idea being, presumably, that, as the designer, he was the only man who thoroughly understood them. Biggles believed him. Indeed, his appearance did much to confirm his story, for he looked thin and ill. He declared, and Algy verified, that the whole area occupied by the secret landing-ground had been burnt out, as well as the equipment, oil, and petrol.

Biggles inquired after von Zoyton, but being told that he was still on the danger list, and not allowed visitors, he did not see him. This had a curious sequel. Weeks later, when Biggles and his comrades were back in London, they learned that not only had von Zoyton recovered from his injuries, but had taken advantage of a *haboob* – one of the local violent sand-storms – to make his escape from hospital. The Egyptian police were looking for him, but so far had been unsuccessful.

'I'm not altogether sorry,' said Biggles, when he heard this news. 'He wasn't a bad chap at heart. Probably it all came from getting mixed up with the wrong crowd when he was a kid. His mother should have warned him.'

BIGGLES IN AUSTRALIA

CHAPTER I

A Pressman Sets a Poser

When Biggles, in answer to a call on the intercom, entered the office of his chief, Air Commodore Raymond of the Special Air Section at Scotland Yard, he was greeted with a smile which he knew from experience was not prompted entirely by humour.

'I'm not much for betting, sir, but I'd risk a small wager that what you're going to tell me isn't really funny,' he observed as he pulled up a chair.

'That would depend on how you looked at it,' answered the Air Commodore drily. 'Serious matters can sometimes provoke an ironical smile. Take a look at this. I thought you'd like to see it.' He pushed across the desk a picture that had obviously been cut from a newspaper.

Biggles studied the photographic reproduction for some time without speaking and without a change of expression. It showed a group of seven men standing on a sandy beach with the sea in the background. The subjects were in tropical kit, creased, dirty, shrunken and generally disreputable. They were hatless, and all needed a hair-cut and a shave.

'Recognize anybody?' asked the Air Commodore, whimsically.

'Of course. Our old friend Erich von Stalhein, no less. He appears to have slipped into the soup – on this occasion without being pushed by me.'

'Do you know any of the others?'

'I fancy I've seen one of them before, but not recently, and on the spur of the moment I can't place him. Where, may I ask, was this fascinating snapshot taken?'

'On the coast of north-west Australia.'

Biggles's eyes opened wide. '*Australia*! For Pete's sake! Where will the ubiquitous Erich turn up next? What was he doing there?'

'That's what I'd like to know. At the time the photo was taken he had just come ashore.'

'What did he *say* he was doing?'

'He said he was, or had been, studying oceanography.'

Biggles smiled cynically. 'Imagine von Stalhein sitting on the sea bed watching the winkles and things. How did this enchanting picture come into your hands?'

'It was spotted by Major Charles of Security Intelligence in a batch of newspapers just in from Australia. Actually, the picture was in several papers. He thought we might like to see it.'

Biggles pushed the paper back across the desk. 'You know, sir, von Stalhein is becoming a nuisance.'

'I'd say he's a menace.'

'Then why don't you do something about it?'

'I've told you before that we've no case against him; nor shall we have while he's clever enough to keep on the right side of the law.'

'With the result that I spend half my time looking for him and the other half dodging him.'

'Of course.'

'What do you mean, of course?'

'While he's engaged in espionage, and you in counter-espionage, it's inevitable that you should always be bumping into each other – in the same way as in football the two centre-forwards are often in collision. He has to earn his living somehow and it's natural that he should stick to the job for which he was trained in one of the most efficient spy schools in the world – the Wilhelmstrasse. He's no more likely to settle down in a routine occupation than you are.' The Air Commodore smiled. 'Don't forget you must be as big a nuisance to him as he is to you.'

Biggles nodded. 'I suppose you're right. At least he keeps us busy and provides us with an excuse for staying in our jobs. How did this Australian affair come about?'

'Quite simply. A few weeks ago north-west Australia was visited by one of those devastating storms which we would call a hurricane but are known locally as willie-willies. They do immense damage, both at sea and ashore. After the one in question, three pearling luggers, out from Broome, failed to return to port, so aircraft of the Royal Australian Air Force were sent out to locate them, or possible survivors should they have been wrecked. One of the rescue aircraft spotted a ship's lifeboat, under sail, making for the mainland miles from anywhere – by which I mean miles from the nearest point where food and water would be available. The pilot radioed the position, whereupon supplies were rushed to the spot where the boat was making its landfall. It seems that a newspaper reporter, scenting a story, also went along in a chartered plane, taking his camera. He got his story, such as it was, and, as you see, a photograph. In the matter of the picture a curious thing happened. At least, it struck the reporter as queer, and he referred to it in his article. When these shipwrecked mariners realized they had been photographed they kicked up a fuss and demanded that the film be destroyed.'

'What reason did they give for that?'

'They said that as scientists they were opposed to any form of publicity.'

'I bet they were,' murmured Biggles, bitingly.

'Actually, that was a mistake, because, as I say, the reporter made a note of it, and certain sceptical editors, in their columns, asked for what possible reason these men should object to being photographed.'

'We could tell them.'

'Of course. Von Stalhein has good reasons for not wanting to see his face in any newspaper.'

'What story did he tell. He'd have to offer some explanation.'

'The spokesman of the party said they were a scientific expedition studying marine life in tropical waters. Their ship, the *See Taube*, out from Hamburg, was caught in the storm and cast ashore on an island. The seven were the sole survivors of a crew of twenty-two. The ship was pounded to pieces on a reef, but by good luck a lifeboat was washed up more or less intact. Having patched it up, they set a course for the mainland. They had, of course, lost everything except the clothes they stood up in. Considering the state they were in their story was not questioned. We can assume that the shipwreck part of it was true.'

'They would remember their names and nationalities – or did they lose those too?' inquired Biggles sarcastically.

'No. They gave their names. You'll find them in the paper. They were four Germans, two Poles, and a Britisher who said he was simply a member of the crew.'

'Did von Stalhein's name appear among them?'

'No.'

'That's what I thought. And I gather they could all speak English.'

'So it seems.'

'Very convenient, if they were going to land in Australia.'

'They said they had no intention of landing in Australia – until they were cast away.'

'Then the fact that they could all speak English must have been one of those curious coincidences we sometimes hear about,' remarked Biggles, with a faint sneer of scepticism. 'Where are they now?'

'No one knows, and, frankly, no one seems to care. They've just disappeared.'

'How could they disappear?'

'They were flown to Darwin and provided with clothes and accommodation pending such time as arrangements could be made for them to return home. It seems that a few days later, an aircraft, chartered by a good Samaritan in the south, turned up and collected them. They just went; and as Darwin is an international port apparently the local people couldn't have cared less.'

'Didn't this sudden departure strike anyone as odd?'

'Evidently not. Darwin is the sort of place where people come and go. After all, von Stalhein and his companions were not under any sort of suspicion. They were not being watched. They had broken no law. The police weren't interested in them. They were free to come and go as they wished.'

'All nice and easy,' muttered Biggles. 'This good Samaritan, as you call him, must have been a contact man. No doubt he saw the picture in the papers, and realizing what had happened, got busy. Which means, in plain English, there was already an enemy agent in Australia.'

'That, as you would say, sticks out like a sore finger.'

'Have you told Australia what we know von Stalhein to be?'

'Not yet.'

'Why not?'

'I don't want to start a spy scare. At the moment von Stalhein is, I imagine, lying low, waiting to see what the outcome of this affair will be. If he decides that it has passed unnoticed by the Security people, both there and here, he may come into the open and proceed with what he went to Australia to do. In which case we may catch up with him.'

'Who do you mean by we?'

'Well – you.'

Biggles reached for a cigarette. 'Surely this is Australia's pigeon.'

'Australia is part of the British Commonwealth, and as such it is also our pigeon. Of this we may be sure. If von Stalhein is in Australia he's not there for our good.'

'I couldn't agree more. No doubt he and the rest of the party quietly faded away because they didn't want to be asked questions which might have been embarrassing. The point is, what questions were they asked when they were rescued. This island on which they were wrecked, for example. What's the name of it?'

'They didn't know.'

'Stuff and nonsense! Of course they knew. Don't ask me to believe that the skipper of a vessel that size didn't know the position of his ship.'

'What size?'

'With a ship's company of twenty-two it was obviously no mere cabin cruiser.'

'There are plenty of islands off that particular coast.'

'How long were they cast away on one.'

'Three weeks – they said.'

'If that's true we should have no great difficulty in finding it, because apart from the wreckage of the ship, seven men in three weeks would leave their mark. But that's a detail that can be gone into later – that's if you think this business is of such importance that it should be followed up.'

'I certainly do.'

'But you're not seriously expecting me to find von Stalhein in a place the size of Australia?'

'If we don't find the man we've got to know what he's doing. Apart from the fact that Australia is a fast-developing continent in which the Iron Curtain brigade would like to get their teeth, there are a lot of things going on there that they would like to know more about. No doubt they would like to have more information than we have released about the new rocket and guided missile ranges. They would like to know more about the present and future production prospects of the newly-discovered uranium deposits.'

'They wouldn't need a ship for that.'

'They'd need a ship to test the strength of any radio-activity persisting in the region of the Montebello Islands, where we exploded atomic bombs.'

'You may have got something there,' admitted Biggles. 'Never mind what the ship was for, it was certainly needed or it wouldn't have been provided. In which case it would seem that an investigation into the purpose of enemy agents in Australia would have to cover not only the mainland but the hundreds of islands within striking distance of it.'

'That, I'm afraid, is what it adds up to.'

'I'm glad to hear you say you're afraid,' said Biggles lugubriously. 'You've good reason to be. So have I. You don't often hear me say that, but the prospect of finding a man, or even a small army of men, in a place the size of Australia, strikes me as having about as much hope of success as a boy looking for a lost peanut on a shingle beach on a dark night. I once had occasion to fly over a stretch of north-west Australia, and what I saw didn't make me pine to see more of it. I know it isn't all like that, but there's plenty that is. No, sir. This isn't a job for one man. It'd be an undertaking for the entire Australian Police Force, and even then I wouldn't bet on them finding an elusive customer like dear Erich, who knows every trick of the game.'

'The police are not likely to take kindly to the idea of looking for a man against whom there is no charge.'

'They could deport him as an undesirable alien.'

'That would only make matters worse. Even if he didn't slip back in he'd be replaced with someone else whom we don't even know. Better the devil you know than the devil you don't know is an old saying, and a true one. See what you can do. I'm not particularly interested in von Stalhein personally; but we must know what he and his party are doing. It's our job to find out. Knowing what we know we can't just let the thing slide.'

Biggles shrugged. 'Very well, sir. You win. I'll do my best to get a line but it's likely to be a slow business.'

'Can I help in any way?'

Biggles thought for a moment. 'You can let me have the name of the reporter who took that photo, the name of the pilot who sent out the S.O.S., and the pinpoint he gave on first spotting the boat at sea. That's where I shall start. It's the only place I can start. If, too, you can identify the aircraft that collected von Stalhein and his party at Darwin it may save me some time there. The control tower should know. It would be something if we knew where that machine came from, who hired it, and where it went. It might also be helpful if you could let me have the name and address of an Australian Security Officer with whom I could get in touch should the need arise.'

'I'll attend to that. Anything else?'

'That's all I can think of at the moment, sir. I'll press on and get ready. It looks as if I shall need two machines, one for marine work and the other for overland. But we can talk about that later.' Biggles got up.

'The Australians are a hospitable lot so you might be going to a worse place,' remarked the Air Commodore comfortingly.

'Then don't be surprised if you hear I've packed up chasing myself round the globe and gone in for sheep raising or something,' was Biggles's last word as he went out.

Returning to the Operations Room he passed on the latest intelligence to his team of pilots.

'What's your own idea of this business,' asked Algy, when he had finished.

'I haven't one,' admitted Biggles. 'Von Stalhein could be engaged on one or more of a dozen shady undertakings – all with an espionage background, of course. We can, however, be reasonably sure of one or two things. He was given a definite assignment, and an important one covering a wide field, or he would be working on his own instead of with a party. It involved, at any rate in the first place, marine work – unless the ship was provided to enable the party to get ashore without passing through a normal port of entry, as would be necessary if they were carrying equipment that would be questioned by the Customs officers.'

'Are we sure they had a ship,' put in Ginger.

'Yes. They wouldn't be likely to start from Europe in a rowing boat. They admitted a crew of twenty-two men. Why did they volunteer that information? I'd say because they knew that the story was more likely to be believed than if they had said they were in those dangerous waters in a small craft. Ships are expensive things, so behind von Stalhein there must be big money; which suggest a foreign government. The ship was the *See Taube* – Sea Pigeon. It came from Hamburg so we can check up on that. The rescue people didn't question it. That's understandable. The first thing they would do would be to get the castaways to civilization, leaving the questions till later; but by that time, the party, as we know, had disappeared.'

Bertie interposed. 'But look here, old boy. If the blighters lost their ship they must have lost their gear, if any.'

'That's what I'm hoping happened,' answered Biggles. 'If the ship broke up, and I think it must have done considering the plight the survivors were in, some of it, or some of the stuff it carried, might have been cast ashore. Working on that assumption I shall start by looking for the island.'

'How many islands are there to be searched,' asked Ginger.

'I don't know,' replied Biggles. 'We shall know more about that when we've studied the chart. Speaking from memory there are quite a lot; but that needn't worry us unduly, because the one with which we're concerned can't be any great distance from the spot where the lifeboat was first seen. As the pilot of the aircraft pinpointed the position it will be on record.'

'This seems to be a more hopeless job than most of those that come our way,' remarked Algy.

'That's what I told the chief. But he argued that it wasn't as sticky as all that because although Australia is a big slice of land there's a limit to the number of places in which von Stalhein would be interested. I hope he's right. But we'd better see about getting organized. We shall need a land plane with plenty of endurance, which means the Halifax; but I've no intention of cruising around the Timor Sea in something that'll sink if we get ditched. I'll take Ginger with me in the Sea Otter we used on that West Indian job. I'd take the Sunderland but there might be difficulties in refuelling. From that angle an amphibian would be safer. Algy, you and Bertie can trundle out to Darwin in the Halifax. We'll travel independently and meet there. Now let's have a look at the chart and see where we're going. When I say going I'm thinking particularly of where we're going to park the machines. There's no dearth of aerodromes, even if they're a long way apart; but except for refuelling I shall endeavour to keep clear of them, for if ever it reaches von Stalhein's ears that we're in Australia he'll know why, and our job will be even more diffi-cult than it is now. And while I think of it, as we're talking about moorings, never forget that on the north-west coast of Australia the difference between high water and low can be up to nearly forty feet. So watch your tides. Now let's look at the map.'

CHAPTER II

Wide Open Spaces

The arrangements made by Biggles for his Australian assignment were rather more involved than usual on account of
the peculiar conditions in which they would have to operate.
Where the quest would eventually lead them was an unknown
quantity, and, as he told the others, it was as well to be prepared
for anything. They were going to a continent, not a country, and
while it was now well provided with aerodromes the distances
between them was a factor that would have to be considered
in conjunction with refuelling. They didn't want to spend half
their time flying to distant points for fuel and oil, much of which
would be exhausted on the return journey, thus hampering their
mobility and putting them in a constant state of anxiety.

The matter was complicated by the employment of a marine
aircraft, although the machine, a Sea Otter, being an amphibian,
could operate from both land or water. The Otter was an ideal
craft for investigating the islands, and it would be able to refuel
at the several landing grounds strung out along the coast
between Perth and Darwin; but it hadn't the endurance range of
the Halifax, with its special tanks, which would in many ways be
more suitable for long-distance overland flights.

Biggles admitted that this question of refuelling worried him, because people would wonder what they were doing and perhaps ask questions. Word of them might be carried by the regular airline pilots to the cities on which they were based, and so reach the ears of von Stalhein or his confederates, who might be anywhere. In order to avoid being seen too often, should the exploration of the islands turn out to be a long business, Biggles had an idea of using the Halifax as a refuelling tender. Working from Port Darwin, it should, he thought, be able to land anywhere on Eighty Mile Beach, which, according to their information, was 'eighty miles of sand without a pebble'. The Otter could refuel from the Halifax and proceed with its work while the Halifax returned to Darwin for a further load of petrol and oil. Whether this would work out as well in practice as in theory could only be ascertained by trial and error. As things turned out this did not arise.

The airfield chosen for a base in the first instance was Broome, a port on the coastal route developed by West Australian Airways. Not only was this the nearest available petrol supply to the area in which von Stalhein's party had first been sighted, but Biggles had a vague hope that he might pick up some information from the crews of the pearling luggers that made the town their home port.

Little news had come to hand, except the information for which Biggles had asked, since his first interview with the Air Commodore. The names given by von Stalhein's party had been checked, and it came as no surprise that they were unknown in Western Europe. The *See Taube* was not known in Hamburg, either.

Biggles had written a personal note to West, one of the control officers he had met on a previous occasion at Port Darwin, asking him to check up on the aircraft in which the 'shipwrecked sailors' had left the town. From where had it come and to where had it gone? He, Biggles, would be along shortly to speak to him about it.

It had been learned that the spot where von Stalhein's boat had first been spotted was about twenty miles seaward from the southern end of the barren stretch of coast, south of Broome, known, and shown on the map, as Eighty Mile Beach, to which reference has already been made. As willie-willies, with their hundred and twenty miles an hour fury, come in broadly from a northerly direction, it was possible to form a rough idea of the most probable direction of the island on which von Stalhein's ship had been cast away. A close study of the chart revealed no lack of islands, and Admiralty Sailing Directions gave descriptions of some of them. Mostly uninhabited, they varied in composition between stark coral reef and the shallow, blown-sand and sea-grass type, like the Lacepedes. Many bore the names of the early explorers or forgotten sea captains. As to the coast of the mainland, Ginger regarded with some concern the thousand miles of sand dunes backed for the most part by desert, with an occasional lonely mine or sheep station. There were towns, but they were few and far between. Ginger's eye followed them round – Derby, Broome, Hedland, Roebourne, Onslow…. He was relieved to note that most of them were served by air.

The Otter arrived first at Port Darwin. Biggles did not go ashore at once, for although his proposed excuse for being there was nothing more romantic than an equipment test in varying overseas conditions, he was afraid he might be thought a fit subject by a press photographer. Publicity was the last thing he wanted.

After dark, taking Ginger with him, he made his way to the airport buildings and reintroduced himself to West, and reminded him of his letter.

'What is it this time – another gold swindle?' inquired West, smiling.

'Nothing like it,' answered Biggles. 'Strictly between ourselves, we're looking for somebody, and we thought he might be in that party I told you about in my letter.'

'Well, I'm sorry, but I haven't much news for you,' was the disappointing reply. 'The machine was a Quantas Airways Lockheed. Came up from Brisbane. I can give you the registration letters if that's any use to you. It went back to Brisbane, but Jimmy Alston, who was flying it, has an idea the people didn't stay there, because he saw them hanging about the airport some time after he'd booked in. He's been here since and I spoke to him about it. He hasn't been able to find out where they went after he unloaded them.'

'Who paid for the flight? It must have been an expensive trip and it's unlikely the passengers had any money.'

'Apparently a fellow named Smith. He paid in ready money. Nobody knew anything about him. Didn't matter much who he was, I reckon, as long as he had the cash.'

'He didn't give any address?'

'If he did no one seems to have made a note of it. All Jimmy could get from the booking clerk was he spoke like a foreigner.'

'Useful name, Smith,' murmured Biggles. 'And that's all you've been able to find out.'

'That's the lot. Do you want me to ask Jimmy, if he comes up again, to try to find out more about this chap Smith?'

Biggles thought for a moment. 'No thanks. It might do more

harm than good. Of course, if he should see any of these people again, and that includes Smith, he might let you know and you could tell me. I expect to be around for a while. Is Alston on a regular run?'

'As a relief. He does most of the charter work. Must know his way round Australia better than anyone.'

'I see. Well, many thanks. We'll get along.'

'How long do you reckon to be here?'

'Not more than a day or two actually in Darwin, but I may be back later on. I'm waiting for a friend of mine to arrive. He's on the same job as I am, in a Halifax. We've arranged to meet here.'

At this point of the conversation the door opened and a man in a captain's uniform came in. 'I'm looking for Bigglesworth,' he announced. 'They tell me he's in the building.'

'That's me,' returned Biggles.

'I've got a message for you. I'm just in from Singapore. There's a friend of yours there, named Lacey, with an old Halifax. He told me to tell you he's hung up with a spot of engine trouble. Nothing serious; but it may be a day or two before he can get away. At the moment everyone's busy on a nasty crack-up on the airfield.'

'Thanks,' acknowledged Biggles. 'Are you going back that way?'

'Day after tomorrow.'

'Well, if he's still there when you get there you might tell him not to get in a flap. There's no hurry. If I'm not here when he gets here he'd better wait.'

'Okay.'

'Thanks a lot.'

The pilot departed and Biggles turned to West. 'If Lacey arrives and I'm not here you might tell him to concentrate on getting his machine a hundred per cent airworthy. This is no country to take chances.'

West grinned. 'Glad you've realized that. Are you thinking of pulling out right away now?'

'As I've nothing to do here I shall probably take a run down the coast to have a general look round. Oh, and that reminds me. Do you happen to know what became of the lifeboat in which those fellows came ashore?'

West shook his head. 'It was never mentioned in my hearing. I gather it had been knocked about so it's unlikely that anyone would trouble to fetch it. I could probably find out for you. Len Seymour, one of our chaps was with the relief party. He'll have gone home now but I could ring him.'

'I wish you would. It's only a detail, but every little helps.'

West put through the call.

'It was left on the beach,' he announced, as he hung up. 'Len says they pulled it high and dry in case it was wanted, and left it there. There was nothing else they could do with it. It wasn't worth much, anyway.'

'Thanks,' acknowledged Biggles. 'Well, we'll get along now. See you later, maybe.'

Leaving the building they returned to the Otter.

'Pity about Algy,' observed Ginger, on the way.

'If he's having trouble it's a good thing he's where he is, and not in the middle of nowhere.'

'Are we going to a hotel for the night?'

'No. We'll sleep on board, then there will be no difficulty in making an early start.'

'You're going straight on to have a look at the islands?'

'We might as well. I don't feel like sitting here doing nothing for perhaps a week. We'll have a wash, get a bite in the town and come back. It's under four miles so if we have to walk it won't do us any harm.'

'Fair enough,' agreed Ginger.

So they had a meal in Darwin, the little town which, practically unknown forty years ago, was 'put on the map' by aviation, and is now the focal point for planes arriving in, or leaving, Australia. A modest monument was erected to the memory of Ross Smith, the airman who, in his Vickers Vimy, first touched down on what was to become the first airport in Australia, with hangars, oil tanks, workshops, and a beacon that can be seen for a hundred miles to guide machines making the night crossing of the Timor Sea.

Early to bed, morning saw Biggles and Ginger deflating their pneumatic mattresses while the stars still gleamed in the sky; and before the town was awake the Otter was droning down a south-westerly course on its six hundred mile run to the scene of its first investigation. To starboard lay the open sea, an indigo plain stretching to infinity in the light of the new-born day. To port, a few feathers of mist were drifting over the purple smudge that was Australia's lonely north-west coast – perhaps the most forsaken stretch of coast in the world.

Ginger knew that Biggles had no clear-cut plan of campaign. Islands, numbers of islands and atolls, any one of which might be the one they sought, were scattered far and wide. They were mostly small and uninhabited, but size was no indication. Biggles had admitted frankly that all they could do was take in turn each square that he had marked on the chart and fly low over any islands that fell within it. This, of course, meant a good deal of dead reckoning navigation for Ginger. The immediate objective was the spot where the rescue pilot had pinpointed the boat. Biggles had not bothered to look him up, feeling sure that he would not be able to tell them more than they already knew. The direction from which the boat had come could only be guesswork, and their guess was as good as his.

It was just after nine o'clock when Ginger announced that they were as near the pinpoint as he would be able to estimate it. The mainland, with its miles of untrodden sand, was a silvery streak on the horizon. The rest was open sea, without a ship, without an island, without a mark of any sort to break its sparkling surface.

Biggles turned the bows of the machine to the north and the search began.

To narrate in detail the hours that followed would be monotonous reiteration. Suffice it to say that several islands were examined without result. Biggles's method was to cruise low over the foreshore while Ginger watched for signs of wreckage. This was really easier than it may sound because most of the islands were low-lying, small and treeless, either coral atolls or banks of sand not more than eight or ten feet high at the highest point. These, Biggles felt sure, would be overwhelmed in severe hurricanes. Once in a while there would be an island worthy of the name, boasting an odd breadfruit tree or a few wind-torn coconut palms.

There were several false alarms when what looked like wreckage was sighted. On one occasion Biggles landed on the tranquil surface of a lagoon; but the wreck turned out to be barnacle and seaweed encrusted remains of an unlucky lugger, lost, no doubt, in one of the notorious willie-willies. They took the opportunity to have a rest, and some food.

'These islets must be death-traps for ships in bad weather,' remarked Ginger.

'We should have taken into account the possibility of sundry wreckage, apart from what we're looking for,' replied Biggles. 'More than once, I believe, the entire pearling fleet has been wiped out. From November to April, when a hurricane can blow up in an hour, pearling must be an anxious business.'

'I imagine you'll go to Broome for the night, and top up the tanks?' supposed Ginger.

'I've been thinking about that,' answered Biggles. 'It may not be necessary. I don't want to be seen there too often. It struck me that we might carry on until near sundown. Then, if we could find a safe anchorage we could sit down for the night and finish this particular area in the morning before heading for Broome. We're still all right for juice.'

Ginger agreed there was no sense in waffling a hundred miles to the coast, only to come back in the morning, if it could be avoided.

It was about four o'clock when Biggles pointed out a lagoon that he thought should suit them. The time was still on the early side, but, as he said, they had had enough flying for one day.

The lagoon was part of a typical coral atoll formation. That is to say, the land that formed the island, at no point more than twenty feet above sea level, was the shape of a horseshoe. The open ends dwindled to mere points, and then, continuing on as reefs of varying width, without quite meeting, encompassed the flat sheet of water that was the lagoon. This might have been half a mile in diameter. The beach, the only beach, was a strip of sand on the inside of the horseshoe. On the outer side, and, indeed, all round the encircling reef, the ocean swell broke in showers of sparkling spray to the accompaniment of a dull continuous rumble. The only vegetation the island could produce was a little sparse scrub and a group of perhaps a dozen palms, their fronds torn and tattered, presumably by the recent willie-willie.

Ginger, who had seen atolls before, was not impressed. He was merely concerned with the safe anchorage it provided, and would provide while the weather remained calm. Ripples surged in through the opening in the reef, but for the most part the lagoon lay like a sheet of glass under a sky serenely blue.

As Biggles made a false run to check the surface for possible obstructions Ginger noticed several small white spots, scattered about the land that he could not identify. Without being more than mildly curious he noted them in passing, recalling that he had seen similar spots on the last island they had surveyed. They hadn't landed, so he had had no opportunity of finding out what they were. The swish of the keel as it kissed the water, cutting a V-shaped ripple, put the objects out of his head; and for the next few minutes, after Biggles had taxied close inshore, they were busy making everything snug.

After that there was nothing more to do. Biggles took the Primus from its locker. 'We'll have a cup of tea and then go ashore to stretch our legs,' he suggested.

'Are you going to sleep on board?' asked Ginger.

'I don't think so. I'd rather sleep on the beach under the stars. We seem to have the place to ourselves and we're not likely to have visitors.'

The only signs of life were, in fact, a few gulls that wheeled around the aircraft mewing their disapproval of it.

Under the water it was different, and although he had seen similar pictures before Ginger hung over the side gazing at that most fascinating of all spectacles, a coral garden. Through it, moving from one growth of coral to another, their shadows falling on the bottom, swam schools of brilliantly coloured fish. Most of these were small, but occasionally a big one would drift lazily into the picture, sending the little fellows darting for their lives.

At Biggles's call of tea-up he turned away reluctantly. 'I'm having a swim when I've had my tea,' he announced.

'That's a pleasant thought,' agreed Biggles. 'I'll keep watch for sharks while you're in; then you can keep watch for me. These seas are stiff with the brutes, but there shouldn't be anything of a dangerous size inside the lagoon. All the same, I'd rather not take a chance.'

Tea finished, Ginger had his dip. Biggles followed, with Ginger standing in the centre-section, watching. But of the dreaded triangular fin he saw no sign.

By the time preparations had been made to spend the night ashore the sun was dropping like a ball of fire beyond the horizon.

CHAPTER III

An Uncomfortable Night

There are few things on earth more beautiful than an atoll on a still, moonlit night. The sunset dies. The colours fade. The palm fronds bow their heads and come silently to rest. Silver stains the eastern sky. The rim of the moon appears, and climbing, broadens, to cast an ethereal radiance across the ocean, the motionless lagoon, and the beach, which seems to float in space. A distant nightgull cries. A land-crab, emerging from its burrow, rattles his shelly legs on a pebble, interrupting for a moment an atmosphere that has taken on the solemnity of a cathedral.

It may have been this atmosphere that prevented Ginger from sleeping. Or it may have been the beauty or the strangeness of the scene. Sitting up on the warm sand he gazed at it, a little annoyed by this unusual wakefulness, particularly as Biggles was already fast asleep beside him. Certainly there was no thought of danger in his head.

In deep meditation he watched a broad ripple surge in through the opening in the reef. It travelled faster and came farther than most of them – the result, he supposed, of an extra big wave. Another followed. There seemed to be something odd about the ripple. Normally the ripples started at once to broaden, and losing their impetus died before they were half-way to the beach. But these particular ripples neither died nor broadened. They maintained a clearly defined arrow-head shape almost to the beach, as if made by an invisible boat. Yet a third of these unnatural ripples came in to set the reflected moonbeams flashing. Then a possible solution struck him. The disturbance could, he thought, be caused by turtles, coming ashore, as is their habit, to lay their eggs in the sand.

He watched for a time, but as there was no further development he lay back, with his head on his hands, to court the sleep without which the following day would find him dull and hot-eyed. But it was no use, and he realized that he had reached that state of wakefulness that made his brain ever more alert. There was only one thing to do, he decided, and that was make a break of some sort. A short walk on the beach might do it.

Sitting up he glanced along the sand, and saw at once that one of the turtles had come ashore. Another was just emerging from the water. Then a frown creased his forehead. These things weren't turtles. They were too big. They were the wrong shape. They looked more like large barrels, tapering at one end. With no other sensation than curiosity he watched, his proposed walk forgotten. He kept still for fear of alarming the creatures and sending them back into the sea before he could identify them.

A third beast now appeared, and it may have been the spider-like way it moved that gave him his first twinge of uneasiness. Whatever the things were, he decided, they were certainly not turtles. No turtle could make a sudden sideways dart. He didn't like the idea of waking Biggles, but when one of the beasts began moving furtively towards them he thought it time he did so. Putting a hand on Biggles's shoulder he gave him a slight shake.

'What is it?' asked Biggles instantly.

'I don't know; but I think you'd better have a look at these things,' answered Ginger. 'I don't like the look of 'em. They came in through the break in the reef – made a big ripple, too.'

Biggles sat up. He looked. He looked for some time without speaking. But when, suddenly, one of the beasts raised itself up and flung out a long snake-like tentacle at something higher up the beach, he not only spoke, but moved fast. 'By thunder!' he exclaimed tersely. 'They're decapods. I don't know much about the ugly brutes but I believe they're dangerous. If they did decide to come for us we wouldn't have much chance. We'd better get into the machine.'

Ginger wasted no time in splashing through the shallow water to the aircraft, which was afloat on about three feet of water ten or twelve yards from the beach. Turning to look back from the cabin door after Biggles had got in he saw one of the beasts moving swiftly, with a sinister gliding motion, towards the place where they had been. In the bright moonlight he could now see tentacles plainly, two long ones, not less than twenty feet in length, held out in front, and a tangle of smaller ones. For the first time he realized too, the bulk of the creature's body. Feeling somewhat shaken he shut the door hurriedly. 'What are you going to do?' he asked Biggles.

*They wasted no time in splashing through
the shallow water.*

'Do? Nothing. They're not likely to come in here. I'm going to sleep.' With that Biggles stretched himself out on the floor.

Ginger didn't feel much like going to sleep; but, naturally, any fears he may have had were allayed by Biggles's casual manner. From which it will be gathered that both of them were in blissful ignorance of the nature of the giant devil-fish, from which natives, who will attack an octopus or shark in its element with a knife, fly in terror.

Ginger had just fetched his mattress with the object of inflating it and trying to get some sleep when the aircraft gave a slight lurch. A flying boat rests very lightly on the water and it takes very little to make it move. A ripple or a gust of wind will do that. But, as Ginger knew well enough, a flying boat doesn't move on calm water of its own accord. He was pondering this strange occurrence when the machine took on a slight list, and instead of recovering remained in that position. This being beyond his understanding he dropped the mattress, and walking through the forward bulkhead door into the cockpit, looked for an explanation. It did not take him long to find it. With its great tentacles over the bows of the machine a giant squid was raising itself out of the water. Even as Ginger stared at a flat luminous eye the size of a tea plate the aircraft heeled over still further under the weight of the beast hanging on one side of it.

Biggles's voice came from the cabin. 'What are you playing at? Why don't you keep still and get some sleep?'

Ginger swayed aft. In a thin, unnatural voice, he said: 'It wasn't me. It's one of those things. It's hanging on the side, as if it's trying to turn us over.'

Biggles was on his feet in an instant, only to stagger as the machine took on a list of forty-five degrees. 'If that thing gets hold of a wing it's liable to tear it off from the root,' he said crisply. 'Can you see the thing from the cockpit?'

'Yes.'

'Load the rifle and bring it to me while I have a dekko.' Biggles went forward. He looked, and, of course, saw what Ginger had seen, except that the beast was clear of the water, hanging across the bows. 'The rifle – quick,' he snapped.

Ginger moved fast. He loaded the rifle and handed it to Biggles. 'Safety catch is on,' he warned.

Very slowly Biggles adjusted his position and brought the rifle to his shoulder. Ginger, nearly sick with loathing and horror, could only watch, his heart behaving oddly. That one awful, cold, expressionless eye seemed to fascinate him, and at the same time take the strength out of his limbs.

The rifle crashed. Simultaneously the eye disappeared, as if it had been an electric lamp switched off. The aircraft righted itself with a jerk, nearly throwing Ginger off his feet. Then, to a great noise of splashing it began to rock, while every now and then something thudded against the hull, the keel, or some other part of the machine.

Clinging to the bulkhead door Ginger stared at Biggles aghast. 'It'll smash us to pieces,' he gasped.

'There's nothing more I can do,' replied Biggles. 'The thing's in the water. I don't know what it takes to kill these beasts, but as I aimed at the eye the bullet must have gone through its brain – if it's got one. This lashing may be its dying convulsions. I'm not going out to see, and perhaps be knocked overboard by one of those threshing tentacles.'

The rocking became less violent, and going to a side window Ginger saw the reason. Twenty yards from the plane and moving away from it was an area of water being churned into foam. More than that, the side of the lagoon nearest to them appeared to have come to life, with ripples racing in all directions and moonlight dancing on the turbulence. Ginger could even see phosphorescent flashes under the water.

'I think other fish, knowing the brute's in its death throes, are rolling up for the feast,' came Biggles's voice from the next window. 'In the sea everything eats everything else.'

'I hope the thing hasn't done any damage,' muttered Ginger.

'I don't think so. We'll see presently. Fortunately it tried to come aboard by the bows. Had it tried to pull itself up on a wing something would certainly have been broken.'

'It must have seen us come aboard, and followed.'

'Possibly. Or it may have taken the aircraft for a new sort of bird, or fish.'

'And to think we were bathing in that water this afternoon,' Ginger shuddered.

'I doubt if the things were here then. I'd say they live in the deep water on the outer side of the reef, but come in at night to play about or look for food – land crabs, for instance.'

'I shall think twice before I try sleeping on any more beaches in this part of the world,' declared Ginger, warmly.

'It looks as if we shall have to swat up our natural history before we start on any more jaunts of this sort,' averred Biggles. 'Matter of fact I've heard of these big brutes but I've never seen one before. We must have struck a colony of 'em. I once had a spot of bother with a big octopus. That was bad enough. I've always been more concerned about sharks, no doubt because they are always around in tropic waters. But I think it's safe now for us to have a look round for any damage.'

The churning had stopped. In fact, the lagoon had settled down, although tiny wavelets still ran up and down the beach. An examination, as far as this was possible in moonlight from the aircraft itself, revealed no sign of damage beyond some peeling of the paint on the bows, caused, it was assumed, by the great squid's suckers.

'Now, perhaps, we'll be allowed to get a little sleep,' said Biggles irritably. 'I don't think those things will trouble us any more tonight. I can see none on the beach, anyway. The danger might be sharks, brought in by the smell of blood – if those horrors have blood. Keep clear of the water.'

'You needn't tell me to do that,' returned Ginger, caustically.

Curiously, whereas before the disturbance he had been unable to sleep, he now dropped off, and when he awoke the sun was pouring an opalescent glaze, lovely to watch, on the ocean. Looking at the lagoon, once more clear and placid, he found it hard to believe that the events of the night were not an evil dream. 'Are you thinking of going ashore again?' he asked Biggles, who was pumping up the Primus.

'There seems to be no point in it. Had there been anything to see we should have seen it.'

'There's just one thing,' returned Ginger. 'As we came in I noticed some white spots that puzzled me. I saw some on another island, too. Thinking it over it struck me that they might be pieces of paper. I can't think of anything else they could be.'

'You can soon settle that,' answered Biggles. 'Slip ashore while I'm making the tea. Five minutes should be enough.'

'Okay,' agreed Ginger.

It is, perhaps, unnecessary to say that he had a good look at the water before he stepped into it. However, seeing nothing he splashed quickly to the beach and made for the nearest of the objects that had aroused his curiosity. Approaching it, he saw that he had been right. He picked up a torn piece of newspaper, printed in German. The next piece was the same, crumpled and stained with salt water. Topping the ridge of the atoll, which brought him facing a shingle beach on which the ocean rollers thundered, he saw there was more waste paper than he had supposed, for here it was less noticeable. First he picked up a typed list of what appeared to be names and addresses. It looked as if it had come adrift from a folio. His next find gave him a shock. All along the high water mark, mixed up with the usual medley of palm fronds, seaweed and shells, were Australian pound notes. He did not stop to collect them all, but picking up a few he hastened back to the aircraft. 'I think we've struck something,' he told Biggles briskly. 'Take a look at these.'

Biggles took the papers and studied them while Ginger poured himself a cup of tea and sat back to await his verdict.

'There's nothing to show what ship these came from,' said Biggles after a while. 'Other ships beside the *Taube* were lost in the hurricane, and these notes may have come from any one of them.'

'But an Australian pearling lugger wouldn't be likely to carry German newspapers.'

'You're right there,' agreed Biggles. 'That, I own, is significant.'

'What is that list?'

'Names and addresses – not in any particular town but several. Very odd. They may mean nothing to us, but if they do, they might mean a lot. The question is, how did these papers get here? There's no sign of a wreck, and these pieces of newspapers couldn't have been in the water very long or they'd have disintegrated.'

'They could have been blown here by the wind.'

'Yes. And on the face of a hundred mile an hour gale they might have travelled a long way. If we're right they must have come from the northerly quadrant.'

'It was on an island north-west of here that I saw what I realize now must have been bits of paper. What about this money? Would a lugger be likely to pay its crew afloat? If not, why take a lot of money to sea? There's nowhere to spend it.'

'I was thinking on the same lines,' answered Biggles thoughtfully. 'We'll go back to that island where you saw the paper. That should give us a direct line on the place this stuff started from. If we find nothing there of interest we'll carry on, following the line. It'll take us farther out to sea than I had reckoned to explore; but then, we've only von Stalhein's word that the party was on an island for three weeks. They could have been at sea longer than they pretended. Get the anchor up and we'll press on as far as we dare. We shall soon have to go to Broome for petrol.'

In a few minutes the Otter was in the air, on the short run back to the last island it had surveyed without landing.

Reaching it, Biggles circled low, twice. 'No sign of a wreck,' he observed. 'Surely there must be one somewhere. I don't think I'll waste time landing here. We'll push on over fresh ground and see if that produces anything.'

Twenty minutes later, by which time he was beginning to look more frequently at his petrol gauge, an island of some size crept up over the horizon. Ginger estimated it to be one of the seldom visited Mandeville Group. Even before they reached it they saw that the beach was strewn with wreckage.

'This looks more like it,' remarked Biggles, with satisfaction in his voice. 'Not much of a lagoon, but the water looks calm enough inside that reef.'

Presently, after following the usual procedure, the Otter rocked gently to a standstill within a few yards of the debris-strewn beach on the sheltered side of the island. It was one of the largest they had visited, being nearly two miles long, about a quarter of a mile wide at the widest part, and better furnished with vegetation than most. There were several stands of coconut palms, although, like the others they had seen, they had suffered severely from the willie-willie.

Finding a bare patch of sand Biggles lowered his wheels and crawled up on to it, so that they could step out onto dry ground. 'I'll tell you something right away,' he said confidently. 'This stuff represents more than one wreck.' He pointed. 'That broken mast with a bit of sail still wrapped round it was never part of a deep sea ship. The mast, and those splintered spars, could have been on a lugger. That reef may have been the one von Stalhein's vessel struck, and broke up, in which case I imagine most of it would go down in the deep water on the far side. I suppose it wouldn't be remarkable if a lugger, caught in the same storm, fell foul of the same island. But let's get busy. We've plenty to do.'

The search began; not for any particular object, but for anything that might indicate the purpose of von Stalhein and his party in Australian waters. At least, Biggles affirmed, they would almost certainly come upon something carrying the names of the vessels that had been cast away.

In this, however, they were to be disappointed.

CHAPTER IV

Island Without a Name

The first sign of tragedy lay on the beach. It was a skeleton. A few shreds of material still clung to it, but gave no clue to the nationality of the dead seaman. Ginger questioned whether it could be a casualty of the last willie-willie, or of a previous one.

'I'd say the last,' replied Biggles. 'I imagine the gulls would soon make short work of a body, human or otherwise. Besides, when the storm was actually on, wind and waves would have broken up a skeleton had it been lying here then.'

They found more skeletons. Aside from these grisly souvenirs of disaster the search went on for an hour or more without producing anything of real interest. There were one or two magazines and scraps of paper but they had been reduced to pulp. Ginger found the stiff covers of a document file, but any papers that it had contained were missing. But a single word, stamped with a rubber stamp on the front, was significant. It was *Vertraulich*.

'Confidential,' translated Biggles. 'Evidently a confidential file. Pity the contents have gone. Anyway, it tells us that a German ship, carrying secret papers, was wrecked here, or near here.'

'That list of addresses I picked up could have come from that file,' said Ginger. 'The size is the same.'

'Could be,' conceded Biggles. 'A file is only used normally to hold several papers, so I suspect that sheet of addresses wasn't the only one. I noticed that of the addresses shown there wasn't one in Sydney or Melbourne. It seems hardly likely that places of that size would be omitted from a complete list, from which I conclude they occurred on pages other than the one we have. But we'll talk about that later. I think we can take it that von Stalhein's story of being shipwrecked was substantially true. But we assumed that already. His party wouldn't have put to sea in an open boat as a matter of choice. It's queer there's nothing with a name on. I have a feeling that anything of that nature was deliberately destroyed. A wooden object, or a cork lifebelt, could easily have been burnt. We've seen the marks of at least one good bonfire. What's this thing?'

A handle stuck up at an angle from the sand. He took hold of it and pulled. The object to which it was attached emerged. He shook the sand from it, and after a brief inspection the face that he turned to Ginger wore a curious smile. 'Now we're getting some-where,' he said softly. 'No lugger would be likely to carry that.'

'A Geiger Counter,'[1] breathed Ginger.

'It looks as if von Stalhein *may* have had some scientists with him; but that isn't to say they were interested in fish. At first sight it looks as if we may have discovered the purpose of that ship in these waters.'

'You mean, to make tests around the Montebello Islands, where we exploded atomic bombs.'

'That could be one of the reasons.'

'How far are we from the islands?'

---

[1] A device for the detection and counting of fast electrical particles, as from radio-active materials.

'For a rough guess four hundred miles.'

'That sounds a long way.'

'The Americans issued a warning to shipping within four hundred and fifty miles of the Marshall Group, where they exploded their bombs. Von Stalhein and his friends may have been going nearer to the Montebello Group for all we know. But let's not jump to conclusions and say the mystery of the spy ship in these waters has been solved. The Geiger Counter is also used for other purposes; for locating uranium deposits in the ground, for instance. Anyway, it's an interesting discovery. We'll take the thing with us when we go.' Biggles raised his head and sniffed. 'Can you smell anything?'

'I've noticed a pretty offensive stink once or twice, if that's what you mean.'

'That's exactly what I mean. It's corruption of some sort. It can only come on the breeze so whatever it is should be in this direction. Let's see.'

A walk of some distance, with the smell becoming stronger, took them inland to an area of scrub that had not been explored, for the search, naturally, had been confined to the foreshore. Biggles approached cautiously – stopped – and then, after taking a few quick paces forward, stopped again, his handkerchief to his nose, bending over something. 'You'd better stay where you are,' he told Ginger. 'This isn't pretty.'

Ginger waited. Minutes passed. Then Biggles, looking a little pale, rejoined him. 'Things outside my calculations have happened here,' he announced grimly.

'What was it?'

'A man. Or what's left of one. I don't think he could have been dead more than a week or ten days.'

'A white man?'

'No. An oriental. I'd say Japanese. He must have been on the lugger. I seem to remember that most of the pearling fleet is manned by Japanese types, Malays, or Asiatics of some sort. I fancy he was the skipper or he wouldn't have had this on him.' Biggles opened a hand to disclose a small tobacco tin. He lifted the lid.

Ginger's eyes went round. 'Pearls!'

'Naturally, that would be the one thing he'd try to save when he knew his ship was done for.'

'But how – why did he stay, when—'

'Just a minute and I'll answer your questions, although, by thunder, they leave more to be answered. He was shot – at least twice. He was hit in the stomach and in the leg. His clothes are stiff with dried blood. And he didn't commit suicide, although he had this gun lying near his hand.' Biggles took the revolver from his pocket, and 'broke' it to show that four shots had been fired. A man determined to kill himself doesn't shoot himself in the leg.'

'He was murdered.'

'He was certainly shot by somebody and that looks mighty like murder. As I see it, hard hit, the poor devil clawed his way into these bushes to escape from whoever was after him.'

'Mutiny.'

Biggles shrugged. 'Could have been; but was this the time and place for a mutiny? Think. The lugger had been battered to death by a hurricane. One man, probably several, managed to get ashore. And here they were, cast away, with little hope, as far as one can see, of ever getting off. I repeat, was that the moment for the survivors to start shooting each other?'

'One would hardly think so.'

'Then how did this shooting come about?'

'There may have been a shortage of food. Some members of the crew shot the others in order to make it go round.'

'Where are they? There's nobody here, alive, or we'd have seen them.'

'They might have got away in a small boat.'

'Would they, do you think, have gone without these?' Biggles held out the pearl tin. 'They must have known about them. Would they have gone knowing that somewhere on the island there was a small fortune to be picked up?'

'Shouldn't think so.'

'On the face of it these pearls might well have been the motive for murder. Yet they were left behind. That doesn't make sense. No, that isn't the answer. If it comes to that, if one man was shot it's possible that others were shot – those on the beach, who we assumed to have been drowned. Were they shot? Let's see.'

Without speaking they returned to the beach, and the nearest skeleton.

Biggles dropped on his knees beside it and began lifting the bones carefully and putting them on one side. A ring fell from a bony finger. A signet ring. He picked it up and looked at the device on it. 'Oriental,' he said. 'Apparently another member of the lugger's crew. Ah! Here we are. This is what I was looking for.' He held out, in the palm of his hand, a bullet, slightly flattened. 'Looks mighty like a Luger to me. I'll keep this. It may tell a tale one day.' Putting it in his pocket he got to his feet.

'There seems to have been a battle here,' said Ginger, looking shaken by this unexpected development.

'We could probably find more bullets if we went through the other skeletons, but I shan't bother. What we have seen tells us enough about that aspect of what happened here.'

'But what could the fighting have been about if it wasn't pearls?'

'You haven't forgotten that another ship went ashore here?'

'No. But as all these survivors would be in the same boat why should they set about each other?'

'That's just it. They weren't in the same boat. There wasn't room for all of them.'

Ginger stared.

'If you were cast away here pearls wouldn't be much use to you. Only one thing could help you.'

'A boat.'

'That's how it looks to me. There was one boat – and more people than could get into it. Von Stalhein's party got possession of it. Whether it was their boat, or a boat belonging to the lugger, I don't know. But we'll soon find out. That boat should still be on Eighty Mile Beach, and it should have a name on it. I say it *should* have. I don't say it has. But if it hasn't we shall know why. Let's go and look. We should have enough fuel to take in the Beach on our way to Broome for a fill-up. Come on. We know where this island is should we decide to return to it. It doesn't appear to have a name.'

As they walked briskly to the Otter, Ginger asked: 'What are you going to do with the pearls?'

'Find the rightful owner and hand them over. We shall have to report what we've seen today even if we don't do it right away. It isn't just a matter of the pearls, although the large pink one in particular should be worth a lot of money. It's a matter of suspected murder, and failure to report a thing like that might subject us to criticism, if nothing worse. For the moment I'll keep an open mind about it.'

The Otter was soon on its way to the mainland, on a course calculated to bring it to Eighty Mile Beach below the estimated position of the abandoned lifeboat. The idea then was to fly along the beach, and after looking at the boat carry on to Broome.

On striking the vast curve of deserted sand, stretching away on either side as far as the eye could see, Biggles made a left hand turn, took the machine to something under a hundred feet and settled down to as slow a cruising speed as was compatible with safe flying. They expected no difficulty in spotting the boat on the flat, unbroken, wind-borne sand. Nor did they, although the sand had silted against it on one side and overflowed into the boat itself. On such a boundless airfield a landing presented no difficulty. Biggles dropped his wheels, put the machine down with hardly a tremor and taxied right up to the little craft that would go to sea no more. In a couple of minutes they were both standing by it.

'No name on the bows or the stern,' muttered Biggles. 'Just what I expected.' On the bows it had been scraped out. On the stern a piece of new timber had been let in. 'Well, that tells us plenty. If the boat had belonged to the *See Taube* there would have been no need to remove the name – always supposing that *See Taube* was really the name of von Stalhein's ship. My guess, and I think it's a pretty safe one, is that this boat belonged to the lost lugger. It was, I fancy, the motive for the murders. Try to carry a description of the boat in your head in case I forget anything. In Broome we should be able to settle any argument. What happened on that island we may never know, but there should be no difficulty in identifying the lost lugger by my description of the dead man. Broome isn't all that big. Let's get along.'

Biggles said little on the short flight to the airfield. Clearly preoccupied with the problems that had arisen, Ginger did not interrupt his thoughts. However, when the white-roofed township appeared ahead Biggles said: 'To save time I'm going to leave you to attend to the refuelling. When you're through, take the small-kit to the Continental Hotel. We'll sleep there tonight. I've some enquiries to make, and I've decided that the safest – and the quickest – way, would be to go to the police. They'll keep quiet if I ask them. Otherwise we might be fiddling about here for days.'

'Okay,' agreed Ginger.

CHAPTER V

A Word With Sergeant Gilson

Leaving Ginger at the airport, Biggles made his way through white-roofed bungalows, palms and poinciana trees, to the Port of Pearls that nestles beside the blue waters of Dampier Creek. With shell-grit crunching under his shoes he sought the police station, where he found Sergeant William Gilson in charge, and introduced himself by putting his credentials on his desk.

The Sergeant, tall, clear-eyed and sun-tanned, a fine figure of a man in his uniform, read the documents. Getting up he closed the door, resumed his seat, and looked enquiringly at Biggles, who was replacing his papers in his breast pocket. 'Take a seat,' he invited. 'It must be something important to bring you all this way,' he observed shrewdly.

'It's important to me, it's important to you, and it may be more important still for Australia,' answered Biggles. 'In fact, it's so important that I thought hard before coming even to you. But you may be able to help me. In all seriousness I warn you that if word of this conversation leaks out, with my name attached to it, you may do your country an immense amount of harm.'

'I can keep my trap shut,' promised Gilson, a trifle curtly.

'Then first I shall have to tell you what brings me to Australia. You will recall, following the recent willie-willie, seven survivors of a wrecked ship came ashore on Eighty Mile Beach?'

'I remember it.'

'One of those men is, and has been for many years, the most notorious enemy agent in Europe. He hates us, which means he hates you. He is now in Australia.'

'What does he want here?'

'That's what I'd like to know, and what I'm here to find out. As he may be anywhere in Australia you'll appreciate I have a job on my hands.'

'You certainly have.'

'I've been having a look round, and it's what I've found that has brought me to you. In answering my questions you may learn a thing or two yourself. How many ships were lost from your fleet here in the last willie-willie?'

'Three. We know where one went ashore so call it two.'

'Was the skipper of one of them a man, probably a Japanese, stockily built, about five foot four in height, with a gold-filled tooth in the upper jaw.'

'He was. That'd be Toto Wada – an Australian-Jap. Nice quiet chap. Used to be a diver till he bought his own lugger.'

'Just to make sure. Did you ever see the thing in which he carried his pearls.'

'Often. It was a two ounce tobacco tin.'

'Like this?' Biggles put the box on the table.

'That's the one.'

'Then you'd better take charge of it for his next of kin.'

'That's his wife. Lives in Sheba Lane.'

The sergeant's eyes opened wide when Biggles held the tin so that the contents could be seen. 'How did you get that? Where's Toto?'

'He won't be coming back. He's dead. His lugger went ashore on an island and broke up. He got ashore, and so did at least one of the crew. This ring may help you to identify him. Both men were subsequently shot. I found the bodies.'

'Shot! How the – who the—'

'A German ship went ashore on the same island. There were Germans in the party that landed on Eighty Mile Beach. You'll see what I'm getting at.'

Gilson's brow was black. 'Yes. I see,' he said slowly.

'That brings us to the boat,' resumed Biggles. 'I've just looked at the boat that brought these foreigners ashore. It's a brown-varnished clinker-built job about twenty-two feet long and four foot beam. Rather high in front, plenty of freeboard—'

'You needn't say any more,' interposed the sergeant. 'I know that boat. It belonged to Toto.'

'That's how I worked it out; and that's why I decided I'd have to tell you about it. Frankly, the fate of this unfortunate pearler is no concern of mine, because it isn't going to help me much in my search for the man I'm looking for. I'd rather you said nothing about it for the moment; but you might keep your ears open, and if you hear any local talk about a strange ship being seen off the coast between, say Wyndham and Perth, let me know. Incidentally, you'd better have these. They may be needed as evidence one day.' Biggles pushed two bullets and a ring across the desk. 'These are two of the shots that did the murders. The ring was on what was left of the finger of one of the crew.'

'And you're asking me to do nothing about this?' Gilson looked doubtful.

'Yes. I'm asking you because there's more at stake than the shooting of one or two pearlers. If you start making inquiries on your own account you may upset my applecart. I know the man I'm looking for. Leave him to me – unless, of course, you hear that I've made a boob and got myself shot.' Biggles smiled. 'Should that happen, and it might, compare the bullet with those on your desk.'

'All right,' agreed Gilson reluctantly. 'If that's how you want it. We'll leave it like that for the time being. You let me know when I can go ahead but don't leave it too long.'

'Not longer than is absolutely necessary,' promised Biggles. 'Now I wonder if by any chance you can help me with this.' He took from his pocket the list of names and addresses Ginger had picked up. 'Do any of those names mean anything to you? I mean, have any of them, to your knowledge, a police record?'

Gilson studied the list. 'No,' he stated, when he came to the end. 'But don't take my word for it. I only deal with local cases, although local in this part of the world covers a pretty wide area – most of it desert, of course. There are two places here I've never even heard of. This Tarracooma Creek is one.'

'It says Tarracooma Creek, Western Australia. We're in West Australia now.'

'All the same I've never heard of it. Must be a small place. But then, Western Australia is a lot of ground and there are probably a lot of places I've never heard of, particularly farther south. I'll ask Old Joe Hopkins when he comes in. He's overdue, so he shouldn't be long. He may know. He used to ride the Fence.[1] He's

[1] The rabbit-proof fence which crosses the continental deserts from north to south. It is patrolled by riders who repair any damage done by the larger wild creatures – kangaroos, wallabies, emus, and the like.

a digger – what you'd call a prospector – now, and knows the country better than most people.'

'What about the name of the man – Roth? Does that mean nothing to you?'

'Not a thing.'

'What about the other place. Daly Flats, Northern Territory?'

'I've never heard of that either. Nor do I know the man's name – Boller. All I know of the Territory is what I read in the papers. I'll tell you what I'll do if you like. I see one of these addresses is in Perth. Chap named Adamsen. I could put a call through to our office there and ask them if they know anything about him.'

'That might save me a trip there.'

'Come through. I'll get the missus to make you a cup of tea while you're waiting.'

'Thanks. That would be very welcome.'

Biggles was shown into the sitting-room where he chatted with the policeman's family for nearly half an hour.

'Not much to tell you,' reported Gilson, when he came back. 'There are no convictions against Adamsen, but they know him for an agitator, trouble-maker, and so on. He's an electrician by trade. Politically he's a red-hot Communist of the loud-mouthed type.'

'Ah,' breathed Biggles. 'That's very interesting. It fits in with what I know.'

'But look here,' went on Gilson. 'Thinking things over while I was waiting for that call, you seem to have put me on a bit of a spot.'

'How so?'

'This business of Wada and his lugger. No offence meant, but I've never seen you before and I've only your word for it. That's okay with me, but a court would want evidence of identification. You didn't know Wada by sight, so your word that he was dead could be disputed.'

'Yes. I see your point,' agreed Biggles pensively.

'What's the name of this island?'

'If it has one I don't know it. It's one of a scattered group, all on the small side, north-east of the Rowley Shoals.'

'How far do you reckon it to be from here?'

'Two hundred miles, more or less.'

'That's a long way.'

'How do you mean?'

'Well, let's be frank about it. I ought to go and look at the body – maybe bring it back here for burial. I knew the man well. There could then be no argument about his death. You've got to produce a body before you can charge anyone with murder.'

'True enough. Very well. Why not go and verify my story?'

'How am I going to do that without bringing you into it? To start with I should have to apply for transport, and as I couldn't do that without giving reasons it would mean letting your cat out of the bag.'

'That is a bit awkward,' agreed Biggles. 'Suppose I flew you out to the island. Would that solve your problems?'

Gilson thought for a moment. 'Yes, that'd do it. I suppose we could do the job in a day?'

'Easily. If that's agreed, the sooner we go the better. What about tomorrow?'

'Suits me.'

'Say, six o'clock tomorrow morning at the airfield.'

'Okay. I'll be there.'

'Good. Then I'll get along. Thanks for being so helpful.'

They shook hands and Biggles departed, thinking hard.

He found Ginger waiting in the hotel lounge. 'Did you get the tanks topped up?' he asked, dropping into the next chair.

'No trouble at all,' Ginger assured him. 'What's your news?'

'In a nutshell: the lugger that went ashore on the island came from here. The body I found was the owner, a Japanese named Wada. The boat that brought von Stalhein and his party ashore belonged to the lugger. That all ties up with what we surmised. But what has set me thinking is this. Gilson, the police-sergeant, was helpful enough to check up on one of the names and addresses on that list you picked up. Adamsen, of Perth. It seems he's a trouble-making agitator. The question is, how does he fit into the von Stalhein set-up?'

'If he isn't actually on the Iron Curtain pay-roll now he may have been listed as a prospective recruit.'

'If that's the case we must assume that the same applies to others on the list. Who compiled that list? There's only one answer. An agent already planted here. With what object?'

'To complete a network of spies against the time they'll be needed.'

'I don't like the sound of that. If you're right, then this is a more dangerous scheme than I had supposed. The trouble is, while these people remain passive they're within the law and there's nothing we can do about it beyond providing the Dominion with the gen so that on the outbreak of a war they could chuck a net over the whole bunch.'

'If the von Stalhein gang intends to contact Adamsen and the others, by watching we might grab them – or tip off the police. We've got a case against them – for murder.'

'We shall have, I hope, by this time tomorrow. We're flying

Gilson out to have a look at things. He knew Wada and will be able to provide evidence of identification. He's meeting us at the airfield at six.'

'While we're there we might have another look round for some more pages from that file.'

'That's a good idea; but we can't spend too long there. Gilson wants to get back and I shall have to find out what Algy's doing. Let's see about something to eat.'

CHAPTER VI

Forestalled

The following morning the Otter left Broome on the hour, and just before seven the Island without a Name crept up over the horizon.

Bill Gilson – for in the easy going Australian manner they were now calling each other by their Christian names – who had evidently done some serious thinking about the affair, was now taking more than a passing interest in it, and posed questions for which so far there was no answer. Naturally, he inclined towards the official police angle. Biggles revealed what he knew, and what he surmised.

'The snag where you're concerned is this,' Biggles told him. 'Putting aside for the moment the question of murder, until you have proof that this gang is working against the interests of Australia there's no point in taking them to court.'

'Murder is plenty of reason,' muttered Bill, grimly.

'All right. Hang the lot – and then where are you? The purpose for which these people came here would be carried on by a fresh gang unknown to us. I believe now that I started off on the wrong foot. The first things that came into my head when I knew von Stalhein was here was the new rocket range, the atom bomb experimental sites and the uranium workings. They, of course, are bound to come into the picture; but I now suspect that the plot goes deeper than that. What I see now is a widespread organization that will not only keep the Iron Curtain countries informed of technical developments here, but might, by fomenting strikes and the like, upset your entire economy.'

'You mean, through Communist propaganda.'

'Call it that if you like; but Communism, in the place where it started, is now a handy political name for a military-minded clique that suffers from the old ambition of world domination. The trouble is, few of the people who get drawn into the thing realize that they're lining up with a potential enemy, or that a cold war is just as deadly as a hot one. They're never likely to get anything out of it, anyway. Of course, there are some who go Red in order to work off a grudge. Von Stalhein is a case in point. With him it's personal. He hates us because Hitler lost the war. When he was a Nazi he hated Communism, and I'd wager he still does. But he'll work for the Iron Curtain brigade because it offers him a way to have another crack at us. For that he has sacrificed his sense of humour, and any pleasure he might have got out of life.'

'I gather he's pretty tough.'

'Tough?' Biggles smiled wanly. 'He's so tough that if you hit him in the face with a stone the stone would go to pieces.'

With the island within gliding distance Biggles cut his engines and idled on. But as the calm water within the reef came into view he stiffened suddenly, staring through the windscreen. 'Do you see what I see?' he asked sharply.

'A ship,' said Ginger tersely.

'Lugger,' observed Bill, laconically, from behind Biggles's shoulder.

'What do you make of that?' queried Biggles, gliding on.

'Your guess is as good as mine. One lugger is much like another. Could be a pearler, put in for some reason or other. All I can say is it isn't one of the Broome fleet.'

'I can see people on the island ... walking about ... blacks as well as whites,' observed Ginger.

'Most luggers carry coloured crews,' said Bill.

'They haven't heard us or they'd be looking up,' said Ginger.

'The rollers on the reef, and on the windward side, would prevent them from hearing anything,' asserted Bill. 'I'd say it's just an odd chance that brought the lugger here.'

'We shall soon know,' murmured Biggles, sideslipping off a little height to glide straight in. 'I shan't run her up on the beach – she might as well stay afloat for the short time we shall be here.'

No more was said. The machine glided on, silently, the steady thunder of the breakers drowning any slight noise it might have made. There was no one on the deck of the lugger. The men ashore did not look up. From water level they were concealed by the scrub and the contours of the ground, so it seemed that the Otter made its landing unobserved. But as soon as Biggles touched his throttle to take the aircraft right on to the lugger a man appeared on deck, hurriedly, and, as it seemed to Ginger, in a state of started agitation – although, in the circumstances, the reason for this might have been natural, and innocent enough. He was a big man, black-bearded, and roughly dressed.

Bill read aloud the name on the vessel's stern, '*Matilda. Darwin.*'

Biggles took the Otter into shallow water near the lugger. Ginger went forward and dropped the anchor.

Bill, who was of course in uniform, hailed the ship. 'Hello, there! Are you all right?'

'Hello, there! Are you all right?'

'Yes,' came the answer.

'What are you doing?'

'Picking up a few fresh nuts.'

'You're a long way from home.'

'With the water picked clean it's time someone looked for new ground.'

Bill turned to Biggles. 'I wouldn't call the man a liar but neither would I bet he's telling the truth,' he said suspiciously. 'Still, his business isn't likely to be ours so let's get on with the job.'

'Just a minute,' returned Biggles. 'There should be two skeletons lying on that beach within forty yards of us. They've gone. Bones don't walk.'

'The *Matilda*'s crew may have buried 'em.'

'Could be,' agreed Biggles dubiously. 'Ginger, there's no need for you to come ashore. Stay here and watch the machine.'

'All right.' Ginger, looking at Biggles's face, knew that he was puzzled by finding the *Matilda* there, and was not entirely satisfied by the explanation given by the man who was presumably the skipper. As Biggles and Bill stepped out and waded ashore he sat in the cockpit to watch events. Blackbeard, too, he noticed, was also watching, leaning on the rail, smoking a pipe; but there was something about his attitude that gave Ginger a feeling that this nonchalance was affected rather than genuine. What, he wondered, were the men ashore doing?

He wondered still more when, a few minutes later, two white and eight coloured men, came into sight from the direction of the thick scrub. Two workmen carried implements that were either spades or shovels. The party, still some distance away, seemed to be in a great hurry, the workmen being urged into a run by another man whose better style of dress suggested that he was in charge – possibly the mate of the lugger.

Ginger realized with a twinge of uneasiness that Biggles and Bill had not seen this procession, for they had already disappeared over the low ridge that formed the backbone of the island when it appeared. The thing struck him as being deliberate rather than accidental – as if the party had been watching, waiting for Bill and Biggles to get out of sight before showing themselves.

Ginger's feeling of uneasiness mounted. Although he told himself that there was no reason for this he became increasingly aware that he was alone, with the others out of earshot. The booming of the breakers on the reef would smother any call for help. It was, therefore, with some anxiety that he watched the shore party hurry on towards their dinghy that had been pulled up on the beach.

He glanced at the lugger, twenty yards away, and saw that Blackbeard was watching him surreptitiously. Did that mean anything – or nothing? There was no answer to that, but he perceived with a sudden wave of apprehension what their position would be if anything happened to the aircraft – a thought that was no doubt prompted by the close proximity of the two craft. He wished fervently that the machine had been moored further away.

Again turning his attention to the shore party he saw that it had now reached the dinghy. Under the directions of the senior man, a big, fierce-looking Malay, it was hauled on to the water. Some of the workmen started to swim to the lugger. The white men moved forward to board the dinghy. One of them, Ginger noticed, walked with a slight limp. Suddenly there was something familiar about his figure. Ginger stared incredulously, telling himself that it was impossible, even though he knew his eyes were not deceiving him. The man was Erich von Stalhein.

For an instant Ginger remained rigid from shock, for the possibility of such an encounter was beyond the limits of his imagination. Recognition, he knew, was largely a matter of time and place. He had not associated von Stalhein with a pearling lugger, or, for that matter, with a desert island; and that, he could only conclude, was why he hadn't recognized him earlier.

By this time the peril of his position had overcome the first stunning shock, and he was moving. What Blackbeard would do when his crew was aboard he didn't know; nor did he waste time guessing. Only one thing mattered, and that was to get the machine well clear of the lugger.

Going forward, trying to behave as if his actions were of no real importance, he hauled in the anchor and returned to the cockpit. Out of the corner of his eye he could see Blackbeard beckoning the dinghy, although it was now nearly alongside. The Malay caught a rope, swarmed up it, and joined Blackbeard in a swift conversation.

Ginger waited for no more. The Otter, fanned by a slight breeze, was already drifting, but nothing like fast enough; for the lugger's anchor was now coming up, and its propeller churning the water into foam set the machine rocking.

The Otter's engines came to life. Even so, Ginger saw that it was going to be touch and go, for the lugger, ostensibly turning, was backing into his tail unit. Instinctively he shouted a warning, although he knew he was wasting his breath. The trouble was, he, too, had to turn to get clear, or run aground.

With teeth clenched, expecting every instant to hear the crash of a collision that would crumple his tail like tissue paper, he brought her bows round to open water. Even when the machine bounded forward under full throttle he was still not sure that he had escaped damage, for the roar of her engines drowned all other sounds and the hull was rocking in the turbulence caused by the lugger's screw.

It was for this reason, because he was not certain that the machine was airworthy, that he did not actually leave the water. As soon as he was sure that he was clear he throttled back and merely skimmed on to the far side of the area of calm water, where he jumped up to ascertain if the aircraft had suffered damage. To his great relief all appeared to be well, so turning to open water, ready to take off should it become necessary, he looked to see what the lugger was doing. His nerves relaxed when he saw that it was heading at full speed for the open sea.

Biggles and Bill were running down the beach.

After waiting for a minute to recover his composure, for he had been badly shaken, he turned again and cruised slowly towards them.

'What on earth are you doing?' was Biggles's greeting.

'You might well ask,' answered Ginger grimly. He jerked a thumb at the retreating lugger. 'Those devils tried to ram me. Nearly got me, too. I recognized him just in time.'

'Recognized who?'

'Von Stalhein.'

It was Biggles turn to stare. 'You mean – he's in that ship?'

'He was on the island at the same time as you – with as pretty a gang of toughs as you ever saw. From the way they ran back to the lugger I have an idea they spotted you. Or if von Stalhein didn't actually recognize you he must have taken a dislike to Bill's uniform.'

'Then what happened?'

'I had a feeling they might try something so I got cracking on a quick move. It took me a minute to get the hook up and by that time the lugger was backing into me. I must have got clear by a whisker. It may have looked like an accident, but it wasn't. They knew what they were doing all right. Had they sunk me, or stove my tail in, we should have been three Robinson Crusoes without even a parrot.'

Biggles looked at Bill. 'So now we know,' he said simply.

'What do you know?' asked Ginger.

'Why Wada's body has disappeared. That goes for the skeleton's, too. No bodies, no murder. Trust von Stalhein to think of that. He came back here to clean up – perhaps look for any papers that were left about. Those lists of names, for instance. It might take him some time to get a duplicate set from where they originated.'

'I take it you didn't find any.'

'We did not. We didn't get much time to look. Your engines starting up brought us back in a hurry.'

'They've buried Wada's body,' said Ginger. 'At any rate, I assume that they've buried something because two of the crew were carrying shovels.'

'Who was with von Stalhein?' asked Biggles.

'There was only one other white man in the party. I can't say I recognized him but I've an idea he was one of the bunch in the photograph. A hair-cut and a shave would alter his appearance.'

Bill stepped into the conversation. 'I could still get this guy von Stalhein. I realize that there's nothing we can do about the lugger at the moment; but we know her name and we shall be home first. What about meeting him when he steps ashore?'

Biggles smiled wanly. 'You don't know von Stalhein. Even if he didn't recognize me he must know that the arrival of an aircraft and a policeman at an out-of-the-way island like this was no mere fluke. Note how he took the precaution of coming back here to clean the place up. No doubt by this time his brain is busy working out what we're likely to do next.'

'I'll get him,' declared Bill doggedly.

'All right. And what are you going to do with him when you've got him? Even if you dug up the whole island and found Wada's body you still wouldn't be able to prove that von Stalhein did the shooting. In fact, knowing how he works, I'd risk a small bet that he didn't pull a trigger. He's a wily bird, and he'd leave that to someone else. Suppose you did grab him, and examined his gun – and found it clean? Or of a different calibre from those bullets I gave you? He'd laugh at you, and you'd have exposed your hand for nothing.'

'Are you suggesting that we let him walk away scot free?'

'Certainly not. I'm merely trying to point out that we may do more harm than good by going off at half cock, whichever way we look at it, yours or mine.'

'What do you mean?'

'You, naturally, are concerned about a murder that has been committed. To me that's only a side issue. I've got to find out what von Stalhein and his gang are doing in Australia, and stop them at it, before they can do worse mischief than murder. To me the important thing about our trip here is the name of that lugger. The owner, or the skipper – probably the same – is in the racket, and that should lead us somewhere. My next step will be to check up on the *Matilda* at Darwin. I own freely that it didn't occur to me that von Stalhein might come back here. It might have been to cover up his tracks, or there may have been other reasons. He may have needed money. We found some notes. He may have hoped to find some instruments that were lost. We found a Geiger Counter. But let's not waste time guessing. The fact remains, he came back, and he has presumably destroyed all evidence of what happened here. I suggest that as we're here we might as well have a look round in case anything was over-looked. Then I'll take you home and push on to Darwin.'

'Okay,' agreed Bill.

They went ashore, but as Biggles had feared, a search of some three hours yielded not a single item of interest. Bill tramped the island from end to end looking for signs of digging, still hoping to find the body of the murdered man; but in the end, to his annoy-ance, he had to give it up.

'I'm afraid von Stalhein made a clean sweep while he was here,' remarked Biggles, as they returned to the aircraft and snatched a makeshift lunch.

'There's still one piece of evidence he may find hard to explain,' growled Bill.

'What's that.'

'The boat. You say it's still on Eighty Mile Beach. How's he going to account for coming ashore in a boat belonging to Wada's lugger? Several witnesses could describe the boat, and that should be good enough.'

'Yes,' agreed Biggles. 'That would certainly take a lot of explaining.'

'I ought to have a look at it. Just where is it?'

'Roughly about sixty miles south of Roebuck Bay. If you like, to save you a journey, we could take it in on the run home. It wouldn't be far out of our way.'

'That'd suit me fine,' declared Bill. 'Save a lot of time and trouble.'

'All right. If we've finished we might as well press on.'

Biggles took the same course as before to the mainland, and again, flying low, cruised up the Beach. But even while he was still short of the position of the boat he was staring hard at it.

'Something's happened down there,' observed Ginger.

'So I see,' returned Biggles, shortly.

'Looks as if someone's had a fire.'

Answered Biggles, in a curious voice: 'It also looks as if another plane has landed since we were here. I can see two sets of wheel tracks and only one of them is mine – the wide, heavy one. There are more footmarks, too, than we made.'

'The boat isn't there!'

'The black spot marks the place where it was. Someone's had a bonfire, and he didn't light it to keep himself warm. Recently, too. It's still smouldering.'

'What's that you're saying?' put in Bill, from behind.

'The boat's gone. Someone has beaten us to it,' replied Biggles.

For a moment Bill was shocked to silence. Then he swore softly.

'Now you see the sort of people we're up against,' Biggles told him, as he glided in to land. 'They leave nothing to chance.'

He put the machine down and taxied up to the still smouldering embers – all that remained of the boat. They got out and looked at it.

'The job was done this morning,' muttered Bill, chagrined. 'And it wasn't done by von Stalhein – unless he's so clever he can be in two places at once.'

'No. He went to the island. Someone came here in a plane –
a light plane. It may not matter much, now that von Stalhein
knows we're on the job, but whoever did this would see that
another plane had been here. We also know *they've* got a plane.
I must confess I'm a bit puzzled by this sudden rush to clean up
every scrap of evidence. It's almost as if they knew I was on my
way here. That could be so, of course. The enemy has spies everywhere, and just as I know von Stalhein's methods, he knows
mine. Maybe that photo did it. Von Stalhein would realize that
once it got into the papers he would almost certainly be spotted
by our Intelligence people – as did, in fact, happen – and take
steps accordingly. Well, it's not much use standing here staring
at the ashes. I'm sorry, Bill, but I'm afraid your last piece of
concrete evidence has gone up in smoke.'

Bill, who had been on his hands and knees studying the footmarks, stood up. 'There were three of 'em in the party that came
here,' he announced. 'Pity I didn't bring my tracker along, or I
could have told you more about 'em.'

'You might measure the width of their wheel track while
you're at it,' requested Biggles. 'As you know people by the size
of their feet, I can sometimes name a plane by the span of its
undercart.'

Bill obliged. 'Six foot, dead,' he said.

'Auster,' murmured Ginger.

'Could have been,' agreed Biggles. 'That would have the accommodation, but I'm not so sure about the endurance range. It must
have come from a distance.'

'The range of the new Auster, if I remember right, is six
hundred miles,' stated Ginger. 'I know that isn't far as distances
go here, but there was nothing to stop it from topping up its

tanks at any airfield along the coast. It might even be doing that at Broome, at this moment.'

'True enough,' conceded Biggles. 'We'll check up on that. If we knew where it refuelled, assuming it did, we should get a line on the direction it came from. If it didn't refuel then it can't be far away – unless it has a private petrol dump. Is there anything more you want to do here, Bill?'

'No.'

'Then we might as well get along.'

They took their places in the Otter and headed for Broome.

CHAPTER VII

Outlook Vague

On arrival at Broome it was soon ascertained that no aircraft had refuelled there that day; but there was a message waiting for them. It was from Algy, to say he had arrived at Darwin, and had urgent news which, had he not turned up, West would have forwarded.

'Which is another way of saying that West has learnt something,' remarked Biggles. 'We'll push right on, Bill, if it's all the same to you. We should just make the trip in daylight.'

'What about this light plane? Would you like me to check up along the coast to find out if a strange machine picked up petrol anywhere?'

'I'd be obliged if you'd do that,' replied Biggles. 'The information would be useful, whether the answer is yes or no. If it did, we should know which way it was travelling, and perhaps pick up some details about who was in it. If it didn't, then we should know that it's based no great distance away.'

That concluded immediate affairs at Broome. Telling Bill that he would let him know any developments that concerned him, and asking him to send a signal to Darwin to let Algy know he was on his way, Biggles took off again on the six hundred mile run to the northern air terminal.

'If Algy's news is from West I can only think that West must have seen, or heard from, Alston,' he opined – correctly, as it transpired. 'It's a relief to know the Halifax is all right again because it begins to look as if we shall need it. At least, I assume it's all right. Algy wouldn't be such a fool as to start across the Timor Sea with a doubtful engine.'

The run was made without incident, and from the air, in the rosy glow of the setting sun, the Halifax could be seen parked beyond the end hangar with Algy and Bertie standing beside it.

Biggles landed, taxied up alongside, switched off and jumped down, Ginger following. 'Everything all right now?' was his greeting.

'Yes,' confirmed Algy. 'The trouble wasn't serious but I didn't feel like taking chances. West tells me you got my message. Any news?'

'Plenty,' returned Biggles. 'But let's have yours first; then we'll give you ours. We needn't stand here. With the weather as it is the machines might as well stay where they are for the night. Let's go over to the canteen. I've been on the go since daylight and I could drink a bucket of tea.'

In the corner of the canteen, almost deserted at an hour when there were no arrivals or departures of aircraft, Algy explained why he had sent the urgent signal to Broome. The news, as Biggles had predicted, emanated from West. Briefly, it was this. Alston had arrived unexpectedly at Darwin the previous day, flying one of the regular services. He had spent the night there and then gone back to Brisbane, leaving before the Halifax had arrived; for which reason, of course, Algy hadn't spoken to him personally. However, Alston had given some information to West, who had passed it on.

'Is West on duty now?' put in Biggles.

'No. He's on night duty tonight. Comes on at ten.'

'I see. Carry on.'

Algy resumed. It appeared that Alston had seen a man named Smith on the airfield at Cloncurry some days earlier, in the process of buying a second-hand aircraft that had been on offer there.

'Was it by any chance an Auster?' inquired Biggles.

Algy looked astonished. 'Yes. An Auster Autocrat. How did you know?'

Biggles smiled faintly. 'We've seen its footprints in the sand. Go ahead.'

Algy concluded his narrative. The Auster's registration was VH-NZZ. With Smith had been a younger man, a qualified pilot who had taken the machine up on a trial run. His name, according to the transfer papers, was Cozens. Alston didn't know him. In fact, he'd never seen or heard of him, although he thought he knew all the professional pilots in the country. When Alston, who was out on a job, returned to Cloncurry, the Auster had gone; no one knew where. Smith had paid for the machine and Cozens had flown it off, taking Smith with him. That was all.

Biggles tapped a cigarette on the back of his hand. 'So the gang has decided to get mobile,' he observed.

'Who's this fellow Smith, anyway?' inquired Algy. 'I'm in the dark. How did he suddenly pop into the picture?'

Biggles answered: 'Smith is the name – or more probably the assumed name – of the chap who chartered the aircraft that collected von Stalhein and his pals from here when they disappeared. He was already in Australia and may turn out to be the big noise. Now he's bought an aircraft, which will save him using public transport.'

'As we know its registration there should be no difficulty in locating it.'

'Maybe not – always supposing it stays on public airfields,' agreed Biggles. 'But short of tearing round the continent ourselves looking for it how are we going to find out where it is? To call in the police, or the civil aviation authorities, would mean explanations and start the sort of hue and cry I'm anxious to avoid. This self-enforced security is really our big handicap. I mean, you couldn't have anything like an official search without von Stalhein getting to hear of it – and he'd know just what to do about that. But I'd better tell you and Bertie what has happened since we came here or we shall be talking at cross purposes. Things have moved faster than I expected.'

For the next half-hour Biggles narrated the events since their arrival in Australia. 'That's how things stand at present,' he concluded. 'Although we've learned quite a lot,' he went on, 'all it has really done is thicken the fog, and left me wondering just what it is we're trying to do. Chasing von Stalhein, or any other members of the gang, round the horizon, isn't going to get us anywhere, as far as I can see. Even if we caught up with them, what then? You can't arrest a man unless you have a case against him. There's no law against buying ships or aeroplanes. You can't prevent a man, in a free country, from cruising round the islands, or from sitting close enough to Woomera to hear the rockets go by – provided he behaves himself.'

Bertie gave his monocle a rub. 'In that case, old boy, would you mind telling me just what we're doing here? Sorry, and all that, but I don't seem to have got it.'

'In a vague sort of way I can see two objectives,' said Biggles. 'The first is to find the headquarters of this man Smith, and the other is to get a complete list of the names that were in that secret file, one page of which we found on the island.'

'And then what?'

'I'd report back to the Air Commodore and suggest the whole thing should be handed over to the Australian Security people for any action they considered necessary. Obviously it would be out of the question for us to watch an unknown number of potential spies.'

'Why not hand the case over as it stands?' suggested Algy. 'Why did the Air Commodore start us on this will-o'-the-wisp hunt?'

'In the first place, I fancy he was actuated by the fact that von Stalhein was in the forefront of the scheme, and we know him and his methods. You must also bear in mind that the Air Commodore didn't know what we know now; or what we suspect; that the ramifications of this business are widespread. Anyway, having started I think we must go on. There are several lines that we could follow.'

'What's the first,' asked Ginger.

'Obviously, we must check on this lugger *Matilda* and see if we can establish how it comes into the set-up. That shouldn't be difficult. The owner must be on the gang's pay-roll or he would not have been taken to the island where Wada was murdered. Nor would he have tried to ram the Otter, with the intention, no doubt, of leaving us marooned on the island.'

'But hold hard, old boy,' interposed Bertie. 'About this ramming effort. I know I'm a bit slow on the uptake, but I don't quite get it. According to Ginger, the wily Erich had a native crew with him. There were only two of you on the island. Why didn't he bump you off while he had the chance?'

'I can think of reasons why that might have been a silly thing to do,' averred Biggles. 'In the first place there was the aircraft. Had there been shooting Ginger could have taken off and radioed an S.O.S. for help; in which case the *Matilda*, on the high seas, wouldn't have had a hope of escaping interception. On top of that, don't forget Bill Gilson was in uniform. I might not have been missed, but Bill would have, and to murder a policeman, in this part of the world particularly, is to start something. For all von Stalhein knew Bill might have left word where he was going. No. Collision with the Otter, which would have left us stuck on the island, certainly long enough for the *Matilda* to reach the mainland, was safer. Had there been trouble it could be said the collision was an accident, and it would have been difficult to prove otherwise.'

Ginger chipped in. 'I had the feeling that Blackbeard, on the lugger, didn't like to act on his own responsibility. He waited for von Stalhein to get aboard – and Erich had already decided what to do.'

'Which brings us to the question, what do we do next?' said Algy. 'Wait here for the *Matilda* to come home?'

'Because *Matilda* is registered in Darwin it doesn't neces- sarily follow that she'll come here,' Biggles pointed out. 'After what's happened von Stalhein wouldn't be likely to overlook the probability of someone being here to meet him. When we've had something to eat I'll take a stroll along the waterfront to see if I can pick up any gen about *Matilda* or her owner.'

'What's the drill for tonight,' enquired Ginger.

'We'll go into the town to get a meal. A walk'll do us good.'

'Taking our small-kit?'

Biggles hesitated. 'I don't think so. I don't like sleeping too far away from the machines. A hotel usually means a delay in the morning. We'd be just as comfortable on our mattresses in the cabins, and on the spot to move off smartly in the morning should we decide to go somewhere. After we've had some food I'll go to the harbour. Don't wait for me. I'll join you here when I'm through.'

One of the airport hands came into the canteen. He looked around, and called: 'Mr. Bigglesworth here?'

'Over here,' answered Biggles.

The man came over and handed him a folded slip of paper. 'From the control room,' he said, and walked away.

Biggles read the message. 'It's from Bill Gilson. Good chap. Does what he says he'll do. This is interesting. Auster VH-NZZ refuelled at Wyndham eleven thirty-five hours. Pilot and two passengers. Came in from south-west. Left heading north-east.'

'Which means it was coming this way,' said Ginger.

'It didn't land here or we should have seen it,' stated Algy.

'I wonder if we could find it,' murmured Biggles, reflectively. He got up. 'Let's stretch our legs and see if we can find a beefsteak. That'll do to go on with.'

CHAPTER VIII

The Opposition Strikes Back

Later, after a good and satisfying meal, eight o'clock saw Biggles, by himself, making his way through the scented tropical night to the harbour, rubbing shoulders with as strange an assortment of humanity as could be found in any port on earth, east or west. Stockmen in sombreros; Chinese vendors of potato chips; pearlers; boys on bicycles; Greek merchants, and seamen of every colour and race under the sun – Malays, Indonesians, Cingalese, Maoris, and Melville Islanders who had paddled their canoes across sixty miles of shark-infested water to go to the cinema.

Biggles soon found what he was looking for, a public house where the customers appeared mostly to be Europeans – or part-European. He went in, and ordering a drink, was soon in conversation with an elderly man whose dress and speech made it clear that his business was connected with salt water. Presently, Biggles said casually: 'You may be able to answer a question for me. There used to be a lugger here named *Matilda*. I don't see her now. Do you know what's happened to her?'

The man saw nothing odd in this question. 'The *Matilda*,' was the ready response. 'Sure I know her. Used to belong to old Greeky

Apergoulos. He sold her to that Dutchman Boller. Leastways he said he was a Dutchman, but I'd say he was a German. Don't see much of her now. They tell me Boller's working something up the Daly.'

Biggles's muscles had tensed at the name Boller; and he was hard put to maintain his pose of indifference when it was followed by the word Daly; for he remembered, of course, that the two words went together on the list of names and addresses in his pocket. 'Boller,' he prompted. 'Who was he? I don't seem to know him.'

'You ain't missed much. Nobody here'd be sorry to see him go for good. Always looking for trouble. Went out of his way to find it.'

'Was he a big fellow with a black beard?'

'That's him.'

'You say he's doing something up the Daly.'

'He's got a place at the head of the river. Cleaning a pandanus swamp to raise peanuts. So they say. I don't believe it. He never struck me as the peanut-growing sort. I know some fellers have done well at it, but it'd take more than peanuts to get me there. The Daly's no place for a Christian. Here it may be hell in the wet, but up there, with every kind of biting bug making yer life miserable, natives waiting for a chance to stick a spear in yer ribs, living on tinned food and native tucker, it must be hell all the time. I ain't never been there, you understand, but I know some who have. Most of 'em stayed – for good.'

Biggles was thinking fast. 'Did you ever hear of a place up the Daly called the Flats?' he asked, although he was anxious not to arouse the man's suspicions by pushing his questions too hard.

'No, can't say as I have. But Taffy Walsh, over there, he'd know.

He used to be on the old *Maroubra*, taking stores along and bringing down the nuts.' Raising his voice the man called, 'Taffy! Come over here.' And when Taffy arrived he went on: 'Here's a feller wants to know what it's like up the Daly.'

The newcomer grinned. 'Thinking of taking a holiday?'

Biggles smiled back. 'No. Just interested.'

'Like crocodiles?'

'I hate 'em.'

'Then keep clear o' the Daly, 'cause scalies are thicker there than fleas on a dog's ear. I've see a dozen or more eighteen-footers crowdin' on a few yards o' mud bank.'

'He was askin' about a place called Daly Flats,' said the first of Biggles's new acquaintances. 'Ever hear of it, Taffy?'

'Yes. It's away up the top of the river; if I remember right, above where the Daly swings north towards Arnhem Land. If you want a spear in your gizzard that's the place to go.'

'Are you serious? You really mean the natives are bad?' queried Biggles, genuinely surprised, for he had supposed that danger-ously hostile aborigines were a thing of the past.

'Not all of 'em; but them as are bad are as bad as they make up. Keep out o' their country. That's my advice.'

The conversation lingered on a little longer, but as soon as he could break away without appearing discourteous, Biggles left the establishment, and well satisfied with his evening's work set about walking back to the airport. He had plenty to think about. Indeed, he had learned more than he expected. Outstanding, of course, was the surprising piece of information that the owner of the lugger was the Boller of Daly Flats, one of the names and addresses on the now important list. He was, apparently, reckoned to be an undesirable character even by Darwin standards, a port which, in its time, must have collected some tough types. Boller was believed to be a German. The man at Tarracooma Creek also had a German name – Roth. Adamsen, of Perth, might also be a German. It began to look as if the spy ring had been infiltrated from East Germany; or maybe von Stalhein and his associates had compiled a list of East Germans already domiciled in Australia. That was not to say, however, that they were active enemy agents. The Iron Curtain experts knew how to put pressure on unwilling, but sometimes helpless, persons. The scheme was beginning to take shape. Thus pondered Biggles as he strode on under a sky ablaze with stars, although occasionally they were partly blotted out by drifting masses of filmy cirro-cumulus cloud.

It was past ten o'clock when he reached the airport. The others would, he knew, be back by now, anxious to hear his news. Well, he had some to give them.

Walking past the hangars there was a minor incident which he was presently to remember, although at the time he didn't give it a second thought, the reason being, no doubt, that the possibility of personal danger, in Darwin, did not enter his head. He stopped to pass the time of night with a mechanic who had been working late in one of the sheds, and as they stood there chatting, the moon, which had been behind a cloud, rode clear.

It so happened, naturally perhaps, although without any conscious reason, Biggles was looking in the direction of the aircraft, and in the blue moonlight he saw, or thought he saw, an object move. What the object was he did not know. He couldn't remember seeing it before. It looked like a hump of something. Had he not gathered an impression that the thing had moved he would have taken it for a bag of freight, or mail, that had by an oversight been dropped and left out. It was as if the object had been moving, but froze into immobility at the precise moment the moon appeared. In the matter of distance it was between thirty and forty yards from the Otter. Not in the least degree concerned beyond the undesirability of having an animal wandering loose on the landing area, to the peril of planes coming in, he merely said to the mechanic: 'What's that thing over there? Is it an animal or has somebody dropped something?'

The mechanic looked, but at that instant the moon was overtaken by another patch of drifting cumulus; and as the object could no longer be distinguished the question was allowed to pass. The mechanic, apparently more concerned about getting home, strode on towards the airport buildings. Biggles went on to the machines.

As he was soon to recall, he had yet another warning, although, still without the slightest suspicion of danger, he ignored it. As he drew close to the Otter, which was the nearer of the two machines, he glanced again at the 'hump', and saw, with faint surprise, that it was not as far away as he had estimated. The distance was less than twenty yards; but he still could not make out what it was.

By this time he could hear the quiet murmur of voices inside the cabin, where the others were presumably together waiting for him, so he walked on to join them, and get a torch to examine the object that had puzzled him. Reaching the cabin door he turned to have a last look at it; and it was with a mild shock that he discovered that the thing, in some mysterious way, had not only closed the distance still more but had somehow flattened itself on the ground. Convinced now that it was an animal he took a pace towards it.

What followed occupied not more than three or four seconds of time.

The object, as black as night, leapt up. An arm went back, and Biggles realized for the first time that it was a man. Seeing that something was about to be thrown, he ducked instinctively. Almost simultaneously something swished over his head and struck the hull of the Otter with a crisp thud.

Biggles's reaction to the attack was to dart forward to seize his assailant; but the man twisted, and turning, raced away across the turf at fantastic speed, dodging and leaping in an extraordinary display of evading tactics. Pursuit was obviously futile. Biggles whipped out a pistol and got as far as raising it; but reluctant to alarm the aerodrome with gunshots he allowed his arm to drop, at the same time looking round to make sure the man had been alone. The moon reappeared. Not a soul was in sight.

Artificial light spread a yellow patch on the grass as the door of the cabin was thrown open. Algy's voice said: 'That you, Biggles?'

'Yes,' answered Biggles, somewhat breathlessly, for the suddenness of the attack had left him a trifle shaken.

'What's going on?'

'I don't quite know.'

'What was that thud? Something hit the cabin.'

'It thundering nearly hit me,' said Biggles grimly. 'Let's see what it was.' Walking up to the hull he seized, and jerked free, a short, triple-barbed spear.

'For heaven's sake,' came Algy's voice, aghast. 'Did someone throw that at you?'

'Yes. A native. And if I hadn't come along, you, or the first person to open that door, would have got it. I saw the devil creeping up to the machine as I came along; but I wasn't expecting anything like this. He may have thought we were all inside. I don't know.'

*Something swished over Biggles' head and struck the
Otter with a crisp thud.*

'He dropped something – or left it behind.' Algy walked out a few yards and came back with a soft mass of something in his hands.

'What is it?' asked Biggles.

'Rag, or tow, or something of that nature. It's wet. My gosh! It's dripping with petrol.'

'It looks as if the idea was to set fire to the machine. As they're so close, if one had caught fire the other would have gone too.'

'And if the door had been jammed we should have been trapped inside.'

A voice from the cabin cried: 'Here, I say, you fellers, What's the flap?'

'Let's get inside,' Biggles told Algy, in a hard voice.

In the cabin the others were told what had happened.

'What do you make of it,' asked Ginger.

'Obviously, somebody was hoping to get rid of us, or at least the machines. Which, equally obviously, means that that person knows we're here, and what we're doing.'

'Von Stalhein.'

Biggles shook his head. 'No. He doesn't work like that. Besides, he must still be at sea. The thing that puzzles me about this is how it has happened so quickly. I don't think von Stalhein could have known we were here till he saw us at the island – wait a minute though! I've got it. The answer's simple. That lugger, the *Matilda*, is fitted with radio. Of course it would be: to enable it to keep in touch with its headquarters. If we accept that, then several things become plain. As I see it now, what happened was this; and I'm pretty sure I'm right. This morning, the first thing that would hit von Stalhein when he realized we were on the job with an Australian police officer, was the boat lying on Eighty

Mile Beach. Up to that moment it wasn't worth bothering about. But now it could be an awkward piece of evidence. He knew perfectly well that if I hadn't already been to look at it I should most certainly do so, and check up on it. It had to be got rid of. He radioed his headquarters, or Smith's headquarters – call it what you like – to warn them. An aircraft – the Auster – was available. Some of the gang got into it, flew to the beach and burnt the boat. If that's correct then the Auster is being kept either in Western Australia or the Northern Territory. What happens next? Smith, or somebody, guessing that we would base ourselves on Darwin, decides that we'd be better out of the way; so he brings along a cut-throat to mop us up.'

'Are you suggesting that he keeps a supply of thugs on hand?' questioned Algy dubiously.

'From what I learnt tonight I see no reason why he shouldn't,' came back Biggles. 'I'd better tell you about that, because it all adds up.'

Biggles then revealed what he had gathered at the harbour. 'So you see, Blackbeard is Boller, one of the names on the list. He's a German who has a place at the headwaters of the Daly. In other words, Daly Flats. Ostensibly, he's been clearing ground for peanuts. What he's *actually* been doing, I suspect, is making a landing strip for an aircraft. Whites, I understand, are few and far between; but there, to Arnhem Land, have apparently retired those aborigines who want no truck with white men. Some of them are bad medicine. So I'm told. I don't know. I've never been there. But as we may have to go we'd better check up on it. West must know the facts. He may be able to tell us the district where they use this type of spear – or put us on to somebody who can. He should be on duty now. I'll walk along and ask him.'

'Here, watch what you're doing old boy,' protested Bertie. 'This beastly bodkin may not be the only one on the airfield.'

'Don't worry,' retorted Biggles grimly. 'If anyone comes close enough to me to chuck one, he'll be the first to meet a piece of metal coming the other way. You watch the machines. From now on it means guard duty. Infernal nuisance; but not such a nuisance as trying to get a bunch of barbs out of your ribs.'

'Well, chase Aunt Lizzie round the haystacks!' exclaimed Bertie. 'This native warrior stuff is all news to me. I thought Australia was civilized – if you get what I mean.'

'So did I,' returned Biggles. 'And so, I imagine it is, except for – well, take a look at that spear. There's nothing civilized about that. I'll see what West has to say about it. I shan't be long.'

Taking the spear Biggles departed.

He was away about half an hour. When he returned the others looked at him expectantly as he held out the spear. 'West says this thing came out of Arnhem Land. He asked me how I got it. When I told him he thought I was kidding. Said that sort of thing didn't happen here. I assured him that it did. He told me this top corner of Australia used to be called the triangle of death on account of the ferocity of the natives. Even today, with native reserves and all that sort of thing, they're not to be trusted. That goes for the half-civilized natives who work up the Daly for the white planters. Incidentally, what struck me as odd – or significant if you like – was this. West said many of the early peanut farmers were Russians. I wonder does that mean anything. Any who are left would certainly employ some native labour. What I'm getting at is, that fellow who had a go at me couldn't have had any personal grudge against me. He could have had no possible reason for wanting to set fire to us, anyway. Somebody sent him; somebody who knows how to handle the locals.'

Biggles was silent for a while, his expression hardening. 'You know, that thought puts an uncomfortable notion into my head.' He paused again, and continued: 'After what West told me I'd decided to do a high reconnaissance over the headwaters of the Daly; but that can wait for a bit. There's no hurry. Airstrips don't run away. And the *Matilda* can't be back there yet, if that's where she's going. I'll tell you what. Tomorrow morning I shall run down to Broome in the Halifax and have a word with Bill Gilson. Ginger can come with me. Algy, you take Bertie with you in the Otter and see if you can spot the *Matilda*. Don't go near it. I'll give you a course from the mouth of the Daly River to the island. If, on that course, you see a lugger heading for the Daly it's pretty certain to be the *Matilda*. Get its position. That's all I want. Take the machine up to the ceiling: the moment you spot the lugger, cut your engines and turn away. It doesn't really matter if they see you, but it'd be better if they didn't. When you've done that make for Broome. We'll wait there for you.'

'Okay,' agreed Algy.

'It's getting late if we're to make an early start. I'll take first watch. The rest of you see about getting some sleep,' concluded Biggles.

CHAPTER IX

Murder in the Outback

It was still only nine o'clock the next morning when Biggles and Ginger arrived at Bill Gilson's house, just in time to catch him going out. The airport superintendent had promised to keep an eye on the machine.

Bill looked surprised to see them. 'You fellers don't waste any time,' he observed cheerfully.

'We've none to waste,' returned Biggles, introducing Ginger. 'Let's go into the office. I want a word with you.'

'Now listen, Bill,' he went on, when they were settled. 'Has Joe Hopkins, your old prospector pal, come in yet?'

'No.'

'You mentioned he was overdue.'

'He is.'

'Is that customary?'

'No. He's usually pretty regular. The tucker he takes with him lasts just so long and no longer. There's nothing to eat in the spinifex. If he isn't soon in I shall have to do something about it.'

'Are there any natives in the district he works?'

Bill stared. 'What's that got to do with it?'

'Are there?'

'Yes. Plenty. But you didn't worry about that. He knows them and they know him.'

'There's never any trouble with them?'

A curious expression dawned on Bill's face. 'Now what made you ask that?'

'Last night, on Darwin airport, one tried to spear me.'

Bill's expression turned to incredulity. 'At *Darwin*! Are you pulling my leg?'

'There was nothing funny about it, believe you me,' retorted Biggles seriously. 'I have reason to believe that the man was an Arnhem Lander. I also have reason to believe that the people I'm looking for, which includes Boller, one of the names on that list I showed you, have an airstrip at the top end of the Daly. They've certainly got one no great distance away. That's where the Auster must have come from with the people who burnt the boat.'

Bill shook his head. 'There's nothing queer in Australia about a private airstrip. Everyone flies – farmers, stockmen, doctors, everybody – and thinks nothing of it. We were about the first people to become what used to be called airminded. No doubt it was a matter of the distances people had to cover to get anywhere. To be fifty or a hundred miles from your nearest neighbour is nothing in this part of the world.'

Biggles nodded. 'I realize that. But you still haven't answered my question about the general behaviour of the natives.'

'Well, since you mention it, there have been reports of – well, if not exactly trouble – difficulties. Of course, some of 'em always have been awkward and unreliable; and lately, instead of getting more friendly, as you'd expect, there's been what you might call a stiffening in their attitudes towards white men. Old Harry Larkin – he's another old timer – told me the other day that a party on what they call walkabout had threatened him. I took it with a pinch of salt, although I must admit that Harry isn't the sort to be easily scared. But what's all this leading up to?'

Biggles lit a cigarette. 'You'll call me an alarmist, I know, but it occurred to me last night that this is just how the trouble began in Malaya and Kenya.'

When Biggles said that Ginger knew just when the thought had struck him, the previous evening, and he had paused in the middle of a sentence.

Bill was staring. 'Do you mean Mau-Mau, and that sort of thing?'

'That's exactly what I mean.'

Bill smiled sceptically. 'But that couldn't happen here.'

'Why couldn't it?'

'Well, it just couldn't, that's all.'

'Tell me why?'

'Most of 'em are in regular touch with whites.'

'So they were in Africa.'

'They've got their own reserves—'

'So they had in Africa.'

Bill shook his head. 'I still don't see how it could happen here.'

'Neither, I imagine, could the settlers who took their wives and kids to outlying farms in Kenya, and now never move without a gun in each hand.' Biggles went on. 'Now look, Bill; I'm not the sort of man to get in a flap easily; and I own freely that I may be barking up a tree with nothing in it. I also own that when I came out here the last thing in my mind was trouble with the natives. I didn't really know what I *was* looking for. But since I've been here one or two things have happened that have made me think hard. Last night, after that man had flung a spear at me, the idea suddenly came to me that the set-up in the sparsely populated areas of Australia is exactly the same as in East Africa. Natives, without settled homes, outnumbering the whites. Isolated homesteads far apart. Stockmen, farmers and prospectors out on their own.... It only needs one or two people to walk about telling the natives that white men are a lot of thieves who have swindled them out of their land, and turned them into slaves, and the next thing is murder.' Biggles made a deprecatory gesture. 'I may be quite wrong, but putting two and two together from what I've learnt since I came here, that was the ugly picture that suddenly crystallized in the fog. This dirty business is all part of the Cold War. It has worked in Malaya, Kenya, Indonesia, Burma and all over the Middle East, so I don't see why it shouldn't happen here. The men who landed in that stolen boat on Eighty Mile Beach came from behind the Iron Curtain, which is the general head-quarters of the Cold War. I know more about them than you do. Whether I'm right or wrong about what they're doing here, don't kid yourself that they can't hurt *you*, or that the technique that has worked in Asia and Africa couldn't work in Australia.' Biggles stubbed his cigarette.

Bill's expression had changed. 'I never looked at it like that,' he admitted soberly.

'Well, it might be worth your while if you bore it in mind and kept an ear to the ground for rumours of agitators. You told me yourself that this fellow Adamsen, in Perth, was known to be one.'

'He's left Perth, they say.'

'Oh he has, has he. I wonder what he's up to. And what about Roth, of Tarracooma Creek – wherever that might be.'

'I've found out where that is.'

'Where is it?'

'It's an old sheep run on the edge of the desert, south-east from here.'

'How far?'

'Roughly, between a hundred and a hundred and fifty miles.'

'Would Hopkins be in that direction?'

'More or less. He's not so far out, of course – mebbe forty miles.'

'Would I be likely to fly over him if I went to Tarracooma?'

'Not unless you made a bit of a dog's leg.'

'Might I see him from the air?'

'I should think so. He's got a mine – or rather, a digging – with a home made crusher. He lives in a wurlie, that's a bough shelter, near what we call a soak, to provide him with water. He scratches enough gold dust to keep him going.'

'Do you know exactly where this place is?'

'Sure. I've called on him there. It's at the foot of the MacLaren Hills.'

'This soak, as you call it. Would that be the only water supply in the district?'

'Yes.'

'Would the natives use it?'

'I expect so.'

'Then it might be a good thing if someone had a look to see if Hopkins is all right.'

'He can take care of himself.'

'I'm glad to hear it, because if Tarracooma is a prospective trouble spot, and being on my list it may be, the natives in that area may be some of the first to get restless.'

'I see what you mean,' replied Bill slowly.

Biggles glanced at his watch. 'While I'm down here I think I'll run out and have a look at this place Tarracooma. I could take in Joe's workings on the way. Would you care to come along?'

'I would, very much.'

'Okay. By the way, whether Joe is all right or not, I wouldn't say anything about my suspicions to anyone just yet. There may be nothing to it. But when a fire is smouldering it only needs one spark to set it alight. That's why I'm hoping you're right about Joe being able to take care of himself; because if he isn't that may be the spark.'

'If he isn't, don't worry; I'll catch the man who did the mischief,' said Bill grimly.

'Exactly,' returned Biggles drily. 'The result of that would be more trouble by way of a reprisal – and up goes the balloon. But let's not talk about that until we have to. Let's go.'

They all walked briskly to the garage where Bill kept his car.

'If you'll keep low I shall be able to pick up my landmarks as we go along,' he averred.

Presently the Halifax, at a few hundred feet, was heading out over the inhospitable terrain that lies behind so much of Western Australia's coast. At the worst it was stark desert, with ribbed sand dunes and tawny hills; at the best, spiky spinifex and salt bush. Salt lakes, as round as saucers, dotted the landscape, reflecting the clear blue of the sky. There was not a living creature in sight. This, brooded Ginger, was the true Australia, still the same as it had been for countless years before the white man came.

'Take a line on the dip between those two humps on the horizon – a bit to your right,' requested Bill, and as Biggles altered course a trifle he resumed his scrutiny of the wilderness for the missing prospector.

The objective took on a more distinct outline as the machine droned on towards it; but of the missing man there was no sign. The scene remained as lifeless as a picture.

'Make for the bottom of the gulley in that hill on your right,' said Bill. 'There's a clump of mulga near it. It's just this side of it that Joe has his wurlie. You'll see the mine. He should be there, or not far away.'

'He isn't there – unless he's deaf,' said Biggles evenly. 'If he was about he'd be looking at us by now.'

The Halifax roared over the mine. Biggles circled it twice, losing height. A hole in the ground, the primitive bough-shelter, a billy-can hanging over a dead fire and some implements lying about, were all that could be seen.

'He should be there,' muttered Bill. 'He hasn't started for home. If he had he would have taken his billy with him.'

'What do you suggest we do?'

'I'd like to go down and have a look. Can you land?'

'It ought to be possible on that bare flat area. Let's see.'

Biggles flew on to the area of desert he had indicated. 'Seems to be all right,' he decided. 'We'll try it. But don't blame me if we have to walk home.'

Actually, the ground was level and devoid of vegetation, and Biggles put the aircraft down without much risk, finishing his run about three hundred yards from the prospector's lonely workings.

'The machine can't take any harm where it is,' remarked Biggles, as they got out, and began walking towards the mine.

The sun was flaying the earth with bars of white heat that made the air quiver and the distant skylines shake; but everything else was still. There was no sound; no song of a bird, no whisper of a breeze. As they drew near the wurlie the silence seemed to take on a sinister quality; for it must have been evident to all that the miner was not there or he would certainly have shown himself by now. Maybe that was why Bill lengthened his stride so that he was the first to reach the shelter.

He took one glance inside, and the face that he turned to the others had lost its colour. 'He's dead,' was all he said.

The old prospector lay in a crumpled heap. He had obviously been dead for some days. There were some ugly black marks on the sand, on which the flies were busy.

'Stay where you are,' said Bill, in a flat voice. 'I'd better attend to this.'

Biggles lit a cigarette and surveyed the sterile landscape.

'He was murdered,' reported Bill, when he had finished his inspection. 'Aborigines. He was clubbed, and stabbed to death with spears. Couldn't have had a chance to defend himself. Came on him in the night, mebbe. Where's his rifle? I don't see it. I know he had one. Kept it in case he got a chance for a shot at a kangaroo. It was an old service .303. Had his initials on the butt, I remember. No cartridges, either. Queer.'

'I see nothing queer about it,' said Biggles. 'When this sort of thing starts that's how it goes. They probably killed him for his rifle. Now, perhaps, you see what I mean,' he concluded, significantly.

Bill tipped his hat on the back of his head. 'I still can't believe it. This sort of thing was common enough years ago but it doesn't often happen now – not in these parts, anyway. Poor old Joe. And to think how many times he's shared his water and tucker with them.'

'We shall have to bury him. It's usual here to bury a perish, as we say, where he's found. We've tools. Then I'll fetch my tracker and see what he has to say about it.'

'You mean, you'll follow up the murderers?'

'To hell and back if necessary. We don't let anybody, black or

'He's dead,' was all Bill said.

white, get away with murder – not even here. Don't tread on more ground than you can help.'

All taking a hand they dug a shallow grave. The body of the old digger was laid in it, after which the earth was replaced and stones piled on it. Bill recited the Lord's Prayer, stuck the spade in the ground at the head of the grave and started to collect the dead man's few simple belongings, putting them in his 'swag' – a coarse canvas holdall. After searching about for a little while in the wurlie he said: 'There's something else missing.'

'What is it?' asked Biggles.

'His dust – gold dust. He wouldn't have stayed here had his claim been worked out. He always managed to get a few ounces. Kept it in a little kangaroo-hide bag he made. I've seen it scores of times.'

'He might have hidden it.'

'Not he. Why should he? He wouldn't be expecting trouble.'

'Seeing the natives—'

'He had no time to hide it, even if he thought of it, which isn't likely. From the way he was killed he hadn't time to do anything.'

'Then if it isn't here the murderer must have taken it.'

Bill nodded. 'That's the only answer.' He fastened the swag and picked it up. 'That's the lot,' he said, and turned to go, only to stop dead, leaning forward, like a dog pointing game.

Ginger did not have to look far for the reason. A hundred yards away a score of naked aborigines were standing in a group, watching them. All carried spears. To say that he was astonished would be to put it mildly. How, and from where, the natives had appeared in a scene that he would have sworn was lifeless, was a mystery.

'Now what?' murmured Biggles.

'I'll have a word with 'em. It may be the mob that murdered Joe.'

'You know more about it than I do, but I'd say not,' replied Biggles. 'The mob that killed Joe, knowing what was bound to follow, would surely make themselves scarce.'

'We'll see.' Bill started walking purposefully towards the aborigines, who remained as rigid as if they had been carved in stone. 'If they didn't do the killing they'll know all about it.'

'Have you got a gun?' queried Biggles.

'I don't need one.'

Biggles shrugged. To Ginger he said quietly: 'There are times when fearlessness can be foolishness.'

Bill stopped at a distance of about twenty yards. 'What name?' he shouted.

There was no answer, no movement.

'Which way country belong you?' demanded Bill.

No answer.

'What yabber-yabber belong you,' persisted Bill. 'You been savvy what happen longa here.'

The aborigines remained like graven images, their black eyes, unwinking, on the policeman.

'Listen, Ginger,' said Biggles tersely. 'He's not going to do anything with that lot, and if he tries there's going to be trouble. Make for the machine. Start up. You may be able to bring it nearer. Behave as if nothing is happening. Above all, don't look scared.'

'Okay.' Ginger started off for the machine, which was not directly behind them but at an angle between the two parties, so that he was able to watch events out of the corner of his eye.

Biggles, with his hands in his pockets, was strolling nearer to

Bill as if nothing unusual was going on. Coming within earshot he said: 'I don't think that's your lot, Bill. I don't see a rifle.'

'They won't talk.'

'If they've decided to take that line you won't make 'em. Push them too hard and we're going to have casualties. We don't want that at this stage.'

'I've never seen 'em in this mood before,' came back Bill, in a voice tense with chagrin.

Biggles realized the position Bill was in. To retire now would look like weakness, loss of face. To go on was to invite open hostility. 'You please yourself what you do; it's your country and you know best,' he said, and lit another cigarette.

The Halifax's engines came to life and the big machine moved slowly and ponderously towards the opposing parties.

Said Bill, reluctantly: 'I suppose you're right, but I hate letting 'em get away with it.' He half turned.

The movement might have been the signal for which the aborigines were waiting. While Bill's eyes were on them, like animals, they hesitated to do anything; but the instant he turned, they acted. With shrill whistles and strange cries they began to fan out.

Bill stared. Not only was he obviously surprised by this behaviour but it was evident that he still had not grasped what was unpleasantly obvious to Biggles; that their lives were in danger. Familiarity with natives normally friendly, had, no doubt, bred contempt, as was understandable. He refused to be intimidated, and it was with reluctance that he moved unhurriedly with Biggles towards the machine.

At the last minute a spear was thrown. It did no harm. But it so enraged Bill that Ginger, who was watching from the cockpit, thought that he was going for the thrower; a course that looked, and probably would have been, suicidal. Biggles had a pistol but he had not drawn it, presumably hoping to avoid hostilities. In any case it would not have been much use against the mob, had they charged.

Ginger decided to take matters into his own hands. Advancing the throttle, as the machine responded he swung it round so that the tail pointed at the natives. The result can be imagined. On the tearing slipstream of the four powerful engines a wall of dust, sand and dead vegetation, struck them like a tidal wave, and for a moment engulfed them. The stuff may well have stung their exposed bodies. At all events, it was more than they could face, and presently vague figures, hands over eyes, could be seen staggering about as they sought to get out of the blast.

Biggles and Bill took the opportunity to get aboard and the immediate danger was past. Ginger relinquished his seat to Biggles, who said, 'Well done.' He did not take off at once, but turning to Bill, asked: 'Now what do you want to do? Do you want to go back to Broome or shall I go back to Tarracooma?'

'I'd rather get back to Broome,' answered Bill; 'Whether it suits your book or not I shall have to report the murder of Joe Hopkins, and the behaviour of those lunatics outside. I can't think what the deuce has come over them.'

'I can,' murmured Biggles. 'I hate saying I told you so, but I did try to give you an idea of what we might expect. We've got to work fast, Bill, or Joe Hopkins won't be the only man to perish. I'll take you home.'

Leaving the naked warriors watching from a distance the Halifax roared into the air.

CHAPTER X

Claws Out at Tarracooma

They got back to Broome to find the Otter there, just in. Algy said they had spotted the *Matilda* about seventy miles out, on a course for the mouth of the Daly.

'That's what I expected, and all I want to know about it for the time being,' said Biggles. He introduced Algy and Bertie to Bill, and then told them the result of their morning's work. 'I'm pretty certain now that whatever else von Stalhein's associates are doing in Australia part of their job is to unsettle the aborigines. Aside from any material damage the natives may do it tends to focus attention on them, which, of course, by employing police and aircraft, makes things easier for the spy ring to operate. How many aborigines have you got in Australia, Bill?'

'As near as can be judged, about fifty thousand. In addition, there are a lot of mixed race.'

Biggles nodded. 'If, as it seems, somebody has been working on the aborigines to antagonize them, we can expect the same conditions in the Territory. In Western Australia the trouble may have started at Tarracooma. In the Territory, up the Daly.' He looked at Bill seriously. 'I realize that you'll have to report the killing of Joe Hopkins, and try to find the murderer; but while you're doing that the trouble may spread. I imagine Hopkins wasn't the only lone prospector out in the wilds.'

'Not by a long chalk. Some fellows work alone, others in pairs. And there are homesteads right off the map.'

'They ought to be warned. The question is how to do it without starting a scare – and being laughed at for alarmists. And while people are laughing, the propaganda agents, realizing that their racket has been rumbled, will work all the harder to set things alight. There's no time to lose. This ugly weed has got to be nipped in the bud. You can see how I'm fixed. I've no authority here to arrest anyone, even if I had a definite charge against him, which I haven't – yet.'

'I might get the fellow who killed Hopkins. I've a good tracker.'

'And while you're looking for him more murders may be committed. You might even be murdered yourself.'

'What do you suggest I do?'

'What do you suggest *I* do? Of course, I could go to Sydney and see one of your Security people whose name has been given me; but that would take time, and it would certainly be some time before anything was done. I should have to convince the man that I wasn't talking through my hat, and he'd have to get instructions before he could take action. All the evidence I have would rest on my unsubstantiated word, and I feel that isn't enough. What I *really* want to do is have a sight of this mystery man Smith, who I suspect is at the root of the trouble. But he's outside your province.' Biggles thought for a moment. 'In view of what's happened I feel inclined to take the bull by the horns and tackle this fellow Roth at Tarracooma. That might stop the rot in this area.'

'How?'

'You could arrest him, and bring him here for questioning.'

'And make myself a laughing stock?'

'That, I must admit, is a chance you'd be taking,' conceded Biggles. 'It's up to you to decide whether it's worth risking your career to save some of your people out there in the blue without a thought of danger in their heads. There is, of course, a possibility that Roth, if he's a guilty party, may panic when he sees us, and do something that would warrant your picking him up. We might find something incriminating in his house. Anyway, it would be worthwhile if we could force him to hold his hand while I got cracking on Daly Flats.'

Bill looked worried, as he had every reason to be. 'This is a free country,' he argued. 'A man can go where he likes and do what he likes as long as he doesn't break the law. And there's no law against talking, to blacks or whites.'

'And that's exactly what the enemy reckons on,' declared Biggles. 'It makes his job easy and ours difficult. Well, I'm going to Tarracooma. You can please yourself whether you come or not.'

'I'll come with you,' decided Bill. 'We could have a look at this feller Roth. No harm in that. On the way I could see what natives were on the move. Give me a minute to report Hopkins' murder and I'll be with you.'

'What about us,' queried Algy, while they were waiting.

'You and Bertie can come along. Anything can happen, and the more witnesses we have the better. The Otter will be all right here.'

'How do you know you'll be able to land at Tarracooma?' inquired Bill, when he returned.

'I don't know. But it's my guess there will be some sort of landing facility. Roth may be only a small fish in the spy outfit but his boss would want to keep in contact with him; and unless I'm off my mark his boss is Mr Smith, who has an aeroplane. Do you think you'll be able to find the place, Bill?'

'I know the general locality. It's unlikely that there's more than one establishment there, so if we see one, that should be it.'

In a few minutes the Halifax was in the air again, on a course a little more to the south than last time. The same sort of country lay below, although there were wide areas of absolute desert, sand or 'gibbers', the rounded stones that look as if they should be on a seaside beach. Later there were broad patches of mulga – a small tree shrub of the acacia family. From one such growth a thin column of smoke was rising. Presently Biggles noticed another, and asked: 'What's that smoke? I don't see anyone about.'

Answered Bill: 'We call 'em mulga wires. Or if you like, bush telegraph. Aborigine talk. Natives signalling.'

'About us?'

'Possibly. Or about the murder. When you're on the ground everyone gets advance notice that you're on the way. But I doubt if the smoke signals can travel as fast as a plane. In the ordinary way I'd say they have no special significance; but I don't like the way the aborigines are keeping out of sight. Of course, if they know a man has been killed that could be enough to send them into hiding. They know jolly well that someone will have to pay for it.'

The aircraft droned on. The only sign of life in the wilderness was a small mob of kangaroos.

'We call that light scrub and sand country ahead, pindan,'

informed Bill. 'If this Tarracooma outfit is really raising sheep we soon ought to see something of 'em. A sheep run can have a frontage of a hundred miles.'

The Halifax droned on, bumping badly in the shimmering heat.

Another twenty minutes passed and Bill said: 'Tarracooma should be about here somewhere. It's new ground to me so I can't say exactly where it is. There's pretty certain to be a billabong – that's a waterhole – so if you climbed a bit higher, and circled, we might spot the light shining on it. Water stands out clear in this sort of country. If there isn't any natural water there should be an iron windmill working an artesian well.'

As it turned out there was a waterhole. As Biggles climbed Ginger spotted it a long way off. He called attention to it, where-upon Biggles cut the engines and began a long glide towards it. Some buildings, made conspicuous only by the shadows they cast, came into view; and a few sheep. Then one or two aborigines appeared, running; one led two horses into a building, presum-ably a stable.

'I can see wheel marks on that sand patch,' said Bill.

'So can I – but there's nothing to show what made them,' replied Biggles. 'Could have been a car, although they look a bit too wide for that. We shall soon see. You'd better do the talking. What line are you going to take?'

'The first thing is to have a look at Roth, and see how he shapes.'

'You'll have to give a reason for calling.'

'I'll ask him if he's had any trouble with his native boys.'

'He'll say no. Which as far as he's concerned will probably be true, because he's one of the very people who's causing the trouble. At least, I think he must be. I can think of no other reason why he should be on von Stalhein's list.'

'I shall bear that in mind,' asserted Bill.

The range of buildings was now almost directly below. The actual house was a long low bungalow of timber and corrugated iron. Ginger thought it looked new. Certainly it had not been there very long.

'No one's come out to have a look at us,' observed Bill.

'They're looking all right, don't make any mistake about that,' returned Biggles, with a suspicion of a sneer in his voice.

He landed down a rather confused line of tracks and ran on as near the bungalow as was practicable, the distance from it being about fifty yards. He switched off. They got down. Ginger could see natives watching them surreptitiously from the outbuildings.

'Somebody had better stay with the machine,' decided Biggles. 'In fact, I think you, Algy, and Bertie, might both stay. You'll be able to see what happens, and you'll be close enough to step in if Mr Roth starts chucking his weight about. I don't think he will, but one never knows.'

Bill, with Biggles and Ginger, strode on to the front door of the building; but before they reached it, it was opened, and a man stood on the threshold. The colour of his skin was enough to reveal at a glance that he was a mixed breed.'

'Mr Roth at home?' began Bill, casually.

'He is. I'm Roth,' was the answer.

For a moment Bill looked somewhat taken aback. As, indeed, was Ginger, and no doubt Biggles too. Naturally, it had been assumed that Roth was a white man. That this was clearly not so put an unexpected factor into the proceedings; but there was of course no opportunity to discuss it.

'May we come in?' questioned Bill, cheerfully, for they had received no invitation to enter. He moved forward.

With some reluctance, it seemed to Ginger, Roth gave way. He gave the impression that he, too, had been caught unprepared – unprepared, that is, for a visit from a police officer. Had Bill been travelling on foot, or on a horse, Roth would probably have had ample warning of his approach.

The door opened directly into what was plainly the living-room. The table was littered with dirty plates and glasses, more than one man would be likely to use at one meal. An empty whisky bottle stood amongst the debris.

'I see you're having a party,' said Bill, evenly. 'I hope I haven't disturbed it?'

This was spoken as a question; but Roth ignored it. 'What do you want?' he asked, in a guttural voice that suggested, as did his name, German parentage on the white side of his pedigree.

'I'm calling on some of the people in the outback, to see if everything's going on all right.'

'Why shouldn't it?'

'One or two of 'em report a little trouble with their aborig-ines.'

'No trouble here.'

'Who have you got in the house?'

'What's that got to do with it.'

'It just struck me that if you've got neighbours here I could speak to them while I'm on the ground. That would save me a journey, mebbe.'

'What visitors would be likely to come here?'

'I don't know. You'd know better than me. I notice one of your friends has a plane.'

Whether this was a shot in the dark, or whether Bill had mentally measured the wheel tracks outside, Ginger did not know. Bill knew the track of the Auster was six feet, for they had told him so on Eighty Mile Beach.

'Friend of mine come up from Perth,' announced Roth, after a momentary hesitation, in which, apparently, he had decided not to deny that a plane had been there. Not that he could very well deny it, with the tracks outside.

'Would I know him?' asked Bill, carelessly.

'Shouldn't think so.'

'What's his name.'

Roth frowned. 'Say, what's the idea of all these questions?'

'I'm just setting my clock right as to who's about in my territory. Have you some objection to answering a few civil questions?'

'Course not.'

'Then why not tell me this man's name?'

Roth scowled. 'All right. If you must know, it's Adamsen.'

Biggles caught Ginger's eye.

'Is he still here?' asked Bill.

'Yes.'

'Anyone else?'

Roth's scowl deepened. 'Why should there be anyone else?'

Bill's manner did not change. 'Only that I notice five people have just had a meal, and I reckon it'd take more than two of you to empty a bottle of whisky.'

That did it. 'What's it got to do with you who I have in my house?' spat Roth. 'Ain't you got nothin' better to do than waste my time with a lot of fool questions? What are you trying to get at, anyhow?'

Bill's voice took on a more brittle quality. 'What I'm trying to get at is the man who murdered Joe Hopkins, the digger.'

Roth stiffened. Alarm showed for a moment in his eyes. He was not a good dissembler.

'So you knew about that,' pressed Bill.

'I didn't say so.'

'But you knew about it.'

'No I didn't.'

Bill strode to a corner of the room picked up a rifle that was leaning against the wall, and holding it by the muzzle pushed the butt forward. 'If you didn't know, how did this get here?' he rasped.

Roth stared. His tongue flicked nervously over his lips.

'This is Joe's rifle and you know it,' challenged Bill.

'I didn't know who it belonged to,' shouted Roth.

'How did it get here?'

'I took it off one of my boys.'

'Why?'

'Because I won't let 'em carry guns.'

'Then let's ask *him* where he got it from,' said Bill firmly. 'Send for him.'

'He ain't here any longer,' muttered Roth.

'Why not?'

'I sacked him a week ago.'

'What was his name?'

'Charlie.'

'Charlie what?'

'How would I know? I can't remember the name of every native who works for me.'

'How many have you got working for you?'

'About a score.'

'What do they all do?'

'What do aborigines usually do on a station?'

'Look after the stock – when there is any,' rapped out Bill, meaningly.

At this juncture the door of an inner room was opened and four men entered. One, the leader, was white; a cadaverous fellow with small dark eyes set close together and a straggling beard. Two were mixed race although one of them had more than a hint of Asiatic in his make-up. The other was a full-blooded aborigine, dressed like the rest.

'What's all the fuss about,' inquired the leader of the newcomers.

'The fuss is about a murder,' answered Bill, shortly. 'Who are you?'

'The name's Adamsen – if that means anything to you.' The man grinned unpleasantly, showing a row of broken discoloured teeth, as if he would make a joke of the business. 'I ain't murdered anyone – so far,' he added.

'I didn't say you had,' retorted Bill curtly. He took out his notebook. 'I'll have the names of the rest of you while I'm here,' he stated. 'I may have to call on you as witnesses.'

A sullen silence settled on the room.

'Come on,' requested Bill, impatiently, pencil in hand.

No one answered.

'I see,' said Bill, coldly. 'So that's how you feel about it. Don't worry, I'll remember your faces. Is there anyone else in that room?' A few quick strides took him to the doorway through which the men had entered. After a glance round he said: 'You got a licence for a wireless transmitter, Roth?'

'I ain't had time. It's only just been put in.'

'Who put it in – Adamsen?'

There was no answer.

Bill came back. 'You're coming with me,' he told Roth.

'Where to?'

'Broome.'

'Like heck I will. What for?'

'To make a statement as to how the property of a dead man came into your possession.'

'I've told you all I know.'

'I'm not satisfied with your explanation.'

'It's as much as you'll get out of me. And I ain't moving from here.'

'You won't gain anything by resisting the police.'

'That's all you know,' sneered Roth, apparently gaining confidence from the presence of his supporters.

At this point, before anyone could stop him, the aborigine dodged across the room to the front door, and putting his fingers to his mouth let out a shrill whistle. Instantly, from where they had been watching, a score of natives came running towards the house.

'I reckon it's time you were going,' scoffed Roth.

Bill's lips came together in a hard line. 'You rat, to drag these poor people into trouble.'

Roth's grin broadened. 'It's you that's in trouble, mister,' he mocked. 'Better get going.'

'Yes, I'm going, and you're coming with me,' said Bill, calmly – surprisingly calmly, Ginger thought, considering he was unarmed.

Roth's right hand began to move slowly towards his side pocket; but it stopped when he found himself looking into the muzzle of Biggles's gun.

'Don't move, anybody,' said Biggles, with ice in his voice. 'Ginger, give Bill your gun, then take the valves out of that radio equipment.'

Ginger handed his gun to Bill and walked to the open door of the inner room. Adamsen half turned as if he would stop him.

Biggles's gun whipped round. 'Stand still,' he grated; and there was something in his manner that brought the man to an abrupt halt, staring.

Ginger went on. He was soon back. 'Okay,' he said.

'You'll pay for this,' stormed Roth.

'We'll talk about who's going to pay later,' said Bill. 'Are you coming with me?'

'No.'

Bill handed his gun to Ginger. 'Hold this,' he said, in a matter-of-fact voice. Turning back to Roth he put out a hand to take his arm – or that was what it looked like. At the same time he said: 'For the last time, are you coming quietly?'

'I'll see you in hell first,' snarled Roth, and struck Bill's arm aside.

Bill's fist flew out. It landed on Roth's jaw and hurled him staggering back against the wall. Before he could recover, moving at a surprising speed for a man of his stature, Bill followed up and hit him again, this time knocking him down. He stooped swiftly. Handcuffs clicked. 'I'll teach you to have a little more respect for the law,' he said trenchantly. 'Come on.'

All this had happened so quickly that the other members of the party hadn't moved, but stood staring, as if finding it difficult to believe their eyes. Biggles, gun in hand, watched them without emotion.

Ginger, wondering why the aborigines did not come in, threw

a glance at the outside door. Algy was standing on the step. The natives had stopped before his automatic.

Bill, grim-faced, and a trifle pale under his tan, pushed Roth towards the door.

Roth, seeing that his friends were not going to help him, flew into a passion. In a voice thin with panic he shouted: 'Gimme a hand some of you. What are you gaping at, you blasted cowards. Charlie—' He broke off abruptly, as if realizing that in his temper he had let something slip.

Bill stopped. 'Charlie,' he repeated, and swung round to face the aborigine, who was backing into the room. 'So you're Charlie?'

'Yes, he's Charlie,' spat Roth vindictively. 'I'm not swinging for any aborigine.'

Charlie moved like lightning. He whipped out a knife. His arm went up.

Biggles hardly moved. His gun crashed. Charlie staggered screaming, clutching his arm. The knife clattered on the floor. Biggles kicked it aside and grabbed the man by the scruff of the neck.

'Mind he hasn't got a gun in his pocket,' warned Bill.

Biggles tapped the man's pockets. Apparently he felt something, for his hand dived into a side pocket. It came out holding a small but bulging bag of kangaroo hide.

'That's it,' cried Bill. 'That's Joe's poke. Bring him along.'

'You won't want me now,' contended Roth.

'You knew all about it,' snapped Bill. 'I'm holding you for an accessory.'

Charlie was groaning. Whether Adamsen and the two half-breeds knew about the murder was questionable. At all events, they were clearly unwilling to be associated with it, for they did nothing. Roth was cursing Charlie luridly for keeping Hopkins' gold, about which he had evidently not been told. Altogether, it was an ugly example of crooks ratting on each other.

'You'll have to give me a minute to fix this man's arm,' Biggles told Bill. 'Get me some rag, Ginger. A towel will do. You'll probably find one in the kitchen.'

There was a delay of a few minutes while a temporary bandage was put on the aborigine's arm. When the job was done Biggles said: 'Go ahead, Bill.'

Carrying Hopkins' rifle Bill took his prisoners through the door. Ginger went with him. Algy was still covering the natives. Biggles was last out of the house. He shut the door behind him.

There were a few critical moments with the aborigines outside. They stirred uneasily and it looked as if they might attempt a rescue; but in the end they did nothing. Maybe it was Bill's uniform that made them hesitate to act. Perhaps it was the old story of everyone leaving the first move to someone else. The fact remains, they stood their ground, wide-eyed and open-mouthed as they watched these unusual events.

The Halifax's engines started. Bertie left them idling and reappeared at the cabin door. Bill pushed his prisoners forward to him, and having handed them over turned about and deliberately walked back to the natives. What he said to them couldn't be heard for the noise of the motors. He made no threatening gestures; he carried no weapon, so the result seemed to be a good example of dominant willpower. The tension relaxed. One of the natives seemed to be explaining something. At the finish, when Bill dismissed them with a wave, they merely walked away.

'Wouldn't do to let 'em think we were scared of 'em,' he remarked, when he rejoined the others. 'I told 'em not to listen to anyone who came along trying to stir up trouble; and if they had any complaint, to make it to me, or the government Protector of Aborigines. Let's get along home.'

Biggles went through to the cockpit, and two minutes later Tarracooma was dropping away astern in a haze of dust.

'What about Adamsen, and that other pair in the house?' asked Ginger.

'There was nothing we could do with them,' answered Biggles. 'They won't do anything. In fact, without their wireless, I don't see that there is much they can do. One thing they will do is think, and think hard. In the first place it must have given them a shock to know we're wise to their game. On top of that they learned about the murder, which I fancy was news to them. It was probably true that Adamsen came up from Perth to fix their wireless. Anyway, we've drawn their teeth for the time being, and that gives us breathing space to decide on our next move.'

The Halifax droned on, kicking the thin desert air behind it.

CHAPTER XI

Move and Countermove

The afternoon was still young when the Halifax got back to Broome, so Biggles, saying he had thought things over on the way, announced his intention of pushing straight on to Darwin with both machines. With Adamsen at Tarracooma there was no point in going to Perth, as he had at one time contemplated; and there was nothing more for them to do at Broome. Bill could be left to deal with the prisoners through ordinary routine channels. This he said he would do, for the time being withholding any reference to the general animosity of the aborigines which, after what had happened at Tarracooma, might fizzle out of its own accord without further trouble.

So after a cup of tea and a snack, thanking Bill for his efficient co-operation, the crews got into their aircraft and flew back together to Darwin without anything of interest happening on the way. As they had to pass over the mouth of the Daly River without deviating from their course they looked for the *Matilda*, but saw nothing of her. As a matter of detail there were several craft on the open sea, but they did not go down to investigate them, Biggles remarking that by this time the lugger was no doubt on the river. This was perhaps a natural assumption; but before long Biggles was to blame himself for assuming too much without supporting evidence.

During the run, he and Ginger discussed the general situation. Ginger was able to tell Biggles that the radio equipment at Tarracooma was very high frequency which pretty well confirmed Biggles's belief that Smith, or whoever the senior member of the spy gang might be, was in direct touch with his operatives regardless of distance. It was some satisfaction to know that as Tarracooma had been silenced it would be several days before he knew what had happened there. He might, Biggles thought, send the Auster down to find out.

The chief topic of conversation was what to do next. It was a problem that presented difficulties. Biggles said he was anxious to have a look at Daly Flats, from the air if not from the ground. But if that was to be done it ought to be done at once, before the lugger got there. He was equally anxious to see Colonel MacEwan, the Australian Security Officer at Sydney, for he felt that the time had come to put their cards on the table. They could not, he asserted, go on tearing about Australia, doing things which, if it was held that they had overstepped their authority, might embarrass everybody concerned. At Tarracooma, by taking a chance and having Bill with them, all had gone well, and they had nipped off one of the ends of the spy network. They couldn't hope to go on doing that sort of thing without the Australian government asking them what the dickens they thought they were up to; and in any case the damage they had done would soon be repaired by Smith, who would carry on with his work.

As he had said before, Biggles went on, what he really wanted was the complete list of enemy agents in the country – or at any rate, those with whom von Stalhein was in touch, or had intended to get in touch on his arrival in Australia. That a duplicate list existed was not to be doubted. Who had it? Possibly Smith, who was certainly a senior member of the spy organization if not the actual head. He now had his own plane for easy transport. It followed, therefore, that where the plane was, so Smith would be. And the most likely place for it to be at that moment, averred Biggles, was at Daly Flats, awaiting the arrival of the *Matilda*, so that Smith could learn at first hand from von Stalhein what had happened on the island. But once he had that information it was unlikely that he would stay there. Taking von Stalhein with him in the Auster, he would depart for an unknown destination. Hence the urgency.

'So you see,' concluded Biggles, 'if I go to Sydney to see Colonel MacEwan, the Security man whose name the Air Commodore gave me, I'd probably miss the boat – or rather, the plane – at Daly Flats. We should then be faced with the job of hunting the whole of Australia for the Auster. All this, of course, is assuming that Smith is at Daly Flats at this moment with the Auster.'

'The Australian government would soon locate the Auster,' declared Ginger confidently.

'I'm not so sure of that,' returned Biggles. 'Smith may keep clear of public airfields. For all we know he may have a dozen hide-outs like Tarracooma, or, as I suspect, Daly Flats.'

'Does this Australian Security Officer know we're here?' queried Ginger.

'I'd say yes, although I haven't confirmed it. But I'm pretty sure the Air Commodore would let him know what was in the wind.'

'Then as you can't go to Sydney *and* Daly Flats why not ring him up?'

Biggles shook his head. 'Fancy trying to explain all this over the phone! Aside from that, on a public telephone service you never know who's listening.'

The debate was resumed later, when they were all on the ground at Darwin, parked as before just beyond the end hangar. By the time they had topped up their tanks it was too late to do any more flying that day. Biggles gave his views as he had given them to Ginger, and the upshot of it all was, he resolved to go to Sydney, in the Halifax, starting at daybreak. The others, in the Otter, could make a cautious reconnaissance of the Daly Flats area, the main objectives being a possible airstrip, the Auster, and the position of the lugger, which, it was supposed, would by that time be well up the river. Having done this the Otter would return to Darwin, there to await Biggles's return.

Biggles said this plan did not entirely please him, but as he couldn't be in two places at once he could think of no alternative. His decision rested on the conviction that they couldn't go on tearing about the continent at the risk, should anything go wrong, of upsetting the Australian government, to say nothing of the government at home.

In pursuance of this plan it was agreed that they should have a meal at the airport and sleep in the machines. Biggles would have a word with West to see if he had any fresh news. In view of the attempt to burn the machines on the previous occasion when they had slept on the airfield it would be necessary to maintain an all-night guard, and the details of this disagreeable duty were arranged, it falling to Ginger's lot to take first watch.

'I don't like leaving the machines unattended even in daylight, so I think Ginger it would be best if you went and had your meal now,' said Biggles. 'We'll go when you come back.'

'Fair enough,' assented Ginger, and set off forthwith. It was still broad daylight although the sun was well on its way down to the horizon. There might be, he thought, three-quarters of an hour of daylight left.

With no other thought in his head than to get a meal as quickly as possible he strode in to the tea-room, which, he found, while not full was fairly well patronized. Some of the airport staff were there, a few air crews, and one or two civilians who he supposed were waiting for the Quantas liner due in shortly from Singapore. His eyes ran over them as he pulled out a chair to sit down, more from habit than any expectation of seeing a person he knew.

Suddenly he stopped dead. Then he pushed the chair back into place, turned about and left the room. For a little way, in order not to attract attention to himself, he walked on; but as soon as he was clear of the building he ran. The others must have seen him coming, for by the time he reached the Otter, in the cabin of which he had left them, Biggles had opened the door and stood waiting.

'What's wrong?' asked Biggles quickly.

'Von Stalhein's in the tea-room,' answered Ginger breathlessly – the breathlessness not being entirely due to exertion.

Biggles looked incredulous. Not for a long time had Ginger seen him so taken aback. But he recovered quickly. 'Is he alone?' he asked, jumping down.

'I think so. He was sitting alone at a table. I didn't stop to check up.'

'Doing what?'

'Looking out of the window as if he was expecting somebody. There were tea things on the table.'

'Did he see you?'

'No – but I wouldn't swear to it. I turned my back as soon as I saw him. I wasn't expecting—'

'Neither was I,' cut in Biggles shortly.

'Well, blow me down!' exclaimed Bertie from the door. 'That blighter is a fair corker. How the deuce did he—'

'Just a minute – let me think,' interposed Biggles curtly. 'This is what comes from taking things for granted. Either the *Matilda* didn't go up the river but came to Darwin instead, or else von Stalhein was put ashore at Wyndham and came up on the regular service. The plane came in from the south while we were sitting here talking.'

'The lugger was heading for the mouth of the Daly when I last saw it,' declared Algy. 'Bertie will confirm that.'

'It could have had its course changed by wireless.'

'But why should von Stalhein come here?'

'For the reason most people go to an airport, I imagine,' answered Biggles drily. 'To catch a plane. You realize that this has knocked my plan sideways. No matter. Let's get things in line. Von Stalhein can't know we're here or he'd hardly be sitting in a public room. We were already here when the plane from the south landed, so if he was on it it's unlikely he'd notice our machines. Or put it the other way round. Had he been here when we landed he would have seen us, and kept out of sight. Not that it matters how he got here. He's here. The question is, where's he going?'

'If he's booked an air passage we can soon answer that,' asserted. Algy.

'I think we'd better have a look at this,' decided Biggles.

'Suppose he sees us?' questioned Ginger.

'I don't see that it matters much. We shan't learn anything by standing here. We must watch what he does. If he sees us – well, maybe that will shake him as much as his arrival here has shaken me. Come on. No – somebody had better stay here to keep an eye on the machines. Bertie, you stay. You may see something from here.'

'Look!' cried Ginger. 'Is that what he's waiting for?' He pointed to the sky.

Gliding in quietly from the south, apparently preparing to land, was an Auster.

'That's it. That's the answer,' replied Biggles crisply. 'Smith's in a hurry to see him. The lugger would be some time chugging up the river against the current. Now listen carefully, everybody,' he went on. 'If that machine collects von Stalhein and takes off again tonight we shall lose track of him. We must stop it somehow. There's only half an hour of daylight left and I doubt if the pilot would risk a night landing on a jungle airstrip – if he's going to Daly Flats. Algy, hurry to the control room and ask West, on any pretext he can think of, to keep that Auster grounded for a quarter of an hour; then join Bertie in the Otter. Bertie, stand by to start up. If the Auster *should* leave the ground, follow it, even if it means a night landing when you get back here. Ginger, you come with me. With luck we may get a glimpse of mister mysterious Smith.'

By the time they had reached the booking hall the Auster was on the ground, taxiing on to the tarmac which, as it happened, was clear of machines. It stopped, but the engine remained ticking over. A man stepped down and waited, looking towards the booking hall. The pilot remained in his seat.

'Do you think that's Smith, waiting by the machine?' asked Ginger.

'No. He looks more like one of these cold-blooded, flat-faced bodyguards, we've seen von Stalhein with before – an Iron-Curtainmonger if ever I saw one. He's here for Erich; we needn't doubt that. Where is he?'

'I saw him in here,' answered Ginger, making a beeline for the tea-room.

As they went to open the door von Stalhein came out, so that they met face to face. If he was surprised to see them he did not show it. The only sign of recognition he gave was a curt nod in passing.

'You're in a great hurry,' bantered Biggles, turning to follow.

On seeing Biggles almost beside him von Stalhein turned impatiently. 'What do you want,' he demanded stiffly.

'Nothing – nothing,' answered Biggles lightly. 'I just wondered who your dour-looking pal was.'

'You don't expect me to tell you?'

'Of course not.' They were still walking towards the Auster.

'I suppose I have to thank that photograph for bringing you here,' muttered von Stalhein savagely.

'Quite right. Naturally, I was interested to see that you were still at the old game. Don't you get tired of playing on the losing side?'

'The game isn't finished yet.'

'Yours is, as far as Australia is concerned.'

Von Stalhein glanced along the hangars as the Halifax's engines started up. 'That, I presume, is Lacey, as busy as ever,' he sneered, as, reaching the Auster, he stopped.

'Of course.'

'Where's he going.'

'I don't know. That depends on where you go.'

Von Stalhein frowned, understanding dawning in his eyes. 'So he's going to follow me.'

'That's the idea. You can't blame us for taking an interest in your movements.'

Von Stalhein hesitated. Ginger could imagine him working out

'You're in a great hurry,' bantered Biggles.

the comparative speeds of the two machines. Actually, there was not much between them.

At this juncture the pilot, a young, good-looking fellow, looked out and stepped into the conversation. 'If you want to get home tonight you'd better get in,' he said, looking a little worried. 'We haven't too much time as it is,' he added.

Biggles gave him a quick, appraising glance, as did Ginger, who felt that this was not the sort of remark likely to be made by a member of the gang. Biggles apparently thought this, too, for in a different tone of voice he said: 'You can't go yet.'

'Why not?'

'Look at the control tower.'

The pilot frowned. 'But they gave me the okay a minute ago.'

'Looks as if they've withdrawn it. There's a Constellation about due in from Singapore.'

'Take no notice,' ordered von Stalhein harshly, moving towards the cabin. 'We must go.'

Biggles addressed the pilot. 'Your name's Cozens, isn't it?'

'Yes.'

'Australian?'

'Yes.'

'Full ticket for commercial flying?'

'Yes.'

'How long have you had it?'

'Three months.'

'How long did it take you to get it?'

'Three years.'

'You ignore control tower signals and you'll lose it in three days,' Biggles told the pilot seriously.

Von Stalhein's escort, who, with a hand in a side pocket, had been listening to this conversation with sullen and ill-concealed impatience, broke in, nodding towards Biggles: 'Who vas he?'

Answered von Stalhein: 'The man I told you about – Bigglesworth.'

'So.'

'So what,' murmured Ginger, well satisfied with the way Biggles's plan for keeping the machine on the ground was working out.

Von Stalhein moved as if to get into the machine.

'I'm sorry, but I daren't leave the ground without an all clear signal,' said Cozens, now looking really worried. After all, he was young, and this may have been his first appointment.

'Wise man,' complimented Biggles. 'It'll be dark in a few minutes, anyway. By the way, I suppose you know the sort of people you're working for?'

'I'm beginning to wonder,' rejoined the pilot, looking hard at Biggles.

'Watch your step,' advised Biggles.

'Who are you?'

Biggles smiled faintly and indicated von Stalhein. 'Ask him – he knows.' He glanced at the northern sky. 'But here comes the Constellation, so I'll leave you to it. So long.' Turning, he walked away.

After a glance at von Stalhein's face, pale with anger, Ginger followed.

'That worked out all right,' said Biggles, as they made for the machines. 'I don't think the Auster will leave tonight.'

'We've shown rather a lot of our hand, haven't we,' asked Ginger anxiously.

'I don't think we've done any harm. Anyhow, there was no other way of keeping them here. I've gained what I wanted – time.'

When they reached the machines Algy and Bertie were there. Algy was smiling. 'West played up. I was sorry I couldn't see von Stalhein's face when the Auster was refused permission to leave.'

Biggles told them what had happened. 'Now look, this is the drill,' he went on. 'Things are about due for a showdown, or they will be if I have my way. I'm going to Sydney in the Halifax, alone, right away. It's close on a two thousand mile run so you needn't expect me back until tomorrow afternoon, however fast I move. If the Auster does take off tonight after all – and West can't hold it indefinitely – there's nothing you can do about it. If it goes in the morning, follow it till it lands, pinpoint the spot, then come back here and wait for me. The place, which I take to be Daly Flats, can't be any great distance away, because working on the daylight factor the Auster could have got there in half an hour or so.'

'Is there any likelihood of the Auster *not* going in the morning?' queried Ginger.

'If this fellow Cozens is the right type, and I think he is, von Stalhein and his frosty-faced pal may find themselves grounded. I don't know. We shall see. Keep your eyes skinned for trouble, because knowing you'll follow him, von Stalhein may well try to keep *you* grounded. For the rest, should any unforeseen situation arise you'll have to act on your own discretion. That's all. As soon as the Constellation has cleared I'll press on to Sydney.'

CHAPTER XII

Disturbing News

Night, fine and warm, with a moon nearly full and a sky spangled with stars, settled silently over the airport. The beacon held aloft its guiding light. Yellow rays lanced the tarmac from windows of buildings where the duty night-staff worked. Strange aromas, the artificial ones familiar, others strange and sometimes exotic, wafted from time to time to Ginger's nostrils as he squatted on the ground, his back to an undercarriage wheel, watching the scene on first guard.

The Halifax and the Constellation had gone, southward bound. The Auster was no longer in sight. For some time, until darkness dimmed the picture, Cozens and his two passengers had stood by it talking, or, as it seemed to those watching, engaged in argument; possibly, it was thought, discussing the hazards of finding and making a night landing on an unofficial airstrip. At the end Cozens had taxied his machine into a hangar and they had all gone off together. Where they had gone was not known. There had been some talk of shadowing them, but it had not been pursued as there seemed no serious reason for this and Algy preferred to keep his party together. The men, it was agreed, would have to return to the airfield sooner or later to get the machine. In short, it was assumed, naturally, that von Stalhein and his associates had gone to look for a bed for the night and would return in the morning. This may have been von Stalhein's intention, but in the event it did not materialize.

About half-past nine Ginger's eyes and muscles were alerted by the silhouette of a man walking quickly from the tarmac towards the Otter. As there was nothing furtive about the approach Ginger's first thought was that it might be West, with news – possibly a radio message from the Halifax. But taking no chances he got up, rapped on the hull – the prearranged warning signal – and awaited the arrival of the visitor.

It turned out to be Cozens, the pilot.

Ginger was astonished, not so much that Cozens should call on them as that he should be allowed to do so; for he could not imagine von Stalhein giving his approval to anything of the sort. It turned out that he had not done so.

'Hello,' greeted Cozens.

'Hello yourself,' answered Ginger. 'You're the last man I expected to see. What can I do for you?'

'You can tell me what your friend meant by that remark of his about watching my step. It's got me worried. This is my first job and I don't want to put a blot on my logbook.'

Algy jumped down. 'Do your people know you've come here?'

'No.'

'So I imagine,' said Algy in a queer voice.

'We had a meal. Then I made the excuse of going to make sure that I'd left everything in the machine all right. I had a feeling they didn't want me to talk to you.'

'How right you were,' murmured Algy.

'They were pretty sore when I refused to ignore the control tower.'

'I can believe that. As a matter of interest where did they want you to go?'

Cozens hesitated. 'Sorry, but when I was offered this job I gave an undertaking to keep my mouth shut.'

'Didn't that strike you as an odd demand?'

'Yes, but beggars can't be choosers. I had nothing to talk about, anyway.'

'Well, I won't press you to go back on that if that's how you feel, even though I realize you don't know what sort of a crowd you've got mixed up with; but I'll do a deal with you. If I tell you, in strict confidence, why you'd be well-advised to watch your step, will you answer a question for me?'

'That's fair enough.'

'Very well. Hold your hat. You're working for an enemy spy outfit.'

Cozens's face was a picture. 'Did you say *spy* outfit?' His voice cracked with incredulity.

'I did. The real stuff, too. The sort you read about in red-hot thrillers. Cloak and dagger work, with all the trimmings – cyanide pistols, gas guns and what have you.'

Cozens clapped a hand to his head. 'I must have been blind,' he muttered. 'This explains a lot of things.'

'Such as landing on Eighty Mile Beach to burn a boat,' suggested Algy.

'You know about *that*?'

'Of course. By the way, did you fly a black in to Darwin recently?'

'I did. I wondered what that was for. I don't mind telling you I didn't think much of it.'

'Neither did we. It may interest you to know that his job was to set fire to this machine.'

Cozen's jaw sagged foolishly. 'Who – who are you,' he stammered.

'British Security Police.'

For a moment Cozens was speechless. Then he blurted: 'Stop! I'm in a spin.'

'Nothing to the spin you'll be in, old boy, if your pals learn that you've been nattering with us,' put in Bertie.

'Are you trying to put the wind up me?'

Algy answered, 'No. Just trying to give you an idea of what may happen to you when your employers no longer have any need of your services.'

'They wouldn't dare to touch me! I'm an Australian.'

Algy smiled sadly. 'Listen, chum,' he said. 'It wouldn't matter if you were King of Australia. When these stiffs have finished with you they'll brush you off like this.' He squashed a mosquito that had landed on the back of his hand.

'They're not likely to do that just yet,' stated Cozens confidently.

'Why not?'

'Because that'd leave 'em with an aircraft and no one to fly it; and they're in a hurry to get home.'

'Where's home?'

Again Cozens hesitated.

'Daly Flats?' suggested Algy.

Cozens started. 'Why ask me if you know?'

'We know quite a lot but you could probably fill in some gaps. I advise you to do that, because when this story breaks in the papers your name's going to appear under some ugly headlines.'

'Okay,' agreed Cozens soberly. 'I'll tell you what I know. Then what do I do?'

'That's a ticklish question. It's up to you. Frankly, I think you'd better carry on as you are for the time being and pick up all the information you can. We'll clear you if you get caught in the net when your police get busy. But we're wasting time. Tell us what you know. How long have you been working for this gang?'

'Just on a month.'

'What on earth made them employ an Australian pilot – that's what beats me.'

'They had another – a foreigner – but he killed himself trying to get into one of these outback landing fields that was too small. I gather they had some urgent business on and had to get a replacement on the spot.'

'They'll replace you, I'll warrant, as soon as another arrives from the Iron Curtain,' declared Algy grimly. 'What have you been doing? Make it snappy. You'd better not stay here too long.'

'I've done a lot of flying,' volunteered Cozens. 'Pretty sticky, some of it, too, landing in out of the way places. Headquarters in the Territory is at Daly Flats. As a result of a radio signal the boss sent me here to pick up a man I didn't know, but who knew I was coming. The other chap came with me to point him out to me – at least, that's what I was told. I'm flying them both to Daly Flats in the morning.'

'Who do you call the boss.'

'He goes by the name of Smith. Actually, he's a foreigner, probably a Russian. Anyhow, he talks a lot to Ivan in a language I don't understand, and Ivan's certainly a Russian. He's the fellow with me now. I didn't see anything strange in that because there are plenty of Russians in Australia. Most of 'em are all right.'

'Tell me more about Daly Flats.'

'It was originally a peanut farm. The man who started it was speared by aborigines – they told me that. I believe Smith bought it cheap and cleared a strip so that he could keep in touch with the outside world by air. He certainly does that. The place is miles from anywhere, and the only other way he could get to and fro would be by river, about two miles away. He's got a lugger for dealing with heavy stuff. Oh yes, everything's laid on, radio and so on. Smith has quite an office there. He employs black labour. I don't know how he manages that because they can be a bad lot. An uncle of mine served in the North-West Mounted, and he told me all about 'em. But somehow Smith keeps in with 'em. Plenty of weapons there in case of trouble.'

'He has other places, I believe.'

'Several. That's true, because I've been to some of them.'

'Tarracooma, for instance.'

'That's right. I was there the other day. Took up a chap from Perth to fix the wireless. Smith says that as a modern pioneer he must keep in touch with his estates. It's the only way in the outback.'

'Would you like to make a sketch map for me showing just where this place, Daly Flats, is? It can only be a question of days before the place is raided and that may save us trouble.'

'Certainly.'

'Then let's go inside. I've pencil and paper there.'

'I shall have to be quick. As it is they may be wondering what I'm doing.'

'You've left it too late,' put in Ginger. 'Here they come now. Fasten your safety belts; we're in for a spot of bumpy weather if I know anything.'

There was no mistaking the two figures, one burly and the other slim and limping slightly, coming towards the machines.

'Cozens, me lad, I'm afraid you're going to find this a bit difficult – if you know what I mean,' observed Bertie.

'Difficult! Why? I'm still doing my job. They can't expect me never to speak to anyone.'

'Can't they, by Jove!' answered Bertie warmly. 'You don't know these blighters.'

'If they start chucking their weight about they'll find I can chuck mine,' declared Cozens.

'You still don't seem to understand that you're dealing with people to whom murder is all part of the day's work,' Algy told him impatiently. 'Get that into your head and never forget it.'

There was no time for more, as the two men were almost upon them.

Von Stalhein spoke first. His voice, as cold and brittle as steel, was an indication of his anger, although he did not show it on his face. 'So here you are, Cozens. You said you were going to look at the machine.'

'So I am. There's plenty of time, isn't there,' retorted the pilot.

'You should have told me where you were going.'

Cozens flared up. 'I like that! Are you telling me who I'm allowed to speak to?'

'While you're in my employ you'll do what you're told. I want to talk to you. Come on.'

Cozens looked at von Stalhein. He looked at Algy. Clearly, he was in a quandary. For some seconds there was an uncomfortable silence. Then Algy said: 'As presumably they are paying your wages you'd better go with them. We all have to take orders – don't we, von Stalhein?'

Von Stalhein didn't answer. What had upset him, and what he wanted to know, Ginger imagined, was how much Cozens had said. Certainly he had no intention of letting him say any more.

'I suppose you're right,' muttered Cozens, answering Algy. 'But this being pushed around as if I was a lackey gets my goat. Be seeing you some time.' He strode away.

Without another word von Stalhein and his companion followed him.

Algy watched them all go. 'What worries me is, Cozens still hasn't grasped the fact that his life is in danger. My only consolation is they're not likely to do anything tonight as they need him to fly them home.'

'We shouldn't have let him go,' asserted Ginger. 'They'll see that he does no more talking, and as soon as they've finished with him he'll disappear.'

'We were in no position to stop him,' averred Algy. 'We set his clock right. The decision was up to him. I know I advised him to go but that was in his own interest. Had he refused, von Stalhein would have known that we'd put him wise, in which case, as he knows too much about them, they certainly would have liquidated him. As it is, von Stalhein has no idea of what was said here so he may hold his hand.'

'Don't you think one of us ought to follow them,' suggested Ginger.

'I don't think that's necessary. They're bound to stay here till daylight now. We'd do better to get some sleep while we can. I have a feeling that things are going to boil over presently.'

Ginger resumed his guard. At midnight, when Algy took over, all was quiet; and so it was when at four o'clock Bertie came on for the dawn watch. Bertie gave the others until six-thirty and then made tea. By the time they had finished a cold breakfast it was broad daylight; but there was still no sign of the Auster's pilot and passengers. The machine remained in its hangar.

'I'd have thought they would have been on the move by now,' said Algy, looking puzzled. 'I can't think what could have happened. I hope they haven't pulled a fast one on us.'

'I don't see how they could, old boy,' opined Bertie. 'The Auster is still in its shed.'

Eight o'clock came. There was still no sign. Ginger walked over to the hangar and returned to report that the Auster was still there.

By nine o'clock Algy was really worried. 'Something's happened. Von Stalhein has given us the slip,' he asserted. 'And I'll tell you why,' he went on. 'He knew that if he used the Auster we'd trail it to its hide-out.'

'The blighter couldn't walk home,' averred Bertie, polishing his eyeglass.

'A horrible thought has just occurred to me,' said Algy, in an inspired tone of voice. 'There's one way he could have got home without walking – or flying. If the *Matilda* brought von Stalhein here, and Biggles considered that possibility, they could have gone off in the lugger. Cozens told us that Daly Flats could be reached by the river.'

'If that's the answer we can say good-bye to Cozens,' asserted Ginger. 'They wouldn't leave him here to come back and talk to us. They'd see him dead first. And if they took him with them it would come to the same thing. They'd never trust him again after what happened last night, and if they didn't need his serv-ices to get home they'd have no further use for him. They could get another pilot to collect the Auster when it suited them.'

'Here, I say, that's a grim thought,' said Bertie. 'How far away is this beastly river?'

'The mouth is a hundred miles south-west of here,' answered Algy. 'I don't know the speed of the lugger and I don't know how far it is up the river to Daly Flats, but if they left here immediately after the row last night, and that's twelve hours ago, they could be on the river by now. Don't forget radio. Von Stalhein might have told Smith what happened here last night and he could have given orders that they were to leave the Auster and come home by the river.'

'The next thing we shall hear is that Cozens's body has been found,' remarked Ginger gloomily. 'We shouldn't have let him go.'

'It's no use talking about that now,' returned Algy. 'Let's do something. The first thing is to confirm what we suspect. Ginger, slip over to the office, ring the harbour master and ask him if the *Matilda* was in last night.'

Ginger hurried off. He was away for twenty minutes and returned at the double. 'You were right,' he reported briefly. 'The *Matilda* came in. It left again just after ten last night.'

'In that case I'd say poor Cozens has had it,' predicted Bertie, lugubriously.

'He isn't in the town,' stated Ginger.

'How do you know that?' asked Algy quickly.

'Because a general order has gone out from Sydney grounding the Auster pending a check on its Certificate of Airworthiness. West had gone off, but the duty officer told me they'd rung up every hotel in the town, looking for Cozens, to warn him that he couldn't leave until lunchtime at the earliest. Biggles must have been responsible for that order. No doubt it struck him as a bright idea to gain time. He wasn't to know that the enemy also had a bright idea, which was to abandon the machine, go home by water, and so give us the slip.'

'If the order was issued by Sydney, the Security man Biggles went to see must have had something to do with it,' averred Algy. 'And his idea, I fancy, was to deprive Smith of his private transport until other orders could be put into effect. It certainly wasn't a coincidence that the Auster had been grounded. Unfortunately it doesn't help us, and it doesn't help Cozens. Incidentally, the order might have been issued to keep him here until Security officers arrived to question him. If that was the scheme it's misfired. He's gone.'

'And gone for good, if I know anything,' murmured Bertie.

Algy paced up and down. 'This is awful. What are we going to do about it?'

'There's a chance that Cozens may not be dead yet. At least, no one has yet reported finding the body, or we'd have heard of it,' remarked Ginger hopefully.

'If he isn't dead he jolly soon will be,' declared Algy. 'Smith won't be the type to keep a man who's no more use to him. Cozens knows too much for them to let him go.'

'How about waffling to Daly Flats and giving it a crack – if you see what I mean,' suggested Bertie.

'Biggles said we were to be here when he got back,' Algy pointed out. 'If we go to Daly Flats, and he gets here before we're back, he'll be completely in the dark as to what's happened.'

'He also said that if a situation arose we were to act on our own initiative,' reminded Ginger.

'You seem to be forgetting that we don't know where this place Daly Flats is!' exclaimed Algy. 'That's my fault, and I ought to be kicked,' he went on savagely. 'Instead of doing so much talking last night when Cozens was here I should have got him to give us the gen right away. He was just going to do it when von Stalhein rolled up. But there, it's easy to be wise after the event. How was I to know that he'd have the brass face to come here?'

'That was a bit of a corker, I must say,' conceded Bertie. 'It's going to be a ghastly bind sitting here all day doing nothing. Biggles won't be back here for hours. We shall have to do something about Cozens.'

'Of course we shall have to do something,' cried Algy desperately. 'Even supposing he's still alive, which I doubt, he'll be on that lugger. How are we going to get hold of him? Luggers don't have landing decks!'

'We don't know for certain where the lugger is, if it comes to that,' contended Ginger. 'For a start we could run down to the Daly to confirm that the *Matilda*'s on her way up.'

'And then what?' requested Algy.

'It'd let the blighters know we're wise to their dirty game,' urged Bertie. 'If we saw Cozens on deck, still alive, that'd be a load off our minds – if you get what I'm driving at.'

'I don't,' rejoined Algy bluntly. 'What I do see is, if that happened, they'd probably knock him on the head and throw him to the crocodiles. I don't want to be responsible for the man's death.'

'We're already responsible for the position he's in, if it comes to that,' argued Ginger critically. 'The one thing that's quite certain is, we shan't save him by standing here yammering about it.'

Algy made up his mind suddenly. 'All right,' he said. 'Let's locate the lugger. Ginger, slip over to the control room and leave word for Biggles about what we're doing in case he gets here before we're back.' Ginger went off at a run.

CHAPTER XIII

Desperate Measures

The Otter was soon in the air, heading south-west for the river which, while of no great size as continental rivers go, has a notorious record of death and disaster out of proportion with its length. The ferocity of its native population, its crocodiles and mosquitoes and its sudden spates, combined for years to discourage visitors.

Algy, at the controls, struck the Daly at its broad mouth, where the muddy water meets the sea between slimy banks sometimes fringed with mangroves; for as he had said, they knew neither the speed of the current against which the lugger would have to force a passage, or of the vessel itself. Anyway, seeing nothing of a ship that looked like the lugger on the sea or in the estuary he turned inland.

For ten miles or so there was no break in the flat, reedy shore, often skirted by mudbanks on which crocodiles in startling numbers lay sunning themselves; but thereafter the river began to narrow, winding sometimes between steep, densely-wooded banks. An occasional wisp of smoke revealed the position of a native village or peanut farm. Waterfowl, white herons, pink cranes, black and white jabiru, geese and ducks, stood in the shallows or flighted up and down in clouds of hundreds.

For another twenty minutes, flying low, the Otter droned on at cruising speed. Then Ginger, who was watching ahead, cried: 'There she is. At all events that looks like her. I'm afraid they'll have heard us.'

'Not necessarily,' answered Algy. 'They themselves will be making a certain amount of noise. I can't see that it matters much if they do spot us. Well, that settles that question. The *Matilda* is on her way up the river. Now what do we do?'

'Go nearer to see if there's any sign of Cozens.'

'Okay.'

'You'll have to buck up. The river narrows.'

Algy cut the engines. 'I'll glide in low. There's a chance we may catch 'em unawares. If Cozens is there it should encourage him to know we're keeping an eye on things.'

The Otter, nose down, glided on at little more than stalling speed but fast overhauling the lugger.

'There are several people on deck,' observed Ginger. 'I don't think they've seen us yet. They're looking ahead. That black-bearded ruffian of a skipper is at the wheel. Von Stalhein is with him. Quite a bunch of natives aft. By gosh! I believe I can see Cozens! Isn't that him sitting on a coil of rope, or something, amidships. Behind the mainmast – with his chin in his hands.'

'I think you're right,' said Algy tersely. 'Yes, that's him. And he's seen us, from the way he jumped up.'

'The natives have seen us, too. They're running forward to tell the skipper.'

All faces on deck were now turned upwards, looking at the aircraft, which was still overtaking from about two hundred yards astern and fast losing height.

'If you go any nearer they'll start shooting at us,' warned Ginger.

Said Bertie, from behind: 'If the dirty dogs start that I've a few things ready to unload on 'em, yes, by Jove!'

'It seems a pity, but I'm afraid we've done all we can do,' said Algy helplessly. 'Case of so near and yet so far.'

No one, either on the ship or in the aircraft, could have been prepared for what happened a moment later. That Cozens himself might do something was a thought that certainly did not enter Ginger's head, for on the face of it he was as helpless as were those in the Otter. Apparently he did not think so. What he did was jump to the rail and dive overboard.

Ginger, remembering the crocodiles, let out a cry of horror.

For a few seconds, Algy, utterly unprepared for such a move, stared unbelievingly; but when Boller raced to the stern of his ship and opened fire with a revolver, blazing shot after shot at the head bobbing in the water, he acted quickly.

What none of those in the aircraft had realized until this moment, although Cozens may have taken it into account, was the speed of the current. Before the *Matilda* had started to turn, the swimmer was forty yards astern, with the gap widening rapidly. Others had joined Boller in the stern and bullets were ripping up feathers of water round Cozens's head; but so far apparently none had touched him, for he continued driving on with a powerful overarm stroke. There was really nothing surprising about this, for to hit a moving target the size of a man's head, at long range, with a revolver, would need all the skill of a superlative marksman.

Another factor that Cozens may have considered when he played his desperate stroke was the position of the *Matilda*. The ship, naturally enough, was ploughing its way up the middle of the stream. This meant, as now became evident, that it had the choice of stopping and then going astern, or edging nearer to one of the banks in order to give itself enough room to do a complete turn about at full speed ahead. When Boller had rushed aft the wheel had been taken over by another man, who seemed to be in some doubt as to which course to take. Then, when he did make up his mind and started to turn he found he had insufficient room, and there was some confusion before he succeeded.

All this had occurred in a matter of only two or three minutes, but in that time others had been busy. Cozens still swimming strongly and striking out diagonally for the nearest bank, was now a good two hundred yards away from the lugger, while Algy, after slamming on full throttle and shoving his nose down for speed, had turned on a wing tip, as indeed was necessary if he was not to hit the trees lining the bank – which in fact he nearly did, missing a tall palm by so narrow a margin that Ginger clapped his hands over his face.

The issue was still in doubt, for in order to pick up the fugitive the trickiest part of the flying was yet to come; and there was no time to be lost, for the current that had given Cozens his early advantage was now on the side of the lugger, and it could be only a matter of minutes before the swimmer was overhauled.

Algy did not commit the folly of trying to land downstream on fast flowing water for reasons which need hardly be explained. Apart from anything else, from his position he would have been bound to overshoot his objective by a wide margin, and he would then have been carried on for some distance before he could get round. He took the only practicable course, which was to tear down the river for half a mile, do another vertical turn, and coming back, land in line with the swimmer in order to catch him as he was swept down by the stream. It would, of course, have been impossible for Cozens, no matter how strong a swimmer he might be, to swim against the current.

Algy carried out the first part of the manoeuvre like the experienced pilot he was; but the next step was complicated by the fact that between the machine and the swimmer was a mudbank. As there was no time for the Otter to get down above it before Cozens reached it, all Algy could do was land below it, and keeping his nose into the stream, engines running, wait for Cozens to come down to him. So far so good. The position now was the Otter fifty yards below the mudbank, nosing into the fierce current at half throttle, rocking and throwing up a bow-wave, the spray of which, splashing on the windscreen, made it none too easy for those behind it to see what was happening in front. Cozens, coming down fast, was near the upper end of the mudbank and striking out to clear it – Algy, of course, keeping lined up with him. A quarter of a mile away was the *Matilda*, travelling at alarming speed. Ginger prayed fervently that it might run aground on the mud, but Boller must have seen it, too, for in the event this did not happen.

At this stage it struck Ginger that Cozens was doing a lot of unnecessary splashing, considering that all he had to do was float; then, with a strangled gasp of horror he saw the reason. What he had taken to be a pile of dead trees on the mudbank were moving, and he realized they were crocodiles – one of them a grey-green brute nearly twenty feet long. No wonder Cozens was splashing, kicking out again towards the middle of the stream, for any attempt now to reach the river bank must have landed him on the mud amongst the beasts he was striving so desperately to avoid.

Algy, trying to keep in line, was nearly swept down the stream broadside on, but by cutting one engine he managed to straighten out.

Ginger, yelling to Bertie to stand by at the cabin door with a line in case Cozens just missed them, watched in a fever of excitement the swimmer's head bearing down on them, expecting every instant to see it disappear as he was dragged under by the beasts in the water.

Forty yards – twenty – ten…. Gasping, Cozens caught the Otter by the bows and hung on, trying to pull himself up. The effort proved beyond him.

'This side,' yelled Ginger, making frantic signals.

Cozens let go, clutching at the smooth hull to check his speed. Leaning out, Bertie grabbed him, first by the hair, then under the arms. A heave and a crash and they were both inside, flat on the floor.

Algy waited for no more, but at once started to turn, for the *Matilda* was now so close that he couldn't have got off upstream without colliding with it. Nor, for that matter, could he take off downstream on such a current without risking disaster at a sharp bend a little lower down. But once round he had the legs of the ship, and those on board must have realized it, for the chatter of a machine gun now added to the general frenzy. One or two bullets hit the Otter. Where, Ginger did not know. Like Algy, he was only concerned with getting clear.

The next minute was to live in his mind for ever. He had, in his time, seen some crazy flying; but none like this. As the Otter tore down the river it seemed certain that they would hit something, if not a log or a crocodile then one of the birds which, disturbed by the noise of the engines and machine-gun fire, rose in multitudes from both banks. If the aircraft did not collide with one of them, he thought, it would be due more to the birds than to Algy, who simply had to take his luck. An aeroplane can't dodge birds when they are all around it.

Not until the Otter had secured a lead of a mile did Algy turn into the stream and take off. Airborne, he sideslipped away from a stream of bullets that came up from the lugger, and then pulled up out of range.

'We've done it!' cried Ginger in a thin voice, relaxing in his seat.

Algy, pale of face, smiled wanly. 'I can't believe it,' he said weakly.

'Where now?'

'Back to Darwin. Better go and see if Cozens is all right.'

Ginger went through the bulkhead door to the cabin to find Cozens sitting in a pool of water taking a tot of brandy that Bertie had given him from the medicine cabinet. He looked as if he needed it.

'Are you raving mad, jumping into a river full of crocodiles?' asked Ginger.

'Rather that than stay on a ship manned by a gang of cold-blooded murderers,' rasped Cozens viciously.

'Oh, so you discovered that, did you?'

'Yes; but don't you worry, pal; I'll get even with 'em if it's the last thing I do. Pushing me around in my own country with a gun poking in my ribs.' Cozens's chief emotion seemed to be anger.

'You can tell us about it presently,' said Ginger. 'We're making for Darwin.'

He returned to the cockpit. 'He's all right,' he told Algy. 'But he seems properly steamed up. On the boil, in fact.'

'He's lucky he isn't stone cold,' answered Algy, briefly.

Half an hour later, at the airport, Cozens, in borrowed clothes – for his own were of course soaking wet – was telling his story to three attentive listeners. Not that there was much to tell. It appeared that the previous night, as he walked away with von Stalhein and Ivan, even before he had reached the airfield boundary a pistol had been pushed into his back. Finding that protests were useless, and perceiving that his life was hanging on a thread, he had been forced to go to the harbour and board the *Matilda*, which had at once set sail. The reason why he had not been killed out of hand, he said, was because he had refused to divulge what he had told Algy, and what Algy had told him. This information had been radioed to Smith at Daly Flats. Smith had given orders for him to be taken there so that he could be questioned. He had been told by Boller that Smith would find means to make him speak. 'They must have been mighty anxious to know what had passed between us,' he concluded. 'As you can imagine, I was feeling pretty sick when you blew along in this kite, and as it was obvious that I was to be bumped off anyway it seemed I had nothing to lose by going overboard. I'm a pretty good swimmer, but I don't mind admitting now, in the excitement of seeing you, and in my haste to get off that lugger, for the moment I clean forgot about the crocs. I remembered them all right when I saw them sliding off that mudbank. Not that it would have made any difference. I'd have gone overboard anyway, if only because those swine were sure I wouldn't. We'd seen crocs on the way up. They'd been pointed out to me. The estuary was swarming with the brutes. Bah! Forget it. Thanks for picking me up. I must say that spot of flying was pretty to watch.'

'It was hair-raising to be in,' alleged Ginger, smiling.

'What are you going to do now,' Algy asked Cozens.

'I'm going to Daly Flats, of course,' was the staggering reply.

Algy started. 'You're *what*?'

'Going to Daly Flats.'

'Are you out of your mind?'

'Certainly not. My kit's there. You don't think I'm going to leave that behind, do you? Besides, these crooks owe me a month's pay. They're not getting away with that, either.'

Algy looked at the others with an expression of startled despair on his face. 'Hark at him!' he said sadly. 'The Voice of Young Australia.' He turned to Cozens. 'We, having been to some trouble to snatch you out of the lions' den, now have the pleasure of watching you leap back into it. Pretty good. How do you reckon to get there?'

'In the Auster, of course.'

'You can't. It's grounded. Or it was when we took off this morning.'

'We'll see about that,' declared Cozens grimly. 'Grounded or not, I'm going. At the moment, with hardly anybody there, I've got a chance. When that mob on the lugger arrives I shall have lost it.'

'He's got something there, old boy,' chipped in Bertie. 'That goes for us, too. Now's the time. Now or never, as they say.'

Algy shook his head. 'This sounds like stark lunacy to me.' He looked at Cozens. 'What time do you reckon the *Matilda* will get to Daly Flats?'

'About three this afternoon, or soon after.'

'As quickly as that?'

'Yes.'

'And how long would it take you to get there in the Auster?'

'Half an hour – not more.'

Bertie looked at Algy. 'How about having a smack at it?'

'You mean, go with him?'

'Of course.'

'What about Biggles?'

'Someone can stay here with the Otter and tell him all about it. The Auster will take three easily, four if necessary.'

'Smith will probably go down to the river to meet the lugger,' put in Cozens. 'The house is some way from the river. Anyway, that's what I'm gambling on – finding the house empty.'

'How many people will be there, not counting Smith?'

'Not more than two or three. Smith's secretary, the cook and a couple of native houseboys who are OK.'

'How many on the lugger?'

'Boller, von Stalhein, Ivan, Boller's Malay bosun and eight or nine aborigines.'

'That would be something to take on,' agreed Algy. 'Pity Biggles isn't here. This seems to be as good a chance as we shall ever get of looking for that list of agents he's so keen to get hold of.'

'And don't forget Cozens knows exactly where the landing strip is,' interposed Ginger. 'He knows his way about the house. And last but not least, after what's happened, which by this time Smith will have been told about by radio, I imagine, the last thing they'll expect at Daly Flats is the Auster, with Cozens in it.'

'I think you're right,' agreed Algy. 'We'll go and have a look at the place. Ginger, slip over to the office with Cozens and find out what the position is with the Auster.'

'That's the stuff,' asserted Bertie. 'Smite while the jolly old iron's hot. That's me, every time.'

Ginger and Cozens went off.

They were not long away, and returned with the information

that the order had not yet been cancelled. The duty officer, who knew them through West, who was on night shift, was sympathetic, but could not give the Auster clearance. They could, however, take the machine off at their own risk as long as they were prepared to accept full responsibility, and take the consequences should Sydney make a fuss about it.

Actually, the only man likely to suffer through a breach of regulations was Cozens, whose licence had been issued in Australia, and could of course be withdrawn by the same authority. It did not take him long to make up his mind, for his blood, as he put it, was up. 'Let's get cracking,' he said.

Algy looked at his watch. The time was one o'clock. 'We have time for a bite of lunch and still be back by the time Biggles gets here,' he proposed. After thinking for a moment he went on: 'No, we can't all go. Someone will have to stay to tell him what's cooking in case he turns up sooner than expected. Cozens will have to go because he knows the way and has to collect his stuff. Which reminds me: Cozens, you might make that sketch map you spoke about, so that whoever is here will know just where we are.'

'That won't take a minute,' assented the Auster pilot.

'Now, who stays?' asked Algy, looking round.

'Let's toss for it,' suggested Ginger. 'Odd man stays.'

'Fair enough.'

They tossed. Algy lost.

'Tough luck, old boy,' sympathized Bertie.

Algy took a spare gun from the magazine and handed it to Cozens. 'You'd better put this in your pocket. I've a feeling you may need it.'

And he was right.

CHAPTER XIV

Good-bye to the Auster

In spite of Bertie's carefree attitude towards the projected raid on Daly Flats, Ginger knew that he was well aware of the dangerous nature of the undertaking. That was merely Bertie's way. Ginger himself had no delusions about it. Only Cozens, in spite of his recent experience, seemed genuinely unconcerned. Whether this was due to lack of imagination, or indignation at the treatment accorded him by what he termed 'a bunch of Reds', Ginger did not know. The fact remained, he was going to collect his kit with no more qualms than if it had been left in a Darwin hotel instead of at the headquarters of a dangerous organization that treated lives as mere pawns in its deadly ambition.

Cozen's purpose was to collect his kit and demand the wages due to him. Just that and no more. Ginger didn't know whether to laugh or be angry at this insistence on behaving as though his late employers were ordinary people. With the political angle, Cozens was not in the least concerned. Nor did he appear to be worried by the repercussions that would probably follow the exposure of the spy plot. In a word, with him the matter was a personal one.

The ostensible reason for Ginger and Bertie going with him was to keep him company and perhaps lend him their support – not that he asked for this. And such was the case up to a point. But their real purpose was, of course, to take what seemed to be a unique opportunity of finding out what was going on at Daly Flats, and possibly gather the evidence Biggles needed to close the affair by exposing the spy plot to the Australian authorities.

As a matter of fact it was not until they were on their way, with Cozens at the controls, that Ginger realized that in the pilot himself lay much of the information Biggles wanted. For instance, as a result of flying the so-called Smith about he knew the locations of several outback landing strips apart from Daly Flats and Tarracooma. He had not of course realized the purpose to which these had been put, or where to be put; being an honest man himself he had without question taken Smith's word for it that they were all part of his commercial enterprises. In view of the distances to be covered it sounded reasonable.

Ginger was already looking down, at country very different from what he had seen east of Broome. Here was the real tropical Australia, a dense tangle of trees and palms and towering grasses cut into jig-saw sections by meandering streams. Clearings were few and far between, for Cozens was not following the Daly. Knowing the ground he took a direct course.

After a pause Cozens went on: 'Come to think of it there may already be a spot of bother going on.'

'What gave you that idea?'

'When I told the traffic manager where I was going he said that if I saw anything of Johnny Bates I could tell him his wife was better. Seems she's been ill.'

'Who's Johnny Bates?'

'A police officer. I've never met him. Apparently a man tried to knife somebody the other day and then bolted into the bush. Bates went after him. Been gone a week or more. But that's nothing. When these Northern Territory cops take the trail they keep going till they get their man. Sometimes they're away for weeks – occasionally months – living hand to mouth. Takes some guts, knowing a spear can come at you out of every bush.'

'You're telling me,' murmured Ginger.

'That's the Fergusson ahead.' Cozens indicated a river. 'We haven't much farther to go.' He altered course slightly, and a few minutes later went on: 'That's the place, straight in front.'

Ginger regarded with curiosity the establishment about which he had heard so much in a few days. There was no mistaking it for it was the only one in sight, comprising a cluster of corrugated-iron-roofed buildings on one side of an area that had been cleared of bush. Originally intended for planting, this was obviously the landing ground.

His doubts as to the reception they were likely to receive returned. No plan had been made, for it was not possible to make one. As he understood it the procedure was for Cozens to land as if nothing unusual had happened, and go in to the house to collect his belongings. He would also demand his back pay, either from Smith, or if he were not there, from the clerk. He seemed quite confident that he would succeed in this, but how it would work out in practice was to Ginger a matter for uncomfortable speculation.

As Cozens began a long glide Bertie remarked, 'If Smith wanted a place off the map, by Jove, he certainly found it.'

'If by that you mean a place well away from white men, you're right,' answered Cozens. 'But don't fool yourself. There are plenty of aborigines down there. They know how to keep out of sight. You could walk about for days and never see one. People who have been into that labyrinth, and were lucky enough to get out, will all tell you that.'

Ginger remembered something. 'Didn't I once read something about an expedition going into Arnhem Land to look for a white woman who was supposed to have been captured by the aborigines – after a shipwreck on the coast, or something?'

'Quite right. The public demanded that something be done about it. An expedition was sent but it found nothing, as the old-timers prophesied. They heard whistles and saw smoke signals – that was all. When a native goes into hiding a white man's wasting his time looking for him.'

By this time the Auster was coming round for its approach run.

'Are you going straight down?' asked Ginger.

'Sure I am. No use fiddling about.'

'I can't see a bally soul,' said Bertie.

'The people in the house may not have heard us – but from the scrub plenty of eyes will be watching us.'

No more was said. Cozens made a neat landing, finishing his run near the house. 'Are you fellows coming with me?' he asked, as he switched off and prepared to get down.

'Of course,' answered Ginger. 'We can keep an eye on the machine from the house. There's not likely to be anyone here able to run off with it, anyway.'

They all got down.

'The door's open,' observed Cozens. 'They must have heard us by now. Queer there's nobody about. Smith will probably have gone to the river to meet the lugger.'

The word queer, Ginger thought, was the right one. Even allowing for the drone of the engine that had for some time filled their ears, the silence that hung over the place was unnatural. The air was heavy. The heat was sultry, with rank unhealthy smells. The whole atmosphere, he felt, as his eyes made a swift reconnaissance, was sombre with a foreboding of evil. A sensation crept over him as of waiting for a bomb to explode.

Even Cozens seemed to be aware of this, for he, too, looked around with a puzzled frown lining his forehead. 'There's something phoney about this,' he said. 'I don't like it.'

'What don't you like?' inquired Ginger.

'The absence of the aborigines. That's a bad sign. There were always some about whenever I've been here.'

'You think they've gone?'

'Not likely. They're watching us.'

'Here, have a heart, laddie,' protested Bertie. 'You're giving me the creeps.'

'Keep your eyes skinned,' warned Cozens.

Ginger pointed. 'Isn't that somebody lying on the ground over there, by that shed? Looks like a native.'

They walked towards the object. It was a native. He was lying flat. He was lying flat because he was dead.

'He was one of the houseboys,' said Cozens. 'I remember his face.'

'There's another over there,' said Bertie.

They didn't go to the second body, which was lying near some scrub. It was, Cozens averred, too near cover, and within easy spear-throw of it. 'Let's get to the house,' he said shortly.

Keeping close together they walked towards the door. At a

distance of a few yards Cozens stopped abruptly, staring at something on the ground, just inside.

The others stopped. They, too, stared at what he had seen.

It was a foot – or rather, a boot. A leather boot.

With slow deliberation Cozens took out his gun. Holding it at the ready he advanced. On the threshold he stopped again. They all stopped.

On the floor lay the dead body of a man. A white man. In uniform.

Cozens, pale as death himself, drew a deep breath. 'Bates,' he said. 'That's who it'll be, Bates.' Swiftly his eyes explored every corner that might conceal the murderer.

'How awful,' was all Ginger could say.

'He must have followed his man here.'

Bertie stooped beside the body of the dead policeman. 'Shot,' he announced. 'Shot in the head, from behind. Where's his gun?'

'They must have taken it.'

'We were just too late,' said Bertie. 'He can't have been dead for more than half an hour.'

'But surely the people in the house wouldn't have been so mad as to shoot a policeman,' opined Ginger.

'No. Bates was after his man. The man ran in here. Bates followed him. He was shot from behind. There might have been more than one man. When the shooting started the house boys bolted. Who killed them I can't imagine. It doesn't matter. We'd better get out of this. It may have stirred up a hornet's nest. Every aborigine on the place will be on the jump. We'll take Bates with us.'

'But what about the white people in the house,' asked Ginger, beginning to recover from the shock of their terrible discovery.

'They may have bolted. Let's see.'

It was soon ascertained that they hadn't bolted. They were dead, killed by spear thrusts; the clerk in his office, the cook in the kitchen and another houseboy in a passage. Everywhere things had been smashed, or lay about in disorder.

'They must still have been at it when they heard us coming,' said Cozens. 'What a shambles.'

'And only on the way here we said it was the sort of thing that might happen,' muttered Ginger. 'What do you suppose could have started them off?'

'Bates. He was after one of them. Come on. The sooner we get word of this to Darwin the better. Be ready to shoot fast. They'll be watching. They may do nothing, but they may come for us. If they do, and get between us and the machine, we've had it.'

Instinctively Ginger walked to the door to look at the aircraft. Near it lay what appeared to be a dead tree stump. It looked natural enough, with broken ends of branches protruding; but what puzzled him was he couldn't remember seeing it before. This was all the more astonishing because it was dead in front of the Auster, which, had it run on a little farther must have collided with it. Cozens, Ginger was sure, would never have taken such a risk had the stump been there.

Had it been there? He stared; but the stump looked as dead as a lump of rock. Turning, he called the others. 'There's something here I don't understand,' he said. 'Cozens, did you nearly run into a tree stump when you landed?'

'Tree stump?' echoed Cozens, hurrying forward.

Ginger turned back. 'Yes,' he answered. 'There's a—' The words died on his lips, for there were now two stumps.

Cozens took one comprehensive look. Raising his gun he began slowly to advance, at the same time saying: 'Stumps my foot. That's two of 'em. Watch out for spears.'

Even though he had been warned Ginger was unprepared for the speed at which the stumps came to life. In a flash they were erect, and two spears were on their way.

The white men ducked or jumped clear, and the spears buried their points in the wooden wall of the house with a crisp double thud. Having thrown, the two men fled in great leaps. Cozens fired. One fell, but he was on his feet again in an instant, and with his fellow disappeared in the jungle.

'Let's go,' said Cozens, briskly. 'There may be scores of them. Keep close. Cover me while I get in. While I'm getting started up blaze away on both sides.'

'What about Bates,' asked Ginger.

'We shall have to leave him. It's going to take us all our time to get aboard without anything to carry.'

The truth of this was soon apparent, for as they moved forward a score of natives burst from the bushes and in a moment the air was full of spears. Several aborigines raced to get between the aircraft and the white men.

'Back,' yelled Cozens. 'Back to the house. It's no use. We can't do it.'

There was a rush to get back to the door, everyone taking it in turns to shoot while the others retired. It was not exactly a dignified withdrawal, but it was at least successful. To Ginger it seemed like a miracle that none of them had been struck. Spears stuck in the ground along their path.

Panting, inside, they looked at each other.

'Let's rattle 'em from the windows,' said Bertie. 'By Jove! I must say that was a bit of a do.'

As they took up positions at the windows a strangled cry broke from Ginger's lips.

There was no need for him to explain.

The Auster was on fire.

CHAPTER XV

The Battle of Daly Flats

For a minute or two those in the house could only watch with helpless resignation and dumb despair the destruction of the Auster. There was no question of trying to save it even if the aborigines had not been there, for one of the spears, with a flaming brand attached, that had been used to fire it had pierced a fuel tank with a result that need not be described. The heat had driven them back but they were still there, doing a follow-my-leader dance in close procession, shaking their spears, yelling, and stamping on the dry earth until the dust flew. Even one who had been wounded joined in, limping as he staggered round. Another lay still. His companions paid no attention to him.

Cozens took aim with his gun, only to lower it with an exclamation of disgust. 'Pah! What's the use. The damage has been done.'

'Pity this couldn't have happened when that stinker Smith was here,' remarked Bertie, wiping condensation from his eyeglass.

'It could have done,' answered Cozens moodily. 'It isn't us in particular that they're mad to kill. Anyone would do. It just happened that we rolled up at the worst possible moment. In another hour, when they'd let off steam and realized what they'd

The aborigines, shaking their spears, yelling and stamping.

done, they would probably have bolted into the bush. We caught them on the boil.'

'What will they do next?' asked Ginger.

'I don't suppose they know themselves. They may have a go at us, or, when the frenzy has worn off, fade away.'

'Thank goodness the house has got a tin roof or they might have tried spearing that with their beastly fireworks,' observed Bertie.

Said Cozens: 'While we're waiting for them to make up their minds what they're going to do we'd better tidy up. We can't leave these bodies lying about. You keep your eye on 'em, Ginger, and yell if they come for us.'

Cozens and Bertie went off, leaving Ginger on guard at the window. They were away about ten minutes. 'What are they doing?' asked Cozens, when they returned.

'They're gone,' Ginger was able to tell him. 'They went into a huddle and then walked away into the bushes.'

'Hm.' Cozens considered the prospect. 'They may be cooling off or they may be planning a trick. They know plenty. Shoot at anything that moves, even if it looks like an animal. How goes the time?'

Ginger glanced at his watch. 'Quarter to three. Biggles might get back to Darwin any time now. When we fail to show up he'll come along in the Otter to find out what's happened.'

'That'll be dandy and no mistake,' said Bertie. 'He'll step right into the custard.'

'We'll have to warn him to keep clear.'

'How?'

'I wonder could I get Darwin on the radio. There's one here, or should be.'

'You mean there was one,' rejoined Bertie. 'The bright boys outside have made it look like a cat's breakfast. The blighters know about radio.'

'In that case we shall have to think of something else,' said Ginger.

Silence fell. The heat was awful. Outside, nothing moved except the smoke still rising into the sultry air from the smouldering remains of the aircraft. Had it not been for that Ginger would have found it hard to believe that this horror had really happened – in a country he had always imagined to be as safe as England.

'Twenty past three,' said Bertie. 'What about Smith, and that bunch on the lugger? According to you, Cozens, they should soon be here.'

'If they come, they're likely to walk right into it, too.'

'Best thing that could happen, absolutely,' declared Bertie. 'It'd tickle me to death to see that swine Smith on the end of a spear. Serve the blighter right. He was responsible for this beastly mess.'

Outside, all remained quiet.

'Do you think they've gone?' asked Ginger.

Cozens shook his head. 'No. They're probably skulking in the scrub, watching for one of us to go out. Time means nothing to them. They might keep it up for days.'

'How jolly!' murmured Bertie.

'I was wondering about putting out a warning signal for Biggles,' explained Ginger. 'He'll come, and I'm scared stiff he'll land.'

'My advice is, wait till you hear him,' replied Cozens. 'At present the aborigines must think they've got us cornered. When they hear another machine coming they may think twice, and push off.'

Ginger looked at Bertie. 'While we're doing nothing we might have a look round Smith's office to see what he's been up to. That was really why we came here.'

'That's an idea,' agreed Bertie. 'This waiting is binding me rigid.'

They found plenty of papers in Smith's office, some of them on the floor, for the natives appeared to have enjoyed making as much mess as possible; but all written matter was in code or in a language neither Ginger nor Bertie could read. They took it to be Russian.

'The back-room boys will be able to sort this out,' predicted Ginger.

'If we can get it to them, which at the moment appears to present difficulties, old boy – if you see what I mean.'

'What's in here, I wonder,' went on Ginger, going over to a closed door. It was locked. He called to Cozens: 'What's in this room leading off Smith's office?'

Cozens replied: 'I don't know. I was never allowed to see inside it. It was always kept locked.'

'Let's unlock it,' suggested Bertie, putting a foot against the lock and throwing his weight on it.

For a moment the door held, but when Ginger added his weight it flew open with a splintering crash.

'Well, blow me down!' ejaculated Bertie, looking round.

The room appeared to be both an armoury and a chemist's shop. Guns and rifles stood in racks with boxes of ammunition at their feet. On a bench were instruments, scales, bottles of chemicals, racks of test tubes and retorts. On a table was a pile of what seemed to be pieces of rock.

'Smith wasn't going to run short of weapons,' observed Bertie.

'He could never have intended to use all these,' declared Ginger. 'A lot of it is cheap stuff, obsolete. I'd say the idea was to dish it out to the aborigines when the time was ripe. That's it,' he went on confidently. 'And I'll tell you something else. I'd bet it was this sort of stuff that von Stalhein's ship was bringing here when it struck the willie-willie and went aground on the island. They'd never have got it through Customs. It would have been unloaded on the lugger and brought up the river. It all fits.'

'That's about the English of it, laddie,' agreed Bertie. 'What's all this junk on the table?'

'Mineral specimens. Couldn't be anything else. Smith, or one of his men, has been prospecting, probably for uranium. There have been some big finds in Australia. We found a Geiger Counter on the island. Now we know what it was for. The ship carried money, too; perhaps to pay the natives, in which case it will most likely turn out to be phoney.'

'Absolutely,' confirmed Bertie. 'Those are the answers. What have we here?' He lifted the lid of a box. 'Bombs! by Jingo. He was all ready for the natives if they turned on him. No, these aren't ordinary grenades. They're tear-gas. The blighter thought of everything.'

'They may come in useful,' said Ginger thoughtfully.

They went back to Cozens, who was cautiously opening a window. 'I'm letting in some air,' he told them. 'This heat is killing me. This is the sort of sticky heat you get here when the wet is on the way; but it isn't due for another week or so.'

'What's the wet,' asked Ginger.

'The rains. You haven't seen it rain till you've seen it raining here. It buckets down, and it keeps on bucketing. Maybe that's what's affecting the aborigines. It gets on everyone's nerves. I'll tell you this: if we don't get out of here before it starts we're likely to be here for some time. With visibility nil there's no question of a plane coming for us.'

'You're a bright and breezy bloke,' remarked Bertie. 'Think of something else to cheer us up.'

Cozens looked critically at the sky. 'I don't like the look of that glare. Something's going to happen. How goes the time?'

'Quarter to four,' answered Ginger. 'If Biggles—'

Cozens stopped him by holding up a hand. 'Listen!'

At last the silence outside was broken. It was broken by the sound of voices, still some distance off, but approaching.

'That's Smith's party,' asserted Cozens. 'I know his voice. He always talks as if everyone was deaf. Looks as if he may get caught in his own trap. We shall soon see.'

'We can't let him do that,' objected Ginger.

'Why not?'

'There's something not nice about standing by doing nothing while people are speared by aborigines.'

'That's pretty good,' sneered Cozens. 'Why, according to you he's the very man who's here to rouse the aborigines against the whites. He's roused 'em. Okay. Now let the skunk see what a good job he's made of it. I'm not forgetting Johnny Bates, in the next room.'

'There's nothing we can do, anyway,' put in Bertie.

'Of course there isn't,' argued Cozens. 'You fellers can do what you like, but I'm not risking a spear in my neck to save a thug who would have bumped me off, and who's about due for hanging, anyway.

'We could at least shout, to give them a chance,' suggested Ginger.

'Okay. Shout if you like. But if it happens that the natives have gone you'll see what Smith'll do to us – if he can.'

Ginger went to the window. 'Von Stalhein,' he shouted.

'That's the way from the river. There's a track, over there,' said Cozens, pointing.

'Von Stalhein,' yelled Ginger.

The voices stopped. Silence fell. Beads of sweat trickled down Ginger's face. 'Go back,' he shouted. 'The aborigines are on the warpath.'

The warning did not achieve its object. What happened would probably have happened in any case. Ginger's shout may merely have expedited things. Smith, actuated more by curiosity than fear, did the most natural thing, as might have been expected.

'There he is. That's Smith,' said Cozens, as a heavily built man appeared from the path he had pointed out. With him was Ivan, another white man, and two natives carrying parcels. They hurried forward, looking about them, apparently for the owner of the voice that had called.

Ginger watched for the crew of the lugger to appear – and, of course, von Stalhein. However, they had not shown up by the time the storm broke.

On seeing the burnt out remains of the aircraft Smith stopped, pointed, said something to the others and hastened towards it. The two natives put down their parcels and waited. There was not a movement in the jungle and Ginger decided that the natives must have gone.

But Cozens must have seen something that aroused his suspicions; or it may have been the very absence of movement that told him what was about to happen; at all events, from the open door towards which they had all moved, he suddenly shouted: 'Look out!'

He was too late. In an instant the air was full of flying spears, thrown by aborigines who had appeared from nowhere, as the saying is.

Ivan and his companion, being behind Smith, fell at once. They hadn't a chance even to draw their guns. Smith ran towards the house.

By this time those in the doorway were shooting; two or three aborigines fell, and it may have been as a result of this that Smith got as far as he did. With only ten yards to go he sprawled forward with a spear between his shoulder blades, hurled by a native who had raced after him. Ginger could see what was going to happen; but Smith and the native were in line, and none of them dare shoot for fear of hitting the wrong man. As Smith collapsed the aborigine also went down, hit perhaps by three bullets, for everyone fired at him.

Of the two natives who had been carrying the parcels, one turned at the first indication of trouble and fled up the path, never to be seen again. The other made for the house and succeeded in reaching it with a spear trailing from his thigh. He fell inside, gasping.

The main body of aborigines were now busy retrieving their weapons, regardless of the sniping that continued from the doorway. At this juncture Ginger remembered something. The tear-gas bombs. Dashing to the box he filled his pockets and returned with one in each hand. Running into the open he threw them all in quick succession as far as he could. What effect they had could not be discerned, for the natives were enveloped in the fast-spreading white vapour of the gas. He turned back to the house to see Cozens and Bertie trying to carry Smith into the house, not very success-fully, for he was a heavy man, and the spear got in the way. Cozens, ashen, pulled it out, and then said it was no use. The man was already dead. The spear had reached his heart.

As if affairs were not sufficiently hectic more confusion was now caused by the drone of a plane, and looking up Ginger saw the Otter burst into view, flying low over the treetops.

'Here's Biggles,' he cried. 'Are we going to let him land?'

Actually, they had no say in the matter, for the Otter's wheels were down and it was already coming in.

'Let's throw some more gas,' shouted Cozens. 'Where did you get it?'

Ginger told him, and a rush was made for the box. A minute later all three of them were hurling bombs into the scrub into which the natives had withdrawn. That the gas was having the desired effect was made clear by the uproar in the bushes.

By now the Otter was on the ground. It rolled to a stop thirty yards away and men began to jump down. First out was Biggles, pale and red-eyed from want of sleep. He did not look too pleased as he snapped: 'What on earth's going on here?'

'The natives have gone mad,' Ginger told him tersely. 'Hark at 'em! They've killed I don't know how many people. We've just driven them back with Smith's tear-gas grenades.'

'Where is Smith.'

Ginger pointed. 'There he is. Dead. Speared.'

Bertie and Cozens came up. From the other side came four men unknown to Ginger. Algy stood by the machine.

Biggles made some brief introductions. The newcomers turned out to be Colonel MacEwan, the Security Officer, and his personal assistant, and two police officials.

'Who started all this?' Biggles, looking worried, wanted to know. 'Algy told us what happened last night and this morning, and why you came on here.'

'We didn't start it you may be sure,' answered Ginger vehemently. 'It had started when we got here. Bates, the policeman from Darwin, had been murdered, and so had everyone else in the house. We walked right into it, and got to the house by the skin of our teeth, whereupon the natives set fire to the Auster.'

Ginger, Cozens and Bertie then took turns to narrate in more detail the sequence of events.

'How many aborigines are there in this mob?' inquired Colonel MacEwan, nodding towards the jungle, now silent.

'There's about a score left,' answered Cozens.

'We should be able to handle them if they come back, which I doubt,' replied the Colonel. 'Now we'll have a look at things.'

From this point the Australian authorities took over.

'I waited at Darwin for a bit, for you to come back,' Biggles told Ginger and Bertie, Cozens having gone to the house with his superiors. 'When you didn't show up I guessed you'd come unstuck and pressed on to see what had happened. This place was due to be raided, anyway. That's why Colonel MacEwan came back with me. By the way, where's von Stalhein?'

'He isn't here,' informed Ginger. 'I don't think any of the people on the lugger came back with Smith from the river. Maybe there was a row about Cozens escaping. I don't know.'

Biggles nodded. 'Von Stalhein usually manages to slip away when Old Man Death's about. No matter. The police will pick up the lugger, no doubt, when it tries to get out of the river – if not before.'

It may be said here that this did not happen, in spite of strenuous efforts to catch the *Matilda*. What saved it was the early arrival of the 'wet', which destroyed visibility for days and must have given the lugger a lucky chance to slip out of the river undetected. Ginger, remembering Smith's native servant who had bolted back down the path when the natives had attacked, thought this man must have reached the river and given the alarm. At all events, his body was not found in the general clean-up. Some weeks later, wreckage thrown up on one of the Melville Islands was believed to be that of the lugger. But this was not proved, and the police are still on the lookout for Boller and his crew.

There is little more to be said. It was only necessary for Colonel MacEwan to walk through the house to satisfy himself of the truth of Biggles's allegations. The Otter went at once to Darwin with a mass of papers, and returned, with the Halifax, bringing a force of police sufficient to prevent any further interference on the part of the aborigines, who, as a matter of detail, when sanity returned must have realized what they had done, for they quietly faded away into their jungle retreats.

Papers revealing the names of enemy agents operating in Australia, including those who had landed in the lifeboat with von Stalhein, were found, and the entire plot exposed, although for security reasons the soft pedal was kept on the story. The native servant who had reached the house with a spear in his thigh recovered, and gave some valuable evidence.

The scheme was much as it had been visualized. The plan was to spread a network of agents and operatives all over the continent both to spy on secret experimental work with atomic and guided missiles, and undermine the country's economy by the infiltration of agitators into the native settlements as had been done elsewhere. When the trouble started certain selected aborigines were to be provided with firearms. Behind the background of disorder scientists were to explore the outback for minerals useful in nuclear research. It was some of these people, with their weapons and equipment, who were on board the ship which was to have met the *Matilda* by appointment, and transferring to it, gone on up the Daly. It was not a matter of bad luck that this failed. Someone blundered in attempting to do it not only in the season of willie-willies, which in North-West Australia can occur at any moment between November and April, but in the most notorious zone of all, between Exmouth Gulf and Eighty Mile Beach.

Biggles and his party returned to Darwin at sundown having handed over to Colonel MacEwan. They never saw Daly Flats again, having no reason, and certainly no desire, to do so. After a rest, during which time Biggles made a full report of his part of the affair for the authorities, they paid a courtesy visit to Bill Gilson at Broome, and then made a leisurely run back to London. They learned later that Bill had received promotion for his handling of the Tarracooma business, which resulted in long prison sentences for his prisoners.

Cozens soon got another job and is now flying a Quantas Constellation. Not only was no action taken over his violation of the regulations with regard to the Auster, which, as had been supposed, Biggles had caused to be grounded, but in view of the part he had played, he was awarded compensation for what he had lost.

So, taking things all round, the only people who came to any harm from Biggles's visit to Australia were those whose sinister conspiracy had taken him there.

Which was as it should be.